British Mystery Multipack Vol. 15

British Mystery Multipack Vol. 15

By

Richard Harding Davis

J. S. Fletcher

Fergus Hume

Carolyn Wells

Enhanced Media
2017

British Mystery Multipack Vol. 15

The Paradise Mystery by J. (Joseph) S. (Smith) Fletcher. First published in 1871.

In the Fog by Richard Harding Davis. First published in 1901.

The Wooden Hand - A Detective Story by Fergus Hume. First published in 1905.

The Maxwell Mystery by Carolyn Wells. First published in 1913.

British Mystery Multipack Vol. 15. Cover, interior design and editing © Copyright 2017 Enhanced Media Publishing. All rights reserved.

Enhanced Media Publishing
Los Angeles, CA.

First Printing: 2017.

ISBN-13: 978-1976465987.

ISBN-10: 1976465982.

Contents

The Paradise Mystery
By J. S. Fletcher 7

In the Fog
By Richard Harding Davis 148

The Wooden Hand
A Detective Story
By Fergus Hume 186

The Maxwell Mystery
By Carolyn Wells 336

The Paradise Mystery

By J. S. Fletcher

I - Only the Guardian

American tourists, sure appreciators of all that is ancient and picturesque in England, invariably come to a halt, holding their breath in a sudden catch of wonder, as they pass through the half-ruinous gateway which admits to the Close of Wrychester. Nowhere else in England is there a fairer prospect of old-world peace. There before their eyes, set in the center of a great green sward, fringed by tall elms and giant beeches, rises the vast fabric of the thirteenth-century Cathedral, its high spire piercing the skies in which rooks are forever circling and calling. The time-worn stone, at a little distance delicate as lacework, is transformed at different hours of the day into shifting shades of color, varying from grey to purple: the massiveness of the great nave and transepts contrasts impressively with the gradual tapering of the spire, rising so high above turret and clerestory that it at last becomes a mere line against the ether. In morning, as in afternoon, or in evening, here is a perpetual atmosphere of rest; and not around the great church alone, but in the quaint and ancient houses which fence in the Close. Little less old than the mighty mass of stone on which their ivy-framed windows look, these houses make the casual observer feel that here, if anywhere in the world, life must needs run smoothly. Under those high gables, behind those mullioned windows, in the beautiful old gardens lying between the stone porches and the elm-shadowed lawn, nothing, one would think, could possibly exist but leisured and pleasant existence: even the busy streets of the old city, outside the crumbling gateway, seem, for the moment, far off.

In one of the oldest of these houses, half hidden behind trees and shrubs in a corner of the Close, three people sat at breakfast one fine May morning. The room in which they sat was in keeping with the old house and its surroundings—a long, low-ceilinged room, with oak paneling around its walls, and oak beams across its roof—a room of old furniture, and, old pictures, and old books, its antique atmosphere relieved by great masses of flowers, set here and there in old china bowls: through its wide windows, the casements of which were thrown wide open, there was an inviting prospect of a high-edged flower garden, and, seen in vistas through the trees and shrubberies, of patches of the west front of the Cathedral, now somber and grey in shadow. But on the garden and into this flower-scented room the sun was shining gaily through the trees, and making gleams of light on the silver and china on the table and on the faces of the three people who sat around it.

Of these three, two were young, and the third was one of those men whose age it is never easy to guess—a tall, clean-shaven, bright-eyed, alert-looking man, good-looking in a clever, professional sort of way, a man whom no one could have taken for anything but a member of one of the learned callings. In some lights he looked no more than forty: a strong light betrayed the fact that his dark hair had a streak of grey in it, and was showing a tendency to whiten about the temples. A strong, intellectually superior man, this, scrupulously groomed and well-dressed, as befitted what he really was—a medical practitioner with an excellent connection amongst the exclusive society of a cathedral town. Around him hung an undeniable air of content and prosperity—as he turned over a pile of letters which stood by his plate, or glanced at the morning newspaper which lay at his elbow, it was easy to see that he had no cares beyond those of the day, and that they—so far as he knew then— were not likely to affect him greatly. Seeing him in these pleasant domestic circumstances, at the head of his table, with abundant evidences of comfort and refinement and modest luxury about him, anyone would have said, without hesitation, that Dr. Mark Ransford was undeniably one of the fortunate folk of this world.

The second person of the three was a boy of apparently seventeen—a well-built, handsome lad of the senior schoolboy type, who was devoting himself in business-like fashion to two widely-differing pursuits—one, the consumption of eggs and bacon and dry toast; the other, the study of a Latin textbook, which he had propped up in front of him against the old-fashioned silver cruet. His quick eyes wandered alternately between his book and his plate; now and then he muttered a line or two to himself. His companions took no notice of these combinations of eating and learning: they knew from experience that it was his way to make up at breakfast-time for the moments he had stolen from his studies the night before.

It was not difficult to see that the third member of the party, a girl of nineteen or twenty, was the boy's sister. Each had a wealth of brown hair, inclining, in the girl's case to a shade that had tints of gold in it; each had grey eyes, in which there was a mixture of blue; each had a bright, vivid color; each was undeniably good-looking and eminently healthy. No one would have doubted that both had lived a good deal of an open-air existence: the boy was already muscular and sinewy: the girl looked as if she was well acquainted with the tennis racket and the golf-stick. Nor would anyone have made the mistake of thinking that these two were blood relations of the man at the head of the table—between them and him there was not the least resemblance of feature, of color, or of manner.

While the boy learnt the last lines of his Latin, and the doctor turned over the newspaper, the girl read a letter—evidently, from the large sprawling handwriting, the missive of some girlish correspondent. She was deep in it when, from one of the turrets of the Cathedral, a bell began to ring. At that, she glanced at her brother.

"There's Martin, Dick!" she said. "You'll have to hurry."

Many a long year before that, in one of the bygone centuries, a worthy citizen of Wrychester, Martin by name, had left a sum of money to the Dean and Chapter of the Cathedral on condition that as long as ever the Cathedral stood, they should cause to be rung a bell from its smaller bell-tower for three minutes before nine o'clock every morning, all the year round. What Martin's object had been no one now knew—but this bell served to remind young gentlemen going to offices, and boys going to school, that the hour of their servitude was near. And Dick Bewery, without a word, bolted half his coffee, snatched up his book, grabbed at a cap which lay with more books on a chair close by, and vanished through the open window. The doctor laughed, laid aside his newspaper, and handed his cup across the table.

"I don't think you need bother yourself about Dick's ever being late, Mary," he said. "You are not quite aware of the power of legs that are only seventeen years old. Dick could get to any given point in just about one-fourth of the time that I could, for instance—moreover, he has a cunning knowledge of every short cut in the city."

Mary Bewery took the empty cup and began to refill it.

"I don't like him to be late," she remarked. "It's the beginning of bad habits."

"Oh, well!" said Ransford indulgently. "He's pretty free from anything of that sort, you know. I haven't even suspected him of smoking, yet."

"That's because he thinks smoking would stop his growth and interfere with his cricket," answered Mary. "He would smoke if it weren't for that."

"That's giving him high praise, then," said Ransford. "You couldn't give him higher! Know how to repress his inclinations. An excellent thing—and most unusual, I fancy. Most people—don't!"

He took his refilled cup, rose from the table, and opened a box of cigarettes which stood on the mantelpiece. And the girl, instead of picking up her letter again, glanced at him a little doubtfully.

"That reminds me of—of something I wanted to say to you," she said. "You're quite right about people not repressing their inclinations. I—I wish some people would!"

Ransford turned quickly from the hearth and gave her a sharp look, beneath which her color heightened. Her eyes shifted their gaze away to her letter, and she picked it up and began to fold it nervously. And at that Ransford rapped out a name, putting a quick suggestion of meaning inquiry into his voice.

"Bryce?" he asked.

The girl nodded her face showing distinct annoyance and dislike. Before saying more, Ransford lighted a cigarette.

"Been at it again?" he said at last. "Since last time?"

"Twice," she answered. "I didn't like to tell you—I've hated to bother you about it. But—what am I to do? I dislike him intensely—I can't tell why, but it's there, and nothing could ever alter the feeling. And though I told him—before—that it was useless—he mentioned it again—yesterday—at Mrs. Folliot's garden-party."

"Confound his impudence!" growled Ransford. "Oh, well!—I'll have to settle with him myself. It's useless trifling with anything like that. I gave him a quiet hint before. And since he won't take it—all right!"

"But—what shall you do?" she asked anxiously. "Not—send him away?"

"If he's any decency about him, he'll go—after what I say to him," answered Ransford. "Don't you trouble yourself about it—I'm not at all keen about him. He's a clever enough fellow, and a good assistant, but I don't like him, personally—never did."

"I don't want to think that anything that I say should lose him his situation—or whatever you call it," she remarked slowly. "That would seem—"

"No need to bother," interrupted Ransford. "He'll get another in two minutes—so to speak. Anyway, we can't have this going on. The fellow must be an ass! When I was young—"

He stopped short at that, and turning away, looked out across the garden as if some recollection had suddenly struck him.

"When you were young—which is, of course, such an awfully long time since!" said the girl, a little teasingly. "What?"

"Only that if a woman said No—unmistakably—once, a man took it as final," replied Ransford. "At least—so I was always given to believe. Nowadays—"

"You forget that Mr. Pemberton Bryce is what most people would call a very pushing young man," said Mary. "If he doesn't get what he wants in this world, it won't be for not asking for it. But—if you must speak to him—and I really think you must!—will you tell him that he is not going to get—me? Perhaps he'll take it finally from you—as my guardian."

"I don't know if parents and guardians count for much in these degenerate days," said Ransford. "But—I won't have him annoying you. And—I suppose it has come to annoyance?"

"It's very annoying to be asked three times by a man whom you've told flatly, once for all, that you don't want him, at any time, ever!" she answered. "It's—irritating!"

"All right," said Ransford quietly. "I'll speak to him. There's going to be no annoyance for you under this roof."

The girl gave him a quick glance, and Ransford turned away from her and picked up his letters.

"Thank you," she said. "But—there's no need to tell me that, because I know it already. Now I wonder if you'll tell me something more?"

Ransford turned back with a sudden apprehension.

"Well?" he asked brusquely. "What?"

"When are you going to tell me all about—Dick and myself?" she asked. "You promised that you would, you know, some day. And—a whole year's gone by since then. And—Dick's seventeen! He won't be satisfied always—just to know no more than that our father and mother died when we were very little, and that you've been guardian—and all that you have been!—to us. Will he, now?"

Ransford laid down his letters again, and thrusting his hands in his pockets, squared his shoulders against the mantelpiece. "Don't you think you might wait until you're twenty-one?" he asked.

"Why?" she said, with a laugh. "I'm just twenty—do you really think I shall be any wiser in twelve months? Of course I shan't!"

"You don't know that," he replied. "You may be—a great deal wiser."

"But what has that got to do with it?" she persisted. "Is there any reason why I shouldn't be told—everything?"

She was looking at him with a certain amount of demand—and Ransford, who had always known that some moment of this sort must inevitably come, felt that she was not going to be put off with ordinary excuses. He hesitated—and she went on speaking.

"You know," she continued, almost pleadingly. "We don't know anything—at all. I never have known, and until lately Dick has been too young to care—"

"Has he begun asking questions?" demanded Ransford hastily.

"Once or twice, lately—yes," replied Mary. "It's only natural." She laughed a little—a forced laugh. "They say," she went on, "that it doesn't matter, nowadays, if you can't tell who your grandfather was—but, just think, we don't know who our father was—except that his name was John Bewery. That doesn't convey much."

"You know more," said Ransford. "I told you—always have told you—that he was an early friend of mine, a man of business, who, with your mother, died young, and I, as their friend, became guardian to you and Dick. Is—is there anything much more that I could tell?"

"There's something I should very much like to know—personally," she answered, after a pause which lasted so long that Ransford began to feel uncomfortable under it. "Don't be angry—or hurt—if I tell you plainly what it is. I'm quite sure it's never even occurred to Dick—but I'm three years ahead of him. It's this—have we been dependent on you?"

Ransford's face flushed and he turned deliberately to the window, and for a moment stood staring out on his garden and the glimpses of the Cathedral. And just as deliberately as he had turned away, he turned back.

"No!" he said. "Since you ask me, I'll tell you that. You've both got money—due to you when you're of age. It—it's in my hands. Not a great lot—but sufficient to—to cover all your expenses. Education—everything. When you're twenty-one, I'll hand over yours—when Dick's twenty-one, his. Perhaps I ought to have told you all that before, but—I didn't think it necessary. I—I dare say I've a tendency to let things slide."

"You've never let things slide about us," she replied quickly, with a sudden glance which made him turn away again. "And I only wanted to know—because I'd got an idea that—well, that we were owing everything to you."

"Not from me!" he exclaimed.

"No—that would never be!" she said. "But—don't you understand? I—wanted to know—something. Thank you. I won't ask more now."

"I've always meant to tell you—a good deal," remarked Ransford, after another pause. "You see, I can scarcely—yet—realize that you're both growing up! You were at school a year ago. And Dick is still very young. Are—are you more satisfied now?" he went on anxiously. "If not—"

"I'm quite satisfied," she answered. "Perhaps—someday—you'll tell me more about our father and mother?—but never mind even that now. You're sure you haven't minded my asking—what I have asked?"

"Of course not—of course not!" he said hastily. "I ought to have remembered. And—but we'll talk again. I must get into the surgery—and have a word with Bryce, too."

"If you could only make him see reason and promise not to offend again," she said. "Wouldn't that solve the difficulty?"

Ransford shook his head and made no answer. He picked up his letters again and went out, and down a long stone-walled passage which led to his surgery at the side of the house. He was alone there when he had shut the door—and he relieved his feelings with a deep groan.

"Heaven help me if the lad ever insists on the real truth and on having proofs and facts given to him!" he muttered. "I shouldn't mind telling her, when she's a bit older—but he wouldn't understand as she would. Anyway, thank God I can keep up the pleasant fiction about the money without her ever knowing that I told her a deliberate lie just now. But—what's in the future? Here's one man to be dismissed already, and there'll be others, and one of them will be the favoured man. That man will have to be told! And—so will she, then. And—my God! she doesn't see, and mustn't see, that I'm madly in love with her myself! She's no idea of it—and she shan't have; I must—must continue to be—only the guardian!"

He laughed a little cynically as he laid his letters down on his desk and proceeded to open them—in which occupation he was presently interrupted by the opening of the side-door and the entrance of Mr. Pemberton Bryce.

II - Making an Enemy

It was characteristic of Pemberton Bryce that he always walked into a room as if its occupant were asleep and he was afraid of waking him. He had a gentle step which was soft without being stealthy, and quiet movements which brought him suddenly to anybody's side before his presence was noticed. He was by Ransford's desk ere Ransford knew he was in the surgery—and Ransford's sudden realization of his presence roused a certain feeling of irritation in his mind, which he instantly endeavored to suppress—it was no use getting cross with a man of whom you were about to rid yourself, he said to himself. And for the moment, after replying to his assistant's greeting—a greeting as quiet as his entrance—he went on reading his letters, and Bryce turned off to that part of the surgery in which the drugs were kept, and busied himself in making up some prescription. Ten minutes went by in silence; then Ransford pushed his correspondence aside, laid a paper-weight on it, and twisting his chair round, looked at the man to whom he was going to say some unpleasant things. Within himself he was revolving a question—how would Bryce take it?

He had never liked this assistant of his, although he had then had him in employment for nearly two years. There was something about Pemberton Bryce which he did not understand and could not fathom. He had come to him with excellent testimonials and good recommendations; he was well up to his work, successful with patients, thoroughly capable as a general practitioner—there was no fault to be found with him on any professional grounds. But to Ransford his personality was objectionable—why, he was not quite sure. Outwardly, Bryce was rather more than presentable—a tall, good-looking man of twenty-eight or thirty, whom some people—women especially—would call handsome; he was the sort of young man who knows the value of good clothes and a smart appearance, and his professional manner was all that could be desired. But Ransford could not help distinguishing between Bryce the doctor and Bryce the man—and Bryce the man he did not like. Outside the professional part of him, Bryce seemed to him to be undoubtedly deep, sly, cunning—he conveyed the impression of being one of those men whose ears are always on the stretch, who take everything in and give little out. There was a curious air of watchfulness and of secrecy about him in private matters which was as repellent—to Ransford's thinking—as it was hard to explain. Anyway, in private affairs, he did not like his assistant, and he liked him less than ever as he glanced at him on this particular occasion.

"I want a word with you," he said curtly. "I'd better say it now."

Bryce, who was slowly pouring some liquid from one bottle into another, looked quietly across the room and did not interrupt himself in his work. Ransford knew that he must have recognized a certain significance in the words just addressed to him—but he showed no outward sign of it, and the liquid went on trickling from one bottle to the other with the same uniform steadiness.

"Yes?" said Bryce inquiringly. "One moment."

He finished his task calmly, put the corks in the bottles, labelled one, restored the other to a shelf, and turned round. Not a man to be easily startled—not easily turned from a purpose, this, thought Ransford as he glanced at Bryce's eyes, which had a trick of fastening their gaze on people with an odd, disconcerting persistency.

"I'm sorry to say what I must say," he began. "But—you've brought it on yourself. I gave you a hint some time ago that your attentions were not welcome to Miss Bewery."

Bryce made no immediate response. Instead, leaning almost carelessly and indifferently against the table at which he had been busy with drugs and bottles, he took a small file from his waistcoat pocket and began to polish his carefully cut nails.

"Yes?" he said, after a pause. "Well?"

"In spite of it," continued Ransford, "you've since addressed her again on the matter—not merely once, but twice."

Bryce put his file away, and thrusting his hands in his pockets, crossed his feet as he leaned back against the table—his whole attitude suggesting, whether intentionally or not, that he was very much at his ease.

"There's a great deal to be said on a point like this," he observed. "If a man wishes a certain young woman to become his wife, what right has any other man—or the young woman herself, for that matter to say that he mustn't express his desires to her?"

"None," said Ransford, "provided he only does it once—and takes the answer he gets as final."

"I disagree with you entirely," retorted Bryce. "On the last particular, at any rate. A man who considers any word of a woman's as being final is a fool. What a woman thinks on Monday she's almost dead certain not to think on Tuesday. The whole history of human relationship is on my side there. It's no opinion—it's a fact."

Ransford stared at this frank remark, and Bryce went on, coolly and imperturbably, as if he had been discussing a medical problem.

"A man who takes a woman's first answer as final," he continued, "is, I repeat, a fool. There are lots of reasons why a woman shouldn't know her own mind at the first time of asking. She may be too surprised. She mayn't be quite decided. She may say one thing when she really means another. That often happens. She isn't much better equipped at the second time of asking. And there are women—young ones—who aren't really certain of themselves at the third time. All that's common sense."

"I'll tell you what it is!" suddenly exclaimed Ransford, after remaining silent for a moment under this flow of philosophy. "I'm not going to discuss theories and ideas. I know one young woman, at any rate, who is certain of herself. Miss Bewery does not feel any inclination to you—now, nor at any time to be! She's told you so three times. And—you should take her answer and behave yourself accordingly!"

Bryce favoured his senior with a searching look.

"How does Miss Bewery know that she mayn't be inclined to—in the future?" he asked. "She may come to regard me with favor."

"No, she won't!" declared Ransford. "Better hear the truth, and be done with it. She doesn't like you—and she doesn't want to, either. Why can't you take your answer like a man?"

"What's your conception of a man?" asked Bryce.

"That!—and a good one," exclaimed Ransford.

"May satisfy you—but not me," said Bryce. "Mine's different. My conception of a man is of a being who's got some perseverance. You can get anything in this world—anything!—by pegging away for it."

"You're not going to get my ward," suddenly said Ransford. "That's flat! She doesn't want you—and she's now said so three times. And—I support her."

"What have you against me?" asked Bryce calmly. "If, as you say, you support her in her resolution not to listen to my proposals, you must have something against me. What is it?"

"That's a question you've no right to put," replied Ransford, "for it's utterly unnecessary. So I'm not going to answer it. I've nothing against you as regards your work—nothing! I'm willing to give you an excellent testimonial."

"Oh!" remarked Bryce quietly. "That means—you wish me to go away?"

"I certainly think it would be best," said Ransford.

"In that case," continued Bryce, more coolly than ever, "I shall certainly want to know what you have against me—or what Miss Bewery has against me. Why am I objected to as a suitor? You, at any rate, know who I am—you know that my father is of our own profession, and a man of reputation and standing, and that I myself came to you on high recommendation. Looked at from my standpoint, I'm a thoroughly eligible young man. And there's a point you forget—there's no mystery about me!"

Ransford turned sharply in his chair as he noticed the emphasis which Bryce put on his last word.

"What do you mean?" he demanded.

"What I've just said," replied Bryce. "There's no mystery attaching to me. Any question about me can be answered. Now, you can't say that as regards your ward. That's a fact, Dr. Ransford."

Ransford, in years gone by, had practiced himself in the art of restraining his temper—naturally a somewhat quick one. And he made a strong effort in that direction now, recognizing that there was something behind his assistant's last remark, and that Bryce meant him to know it was there.

"I'll repeat what I've just said," he answered. "What do you mean by that?"

"I hear things," said Bryce. "People will talk—even a doctor can't refuse to hear what gossiping and garrulous patients say. Since she came to you from school, a year ago, Wrychester people have been much interested in Miss Bewery, and in her brother, too. And there are a good many residents of the Close—you know their nice, inquisitive ways!—who want to know who the sister and brother really are—and what your relationship is to them!"

"Confound their impudence!" growled Ransford.

"By all means," agreed Bryce. "And—for all I care—let them be confounded, too. But if you imagine that the choice and select coteries of a cathedral town, consisting mainly of the relicts of deceased deans, canons, prebendaries and the like, and of maiden aunts, elderly spinsters, and tea-table-haunting curates, are free from gossip—why, you're a singularly innocent person!"

"They'd better not begin gossiping about my affairs," said Ransford. "Otherwise—"

"You can't stop them from gossiping about your affairs," interrupted Bryce cheerfully. "Of course they gossip about your affairs; have gossiped about them; will continue to gossip about them. It's human nature!"

"You've heard them?" asked Ransford, who was too vexed to keep back his curiosity. "You yourself?"

"As you are aware, I am often asked out to tea," replied Bryce, "and to garden-parties, and tennis-parties, and choice and cozy functions patronized by curates and associated with crumpets. I have heard—with these ears. I can even repeat the sort of thing I have heard. 'That dear, delightful Miss Bewery—what a charming girl! And that good-looking boy, her brother—quite a dear! Now I wonder who they really are? Wards of Dr. Ransford, of course! Really, how very romantic!—and just a little—eh?—unusual? Such a comparatively young man to have such a really charming girl as his ward! Can't be more than forty-five himself, and she's twenty—how very, very romantic! Really, one would think there ought to be a chaperon!'"

"Damn!" said Ransford under his breath.

"Just so," agreed Bryce. "But—that's the sort of thing. Do you want more? I can supply an unlimited quantity in the piece if you like. But it's all according to sample."

"So—in addition to your other qualities," remarked Ransford, "you're a gossiper?"

Bryce smiled slowly and shook his head.

"No," he replied. "I'm a listener. A good one, too. But do you see my point? I say—there's no mystery about me. If Miss Bewery will honor me with her hand, she'll get a man whose antecedents will bear the strictest investigation."

"Are you inferring that hers won't?" demanded Ransford.

"I'm not inferring anything," said Bryce. "I am speaking for myself, of myself. Pressing my own claim, if you like, on you, the guardian. You might do much worse than support my claims, Dr. Ransford."

"Claims, man!" retorted Ransford. "You've got no claims! What are you talking about? Claims!"

"My pretensions, then," answered Bryce. "If there is a mystery—as Wrychester people say there is—about Miss Bewery, it would be safe with me. Whatever you may think, I'm a thoroughly dependable man—when it's in my own interest."

"And—when it isn't?" asked Ransford. "What are you then?—as you're so candid."

"I could be a very bad enemy," replied Bryce.

There was a moment's silence, during which the two men looked attentively at each other.

"I've told you the truth," said Ransford at last. "Miss Bewery flatly refuses to entertain any idea whatever of ever marrying you. She earnestly hopes that that eventuality may never be mentioned to her again. Will you give me your word of honor to respect her wishes?"

"No!" answered Bryce. "I won't!"

"Why not?" asked Ransford, with a faint show of anger. "A woman's wishes!"

"Because I may consider that I see signs of a changed mind in her," said Bryce. "That's why."

"You'll never see any change of mind," declared Ransford. "That's certain. Is that your fixed determination?"

"It is," answered Bryce. "I'm not the sort of man who is easily repelled."

"Then, in that case," said Ransford, "we had better part company." He rose from his desk, and going over to a safe which stood in a corner, unlocked it and took some papers from an inside drawer. He consulted one of these and turned to Bryce. "You remember our agreement?" he continued. "Your engagement was to be determined by a three months' notice on either side, or, at my will, at any time by payment of three months' salary?"

"Quite right," agreed Bryce. "I remember, of course."

"Then I'll give you a cheque for three months' salary—now," said Ransford, and sat down again at his desk. "That will settle matters definitely—and, I hope, agreeably."

Bryce made no reply. He remained leaning against the table, watching Ransford write the cheque. And when Ransford laid the cheque down at the edge of the desk he made no movement towards it.

"You must see," remarked Ransford, half apologetically, "that it's the only thing I can do. I can't have any man who's not—not welcome to her, to put it plainly—causing any annoyance to my ward. I repeat, Bryce—you must see it!"

"I have nothing to do with what you see," answered Bryce. "Your opinions are not mine, and mine aren't yours. You're really turning me away—as if I were a dishonest foreman!—because in my opinion it would be a very excellent thing for her and for myself if Miss Bewery would consent to marry me. That's the plain truth."

Ransford allowed himself to take a long and steady look at Bryce. The thing was done now, and his dismissed assistant seemed to be taking it quietly—and Ransford's curiosity was aroused.

"I can't make you out!" he exclaimed. "I don't know whether you're the most cynical young man I ever met, or whether you're the most obtuse—"

"Not the last, anyway," interrupted Bryce. "I assure you of that!"

"Can't you see for yourself, then, man, that the girl doesn't want you!" said Ransford. "Hang it!—for anything you know to the contrary, she may have—might have—other ideas!"

Bryce, who had been staring out of a side window for the last minute or two, suddenly laughed, and, lifting a hand, pointed into the garden. And Ransford turned—and saw Mary Bewery walking there with a tall lad, whom he recognized as one Sackville Bonham, stepson of Mr. Folliot, a wealthy resident of the Close. The two young people were laughing and chatting together with evident great friendliness.

"Perhaps," remarked Bryce quietly, "her ideas run in—that direction? In which case, Dr. Ransford, you'll have trouble. For Mrs. Folliot, mother of yonder callow youth, who's the apple of her eye, is one of the inquisitive ladies of whom I've just told you, and if her son unites himself with anybody, she'll want to know exactly who that anybody is. You'd far better have supported me as an aspirant! However—I suppose there's no more to say."

"Nothing!" answered Ransford. "Except to say good-day—and good-bye to you. You needn't remain—I'll see to everything. And I'm going out now. I think you'd better not exchange any farewells with anyone."

Bryce nodded silently, and Ransford, picking up his hat and gloves, left the surgery by the side door. A moment later, Bryce saw him crossing the Close.

III - St. Wrytha's Stair

The summarily dismissed assistant, thus left alone, stood for a moment in evident deep thought before he moved towards Ransford's desk and picked up the cheque. He looked at it carefully, folded it neatly, and put it away in his pocket-book; after that he proceeded to collect a few possessions of his own, instruments, books from various drawers and shelves. He was placing these things in a small hand-bag when a gentle tap sounded on the door by which patients approached the surgery.

"Come in!" he called.

There was no response, although the door was slightly ajar; instead, the knock was repeated, and at that Bryce crossed the room and flung the door open.

A man stood outside—an elderly, slight-figured, quiet-looking man, who looked at Bryce with a half-deprecating, half-nervous air; the air of a man who was shy in manner and evidently fearful of seeming to intrude. Bryce's quick, observant eyes took him in at a glance, noting a much worn and lined face, thin grey hair and tired eyes; this was a man, he said to himself, who had seen trouble. Nevertheless, not a poor man, if his general appearance was anything to go by—he was well and even expensively dressed, in the style generally affected by well-to-do merchants and city men; his clothes were fashionably cut, his silk hat was new, his linen and boots irreproachable; a fine diamond pin gleamed in his carefully arranged cravat.

Why, then, this unmistakably furtive and half-frightened manner—which seemed to be somewhat relieved at the sight of Bryce?

"Is this—is Dr. Ransford within?" asked the stranger. "I was told this is his house."

"Dr. Ransford is out," replied Bryce. "Just gone out—not five minutes ago. This is his surgery. Can I be of use?"

The man hesitated, looking beyond Bryce into the room.

"No, thank you," he said at last. "I—no, I don't want professional services—I just called to see Dr. Ransford—I—the fact is, I once knew someone of that name. It's no matter—at present."

Bryce stepped outside and pointed across the Close.

"Dr. Ransford," he said, "went over there—I rather fancy he's gone to the Deanery—he has a case there. If you went through Paradise, you'd very likely meet him coming back—the Deanery is the big house in the far corner yonder."

The stranger followed Bryce's outstretched finger.

"Paradise?" he said, wonderingly. "What's that?"

Bryce pointed to a long stretch of grey wall which projected from the south wall of the Cathedral into the Close.

"It's an enclosure—between the south porch and the transept," he said. "Full of old tombs and trees—a sort of wilderness—why called Paradise I don't know. There's a short cut across it to the Deanery and that part of the Close—through that archway you see over there. If you go across, you're almost sure to meet Dr. Ransford."

"I'm much obliged to you," said the stranger. "Thank you."

He turned away in the direction which Bryce had indicated, and Bryce went back—only to go out again and call after him.

"If you don't meet him, shall I say you'll call again?" he asked. "And—what name?"

The stranger shook his head.

"It's immaterial," he answered. "I'll see him—somewhere—or later. Many thanks."

He went on his way towards Paradise, and Bryce returned to the surgery and completed his preparations for departure. And in the course of things, he more than once looked through the window into the garden and saw Mary Bewery still walking and talking with young Sackville Bonham.

"No," he muttered to himself. "I won't trouble to exchange any farewells—not because of Ransford's hint, but because there's no need. If Ransford thinks he's going to drive me out of Wrychester before I choose to go he's badly mistaken—it'll be time enough to say farewell when I take my departure—and that won't be just yet. Now I wonder who that old chap was? Knew someone of Ransford's name once, did he? Probably Ransford himself—in which case he knows more of Ransford than anybody in Wrychester knows—for nobody in Wrychester knows anything beyond a few years back. No, Dr. Ransford!—no farewells—to anybody! A mere departure—till I turn up again."

But Bryce was not to get away from the old house without something in the nature of a farewell. As he walked out of the surgery by the side entrance, Mary Bewery, who had just parted from young Bonham in the garden and was about to visit her dogs in the stable yard, came along: she and Bryce met, face to face. The girl flushed, not so much from embarrassment as from vexation; Bryce, cool as ever, showed no sign of any embarrassment. Instead, he laughed, tapping the hand-bag which he carried under one arm.

"Summarily turned out—as if I had been stealing the spoons," he remarked. "I go—with my small belongings. This is my first reward—for devotion."

"I have nothing to say to you," answered Mary, sweeping by him with a highly displeased glance. "Except that you have brought it on yourself."

"A very feminine retort!" observed Bryce. "But—there is no malice in it? Your anger won't last more than—shall we say a day?"

"You may say what you like," she replied. "As I just said, I have nothing to say—now or at any time."

"That remains to be proved," remarked Bryce. "The phrase is one of much elasticity. But for the present—I go!"

He walked out into the Close, and without as much as a backward look struck off across the sward in the direction in which, ten minutes before, he had sent the strange man. He had rooms in a quiet lane on the farther side of the Cathedral precinct, and his present intention was to go to them to leave his bag and make some further arrangements. He had no idea of leaving Wrychester—he knew of another doctor in the city who was badly in need of help: he would go to him—would tell him, if need be, why he had left Ransford. He had a multiplicity of schemes and ideas in his head, and he began to consider some of them as he stepped out of the Close into the ancient enclosure which all Wrychester folk knew by its time-honored name of Paradise. This was really an outer court of the old cloisters; its high walls, half-ruinous, almost wholly covered with ivy, shut in an expanse of turf, liberally furnished with yew and cypress and studded with tombs and gravestones. In one corner rose a gigantic elm; in another a broken stairway of stone led to a doorway set high in the walls of the nave; across the enclosure itself was a pathway which led towards the houses in the south-east corner of the Close. It was a curious, gloomy spot, little frequented save by people who went across it rather than follow the graveled paths outside, and it was untenanted when Bryce stepped into it. But just as he walked through the archway he saw Ransford. Ransford was emerging hastily from a postern door in the west porch—so hastily that Bryce checked himself to look at him. And though they were twenty yards apart, Bryce saw that Ransford's face was very pale, almost to whiteness, and that he was unmistakably agitated. Instantly he connected that agitation with the man who had come to the surgery door.

"They've met!" mused Bryce, and stopped, staring after Ransford's retreating figure. "Now what is it in that man's mere presence that's upset Ransford? He looks like a man who's had a nasty, unexpected shock—a bad 'un!"

He remained standing in the archway, gazing after the retreating figure, until Ransford had disappeared within his own garden; still wondering and speculating, but not about his own affairs, he turned across Paradise at last and made his way towards the farther corner. There was a little wicket-gate there, set in the ivied wall; as Bryce opened it, a man in the working dress of a stone-mason, whom he recognized as being one of the master-mason's staff, came running out of the bushes. His face, too, was white, and his eyes were big with excitement. And recognizing Bryce, he halted, panting.

"What is it, Varner?" asked Bryce calmly. "Something happened?"

The man swept his hand across his forehead as if he were dazed, and then jerked his thumb over his shoulder.

"A man!" he gasped. "Foot of St. Wrytha's Stair there, doctor. Dead—or if not dead, near it. I saw it!"

Bryce seized Varner's arm and gave it a shake.

"You saw—what?" he demanded.

"Saw him—fall. Or rather—flung!" panted Varner. "Somebody—couldn't see who, no how—flung him right through yon doorway, up there. He fell right over the steps—crash!" Bryce looked over the tops of the yews and cypresses at the doorway in the clerestory to which Varner pointed—a low, open archway gained by the half-ruinous stair. It was forty feet at least from the ground.

"You saw him—thrown!" he exclaimed. "Thrown—down there? Impossible, man!"

"Tell you I saw it!" asserted Varner doggedly. "I was looking at one of those old tombs yonder—somebody wants some repairs doing—and the jackdaws were making such a to-do up there by the roof I glanced up at them. And I saw this man thrown through that door—fairly flung through it! God!—do you think I could mistake my own eyes?"

"Did you see who flung him?" asked Bryce.

"No; I saw a hand—just for one second, as it might be—by the edge of the doorway," answered Varner. "I was more for watching him! He sort of tottered for a second on the step outside the door, turned over and screamed—I can hear it now!—and crashed down on the flags beneath."

"How long since?" demanded Bryce.

"Five or six minutes," said Varner. "I rushed to him—I've been doing what I could. But I saw it was no good, so I was running for help—"

Bryce pushed him towards the bushes by which they were standing.

"Take me to him," he said. "Come on!"

Varner turned back, making a way through the cypresses. He led Bryce to the foot of the great wall of the nave. There in the corner formed by the angle of nave and transept, on a broad pavement of flagstones, lay the body of a man crumpled up in a curiously twisted position. And with one glance, even before he reached it, Bryce knew what body it was—that of the man who had come, shyly and furtively, to Ransford's door.

"Look!" exclaimed Varner, suddenly pointing. "He's stirring!"

Bryce, whose gaze was fastened on the twisted figure, saw a slight movement which relaxed as suddenly as it had occurred. Then came stillness. "That's the end!" he muttered. "The man's dead! I'll guarantee that before I put a hand on him. Dead enough!" he went on, as he reached the body and dropped on one knee by it. "His neck's broken."

The mason bent down and looked, half-curiously, half-fearfully, at the dead man. Then he glanced upward—at the open door high above them in the walls.

"It's a fearful drop, that, sir," he said. "And he came down with such violence. You're sure it's over with him?"

"He died just as we came up," answered Bryce. "That movement we saw was the last effort—involuntary, of course. Look here, Varner!—you'll have to get help. You'd better fetch some of the cathedral people—some of the vergers. No!" he broke off suddenly, as the low strains of an organ came from within the great building. "They're just beginning the morning service—of course, it's ten o'clock. Never mind them—go straight to the police. Bring them back—I'll stay here."

The mason turned off towards the gateway of the Close, and while the strains of the organ grew louder, Bryce bent over the dead man, wondering what had really happened. Thrown from an open doorway in the clerestory over St. Wrytha's Stair?—it seemed almost impossible! But a sudden thought struck him: supposing two men, wishing to talk in privacy unobserved, had gone up into the clerestory of the Cathedral—as they easily could, by more than one door, by more than one stair—and supposing they had quarreled, and one of them had flung or pushed the other through the door above—what then? And on the heels of that thought hurried another—this man, now lying dead, had come to the surgery, seeking Ransford, and had subsequently gone away, presumably in search of him, and Bryce himself had just seen Ransford, obviously agitated and pale of cheek, leaving the west porch; what did it all mean? what was the apparently obvious inference to be drawn? Here was the stranger dead—and Varner was ready to swear that he had seen him thrown, flung violently, through the door forty feet above. That was—murder! Then—who was the murderer?

Bryce looked carefully and narrowly around him. Now that Varner had gone away, there was not a human being in sight, nor anywhere near, so far as he knew. On one side of him and the dead man rose the grey walls of nave and transept; on the other, the cypresses and yews rising amongst the old tombs and monuments. Assuring himself that no one was near, no eye watching, he slipped his hand into the inner breast pocket of the dead man's smart morning coat. Such a man must carry papers—papers would reveal something. And Bryce wanted to know anything—anything that would give information and let him into whatever secret there might be between this unlucky stranger and Ransford.

But the breast pocket was empty; there was no pocket-book there; there were no papers there. Nor were there any papers elsewhere in the other pockets which he hastily searched: there was not even a card with a name on it. But he found a purse, full of money—banknotes, gold, silver—and in one of its compartments a scrap of paper folded curiously, after the fashion of the cocked-hat missives of another age in which envelopes had not been invented. Bryce hurriedly unfolded this, and after one glance at its contents, made haste to secrete it in his own pocket. He had only just done this and put back the purse when he heard Varner's voice, and a second later the voice of Inspector Mitchington, a well-known police official. And at that

Bryce sprang to his feet, and when the mason and his companions emerged from the bushes was standing looking thoughtfully at the dead man. He turned to Mitchington with a shake of the head.

"Dead!" he said in a hushed voice. "Died as we got to him. Broken—all to pieces, I should say—neck and spine certainly. I suppose Varner's told you what he saw."

Mitchington, a sharp-eyed, dark-complexioned man, quick of movement, nodded, and after one glance at the body, looked up at the open doorway high above them.

"That the door?" he asked, turning to Varner. "And—it was open?"

"It's always open," answered Varner. "Least-ways, it's been open, like that, all this spring, to my knowledge."

"What is there behind it?" inquired Mitchington.

"Sort of gallery, that runs all-round the nave," replied Varner. "Clerestory gallery—that's what it is. People can go up there and walk around—lots of 'em do—tourists, you know. There's two or three ways up to it—staircases in the turrets."

Mitchington turned to one of the two constables who had followed him.

"Let Varner show you the way up there," he said. "Go quietly—don't make any fuss—the morning service is just beginning. Say nothing to anybody—just take a quiet look around, along that gallery, especially near the door there—and come back here." He looked down at the dead man again as the mason and the constable went away. "A stranger, I should think, doctor—tourist, most likely. But—thrown down! That man Varner is positive. That looks like foul play."

"Oh, there's no doubt of that!" asserted Bryce. "You'll have to go into that pretty deeply. But the inside of the Cathedral's like a rabbit-warren, and whoever threw the man through that doorway no doubt knew how to slip away unobserved. Now, you'll have to remove the body to the mortuary, of course—but just let me fetch Dr. Ransford first. I'd like some other medical man than myself to see him before he's moved—I'll have him here in five minutes."

He turned away through the bushes and emerging upon the Close ran across the lawns in the direction of the house which he had left not twenty minutes before. He had but one idea as he ran—he wanted to see Ransford face to face with the dead man—wanted to watch him, to observe him, to see how he looked, how he behaved. Then he, Bryce, would know—something.

But he was to know something before that. He opened the door of the surgery suddenly, but with his usual quietness of touch. And on the threshold he paused. Ransford, the very picture of despair, stood just within, his face convulsed, beating one hand upon the other.

IV - The Room at the Mitre

In the few seconds which elapsed before Ransford recognized Bryce's presence, Bryce took a careful, if swift, observation of his late employer. That Ransford was visibly upset by something was plain enough to see; his face was still pale, he was muttering to himself, one clenched fist was pounding the open palm of the other hand—altogether, he looked like a man who is suddenly confronted with some fearful difficulty. And when Bryce, having looked long enough to satisfy his wishes, coughed gently, he started in such a fashion as to suggest that his nerves had become unstrung.

"What is it?—what are you doing there?" he demanded almost fiercely. "What do you mean by coming in like that?"

Bryce affected to have seen nothing.

"I came to fetch you," he answered. "There's been an accident in Paradise—man fallen from that door at the head of St. Wrytha's Stair. I wish you'd come—but I may as well tell you that he's past help—dead!"

"Dead! A man?" exclaimed Ransford. "What man? A workman?"

Bryce had already made up his mind about telling Ransford of the stranger's call at the surgery. He would say nothing—at that time at any rate. It was improbable that anyone but himself knew of the call; the side entrance to the surgery was screened from the Close by a shrubbery; it was very unlikely that any passer-by had seen the man call or go away. No—he would keep his knowledge secret until it could be made better use of.

"Not a workman—not a townsman—a stranger," he answered. "Looks like a well-to-do tourist. A slightly-built, elderly man—grey-haired."

Ransford, who had turned to his desk to master himself, looked round with a sudden sharp glance—and for the moment Bryce was taken aback. For he had condemned Ransford—and yet that glance was one of apparently genuine surprise, a glance which almost convinced him, against his will, against only too evident facts, that Ransford was hearing of the Paradise affair for the first time.

"An elderly man—grey-haired—slightly built?" said Ransford. "Dark clothes—silk hat?"

"Precisely," replied Bryce, who was now considerably astonished. "Do you know him?"

"I saw such a man entering the Cathedral, a while ago," answered Ransford. "A stranger, certainly. Come along, then."

He had fully recovered his self-possession by that time, and he led the way from the surgery and across the Close as if he were going on an ordinary professional visit. He kept silence as they walked rapidly towards Paradise, and Bryce was silent, too. He had studied Ransford a good deal during their two years' acquaintanceship, and he knew Ransford's power of repressing and commanding his feelings and concealing his thoughts. And now he decided that the look and start which he had at first taken to be of the nature of genuine astonishment were cunningly assumed, and he was not surprised when, having reached the group of men gathered around the body, Ransford showed nothing but professional interest.

"Have you done anything towards finding out who this unfortunate man is?" asked Ransford, after a brief examination, as he turned to Mitchington. "Evidently a stranger—but he probably has papers on him."

"There's nothing on him—except a purse, with plenty of money in it," answered Mitchington. "I've been through his pockets myself: there isn't a scrap of paper—not even as much as an old letter. But he's evidently a tourist, or something of the sort, and so he'll probably have stayed in the city all night, and I'm going to inquire at the hotels."

"There'll be an inquest, of course," remarked Ransford mechanically. "Well—we can do nothing, Mitchington. You'd better have the body removed to the mortuary." He turned and looked up the broken stairway at the foot of which they were standing. "You say he fell down that?" he asked. "Whatever was he doing up there?"

Mitchington looked at Bryce.

"Haven't you told Dr. Ransford how it was?" he asked.

"No," answered Bryce. He glanced at Ransford, indicating Varner, who had come back with the constable and was standing by. "He didn't fall," he went on, watching Ransford narrowly. "He was violently flung out of that doorway. Varner here saw it."

Ransford's cheek flushed, and he was unable to repress a slight start. He looked at the mason.

"You actually saw it!" he exclaimed. "Why, what did you see?"

"Him!" answered Varner, nodding at the dead man. "Flung, head and heels, clean through that doorway up there. Hadn't a chance to save himself, he hadn't! Just grabbed at—nothing!—and came down. Give a year's wages if I hadn't seen it—and heard him scream."

Ransford was watching Varner with a set, concentrated look.

"Who—flung him?" he asked suddenly. "You say you saw!"

"Aye, sir, but not as much as all that!" replied the mason. "I just saw a hand—and that was all. But," he added, turning to the police with a knowing look, "there's one thing I can swear to—it was a gentleman's hand! I saw the white shirt cuff and a bit of a black sleeve!"

Ransford turned away. But he just as suddenly turned back to the inspector.

"You'll have to let the Cathedral authorities know, Mitchington," he said. "Better get the body removed, though, first—do it now before the morning service is over. And—let me hear what you find out about his identity, if you can discover anything in the city."

He went away then, without another word or a further glance at the dead man. But Bryce had already assured himself of what he was certain was a fact—that a look of unmistakable relief had swept across Ransford's face for the fraction of a second when he knew that there were no papers on the dead man. He himself waited after Ransford had gone; waited until the police had fetched a stretcher, when he personally superintended the removal of the body to the mortuary outside the Close. And there a constable who had come over from the police-station gave a faint hint as to further investigation.

"I saw that poor gentleman last night, sir," he said to the inspector. "He was standing at the door of the Mitre, talking to another gentleman—a tallish man."

"Then I'll go across there," said Mitchington. "Come with me, if you like, Dr. Bryce."

This was precisely what Bryce desired—he was already anxious to acquire all the information he could get. And he walked over the way with the inspector, to the quaint old-world inn which filled almost one side of the little square known as Monday Market, and in at the courtyard, where, looking out of the bow window which had served as an outer bar in the coaching days, they found the landlady of the Mitre, Mrs. Partingley. Bryce saw at once that she had heard the news.

"What's this, Mr. Mitchington?" she demanded as they drew near across the cobble-paved yard. "Somebody's been in to say there's been an accident to a gentleman, a stranger—I hope it isn't one of the two we've got in the house?"

"I should say it is, ma'am," answered the inspector. "He was seen outside here last night by one of our men, anyway."

The landlady uttered an expression of distress, and opening a side-door, motioned them to step into her parlor.

"Which of them is it?" she asked anxiously. "There's two—came together last night, they did—a tall one and a short one. Dear, dear me!—is it a bad accident, now, inspector?"

"The man's dead, ma'am," replied Mitchington grimly. "And we want to know who he is. Have you got his name—and the other gentleman's?"

Mrs. Partingley uttered another exclamation of distress and astonishment, lifting her plump hands in horror. But her business faculties remained alive, and she made haste to produce a big visitors' book and to spread it open before her callers.

"There it is!" she said, pointing to the two last entries. "That's the short gentleman's name—Mr. John Braden, London. And that's the tall one's—Mr. Christopher Dellingham—also London. Tourists, of course—we've never seen either of them before."

"Came together, you say, Mrs. Partingley?" asked Mitchington. "When was that, now?"

"Just before dinner, last night," answered the landlady. "They'd evidently come in by the London train—that gets in at six-forty, as you know. They came here together, and they'd dinner together, and spent the evening together. Of course, we took them for friends. But they didn't go out together this morning, though they'd breakfast together. After breakfast, Mr. Dellingham asked me the way to the old Manor Mill, and he went off there, so I concluded. Mr. Braden, he hung about a bit, studying a local directory I'd lent him, and after a while he asked me if he could hire a trap to take him out to Saxonsteade this afternoon. Of course, I said he could, and he arranged for it to be ready at two-thirty. Then he went out, and across the market towards the Cathedral. And that," concluded Mrs. Partingley, "is about all I know, gentlemen."

"Saxonsteade, eh?" remarked Mitchington. "Did he say anything about his reasons for going there?"

"Well, yes, he did," replied the landlady. "For he asked me if I thought he'd be likely to find the Duke at home at that time of day. I said I knew his Grace was at Saxonsteade just now, and that I should think the middle of the afternoon would be a good time."

"He didn't tell you his business with the Duke?" asked Mitchington.

"Not a word!" said the landlady. "Oh, no!—just that, and no more. But—here's Mr. Dellingham."

Bryce turned to see a tall, broad-shouldered, bearded man pass the window—the door opened and he walked in, to glance inquisitively at the inspector. He turned at once to Mrs. Partingley.

"I hear there's been an accident to that gentleman I came in with last night?" he said. "Is it anything serious? Your ostler says—"

"These gentlemen have just come about it, sir," answered the landlady. She glanced at Mitchington. "Perhaps you'll tell—" she began.

"Was he a friend of yours, sir?" asked Mitchington. "A personal friend?"

"Never saw him in my life before last night!" replied the tall man. "We just chanced to meet in the train coming down from London, got talking, and discovered we were both coming to the same place—Wrychester. So—we came to this house together. No—no friend of mine—not even an acquaintance—previous, of course, to last night. Is—is it anything serious?"

"He's dead, sir," replied Mitchington. "And now we want to know who he is."

"God bless my soul! Dead? You don't say so!" exclaimed Mr. Dellingham. "Dear, dear! Well, I can't help you—don't know him from Adam. Pleasant, well-informed man—seemed to have travelled a great deal in foreign countries. I can tell you this much, though," he went on, as if a sudden recollection had come to him; "I gathered that he'd only just arrived in England—in fact, now I come to think of it, he said as much. Made some remark in the train about the pleasantness of the English landscape, don't you know?—I got an idea that he'd recently come from some country where trees and hedges and green fields aren't much in evidence. But—if you want to know who he is, officer, why don't you search him? He's sure to have papers, cards, and so on about him."

"We have searched him," answered Mitchington. "There isn't a paper, a letter, or even a visiting card on him."

Mr. Dellingham looked at the landlady.

"Bless me!" he said. "Remarkable! But he'd a suit-case, or something of the sort—something light—which he carried up from the railway station himself. Perhaps in that—"

"I should like to see whatever he had," said Mitchington. "We'd better examine his room, Mrs. Partingley."

Bryce presently followed the landlady and the inspector upstairs—Mr. Dellingham followed him. All four went into a bedroom which looked out on Monday Market. And there, on a side-table, lay a small leather suit-case, one which could easily be carried, with its upper half thrown open and back against the wall behind.

The landlady, Mr. Dellingham and Bryce stood silently by while the inspector examined the contents of this the only piece of luggage in the room. There was very little to see—what toilet articles the visitor brought were spread out on the dressing-table—brushes, combs, a case of razors, and the like. And Mitchington nodded sidewise at them as he began to take the articles out of the suit-case.

"There's one thing strikes me at once," he said. "I dare say you gentlemen notice it. All these things are new! This suit-case hasn't been in use very long—see, the leather's almost unworn—and those things on the dressing-table are new. And what there is here looks new, too. There's not much, you see—he evidently had no intention of a long stop. An extra pair of trousers—some shirts—socks—collars—neckties—slippers—handkerchiefs—that's about all. And the first thing to do is to see if the linen's marked with name or initials."

He deftly examined the various articles as he took them out, and in the end shook his head.

"No name—no initials," he said. "But look here—do you see, gentlemen, where these collars were bought? Half a dozen of them, in a box. Paris! There you are—the seller's name, inside the collar, just as in England. Aristide Pujol, 82, Rue des Capucines. And—judging by the look of 'em—I should say these shirts were bought there, too—and the handkerchiefs—and the neckwear—they all have a foreign look. There may be a clue in that—we might trace him in France if we can't in England. Perhaps he is a Frenchman."

"I'll take my oath he isn't!" exclaimed Mr. Dellingham. "However long he'd been out of England he hadn't lost a North-Country accent! He was some sort of a North-Countryman—Yorkshire or Lancashire, I'll go bail. No Frenchman, officer—not he!"

"Well, there's no papers here, anyway," said Mitchington, who had now emptied the suit-case. "Nothing to show who he was. Nothing here, you see, in the way of paper but this old book—what is it—History of Barthorpe."

"He showed me that in the train," remarked Mr. Dellingham. "I'm interested in antiquities and archaeology, and anybody who's long in my society finds it out. We got talking of such things, and he pulled out that book, and told me with great pride, that he'd picked it up from a book-barrow in the street, somewhere in London, for one-and-six. I think," he added musingly, "that what attracted him in it was the old calf binding and the steel frontispiece—I'm sure he'd no great knowledge of antiquities."

Mitchington laid the book down, and Bryce picked it up, examined the title-page, and made a mental note of the fact that Barthorpe was a market-town in the Midlands. And it was on the tip of his tongue to say that if the dead man had no particular interest in antiquities and archaeology, it was somewhat strange that he should have bought a book which was mainly antiquarian, and that it might be that he had so bought it because of a connection between Barthorpe and himself. But he remembered that it was his own policy to keep pertinent facts for his own private consideration, so he said nothing. And Mitchington presently remarking that there was no more to be done there, and ascertaining from Mr. Dellingham that it was his intention to remain in Wrychester for at any rate a few days, they went downstairs again, and Bryce and the inspector crossed over to the police-station.

The news had spread through the heart of the city, and at the police-station doors a crowd had gathered. Just inside two or three principal citizens were talking to the Superintendent—amongst them was Mr. Stephen Folliot, the stepfather of young Bonham—a big, heavy-faced man who had been a resident in the Close for some years, was known to be of great wealth, and had a reputation as a grower of rare roses. He was telling the Superintendent something—and the Superintendent beckoned to Mitchington.

"Mr. Folliot says he saw this gentleman in the Cathedral," he said. "Can't have been so very long before the accident happened, Mr. Folliot, from what you say."

"As near as I can reckon, it would be five minutes to ten," answered Mr. Folliot. "I put it at that because I'd gone in for the morning service, which is at ten. I saw him go up the inside stair to the clerestory gallery—he was looking about him. Five minutes to ten—and it must have happened immediately afterwards."

Bryce heard this and turned away, making a calculation for himself. It had been on the stroke of ten when he saw Ransford hurrying out of the west porch. There was a stairway from the gallery down to that west porch. What, then, was the inference? But for the moment he drew none—instead, he went home to his rooms in Friary Lane, and shutting himself up, drew from his pocket the scrap of paper he had taken from the dead man.

V - The Scrap of Paper

When Bryce, in his locked room, drew that bit of paper from his pocket, it was with the conviction that in it he held a clue to the secret of the morning's adventure. He had only taken a mere glance at it as he withdrew it from the dead man's purse, but he had seen enough of what was written on it to make him certain that it was a document—if such a mere fragment could be called a document—of no ordinary importance. And now he unfolded and laid it flat on his table and looked at it carefully, asking himself what was the real meaning of what he saw.

There was not much to see. The scrap of paper itself was evidently a quarter of a leaf of old-fashioned, stoutish notepaper, somewhat yellow with age, and bearing evidence of having been folded and kept flat in the dead man's purse for some time—the creases were well-defined, the edges were worn and slightly stained by long rubbing against the leather. And in its center were a few words, or, rather abbreviations of words, in Latin, and some figures:

> In Para. Wrycestr. juxt. tumb.
> Ric. Jenk. ex cap. xxiii. xv.

Bryce at first sight took them to be a copy of some inscription but his knowledge of Latin told him, a moment later, that instead of being an inscription, it was a direction. And a very plain direction, too!—he read it easily. In Paradise, at Wrychester, next to, or near, the tomb of Richard Jenkins, or, possibly, Jenkinson, from, or behind, the head, twenty-three, fifteen—inches, most likely. There was no doubt that there was the meaning of the words. What, now, was it that lay behind the tomb of Richard Jenkins, or Jenkinson, in Wrychester Paradise?—in all probability twenty-three inches from the head-stone, and fifteen inches beneath the surface. That was a question which Bryce immediately resolved to find a satisfactory answer to; in the meantime there were other questions which he set down in order on his mental tablets. They were these:

1. Who, really, was the man who had registered at the Mitre under the name of John Braden?
2. Why did he wish to make a personal call on the Duke of Saxonsteade?
3. Was he some man who had known Ransford in time past—and whom Ransford had no desire to meet again?
4. Did Ransford meet him—in the Cathedral?
5. Was it Ransford who flung him to his death down St. Wrytha's Stair?
6. Was that the real reason of the agitation in which he, Bryce, had found Ransford a few moments after the discovery of the body?

There was plenty of time before him for the due solution of these mysteries, reflected Bryce—and for solving another problem which might possibly have some relationship to them—that of the exact connection between Ransford and his two wards. Bryce, in telling Ransford that morning of what was being said amongst the tea-table circles of the old cathedral city, had purposely only told him half a tale. He knew, and had known for months, that the society of the Close was greatly exercised over the position of the Ransford menage. Ransford, a bachelor, a well-preserved, active, alert man who was certainly of no more than middle age and did not look his years, had come to Wrychester only a few years previously, and had never shown any signs of forsaking his single state. No one had ever heard him mention his family or relations; then, suddenly, without warning, he had brought into his house Mary Bewery, a handsome young woman of nineteen, who was said to have only just left school, and her brother Richard, then a boy of sixteen, who had certainly been at a public school of repute and was entered at the famous Dean's School of Wrychester as soon as he came to his new home. Dr. Ransford spoke of these two as his wards, without further explanation; the society of the Close was beginning to want much more explanation. Who were they—these two young people? Was Dr. Ransford their uncle, their cousin—what was he to them? In any case, in the opinion of the elderly ladies who set the tone of society in Wrychester, Miss Bewery was much too young, and far too pretty, to be left without a chaperon. But, up to then, no one had dared to say as much to Dr. Ransford—instead, everybody said it freely behind his back.

Bryce had used eyes and ears in relation to the two young people. He had been with Ransford a year when they arrived; admitted freely to their company, he had soon discovered that whatever relationship existed between them and Ransford, they had none with anybody else—that they knew of. No letters came for them from uncles, aunts, cousins, grandfathers, grandmothers. They appeared to have no memories or reminiscences of relatives, nor of father or mother; there was a curious atmosphere of isolation about them. They had plenty of talk about what might be called their present—their recent schooldays, their youthful experiences, games, pursuits—but none of what, under any circumstances, could have been a very far-distant past. Bryce's quick and attentive ears discovered things—for instance that for many years past Ransford had been in the habit of spending his annual two months' holiday with these two. Year after year—at any rate since the boy's tenth year—he had taken them travelling; Bryce heard scraps of reminiscences of tours in

France, and in Switzerland, and in Ireland, and in Scotland—even as far afield as the far north of Norway. It was easy to see that both boy and girl had a mighty veneration for Ransford; just as easy to see that Ransford took infinite pains to make life something more than happy and comfortable for both. And Bryce, who was one of those men who firmly believe that no man ever does anything for nothing and that self-interest is the mainspring of Life, asked himself over and over again the question which agitated the ladies of the Close: Who are these two, and what is the bond between them and this sort of fairy-godfather-guardian?

And now, as he put away the scrap of paper in a safely-locked desk, Bryce asked himself another question: Had the events of that morning anything to do with the mystery which hung around Dr. Ransford's wards? If it had, then all the more reason why he should solve it. For Bryce had made up his mind that, by hook or by crook, he would marry Mary Bewery, and he was only too eager to lay hands on anything that would help him to achieve that ambition. If he could only get Ransford into his power—if he could get Mary Bewery herself into his power—well and good. Once he had got her, he would be good enough to her—in his way.

Having nothing to do, Bryce went out after a while and strolled round to the Wrychester Club—an exclusive institution, the members of which were drawn from the leisured, the professional, the clerical, and the military circles of the old city. And there, as he expected, he found small groups discussing the morning's tragedy, and he joined one of them, in which was Sackville Bonham, his presumptive rival, who was busily telling three or four other young men what his stepfather, Mr. Folliot, had to say about the event.

"My stepfather says—and I tell you he saw the man," said Sackville, who was noted in Wrychester circles as a loquacious and forward youth; "he says that whatever happened must have happened as soon as ever the old chap got up into that clerestory gallery. Look here!—it's like this. My stepfather had gone in there for the morning service—strict old church-goer he is, you know—and he saw this stranger going up the stairway. He's positive, Mr. Folliot, that it was then five minutes to ten. Now, then, I ask you—isn't he right, my stepfather, when he says that it must have happened at once—immediately?"

"Because that man, Varner, the mason, says he saw the man fall before ten. What?"

One of the group nodded at Bryce.

"I should think Bryce knows what time it happened as well as anybody," he said. "You were first on the spot, Bryce, weren't you?"

"After Varner," answered Bryce laconically. "As to the time—I could fix it in this way—the organist was just beginning a voluntary or something of the sort."

"That means ten o'clock—to the minute—when he was found!" exclaimed Sackville triumphantly. "Of course, he'd fallen a minute or two before that—which proves Mr. Folliot to be right. Now what does that prove? Why, that the old chap's assailant, whoever he was, dogged him along that gallery as soon as he entered, seized him when he got to the open doorway, and flung him through! Clear as—as noonday!"

One of the group, a rather older man than the rest, who was leaning back in a tilted chair, hands in pockets, watching Sackville Bonham smilingly, shook his head and laughed a little.

"You're taking something for granted, Sackie, my son!" he said. "You're adopting the mason's tale as true. But I don't believe the poor man was thrown through that doorway at all—not I!"

Bryce turned sharply on this speaker—young Archdale, a member of a well-known firm of architects.

"You don't?" he exclaimed. "But Varner says he saw him thrown!"

"Very likely," answered Archdale. "But it would all happen so quickly that Varner might easily be mistaken. I'm speaking of something I know. I know every inch of the Cathedral fabric—ought to, as we're always going over it, professionally. Just at that doorway, at the head of St. Wrytha's Stair, the flooring of the clerestory gallery is worn so smooth that it's like a piece of glass—and it slopes! Slopes at a very steep angle, too, to the doorway itself. A stranger walking along there might easily slip, and if the door was open, as it was, he'd be shot out and into space before he knew what was happening."

This theory produced a moment's silence—broken at last by Sackville Bonham.

"Varner says he saw—saw!—a man's hand, a gentleman's hand," insisted Sackville. "He saw a white shirt cuff, a bit of the sleeve of a coat. You're not going to get over that, you know. He's certain of it!"

"Varner may be as certain of it as he likes," answered Archdale, almost indifferently, "and still he may be mistaken. The probability is that Varner was confused by what he saw. He may have had a white shirt cuff and the sleeve of a black coat impressed upon him, as in a flash—and they were probably those of the man who was killed. If, as I suggest, the man slipped, and was shot out of that open doorway, he would execute some violent and curious movements in the effort to save himself in which his arms would play an important part. For one thing, he would certainly throw out an arm—to clutch at anything. That's what Varner most probably saw. There's no evidence whatever that the man was flung down."

Bryce turned away from the group of talkers to think over Archdale's suggestion. If that suggestion had a basis of fact, it destroyed his own theory that Ransford was responsible for the stranger's death. In that case, what was the reason of Ransford's unmistakable agitation on leaving the west porch, and of his attack—equally unmistakable—of nerves in the surgery? But what Archdale had said made him inquisitive, and after he had treated himself—in celebration of his freedom—to an unusually good lunch at the Club, he went round to the Cathedral to make a personal inspection of the gallery in the clerestory.

There was a stairway to that gallery in the corner of the south transept, and Bryce made straight for it—only to find a policeman there, who pointed to a placard on the turret door. "Closed, doctor—by order of the Dean and Chapter," he announced. "Till further orders. The fact was, sir," he went on confidentially, "after the news got out, so many people came crowding in here and up to that gallery that the Dean ordered all the entrances to be shut up at once—nobody's been allowed up since noon."

"I suppose you haven't heard anything of any strange person being seen lurking about up there this morning?" asked Bryce.

"No, sir. But I've had a bit of a talk with some of the vergers," replied the policeman, "and they say it's a most extraordinary thing that none of them ever saw this strange gentleman go up there, nor even heard any scuffle. They say—the vergers—that they were all about at the time, getting ready for the morning service, and they neither saw nor heard. Odd, sir, ain't it?"

"The whole thing's odd," agreed Bryce, and left the Cathedral. He walked round to the wicket gate which admitted to that side of Paradise—to find another policeman posted there. "What!—is this closed, too?" he asked.

"And time, sir," said the man. "They'd ha' broken down all the shrubs in the place if orders hadn't been given! They were mad to see where the gentleman fell—came in crowds at dinnertime."

Bryce nodded, and was turning away, when Dick Bewery came round a corner from the Deanery Walk, evidently keenly excited. With him was a girl of about his own age—a certain characterful young lady whom Bryce knew as Betty Campany, daughter of the librarian to the Dean and Chapter and therefore custodian of one of the most famous cathedral libraries in the country. She, too, was apparently brimming with excitement, and her pretty and vivacious face puckered itself into a frown as the policeman smiled and shook his head.

"Oh, I say, what's that for?" exclaimed Dick Bewery. "Shut up?—what a lot of rot! I say!—can't you let us go in—just for a minute?"

"Not for a pension, sir!" answered the policeman good-naturedly. "Don't you see the notice? The Dean 'ud have me out of the force by tomorrow if I disobeyed orders. No admittance, nowhere, no how! But lor' bless yer!" he added, glancing at the two young people. "There's nothing to see—nothing!—as Dr. Bryce there can tell you."

Dick, who knew nothing of the recent passages between his guardian and the dismissed assistant, glanced at Bryce with interest.

"You were on the spot first, weren't you?" he asked: "Do you think it really was murder?"

"I don't know what it was," answered Bryce. "And I wasn't first on the spot. That was Varner, the mason—he called me." He turned from the lad to glance at the girl, who was peeping curiously over the gate into the yews and cypresses. "Do you think your father's at the Library just now?" he asked. "Shall I find him there?"

"I should think he is," answered Betty Campany. "He generally goes down about this time." She turned and pulled Dick Bewery's sleeve. "Let's go up in the clerestory," she said. "We can see that, anyway."

"Also closed, miss," said the policeman, shaking his head. "No admittance there, neither. The public firmly warned off—so to speak. 'I won't have the Cathedral turned into a peepshow!' that's precisely what I heard the Dean say with my own ears. So—closed!"

The boy and the girl turned away and went off across the Close, and the policeman looked after them and laughed.

"Lively young couple, that, sir!" he said. "What they call healthy curiosity, I suppose? Plenty o' that knocking around in the city today."

Bryce, who had half-turned in the direction of the Library, at the other side of the Close, turned round again.

"Do you know if your people are doing anything about identifying the dead man?" he asked. "Did you hear anything at noon?"

"Nothing but that there'll be inquiries through the newspapers, sir," replied the policeman. "That's the surest way of finding something out. And I did hear Inspector Mitchington say that they'd have to ask the Duke if he knew anything about the poor man—I suppose he'd let fall something about wanting to go over to Saxonsteade."

Bryce went off in the direction of the Library thinking. The newspapers?—yes, no better channel for spreading the news. If Mr. John Braden had relations and friends, they would learn of his sad death through the newspapers, and would come forward. And in that case—

"But it wouldn't surprise me," mused Bryce, "if the name given at the Mitre is an assumed name. I wonder if that theory of Archdale's is a correct one?—however, there'll be more of that at the inquest tomorrow. And in the meantime—let me find out something about the tomb of Richard Jenkins, or Jenkinson—whoever he was."

The famous Library of the Dean and Chapter of Wrychester was housed in an ancient picturesque building in one corner of the Close, wherein, day in and day out, amidst priceless volumes and manuscripts, huge folios and weighty quartos, old prints, and relics of the mediaeval ages, Ambrose Campany, the librarian, was pretty nearly always to be found, ready to show his treasures to the visitors and tourists who came from all parts of the world to see a collection well known to bibliophiles. And Ambrose Campany, a cheery-faced, middle-aged man, with booklover and antiquary written all over him, shock headed, blue-spectacled, was there now, talking to an old man whom Bryce knew as a neighbour of his in Friary Lane—one Simpson Barker, a quiet, meditative old fellow, believed to be a retired tradesman who spent his time in gentle pottering about the city. Bryce, as he entered, caught what Campany was just then saying.

"The most important thing I've heard about it," said Campany, "is—that book they found in the man's suit-case at the Mitre. I'm not a detective—but there's a clue!"

VI - By Misadventure

Old Simpson Harker, who sat near the librarian's table, his hands folded on the crook of his stout walking stick, glanced out of a pair of unusually shrewd and bright eyes at Bryce as he crossed the room and approached the pair of gossipers.

"I think the doctor was there when that book you're speaking of was found," he remarked. "So I understood from Mitchington."

"Yes, I was there," said Bryce, who was not unwilling to join in the talk. He turned to Campany. "What makes you think there's a clue—in that?" he asked.

"Why this," answered the librarian. "Here's a man in possession of an old history of Barthorpe. Barthorpe is a small market-town in the Midlands—Leicestershire, I believe, of no particular importance that I know of, but doubtless with a story of its own. Why should anyone but a Barthorpe man, past or present, be interested in that story so far as to carry an old account of it with him? Therefore, I conclude this stranger was a Barthorpe man. And it's at Barthorpe that I should make inquiries about him."

Simpson Harker made no remark, and Bryce remembered what Mr. Dellingham had said when the book was found.

"Oh, I don't know!" he replied carelessly. "I don't see that that follows. I saw the book—a curious old binding and queer old copper-plates. The man may have picked it up for that reason—I've bought old books myself for less."

"All the same," retorted Campany, "I should make inquiry at Barthorpe. You've got to go on probabilities. The probabilities in this case are that the man was interested in the book because it dealt with his own town."

Bryce turned away towards a wall on which hung a number of charts and plans of Wrychester Cathedral and its precincts—it was to inspect one of these that he had come to the Library. But suddenly remembering that there was a question which he could ask without exciting any suspicion or surmise, he faced round again on the librarian.

"Isn't there a register of burials within the Cathedral?" he inquired. "Some book in which they're put down? I was looking in the Memorials of Wrychester the other day, and I saw some names I want to trace."

Campany lifted his quill pen and pointed to a case of big leather-bound volumes in a far corner of the room.

"Third shelf from the bottom, doctor," he replied. "You'll see two books there—one's the register of all burials within the Cathedral itself up to date: the other's the register of those in Paradise and the cloisters. What names are you wanting to trace?"

But Bryce affected not to hear the last question; he walked over to the place which Campany had indicated, and taking down the second book carried it to an adjacent table. Campany called across the room to him.

"You'll find useful indexes at the end," he said. "They're all brought up to the present time—from four hundred years ago, nearly."

Bryce turned to the index at the end of his book—an index written out in various styles of handwriting. And within a minute he found the name he wanted—there it was plainly before him—Richard Jenkins, died March 8th, 1715: buried, in Paradise, March 10th. He nearly laughed aloud at the ease with which he was tracing out what at first had seemed a difficult matter to investigate. But lest his task should seem too easy, he continued to turn over the leaves of the big folio, and in order to have an excuse if the librarian should ask him any further questions, he memorized some of the names which he saw. And after a while he took the book back to its shelf, and turned to the wall on which the charts and maps were hung. There was one there of Paradise, whereon was marked the site and names of all the tombs and graves in that ancient enclosure; from it he hoped to ascertain the exact position and whereabouts of Richard Jenkins's grave.

But here Bryce met his first check. Down each side of the old chart—dated 1850—there was a tabulated list of the tombs in Paradise. The names of families and persons were given in this list—against each name was a number corresponding with the same number, marked on the various divisions of the chart. And there was no Richard Jenkins on that list—he went over it carefully twice, thrice. It was not there. Obviously, if the tomb of Richard Jenkins, who was buried in Paradise in 1715, was still there, amongst the cypresses and yew trees, the name and inscription on it had vanished, worn away by time and weather, when that chart had been made, a hundred and thirty-five years later. And in that case, what did the memorandum mean which Bryce had found in the dead man's purse?

He turned away at last from the chart, at a loss—and Campany glanced at him.

"Found what you wanted?" he asked.

"Oh, yes!" replied Bryce, primed with a ready answer. "I just wanted to see where the Spelbanks were buried—quite a lot of them, I see."

"Southeast corner of Paradise," said Campany. "Several tombs. I could have spared you the trouble of looking."

"You're a regular encyclopedia about the place," laughed Bryce. "I suppose you know every spout and gargoyle!"

"Ought to," answered the librarian. "I've been fed on it, man and boy, for five-and-forty years."

Bryce made some fitting remark and went out and home to his rooms—there to spend most of the ensuing evening in trying to puzzle out the various mysteries of the day. He got no more light on them then, and he was still exercising his brains on them when he went to the inquest next morning—to find the Coroner's court packed to the doors with an assemblage of townsfolk just as curious as he was. And as he sat there, listening to the preliminaries, and to the evidence of the first witnesses, his active and scheming mind figured to itself, not without much cynical amusement, how a word or two from his lips would go far to solve matters. He thought of what he might tell—if he told all the truth. He thought of what he might get out of Ransford if he, Bryce, were Coroner, or solicitor, and had Ransford in that witness-box. He would ask him on his oath if he knew that dead man—if he had had dealings with him in times past—if he had met and spoken to him on that eventful morning—he would ask him, point-blank, if it was not his hand that had thrown him to his death. But Bryce had no intention of making any revelations just then—as for himself he was going to tell just as much as he pleased and no more. And so he sat and heard—and knew from what he heard that everybody there was in a hopeless fog, and that in all that crowd there was but one man who had any real suspicion of the truth, and that that man was himself.

The evidence given in the first stages of the inquiry was all known to Bryce, and to most people in the court, already. Mr. Dellingham told how he had met the dead man in the train, journeying from London to Wrychester. Mrs. Partingley told how he had arrived at the Mitre, registered in her book as Mr. John Braden, and had next morning asked if he could get a conveyance for Saxonsteade in the afternoon, as he wished to see the Duke. Mr. Folliot testified to having seen him in the Cathedral, going towards one of the stairways leading to the gallery. Varner—most important witness of all up to that point—told of what he had seen. Bryce himself, followed by Ransford, gave medical evidence; Mitchington told of his examination of the dead man's clothing and effects in his room at the Mitre. And Mitchington added the first information which was new to Bryce.

"In consequence of finding the book about Barthorpe in the suit-case," said Mitchington, "we sent a long telegram yesterday to the police there, telling them what had happened, and asking them to make the most careful inquiries at once about any townsman of theirs of the name of John Braden, and to wire us the result of such inquiries this morning. This is their reply, received by us an hour ago. Nothing whatever is known at Barthorpe—which is a very small town—of any person of that name."

So much for that, thought Bryce. He turned with more interest to the next witness—the Duke of Saxonsteade, the great local magnate, a big, bluff man who had been present in court since the beginning of the proceedings, in which he was manifestly highly interested. It was possible that he might be able to tell something of moment—he might, after all, know something of this apparently mysterious stranger, who, for anything that Mrs. Partingley or anybody else could say to the contrary, might have had an appointment and business with him.

But his Grace knew nothing. He had never heard the name of John Braden in his life—so far as he remembered. He had just seen the body of the unfortunate man and had looked carefully at the features. He was not a man of whom he had any knowledge whatever—he could not recollect ever having seen him anywhere at any time. He knew literally nothing of him—could not think of any reason at all why this Mr. John Braden should wish to see him.

"Your Grace has, no doubt, had business dealings with a good many people at one time or another," suggested the Coroner. "Some of them, perhaps, with men whom your Grace only saw for a brief space of time—a few minutes, possibly. You don't remember ever seeing this man in that way?"

"I'm credited with having an unusually good memory for faces," answered the Duke. "And—if I may say so—rightly. But I don't remember this man at all—in fact, I'd go as far as to say that I'm positive I've never—knowingly—set eyes on him in my life."

"Can your Grace suggest any reason at all why he should wish to call on you?" asked the Coroner.

"None! But then," replied the Duke, "there might be many reasons—unknown to me, but at which I can make a guess. If he was an antiquary, there are lots of old things at Saxonsteade which he might wish to see. Or he might be a lover of pictures—our collection is a bit famous, you know. Perhaps he was a bookman—we have some rare editions. I could go on multiplying reasons—but to what purpose?"

"The fact is, your Grace doesn't know him and knows nothing about him," observed the Coroner.

"Just so—nothing!" agreed the Duke and stepped down again.

It was at this stage that the Coroner sent the jurymen away in charge of his officer to make a careful personal inspection of the gallery in the clerestory. And while they were gone there was some commotion caused in the court by the entrance of a police official who conducted to the Coroner a middle-aged, well-dressed man whom Bryce at once set down as a London commercial magnate of some quality. Between the new arrival and the Coroner an interchange of remarks was at once made, shared in presently by some of the officials at the table. And when the jury came back the stranger was at once ushered into the witness-box, and the Coroner turned to the jury and the court.

"We are unexpectedly able to get some evidence of identity, gentlemen," he observed. "The gentleman who has just stepped into the witness-box is Mr. Alexander Chilstone, manager of the London & Colonies Bank, in Threadneedle Street. Mr. Chilstone saw particulars of this matter in the newspapers this morning, and he at once set off to Wrychester to tell us what he knows of the dead man. We are very much obliged to Mr. Chilstone—and when he has been sworn he will perhaps kindly tell us what he can."

In the midst of the murmur of sensation which ran round the court, Bryce indulged himself with a covert look at Ransford who was sitting opposite to him, beyond the table in the center of the room. He saw at once that Ransford, however strenuously he might be fighting to keep his face under control, was most certainly agitated by the Coroner's announcement. His cheeks had paled, his eyes were a little dilated, his lips parted as he stared at the bank-manager—altogether, it was more than mere curiosity that was indicated on his features. And Bryce, satisfied and secretly elated, turned to hear what Mr. Alexander Chilstone had to tell.

That was not much—but it was of considerable importance. Only two days before, said Mr. Chilstone—that was, on the day previous to his death—Mr. John Braden had called at the London & Colonies Bank, of which he, Mr. Chilstone, was manager, and introducing himself as having just arrived in England from Australia, where, he said, he had been living for some years, had asked to be allowed to open an account. He produced some references from agents of the London & Colonies Bank, in Melbourne, which were highly satisfactory; the account being opened, he paid into it a sum of ten thousand pounds in a draft at sight drawn by one of those agents. He drew nothing against this, remarking casually that he had plenty of money in his pocket for the present: he did not even take the cheque-book which was offered him, saying that he would call for it later.

"He did not give us any address in London, nor in England," continued the witness. "He told me that he had only arrived at Charing Cross that very morning, having travelled from Paris during the night. He said that he should settle down for a time at some residential hotel in London, and in the meantime he had one or two calls, or visits, to make in the country: when he returned from them, he said, he would call on me again. He gave me very little information about himself: it was not necessary, for his references from our agents in Australia were quite satisfactory. But he did mention that he had been out there for some years, and had speculated in landed property—he also said that he was now going to settle in England for good. That," concluded Mr. Chilstone, "is all I can tell of my own knowledge. But," he added, drawing a newspaper from his pocket, "here is an advertisement which I noticed in this morning's Times as I came down. You will observe," he said, as he passed it to the Coroner, "that it has certainly been inserted by our unfortunate customer."

The Coroner glanced at a marked passage in the personal column of the Times, and read it aloud:

"The advertisement is as follows," he announced. "'If this meets the eye of old friend Marco, he will learn that Sticker wishes to see him again. Write J. Braden, c/o London & Colonies Bank, Threadneedle Street, London.'"

Bryce was keeping a quiet eye on Ransford. Was he mistaken in believing that he saw him start; that he saw his cheek flush as he heard the advertisement read out? He believed he was not mistaken—but if he was right, Ransford the next instant regained full control of himself and made no sign. And Bryce turned again to Coroner and witness.

But the witness had no more to say—except to suggest that the bank's Melbourne agents should be cabled to for information, since it was unlikely that much more could be got in England. And with that the middle stage of the proceedings ended—and the last one came, watched by Bryce with increasing anxiety. For it was soon evident, from certain remarks made by the Coroner, that the theory which Archdale had put forward at the club in Bryce's hearing the previous day had gained favor with the authorities, and that the visit of the jurymen to the scene of the disaster had been intended by the Coroner to predispose them in behalf of it. And now Archdale himself, as representing the architects who held a retaining fee in connection with the Cathedral, was called to give his opinion—and he gave it in almost the same words which Bryce had heard him use twenty-four hours previously. After him came the master-mason, expressing the same decided conviction—that the real truth was that the pavement of the gallery had at that particular place become so smooth, and was inclined towards the open doorway at such a sharp angle, that the unfortunate man had lost his footing on it, and before he could recover it had been shot out of the arch and over the broken head of St. Wrytha's Stair. And though, at a juryman's wish, Varner was recalled, and stuck stoutly to his original story of having seen a hand which, he protested, was certainly not that of the dead man, it soon became plain that the jury shared the Coroner's belief that Varner in his fright and excitement had been mistaken, and no one was surprised when the foreman, after a very brief consultation with his fellows, announced a verdict of death by misadventure.

"So the city's cleared of the stain of murder!" said a man who sat next to Bryce. "That's a good job, anyway! Nasty thing, doctor, to think of a murder being committed in a cathedral. There'd be a question of sacrilege, of course—and all sorts of complications."

Bryce made no answer. He was watching Ransford, who was talking to the Coroner. And he was not mistaken now—Ransford's face bore all the signs of infinite relief. From—what? Bryce turned, to leave the stuffy, rapidly-emptying court. And as he passed the center table he saw old Simpson Harker, who, after sitting in attentive silence for three hours had come up to it, picked up the "History of

Barthorpe" which had been found in Braden's suit-case and was inquisitively peering at its title-page.

VII - The Double Trail

Pemberton Bryce was not the only person in Wrychester who was watching Ransford with keen attention during these events. Mary Bewery, a young woman of more than usual powers of observation and penetration, had been quick to see that her guardian's distress over the affair in Paradise was something out of the common. She knew Ransford for an exceedingly tender-hearted man, with a considerable spice of sentiment in his composition: he was noted for his more than professional interest in the poorer sort of his patients and had gained a deserved reputation in the town for his care of them. But it was somewhat surprising, even to Mary, that he should be so much upset by the death of a total stranger as to lose his appetite, and, for at any rate a couple of days, be so restless that his conduct could not fail to be noticed by herself and her brother. His remarks on the tragedy were conventional enough—a most distressing affair—a sad fate for the poor fellow—most unexplainable and mysterious, and so on—but his concern obviously went beyond that. He was ill at ease when she questioned him about the facts; almost irritable when Dick Bewery, schoolboy-like, asked him concerning professional details; she was sure, from the lines about his eyes and a worn look on his face, that he had passed a restless night when he came down to breakfast on the morning of the inquest. But when he returned from the inquest she noticed a change—it was evident, to her ready wits, that Ransford had experienced a great relief. He spoke of relief, indeed, that night at dinner, observing that the verdict which the jury had returned had cleared the air of a foul suspicion; it would have been no pleasant matter, he said, if Wrychester Cathedral had gained an unenviable notoriety as the scene of a murder.

"All the same," remarked Dick, who knew all the talk of the town, "Varner persists in sticking to what he's said all along. Varner says—said this afternoon, after the inquest was over—that he's absolutely certain of what he saw, and that he not only saw a hand in a white cuff and black coat sleeve, but that he saw the sun gleam for a second on the links in the cuff, as if they were gold or diamonds. Pretty stiff evidence that, sir, isn't it?"

"In the state of mind in which Varner was at that moment," replied Ransford, "he wouldn't be very well able to decide definitely on what he really did see. His vision would retain confused images. Probably he saw the dead man's hand—he was wearing a black coat and white linen. The verdict was a most sensible one."

No more was said after that, and that evening Ransford was almost himself again. But not quite himself. Mary caught him looking very grave, in evident abstraction, more than once; more than once she heard him sigh heavily. But he said no more of the matter until two days later, when, at breakfast, he announced his intention of attending John Braden's funeral, which was to take place that morning.

"I've ordered the brougham for eleven," he said, "and I've arranged with Dr. Nicholson to attend to any urgent call that comes in between that and noon—so, if there is any such call, you can telephone to him. A few of us are going to attend this poor man's funeral—it would be too bad to allow a stranger to go to his grave unattended, especially after such a fate. There'll be somebody representing the Dean and Chapter, and three or four principal townsmen, so he'll not be quite neglected. And"—here he hesitated and looked a little nervously at Mary, to whom he was telling all this, Dick having departed for school—"there's a little matter I wish you'd attend to—you'll do it better than I should. The man seems to have been friendless; here, at any rate—no relations have come forward, in spite of the publicity—so—don't you think it would be rather—considerate, eh?—to put a wreath, or a cross, or something of that sort on his grave—just to show—you know?"

"Very kind of you to think of it," said Mary. "What do you wish me to do?"

"If you'd go to Gardales', the florists, and order—something fitting, you know," replied Ransford, "and afterwards—later in the day—take it to St. Wigbert's Churchyard—he's to be buried there—take it—if you don't mind—yourself, you know."

"Certainly," answered Mary. "I'll see that it's done."

She would do anything that seemed good to Ransford—but all the same she wondered at this somewhat unusual show of interest in a total stranger. She put it down at last to Ransford's undoubted sentimentality—the man's sad fate had impressed him. And that afternoon the sexton at St. Wigbert's pointed out the new grave to Miss Bewery and Mr. Sackville Bonham, one carrying a wreath and the other a large bunch of lilies. Sackville, chancing to encounter Mary at the florist's, whither he had repaired to execute a commission for his mother, had heard her business, and had been so struck by the notion—or by a desire to ingratiate himself with Miss Bewery—that he had immediately bought flowers himself—to be put down to her account—and insisted on accompanying Mary to the churchyard.

Bryce heard of this tribute to John Braden next day—from Mrs. Folliot, Sackville Bonham's mother, a large lady who dominated certain circles of Wrychester society in several senses. Mrs. Folliot was one of those women who have been gifted by nature with capacity—she was conspicuous in many ways. Her voice was masculine; she stood nearly six feet in her stoutly-soled shoes; her breadth corresponded to her height; her eyes were piercing, her nose Roman; there was not a curate in Wrychester who was not under her thumb, and if the Dean himself saw her coming, he turned hastily into the nearest shop, sweating with fear lest she should follow him. Endued with riches and fortified by assurance, Mrs. Folliot was the presiding spirit in many movements of charity and benevolence; there were people in Wrychester who were unkind enough to say—behind her back—that she was as meddlesome as she was most undoubtedly autocratic, but, as one of her staunchest clerical defenders once pointed out, these grumblers were what might be contemptuously dismissed as five-shilling subscribers. Mrs. Folliot, in her way, was undoubtedly a power—and for reasons of his own Pemberton Bryce, whenever he met her—which was fairly often—was invariably suave and polite.

"Most mysterious thing, this, Dr. Bryce," remarked Mrs. Folliot in her deepest tones, encountering Bryce, the day after the funeral, at the corner of a back street down which she was about to sail on one of her charitable missions, to the terror of any of the women who happened to be caught gossiping. "What, now, should make Dr. Ransford cause flowers to be laid on the grave of a total stranger? A sentimental feeling? Fiddle-de-dee! There must be some reason."

"I'm afraid I don't know what you're talking about, Mrs. Folliot," answered Bryce, whose ears had already lengthened. "Has Dr. Ransford been laying flowers on a grave?—I didn't know of it. My engagement with Dr. Ransford terminated two days ago—so I've seen nothing of him."

"My son, Mr. Sackville Bonham," said Mrs. Folliot, "tells me that yesterday Miss Bewery came into Gardales' and spent a sovereign—actually a sovereign!—on a wreath, which, she told Sackville, she was about to carry, at her guardian's desire, to this strange man's grave. Sackville, who is a warm-hearted boy, was touched—he, too, bought flowers and accompanied Miss Bewery. Most extraordinary! A perfect stranger! Dear me—why, nobody knows who the man was!"

"Except his bank-manager," remarked Bryce, "who says he's holding ten thousand pounds of his."

"That," admitted Mrs. Folliot gravely, "is certainly a consideration. But then, who knows?—the money may have been stolen. Now, really, did you ever hear of a quite respectable man who hadn't even a visiting-card or a letter upon him? And from Australia, too!—where all the people that are wanted run away to! I have actually been tempted to wonder, Dr. Bryce, if Dr. Ransford knew this man—in years gone by? He might have, you know, he might have—certainly! And that, of course, would explain the flowers."

"There is a great deal in the matter that requires explanation, Mrs. Folliot," said Bryce. He was wondering if it would be wise to instill some minute drop of poison into the lady's mind, there to increase in potency and in due course to spread. "I—of course, I may have been mistaken—I certainly thought Dr. Ransford seemed unusually agitated by this affair—it appeared to upset him greatly."

"So I have heard—from others who were at the inquest," responded Mrs. Folliot. "In my opinion our Coroner—a worthy man otherwise—is not sufficiently particular. I said to Mr. Folliot this morning, on reading the newspaper, that in my view that inquest should have been adjourned for further particulars. Now I know of one particular that was never mentioned at the inquest!"

"Oh?" said Bryce. "And what?"

"Mrs. Deramore, who lives, as you know, next to Dr. Ransford," replied Mrs. Folliot, "told me this morning that on the morning of the accident, happening to look out of one of her upper windows, she saw a man whom, from the description given in the newspapers, was, Mrs. Deramore feels assured, was the mysterious stranger, crossing the Close towards the Cathedral in, Mrs. Deramore is positive, a dead straight line from Dr. Ransford's garden—as if he had been there. Dr. Bryce!—a direct question should have been asked of Dr. Ransford—had he ever seen that man before?"

"Ah, but you see, Mrs. Folliot, the Coroner didn't know what Mrs. Deramore saw, so he couldn't ask such a question, nor could anyone else," remarked Bryce, who was wondering how long Mrs. Deramore remained at her upper window and if she saw him follow Braden. "But there are circumstances, no doubt, which ought to be inquired into. And it's certainly very curious that Dr. Ransford should send a wreath to the grave of—a stranger."

He went away convinced that Mrs. Folliot's inquisitiveness had been aroused, and that her tongue would not be idle: Mrs. Folliot, left to herself, had the gift of creating an atmosphere, and if she once got it into her head that there was some mysterious connection between Dr. Ransford and the dead man, she would never rest until she had spread her suspicions. But as for Bryce himself, he wanted more than suspicions—he wanted facts, particulars, data. And once more he began to go over the sum of evidence which had accrued.

The question of the scrap of paper found in Braden's purse, and of the exact whereabouts of Richard Jenkins's grave in Paradise, he left for the time being. What was now interesting him chiefly was the advertisement in the Times to which the bank-manager from London had drawn attention. He had made haste to buy a copy of the Times and to cut out the advertisement. There it was—old friend Marco was wanted by (presumably old friend) Sticker, and whoever Sticker might be he could certainly be found under care of J. Braden. It had never been in doubt a moment, in Bryce's mind, that Sticker was J. Braden himself. Who, now, was Marco? Who—a million to one on it!—but Ransford, whose Christian name was Mark?

He reckoned up his chances of getting at the truth of the affair anew that night. As things were, it seemed unlikely that any relations of Braden would now turn up. The Wrychester Paradise case, as the reporters had aptly named it, had figured largely in the newspapers, London and provincial; it could scarcely have had more publicity—yet no one, save this bank-manager, had come forward. If there had been any one to come forward the bank-manager's evidence would surely have proved an incentive to speed—for there was a sum of ten thousand pounds awaiting John Braden's next-of-kin. In Bryce's opinion the chance of putting in a claim to ten thousand pounds is not left waiting forty-eight hours—whoever saw such a chance would make instant use of telegraph or telephone. But no message from anybody professing relationship with the dead man had so far reached the Wrychester police.

When everything had been taken into account, Bryce saw no better clue for the moment than that suggested by Ambrose Campany—Barthorpe. Ambrose Campany, bookworm though he was, was a shrewd, sharp fellow, said Bryce—a man of ideas. There was certainly much in his suggestion that a man wasn't likely to buy an old book about a little insignificant town like Barthorpe unless he had some interest in it—Barthorpe, if Campany's theory were true, was probably the place of John Braden's origin.

Therefore, information about Braden, leading to knowledge of his association or connection with Ransford, might be found at Barthorpe. True, the Barthorpe police had already reported that they could tell nothing about any Braden, but that, in Bryce's opinion, was neither here nor there—he had already come to the conclusion that Braden was an assumed name. And if he went to Barthorpe, he was not going to trouble the police—he knew better methods than that of finding things out. Was he going? was it worth his while? A moment's reflection decided that matter—anything was worth his while which would help him to get a strong hold on Mark Ransford. And always practical in his doings, he walked round to the Free Library, obtained a gazetteer, and looked up particulars of Barthorpe. There he learnt that Barthorpe was an ancient market-town of two thousand inhabitants in the north of Leicestershire, famous for nothing except that it had been the scene of a battle at the time of the Wars of the Roses, and that its trade was mainly in agriculture and stocking-making—evidently a slow, sleepy old place.

That night Bryce packed a hand-bag with small necessaries for a few days' excursion, and next morning he took an early train to London; the end of that afternoon found him in a Midland northern-bound express, looking out on the undulating, green acres of Leicestershire. And while his train was making a three minutes' stop at Leicester itself, the purpose of his journey was suddenly recalled to him by hearing the strident voices of the porters on the platform.

"Barthorpe next stop!—next stop Barthorpe!"

One of two other men who shared a smoking compartment with Bryce turned to his companion as the train moved off again.

"Barthorpe?" he remarked. "That's the place that was mentioned in connection with that very queer affair at Wrychester, that's been reported in the papers so much these last few days. The mysterious stranger who kept ten thousand in a London bank, and of whom nobody seems to know anything, had nothing on him but a history of Barthorpe. Odd! And yet, though you'd think he'd some connection with the place, or had known it, they say nobody at Barthorpe knows anything about anybody of his name."

"Well, I don't know that there is anything so very odd about it, after all," replied the other man. "He may have picked up that old book for one of many reasons that could be suggested. No—I read all that case in the papers, and I wasn't so much impressed by the old book feature of it. But I'll tell you what—there was a thing struck me. I know this Barthorpe district—we shall be in it in a few minutes—I've been a good deal over it. This strange man's name was given in the papers as John Braden. Now close to Barthorpe—a mile or two outside it, there's a village of that name—Braden Medworth. That's a curious coincidence—and taken in conjunction with the man's possession of an old book about Barthorpe—why, perhaps there's something in it—possibly more than I thought for at first."

"Well—it's an odd case—a very odd case," said the first speaker. "And—as there's ten thousand pounds in question, more will be heard of it. Somebody'll be after that, you may be sure!"

Bryce left the train at Barthorpe thanking his good luck—the man in the far corner had unwittingly given him a hint. He would pay a visit to Braden Medworth—the coincidence was too striking to be neglected. But first Barthorpe itself— a quaint old-world little market-town, in which some of even the principal houses still wore roofs of thatch, and wherein the old custom of ringing the curfew bell was kept up. He found an old-fashioned hotel in the marketplace, under the shadow of the parish church, and in its oak-paneled dining-room, hung about with portraits of masters of foxhounds and queer old prints of sporting and coaching days, he dined comfortably and well.

It was too late to attempt any investigations that evening, and when Bryce had finished his leisurely dinner he strolled into the smoking-room—an even older and quainter apartment than that which he had just left. It was one of those rooms only found in very old houses—a room of nooks and corners, with a great open fireplace, and old furniture and old pictures and curiosities—the sort of place to which the old-fashioned tradesmen of the small provincial towns still resort of an evening rather than patronize the modern political clubs. There were several men of this sort in the room when Bryce entered, talking local politics amongst themselves, and he found a quiet corner and sat down in it to smoke, promising himself some amusement from the conversation around him; it was his way to find interest and amusement in anything that offered. But he had scarcely settled down in a comfortably cushioned elbow chair when the door opened again and into the room walked old Simpson Harker.

VIII - The Best Man

Old Harker's shrewd eyes, travelling round the room as if to inspect the company in which he found himself, fell almost immediately on Bryce—but not before Bryce had had time to assume an air and look of innocent and genuine surprise. Harker affected no surprise at all—he looked the astonishment he felt as the younger man rose and motioned him to the comfortable easy-chair which he himself had just previously taken.

"Dear me!" he exclaimed, nodding his thanks. "I'd no idea that I should meet you in these far-off parts, Dr. Bryce! This is a long way from Wrychester, sir, for Wrychester folk to meet in."

"I'd no idea of meeting you, Mr. Harker," responded Bryce. "But it's a small world, you know, and there are a good many coincidences in it. There's nothing very wonderful in my presence here, though—I ran down to see after a country practice—I've left Dr. Ransford."

He had the lie ready as soon as he set eyes on Harker, and whether the old man believed it or not, he showed no sign of either belief or disbelief. He took the chair which Bryce drew forward and pulled out an old-fashioned cigar-case, offering it to his companion.

"Will you try one, doctor?" he asked. "Genuine stuff that, sir—I've a friend in Cuba who remembers me now and then. No," he went on, as Bryce thanked him and took a cigar, "I didn't know you'd finished with the doctor. Quietish place this to practice in, I should think—much quieter even than our sleepy old city."

"You know it?" inquired Bryce.

"I've a friend lives here—old friend of mine," answered Harker. "I come down to see him now and then—I've been here since yesterday. He does a bit of business for me. Stopping long, doctor?"

"Only just to look round," answered Bryce.

"I'm off tomorrow morning—eleven o'clock," said Harker. "It's a longish journey to Wrychester—for old bones like mine."

"Oh, you're all right!—worth half a dozen younger men," responded Bryce. "You'll see a lot of your contemporaries out, Mr. Harker. Well—as you've treated me to a very fine cigar, now you'll let me treat you to a drop of whisky?—they generally have something of pretty good quality in these old-fashioned establishments, I believe."

The two travelers sat talking until bedtime—but neither made any mention of the affair which had recently set all Wrychester agog with excitement. But Bryce was wondering all the time if his companion's story of having a friend at Barthorpe was no more than an excuse, and when he was alone in his own bedroom and reflecting more seriously he came to the conclusion that old Harker was up to some game of his own in connection with the Paradise mystery.

"The old chap was in the Library when Ambrose Campany said that there was a clue in that Barthorpe history," he mused. "I saw him myself examining the book after the inquest. No, no, Mr. Harker!—the facts are too plain—the evidences too obvious. And yet—what interest has a retired old tradesman of Wrychester got in this affair? I'd give a good deal to know what Harker really is doing here—and who his Barthorpe friend is."

If Bryce had risen earlier next morning, and had taken the trouble to track old Harker's movements, he would have learnt something that would have made him still more suspicious. But Bryce, seeing no reason for hurry, lay in bed till well past nine o'clock, and did not present himself in the coffee-room until nearly half-past ten. And at that hour Simpson Harker, who had breakfasted before nine, was in close consultation with his friend—that friend being none other than the local superintendent of police, who was confidentially closeted with the old man in his private house, whither Harker, by previous arrangement, had repaired as soon as his breakfast was over. Had Bryce been able to see through walls or hear through windows, he would have been surprised to find that the Harker of this consultation was not the quiet, easy-going, gossipy old gentleman of Wrychester, but an eminently practical and business-like man of affairs.

"And now as regards this young fellow who's staying across there at the Peacock," he was saying in conclusion, at the very time that Bryce was leisurely munching his second mutton chop in the Peacock coffee-room, "he's after something or other—his talk about coming here to see after a practice is all lies!—and you'll keep an eye on him while he's in your neighborhood. Put your best plain-clothes man on to him at once—he'll easily know him from the description I gave you—and let him shadow him wherever he goes. And then let me know of his movement—he's certainly on the track of something, and what he does may be useful to me—I can link it up with my own work. And as regards the other matter—keep me informed if you come on anything further. Now I'll go out by your garden and down the back of the town to the station. Let me know, by the by, when this young man at the Peacock leaves here, and, if possible—and you can find out—for where."

Bryce was all unconscious that anyone was interested in his movements when he strolled out into Barthorpe market-place just after eleven. He had asked a casual question of the waiter and found that the old gentleman had departed—he accordingly believed himself free from observation. And forthwith he set about his work of inquiry in his own fashion. He was not going to draw any attention to himself by asking questions of present-day inhabitants, whose curiosity might then be aroused;

he knew better methods than that. Every town, said Bryce to himself, possesses public records—parish registers, burgess rolls, lists of voters; even small towns have directories which are more or less complete—he could search these for any mention or record of anybody or any family of the name of Braden. And he spent all that day in that search, inspecting numerous documents and registers and books, and when evening came he had a very complete acquaintance with the family nomenclature of Barthorpe, and he was prepared to bet odds against any one of the name of Braden having lived there during the past half-century. In all his searching he had not once come across the name.

The man who had spent a very lazy day in keeping an eye on Bryce, as he visited the various public places whereat he made his researches, was also keeping an eye upon him next morning, when Bryce, breakfasting earlier than usual, prepared for a second day's labours. He followed his quarry away from the little town: Bryce was walking out to Braden Medworth. In Bryce's opinion, it was something of a wild-goose chase to go there, but the similarity in the name of the village and of the dead man at Wrychester might have its significance, and it was but a two miles' stroll from Barthorpe. He found Braden Medworth a very small, quiet, and picturesque place, with an old church on the banks of a river which promised good sport to anglers. And there he pursued his tactics of the day before and went straight to the vicarage and its vicar, with a request to be allowed to inspect the parish registers. The vicar, having no objection to earning the resultant fees, hastened to comply with Bryce's request, and inquired how far back he wanted to search and for what particular entry.

"No particular entry," answered Bryce, "and as to period—fairly recent. The fact is, I am interested in names. I am thinking"—here he used one more of his easily found inventions—"of writing a book on English surnames, and am just now inspecting parish registers in the Midlands for that purpose."

"Then I can considerably simplify your labours," said the vicar, taking down a book from one of his shelves. "Our parish registers have been copied and printed, and here is the volume—everything is in there from 1570 to ten years ago, and there is a very full index. Are you staying in the neighborhood—or the village?"

"In the neighborhood, yes; in the village, no longer than the time I shall spend in getting some lunch at the inn yonder," answered Bryce, nodding through an open window at an ancient tavern which stood in the valley beneath, close to an old stone bridge. "Perhaps you will kindly lend me this book for an hour?—then, if I see anything very noteworthy in the index, I can look at the actual registers when I bring it back."

The vicar replied that that was precisely what he had been about to suggest, and Bryce carried the book away. And while he sat in the inn parlor awaiting his lunch, he turned to the carefully-compiled index, glancing it through rapidly. On the third page he saw the name Bewery.

If the man who had followed Bryce from Barthorpe to Braden Medworth had been with him in the quiet inn parlor he would have seen his quarry start, and heard him let a stifled exclamation escape his lips. But the follower, knowing his man was safe for an hour, was in the bar outside eating bread and cheese and drinking ale, and Bryce's surprise was witnessed by no one. Yet he had been so much surprised that if all Wrychester had been there he could not, despite his self-training in watchfulness, have kept back either start or exclamation.

Bewery! A name so uncommon that here—here, in this out-of-the-way Midland village!—there must be some connection with the object of his search. There the name stood out before him, to the exclusion of all others—Bewery—with just one entry of figures against it. He turned to page 387 with a sense of sure discovery.

And there an entry caught his eye at once—and he knew that he had discovered more than he had ever hoped for. He read it again and again, gloating over his wonderful luck.

June 19th, 1891. John Brake, bachelor, of the parish of St. Pancreas, London, to Mary Bewery, spinster, of this parish, by the Vicar. Witnesses, Charles Claybourne, Selina Womersley, Mark Ransford.

Twenty-two years ago! The Mary Bewery whom Bryce knew in Wrychester was just about twenty—this Mary Bewery, spinster, of Braden Medworth, was, then, in all probability, her mother. But John Brake who married that Mary Bewery—who was he? Who indeed, laughed Bryce, but John Braden, who had just come by his death in Wrychester Paradise? And there was the name of Mark Ransford as witness. What was the further probability? That Mark Ransford had been John Brake's best man; that he was the Marco of the recent Times advertisement; that John Braden, or Brake, was the Sticker of the same advertisement. Clear!—clear as noonday! And—what did it all mean, and imply, and what bearing had it on Braden or Brake's death?

Before he ate his cold beef, Bryce had copied the entry from the reprinted register, and had satisfied himself that Ransford was not a name known to that village—Mark Ransford was the only person of the name mentioned in the register. And his lunch done, he set off for the vicarage again, intent on getting further information, and before he reached the vicarage gates noticed, by accident, a place whereat he was more likely to get it than from the vicar—who was a youngish man. At the end of the few houses between the inn and the bridge he saw a little shop with the name Charles Claybourne painted roughly above its open window. In that open window sat an old, cheery-faced man, mending shoes, who blinked at the stranger through his big spectacles.

Bryce saw his chance and turned in—to open the book and point out the marriage entry.

"Are you the Charles Claybourne mentioned there?" he asked, without ceremony.

"That's me, sir!" replied the old shoemaker briskly, after a glance. "Yes—right enough!"

"How came you to witness that marriage?" inquired Bryce.

The old man nodded at the church across the way.

"I've been sexton and parish clerk two-and-thirty years, sir," he said. "And I took it on from my father—and he had the job from his father."

"Do you remember this marriage?" asked Bryce, perching himself on the bench at which the shoemaker was working. "Twenty-two years since, I see."

"Aye, as if it was yesterday!" answered the old man with a smile. "Miss Bewery's marriage?—why, of course!"

"Who was she?" demanded Bryce.

"Governess at the vicarage," replied Claybourne. "Nice, sweet young lady."

"And the man she married?—Mr. Brake," continued Bryce. "Who was he?"

"A young gentleman that used to come here for the fishing, now and then," answered Claybourne, pointing at the river. "Famous for our trout we are here, you know, sir. And Brake had come here for three years before they were married—him and his friend Mr. Ransford."

"You remember him, too?" asked Bryce.

"Remember both of 'em very well indeed," said Claybourne, "though I never set eyes on either after Miss Mary was wed to Mr. Brake. But I saw plenty of 'em both before that. They used to put up at the inn there—that I saw you come out of just now. They came two or three times a year—and they were a bit thick with our parson of that time—not this one: his predecessor—and they used to go up to the vicarage and smoke their pipes and cigars with him—and of course, Mr. Brake and the governess fixed it up. Though, you know, at one time it was considered it was going to be her and the other young gentleman, Mr. Ransford—yes! But, in the end, it was Brake—and Ransford stood best man for him."

Bruce assimilated all this information greedily—and asked for more.

"I'm interested in that entry," he said, tapping the open book. "I know some people of the name of Bewery—they may be relatives."

The shoemaker shook his head as if doubtful.

"I remember hearing it said," he remarked, "that Miss Mary had no relations. She'd been with the old vicar some time, and I don't remember any relations ever coming to see her, nor her going away to see any."

"Do you know what Brake was?" asked Bryce. "As you say he came here for a good many times before the marriage, I suppose you'd hear something about his profession, or trade, or whatever it was?"

"He was a banker, that one," replied Claybourne. "A banker—that was his trade, sir. T'other gentleman, Mr. Ransford, he was a doctor—I mind that well enough, because once when him and Mr. Brake were fishing here, Thomas Joynt's wife fell downstairs and broke her leg, and they fetched him to her—he'd got it set before they'd got the reg'lar doctor out from Barthorpe yonder."

Bryce had now got all the information he wanted, and he made the old parish clerk a small present and turned to go. But another question presented itself to his mind and he reentered the little shop.

"Your late vicar?" he said. "The one in whose family Miss Bewery was governess—where is he now? Dead?"

"Can't say whether he's dead or alive, sir," replied Claybourne. "He left this parish for another—a living in a different part of England—some years since, and I haven't heard much of him from that time to this—he never came back here once, not even to pay us a friendly visit—he was a queerish sort. But I'll tell you what, sir," he added, evidently anxious to give his visitor good value for his half-crown, "our present vicar has one of those books with the names of all the clergymen in 'em, and he'd tell you where his predecessor is now, if he's alive—name of Reverend Thomas Gilwaters, M.A.—an Oxford college man he was, and very high learned."

Bryce went back to the vicarage, returned the borrowed book, and asked to look at the registers for the year 1891. He verified his copy and turned to the vicar.

"I accidentally came across the record of a marriage there in which I'm interested," he said as he paid the search fees. "Celebrated by your predecessor, Mr. Gilwaters. I should be glad to know where Mr. Gilwaters is to be found. Do you happen to possess a clerical directory?"

The vicar produced a "Crockford" and Bryce turned over its pages. Mr. Gilwaters, who from the account there given appeared to be an elderly man who had now retired, lived in London, in Bayswater, and Bryce made a note of his address and prepared to depart.

"Find any names that interested you?" asked the vicar as his caller left. "Anything noteworthy?"

"I found two or three names which interested me immensely," answered Bryce from the foot of the vicarage steps. "They were well worth searching for."

And without further explanation he marched off to Barthorpe duly followed by his shadow, who saw him safely into the Peacock an hour later—and, an hour after that, went to the police superintendent with his report.

"Gone, sir," he said. "Left by the five-thirty express for London."

IX - The House of His Friend

Bryce found himself at eleven o'clock next morning in a small book-lined parlor in a little house which stood in a quiet street in the neighborhood of Westbourne Grove. Over the mantelpiece, amongst other odds and ends of pictures and photographs, hung a watercolor drawing of Braden Medworth—and to him presently entered an old, silver-haired clergyman whom he at once took to be Braden Medworth's former vicar, and who glanced inquisitively at his visitor and then at the card which Bryce had sent in with a request for an interview.

"Dr. Bryce?" he said inquiringly. "Dr. Pemberton Bryce?"

Bryce made his best bow and assumed his suavest and most ingratiating manner.

"I hope I am not intruding on your time, Mr. Gilwaters?" he said. "The fact is, I was referred to you, yesterday, by the present vicar of Braden Medworth—both he, and the sexton there, Claybourne, whom you, of course, remember, thought you would be able to give me some information on a subject which is of great importance—to me."

"I don't know the present vicar," remarked Mr. Gilwaters, motioning Bryce to a chair, and taking another close by. "Clayborne, of course, I remember very well indeed—he must be getting an old man now—like myself! What is it you want to know, now?"

"I shall have to take you into my confidence," replied Bryce, who had carefully laid his plans and prepared his story, "and you, I am sure, Mr. Gilwaters, will respect mine. I have for two years been in practice at Wrychester, and have there made the acquaintance of a young lady whom I earnestly desire to marry. She is the ward of the man to whom I have been assistant. And I think you will begin to see why I have come to you when I say that this young lady's name is—Mary Bewery."

The old clergyman started, and looked at his visitor with unusual interest. He grasped the arm of his elbow chair and leaned forward.

"Mary Bewery!" he said in a low whisper. "What—what is the name of the man who is her—guardian?"

"Dr. Mark Ransford," answered Bryce promptly.

The old man sat upright again, with a little toss of his head.

"Bless my soul!" he exclaimed. "Mark Ransford! Then—it must have been as I feared—and suspected!"

Bryce made no remark. He knew at once that he had struck on something, and it was his method to let people take their own time. Mr. Gilwaters had already fallen into something closely resembling a reverie: Bryce sat silently waiting and expectant. And at last the old man leaned forward again, almost eagerly.

"What is it you want to know?" he asked, repeating his first question. "Is—is there some—some mystery?"

"Yes!" replied Bryce. "A mystery that I want to solve, sir. And I dare say that you can help me, if you'll be so good. I am convinced—in fact, I know!—that this young lady is in ignorance of her parentage, that Ransford is keeping some fact, some truth back from her—and I want to find things out. By the merest chance—accident, in fact—I discovered yesterday at Braden Medworth that some twenty-two years ago you married one Mary Bewery, who, I learnt there, was your governess, to a John Brake, and that Mark Ransford was John Brake's best man and a witness of the marriage. Now, Mr. Gilwaters, the similarity in names is too striking to be devoid of significance. So—it's of the utmost importance to me!—can or will you tell me—who was the Mary Bewery you married to John Brake? Who was John Brake? And what was Mark Ransford to either, or to both?"

He was wondering, all the time during which he reeled off these questions, if Mr. Gilwaters was wholly ignorant of the recent affair at Wrychester. He might be—a glance round his book-filled room had suggested to Bryce that he was much more likely to be a bookworm than a newspaper reader, and it was quite possible that the events of the day had small interest for him. And his first words in reply to Bryce's questions convinced Bryce that his surmise was correct and that the old man had read nothing of the Wrychester Paradise mystery, in which Ransford's name had, of course, figured as a witness at the inquest.

"It is nearly twenty years since I heard any of their names," remarked Mr. Gilwaters. "Nearly twenty years—a long time! But, of course, I can answer you. Mary Bewery was our governess at Braden Medworth. She came to us when she was nineteen—she was married four years later. She was a girl who had no friends or relatives—she had been educated at a school in the North—I engaged her from that school, where, I understood, she had lived since infancy. Now then, as to Brake and Ransford. They were two young men from London, who used to come fishing in Leicestershire. Ransford was a few years the younger—he was either a medical student in his last year, or he was an assistant somewhere in London. Brake—was a bank manager in London—of a branch of one of the big banks. They were pleasant young fellows, and I used to ask them to the vicarage. Eventually, Mary Bewery and John Brake became engaged to be married. My wife and I were a good deal surprised—we had believed, somehow, that the favoured man would be Ransford. However, it was Brake—and Brake she married, and, as you say, Ransford was best man. Of course, Brake took his wife off to London—and from the day of her wedding, I never saw her again."

"Did you ever see Brake again?" asked Bryce. The old clergyman shook his head.

"Yes!" he said sadly. "I did see Brake again—under grievous, grievous circumstances!"

"You won't mind telling me what circumstances?" suggested Bryce. "I will keep your confidence, Mr. Gilwaters."

"There is really no secret in it—if it comes to that," answered the old man. "I saw John Brake again just once. In a prison cell!"

"A prison cell!" exclaimed Bryce. "And he—a prisoner?"

"He had just been sentenced to ten years' penal servitude," replied Mr. Gilwaters. "I had heard the sentence—I was present. I got leave to see him. Ten years' penal servitude!—a terrible punishment. He must have been released long ago—but I never heard more."

Bryce reflected in silence for a moment—reckoning and calculating.

"When was this—the trial?" he asked.

"It was five years after the marriage—seventeen years ago," replied Mr. Gilwaters.

"And—what had he been doing?" inquired Bryce.

"Stealing the bank's money," answered the old man. "I forget what the technical offence was—embezzlement, or something of that sort. There was not much evidence came out, for it was impossible to offer any defense, and he pleaded guilty. But I gathered from what I heard that something of this sort occurred. Brake was a branch manager. He was, as it were, pounced upon one morning by an inspector, who found that his cash was short by two or three thousand pounds. The bank people seemed to have been unusually strict and even severe—Brake, it was said, had some explanation, but it was swept aside and he was given in charge. And the sentence was as I said just now—a very savage one, I thought. But there had recently been some bad cases of that sort in the banking world, and I suppose the judge felt that he must make an example. Yes—a most trying affair!—I have a report of the case somewhere, which I cut out of a London newspaper at the time."

Mr. Gilwaters rose and turned to an old desk in the corner of his room, and after some rummaging of papers in a drawer, produced a newspaper-cutting book and traced an insertion in its pages. He handed the book to his visitor.

"There is the account," he said. "You can read it for yourself. You will notice that in what Brake's counsel said on his behalf there are one or two curious and mysterious hints as to what might have been said if it had been of any use or advantage to say it. A strange case!"

Bryce turned eagerly to the faded scrap of newspaper.

BANK MANAGER'S DEFALCATION

At the Central Criminal Court yesterday, John Brake, thirty-three, formerly manager of the Upper Tooting branch of the London & Home Counties Bank, Ltd., pleaded guilty to embezzling certain sums, the property of his employers. Mr. Walkinshaw, Q.C., addressing the court on behalf of the prisoner, said that while it was impossible for his client to offer any defense, there were circumstances in the case which, if it had been worthwhile to put them in evidence, would have shown that the prisoner was a wronged and deceived man. To use a Scriptural phrase, Brake had been wounded in the house of his friend. The man who was really guilty in this affair had cleverly escaped all consequences, nor would it be of the least use to enter into any details respecting him. Not one penny of the money in question had been used by the prisoner for his own purposes. It was doubtless a wrong and improper thing that his client had done, and he had pleaded guilty and would submit to the consequences. But if everything in connection with the case could have been told, if it would have served any useful purpose to tell it, it would have been seen that what the prisoner really was guilty of was a foolish and serious error of judgment. He himself, concluded the learned counsel, would go so far as to say that, knowing what he did, knowing what had been told him by his client in strict confidence, the prisoner, though technically guilty, was morally innocent. His Lordship, merely remarking that no excuse of any sort could be offered in a case of this sort, sentenced the prisoner to ten years' penal servitude.

Bryce read this over twice before handing back the book.
"Very strange and mysterious, Mr. Gilwaters," he remarked. "You say that you saw Brake after the case was over. Did you learn anything?"
"Nothing whatever!" answered the old clergyman. "I got permission to see him before he was taken away. He did not seem particularly pleased or disposed to see me. I begged him to tell me what the real truth was. He was, I think, somewhat dazed by the sentence—but he was also sullen and morose. I asked him where his wife and two children—one, a mere infant—were. For I had already been to his private address and had found that Mrs. Brake had sold all the furniture and disappeared—completely. No one—thereabouts, at any rate—knew where she was, or would tell me anything. On my asking this, he refused to answer. I pressed him—he said finally that he was only speaking the truth when he replied that he did not know

where his wife was. I said I must find her. He forbade me to make any attempt. Then I begged him to tell me if she was with friends. I remember very well what he replied.—'I'm not going to say one word more to any man living, Mr. Gilwaters,' he answered determinedly. 'I shall be dead to the world—only because I've been a trusting fool!—for ten years or thereabouts, but, when I come back to it, I'll let the world see what revenge means! Go away!' he concluded. 'I won't say one word more.' And—I left him."

"And—you made no more inquiries?—about the wife?" asked Bryce.

"I did what I could," replied Mr. Gilwaters. "I made some inquiry in the neighborhood in which they had lived. All I could discover was that Mrs. Brake had disappeared under extraordinarily mysterious circumstances. There was no trace whatever of her. And I speedily found that things were being said—the usual cruel suspicions, you know."

"Such as—what?" asked Bryce.

"That the amount of the defalcations was much larger than had been allowed to appear," replied Mr. Gilwaters. "That Brake was a very clever rogue who had got the money safely planted somewhere abroad, and that his wife had gone off somewhere—Australia, or Canada, or some other far-off region—to await his release. Of course, I didn't believe one word of all that. But there was the fact—she had vanished! And eventually, I thought of Ransford, as having been Brake's great friend, so I tried to find him. And then I found that he, too, who up to that time had been practicing in a London suburb—Streatham—had also disappeared. Just after Brake's arrest, Ransford had suddenly sold his practice and gone—no one knew where, but it was believed—abroad. I couldn't trace him, anyway. And soon after that I had a long illness, and for two or three years was an invalid, and—well, the thing was over and done with, and, as I said just now, I have never heard anything of any of them for all these years. And now!—now you tell me that there is a Mary Bewery who is a ward of a Dr. Mark Ransford at—where did you say?"

"At Wrychester," answered Bryce. "She is a young woman of twenty, and she has a brother, Richard, who is between seventeen and eighteen."

"Without a doubt those are Brake's children!" exclaimed the old man. "The infant I spoke of was a boy. Bless me!—how extraordinary. How long have they been at Wrychester?"

"Ransford has been in practice there some years—a few years," replied Bryce. "These two young people joined him there definitely two years ago. But from what I have learnt, he has acted as their guardian ever since they were mere children."

"And—their mother?" asked Mr. Gilwaters.

"Said to be dead—long since," answered Bryce. "And their father, too. They know nothing. Ransford won't tell them anything. But, as you say—I've no doubt of it myself now—they must be the children of John Brake."

"And have taken the name of their mother!" remarked the old man.

"Had it given to them," said Bryce. "They don't know that it isn't their real name. Of course, Ransford has given it to them! But now—the mother?"

"Ah, yes, the mother!" said Mr. Gilwaters. "Our old governess! Dear me!"

"I'm going to put a question to you," continued Bryce, leaning nearer and speaking in a low, confidential tone. "You must have seen much of the world, Mr. Gilwaters—men of your profession know the world, and human nature, too. Call to mind all the mysterious circumstances, the veiled hints, of that trial. Do you think—have you ever thought—that the false friend whom the counsel referred to was—Ransford? Come, now!"

The old clergyman lifted his hands and let them fall on his knees.

"I do not know what to say!" he exclaimed. "To tell you the truth, I have often wondered if—if that was what really did happen. There is the fact that Brake's wife disappeared mysteriously—that Ransford made a similar mysterious disappearance about the same time—that Brake was obviously suffering from intense and bitter hatred when I saw him after the trial—hatred of some person on whom he meant to be revenged—and that his counsel hinted that he had been deceived and betrayed by a friend. Now, to my knowledge, he and Ransford were the closest of friends—in the old days, before Brake married our governess. And I suppose the friendship continued—certainly Ransford acted as best man at the wedding! But how account for that strange double disappearance?"

Bryce had already accounted for that, in his own secret mind. And now, having got all that he wanted out of the old clergyman, he rose to take his leave.

"You will regard this interview as having been of a strictly private nature, Mr. Gilwaters?" he said.

"Certainly!" responded the old man. "But—you mentioned that you wished to marry the daughter? Now that you know about her father's past—for I am sure she must be John Brake's child—you won't allow that to—eh?"

"Not for a moment!" answered Bryce, with a fair show of magnanimity. "I am not a man of that complexion, sir. No!—I only wished to clear up certain things, you understand."

"And—since she is apparently—from what you say—in ignorance of her real father's past—what then?" asked Mr. Gilwaters anxiously. "Shall you—"

"I shall do nothing whatever in any haste," replied Bryce. "Rely upon me to consider her feelings in everything. As you have been so kind, I will let you know, later, how matters go."

This was one of Pemberton Bryce's ready inventions. He had not the least intention of ever seeing or communicating with the late vicar of Braden Medworth again; Mr. Gilwaters had served his purpose for the time being. He went away from Bayswater, and, an hour later, from London, highly satisfied. In his opinion, Mark Ransford, seventeen years before, had taken advantage of his friend's misfortunes to run away with his wife, and when Brake, alias Braden, had unexpectedly turned up at Wrychester, he had added to his former wrong by the commission of a far greater one.

X - Diplomacy

Bryce went back to Wrychester firmly convinced that Mark Ransford had killed John Braden. He reckoned things up in his own fashion. Some years must have elapsed since Braden, or rather Brake's release. He had probably heard, on his release, that Ransford and his, Brake's, wife had gone abroad—in that case he would certainly follow them. He might have lost all trace of them; he might have lost his original interest in his first schemes of revenge; he might have begun a new life for himself in Australia, whence he had undoubtedly come to England recently. But he had come, at last, and he had evidently tracked Ransford to Wrychester—why, otherwise, had he presented himself at Ransford's door on that eventful morning which was to witness his death? Nothing, in Bryce's opinion, could be clearer. Brake had turned up. He and Ransford had met—most likely in the precincts of the Cathedral. Ransford, who knew all the quiet corners of the old place, had in all probability induced Brake to walk up into the gallery with him, had noticed the open doorway, had thrown Brake through it. All the facts pointed to that conclusion—it was a theory which, so far as Bryce could see, was perfect. It ought to be enough—proved—to put Ransford in a criminal dock. Bryce resolved it in his own mind over and over again as he sped home to Wrychester—he pictured the police listening greedily to all that he could tell them if he liked. There was only one factor in the whole sum of the affair which seemed against him—the advertisement in the Times. If Brake desired to find Ransford in order to be revenged on him, why did he insert that advertisement, as if he were longing to meet a cherished friend again? But Bryce gaily surmounted that obstacle—full of shifts and subtleties himself, he was ever ready to credit others with trading in them, and he put the advertisement down as a clever ruse to attract, not Ransford, but some person who could give information about Ransford. Whatever its exact meaning might have been, its existence made no difference to Bryce's firm opinion that it was Mark Ransford who flung John Brake down St. Wrytha's Stair and killed him. He was as sure of that as he was certain that Braden was Brake. And he was not going to tell the police of his discoveries—he was not going to tell anybody. The one thing that concerned him was—how best to make use of his knowledge with a view to bringing about a marriage between himself and Mark Ransford's ward. He had set his mind on that for twelve months past, and he was not a man to be baulked of his purpose. By fair means, or foul—he himself ignored the last word and would have substituted the term skillful for it—Pemberton Bryce meant to have Mary Bewery.

Mary Bewery herself had no thought of Bryce in her head when, the morning after that worthy's return to Wrychester, she set out, alone, for the Wrychester Golf Club. It was her habit to go there almost every day, and Bryce was well acquainted with her movements and knew precisely where to waylay her. And empty of Bryce though her mind was, she was not surprised when, at a lonely place on Wrychester Common, Bryce turned the corner of a spinny and met her face to face.

Mary would have passed on with no more than a silent recognition—she had made up her mind to have no further speech with her guardian's dismissed assistant. But she had to pass through a wicket gate at that point, and Bryce barred the way, with unmistakable purpose. It was plain to the girl that he had laid in wait for her. She was not without a temper of her own, and she suddenly let it out on the offender.

"Do you call this manly conduct, Dr. Bryce?" she demanded, turning an indignant and flushed face on him. "To waylay me here, when you know that I don't want to have anything more to do with you. Let me through, please—and go away!"

But Bryce kept a hand on the little gate, and when he spoke there was that in his voice which made the girl listen in spite of herself.

"I'm not here on my own behalf," he said quickly. "I give you my word I won't say a thing that need offend you. It's true I waited here for you—it's the only place in which I thought I could meet you, alone. I want to speak to you. It's this—do you know your guardian is in danger?"

Bryce had the gift of plausibility—he could convince people, against their instincts, even against their wills, that he was telling the truth. And Mary, after a swift glance, believed him.

"What danger?" she asked. "And if he is, and if you know he is—why don't you go direct to him?"

"The most fatal thing in the world to do!" exclaimed Bryce. "You know him—he can be nasty. That would bring matters to a crisis. And that, in his interest, is just what mustn't happen."

"I don't understand you," said Mary.

Bryce leaned nearer to her—across the gate.

"You know what happened last week," he said in a low voice. "The strange death of that man—Braden."

"Well?" she asked, with a sudden look of uneasiness. "What of it?"

"It's being rumored—whispered—in the town that Dr. Ransford had something to do with that affair," answered Bryce. "Unpleasant—unfortunate—but it's a fact."

"Impossible!" exclaimed Mary with a heightening color. "What could he have to do with it? What could give rise to such foolish—wicked—rumors?"

"You know as well as I do how people talk, how they will talk," said Bryce. "You can't stop them, in a place like Wrychester, where everybody knows everybody. There's a mystery around Braden's death—it's no use denying it. Nobody knows who he was, where he came from, why he came. And it's being hinted—I'm only telling you what I've gathered—that Dr. Ransford knows more than he's ever told. There are, I'm afraid, grounds."

"What grounds?" demanded Mary. While Bryce had been speaking, in his usual slow, careful fashion, she had been reflecting—and remembering Ransford's evident agitation at the time of the Paradise affair—and his relief when the inquest was over—and his sending her with flowers to the dead man's grave and she began to experience a sense of uneasiness and even of fear. "What grounds can there be?" she added. "Dr. Ransford didn't know that man—had never seen him!"

"That's not certain," replied Bryce. "It's said—remember, I'm only repeating things—it's said that just before the body was discovered, Dr. Ransford was seen—seen, mind you!—leaving the west porch of the Cathedral, looking as if he had just been very much upset. Two persons saw this."

"Who are they?" asked Mary.

"That I'm not allowed to tell you," said Bryce, who had no intention of informing her that one person was himself and the other imaginary. "But I can assure you that I am certain—absolutely certain!—that their story is true. The fact is—I can corroborate it."

"You!" she exclaimed.

"I!" replied Bryce. "I will tell you something that I have never told anybody—up to now. I shan't ask you to respect my confidence—I've sufficient trust in you to know that you will, without any asking. Listen!—on that morning, Dr. Ransford went out of the surgery in the direction of the Deanery, leaving me alone there. A few minutes later, a tap came at the door. I opened it—and found—a man standing outside!"

"Not—that man?" asked Mary fearfully.

"That man—Braden," replied Bryce. "He asked for Dr. Ransford. I said he was out—would the caller leave his name? He said no—he had called because he had once known a Dr. Ransford, years before. He added something about calling again, and he went away—across the Close towards the Cathedral. I saw him again—not very long afterwards—lying in the corner of Paradise—dead!"

Mary Bewery was by this time pale and trembling—and Bryce continued to watch her steadily. She stole a furtive look at him.

"Why didn't you tell all this at the inquest?" she asked in a whisper.

"Because I knew how damning it would be to—Ransford," replied Bryce promptly. "It would have excited suspicion. I was certain that no one but myself knew that Braden had been to the surgery door—therefore, I thought that if I kept silence, his calling there would never be known. But—I have since found that I was mistaken. Braden was seen—going away from Dr. Ransford's."

"By—whom?" asked Mary.

"Mrs. Deramore—at the next house," answered Bryce. "She happened to be looking out of an upstairs window. She saw him go away and cross the Close."

"Did she tell you that?" demanded Mary, who knew Mrs. Deramore for a gossip.

"Between ourselves," said Bryce, "she did not! She told Mrs. Folliot—Mrs. Folliot told me."

"So—it is talked about!" exclaimed Mary.

"I said so," assented Bryce. "You know what Mrs. Folliot's tongue is."

"Then Dr. Ransford will get to hear of it," said Mary.

"He will be the last person to get to hear of it," affirmed Bryce. "These things are talked of, hole-and-corner fashion, a long time before they reach the ears of the person chiefly concerned."

Mary hesitated a moment before she asked her next question.

"Why have you told me all this?" she demanded at last.

"Because I didn't want you to be suddenly surprised," answered Bryce. "This—whatever it is—may come to a sudden head—of an unpleasant sort. These rumors spread—and the police are still keen about finding out things concerning this dead man. If they once get it into their heads that Dr. Ransford knew him—"

Mary laid her hand on the gate between them—and Bryce, who had done all he wished to do at that time, instantly opened it, and she passed through.

"I am much obliged to you," she said. "I don't know what it all means—but it is Dr. Ransford's affair—if there is any affair, which I doubt. Will you let me go now, please?"

Bryce stood aside and lifted his hat, and Mary, with no more than a nod, walked on towards the golf club-house across the Common, while Bryce turned off to the town, highly elated with his morning's work. He had sown the seeds of uneasiness and suspicion broadcast—some of them, he knew, would mature.

Mary Bewery played no golf that morning. In fact, she only went on to the club-house to rid herself of Bryce, and presently she returned home, thinking. And indeed, she said to herself, she had abundant food for thought. Naturally candid and honest, she did not at that moment doubt Bryce's good faith; much as she disliked him in most ways she knew that he had certain commendable qualities, and she was inclined to believe him when he said that he had kept silence in order to ward off consequences which might indirectly be unpleasant for her. But of him and his news she thought little—what occupied her mind was the possible connection between the stranger who had come so suddenly and disappeared so suddenly—and forever!—and Mark Ransford. Was it possible—really possible—that there had been some meeting between them in or about the Cathedral precincts that morning? She knew, after a moment's reflection, that it was very possible—why not? And from that her thoughts followed a natural trend—was the mystery surrounding this man connected in any way with the mystery about herself and her brother?—that mystery of which (as it seemed to her) Ransford was so shy of speaking. And again—and for the hundredth time—she asked herself why he was so reticent, so evidently full of dislike of the subject, why he could not tell her and Dick whatever there was to tell, once for all?

She had to pass the Folliots' house in the far corner of the Close on her way home—a fine old mansion set in well-wooded grounds, enclosed by a high wall of old red brick. A door in that wall stood open, and inside it, talking to one of his gardeners, was Mr. Folliot—the vistas behind him were gay with flowers and rich with the roses which he passed all his days in cultivating. He caught sight of Mary as she passed the open doorway and called her back.

"Come in and have a look at some new roses I've got," he said. "Beauties! I'll give you a handful to carry home."

Mary rather liked Mr. Folliot. He was a big, half-asleep sort of man, who had few words and could talk about little else than his hobby. But he was a passionate lover of flowers and plants, and had a positive genius for rose-culture, and was at all times highly delighted to take flower-lovers round his garden. She turned at once and walked in, and Folliot led her away down the scented paths.

"It's an experiment I've been trying," he said, leading her up to a cluster of blooms of a color and size which she had never seen before. "What do you think of the results?"

"Magnificent!" exclaimed Mary. "I never saw anything so fine!"

"No!" agreed Folliot, with a quiet chuckle. "Nor anybody else—because there's no such rose in England. I shall have to go to some of these learned parsons in the Close to invent me a Latin name for this—it's the result of careful experiments in grafting—took me three years to get at it. And see how it blooms,—scores on one standard."

He pulled out a knife and began to select a handful of the finest blooms, which he presently pressed into Mary's hand.

"By the by," he remarked as she thanked him and they turned away along the path, "I wanted to have a word with you—or with Ransford. Do you know—does he know—that that confounded silly woman who lives near to your house—Mrs. Deramore—has been saying some things—or a thing—which—to put it plainly—might make some unpleasantness for him?"

Mary kept a firm hand on her wits—and gave him an answer which was true enough, so far as she was aware.

"I'm sure he knows nothing," she said. "What is it, Mr. Folliot?"

"Why, you know what happened last week," continued Folliot, glancing knowingly at her. "The accident to that stranger. This Mrs. Deramore, who's nothing but an old chatterer, has been saying, here and there, that it's a very queer thing Dr. Ransford doesn't know anything about him, and can't say anything, for she herself, she says, saw the very man going away from Dr. Ransford's house not so long before the accident."

"I am not aware that he ever called at Dr. Ransford's," said Mary. "I never saw him—and I was in the garden, about that very time, with your stepson, Mr. Folliot."

"So Sackville told me," remarked Folliot. "He was present—and so was I—when Mrs. Deramore was tattling about it in our house yesterday. He said, then, that he'd never seen the man go to your house. You never heard your servants make any remark about it?"

"Never!" answered Mary.

"I told Mrs. Deramore she'd far better hold her tongue," continued Folliot. "Tittle-tattle of that sort is apt to lead to unpleasantness. And when it came to it, it turned out that all she had seen was this stranger strolling across the Close as if he'd just left your house. If—there's always some if! But I'll tell you why I mentioned it to you," he continued, nudging Mary's elbow and glancing covertly first at her and then at his house on the far side of the garden. "Ladies that are—getting on a bit in years, you know—like my wife, are apt to let their tongues wag, and between you and me, I shouldn't wonder if Mrs. Folliot has repeated what Mrs. Deramore said—eh? And I don't want the doctor to think that—if he hears anything, you know, which he may, and, again, he might—to think that it originated here. So, if he should ever mention it to you, you can say it sprang from his next-door neighbour. Bah!—they're a lot of old gossips, these Close ladies!"

"Thank you," said Mary. "But—supposing this man had been to our house—what difference would that make? He might have been for half a dozen reasons."

Folliot looked at her out of his half-shut eyes.

"Some people would want to know why Ransford didn't tell that—at the inquest," he answered. "That's all. When there's a bit of mystery, you know—eh?"

He nodded—as if reassuringly—and went off to rejoin his gardener, and Mary walked home with her roses, more thoughtful than ever. Mystery?—a bit of mystery? There was a vast and heavy cloud of mystery, and she knew she could have no peace until it was lifted.

XI - The Back Room

In the midst of all her perplexity at that moment, Mary Bewery was certain of one fact about which she had no perplexity nor any doubt—it would not be long before the rumors of which Bryce and Mr. Folliot had spoken. Although she had only lived in Wrychester a comparatively short time she had seen and learned enough of it to know that the place was a hotbed of gossip. Once gossip was started there, it spread, widening in circle after circle. And though Bryce was probably right when he said that the person chiefly concerned was usually the last person to hear what was being whispered, she knew well enough that sooner or later this talk about Ransford would come to Ransford's own ears. But she had no idea that it was to come so soon, nor from her own brother.

Lunch in the Ransford menage was an informal meal. At a quarter past one every day, it was on the table—a cold lunch to which the three members of the household helped themselves as they liked, independent of the services of servants. Sometimes all three were there at the same moment; sometimes Ransford was half an hour late; the one member who was always there to the moment was Dick Bewery, who fortified himself sedulously after his morning's school labours. On this particular day all three met in the dining-room at once, and sat down together. And before Dick had eaten many mouthfuls of a cold pie to which he had just liberally helped himself he bent confidentially across the table towards his guardian.

"There's something I think you ought to be told about, sir," he remarked with a side-glance at Mary. "Something I heard this morning at school. You know, we've a lot of fellows—town boys—who talk."

"I daresay," responded Ransford dryly. "Following the example of their mothers, no doubt. Well—what is it?"

He, too, glanced at Mary—and the girl had her work set to look unconscious.

"It's this," replied Dick, lowering his voice in spite of the fact that all three were alone. "They're saying in the town that you know something which you won't tell about that affair last week. It's being talked of."

Ransford laughed—a little cynically.

"Are you quite sure, my boy, that they aren't saying that I daren't tell?" he asked. "Daren't is a much more likely word than won't, I think."

"Well—about that, sir," acknowledged Dick. "Comes to that, anyhow."

"And what are their grounds?" inquired Ransford. "You've heard them, I'll be bound!"

"They say that man—Braden—had been here—here, to the house!—that morning, not long before he was found dead," answered Dick. "Of course, I said that was all bosh!—I said that if he'd been here and seen you, I'd have heard of it, dead certain."

"That's not quite so dead certain, Dick, as that I have no knowledge of his ever having been here," said Ransford. "But who says he came here?"

"Mrs. Deramore," replied Dick promptly. "She says she saw him go away from the house and across the Close, a little before ten. So Jim Deramore says, anyway—and he says his mother's eyes are as good as another's."

"Doubtless!" assented Ransford. He looked at Mary again, and saw that she was keeping hers fixed on her plate. "Well," he continued, "if it will give you any satisfaction, Dick, you can tell the gossips that Dr. Ransford never saw any man, Braden or anybody else, at his house that morning, and that he never exchanged a word with Braden. So much for that! But," he added, "you needn't expect them to believe you. I know these people—if they've got an idea into their heads they'll ride it to death. Nevertheless, what I say is a fact."

Dick presently went off—and once more Ransford looked at Mary. And this time, Mary had to meet her guardian's inquiring glance.

"Have you heard anything of this?" he asked.

"That there was a rumor—yes," she replied without hesitation. "But—not until just now—this morning."

"Who told you of it?" inquired Ransford.

Mary hesitated. Then she remembered that Mr. Folliot, at any rate, had not bound her to secrecy.

"Mr. Folliot," she replied. "He called me into his garden, to give me those roses, and he mentioned that Mrs. Deramore had said these things to Mrs. Folliot, and as he seemed to think it highly probable that Mrs. Folliot would repeat them, he told me because he didn't want you to think that the rumor had originally arisen at his house."

"Very good of him, I'm sure," remarked Ransford dryly. "They all like to shift the blame from one to another! But," he added, looking searchingly at her, "you don't know anything about—Braden's having come here?"

He saw at once that she did, and Mary saw a slight shade of anxiety come over his face.

"Yes, I do!" she replied. "That morning. But—it was told to me, only today, in strict confidence."

"In strict confidence!" he repeated. "May I know—by whom?"

"Dr. Bryce," she answered. "I met him this morning. And I think you ought to know. Only—it was in confidence." She paused for a moment, looking at him, and her face grew troubled. "I hate to suggest it," she continued, "but—will you come with me to see him, and I'll ask him—things being as they are—to tell you what he told me. I can't—without his permission."

Ransford shook his head and frowned.

"I dislike it!" he said. "It's—it's putting ourselves in his power, as it were. But—I'm not going to be left in the dark. Put on your hat, then."

Bryce, ever since his coming to Wrychester, had occupied rooms in an old house in Friary Lane, at the back of the Close. He was comfortably lodged. Downstairs he had a double sitting-room, extending from the front to the back of the house; his front window looked out on one garden, his back window on another. He had just finished lunch in the front part of his room, and was looking out of his window, wondering what to do with himself that afternoon, when he saw Ransford and Mary Bewery approaching. He guessed the reason of their visit at once, and went straight to the front door to meet them, and without a word motioned them to follow him into his own quarters. It was characteristic of him that he took the first word—before either of his visitors could speak.

"I know why you've come," he said, as he closed the door and glanced at Mary. "You either want my permission that you should tell Dr. Ransford what I told you this morning, or, you want me to tell him myself. Am I right?"

"I should be glad if you would tell him," replied Mary. "The rumor you spoke of has reached him—he ought to know what you can tell. I have respected your confidence, so far."

The two men looked at each other. And this time it was Ransford who spoke first.

"It seems to me," he said, "that there is no great reason for privacy. If rumors are flying about in Wrychester, there is an end of privacy. Dick tells me they are saying at the school that it is known that Braden called on me at my house shortly before he was found dead. I know nothing whatever of any such call! But—I left you in my surgery that morning. Do you know if he came there?"

"Yes!" answered Bryce. "He did come. Soon after you'd gone out."

"Why did you keep that secret?" demanded Ransford. "You could have told it to the police—or to the Coroner—or to me. Why didn't you?"

Before Bryce could answer, all three heard a sharp click of the front garden gate, and looking round, saw Mitchington coming up the walk.

"Here's one of the police, now," said Bryce calmly. "Probably come to extract information. I would much rather he didn't see you here—but I'd also like you to hear what I shall say to him. Step inside there," he continued, drawing aside the curtains which shut off the back room. "Don't stick at trifles!—you don't know what may be afoot."

He almost forced them away, drew the curtains again, and hurrying to the front door, returned almost immediately with Mitchington.

"Hope I'm not disturbing you, doctor," said the inspector, as Bryce brought him in and again closed the door. "Not? All right, then—I came round to ask you a question. There's a queer rumor getting out in the town, about that affair last week. Seems to have sprung from some of those old dowagers in the Close."

"Of course!" said Bryce. He was mixing a whisky-and-soda for his caller, and his laugh mingled with the splash of the siphon. "Of course! I've heard it."

"You've heard?" remarked Mitchington. "Um! Good health, sir!—heard, of course, that—"

"That Braden called on Dr. Ransford not long before the accident, or murder, or whatever it was, happened," said Bryce. "That's it—eh?"

"Something of that sort," agreed Mitchington. "It's being said, anyway, that Braden was at Ransford's house, and presumably saw him, and that Ransford, accordingly, knows something about him which he hasn't told. Now—what do you know? Do you know if Ransford and Braden did meet that morning?"

"Not at Ransford's house, anyway," answered Bryce promptly. "I can prove that. But since this rumor has got out, I'll tell you what I do know, and what the truth is. Braden did come to Ransford's—not to the house, but to the surgery. He didn't see Ransford—Ransford had gone out, across the Close. Braden saw—me!"

"Bless me!—I didn't know that," remarked Mitchington. "You never mentioned it."

"You'll not wonder that I didn't," said Bryce, laughing lightly, "when I tell you what the man wanted."

"What did he want, then?" asked Mitchington.

"Merely to be told where the Cathedral Library was," answered Bryce.

Ransford, watching Mary Bewery, saw her cheeks flush, and knew that Bryce was cheerfully telling lies. But Mitchington evidently had no suspicion.

"That all?" he asked. "Just a question?"

"Just a question—that question," replied Bryce. "I pointed out the Library—and he walked away. I never saw him again until I was fetched to him—dead. And I thought so little of the matter that—well, it never even occurred to me to mention it."

"Then—though he did call—he never saw Ransford?" asked the inspector.

"I tell you Ransford was already gone out," answered Bryce. "He saw no one but myself. Where Mrs. Deramore made her mistake—I happen to know, Mitchington, that she started this rumor—was in trying to make two and two into five. She saw this man crossing the Close, as if from Ransford's house and she at once imagined he'd seen and been talking with Ransford."

"Old fool!" said Mitchington. "Of course, that's how these tales get about. However, there's more than that in the air."

The two listeners behind the curtains glanced at each other. Ransford's glance showed that he was already chafing at the unpleasantness of his position—but Mary's only betokened apprehension. And suddenly, as if she feared that Ransford would throw the curtains aside and walk into the front room, she laid a hand on his arm and motioned him to be patient—and silent.

"Oh?" said Bryce. "More in the air? About that business?"

"Just so," assented Mitchington. "To start with, that man Varner, the mason, has never ceased talking. They say he's always at it—to the effect that the verdict of the jury at the inquest was all wrong, and that his evidence was put clean aside. He persists that he did see—what he swore he saw."

"He'll persist in that to his dying day," said Bryce carelessly. "If that's all there is—"

"It isn't," interrupted the inspector. "Not by a long chalk! But Varner's is a direct affirmation—the other matter's a sort of ugly hint. There's a man named Collishaw, a townsman, who's been employed as a mason's laborer about the Cathedral of late. This Collishaw, it seems, was at work somewhere up in the galleries, ambulatories, or whatever they call those upper regions, on the very morning of the affair. And the other night, being somewhat under the influence of drink, and talking the matter over with his mates at a tavern, he let out some dark hints that he could tell something if he liked. Of course, he was pressed to tell them—and wouldn't. Then—so my informant tells me—he was dared to tell, and became surlily silent. That, of course, spread, and got to my ears. I've seen Collishaw."

"Well?" asked Bryce.

"I believe the man does know something," answered Mitchington. "That's the impression I carried away, anyhow. But—he won't speak. I charged him straight out with knowing something—but it was no good. I told him of what I'd heard. All he would say was that whatever he might have said when he'd got a glass of beer or so too much, he wasn't going to say anything now neither for me nor for anybody!"

"Just so!" remarked Bryce. "But—he'll be getting a glass too much again, some day, and then—then, perhaps he'll add to what he said before. And—you'll be sure to hear of it."

"I'm not certain of that," answered Mitchington. "I made some inquiry and I find that Collishaw is usually a very sober and retiring sort of chap—he'd been lured on to drink when he let out what he did. Besides, whether I'm right or wrong, I got the idea into my head that he'd already been—squared!"

"Squared!" exclaimed Bryce. "Why, then, if that affair was really murder, he'd be liable to being charged as an accessory after the fact!"

"I warned him of that," replied Mitchington. "Yes, I warned him solemnly."

"With no effect?" asked Bryce.

"He's a surly sort of man," said Mitchington. "The sort that takes refuge in silence. He made no answer beyond a growl."

"You really think he knows something?" suggested Bryce. "Well—if there is anything, it'll come out—in time."

"Oh, it'll come out!" assented Mitchington. "I'm by no means satisfied with that verdict of the coroner's inquiry. I believe there was foul play—of some sort. I'm still following things up—quietly. And—I'll tell you something—between ourselves—I've made an important discovery. It's this. On the evening of Braden's arrival at the Mitre he was out, somewhere, for a whole two hours—by himself."

"I thought we learned from Mrs. Partingley that he and the other man, Dellingham, spent the evening together?" said Bryce.

"So we did—but that was not quite so," replied Mitchington. "Braden went out of the Mitre just before nine o'clock and he didn't return until a few minutes after eleven. Now, then, where did he go?"

"I suppose you're trying to find that out?" asked Bryce, after a pause, during which the listeners heard the caller rise and make for the door.

"Of course!" replied Mitchington, with a confident laugh. "And—I shall! Keep it to yourself, doctor."

When Bryce had let the inspector out and returned to his sitting-room, Ransford and Mary had come from behind the curtains. He looked at them and shook his head.

"You heard—a good deal, you see," he observed.

"Look here!" said Ransford peremptorily. "You put that man off about the call at my surgery. You didn't tell him the truth."

"Quite right," assented Bryce. "I didn't. Why should I?"

"What did Braden ask you?" demanded Ransford. "Come, now?"

"Merely if Dr. Ransford was in," answered Bryce, "remarking that he had once known a Dr. Ransford. That was—literally—all. I replied that you were not in."

Ransford stood silently thinking for a moment or two. Then he moved towards the door.

"I don't see that any good will come of more talk about this," he said. "We three, at any rate, know this—I never saw Braden when he came to my house."

Then he motioned Mary to follow him, and they went away, and Bryce, having watched them out of sight, smiled at himself in his mirror—with full satisfaction.

XII - Murder of the Mason's Laborer

It was towards noon of the very next day that Bryce made a forward step in the matter of solving the problem of Richard Jenkins and his tomb in Paradise. Ever since his return from Barthorpe he had been making attempts to get at the true meaning of this mystery. He had paid so many visits to the Cathedral Library that Ambrose Campany had asked him jestingly if he was going in for archaeology; Bryce had replied that having nothing to do just then he saw no reason why he shouldn't improve his knowledge of the antiquities of Wrychester. But he was scrupulously careful not to let the librarian know the real object of his prying and peeping into the old books and documents. Campany, as Bryce was very well aware, was a walking encyclopedia of information about Wrychester Cathedral: he was, in fact, at that time, engaged in completing a history of it. And it was through that history that Bryce accidentally got his precious information. For on the day following the interview with Mary Bewery and Ransford, Bryce being in the library was treated by Campany to an inspection of certain drawings which the librarian had made for illustrating his work-drawings, most of them, of old brasses, coats of arms, and the like,—And at the foot of one of these, a drawing of a shield on which was sculptured three crows, Bryce saw the name Richard Jenkins, armiger. It was all he could do to repress a start and to check his tongue. But Campany, knowing nothing, quickly gave him the information he wanted.

"All these drawings," he said, "are of old things in and about the Cathedral. Some of them, like that, for instance, that Jenkins shield, are of ornamentations on tombs which are so old that the inscriptions have completely disappeared—tombs in the Cloisters, and in Paradise. Some of those tombs can only be identified by these sculptures and ornaments."

"How do you know, for instance, that any particular tomb or monument is, we'll say, Jenkins's?" asked Bryce, feeling that he was on safe ground. "Must be a matter of doubt if there's no inscription left, isn't it?"

"No!" replied Campany. "No doubt at all. In that particular case, there's no doubt that a certain tomb out there in the corner of Paradise, near the east wall of the south porch, is that of one Richard Jenkins, because it bears his coat-of-arms, which, as you see, bore these birds—intended either as crows or ravens. The inscription's clean gone from that tomb—which is why it isn't particularized in that chart of burials in Paradise—the man who prepared that chart didn't know how to trace things as we do nowadays. Richard Jenkins was, as you may guess, a Welshman, who settled here in Wrychester in the seventeenth century: he left some money to St. Hedwige's Church, outside the walls, but he was buried here. There are more instances—look at this, now—this coat-of-arms—that's the only means there is of identifying another tomb in Paradise—that of Gervase Tyrrwhit. You see his armorial bearings in this drawing? Now those—"

Bryce let the librarian go on talking and explaining, and heard all he had to say as a man hears things in a dream—what was really active in his own mind was joy at this unexpected stroke of luck: he himself might have searched for many a year and never found the last resting-place of Richard Jenkins. And when, soon after the great clock of the Cathedral had struck the hour of noon, he left Campany and quitted the Library, he walked over to Paradise and plunged in amongst its yews and cypresses, intent on seeing the Jenkins tomb for himself. No one could suspect anything from merely seeing him there, and all he wanted was one glance at the ancient monument.

But Bryce was not to give even one look at Richard Jenkins's tomb that day, nor the next, nor for many days—death met him in another form before he had taken many steps in the quiet enclosure where so much of Wrychester mortality lay sleeping.

From over the topmost branches of the old yew trees a great shaft of noontide sunlight fell full on a patch of the grey walls of the high-roofed nave. At the foot of it, his back comfortably planted against the angle of a projecting buttress, sat a man, evidently fast asleep in the warmth of those powerful rays. His head leaned down and forward over his chest, his hands were folded across his waist, his whole attitude was that of a man who, having eaten and drunken in the open air, has dropped off to sleep. That he had so dropped off while in the very act of smoking was evident from the presence of a short, well-blackened clay pipe which had fallen from his lips and lay in the grass beside him. Near the pipe, spread on a colored handkerchief, were the remains of his dinner—Bryce's quick eye noticed fragments of bread, cheese, onions. And close by stood one of those tin bottles in which laboring men carry their drink; its cork, tied to the neck by a piece of string, dangled against the side. A few yards away, a mass of fallen rubbish and a shovel and wheelbarrow showed at what the sleeper had been working when his dinner-hour and time for rest had arrived.

Something unusual, something curiously noticeable—yet he could not exactly tell what—made Bryce go closer to the sleeping man. There was a strange stillness about him—a rigidity which seemed to suggest something more than sleep. And suddenly, with a stifled exclamation, he bent forward and lifted one of the folded hands. It dropped like a leaden weight when Bryce released it, and he pushed back the man's face and looked searchingly into it. And in that instant he knew that for the second time within a fortnight he had found a dead man in Wrychester Paradise.

There was no doubt whatever that the man was dead. His hands and body were warm enough—but there was not a flicker of breath; he was as dead as any of the folk who lay six feet beneath the old gravestones around him. And Bryce's practiced touch and eye knew that he was only just dead—and that he had died in his sleep. Everything there pointed unmistakably to what had happened. The man had eaten his frugal dinner, washed it down from his tin bottle, lighted his pipe, leaned back in the warm sunlight, dropped asleep—and died as quietly as a child taken from its play to its slumbers.

After one more careful look, Bryce turned and made through the trees to the path which crossed the old graveyard. And there, going leisurely home to lunch, was Dick Bewery, who glanced at the young doctor inquisitively.

"Hullo!" he exclaimed with the freedom of youth towards something not much older. "You there? Anything on?"

Then he looked more clearly, seeing Bryce to be pale and excited. Bryce laid a hand on the lad's arm.

"Look here!" he said. "There's something wrong—again!—in here. Run down to the police-station—get hold of Mitchington—quietly, you understand!—bring him here at once. If he's not there, bring somebody else—any of the police. But—say nothing to anybody but them."

Dick gave him another swift look, turned, and ran. And Bryce went back to the dead man—and picked up the tin bottle, and making a cup of his left hand poured out a trickle of the contents. Cold tea!—and, as far as he could judge, nothing else. He put the tip of his little finger into the weak-looking stuff, and tasted—it tasted of nothing but a super-abundance of sugar.

He stood there, watching the dead man until the sound of footsteps behind him gave warning of the return of Dick Bewery, who, in another minute, hurried through the bushes, followed by Mitchington. The boy stared in silence at the still figure, but the inspector, after a hasty glance, turned a horrified face on Bryce.

"Good Lord!" he gasped. "It's Collishaw!"

Bryce for the moment failed to comprehend this, and Mitchington shook his head.

"Collishaw!" he repeated. "Collishaw, you know! The man I told you about yesterday afternoon. The man that said—"

Mitchington suddenly checked himself, with a glance at Dick Bewery.

"I remember—now," said Bryce. "The mason's laborer! So—this is the man, eh? Well, Mitchington, he's dead!—I found him dead, just now. I should say he'd been dead five to ten minutes—not more. You'd better get help—and I'd like another medical man to see him before he's removed."

Mitchington looked again at Dick.

"Perhaps you'd fetch Dr. Ransford, Mr—Richard?" he asked. "He's nearest."

"Dr. Ransford's not at home," said Dick. "He went to Highminster—some County Council business or other—at ten this morning, and he won't be back until four—I happen to know that. Shall I run for Dr. Coates?"

"If you wouldn't mind," said Mitchington, "and as it's close by, drop in at the station again and tell the sergeant to come here with a couple of men. I say!" he went on, when the boy had hurried off, "this is a queer business, Dr. Bryce! What do you think?"

"I think this," answered Bryce. "That man!—look at him!—a strong, healthy-looking fellow, in the very prime of life—that man has met his death by foul means.

You take particular care of those dinner things of his—the remains of his dinner, every scrap—and of that tin bottle. That, especially. Take all these things yourself, Mitchington, and lock them up—they'll be wanted for examination."

Mitchington glanced at the simple matters which Bryce indicated. And suddenly he turned a half-frightened glance on his companion.

"You don't mean to say that—that you suspect he's been poisoned?" he asked. "Good Lord, if that is so—"

"I don't think you'll find that there's much doubt about it," answered Bryce. "But that's a point that will soon be settled. You'd better tell the Coroner at once, Mitchington, and he'll issue a formal order to Dr. Coates to make a post-mortem. And," he added significantly, "I shall be surprised if it isn't as I say—poison!"

"If that's so," observed Mitchington, with a grim shake of his head, "if that really is so, then I know what I shall think! This!" he went on, pointing to the dead man, "this is—a sort of sequel to the other affair. There's been something in what the poor chap said—he did know something against somebody, and that somebody's got to hear of it—and silenced him. But, Lord, doctor, how can it have been done?"

"I can see how it can have been done, easy enough," said Bryce. "This man has evidently been at work here, by himself, all the morning. He of course brought his dinner with him. He no doubt put his basket and his bottle down somewhere, while he did his work. What easier than for someone to approach through these trees and shrubs while the man's back was turned, or he was busy round one of these corners, and put some deadly poison into that bottle? Nothing!"

"Well," remarked Mitchington, "if that's so, it proves something else—to my mind."

"What!" asked Bryce.

"Why, that whoever it was who did it was somebody who had a knowledge of poison!" answered Mitchington. "And I should say there aren't many people in Wrychester who have such knowledge outside yourselves and the chemists. It's a black business, this!"

Bryce nodded silently. He waited until Dr. Coates, an elderly man who was the leading practitioner in the town, arrived, and to him he gave a careful account of his discovery. And after the police had taken the body away, and he had accompanied Mitchington to the police-station and seen the tin bottle and the remains of Collishaw's dinner safely locked up, he went home to lunch, and to wonder at this strange development. The inspector was doubtless right in saying that Collishaw had been done to death by somebody who wanted to silence him—but who could that somebody be? Bryce's thoughts immediately turned to the fact that Ransford had overheard all that Mitchington had said, in that very room in which he, Bryce, was then lunching—Ransford! Was it possible that Ransford had realized a danger in Collishaw's knowledge, and had—

He was interrupted at this stage by Mitchington, who came hurriedly in with a scared face.

"I say, I say!" he whispered as soon as Bryce's landlady had shut the door on them. "Here's a fine business! I've heard something—something I can hardly credit—but it's true. I've been to tell Collishaw's family what's happened. And—I'm fairly dazed by it—yet it's there—it is so!"

"What's so?" demanded Bryce. "What is it that's true?"

Mitchington bent closer over the table.

"Dr. Ransford was fetched to Collishaw's cottage at six o'clock this morning!" he said. "It seems that Collishaw's wife has been in a poor way about her health of late, and Dr. Ransford has attended her, off and on. She had some sort of a seizure this morning—early—and Ransford was sent for. He was there some little time—and I've heard some queer things."

"What sort of queer things?" demanded Bryce. "Don't be afraid of speaking out, man!—there's no one to hear but myself."

"Well, things that look suspicious, on the face of it," continued Mitchington, who was obviously much upset. "As you'll acknowledge when you hear them. I got my information from the next-door neighbour, Mrs. Batts. Mrs. Batts says that when Ransford—who'd been fetched by Mrs. Batts's eldest lad—came to Collishaw's house, Collishaw was putting up his dinner to take to his work—"

"What on earth made Mrs. Batts tell you that?" interrupted Bryce.

"Oh, well, to tell you the truth, I put a few questions to her as to what went on while Ransford was in the house," answered Mitchington. "When I'd once found that he had been there, you know, I naturally wanted to know all I could."

"Well?" asked Bryce.

"Collishaw, I say, was putting up his dinner to take to his work," continued Mitchington. "Mrs. Batts was doing a thing or two about the house. Ransford went upstairs to see Mrs. Collishaw. After a while he came down and said he would have to remain a little. Collishaw went up to speak to his wife before going out. And then Ransford asked Mrs. Batts for something—I forget what—some small matter which the Collishaw's hadn't got and she had, and she went next door to fetch it. Therefore—do you see?—Ransford was left alone with—Collishaw's tin bottle!"

Bryce, who had been listening attentively, looked steadily at the inspector.

"You're suspecting Ransford already!" he said.

Mitchington shook his head.

"What's it look like?" he answered, almost appealingly. "I put it to you, now!—what does it look like? Here's this man been poisoned without a doubt—I'm certain of it. And—there were those rumors—it's idle to deny that they centered in Ransford. And—this morning Ransford had the chance!"

"That's arguing that Ransford purposely carried a dose of poison to put into Collishaw's tin bottle!" said Bryce half-sneeringly. "Not very probable, you know, Mitchington."

Mitchington spread out his hands.

"Well, there it is!" he said. "As I say, there's no denying the suspicious look of it. If I were only certain that those rumors about what Collishaw hinted he could say had got to Ransford's ears!—why, then—"

"What's being done about that post-mortem?" asked Bryce.

"Dr. Coates and Dr. Everest are going to do it this afternoon," replied Mitchington. "The Coroner went to them at once, as soon as I told him."

"They'll probably have to call in an expert from London," said Bryce. "However, you can't do anything definite, you know, until the result's known. Don't say anything of this to anybody. I'll drop in at your place later and hear if Coates can say anything really certain."

Mitchington went away, and Bryce spent the rest of the afternoon wondering, speculating and scheming. If Ransford had really got rid of this man who knew something—why, then, it was certainly Ransford who killed Braden.

He went round to the police-station at five o'clock. Mitchington drew him aside.

"Coates says there's no doubt about it!" he whispered. "Poisoned! Hydrocyanic acid!"

XIII - Bryce is Asked a Question

Mitchington stepped aside into a private room, motioning Bryce to follow him. He carefully closed the door, and looking significantly at his companion, repeated his last words, with a shake of the head.

"Poisoned!—without the very least doubt," he whispered. "Hydrocyanic acid—which, I understand, is the same thing as what's commonly called prussic acid. They say then hadn't the least difficulty in finding that out! so there you are."

"That's what Coates has told you, of course?" asked Bryce. "After the autopsy?"

"Both of 'em told me—Coates, and Everest, who helped him," replied Mitchington. "They said it was obvious from the very start. And—I say!"

"Well?" said Bryce.

"It wasn't in that tin bottle, anyway," remarked Mitchington, who was evidently greatly weighted with mystery.

"No!—of course it wasn't!" affirmed Bryce. "Good Heavens, man—I know that!"

"How do you know?" asked Mitchington.

"Because I poured a few drops from that bottle into my hand when I first found Collishaw and tasted the stuff," answered Bryce readily. "Cold tea! with too much sugar in it. There was no H.C.N. in that besides, wherever it is, there's always a smell stronger or fainter—of bitter almonds. There was none about that bottle."

"Yet you were very anxious that we should take care of the bottle?" observed Mitchington.

"Of course!—because I suspected the use of some much rarer poison than that," retorted Bryce. "Pooh!—it's a clumsy way of poisoning anybody!—quick though it is."

"Well, there's where it is!" said Mitchington. "That'll be the medical evidence at the inquest, anyway. That's how it was done. And the question now is—"

"Who did it?" interrupted Bryce. "Precisely! Well—I'll say this much at once, Mitchington. Whoever did it was either a big bungler—or damned clever! That's what I say!"

"I don't understand you," said Mitchington.

"Plain enough—my meaning," replied Bryce, smiling. "To finish anybody with that stuff is easy enough—but no poison is more easily detected. It's an amateurish way of poisoning anybody—unless you can do it in such a fashion that no suspicion can attach you to. And in this case it's here—whoever administered that poison to Collishaw must have been certain—absolutely certain, mind you!—that it was impossible for anyone to find out that he'd done so. Therefore, I say what I said—the man must be damned clever. Otherwise, he'd be found out pretty quick. And all that puzzles me is—how was it administered?"

"How much would kill anybody—pretty quick?" asked Mitchington.

"How much? One drop would cause instantaneous death!" answered Bryce. "Cause paralysis of the heart, there and then, instantly!"

Mitchington remained silent awhile, looking meditatively at Bryce. Then he turned to a locked drawer, produced a key, and took something out of the drawer—a small object, wrapped in paper.

"I'm telling you a good deal, doctor," he said. "But as you know so much already, I'll tell you a bit more. Look at this!"

He opened his hand and showed Bryce a small cardboard pill-box, across the face of which a few words were written—One after meals—Mr. Collishaw.

"Whose handwriting's that?" demanded Mitchington.

Bryce looked closer, and started.

"Ransford's!" he muttered. "Ransford—of course!"

"That box was in Collishaw's waistcoat pocket," said Mitchington. "There are pills inside it, now. See!" He took off the lid of the box and revealed four sugar-coated pills. "It wouldn't hold more than six, this," he observed.

Bryce extracted a pill and put his nose to it, after scratching a little of the sugar coating away.

"Mere digestive pills," he announced.

"Could—it!—have been given in one of these?" asked Mitchington.

"Possible," replied Bryce. He stood thinking for a moment. "Have you shown those things to Coates and Everest?" he asked at last.

"Not yet," replied Mitchington. "I wanted to find out, first, if Ransford gave this box to Collishaw, and when. I'm going to Collishaw's house presently—I've certain inquiries to make. His widow'll know about these pills."

"You're suspecting Ransford," said Bryce. "That's certain!"

Mitchington carefully put away the pill-box and relocked the drawer.

"I've got some decidedly uncomfortable ideas—which I'd much rather not have—about Dr. Ransford," he said. "When one thing seems to fit into another, what is one to think. If I were certain that that rumor which spread, about Collishaw's knowledge of something—you know, had got to Ransford's ears—why, I should say it looked very much as if Ransford wanted to stop Collishaw's tongue for good before it could say more—and next time, perhaps, something definite. If men once begin to hint that they know something, they don't stop at hinting. Collishaw might have spoken plainly before long—to us!"

Bryce asked a question about the holding of the inquest and went away. And after thinking things over, he turned in the direction of the Cathedral, and made his way through the Cloisters to the Close. He was going to make another move in his own game, while there was a good chance. Everything at this juncture was throwing excellent cards into his hand—he would be foolish, he thought, not to play them to advantage. And so he made straight for Ransford's house, and before he reached it, met Ransford and Mary Bewery, who were crossing the Close from another point, on their way from the railway station, whither Mary had gone especially to meet her guardian. They were in such deep conversation that Bryce was close upon them before they observed his presence. When Ransford saw his late assistant, he scowled unconsciously—Bryce, and the interview of the previous afternoon, had been much in his thoughts all day, and he had an uneasy feeling that Bryce was playing some game. Bryce was quick to see that scowl—and to observe the sudden start which Mary could not repress—and he was just as quick to speak.

"I was going to your house, Dr. Ransford," he remarked quietly. "I don't want to force my presence on you, now or at any time—but I think you'd better give me a few minutes."

They were at Ransford's garden gate by that time, and Ransford flung it open and motioned Bryce to follow. He led the way into the dining-room, closed the door on the three, and looked at Bryce. Bryce took the glance as a question, and put another, in words.

"You've heard of what's happened during the day?" he said.

"About Collishaw—yes," answered Ransford. "Miss Bewery has just told me—what her brother told her. What of it?"

"I have just come from the police-station," said Bryce. "Coates and Everest have carried out an autopsy this afternoon. Mitchington told me the result."

"Well?" demanded Ransford, with no attempt to conceal his impatience. "And what then?"

"Collishaw was poisoned," replied Bryce, watching Ransford with a closeness which Mary did not fail to observe. "H.C.N. No doubt at all about it."

"Well—and what then?" asked Ransford, still more impatiently. "To be explicit—what's all this to do with me?"

"I came here to do you a service," answered Bryce. "Whether you like to take it or not is your look-out. You may as well know it you're in danger. Collishaw is the man who hinted—as you heard yesterday in my rooms—that he could say something definite about the Braden affair—if he liked."

"Well?" said Ransford.

"It's known—to the police—that you were at Collishaw's house early this morning," said Bryce. "Mitchington knows it."

Ransford laughed.

"Does Mitchington know that I overheard what he said to you, yesterday afternoon?" he inquired.

"No, he doesn't," answered Bryce. "He couldn't possibly know unless I told him. I haven't told him—I'm not going to tell him. But—he's suspicious already."

"Of me, of course," suggested Ransford, with another laugh. He took a turn across the room and suddenly faced round on Bryce, who had remained standing near the door. "Do you really mean to tell me that Mitchington is such a fool as to believe that I would poison a poor working man—and in that clumsy fashion?" he burst out. "Of course you don't."

"I never said I did," answered Bryce. "I'm only telling you what Mitchington thinks his grounds for suspecting. He confided in me because—well, it was I who found Collishaw. Mitchington is in possession of a box of digestive pills which you evidently gave Collishaw."

"Bah!" exclaimed Ransford. "The man's a fool! Let him come and talk to me."

"He won't do that—yet," said Bryce. "But—I'm afraid he'll bring all this out at the inquest. The fact is—he's suspicious—what with one thing or another—about the former affair. He thinks you concealed the truth—whatever it may be—as regards any knowledge of Braden which you may or mayn't have."

"I'll tell you what it is!" said Ransford suddenly. "It just comes to this—I'm suspected of having had a hand—the hand, if you like!—in Braden's death, and now of getting rid of Collishaw because Collishaw could prove that I had that hand. That's about it!"

"A clear way of putting it, certainly," assented Bryce. "But—there's a very clear way, too, of dissipating any such ideas."

"What way?" demanded Ransford.

"If you do know anything about the Braden affair—why not reveal it, and be done with the whole thing," suggested Bryce. "That would finish matters."

Ransford took a long, silent look at his questioner. And Bryce looked steadily back—and Mary Bewery anxiously watched both men.

"That's my business," said Ransford at last. "I'm neither to be coerced, bullied, or cajoled. I'm obliged to you for giving me a hint of my—danger, I suppose! And—I don't propose to say any more."

"Neither do I," said Bryce. "I only came to tell you."

And therewith, having successfully done all that he wanted to do, he walked out of the room and the house, and Ransford, standing in the window, his hands thrust in his pockets, watched him go away across the Close.

"Guardian!" said Mary softly.

Ransford turned sharply.

"Wouldn't it be best," she continued, speaking nervously, "if—if you do know anything about that unfortunate man—if you told it? Why have this suspicion fastening itself on you? You!"

Ransford made an effort to calm himself. He was furiously angry—angry with Bryce, angry with Mitchington, angry with the cloud of foolishness and stupidity that seemed to be gathering.

"Why should I—supposing that I do know something, which I don't admit—why should I allow myself to be coerced and frightened by these fools?" he asked. "No man can prevent suspicion falling on him—it's my bad luck in this instance. Why should I rush to the police-station and say, 'Here—I'll blurt out all I know—everything!' Why?"

"Wouldn't that be better than knowing that people are saying things?" she asked.

"As to that," replied Ransford, "you can't prevent people saying things—especially in a town like this. If it hadn't been for the unfortunate fact that Braden came to the surgery door, nothing would have been said. But what of that?—I have known hundreds of men in my time—aye, and forgotten them! No!—I am not going to fall a victim to this device—it all springs out of curiosity. As to this last affair—it's all nonsense!"

"But—if the man was really poisoned?" suggested Mary.

"Let the police find the poisoner!" said Ransford, with a grim smile. "That's their job."

Mary said nothing for a moment, and Ransford moved restlessly about the room.

"I don't trust that fellow Bryce," he said suddenly. "He's up to something. I don't forget what he said when I bundled him out that morning."

"What?" she asked.

"That he would be a bad enemy," answered Ransford. "He's posing now as a friend—but a man's never to be so much suspected as when he comes doing what you may call unnecessary acts of friendship. I'd rather that anybody was mixed up in my affairs—your affairs—than Pemberton Bryce!"

"So would I!" she said. "But—"

She paused there a moment and then looked appealingly at Ransford.

"I do wish you'd tell me—what you promised to tell me," she said. "You know what I mean—about me and Dick. Somehow—I don't quite know how or why—I've an uneasy feeling that Bryce knows something, and that he's mixing it all up with—this! Why not tell me—please!"

Ransford, who was still marching about the room, came to a halt, and leaning his hands on the table between them, looked earnestly at her.

"Don't ask that—now!" he said. "I can't—yet. The fact is, I'm waiting for something—some particulars. As soon as I get them, I'll speak to you—and to Dick. In the meantime—don't ask me again—and don't be afraid. And as to this affair, leave it to me—and if you meet Bryce again, refuse to discuss anything with him. Look here!—there's only one reason why he professes friendliness and a desire to save me annoyance. He thinks he can ingratiate himself with—you!"

"Mistaken!" murmured Mary, shaking her head. "I don't trust him. And—less than ever because of yesterday. Would an honest man have done what he did? Let that police inspector talk freely, as he did, with people concealed behind a curtain? And—he laughed about it! I hated myself for being there—yet could we help it?"

"I'm not going to hate myself on Pemberton Bryce's account," said Ransford. "Let him play his game—that he has one, I'm certain."

Bryce had gone away to continue his game—or another line of it. The Collishaw matter had not made him forget the Richard Jenkins tomb, and now, after leaving Ransford's house, he crossed the Close to Paradise with the object of doing a little more investigation. But at the archway of the ancient enclosure he met old Simpson Harker, pottering about in his usual apparently aimless fashion. Harker smiled at sight of Bryce.

"Ah, I was wanting to have a word with you, doctor!" he said. "Something important. Have you got a minute or two to spare, sir? Come round to my little place, then—we shall be quiet there."

Bryce had any amount of time to spare for an interesting person like Harker, and he followed the old man to his house—a tiny place set in a nest of similar old-world buildings behind the Close. Harker led him into a little parlor, comfortable and snug, wherein were several shelves of books of a curiously legal and professional-looking aspect, some old pictures, and a cabinet of odds and ends, stowed away in of dark corner. The old man motioned him to an easy chair, and going over to a cupboard, produced a decanter of whisky and a box of cigars.

"We can have a peaceful and comfortable talk here, doctor," he remarked, as he sat down near Bryce, after fetching glasses and soda-water. "I live all alone, like a hermit—my bit of work's done by a woman who only looks in of a morning. So we're all by ourselves. Light your cigar!—same as that I gave you at Barthorpe. Um—well, now," he continued, as Bryce settled down to listen. "There's a question I want to put to you—strictly between ourselves—strictest of confidence, you know. It was you who was called to Braden by Varner, and you were left alone with Braden's body?"

"Well?" admitted Bryce, suddenly growing suspicious. "What of it?"

Harker edged his chair a little closer to his guest's, and leaned towards him.

"What," he asked in a whisper, "what have you done with that scrap of paper that you took out of Braden's purse?"

XIV - From the Past

If any remarkably keen and able observer of the odd characteristics of humanity had been present in Harker's little parlor at that moment, watching him and his visitor, he would have been struck by what happened when the old man put this sudden and point-blank question to the young one. For Harker put the question, though in a whisper, in no more than a casual, almost friendlily-confidential way, and Bryce never showed by the start of a finger or the flicker of an eyelash that he felt it to be what he really knew it to be—the most surprising and startling question he had ever had put to him. Instead, he looked his questioner calmly in the eyes, and put a question in his turn.

"Who are you, Mr. Harker?" asked Bryce quietly.

Harker laughed—almost gleefully.

"Yes, you've a right to ask that!" he said. "Of course!—glad you take it that way. You'll do!"

"I'll qualify it, then," added Bryce. "It's not who—it's what are you!"

Harker waved his cigar at the book-shelves in front of which his visitor sat.

"Take a look at my collection of literature, doctor," he said. "What d'ye think of it?"

Bryce turned and leisurely inspected one shelf after another.

"Seems to consist of little else but criminal cases and legal handbooks," he remarked quietly. "I begin to suspect you, Mr. Harker. They say here in Wrychester that you're a retired tradesman. I think you're a retired policeman—of the detective branch."

Harker laughed again.

"No Wrychester man has ever crossed my threshold since I came to settle down here," he said. "You're the first person I've ever asked in—with one notable exception. I've never even had Campany, the librarian, here. I'm a hermit."

"But—you were a detective?" suggested Bryce.

"Aye, for a good five-and-twenty years!" replied Harker. "And pretty well known, too, sir. But—my question, doctor. All between ourselves!"

"I'll ask you one, then," said Bryce. "How do you know I took a scrap of paper from Braden's purse?"

"Because I know that he had such a paper in his purse the night he came to the Mitre," answered Harker, "and was certain to have it there next morning, and because I also know that you were left alone with the body for some minutes after Varner fetched you to it, and that when Braden's clothing and effects were searched by Mitchington, the paper wasn't there. So, of course, you took it! Doesn't matter to me that ye did—except that I know, from knowing that, that you're on a similar game to my own—which is why you went down to Leicestershire."

"You knew Braden?" asked Bryce.

"I knew him!" answered Harker.

"You saw him—spoke with him—here in Wrychester?" suggested Bryce.

"He was here—in this room—in that chair—from five minutes past nine to close on ten o'clock the night before his death," replied Harker.

Bryce, who was quietly appreciating the Havana cigar which the old man had given him, picked up his glass, took a drink, and settled himself in his easy chair as if he meant to stay there awhile.

"I think we'd better talk confidentially, Mr. Harker," he said.

"Precisely what we are doing, Dr. Bryce," replied Harker.

"All right, my friend," said Bryce, laconically. "Now we understand each other. So—do you know who John Braden really was?"

"Yes!" replied Harker, promptly. "He was in reality John Brake, ex-bank manager, ex-convict."

"Do you know if he's any relatives here in Wrychester?" inquired Bryce.

"Yes," said Harker. "The boy and girl who live with Ransford—they're Brake's son and daughter."

"Did Brake know that—when he came here?" continued Bryce.

"No, he didn't—he hadn't the least idea of it," responded Harker.

"Had you—then?" asked Bryce.

"No—not until later—a little later," replied Harker.

"You found it out at Barthorpe?" suggested Bryce.

"Not a bit of it; I worked it out here—after Brake was dead," said Harker. "I went to Barthorpe on quite different business—Brake's business."

"Ah!" said Bryce. He looked the old detective quietly in the eyes. "You'd better tell me all about it," he added.

"If we're both going to tell each other—all about it," stipulated Harker.

"That's settled," assented Bryce.

Harker smoked thoughtfully for a moment and seemed to be thinking.

"I'd better go back to the beginning," he said. "But, first—what do you know about Brake? I know you went down to Barthorpe to find out what you could—how far did your searches take you?"

"I know that Brake married a girl from Braden Medworth, that he took her to London, where he was manager of a branch bank, that he got into trouble, and was sentenced to ten years' penal servitude," answered Bryce, "together with some small details into which we needn't go at present."

"Well, as long as you know all that, there's a common basis and a common starting-point," remarked Harker, "so I'll begin at Brake's trial. It was I who arrested Brake. There was no trouble, no bother. He'd been taken unawares, by an inspector of the bank. He'd a considerable deficiency—couldn't make it good—couldn't or wouldn't explain except by half-sullen hints that he'd been cruelly deceived. There was no defense—couldn't be. His counsel said that he could—"

"I've read the account of the trial," interrupted Bryce.

"All right—then you know as much as I can tell you on that point," said Harker. "He got, as you say, ten years. I saw him just before he was removed and asked him if there was anything I could do for him about his wife and children. I'd never seen them—I arrested him at the bank, and, of course, he was never out of custody after that. He answered in a queer, curt way that his wife and children were being looked after. I heard, incidentally, that his wife had left home, or was from home—there was something mysterious about it—either as soon as he was arrested or before. Anyway, he said nothing, and from that moment I never set eyes on him again until I met him in the street here in Wrychester, the other night, when he came to the Mitre. I knew him at once—and he knew me. We met under one of those big standard lamps in the Market Place—I was following my usual practice of having an evening walk, last thing before going to bed. And we stopped and stared at each other. Then he came forward with his hand out, and we shook hands. 'This is an odd thing!' he said. 'You're the very man I wanted to find! Come somewhere, where it's quiet, and let me have a word with you.' So—I brought him here."

Bryce was all attention now—for once he was devoting all his faculties to tense and absorbed concentration on what another man could tell, leaving reflections and conclusions on what he heard until all had been told.

"I brought him here," repeated Harker. "I told him I'd been retired and was living here, as he saw, alone. I asked him no questions about himself—I could see he was a well-dressed, apparently well-to-do man. And presently he began to tell me about himself. He said that after he'd finished his term he left England and for some time travelled in Canada and the United States, and had gone then—on to New Zealand and afterwards to Australia, where he'd settled down and begun speculating in wool. I said I hoped he'd done well. Yes, he said, he'd done very nicely—and then he gave me a quiet dig in the ribs. 'I'll tell you one thing I've done, Harker,' he said. 'You were very polite and considerate to me when I'd my trouble, so I don't mind telling you. I paid the bank every penny of that money they lost through my foolishness at that time—every penny, four years ago, with interest, and

I've got their receipt.' 'Delighted to hear it, Mr.—Is it the same name still?' I said. 'My name ever since I left England,' he said, giving me a look, 'is Braden—John Braden.' 'Yes,' he went on, 'I paid 'em—though I never had one penny of the money I was fool enough to take for the time being—not one halfpenny!' 'Who had it, Mr. Braden?' I asked him, thinking that he'd perhaps tell after all that time. 'Never mind, my lad!' he answered. 'It'll come out—yet. Never mind that, now. I'll tell you why I wanted to see you. The fact is, I've only been a few hours in England, so to speak, but I'd thought of you, and wondered where I could get hold of you—you're the only man of your profession I ever met, you see,' he added, with a laugh. 'And I want a bit of help in that way.' 'Well, Mr. Braden,' I said, 'I've retired, but if it's an easy job—' 'It's one you can do, easy enough,' he said. 'It's just this—I met a man in Australia who's extremely anxious to get some news of another man, named Falkiner Wraye, who hails from Barthorpe, in Leicestershire. I promised to make inquiries for him. Now, I have strong reasons why I don't want to go near Barthorpe—Barthorpe has unpleasant memories and associations for me, and I don't want to be seen there. But this thing's got to be personal investigation—will you go here, for me? I'll make it worth your while. All you've got to do,' he went on, 'is to go there—see the police authorities, town officials, anybody that knows the place, and ask them if they can tell you anything of one Falkiner Wraye, who was at one time a small estate agent in Barthorpe, left the place about seventeen years ago—maybe eighteen—and is believed to have recently gone back to the neighborhood. That's all. Get what information you can, and write it to me, care of my bankers in London. Give me a sheet of paper and I'll put down particulars for you.'"

Harker paused at this point and nodded his head at an old bureau which stood in a corner of his room.

"The sheet of paper's there," he said. "It's got on it, in his writing, a brief memorandum of what he wanted and the address of his bankers. When he'd given it to me, he put his hand in his pocket and pulled out a purse in which I could see he was carrying plenty of money. He took out some notes. 'Here's five-and-twenty pounds on account, Harker,' he said. 'You might have to spend a bit. Don't be afraid—plenty more where that comes from. You'll do it soon?' he asked. 'Yes, I'll do it, Mr. Braden,' I answered. 'It'll be a bit of a holiday for me.' 'That's all right,' he said. 'I'm delighted I came across you.' 'Well, you couldn't be more delighted than I was surprised,' I said. 'I never thought to see you in Wrychester. What brought you here, if one may ask—sight-seeing?' He laughed at that, and he pulled out his purse again. 'I'll show you something—a secret,' he said, and he took a bit of folded paper out of his purse. 'What do you make of that?' he asked. 'Can you read Latin?' 'No—except a word or two,' I said, 'but I know a man who can.' 'Ah, never mind,' said he. 'I know enough Latin for this—and it's a secret. However, it won't be a secret long, and you'll hear all about it.' And with that he put the bit of paper in his purse again, and we began talking about other matters, and before long he said he'd promised to have a chat with a gentleman at the Mitre whom he'd come along with in the train, and away he went, saying he'd see me before he left the town."

"Did he say how long he was going to stop here?" asked Bryce.

"Two or three days," replied Harker.

"Did he mention Ransford?" inquired Bryce.

"Never!" said Harker.

"Did he make any reference to his wife and children?"

"Not the slightest!"

"Nor to the hint that his counsel threw out at the trial?"

"Never referred to that time except in the way I told you—that he hadn't a penny of the money, himself and that he'd himself refunded it."

Bryce meditated awhile. He was somewhat puzzled by certain points in the old detective's story, and he saw now that there was much more mystery in the Braden affair than he had at first believed.

"Well," he asked, after a while, "did you see him again?"

"Not alive!" replied Harker. "I saw him dead—and I held my tongue, and have held it. But—something happened that day. After I heard of the accident, I went into the Crown and Cushion tavern—the fact was, I went to get a taste of whisky, for the news had upset me. And in that long bar of theirs, I saw a man whom I knew—a man whom I knew, for a fact, to have been a fellow convict of Brake's. Name of Glassdale—forgery. He got the same sentence that Brake got, about the same time, was in the same convict prison with Brake, and he and Brake would be released about the same date. There was no doubt about his identity—I never forget a face, even after thirty years I'd tell one. I saw him in that bar before he saw me, and I took a careful look at him. He, too, like Brake, was very well dressed, and very prosperous looking. He turned as he set down his glass, and caught sight of me—and he knew me. Mind you, he'd been through my hands in times past! And he instantly moved to a side-door and—vanished. I went out and looked up and down—he'd gone. I found out afterwards, by a little quiet inquiry, that he'd gone straight to the station, boarded the first train—there was one just giving out, to the junction—and left the city. But I can lay hands on him!"

"You've kept this quiet, too?" asked Bryce.

"Just so—I've my own game to play," replied Harker. "This talk with you is part of it—you come in, now—I'll tell you why, presently. But first, as you know, I went to Barthorpe. For, though Brake was dead, I felt I must go—for this reason. I was certain that he wanted that information for himself—the man in Australia was a fiction. I went, then—and learned nothing. Except that this Falkiner Wraye had been, as Brake said, a Barthorpe man, years ago. He'd left the town eighteen years since, and nobody knew anything about him. So I came home. And now then, doctor—your turn! What were you after, down there at Barthorpe?"

Bryce meditated his answer for a good five minutes. He had always intended to play the game off his own bat, but he had heard and seen enough since entering Harker's little room to know that he was in company with an intellect which was keener and more subtle than his, and that it would be all to his advantage to go in with the man who had vast and deep experience. And so he made a clean breast of all he had done in the way of investigation, leaving his motive completely aside.

"You've got a theory, of course?" observed Harker, after listening quietly to all that Bryce could tell. "Naturally, you have! You couldn't accumulate all that without getting one."

"Well," admitted Bryce, "honestly, I can't say that I have. But I can see what theory there might be. This—that Ransford was the man who deceived Brake, that he ran away with Brake's wife, that she's dead, and that he's brought up the children in ignorance of all that—and therefore—"

"And therefore," interrupted Harker with a smile, "that when he and Brake met—as you seem to think they did—Ransford flung Brake through that open doorway; that Collishaw witnessed it, that Ransford's found out about Collishaw, and that Collishaw has been poisoned by Ransford. Eh?"

"That's a theory that seems to be supported by facts," said Bryce.

"It's a theory that would doubtless suit men like Mitchington," said the old detective, with another smile. "But—not me, sir! Mind you, I don't say there isn't something in it—there's doubtless a lot. But—the mystery's a lot thicker than just that. And Brake didn't come here to find Ransford. He came because of the secret in that scrap of paper. And as you've got it, doctor—out with it!"

Bryce saw no reason for concealment and producing the scrap of paper laid it on the table between himself and his host. Harker peered inquisitively at it.

"Latin!" he said. "You can read it, of course. What does it say?"

Bryce repeated a literal translation.

"I've found the place," he added. "I found it this morning. Now, what do you suppose this means?"

Harker was looking hard at the two lines of writing.

"That's a big question, doctor," he answered. "But I'll go so far as to say this—when we've found out what it does mean, we shall know a lot more than we know now!"

XV - The Double Offer

Bryce, who was deriving a considerable and peculiar pleasure from his secret interview with the old detective, smiled at Harker's last remark.

"That's a bit of a platitude, isn't it?" he suggested. "Of course we shall know a lot more—when we do know a lot more!"

"I set store by platitudes, sir," retorted Harker. "You can't repeat an established platitude too often—it's got the hallmark of good use on it. But now, till we do know more—you've no doubt been thinking a lot about this matter, Dr. Bryce—hasn't it struck you that there's one feature in connection with Brake, or Braden's visit to Wrychester to which nobody's given any particular attention up to now—so far as we know, at any rate?"

"What?" demanded Bryce.

"This," replied Harker. "Why did he wish to see the Duke of Saxonsteade? He certainly did want to see him—and as soon as possible. You'll remember that his Grace was questioned about that at the inquest and could give no explanation—he knew nothing of Brake, and couldn't suggest any reason why Brake should wish to have an interview with him. But—I can!"

"You?" exclaimed Bryce.

"I," answered Harker. "And it's this—I spoke just now of that man Glassdale. Now you, of course; have no knowledge of him, and as you don't keep yourself posted in criminal history, you don't know what his offence was?"

"You said—forgery?" replied Bryce.

"Just so—forgery," assented Harker. "And the signature that he forged was—the Duke of Saxonsteade's! As a matter of fact, he was the Duke's London estate agent. He got wrong, somehow, and he forged the Duke's name to a cheque. Now, then, considering who Glassdale is, and that he was certainly a fellow-convict of Brake's, and that I myself saw him here in Wrychester on the day of Brake's death—what's the conclusion to be drawn? That Brake wanted to see the Duke on some business of Glassdale's! Without a doubt! It may have been that he and Glassdale wanted to visit the Duke, together."

Bryce silently considered this suggestion for a while.

"You said, just now, that Glassdale could be traced?" he remarked at last.

"Traced—yes," replied Harker. "So long as he's in England."

"Why not set about it?" suggested Bryce.

"Not yet," said Harker. "There's things to do before that. And the first thing is—let's get to know what the mystery of that scrap of paper is. You say you've found Richard Jenkins's tomb? Very well—then the thing to do is to find out if anything is hidden there. Try it tomorrow night. Better go by yourself—after dark. If you find anything, let me know. And then—then we can decide on a next step. But between now and then, there'll be the inquest on this man Collishaw. And, about that—a word in your ear! Say as little as ever you can!—after all, you know nothing beyond what you saw. And—we mustn't meet and talk in public—after you've done that bit of exploring in Paradise tomorrow night, come round here and we'll consider matters."

There was little that Bryce could say or could be asked to say at the inquest on the mason's laborer next morning. Public interest and excitement was as keen about Collishaw's mysterious death as about Braden's, for it was already rumored through the town that if Braden had not met with his death when he came to Wrychester, Collishaw would still be alive. The Coroner's court was once more packed; once more there was the same atmosphere of mystery. But the proceedings were of a very different nature to those which had attended the inquest on Braden. The foreman under whose orders Collishaw had been working gave particulars of the dead man's work on the morning of his death. He had been instructed to clear away an accumulation of rubbish which had gathered at the foot of the south wall of the nave in consequence of some recent repairs to the masonry—there was a full day's work before him. All day he would be in and out of Paradise with his barrow, wheeling away the rubbish he gathered up. The foreman had looked in on him once or twice; he had seen him just before noon, when he appeared to be in his usual health—he had made no complaint, at any rate. Asked if he had happened to notice where Collishaw had set down his dinner basket and his tin bottle while he worked, he replied that it so happened that he had—he remembered seeing both bottle and basket and the man's jacket deposited on one of the box-tombs under a certain yew-tree—which he could point out, if necessary.

Bryce's account of his finding of Collishaw amounted to no more than a bare recital of facts. Nor was much time spent in questioning the two doctors who had conducted the post-mortem examination. Their evidence, terse and particular, referred solely to the cause of death. The man had been poisoned by a dose of hydrocyanic acid, which, in their opinion, had been taken only a few minutes before his body was discovered by Dr. Bryce. It had probably been a dose which would cause instantaneous death. There were no traces of the poison in the remains of his dinner, nor in the liquid in his tin bottle, which was old tea. But of the cause of his sudden death there was no more doubt than of the effects. Ransford had been in the court from the outset of the proceedings, and when the medical evidence had been given he was called. Bryce, watching him narrowly, saw that he was suffering from repressed excitement—and that that excitement was as much due to anger as to anything else. His face was set and stern, and he looked at the Coroner with an expression which portended something not precisely clear at that moment. Bryce, trying to analyze it, said to himself that he shouldn't be surprised if a scene followed—Ransford looked like a man who is bursting to say something in no unmistakable fashion. But at first he answered the questions put to him calmly and decisively.

"When this man's clothing was searched," observed the Coroner, "a box of pills was found, Dr. Ransford, on which your writing appears. Had you been attending him—professionally?"

"Yes," replied Ransford. "Both Collishaw and his wife. Or, rather, to be exact, I had been in attendance on the wife, for some weeks. A day or two before his death, Collishaw complained to me of indigestion, following on his meals. I gave him some digestive pills—the pills you speak of, no doubt."

"These?" asked the Coroner, passing over the box which Mitchington had found.

"Precisely!" agreed Ransford. "That, at any rate, is the box, and I suppose those to be the pills."

"You made them up yourself?" inquired the Coroner.

"I did—I dispense all my own medicines."

"Is it possible that the poison we have heard of, just now, could get into one of those pills—by accident?"

"Utterly impossible!—under my hands, at any rate," answered Ransford.

"Still, I suppose, it could have been administered in a pill?" suggested the Coroner.

"It might," agreed Ransford. "But," he added, with a significant glance at the medical men who had just given evidence. "It was not so administered in this case, as the previous witnesses very well know!"

The Coroner looked round him, and waited a moment.

"You are at liberty to explain—that last remark," he said at last. "That is—if you wish to do so." "Certainly!" answered Ransford, with alacrity. "Those pills are, as you will observe, coated, and the man would swallow them whole—immediately after his food. Now, it would take some little time for a pill to dissolve, to disintegrate, to be digested. If Collishaw took one of my pills as soon as he had eaten his dinner, according to instructions, and if poison had been in that pill, he would not have died at once—as he evidently did. Death would probably have been delayed some little time until the pill had dissolved. But, according to the evidence you have had before you, he died quite suddenly while eating his dinner—or immediately after it. I am not legally represented here—I don't consider it at all necessary—but I ask you to recall Dr. Coates and to put this question to him: Did he find one of those digestive pills in this man's stomach?"

The Coroner turned, somewhat dubiously, to the two doctors who had performed the autopsy. But before he could speak, the superintendent of police rose and began to whisper to him, and after a conversation between them, he looked round at the jury, every member of which had evidently been much struck by Ransford's suggestion.

"At this stage," he said, "it will be necessary to adjourn. I shall adjourn the inquiry for a week, gentlemen. You will—" Ransford, still standing in the witness-box, suddenly lost control of himself. He uttered a sharp exclamation and smote the ledge before him smartly with his open hand.

"I protest against that!" he said vehemently. "Emphatically, I protest! You first of all make a suggestion which tells against me—then, when I demand that a question shall be put which is of immense importance to my interests, you close down the inquiry—even if only for the moment. That is grossly unfair and unjust!"

"You are mistaken," said the Coroner. "At the adjourned inquiry, the two medical men can be recalled, and you will have the opportunity—or your solicitor will have—of asking any questions you like for the present—"

"For the present you have me under suspicion!" interrupted Ransford hotly. "You know it—I say this with due respect to your office—as well as I do. Suspicion is rife in the city against me. Rumor is being spread—secretly—and, I am certain—from the police, who ought to know better. And—I will not be silenced, Mr. Coroner!—I take this public opportunity, as I am on oath, of saying that I know nothing whatever of the causes of the deaths of either Collishaw or of Braden—upon my solemn oath!"

"The inquest is adjourned to this day week," said the Coroner quietly.

Ransford suddenly stepped down from the witness-box and without word or glance at any one there, walked with set face and determined look out of the court, and the excited spectators, gathering into groups, immediately began to discuss his vigorous outburst and to take sides for and against him.

Bryce, judging it advisable to keep away from Mitchington just then, and, for similar reasons, keeping away from Harker also, went out of the crowded building alone—to be joined in the street outside by Sackville Bonham, whom he had noticed in court, in company with his stepfather, Mr. Folliot.

Folliot, Bryce had observed, had stopped behind, exchanging some conversation with the Coroner. Sackville came up to Bryce with a knowing shake of the hand. He was one of those very young men who have a habit of suggesting that their fund of knowledge is extensive and peculiar, and Bryce waited for a manifestation.

"Queer business, all that, Bryce!" observed Sackville confidentially. "Of course, Ransford is a perfect ass!"

"Think so?" remarked Bryce, with an inflection which suggested that Sackville's opinion on anything was as valuable as the Attorney-General's. "That's how it strikes you, is it?"

"Impossible that it could strike one in any other way, you know," answered Sackville with fine and lofty superiority. "Ransford should have taken immediate steps to clear himself of any suspicion. It's ridiculous, considering his position—guardian to—to Miss Bewery, for instance—that he should allow such rumors to circulate. By God, sir, if it had been me, I'd have stopped 'em!—before they left the parish pump!"

"Ah?" said Bryce. "And—how?"

"Made an example of somebody," replied Sackville, with emphasis. "I believe there's law in this country, isn't there?—law against libel and slander, and that sort of thing, eh? Oh, yes!"

"Not been much time for that—yet," remarked Bryce.

"Piles of time," retorted Sackville, swinging his stick vigorously. "No, sir, Ransford is an ass! However, if a man won't do things for himself, well, his friends must do something for him. Ransford, of course, must be pulled—dragged!—out of this infernal hole. Of course he's suspected! But my stepfather—he's going to take a hand. And my stepfather, Bryce, is a devilish cute old hand at a game of this sort!"

"Nobody doubts Mr. Folliot's abilities, I'm sure," said Bryce. "But—you don't mind saying—how is he going to take a hand?"

"Stir things towards a clearing-up," announced Sackville promptly. "Have the whole thing gone into—thoroughly. There are matters that haven't been touched on, yet. You'll see, my boy!"

"Glad to hear it," said Bryce. "But—why should Mr. Folliot be so particular about clearing Ransford?"

Sackville swung his stick, and pulled up his collar, and jerked his nose a trifle higher.

"Oh, well," he said. "Of course, it's—it's a pretty well understood thing, don't you know—between myself and Miss Bewery, you know—and of course, we couldn't have any suspicions attaching to her guardian, could we, now? Family interest, don't you know—Caesar's wife, and all that sort of thing, eh?"

"I see," answered Bryce, quietly,—"sort of family arrangement. With Ransford's consent and knowledge, of course?"

"Ransford won't even be consulted," said Sackville, airily. "My stepfather—sharp man, that, Bryce!—he'll do things in his own fashion. You look out for sudden revelations!"

"I will," replied Bryce. "By-bye!"

He turned off to his rooms, wondering how much of truth there was in the fatuous Sackville's remarks. And—was there some mystery still undreamt of by himself and Harker? There might be—he was still under the influence of Ransford's indignant and dramatic assertion of his innocence. Would Ransford have allowed himself an outburst of that sort if he had not been, as he said, utterly ignorant of the immediate cause of Braden's death? Now Bryce, all through, was calculating, for his own purposes, on Ransford's share, full or partial, in that death—if Ransford really knew nothing whatever about it, where did his, Bryce's theory, come in—and how would his present machinations result? And, more—if Ransford's assertion were true, and if Varner's story of the hand, seen for an instant in the archway, were also true—and Varner was persisting in it—then, who was the man who flung Braden to his death that morning? He realized that, instead of straightening out, things were becoming more and more complicated.

But he realized something else. On the surface, there was a strong case of suspicion against Ransford. It had been suggested that very morning before a coroner and his jury; it would grow; the police were already permeated with suspicion and distrust. Would it not pay him, Bryce, to encourage, to help it? He had his own score to pay off against Ransford; he had his own schemes as regards Mary Bewery. Anyway, he was not going to share in any attempts to clear the man who had bundled him out of his house unceremoniously—he would bide his time. And in the meantime there were other things to be done—one of them that very night.

But before Bryce could engage in his secret task of excavating a small portion of Paradise in the rear of Richard Jenkins's tomb, another strange development came. As the dark fell over the old city that night and he was thinking of setting out on his mission, Mitchington came in, carrying two sheets of paper, obviously damp from the press, in his hand. He looked at Bryce with an expression of wonder.

"Here's a queer go!" he said. "I can't make this out at all! Look at these big handbills—but perhaps you've seen 'em? They're being posted all over the city—we've had a bundle of 'em thrown in on us."

"I haven't been out since lunch," remarked Bryce. "What are they?"

Mitchington spread out the two papers on the table, pointing from one to the other.

"You see?" he said. "Five Hundred Pounds Reward!—One Thousand Pounds Reward! And—both out at the same time, from different sources!"

"What sources?" asked Bryce, bending over the bills. "Ah—I see. One signed by Phipps & Maynard, the other by Beachcroft. Odd, certainly!"

"Odd?" exclaimed Mitchington. "I should think so! But, do you see, doctor? that one—five hundred reward—is offered for information of any nature relative to the deaths of John Braden and James Collishaw, both or either. That amount will be paid for satisfactory information by Phipps & Maynard. And Phipps & Maynard are Ransford's solicitors! That bill, sir, comes from him! And now the other, the thousand pound one, that offers the reward to anyone who can give definite information as to the circumstances attending the death of John Braden—to be paid by Mr. Beachcroft. And he's Mr. Folliot's solicitor! So—that comes from Mr. Folliot. What has he to do with it? And are these two putting their heads together—or are these bills quite independent of each other? Hang me if I understand it!"

Bryce read and re-read the contents of the two bills. And then he thought for a while before speaking.

"Well," he said at last, "there's probably this in it—the Folliots are very wealthy people. Mrs. Folliot, it's pretty well known, wants her son to marry Miss Bewery—Dr. Ransford's ward. Probably she doesn't wish any suspicion to hang over the family. That's all I can suggest. In the other case, Ransford wants to clear himself. For don't forget this, Mitchington!—somewhere, somebody may know something! Only something. But that something might clear Ransford of the suspicion that's undoubtedly been cast upon him. If you're thinking to get a strong case against Ransford, you've got your work set. He gave your theory a nasty knock this morning by his few words about that pill. Did Coates and Everest find a pill, now?"

"Not at liberty to say, sir," answered Mitchington. "At present, anyway. Um! I dislike these private offers of reward—it means that those who make 'em get hold of information which is kept back from us, d'you see! They're inconvenient."

Then he went away, and Bryce, after waiting awhile, until night had settled down, slipped quietly out of the house and set off for the gloom of Paradise.

XVI - Beforehand

In accordance with his undeniable capacity for contriving and scheming, Bryce had made due and careful preparations for his visit to the tomb of Richard Jenkins. Even in the momentary confusion following upon his discovery of Collishaw's dead body, he had been sufficiently alive to his own immediate purposes to notice that the tomb—a very ancient and dilapidated structure—stood in the midst of a small expanse of stone pavement between the yew-trees and the wall of the nave; he had noticed also that the pavement consisted of small squares of stone, some of which bore initials and dates. A sharp glance at the presumed whereabouts of the particular spot which he wanted, as indicated in the scrap of paper taken from Braden's purse, showed him that he would have to raise one of those small squares—possibly two or three of them. And so he had furnished himself with a short crowbar of tempered steel, specially purchased at the iron-monger's, and with a small bull's-eye lantern. Had he been arrested and searched as he made his way towards the cathedral precincts he might reasonably have been suspected of a design to break into the treasury and appropriate the various ornaments for which Wrychester was famous. But Bryce feared neither arrest nor observation. During his residence in Wrychester he had done a good deal of prowling about the old city at night, and he knew that Paradise, at any time after dark, was a deserted place. Folk might cross from the close archway to the wicket-gate by the outer path, but no one would penetrate within the thick screen of yew and cypress when night had fallen. And now, in early summer, the screen of trees and bushes was so thick in leaf, that once within it, foliage on one side, the great walls of the nave on the other, there was little likelihood of any person overlooking his doings while he made his investigation. He anticipated a swift and quiet job, to be done in a few minutes.

But there was another individual in Wrychester who knew just as much of the geography of Paradise as Pemberton Bryce knew. Dick Bewery and Betty Campany had of late progressed out of the schoolboy and schoolgirl hail-fellow-well-met stage to the first dawnings of love, and in spite of their frequent meetings had begun a romantic correspondence between each other, the joy and mystery of which was increased a hundredfold by a secret method of exchange of these missives. Just within the wicket-gate entrance of Paradise there was an old monument wherein was a convenient cavity—Dick Bewery's ready wits transformed this into love's post-office. In it he regularly placed letters for Betty: Betty stuffed into it letters for him. And on this particular evening Dick had gone to Paradise to collect a possible mail, and as Bryce walked leisurely up the narrow path, enclosed by trees and old masonry which led from Friary Lane to the ancient enclosure, Dick turned a corner and ran full into him. In the light of the single lamp which illumined the path, the two recovered themselves and looked at each other.

"Hullo!" said Bryce. "What's your hurry, young Bewery?"

Dick, who was panting for breath, more from excitement than haste, drew back and looked at Bryce. Up to then he knew nothing much against Bryce, whom he had rather liked in the fashion in which boys sometimes like their seniors, and he was not indisposed to confide in him.

"Hullo!" he replied. "I say! Where are you off to?"

"Nowhere!—strolling round," answered Bryce. "No particular purpose, why?"

"You weren't going in—there?" asked Dick, jerking a thumb towards Paradise.

"In—there!" exclaimed Bryce. "Good Lord, no!—dreary enough in the daytime! What should I be going in there for?"

Dick seized Bryce's coat-sleeve and dragged him aside.

"I say!" he whispered. "There's something up in there—a search of some sort!"

Bryce started in spite of an effort to keep unconcerned.

"A search? In there?" he said. "What do you mean?"

Dick pointed amongst the trees, and Bryce saw the faint glimmer of a light.

"I was in there—just now," said Dick. "And some men—three or four—came along. They're in there, close up by the nave, just where you found that chap Collishaw. They're—digging—or something of that sort!"

"Digging!" muttered Bryce. "Digging?"

"Something like it, anyhow," replied Dick. "Listen."

Bryce heard the ring of metal on stone. And an unpleasant conviction stole over him that he was being forestalled, that somebody was beforehand with him, and he cursed himself for not having done the previous night what he had left undone till this night.

"Who are they?" he asked. "Did you see them—their faces?"

"Not their faces," answered Dick. "Only their figures in the gloom. But I heard Mitchington's voice."

"Police, then!" said Bryce. "What on earth are they after?"

"Look here!" whispered Dick, pulling at Bryce's arm again. "Come on! I know how to get in there without their seeing us. You follow me."

Bryce followed readily, and Dick stepping through the wicket-gate, seized his companion's wrist and led him amongst the bushes in the direction of the spot from whence came the metallic sounds. He walked with the step of a cat, and Bryce took pains to follow his example. And presently from behind a screen of cypresses they looked out on the expanse of flagging in the midst of which stood the tomb of Richard Jenkins.

Round about that tomb were five men whose faces were visible enough in the light thrown by a couple of strong lamps, one of which stood on the tomb itself, while the other was set on the ground. Four out of the five the two watchers recognized at once. One, kneeling on the flags, and busy with a small crowbar similar to that which Bryce carried inside his overcoat, was the master-mason of the cathedral. Another, standing near him, was Mitchington. A third was a clergyman—one of the lesser dignitaries of the Chapter. A fourth—whose presence made Bryce start for the second time that evening—was the Duke of Saxonsteade. But the fifth was a stranger—a tall man who stood between Mitchington and the Duke, evidently paying anxious attention to the master-mason's proceedings. He was no Wrychester man—Bryce was convinced of that.

And a moment later he was convinced of another equally certain fact. Whatever these five men were searching for, they had no clear or accurate idea of its exact whereabouts. The master-mason was taking up the small squares of flagstone with his crowbar one by one, from the outer edge of the foot of the old box-tomb; as he removed each, he probed the earth beneath it. And Bryce, who had instinctively realized what was happening, and knew that somebody else than himself was in possession of the secret of the scrap of paper, saw that it would be some time before they arrived at the precise spot indicated in the Latin directions. He quietly drew back and tugged at Dick Bewery.

"Stop here, and keep quiet!" he whispered when they had retreated out of all danger of being overheard. "Watch 'em! I want to fetch somebody—want to know who that stranger is. You don't know him?"

"Never seen him before," replied Dick. "I say!—come quietly back—don't give it away. I want to know what it's all about."

Bryce squeezed the lad's arm by way of assurance and made his way back through the bushes. He wanted to get hold of Harker, and at once, and he hurried round to the old man's house and without ceremony walked into his parlor. Harker, evidently expecting him, and meanwhile amusing himself with his pipe and book, rose from his chair as the younger man entered.

"Found anything?" he asked.

"We're done!" answered Bryce. "I was a fool not to go last night! We're forestalled, my friend!—that's about it!"

"By—whom?" inquired Harker.

"There are five of them at it, now," replied Bryce. "Mitchington, a mason, one of the cathedral clergy, a stranger, and the Duke of Saxonsteade! What do you think of that?"

Harker suddenly started as if a new light had dawned on him.

"The Duke!" he exclaimed. "You don't say so! My conscience!—now, I wonder if that can really be? Upon my word, I'd never thought of it!"

"Thought of what?" demanded Bryce.

"Never mind! tell you later," said Harker. "At present, is there any chance of getting a look at them?"

"That's what I came for," retorted Bryce. "I've been watching them, with young Bewery. He put me up to it. Come on! I want to see if you know the man who's a stranger."

Harker crossed the room to a chest of drawers, and after some rummaging pulled something out.

"Here!" he said, handing some articles to Bryce. "Put those on over your boots. Thick felt overshoes—you could walk round your own mother's bedroom in those and she'd never hear you. I'll do the same. A stranger, you say? Well, this is a proof that somebody knows the secret of that scrap of paper besides us, doctor!"

"They don't know the exact spot," growled Bryce, who was chafing at having been done out of his discovery. "But, they'll find it, whatever may be there."

He led Harker back to Paradise and to the place where he had left Dick Bewery, whom they approached so quietly that Bryce was by the lad's side before Dick knew he was there. And Harker, after one glance at the ring of faces, drew Bryce back and put his lips close to his ear and breathed a name in an almost imperceptible yet clear whisper.

"Glassdale!"

Bryce started for the third time. Glassdale!—the man whom Harker had seen in Wrychester within an hour or so of Braden's death: the ex-convict, the forger, who had forged the Duke of Saxonsteade's name! And there! standing, apparently quite at his ease, by the Duke's side. What did it all mean?

There was no explanation of what it meant to be had from the man whom Bryce and Harker and Dick Bewery secretly watched from behind the screen of cypress trees. Four of them watched in silence, or with no more than a whispered word now and then while the fifth worked. This man worked methodically, replacing each stone as he took it up and examined the soil beneath it. So far nothing had resulted, but he was by that time working at some distance from the tomb, and Bryce, who had an exceedingly accurate idea of where the spot might be, as indicated in the measurements on the scrap of paper, nudged Harker as the master-mason began to take up the last of the small flags. And suddenly there was a movement amongst the watchers, and the master-mason looked up from his job and motioned Mitchington to pass him a trowel which lay at a little distance.

"Something here!" he said, loudly enough to reach the ears of Bryce and his companions. "Not so deep down, neither, gentlemen!"

A few vigorous applications of the trowel, a few lumps of earth cast out of the cavity, and the master-mason put in his hand and drew forth a small parcel, which in the light of the lamp held close to it by Mitchington looked to be done up in coarse sacking, secured by great blotches of black sealing wax. And now it was Harker who nudged Bryce, drawing his attention to the fact that the parcel, handed by the master-mason to Mitchington was at once passed on by Mitchington to the Duke of Saxonsteade, who, it was very plain to see, appeared to be as much delighted as surprised at receiving it.

"Let us go to your office, inspector," he said. "We'll examine the contents there. Let us all go at once!"

The three figures behind the cypress trees remained immovable and silent until the five searchers had gone away with their lamps and tools and the sound of their retreating footsteps in Friary Lane had died out. Then Dick Bewery moved and began to slip off, and Bryce reached out a hand and took him by the shoulder.

"I say, Bewery!" he said. "Going to tell all that?"

Harker got in a word before Dick could answer.

"No matter if he does, doctor," he remarked quietly. "Whatever it is, the whole town'll know of it by tomorrow. They'll not keep it back."

Bryce let Dick go, and the boy immediately darted off in the direction of the close, while the two men went towards Harker's house. Neither spoke until they were safe in the old detective's little parlor, then Harker, turning up his lamp, looked at Bryce and shook his head.

"It's a good job I've retired!" he said, almost sadly. "I'm getting too old for my trade, doctor. Once upon a time I should have been fit to kick myself for not having twigged the meaning of this business sooner than I have done!"

"Have you twigged it?" demanded Bryce, almost scornfully. "You're a good deal cleverer than I am if you have. For hang me if I know what it means!"

"I do!" answered Harker. He opened a drawer in his desk and drew out a scrap-book, filled, as Bryce saw a moment later, with cuttings from newspapers, all duly arranged and indexed. The old man glanced at the index, turned to a certain page, and put his finger on an entry. "There you are!" he said. "And that's only one—there are several more. They'll tell you in detail what I can tell you in a few words and what I ought to have remembered. It's fifteen years since the famous robbery at Saxonsteade which has never been accounted for—robbery of the Duchess's diamonds—one of the cleverest burglaries ever known, doctor. They were got one night after a grand ball there; no arrest was ever made, they were never traced. And I'll lay all I'm worth to a penny-piece that the Duke and those men are gladding their eyes with the sight of them just now!—in Mitchington's office—and that the information that they were where they've just been found was given to the Duke by—Glassdale!"

"Glassdale! That man!" exclaimed Bryce, who was puzzling his brain over possible developments.

"That man, sir!" repeated Harker. "That's why Glassdale was in Wrychester the day of Braden's death. And that's why Braden, or Brake, came to Wrychester at all. He and Glassdale, of course, had somehow come into possession of the secret, and no doubt meant to tell the Duke together, and get the reward—there was 95,000 offered! And as Brake's dead, Glassdale's spoken, but"—here the old man paused and gave his companion a shrewd look—"the question still remains: How did Brake come to his end?"

XVII - To Be Shadowed

Dick Bewery burst in upon his sister and Ransford with a budget of news such as it rarely fell to the lot of romance-loving seventeen to tell. Secret and mysterious digging up of grave-yards by night—discovery of sealed packets, the contents of which might only be guessed at—the whole thing observed by hidden spectators—these were things he had read of in fiction, but had never expected to have the luck to see in real life. And being gifted with some powers of imagination and of narrative, he made the most of his story to a pair of highly attentive listeners, each of whom had his, and her, own reasons for particular attention.

"More mystery!" remarked Mary when Dick's story had come to an end. "What a pity they didn't open the parcel!" She looked at Ransford, who was evidently in deep thought. "I suppose it will all come out?" she suggested.

"Sure to!" he answered, and turned to Dick. "You say Bryce fetched old Harker—after you and Bryce had watched these operations a bit? Did he say why he fetched him?"

"Never said anything as to his reasons," answered Dick. "But, I rather guessed, at the end, that Bryce wanted me to keep quiet about it, only old Harker said there was no need."

Ransford made no comment on this, and Dick, having exhausted his stock of news, presently went off to bed.

"Master Bryce," observed Ransford, after a period of silence, "is playing a game! What it is, I don't know—but I'm certain of it. Well, we shall see! You've been much upset by all this," he went on, after another pause, "and the knowledge that you have has distressed me beyond measure! But just have a little—a very little—more patience, and things will be cleared—I can't tell all that's in my mind, even to you."

Mary, who had been sewing while Ransford, as was customary with him in an evening, read the Times to her, looked down at her work.

"I shouldn't care, if only these rumors in the town—about you—could be crushed!" she said. "It's so cruel, so vile, that such things—"

Ransford snapped his fingers.

"I don't care that about the rumors!" he answered, contemptuously. "They'll be crushed out just as suddenly as they arose—and then, perhaps, I'll let certain folk in Wrychester know what I think of them. And as regards the suspicion against me, I know already that the only people in the town for whose opinion I carefully accept what I said before the Coroner. As to the others, let them talk! If the thing comes to a head before its due time—"

"You make me think that you know more—much more!—than you've ever told me!" interrupted Mary.

"So I do!" he replied. "And you'll see in the end why I've kept silence. Of course, if people who don't know as much will interfere—"

He was interrupted there by the ringing of the front door bell, at the sound of which he and Mary looked at each other.

"Who can that be?" said Mary. "It's past ten o'clock."

Ransford offered no suggestion. He sat silently waiting, until the parlor maid entered.

"Inspector Mitchington would be much obliged if you could give him a few minutes, sir," she said.

Ransford got up from his chair.

"Take Inspector Mitchington into the study," he said. "Is he alone?"

"No, sir—there's a gentleman with him," replied the girl.

"All right—I'll be with them presently," answered Ransford. "Take them both in there and light the gas. Police!" he went on, when the parlor maid had gone. "They get hold of the first idea that strikes them, and never even look round for another, You're not frightened?"

"Frightened—no! Uneasy—yes!" replied Mary. "What can they want, this time of night?"

"Probably to tell me something about this romantic tale of Dick's," answered Ransford, as he left the room. "It'll be nothing more serious, I assure you."

But he was not so sure of that. He was very well aware that the Wrychester police authorities had a definite suspicion of his guilt in the Braden and Collishaw matters, and he knew from experience that police suspicion is a difficult matter to dissipate. And before he opened the door of the little room which he used as a study he warned himself to be careful—and silent.

The two visitors stood near the hearth—Ransford took a good look at them as he closed the door behind him. Mitchington he knew well enough; he was more interested in the other man, a stranger. A quiet-looking, very ordinary individual, who might have been half a dozen things—but Ransford instantly set him down as a detective. He turned from this man to the inspector.

"Well?" he said, a little brusquely. "What is it?"

"Sorry to intrude so late, Dr. Ransford," answered Mitchington, "but I should be much obliged if you would give us a bit of information—badly wanted, doctor, in view of recent events," he added, with a smile which was meant to be reassuring. "I'm sure you can—if you will."

"Sit down," said Ransford, pointing to chairs. He took one himself and again glanced at the stranger. "To whom am I speaking, in addition to yourself, Inspector?" he asked. "I'm not going to talk to strangers."

"Oh, well!" said Mitchington, a little awkwardly. "Of course, doctor, we've had to get a bit of professional help in these unpleasant matters. This gentleman's Detective-Sergeant Jettison, from the Yard."

"What information do you want?" asked Ransford.

Mitchington glanced at the door and lowered his voice. "I may as well tell you, doctor," he said confidentially, "there's been a most extraordinary discovery made tonight, which has a bearing on the Braden case. I dare say you've heard of the great jewel robbery which took place at the Duke of Saxonsteade's some years ago, which has been a mystery to this very day?"

"I have heard of it," answered Ransford.

"Very well—tonight those jewels—the whole lot!—have been discovered in Paradise yonder, where they'd been buried, at the time of the robbery, by the thief," continued Mitchington. "They've just been examined, and they're now in the Duke's own hands again—after all these years! And—I may as well tell you—we now know that the object of Braden's visit to Wrychester was to tell the Duke where those jewels were hidden. Braden—and another man—had learned the secret, from the real thief, who's dead in Australia. All that I may tell you, doctor—for it'll be public property tomorrow."

"Well?" said Ransford.

Mitchington hesitated a moment, as if searching for his next words. He glanced at the detective; the detective remained immobile; he glanced at Ransford; Ransford gave him no encouragement.

"Now look here, doctor!" he exclaimed, suddenly. "Why not tell us something? We know now who Braden really was! That's settled. Do you understand?"

"Who was he, then?" asked Ransford, quietly.

"He was one John Brake, sometime manager of a branch of a London bank, who, seventeen years ago, got ten years' penal servitude for embezzlement," answered Mitchington, watching Ransford steadily. "That's dead certain—we know it! The man who shared this secret with him about the Saxonsteade jewels has told us that much, today. John Brake!"

"What have you come here for?" asked Ransford.

"To ask you—between ourselves—if you can tell us anything about Brake's earlier days—antecedents—that'll help us," replied Mitchington. "It may be—Jettison here—a man of experience—thinks it'll be found to be—that Brake, or Braden as we call him—was murdered because of his possession of that secret about the jewels. Our informant tells us that Braden certainly had on him, when he came to Wrychester, a sort of diagram showing the exact location of the spot where the jewels were hidden—that diagram was most assuredly not found on Braden when we examined his clothing and effects. It may be that it was wrested from him in the gallery of the clerestory that morning, and that his assailant, or assailants—for there may have been two men at the job—afterwards pitched him through that open doorway, after half-stifling him. And if that theory's correct—and I, personally, am now quite inclined to it—it'll help a lot if you'll tell us what you know of Braden's—Brake's—antecedents. Come now, doctor!—you know very well that Braden, or Brake, did come to your surgery that morning and said to your assistant that he'd known a Dr. Ransford in times past! Why not speak?"

Ransford, instead of answering Mitchington's evidently genuine appeal, looked at the New Scotland Yard man.

"Is that your theory?" he asked.

Jettison nodded his head, with a movement indicative of conviction.

"Yes, sir!" he replied. "Having regard to all the circumstances of the case, as they've been put before me since I came here, and with special regard to the revelations which have resulted in the discovery of these jewels, it is! Of course, today's events have altered everything. If it hadn't been for our informant—"

"Who is your informant?" inquired Ransford.

The two callers looked at each other—the detective nodded at the inspector.

"Oh, well!" said Mitchington. "No harm in telling you, doctor. A man named Glassdale—once a fellow-convict with Brake. It seems they left England together after their time was up, emigrated together, prospered, even went so far—both of 'em!—as to make good the money they'd appropriated, and eventually came back together—in possession of this secret. Brake came specially to Wrychester to tell the Duke—Glassdale was to join him on the very morning Brake met his death. Glassdale did come to the town that morning—and as soon as he got here, heard of Brake's strange death. That upset him—and he went away—only to come back to-day, go to Saxonsteade, and tell everything to the Duke—with the result we've told you of."

"Which result," remarked Ransford, steadily regarding Mitchington, "has apparently altered all your ideas about—me!"

Mitchington laughed a little awkwardly.

"Oh, well, come, now, doctor!" he said. "Why, yes—frankly, I'm inclined to Jettison's theory—in fact, I'm certain that's the truth."

"And your theory," inquired Ransford, turning to the detective, "is—put it in a few words."

"My theory—and I'll lay anything it's the correct one!—is this," replied Jettison. "Brake came to Wrychester with his secret. That secret wasn't confined to him and Glassdale—either he let it out to somebody, or it was known to somebody. I understand from Inspector Mitchington here that on the evening of his arrival Brake was away from the Mitre Hotel for two hours. During that time, he was somewhere—with whom? Probably with somebody who got the secret out of him, or to whom he communicated it. For, think!—according to Glassdale, who, we are quite sure, has told the exact truth about everything, Brake had on him a scrap of paper, on which were instructions, in Latin, for finding the exact spot whereat the missing Saxonsteade jewels had been hidden, years before, by the actual thief—who, I may tell you, sir, never had the opportunity of returning to re-possess himself of them. Now, after Brake's death, the police examined his clothes and effects—they never found that scrap of paper! And I work things out this way. Brake was followed into that gallery—a lonely, quiet place—by the man or men who had got possession of the secret; he was, I'm told, a slightly-built, not over-strong man—he was seized and robbed of that paper and flung to his death. And all that fits in with the second mystery of Collishaw—who probably knew, if not everything, then something, of the exact circumstances of Brake's death, and let his knowledge get to the ears of—Brake's assailant!—who cleverly got rid of him. That's my notion," concluded the detective. "And—I shall be surprised if it isn't a correct one!"

"And, as I've said, doctor," chimed in Mitchington, "can't you give us a bit of information, now? You see the line we're on? Now, as it's evident you once knew Braden, or Brake—"

"I have never said so!" interrupted Ransford sharply.

"Well—we infer it, from the undoubted fact that he called here," remarked Mitchington. "And if—"

"Wait!" said Ransford. He had been listening with absorbed attention to Jettison's theory, and he now rose from his chair and began to pace the room, hands in pockets, as if in deep thought. Suddenly he paused and looked at Mitchington. "This needs some reflection," he said. "Are you pressed for time?"

"Not in the least," answered Mitchington, readily. "Our time's yours, sir. Take as long as you like."

Ransford touched a bell and summoning the parlor maid told her to fetch whisky, soda, and cigars. He pressed these things on the two men, lighted a cigar himself, and for a long time continued to walk up and down his end of the room, smoking and evidently in very deep thought. The visitors left him alone, watching him curiously now and then—until, when quite ten minutes had gone by, he suddenly drew a chair close to them and sat down again.

"Now, listen to me!" he said. "If I give my confidence to you, as police officials, will you give me your word that you won't make use of my information until I give you leave—or until you have consulted me further? I shall rely on your word, mind!"

"I say yes to that, doctor," answered Mitchington.

"The same here, sir," said the detective.

"Very well," continued Ransford. "Then—this is between ourselves, until such time as I say something more about it. First of all, I am not going to tell you anything whatever about Braden's antecedents—at present! Secondly—I am not sure that your theory, Mr. Jettison, is entirely correct, though I think it is by way of coming very near to the right one—which is sure to be worked out before long. But—on the understanding of secrecy for the present I can tell you something which I should not have been able to tell you but for the events of tonight, which have made me put together certain facts. Now attention! To begin with, I know where Braden was for at any rate some time on the evening of the day on which he came to Wrychester. He was with the old man whom we all know as Simpson Harker."

Mitchington whistled; the detective, who knew nothing of Simpson Harker, glanced at him as if for information. But Mitchington nodded at Ransford, and Ransford went on.

"I know this for this reason," he continued. "You know where Harker lives. I was in attendance for nearly two hours that evening on a patient in a house opposite—I spent a good deal of time in looking out of the window. I saw Harker take a man into his house: I saw the man leave the house nearly an hour later: I recognized that man next day as the man who met his death at the Cathedral. So much for that."

"Good!" muttered Mitchington. "Good! Explains a lot."

"But," continued Ransford, "what I have to tell you now is of a much more serious—and confidential—nature. Now, do you know—but, of course, you don't!—that your proceedings tonight were watched?"

"Watched!" exclaimed Mitchington. "Who watched us?"

"Harker, for one," answered Ransford. "And—for another—my late assistant, Mr. Pemberton Bryce."

Mitchington's jaw dropped.

"God bless my soul!" he said. "You don't mean it, doctor! Why, how did you—"

"Wait a minute," interrupted Ransford. He left the room, and the two callers looked at each other.

"This chap knows more than you think," observed Jettison in a whisper. "More than he's telling now!"

"Let's get all we can, then," said Mitchington, who was obviously much surprised by Ransford's last information. "Get it while he's in the mood."

"Let him take his own time," advised Jettison. "But—you mark me!—he knows a lot! This is only an instalment."

Ransford came back—with Dick Bewery, clad in a loud patterned and gaily colored suit of pajamas.

"Now, Dick," said Ransford. "Tell Inspector Mitchington precisely what happened this evening, within your own knowledge."

Dick was nothing loth to tell his story for the second time—especially to a couple of professional listeners. And he told it in full detail, from the moment of his sudden encounter with Bryce to that in which he parted with Bryce and Harker. Ransford, watching the official faces, saw what it was in the story that caught the official attention and excited the official mind.

"Dr. Bryce went off at once to fetch Harker, did he?" asked Mitchington, when Dick had made a end.

"At once," answered Dick. "And was jolly quick back with him!"

"And Harker said it didn't matter about your telling as it would be public news soon enough?" continued Mitchington.

"Just that," said Dick.

Mitchington looked at Ransford, and Ransford nodded to his ward.

"All right, Dick," he said. "That'll do."

The boy went off again, and Mitchington shook his head.

"Queer!" he said. "Now what have those two been up to?—something, that's certain. Can you tell us more, doctor?"

"Under the same conditions—yes," answered Ransford, taking his seat again. "The fact is, affairs have got to a stage where I consider it my duty to tell you more. Some of what I shall tell you is hearsay—but it's hearsay that you can easily verify for yourselves when the right moment comes. Mr. Campany, the librarian, lately remarked to me that my old assistant, Mr. Bryce, seemed to be taking an extraordinary interest in archaeological matters since he left me—he was now, said Campany, always examining documents about the old tombs and monuments of the Cathedral and its precincts."

"Ah—just so!" exclaimed Mitchington. "To be sure!—I'm beginning to see!"

"And," continued Ransford, "Campany further remarked, as a matter for humorous comment, that Bryce was also spending much time looking round our old tombs. Now you made this discovery near an old tomb, I understand?"

"Close by one—yes," assented the inspector.

"Then let me draw your attention to one or two strange facts—which are undoubted facts," continued Ransford. "Bryce was left alone with the dead body of Braden for some minutes, while Varner went to fetch the police. That's one."

"That's true," muttered Mitchington. "He was—several minutes!"

"Bryce it was who discovered Collishaw—in Paradise," said Ransford. "That's fact two. And fact three—Bryce evidently had a motive in fetching Harker tonight—to overlook your operations. What was his motive? And taking things altogether; what are, or have been, these secret affairs which Bryce and Harker have evidently been engaged in?"

Jettison suddenly rose, buttoning his light overcoat. The action seemed to indicate a newly-formed idea, a definite conclusion. He turned sharply to Mitchington.

"There's one thing certain, inspector," he said. "You'll keep an eye on those two from this out! From—just now!"

"I shall!" assented Mitchington. "I'll have both of 'em shadowed wherever they go or are, day or night. Harker, now, has always been a bit of a mystery, but Bryce—hang me if I don't believe he's been having me! Double game!—but, never mind. There's no more, doctor?"

"Not yet," replied Ransford. "And I don't know the real meaning or value of what I have told you. But—in two days from now, I can tell you more. In the meantime—remember your promise!"

He let his visitors out then, and went back to Mary.

"You'll not have to wait long for things to clear," he said. "The mystery's nearly over!"

XVIII - Surprise

Mitchington and the man from New Scotland Yard walked away in silence from Ransford's house and kept the silence up until they were in the middle of the Close and accordingly in solitude. Then Mitchington turned to his companion.

"What d'ye think of that?" he asked, with a half laugh. "Different complexion it puts on things, eh?"

"I think just what I said before—in there," replied the detective. "That man knows more than he's told, even now!"

"Why hasn't he spoken sooner, then?" demanded Mitchington. "He's had two good chances—at the inquests."

"From what I saw of him, just now," said Jettison, "I should say he's the sort of man who can keep his own counsel till he considers the right time has come for speaking. Not the sort of man who'll care twopence whatever's said about him, you understand? I should say he's known a good lot all along, and is just keeping it back till he can put a finishing touch to it. Two days, didn't he say? Aye, well, a lot can happen in two days!"

"But about your theory?" questioned Mitchington. "What do you think of it now—in relation to what we've just heard?"

"I'll tell you what I can see," answered Jettison. "I can see how one bit of this puzzle fits into another—in view of what Ransford has just told us. Of course, one's got to do a good deal of supposing—it's unavoidable in these cases. Now supposing Braden let this man Harker into the secret of the hidden jewels that night, and supposing that Harker and Bryce are in collusion—as they evidently are, from what that boy told us—and supposing they between them, together or separately, had to do with Braden's death, and supposing that man Collishaw saw something that would incriminate one or both—eh?"

"Well?" asked Mitchington.

"Bryce is a medical man," observed Jettison. "It would be an easy thing for a medical man to get rid of Collishaw as he undoubtedly was got rid of. Do you see my point?"

"Aye—and I can see that Bryce is a clever hand at throwing dust in anybody's eyes!" muttered Mitchington. "I've had some dealings with him over this affair and I'm beginning to think—only now!—that he's been having me for the mug! He's evidently a deep 'un—and so's the other man."

"I wanted to ask you that," said Jettison. "Now, exactly who are these two?—tell me about them—both."

"Not so much to tell," answered Mitchington. "Harker's a quiet old chap who lives in a little house over there—just off that far corner of this Close. Said to be a retired tradesman, from London. Came here a few years ago, to settle down. Inoffensive, pleasant old chap. Potters about the town—puts in his time as such old chaps do—bit of reading at the libraries—bit of gossip here and—there you know the sort. Last man in the world I should have thought would have been mixed up in an affair of this sort!"

"And therefore all the more likely to be!" said Jettison. "Well—the other?"

"Bryce was until the very day of Braden's appearance, Ransford's assistant," continued Mitchington. "Been with Ransford about two years. Clever chap, undoubtedly, but certainly deep and, in a way, reserved, though he can talk plenty if he's so minded and it's to his own advantage. He left Ransford suddenly—that very morning. I don't know why. Since then he's remained in the town. I've heard that he's pretty keen on Ransford's ward—sister of that lad we saw tonight. I don't know myself, if it's true—but I've wondered if that had anything to do with his leaving Ransford so suddenly."

"Very likely," said Jettison. They had crossed the Close by that time and come to a gas-lamp which stood at the entrance, and the detective pulled out his watch and glanced at it. "Ten past eleven," he said. "You say you know this Bryce pretty well? Now, would it be too late—if he's up still—to take a look at him! If you and he are on good terms, you could make an excuse. After what I've heard, I'd like to get at close quarters with this gentleman."

"Easy enough," assented Mitchington. "I've been there as late as this—he's one of the sort that never goes to bed before midnight. Come on!—it's close by. But—not a word of where we've been. I'll say I've dropped in to give him a bit of news. We'll tell him about the jewel business—and see how he takes it. And while we're there—size him up!"

Mitchington was right in his description of Bryce's habits—Bryce rarely went to bed before one o'clock in the morning. He liked to sit up, reading. His favorite mental food was found in the lives of statesmen and diplomatists, most of them of the sort famous for trickery and chicanery—he not only made a close study of the ways of these gentry but wrote down notes and abstracts of passages which particularly appealed to him. His lamp was burning when Mitchington and Jettison came in view of his windows—but that night Bryce was doing no thinking about statecraft: his mind was fixed on his own affairs. He had lighted his fire on going home and for an hour had sat with his legs stretched out on the fender, carefully weighing things up. The event of the night had convinced him that he was at a critical phase of his present adventure, and it behoved him, as a good general, to review his forces.

The forestalling of his plans about the hiding-place in Paradise had upset Bryce's schemes—he had figured on being able to turn that secret, whatever it was, to his own advantage. It struck him now, as he meditated, that he had never known exactly what he expected to get out of that secret—but he had hoped that it would have been something which would make a few more considerable and tightly-strung meshes in the net which he was endeavoring to weave around Ransford. Now he was faced by the fact that it was not going to yield anything in the way of help—it was a secret no longer, and it had yielded nothing beyond the mere knowledge that John Braden, who was in reality John Brake, had carried the secret to Wrychester—to reveal it in the proper quarter. That helped Bryce in no way—so far as he could see. And therefore it was necessary to re-state his case to himself; to take stock; to see where he stood—and more than all, to put plainly before his own mind exactly what he wanted.

And just before Mitchington and the detective came up the path to his door, Bryce had put his notions into clear phraseology. His aim was definite—he wanted to get Ransford completely into his power, through suspicion of Ransford's guilt in the affairs of Braden and Collishaw. He wanted, at the same time, to have the means of exonerating him—whether by fact or by craft—so that, as an ultimate method of success for his own projects he would be able to go to Mary Bewery and say "Ransford's very life is at my mercy: if I keep silence, he's lost: if I speak, he's saved: it's now for you to say whether I'm to speak or hold my tongue—and you're the price I want for my speaking to save him!" It was in accordance with his views of human nature that Mary Bewery would accede to his terms: he had not known her and Ransford for nothing, and he was aware that she had a profound gratitude for her guardian, which might even be akin to a yet unawakened warmer feeling. The probability was that she would willingly sacrifice herself to save Ransford—and Bryce cared little by what means he won her, fair or foul, so long as he was successful. So now, he said to himself, he must make a still more definite move against Ransford. He must strengthen and deepen the suspicions which the police already had: he must give them chapter and verse and supply them with information, and get Ransford into the tightest of corners, solely that, in order to win Mary Bewery, he might have the credit of pulling him out again. That, he felt certain, he could do—if he could make a net in which to enclose Ransford he could also invent a two-edged sword which would cut every mesh of that net into fragments. That would be—child's play—mere statecraft—elementary diplomacy. But first—to get Ransford fairly bottled up—that was the thing! He determined to lose no more time—and he was thinking of visiting Mitchington immediately after breakfast next morning when Mitchington knocked at his door.

Bryce was rarely taken back, and on seeing Mitchington and a companion, he forthwith invited them into his parlor, put out his whisky and cigars, and pressed both on them as if their late call were a matter of usual occurrence. And when he had helped both to a drink, he took one himself, and tumbler in hand, dropped into his easy chair again.

"We saw your light, doctor—so I took the liberty of dropping into tell you a bit of news," observed the inspector. "But I haven't introduced my friend—this is Detective-Sergeant Jettison, of the Yard—we've got him down about this business—must have help, you know."

Bryce gave the detective a half-sharp, half-careless look and nodded.

"Mr. Jettison will have abundant opportunities for the exercise of his talents!" he observed in his best cynical manner. "I dare say he's found that out already."

"Not an easy affair, sir, to be sure," assented Jettison. "Complicated!"

"Highly so!" agreed Bryce. He yawned, and glanced at the inspector. "What's your news, Mitchington?" he asked, almost indifferently.

"Oh, well!" answered Mitchington. "As the Herald's published tomorrow you'll see it in there, doctor—I've supplied an account for this week's issue; just a short one—but I thought you'd like to know. You've heard of the famous jewel robbery at the Duke's, some years ago? Yes?—well, we've found all the whole bundle tonight—buried in Paradise! And how do you think the secret came out?"

"No good at guessing," said Bryce.

"It came out," continued Mitchington, "through a man who, with Braden—Braden, mark you!—got in possession of it—it's a long story—and, with Braden, was going to reveal it to the Duke that very day Braden was killed. This man waited until this very morning and then told his Grace—his Grace came with him to us this afternoon, and tonight we made a search and found—everything! Buried—there in Paradise! Dug 'em up, doctor!"

Bryce showed no great interest. He took a leisurely sip at his liquor and set down the glass and pulled out his cigarette case. The two men, watching him narrowly, saw that his fingers were steady as rocks as he struck the match.

"Yes," he said as he threw the match away. "I saw you busy."

In spite of himself Mitchington could not repress a start nor a glance at Jettison. But Jettison was as imperturbable as Bryce himself, and Mitchington raised a forced laugh.

"You did!" he said, incredulously. "And we thought we had it all to ourselves! How did you come to know, doctor?"

"Young Bewery told me what was going on," replied Bryce, "so I took a look at you. And I fetched old Harker to take a look, too. We all watched you—the boy, Harker, and I—out of sheer curiosity, of course. We saw you get up the parcel. But, naturally, I didn't know what was in it—till now."

Mitchington, thoroughly taken aback by this candid statement, was at a loss for words, and again he glanced at Jettison. But Jettison gave no help, and Mitchington fell back on himself.

"So you fetched old Harker?" he said. "What—what for, doctor? If one may ask, you know."

Bryce made a careless gesture with his cigarette.

"Oh—old Harker's deeply interested in what's going on," he answered. "And as young Bewery drew my attention to your proceedings, why, I thought I'd draw Harker's. And Harker was—interested."

Mitchington hesitated before saying more. But eventually he risked a leading question.

"Any special reason why he should be, doctor?" he asked.

Bryce put his thumbs in the armholes of his waistcoat and looked half-lazily at his questioner.

"Do you know who old Harker really is?" he inquired.

"No!" answered Mitchington. "I know nothing about him—except that he's said to be a retired tradesman, from London, who settled down here some time ago."

Bryce suddenly turned on Jettison.

"Do you?" he asked.

"I, sir!" exclaimed Jettison. "I don't know this gentleman—at all!"

Bryce laughed—with his usual touch of cynical sneering.

"I'll tell you—now—who old Harker is, Mitchington," he said. "You may as well know. I thought Mr. Jettison might recognize the name. Harker is no retired London tradesman—he's a retired member of your profession, Mr. Jettison. He was in his day one of the smartest men in the service of your department. Only he's transposed his name—ask them at the Yard if they remember Harker Simpson? That seems to startle you, Mitchington! Well, as you're here, perhaps I'd better startle you a bit more."

XIX - The Subtlety of the Devil

There was a sudden determination and alertness in Bryce's last words which contrasted strongly, and even strangely, with the almost cynical indifference that had characterized him since his visitors came in, and the two men recognized it and glanced questioningly at each other. There was an alteration, too, in his manner; instead of lounging lazily in his chair, as if he had no other thought than of personal ease, he was now sitting erect, looking sharply from one man to the other; his whole attitude, bearing, speech seemed to indicate that he had suddenly made up his mind to adopt some definite course of action.

"I'll tell you more!" he repeated. "And, since you're here—now!"

Mitchington, who felt a curious uneasiness, gave Jettison another glance. And this time it was Jettison who spoke.

"I should say," he remarked quietly, "knowing what I've gathered of the matter, that we ought to be glad of any information Dr. Bryce can give us."

"Oh, to be sure!" assented Mitchington. "You know more, then, doctor?"

Bryce motioned his visitors to draw their chairs nearer to his, and when he spoke it was in the low, concentrated tones of a man who means business—and confidential business.

"Now look here, Mitchington," he said, "and you, too, Mr. Jettison, as you're on this job—I'm going to talk straight to both of you. And to begin with, I'll make a bold assertion—I know more of this Wrychester Paradise mystery—involving the deaths of both Braden and Collishaw, than any man living—because, though you don't know it, Mitchington, I've gone right into it. And I'll tell you in confidence why I went into it—I want to marry Dr. Ransford's ward, Miss Bewery!"

Bryce accompanied this candid admission with a look which seemed to say: Here we are, three men of the world, who know what things are—we understand each other! And while Jettison merely nodded comprehendingly, Mitchington put his thoughts into words.

"To be sure, doctor, to be sure!" he said. "And accordingly—what's their affair, is yours! Of course!"

"Something like that," assented Bryce. "Naturally no man wishes to marry unless he knows as much as he can get to know about the woman he wants, her family, her antecedents—and all that. Now, pretty nearly everybody in Wrychester who knows them, knows that there's a mystery about Dr. Ransford and his two wards—it's been talked of, no end, amongst the old dowagers and gossips of the Close, particularly—you know what they are! Miss Bewery herself, and her brother, young Dick, in a lesser degree, know there's a mystery. And if there's one man in the world who knows the secret, it's Ransford. And, up to now, Ransford won't tell—he won't even tell Miss Bewery. I know that she's asked him—he keeps up an obstinate silence. And so—I determined to find things out for myself."

"Aye—and when did you start on that little game, now, doctor?" asked Mitchington. "Was it before, or since, this affair developed?"

"In a really serious way—since," replied Bryce. "What happened on the day of Braden's death made me go thoroughly into the whole matter. Now, what did happen? I'll tell you frankly, now, Mitchington, that when we talked once before about this affair, I didn't tell you all I might have told. I'd my reasons for reticence. But now I'll give you full particulars of what happened that morning within my knowledge—pay attention, both of you, and you'll see how one thing fits into another. That morning, about half-past nine, Ransford left his surgery and went across the Close. Not long after he'd gone, this man Braden came to the door, and asked me if Dr. Ransford was in? I said he wasn't—he'd just gone out, and I showed the man in which direction. He said he'd once known a Dr. Ransford, and went away. A little later, I followed. Near the entrance of Paradise, I saw Ransford leaving the west porch of the Cathedral. He was undeniably in a state of agitation—pale, nervous. He didn't see me. I went on and met Varner, who told me of the accident. I went with him to the foot of St. Wrytha's Stair and found the man who had recently called at the surgery. He died just as I reached him. I sent for you. When you came, I went back to the surgery—I found Ransford there in a state of most unusual agitation—he looked like a man who has had a terrible shock. So much for these events. Put them together."

Bryce paused awhile, as if marshalling his facts.

"Now, after that," he continued presently, "I began to investigate matters myself—for my own satisfaction. And very soon I found out certain things—which I'll summarize, briefly, because some of my facts are doubtless known to you already. First of all—the man who came here as John Braden was, in reality, one John

Brake. He was at one time manager of a branch of a well-known London banking company. He appropriated money from them under apparently mysterious circumstances of which I, as yet, knew nothing; he was prosecuted, convicted, and sentenced to ten years' penal servitude. And those two wards of Ransford's, Mary and Richard Bewery, as they are called, are, in reality, Mary and Richard Brake—his children."

"You've established that as a fact?" asked Jettison, who was listening with close attention. "It's not a surmise on your part?"

Bryce hesitated before replying to this question. After all, he reflected, it was a surmise. He could not positively prove his assertion.

"Well," he answered after a moment's thought, "I'll qualify that by saying that from the evidence I have, and from what I know, I believe it to be an indisputable fact. What I do know of fact, hard, positive fact, is this:—John Brake married a Mary Bewery at the parish church of Braden Medworth, near Barthorpe, in Leicestershire: I've seen the entry in the register with my own eyes. His best man, who signed the register as a witness, was Mark Ransford. Brake and Ransford, as young men, had been in the habit of going to Braden Medworth to fish; Mary Bewery was governess at the vicarage there. It was always supposed she would marry Ransford; instead, she married Brake, who, of course, took her off to London. Of their married life, I know nothing. But within a few years, Brake was in trouble, for the reason I have told you. He was arrested—and Harker was the man who arrested him."

"Dear me!" exclaimed Mitchington. "Now, if I'd only known—"

"You'll know a lot before I'm through," said Bryce. "Now, Harker, of course, can tell a lot—yet it's unsatisfying. Brake could make no defense—but his counsel threw out strange hints and suggestions—all to the effect that Brake had been cruelly and wickedly deceived—in fact, as it were, trapped into doing what he did. And—by a man whom he'd trusted as a close friend. So much came to Harker's ears—but no more, and on that particular point I've no light. Go on from that to Brake's private affairs. At the time of his arrest he had a wife and two very young children. Either just before, or at, or immediately after his arrest they completely disappeared—and Brake himself utterly refused to say one single word about them. Harker asked if he could do anything—Brake's answer was that no one was to concern himself. He preserved an obstinate silence on that point. The clergyman in whose family Mrs. Brake had been governess saw Brake, after his conviction—Brake would say nothing to him. Of Mrs. Brake, nothing more is known—to me at any rate. What was known at the time is this—Brake communicated to all who came in contact with him, just then, the idea of a man who has been cruelly wronged and deceived, who takes refuge in sullen silence, and who is already planning and cherishing—revenge!"

"Aye, aye!" muttered Mitchington. "Revenge?—just so!"

"Brake, then," continued Bryce, "goes off to his term of penal servitude, and so disappears—until he reappears here in Wrychester. Leave him for a moment, and go back. And—it's a going back, no doubt, to supposition and to theory—but there's reason in what I shall advance. We know—beyond doubt—that Brake had been tricked and deceived, in some money matter, by some man—some mysterious man—whom he referred to as having been his closest friend. We know, too, that there was extraordinary mystery in the disappearance of his wife and children. Now, from all that has been found out, who was Brake's closest friend? Ransford! And of Ransford, at that time, there's no trace. He, too, disappeared—that's a fact which I've established. Years later, he reappears—here at Wrychester, where he's bought a practice. Eventually he has two young people, who are represented as his wards, come to live with him. Their name is Bewery. The name of the young woman whom John Brake married was Bewery. What's the inference? That their mother's dead—that they're known under her maiden name: that they, without a shadow of doubt, are John Brake's children. And that leads up to my theory—which I'll now tell you in confidence—if you wish for it."

"It's what I particularly wish for," observed Jettison quietly. "The very thing!"

"Then, it's this," said Bryce. "Ransford was the close friend who tricked and deceived Brake:

"He probably tricked him in some money affair, and deceived him in his domestic affairs. I take it that Ransford ran away with Brake's wife, and that Brake, sooner than air all his grievance to the world, took it silently and began to concoct his ideas of revenge. I put the whole thing this way. Ransford ran away with Mrs. Brake and the two children—mere infants—and disappeared. Brake, when he came out of prison, went abroad—possibly with the idea of tracking them. Meanwhile, as is quite evident, he engaged in business and did well. He came back to England as John Braden, and, for the reason of which you're aware, he paid a visit to Wrychester, utterly unaware that anyone known to him lived here. Now, try to reconstruct what happened. He looks round the Close that morning. He sees the name of Dr. Mark Ransford on the brass plate of a surgery door. He goes to the surgery, asks a question, makes a remark, goes away. What is the probable sequence of events? He meets Ransford near the Cathedral—where Ransford certainly was. They recognize each other—most likely they turn aside, go up to that gallery as a quiet place, to talk—there is an altercation—blows—somehow or other, probably from accident, Braden is thrown through that open doorway, to his death. And—Collishaw saw what happened!"

Bryce was watching his listeners, turning alternately from one to the other. But it needed little attention on his part to see that theirs was already closely strained; each man was eagerly taking in all that he said and suggested. And he went on emphasizing every point as he made it.

"Collishaw saw what happened?" he repeated. "That, of course, is theory—supposition. But now we pass from theory back to actual fact. I'll tell you something now, Mitchington, which you've never heard of, I'm certain. I made it in my way, after Collishaw's death, to get some information, secretly, from his widow, who's a fairly shrewd, intelligent woman for her class. Now, the widow, in looking over her husband's effects, in a certain drawer in which he kept various personal matters, came across the deposit book of a Friendly Society of which Collishaw had been a member for some years. It appears that he, Collishaw, was something of a saving man, and every year he managed to put by a bit of money out of his wages, and twice or thrice in the year he took these savings—never very much; merely a pound or two—to this Friendly Society, which, it seems, takes deposits in that way from its members. Now, in this book is an entry—I saw it—which shows that only two days before his death, Collishaw paid fifty pounds—fifty pounds, mark you!—into the Friendly Society. Where should Collishaw get fifty pounds, all of a sudden! He was a mason's laborer, earning at the very outside twenty-six or eight shillings a week. According to his wife, there was no one to leave him a legacy. She never heard of his receipt of this money from any source. But—there's the fact! What explains it? My theory—that the rumor that Collishaw, with a pint too much ale in him, had hinted that he could say something about Braden's death if he chose, had reached Braden's assailant; that he had made it his business to see Collishaw and had paid him that fifty pounds as hush-money—and, later, had decided to rid himself of Collishaw altogether, as he undoubtedly did, by poison."

Once more Bryce paused—and once more the two listeners showed their attention by complete silence.

"Now we come to the question—how was Collishaw poisoned?" continued Bryce. "For poisoned he was, without doubt. Here we go back to theory and supposition once more. I haven't the least doubt that the hydrocyanic acid which caused his death was taken by him in a pill—a pill that was in that box which they found on him, Mitchington, and showed me. But that particular pill, though precisely similar in appearance, could not be made up of the same ingredients which were in the other pills. It was probably a thickly coated pill which contained the poison;—in solution of course. The coating would melt almost as soon as the man had swallowed it—and death would result instantaneously. Collishaw, you may say, was condemned to death when he put that box of pills in his waistcoat pocket. It was mere chance, mere luck, as to when the exact moment of death came to him. There had been six pills in that box—there were five left. So Collishaw picked out the poisoned pill—first! It might have been delayed till the sixth dose, you see—but he was doomed."

Mitchington showed a desire to speak, and Bryce paused.

"What about what Ransford said before the Coroner?" asked Mitchington. "He demanded certain information about the post-mortem, you know, which, he said, ought to have shown that there was nothing poisonous in those pills."

"Pooh!" exclaimed Bryce contemptuously. "Mere bluff! Of such a pill as that I've described there'd be no trace but the sugar coating—and the poison. I tell you, I haven't the least doubt that that was how the poison was administered. It was easy. And—who is there that would know how easily it could be administered but—a medical man?"

Mitchington and Jettison exchanged glances. Then Jettison leaned nearer to Bryce.

"So your theory is that Ransford got rid of both Braden and Collishaw—murdered both of them, in fact?" he suggested. "Do I understand that's what it really comes to—in plain words?"

"Not quite," replied Bryce. "I don't say that Ransford meant to kill Braden—my notion is that they met, had an altercation, probably a struggle, and that Braden lost his life in it. But as regards Collishaw …"

"Don't forget!" interrupted Mitchington. "Varner swore that he saw Braden flung through that doorway! Flung out! He saw a hand."

"For everything that Varner could prove to the contrary," answered Bryce, "the hand might have been stretched out to pull Braden back. No—I think there may have been accident in that affair. But, as regards Collishaw—murder, without doubt—deliberate!"

He lighted another cigarette, with the air of a man who had spoken his mind, and Mitchington, realizing that he had said all he had to say, got up from his seat.

"Well—it's all very interesting and very clever, doctor," he said, glancing at Jettison. "And we shall keep it all in mind. Of course, you've talked all this over with Harker? I should like to know what he has to say. Now that you've told us who he is, I suppose we can talk to him?"

"You'll have to wait a few days, then," said Bryce. "He's gone to town—by the last train tonight—on this business. I've sent him. I had some information today about Ransford's whereabouts during the time of disappearance, and I've commissioned Harker to examine into it. When I hear what he's found out, I'll let you know."

"You're taking some trouble," remarked Mitchington.

"I've told you the reason," answered Bryce.

Mitchington hesitated a little; then, with a motion of his head towards the door, beckoned Jettison to follow him.

"All right," he said. "There's plenty for us to see into, I'm thinking!"

Bryce laughed and pointed to a shelf of books near the fireplace.

"Do you know what Napoleon Bonaparte once gave as sound advice to police?" he asked. "No! Then I'll tell you. 'The art of the police,' he said, 'is not to see that which it is useless for it to see.' Good counsel, Mitchington!"

The two men went away through the midnight streets, and kept silence until they were near the door of Jettison's hotel. Then Mitchington spoke.

"Well!" he said. "We've had a couple of tales, anyhow! What do you think of things, now?"

Jettison threw back his head with a dry laugh.

"Never been better puzzled in all my time!" he said. "Never! But—if that young doctor's playing a game—then, by the Lord Harry, inspector, it's a damned deep 'un! And my advice is—watch the lot!"

XX - Jettison Takes a Hand

By breakfast time next morning the man from New Scotland Yard had accomplished a series of meditations on the confidences made to him and Mitchington the night before and had determined on at least one course of action. But before entering upon it he had one or two important letters to write, the composition of which required much thought and trouble, and by the time he had finished them, and deposited them by his own hand in the General Post Office, it was drawing near to noon—the great bell of the Cathedral, indeed, was proclaiming noontide to Wrychester as Jettison turned into the police-station and sought Mitchington in his office.

"I was just coming round to see if you'd overslept yourself," said Mitchington good-humoredly. "We were up pretty late last night, or, rather, this morning."

"I've had letters to write," said Jettison. He sat down and picked up a newspaper and cast a casual glance over it. "Got anything fresh?"

"Well, this much," answered Mitchington. "The two gentlemen who told us so much last night are both out of town. I made an excuse to call on them both early this morning—just on nine o'clock. Dr. Ransford went up to London by the eight-fifteen.

"Dr. Bryce, says his landlady, went out on his bicycle at half-past eight—where, she didn't know, but, she fancied, into the country. However, I ascertained that Ransford is expected back this evening, and Bryce gave orders for his usual dinner to be ready at seven o'clock, and so—"

Jettison flung away the newspaper and pulled out his pipe.

"Oh, I don't think they'll run away—either of 'em," he remarked indifferently. "They're both too cock-sure of their own ways of looking at things."

"You looked at 'em anymore?" asked Mitchington.

"Done a bit of reflecting—yes," replied the detective. "Complicated affair, my lad! More in it than one would think at first sight. I'm certain of this quite apart from whatever mystery there is about the Braden affair and the Collishaw murder, there's a lot of scheming and contriving been going on—and is going on!—somewhere, by somebody. Underhand work, you understand? However, my particular job is the Collishaw business—and there's a bit of information I'd like to get hold of at once. Where's the office of that Friendly Society we heard about last night?"

"That'll be the Wrychester Second Friendly," answered Mitchington. "There are two such societies in the town—the first's patronized by small tradesmen and the like; the second by workingmen. The second does take deposits from its members. The office is in Fladgate—secretary's name outside—Mr. Stebbing. What are you after?"

"Tell you later," said Jettison. "Just an idea."

He went leisurely out and across the market square and into the narrow, old-world street called Fladgate, along which he strolled as if doing no more than looking about him until he came to an ancient shop which had been converted into an office, and had a wire blind over the lower half of its front window, wherein was woven in conspicuous gilt letters Wrychester Second Friendly Society—George Stebbing, Secretary. Nothing betokened romance or mystery in that essentially humble place, but it was in Jettison's mind that when he crossed its threshold he was on his way to discovering something that would possibly clear up the problem on which he was engaged.

The staff of the Second Friendly was inconsiderable in numbers—an outer office harbored a small boy and a tall young man; an inner one accommodated Mr. Stebbing, also a young man, sandy-haired and freckled, who, having inspected Detective-Sergeant Jettison's professional card, gave him the best chair in the room and stared at him with a mingling of awe and curiosity which plainly showed that he had never entertained a detective before. And as if to show his visitor that he realized the seriousness of the occasion, he nodded meaningly at his door.

"All safe, here, sir!" he whispered. "Well fitting doors in these old houses—knew how to make 'em in those days. No chance of being overheard here—what can I do for you, sir?"

"Thank you—much obliged to you," said Jettison. "No objection to my pipe, I suppose? Just so. Ah!—well, between you and me, Mr. Stebbing, I'm down here in connection with that Collishaw case—you know."

"I know, sir—poor fellow!" said the secretary. "Cruel thing, sir, if the man was put an end to. One of our members, was Collishaw, sir."

"So I understand," remarked Jettison. "That's what I've come about. Bit of information, on the quiet, eh? Strictly between our two selves—for the present."

Stebbing nodded and winked, as if he had been doing business with detectives all his life. "To be sure, sir, to be sure!" he responded with alacrity. "Just between you and me and the door post!—all right. Anything I can do, Mr. Jettison, shall be done. But it's more in the way of what I can tell, I suppose?"

"Something of that sort," replied Jettison in his slow, easy-going fashion. "I want to know a thing or two. Yours is a working-man's society, I think? Aye—and I understand you've a system whereby such a man can put his bits of savings by in your hands?"

"A capital system, too!" answered the secretary, seizing on a pamphlet and pushing it into his visitor's hand. "I don't believe there's better in England! If you read that—"

"I'll take a look at it some time," said Jettison, putting the pamphlet in his pocket. "Well, now, I also understand that Collishaw was in the habit of bringing you a bit of saved money now and then a sort of saving fellow, wasn't he?" Stebbing nodded assent and reached for a ledger which lay on the farther side of his desk.

"Collishaw," he answered, "had been a member of our society ever since it started—fourteen years ago. And he'd been putting in savings for some eight or nine years. Not much, you'll understand. Say, as an average, two to three pounds every half-year—never more. But, just before his death, or murder, or whatever you like to call it, he came in here one day with fifty pounds! Fairly astounded me, sir! Fifty pounds—all in a lump!"

"It's about that fifty pounds I want to know something," said Jettison. "He didn't tell you how he'd come by it? Wasn't a legacy, for instance?"

"He didn't say anything but that he'd had a bit of luck," answered Stebbing. "I asked no questions. Legacy, now?—no, he didn't mention that. Here it is," he continued, turning over the pages of the ledger. "There! 50 pounds. You see the date—that 'ud be two days before his death."

Jettison glanced at the ledger and resumed his seat.

"Now, then, Mr. Stebbing, I want you to tell me something very definite," he said. "It's not so long since this happened, so you'll not have to tag your memory to any great extent. In what form did Collishaw pay that fifty pounds to you?"

"That's easy answered, sir," said the secretary. "It was in gold. Fifty sovereigns—he had 'em in a bit of a bag." Jettison reflected on this information for a moment or two. Then he rose.

"Much obliged to you, Mr. Stebbing," he said. "That's something worth knowing. Now there's something else you can tell me as long as I'm here—though, to be sure, I could save you the trouble by using my own eyes. How many banks are there in this little city of yours?"

"Three," answered Stebbing promptly. "Old Bank, in Monday Market; Popham & Hargreaves, in the Square; Wrychester Bank, in Spurriergate. That's the lot."

"Much obliged," said Jettison. "And—for the present—not a word of what we've talked about. You'll be hearing more—later."

He went away, memorizing the names of the three banking establishments—ten minutes later he was in the private parlor of the first, in serious conversation with its manager. Here it was necessary to be more secret, and to insist on more secrecy than with the secretary of the Second Friendly, and to produce all his credentials and give all his reasons. But Jettison drew that covert blank, and the next, too, and it was not until he had been closeted for some time with the authorities of the third bank that he got the information he wanted. And when he had got it, he impressed secrecy and silence on his informants in a fashion which showed them that however easy-going his manner might be, he knew his business as thoroughly as they knew theirs.

It was by that time past one o'clock, and Jettison turned into the small hotel at which he had lodged himself. He thought much and gravely while he ate his dinner; he thought still more while he smoked his after-dinner pipe. And his face was still heavy with thought when, at three o'clock, he walked into Mitchington's office and finding the inspector alone shut the door and drew a chair to Mitchington's desk.

"Now then," he said. "I've had a rare morning's work, and made a discovery, and you and me, my lad, have got to have about as serious a bit of talk as we've had since I came here."

Mitchington pushed his papers aside and showed his keen attention.

"You remember what that young fellow told us last night about that man Collishaw paying in fifty pounds to the Second Friendly two days before his death," said Jettison. "Well, I thought over that business a lot, early this morning, and I fancied I saw how I could find something out about it. So I have—on the strict quiet. That's why I went to the Friendly Society. The fact was—I wanted to know in what form Collishaw handed in that fifty pounds. I got to know. Gold!"

Mitchington, whose work hitherto had not led him into the mysteries of detective enterprise, nodded delightedly.

"Good!" he said. "Rare idea! I should never have thought of it! And—what do you make out of that, now?"

"Nothing," replied Jettison. "But—a good deal out of what I've learned since that bit of a discovery. Now, put it to yourself—whoever it was that paid Collishaw that fifty pounds in gold did it with a motive. More than one motive, to be exact—but we'll stick to one, to begin with. The motive for paying in gold was—avoidance of discovery. A cheque can be readily traced. So can banknotes. But gold is not easily traced. Therefore the man who paid Collishaw fifty pounds took care to provide himself with gold. Now then—how many men are there in a small place like this who are likely to carry fifty pounds in gold in their pockets, or to have it at hand?"

"Not many," agreed Mitchington.

"Just so—and therefore I've been doing a bit of secret inquiry amongst the bankers, as to who supplied himself with gold about that date," continued Jettison. "I'd to convince 'em of the absolute necessity of information, too, before I got any! But I got some—at the third attempt. On the day previous to that on which Collishaw handed that fifty pounds to Stebbing, a certain Wrychester man drew fifty pounds in gold at his bank. Who do you think he was?"

"Who—who?" demanded Mitchington.

Jettison leaned half-across the desk.

"Bryce!" he said in a whisper. "Bryce!"

Mitchington sat up in his chair and opened his mouth in sheer astonishment.

"Good heavens!" he muttered after a moment's silence. "You don't mean it?"

"Fact!" answered Jettison. "Plain, incontestable fact, my lad. Dr. Bryce keeps an account at the Wrychester bank. On the day I'm speaking of he cashed a cheque to self for fifty pounds and took it all in gold."

The two men looked at each other as if each were asking his companion a question.

"Well?" said Mitchington at last. "You're a cut above me, Jettison. What do you make of it?"

"I said last night that the young man was playing a deep game," replied Jettison. "But—what game? What's he building up? For mark you, Mitchington, if—I say if, mind!—if that fifty pounds which he drew in gold is the identical fifty paid to Collishaw, Bryce didn't pay it as hush-money!"

"Think not?" said Mitchington, evidently surprised. "Now, that was my first impression. If it wasn't hush-money—"

"It wasn't hush-money, for this reason," interrupted Jettison. "We know that whatever else he knew, Bryce didn't know of the accident to Braden until Varner fetched him to Braden. That's established—on what you've put before me. Therefore, whatever Collishaw saw, before or at the time that accident happened, it wasn't Bryce who was mixed up in it. Therefore, why should Bryce pay Collishaw hush-money?"

Mitchington, who had evidently been thinking, suddenly pulled out a drawer in his desk and took some papers from it which he began to turn over.

"Wait a minute," he said. "I've an abstract here—of what the foreman at the Cathedral mason's yard told me of what he knew as to where Collishaw was working that morning when the accident happened—I made a note of it when I questioned him after Collishaw's death. Here you are:

'Foreman says that on morning of Braden's accident, Collishaw was at work in the north gallery of the clerestory, clearing away some timber which the carpenters had left there. Collishaw was certainly thus engaged from nine o'clock until past eleven that morning. Mem. Have investigated this myself. From the exact spot where C. was clearing the timber, there is an uninterrupted view of the gallery on the south side of the nave, and of the arched doorway at the head of St. Wrytha's Stair.'"

"'Well,' observed Jettison, 'that proves what I'm saying. It wasn't hush-money. For whoever it was that Collishaw saw lay hands on Braden, it wasn't Bryce—Bryce, we know, was at that time coming across the Close or crossing that path through the part you call Paradise: Varner's evidence proves that. So—if the fifty pounds wasn't paid for hush-money, what was it paid for?"

"Do you suggest anything?" asked Mitchington.

"I've thought of two or three things," answered the detective. "One's this—was the fifty pounds paid for information? If so, and Bryce has that information, why doesn't he show his hand more plainly? If he bribed Collishaw with fifty pounds: to tell him who Braden's assailant was, he now knows!—so why doesn't he let it out, and have done with it?"

"Part of his game—if that theory's right," murmured Mitchington.

"It mayn't be right," said Jettison. "But it's one. And there's another—supposing he paid Collishaw that money on behalf of somebody else? I've thought this business out right and left, top-side and bottom-side, and hang me if I don't feel certain there is somebody else! What did Ransford tell us about Bryce and this old Harker—think of that! And yet, according to Bryce, Harker is one of our old Yard men!—and therefore ought to be above suspicion."

Mitchington suddenly started as if an idea had occurred to him.

"I say, you know!" he exclaimed. "We've only Bryce's word for it that Harker is an ex-detective. I never heard that he was—if he is, he's kept it strangely quiet. You'd have thought that he'd have let us know, here, of his previous calling—I never heard of a policeman of any rank who didn't like to have a bit of talk with his own sort about professional matters."

"Nor me," assented Jettison. "And as you say, we've only Bryce's word. And, the more I think of it, the more I'm convinced there's somebody—some man of whom you don't seem to have the least idea—who's in this. And it may be that Bryce is in with him. However—here's one thing I'm going to do at once. Bryce gave us that information about the fifty pounds. Now I'm going to tell Bryce straight out that I've gone into that matter in my own fashion—a fashion he evidently never thought of—and ask him to explain why he drew a similar amount in gold. Come on round to his rooms."

But Bryce was not to be found at his rooms—had not been back to his rooms, said his landlady, since he had ridden away early in the morning: all she knew was that he had ordered his dinner to be ready at his usual time that evening. With that the two men had to be content, and they went back to the police-station still discussing the situation. And they were still discussing it an hour later when a telegram was handed to Mitchington, who tore it open, glanced over its contents and passed it to his companion who read it aloud.

"Meet me with Jettison Wrychester Station on arrival of five-twenty express from London mystery cleared up guilty men known—Ransford."

Jettison handed the telegram back.

"A man of his word!" he said. "He mentioned two days—he's done it in one! And now, my lad—do you notice?—he says men, not man! It's as I said—there's been more than one of 'em in this affair. Now then—who are they?"

XXI - The Saxonsteade Arms

Bryce had ridden away on his bicycle from Wrychester that morning intent on a new piece of diplomacy. He had sat up thinking for some time after the two police officials had left him at midnight, and it had occurred to him that there was a man from whom information could be had of whose services he had as yet made no use but who must be somewhere in the neighborhood—the man Glassdale. Glassdale had been in Wrychester the previous evening; he could scarcely be far away now; there was certainly one person who would know where he could be found, and that person was the Duke of Saxonsteade. Bryce knew the Duke to be an extremely approachable man, a talkative, even a garrulous man, given to holding converse with anybody about anything, and he speedily made up his mind to ride over to Saxonsteade, invent a plausible excuse for his call, and get some news out of his Grace. Even if Glassdale had left the neighborhood, there might be fragments of evidence to pick up from the Duke, for Glassdale, he knew, had given his former employer the information about the stolen jewels and would, no doubt, have added more about his acquaintance with Braden. And before Bryce came to his dreamed-of master-stroke in that matter, there were one or two things he wanted to clear up, to complete his double net, and he had an idea that an hour's chat with Glassdale would yield all that he desired.

The active brain that had stood Bryce in good stead while he spun his meshes and devised his schemes was more active than ever that early summer morning. It was a ten-mile ride through woods and valleys to Saxonsteade, and there were sights and beauties of nature on either side of him which any other man would have lingered to admire and most men would have been influenced by. But Bryce had no eyes for the clouds over the copper-crowned hills or the mystic shadows in the deep valleys or the new buds in the hedgerows, and no thought for the rustic folk whose cottages he passed here and there in a sparsely populated country. All his thoughts were fixed on his schemes, almost as mechanically as his eyes followed the white road in front of his wheel. Ever since he had set out on his campaign he had regularly taken stock of his position; he was forever reckoning it up. And now, in his opinion, everything looked very promising. He had—so far as he was aware—created a definite atmosphere of suspicion around and against Ransford—it needed only a little more suggestion, perhaps a little more evidence to bring about Ransford's arrest. And the only question which at all troubled Bryce was—should he let matters go to that length before putting his ultimatum before Mary Bewery, or should he show her his hand first? For Bryce had so worked matters that a word from him to the police would damn Ransford or save him—and now it all depended, so far as Bryce himself was concerned, on Mary Bewery as to which word should be said. Elaborate as the toils were which he had laid out for Ransford to the police, he could sweep them up and tear them away with a sentence of added knowledge—

if Mary Bewery made it worth his while. But first—before coming to the critical point—there was yet certain information which he desired to get, and he felt sure of getting it if he could find Glassdale. For Glassdale, according to all accounts, had known Braden intimately of late years, and was most likely in possession of facts about him—and Bryce had full confidence in himself as an interviewer of other men and a supreme belief that he could wheedle a secret out of anybody with whom he could procure an hour's quiet conversation.

As luck would have it, Bryce had no need to make a call upon the approachable and friendly Duke. Outside the little village at Saxonsteade, on the edge of the deep woods which fringed the ducal park, stood an old wayside inn, a relic of the coaching days, which bore on its sign the ducal arms. Into its old stone hall marched Bryce to refresh himself after his ride, and as he stood at the bow-windowed bar, he glanced into the garden beyond and there saw, comfortably smoking his pipe and reading the newspaper, the very man he was looking for.

Bryce had no spice of bashfulness, no want of confidence anywhere in his nature; he determined to attack Glassdale there and then. But he took a good look at his man before going out into the garden to him. A plain and ordinary sort of fellow, he thought; rather over middle age, with a tinge of grey in his hair and moustache; prosperous looking and well-dressed, and at that moment of the appearance of what he was probably taken for by the inn people—a tourist. Whether he was the sort who would be communicative or not, Bryce could not tell from outward signs, but he was going to try, and he presently found his card-case, took out a card, and strolling down the garden to the shady spot in which Glassdale sat, assumed his politest and suavest manner and presented himself.

"Allow me, sir," he said, carefully abstaining from any mention of names. "May I have the pleasure of a few minutes' conversation with you?"

Glassdale cast a swift glance of surprise, not unmingled with suspicion, at the intruder—the sort of glance that a man used to watchfulness would throw at anybody, thought Bryce. But his face cleared as he read the card, though it was still doubtful as he lifted it again.

"You've the advantage of me, sir," he said. "Dr. Bryce, I see. But—"

Bryce smiled and dropped into a garden chair at Glassdale's side.

"You needn't be afraid of talking to me," he answered. "I'm well known in Wrychester. The Duke," he went on, nodding his head in the direction of the great house which lay behind the woods at the foot of the garden, "knows me well enough—in fact, I was on my way to see his Grace now, to ask him if he could tell me where you could be found. The fact is, I'm aware of what happened last night—the jewel affair, you know—Mitchington told me—and of your friendship with Braden, and I want to ask you a question or two about Braden."

Glassdale, who had looked somewhat mystified at the beginning of this address, seemed to understand matters better by the end of it.

"Oh, well, of course, doctor," he said, "if that's it—but, of course—a word first!—these folk here at the inn don't know who I am or that I've any connection with the Duke on that affair. I'm Mr. Gordon here—just staying for a bit."

"That's all right," answered Bryce with a smile of understanding. "All this is between ourselves. I saw you with the Duke and the rest of them last night, and I recognized you just now. And all I want is a bit of talk about Braden. You knew him pretty well of late years?"

"Knew him for a good many years," replied Glassdale. He looked narrowly at his visitor. "I suppose you know his story—and mine?" he asked. "Bygone affairs, eh?"

"Yes, yes!" answered Bryce reassuringly. "No need to go into that—that's all done with."

"Aye—well, we both put things right," said Glassdale. "Made restitution—both of us, you understand. So that is done with? And you know, then, of course, who Braden really was?"

"John Brake, ex bank-manager," answered Bryce promptly. "I know all about it. I've been deeply interested and concerned in his death. And I'll tell you why. I want to marry his daughter."

Glassdale turned and stared at his companion.

"His daughter!" he exclaimed. "Brake's daughter! God bless my soul! I never knew he had a daughter!"

It was Bryce's turn to stare now. He looked at Glassdale incredulously.

"Do you mean to tell me that you knew Brake all those years and that he never mentioned his children?" he exclaimed.

"Never a word of 'em!" replied Glassdale. "Never knew he had any!"

"Did he never speak of his past?" asked Bryce.

"Not in that respect," answered Glassdale. "I'd no idea that he was—or had been—a married man. He certainly never mentioned wife nor children to me, sir, and yet I knew Brake about as intimately as two men can know each other for some years before we came back to England."

Bryce fell into one of his fits of musing. What could be the meaning of this extraordinary silence on Brake's part? Was there still some hidden secret, some other mystery at which he had not yet guessed?

"Odd!" he remarked at last after a long pause during which Glassdale had watched him curiously. "But, did he ever speak to you of an old friend of his named Ransford—a doctor?"

"Never!" said Glassdale. "Never mentioned such a man!"

Bryce reflected again, and suddenly determined to be explicit.

"John Brake, the bank manager," he said, "was married at a place called Braden Medworth, in Leicestershire, to a girl named Mary Bewery. He had two children, who would be, respectively, about four and one years of age when his—we'll call it misfortune—happened. That's a fact!"

"First I ever heard of it, then," said Glassdale. "And that's a fact, too!"

"He'd also a very close friend named Ransford—Mark Ransford," continued Bryce. "This Ransford was best man at Brake's wedding."

"Never heard him speak of Ransford, nor of any wedding!" affirmed Glassdale. "All news to me, doctor."

"This Ransford is now in practice in Wrychester," said Bryce. "And he has two young people living with him as his wards—a girl of twenty, a boy of seventeen—who are, without doubt, John Brake's children. It is the daughter that I want to marry."

Glassdale shook his head as if in sheer perplexity.

"Well, all I can say is, you surprise me!" he remarked. "I'd no idea of any such thing."

"Do you think Brake came to Wrychester because of that?" asked Bryce.

"How can I answer that, sir, when I tell you that I never heard him breathe one word of any children?" exclaimed Glassdale. "No! I know his reason for coming to Wrychester. It was wholly and solely—as far as I know—to tell the Duke here about that jewel business, the secret of which had been entrusted to Brake and me by a man on his death-bed in Australia. Brake came to Wrychester by himself—I was to join him next morning: we were then to go to see the Duke together. When I got to Wrychester, I heard of Brake's accident, and being upset by it, I went away again and waited some days until yesterday, when I made up my mind to tell the Duke myself, as I did, with very fortunate results. No, that's the only reason I know of why Brake came this way. I tell you I knew nothing at all of his family affairs! He was a very close man, Brake, and apart from his business matters, he'd only one idea in his head, and that was lodged there pretty firmly, I can assure you!"

"What was it?" asked Bryce.

"He wanted to find a certain man—or, rather, two men—who'd cruelly deceived and wronged him, but one of 'em in particular," answered Glassdale. "The particular one he believed to be in Australia, until near the end, when he got an idea that he'd left for England; as for the other, he didn't bother much about him. But the man that he did want!—ah, he wanted him badly!"

"Who was that man?" asked Bryce.

"A man of the name of Falkiner Wraye," answered Glassdale promptly. "A man he'd known in London. This Wraye, together with his partner, a man called Flood, tricked Brake into lending 'em several thousand pounds—bank's money, of course—for a couple of days—no more—and then clean disappeared, leaving him to pay the piper! He was a fool, no doubt, but he'd been mixed up with them; he'd done it before, and they'd always kept their promises, and he did it once too often. He let 'em have some thousands; they disappeared, and the bank inspector happened to call at Brake's bank and ask for his balances. And—there he was. And—that's why he'd Falkiner Wraye on his mind—as his one big idea. T'other man was a lesser consideration, Wraye was the chief offender."

"I wish you'd tell me all you know about Brake," said Bryce after a pause during which he had done some thinking. "Between ourselves, of course."

"Oh—I don't know that there's so much secrecy!" replied Glassdale almost indifferently. "Of course, I knew him first when we were both inmates of—you understand where; no need for particulars. But after we left that place, I never saw him again until we met in Australia a few years ago. We were both in the same trade—speculating in wool. We got pretty thick and used to see each other a great deal, and of course, grew confidential. He told me in time about his affair, and how he'd traced this Wraye to the United States, and then, I think, to New Zealand, and afterwards to Australia, and as I was knocking about the country a great deal buying up wool, he asked me to help him, and gave me a description of Wraye, of whom, he said, he'd certainly heard something when he first landed at Sydney, but had never been able to trace afterwards. But it was no good—I never either saw or heard of Wraye—and Brake came to the conclusion he'd left Australia. And I know he hoped to get news of him, somehow, when we returned to England."

"That description, now?—what was it?" asked Bryce.

"Oh!" said Glassdale. "I can't remember it all, now—big man, clean shaven, nothing very particular except one thing. Wraye, according to Brake, had a bad scar on his left jaw and had lost the middle finger of his left hand—all from a gun accident. He—what's the matter, sir?"

Bryce had suddenly let his pipe fall from his lips. He took some time in picking it up. When he raised himself again his face was calm if a little flushed from stooping.

"Bit my pipe on a bad tooth!" he muttered. "I must have that tooth seen to. So you never heard or saw anything of this man?"

"Never!" answered Glassdale. "But I've wondered since this Wrychester affair if Brake accidentally came across one or other of those men, and if his death arose out of it. Now, look here, doctor! I read the accounts of the inquest on Brake—I'd have gone to it if I'd dared, but just then I hadn't made up my mind about seeing the Duke; I didn't know what to do, so I kept away, and there's a thing has struck me that I don't believe the police have ever taken the slightest notice of."

"What's that?" demanded Bryce.

"Why, this!" answered Glassdale. "That man who called himself Dellingham—who came with Brake to the Mitre Hotel at Wrychester—who is he? Where did Brake meet him? Where did he go? Seems to me the police have been strangely negligent about that! According to the accounts I've read, everybody just accepted this Dellingham's first statement, took his word, and let him—vanish! No one, as far as I know, ever verified his account of himself. A stranger!"

Bryce, who was already in one of his deep moods of reflection, got up from his chair as if to go.

"Yes," he said. "There may be something in your suggestion. They certainly did take his word without inquiry. It's true—he mightn't be what he said he was."

"Aye, and from what I read, they never followed his movements that morning!" observed Glassdale. "Queer business altogether! Isn't there some reward offered, doctor? I heard of some placards or something, but I've never seen them; of course, I've only been here since yesterday morning."

Bryce silently drew some papers from his pocket. From them he extracted the two handbills which Mitchington had given him and handed them over.

"Well, I must go," he said. "I shall no doubt see you again in Wrychester, over this affair. For the present, all this is between ourselves, of course?"

"Oh, of course, doctor!" answered Glassdale. "Quite so!" Bryce went off and got his bicycle and rode away in the direction of Wrychester. Had he remained in that garden he would have seen Glassdale, after reading both the handbills, go into the house and have heard him ask the landlady at the bar to get him a trap and a good horse in it as soon as possible; he, too, now wanted to go to Wrychester and at once. But Bryce was riding down the road, muttering certain words to himself over and over again.

"The left jaw—and the left hand!" he repeated. "Left hand—left jaw! Unmistakable!"

XXII - Other People's Notions

The great towers of Wrychester Cathedral had come within Bryce's view before he had made up his mind as to the next step in this last stage of his campaign. He had ridden away from the Saxonsteade Arms feeling that he had got to do something at once, but he was not quite clear in his mind as to what that something exactly was. But now, as he topped a rise in the road, and saw Wrychester lying in its hollow beneath him, the summer sun shining on its red roofs and grey walls, he suddenly came to a decision, and instead of riding straight ahead into the old city he turned off at a by-road, made a line across the northern outskirts, and headed for the golf-links. He was almost certain to find Mary Bewery there at that hour, and he wanted to see her at once. The time for his great stroke had come.

But Mary Bewery was not there—had not been there that morning said the caddy-master. There were only a few players out. In one of them, coming towards the club-house, Bryce recognized Sackville Bonham. And at sight of Sackville, Bryce had an inspiration. Mary Bewery would not come up to the links now before afternoon; he, Bryce, would lunch there and then go towards Wrychester to meet her by the path across the fields on which he had waylaid her after his visit to Leicestershire. And meanwhile he would inveigle Sackville Bonham into conversation. Sackville fell readily into Bryce's trap. He was the sort of youth who loves to talk, especially in a hinting and mysterious fashion. And when Bryce, after treating him to an appetizer in the bar of the club-house, had suggested that they should lunch together and got him into a quiet corner of the dining-room, he launched forth at once on the pertinent matter of the day.

"Heard all about this discovery of those missing Saxonsteade diamonds?" he asked as he and Bryce picked up their knives and forks. "Queer business that, isn't it? Of course, it's got to do with those murders!"

"Think so?" asked Bryce.

"Can anybody think anything else?" said Sackville in his best dogmatic manner. "Why, the thing's plain. From what's been let out—not much, certainly, but enough—it's quite evident."

"What's your theory?" inquired Bryce.

"My stepfather—knowing old bird he is, too!—sums the whole thing up to a nicety," answered Sackville. "That old chap, Braden, you know, is in possession of that secret. He comes to Wrychester about it. But somebody else knows. That somebody gets rid of Braden. Why? So that the secret'll be known then only to one—the murderer! See! And why? Why?"

"Well, why?" repeated Bryce. "Don't see, so far."

"You must be dense, then," said Sackville with the lofty superiority of youth. "Because of the reward, of course! Don't you know that there's been a standing offer—never withdrawn!—of five thousand pounds for news of those jewels?"

"No, I didn't," answered Bryce.

"Fact, sir—pure fact," continued Sackville. "Now, five thousand, divided in two, is two thousand five hundred each. But five thousand, undivided, is—what?"

"Five thousand—apparently," said Bryce.

"Just so! And," remarked Sackville knowingly, "a man'll do a lot for five thousand."

"Or—according to your argument—for half of it," said Bryce. "What you—or your stepfather's—aiming at comes to this, that suspicion rests on Braden's sharer in the secret. That it?"

"And why not?" asked Sackville. "Look at what we know—from the account in the paper this morning. This other chap, Glassdale, waits a bit until the first excitement about Braden is over, then he comes forward and tells the Duke where the Duchess's diamonds are planted. Why? So that he can get the five thousand pound reward! Plain as a pikestaff! Only, the police are such fools."

"And what about Collishaw?" asked Bryce, willing to absorb all his companion's ideas.

"Part of the game," declared Sackville. "Same man that got rid of Braden got rid of that chap! Probably Collishaw knew a bit and had to be silenced. But, whether that Glassdale did it all off his own bat or whether he's somebody in with him, that's where the guilt'll be fastened in the end, my stepfather says. And—it'll be so. Stands to reason!"

"Anybody come forward about that reward your stepfather offered?" asked Bryce.

"I'm not permitted to say," answered Sackville. "But," he added, leaning closer to his companion across the table, "I can tell you this—there's wheels within wheels! You understand! And things'll be coming out. Got to! We can't—as a family—let Ransford lie under that cloud, don't you know. We must clear him. That's precisely why Mr. Folliot offered his reward. Ransford, of course, you know, Bryce, is very much to blame—he ought to have done more himself. And, of course, as my mother and my stepfather say, if Ransford won't do things for himself, well, we must do 'em for him! We couldn't think of anything else."

"Very good of you all, I'm sure," assented Bryce. "Very thoughtful and kindly."

"Oh, well!" said Sackville, who was incapable of perceiving a sneer or of knowing when older men were laughing at him. "It's one of those things that one's got to do—under the circumstances. Of course, Miss Bewery isn't Dr. Ransford's daughter, but she's his ward, and we can't allow suspicion to rest on her guardian. You leave it to me, my boy, and you'll see how things will be cleared!"

"Doing a bit underground, eh?" asked Bryce.

"Wait a bit!" answered Sackville with a knowing wink. "It's the least expected that happens—what?"

Bryce replied that Sackville was no doubt right, and began to talk of other matters. He hung about the club-house until past three o'clock, and then, being well acquainted with Mary Bewery's movements from long observation of them, set out to walk down towards Wrychester, leaving his bicycle behind him. If he did not meet Mary on the way, he meant to go to the house. Ransford would be out on his afternoon round of calls; Dick Bewery would be at school; he would find Mary alone. And it was necessary that he should see her alone, and at once, for since morning an entirely new view of affairs had come to him, based on added knowledge, and he now saw a chance which he had never seen before. True, he said to himself, as he walked across the links and over the country which lay between their edge and Wrychester, he had not, even now, the accurate knowledge as to the actual murderer of either Braden or Collishaw that he would have liked, but he knew something that would enable him to ask Mary Bewery point-blank whether he was to be friend or enemy. And he was still considering the best way of putting his case to her when, having failed to meet her on the way, he at last turned into the Close, and as he approached Ransford's house, saw Mrs. Folliot leaving it.

Mary Bewery, like Bryce, had been having a day of events. To begin with, Ransford had received a wire from London, first thing in the morning, which had made him run, breakfastless, to catch the next express. He had left Mary to make arrangements about his day's work, for he had not yet replaced Bryce, and she had been obliged to seek out another practitioner who could find time from his own duties to attend to Ransford's urgent patients. Then she had had to see callers who came to the surgery expecting to find Ransford there; and in the middle of a busy morning, Mr. Folliot had dropped in, to bring her a bunch of roses, and, once admitted, had shown unmistakable signs of a desire to gossip.

"Ransford out?" he asked as he sat down in the dining-room. "Suppose he is, this time of day."

"He's away," replied Mary. "He went to town by the first express, and I have had a lot of bother arranging about his patients."

"Did he hear about this discovery of the Saxonsteade jewels before he went?" asked Folliot. "Suppose he wouldn't though—wasn't known until the weekly paper came out this morning. Queer business! You've heard, of course?"

"Dr. Short told me," answered Mary. "I don't know any details."

Folliot looked meditatively at her a moment.

"Got something to do with those other matters, you know," he remarked. "I say! What's Ransford doing about all that?"

"About all what, Mr. Folliot?" asked Mary, at once on her guard. "I don't understand you."

"You know—all that suspicion—and so on," said Folliot. "Bad position for a professional man, you know—ought to clear himself. Anybody been applying for that reward Ransford offered?"

"I don't know anything about it," replied Mary. "Dr. Ransford is very well able to take care of himself, I think. Has anybody applied for yours?"

Folliot rose from his chair again, as if he had changed his mind about lingering, and shook his head.

"Can't say what my solicitors may or may not have heard—or done," he answered. "But—queer business, you know—and ought to be settled. Bad for Ransford to have any sort of a cloud over him. Sorry to see it."

"Is that why you came forward with a reward?" asked Mary.

But to this direct question Folliot made no answer. He muttered something about the advisability of somebody doing something and went away, to Mary's relief. She had no desire to discuss the Paradise mysteries with anybody, especially after Ransford's assurance of the previous evening. But in the middle of the afternoon in walked Mrs. Folliot, a rare caller, and before she had been closeted with Mary five minutes brought up the subject again.

"I want to speak to you on a very serious matter, my dear Miss Bewery," she said. "You must allow me to speak plainly on account of—of several things. My—my superiority in—in age, you know, and all that!"

"What's the matter, Mrs. Folliot?" asked Mary, steeling herself against what she felt sure was coming. "Is it—very serious? And—pardon me—is it about what Mr. Folliot mentioned to me this morning? Because if it is, I'm not going to discuss that with you or with anybody!"

"I had no idea that my husband had been here this morning," answered Mrs. Folliot in genuine surprise. "What did he want to talk about?"

"In that case, what do you want to talk about?" asked Mary. "Though that doesn't mean that I'm going to talk about it with you."

Mrs. Folliot made an effort to understand this remark, and after inspecting her hostess critically for a moment, proceeded in her most judicial manner.

"You must see, my dear Miss Bewery, that it is highly necessary that someone should use the utmost persuasion on Dr. Ransford," she said. "He is placing all of you—himself, yourself, your young brother—in most invidious positions by his silence! In society such as—well, such as you get in a cathedral town, you know, no man of reputation can afford to keep silence when his—his character is affected."

Mary picked up some needlework and began to be much occupied with it.

"Is Dr. Ransford's character affected?" she asked. "I wasn't aware of it, Mrs. Folliot."

"Oh, my dear, you can't be quite so very—so very, shall we say ingenuous?—as all that!" exclaimed Mrs. Folliot. "These rumors!—of course, they are very wicked and cruel ones, but you know they have spread. Dear me!—why, they have been common talk!"

"I don't think my guardian cares twopence for common talk, Mrs. Folliot," answered Mary. "And I am quite sure I don't."

"None of us—especially people in our position—can afford to ignore rumors and common talk," said Mrs. Folliot in her loftiest manner. "If we are, unfortunately, talked about, then it is our solemn, bounden duty to put ourselves right in the eyes of our friends—and of society. If I for instance, my dear, heard anything affecting my—let me say, moral-character, I should take steps, the most stringent, drastic, and forceful steps, to put matters to the test. I would not remain under a stigma—no, not for one minute!"

"I hope you will never have occasion to rehabilitate your moral character, Mrs. Folliot," remarked Mary, bending closely over her work. "Such a necessity would indeed be dreadful."

"And yet you do not insist—yes, insist!—on Dr. Ransford's taking strong steps to clear himself!" exclaimed Mrs. Folliot. "Now that, indeed, is a dreadful necessity!"

"Dr. Ransford," answered Mary, "is quite able to defend and to take care of himself. It is not for me to tell him what to do, or even to advise him what to do. And—since you will talk of this matter, I tell you frankly, Mrs. Folliot, that I don't believe any decent person in Wrychester has the least suspicion or doubt of Dr. Ransford. His denial of any share or complicity in those sad affairs—the mere idea of it as ridiculous as it's wicked—was quite sufficient. You know very well that at that second inquest he said—on oath, too—that he knew nothing of these affairs. I repeat, there isn't a decent soul in the city doubts that!"

"Oh, but you're quite wrong!" said Mrs. Folliot, hurriedly. "Quite wrong, I assure you, my dear. Of course, everybody knows what Dr. Ransford said—very excitedly, poor man, I'm given to understand on the occasion you refer to, but then, what else could he have said in his own interest? What people want is the proof of his innocence. I could—but I won't—tell you of many of the very best people who are—well, very much exercised over the matter—I could indeed!"

"Do you count yourself among them?" asked Mary in a cold fashion which would have been a warning to anyone but her visitor. "Am I to understand that, Mrs. Folliot?"

"Certainly not, my dear," answered Mrs. Folliot promptly. "Otherwise I should not have done what I have done towards establishing the foolish man's innocence!"

Mary dropped her work and turned a pair of astonished eyes on Mrs. Folliot's large countenance.

"You!" she exclaimed. "To establish—Dr. Ransford's innocence? Why, Mrs. Folliot, what have you done?"

Mrs. Folliot toyed a little with the jeweled head of her sunshade. Her expression became almost coy.

"Oh, well!" she answered after a brief spell of indecision. "Perhaps it is as well that you should know, Miss Bewery. Of course, when all this sad trouble was made far worse by that second affair—the working-man's death, you know, I said to my husband that really one must do something, seeing that Dr. Ransford was so very, very obdurate and wouldn't speak. And as money is nothing—at least as things go—to me or to Mr. Folliot, I insisted that he should offer a thousand pounds reward to have the thing cleared up. He's a generous and open-handed man, and he agreed with me entirely, and put the thing in hand through his solicitors. And nothing would please us more, my dear, than to have that thousand pounds claimed! For of course, if there is to be—as I suppose there is—a union between our families, it would be utterly impossible that any cloud could rest on Dr. Ransford, even if he is only your guardian. My son's future wife cannot, of course—"

Mary laid down her work again and for a full minute stared Mrs. Folliot in the face.

"Mrs. Folliot!" she said at last. "Are you under the impression that I'm thinking of marrying your son?"

"I think I've every good reason for believing it!" replied Mrs. Folliot.

"You've none!" retorted Mary, gathering up her work and moving towards the door. "I've no more intention of marrying Mr. Sackville Bonham than of eloping with the Bishop! The idea's too absurd to—even be thought of!"

Five minutes later Mrs. Folliot, heightened in color, had gone. And presently Mary, glancing after her across the Close, saw Bryce approaching the gate of the garden.

XXIII - The Unexpected

Mary's first instinct on seeing the approach of Pemberton Bryce, the one man she least desired to see, was to retreat to the back of the house and send the parlor maid to the door to say her mistress was not at home. But she had lately become aware of Bryce's curiously dogged persistence in following up whatever he had in view, and she reflected that if he were sent away then he would be sure to come back and come back until he had got whatever it was that he wanted. And after a moment's further consideration, she walked out of the front door and confronted him resolutely in the garden.

"Dr. Ransford is away," she said with almost unnecessary brusqueness. "He's away until evening."

"I don't want him," replied Bryce just as brusquely. "I came to see you."

Mary hesitated. She continued to regard Bryce steadily, and Bryce did not like the way in which she was looking at him. He made haste to speak before she could either leave or dismiss him.

"You'd better give me a few minutes," he said, with a note of warning. "I'm here in your interests—or in Ransford's. I may as well tell you, straight out, Ransford's in serious and imminent danger! That's a fact."

"Danger of what?" she demanded.

"Arrest—instant arrest!" replied Bryce. "I'm telling you the truth. He'll probably be arrested tonight, on his return. There's no imagination in all this—I'm speaking of what I know. I've—curiously enough—got mixed up with these affairs, through no seeking of my own, and I know what's behind the scenes. If it were known that I'm letting out secrets to you, I should get into trouble. But, I want to warn you!"

Mary stood before him on the path, hesitating. She knew enough to know that Bryce was telling some sort of truth: it was plain that he had been mixed up in the recent mysteries, and there was a ring of conviction in his voice which impressed her. And suddenly she had visions of Ransford's arrest, of his being dragged off to prison to meet a cruel accusation, of the shame and disgrace, and she hesitated further.

"But if that's so," she said at last, "what's the good of coming to me? I can't do anything!"

"I can!" said Bryce significantly. "I know more—much more—than the police know—more than anybody knows. I can save Ransford. Understand that!"

"What do you want now?" she asked.

"To talk to you—to tell you how things are," answered Bryce. "What harm is there in that? To make you see how matters stand, and then to show you what I can do to put things right."

Mary glanced at an open summer-house which stood beneath the beech trees on one side of the garden. She moved towards it and sat down there, and Bryce followed her and seated himself.

"Well—" she said.

Bryce realized that his moment had arrived. He paused, endeavoring to remember the careful preparations he had made for putting his case. Somehow, he was not so clear as to his line of attack as he had been ten minutes previously—he realized that he had to deal with a young woman who was not likely to be taken in nor easily deceived. And suddenly he plunged into what he felt to be the thick of things.

"Whether you, or whether Ransford—whether both or either of you, know it or not," he said, "the police have been on to Ransford ever since that Collishaw affair! Underground work, you know. Mitchington has been digging into things ever since then, and lately he's had a London detective helping him."

Mary, who had carried her work into the garden, had now resumed it, and as Bryce began to talk she bent over it steadily stitching.

"Well?" she said.

"Look here!" continued Bryce. "Has it never struck you—it must have done!—that there's considerable mystery about Ransford? But whether it has struck you or not, it's there, and it's struck the police forcibly. Mystery connected with him before—long before—he ever came here. And associated, in some way, with that man Braden. Not of late—in years past. And, naturally, the police have tried to find out what that was."

"What have they found out?" asked Mary quietly.

"That I'm not at liberty to tell," replied Bryce. "But I can tell you this—they know, Mitchington and the London man, that there were passages between Ransford and Braden years ago."

"How many years ago?" interrupted Mary.

Bryce hesitated a moment. He had a suspicion that this self-possessed young woman who was taking everything more quietly than he had anticipated, might possibly know more than he gave her credit for knowing. He had been watching her fingers since they sat down in the summer-house, and his sharp eyes saw that they were as steady as the spire of the cathedral above the trees—he knew from that that she was neither frightened nor anxious.

"Oh, well—seventeen to twenty years ago," he answered. "About that time. There were passages, I say, and they were of a nature which suggests that the reappearance of Braden on Ransford's present stage of life would be, extremely unpleasant and unwelcome to Ransford."

"Vague!" murmured Mary. "Extremely vague!"

"But quite enough," retorted Bryce, "to give the police the suggestion of motive. I tell you the police know quite enough to know that Braden was, of all men in the world, the last man Ransford desired to see cross his path again. And—on that morning on which the Paradise affair occurred—Braden did cross his path. Therefore, in the conventional police way of thinking and looking at things, there's motive."

"Motive for what?" asked Mary.

Bryce arrived here at one of his critical stages, and he paused a moment in order to choose his words.

"Don't get any false ideas or impressions," he said at last. "I'm not accusing Ransford of anything. I'm only telling you what I know the police think and are on the very edge of accusing him of. To put it plainly—of murder. They say he'd a motive for murdering Braden—and with them motive is everything. It's the first thing they seem to think of; they first question they ask themselves. 'Why should this man have murdered that man?'—do you see! 'What motive had he?—that's the point. And they think—these chaps like Mitchington and the London man—that Ransford certainly had a motive for getting rid of Braden when they met."

"What was the motive?" asked Mary.

"They've found out something—perhaps a good deal—about what happened between Braden and Ransford some years ago," replied Bryce. "And their theory is—if you want to know the truth—that Ransford ran away with Braden's wife, and that Braden had been looking for him ever since."

Bryce had kept his eyes on Mary's hands, and now at last he saw the girl's fingers tremble. But her voice was steady enough when she spoke.

"Is that mere conjecture on their part, or is it based on any fact?" she asked.

"I'm not in full knowledge of all their secrets," answered Bryce, "but I've heard enough to know that there's a basis of undeniable fact on which they're going. I know for instance, beyond doubt, that Braden and Ransford were bosom friends, years ago, that Braden was married to a girl whom Ransford had wanted to marry, that Braden's wife suddenly left him, mysteriously, a few years later, and that, at the same time, Ransford made an equally mysterious disappearance. The police know all that. What is the inference to be drawn? What inference would anyone—you yourself, for example—draw?"

"None, till I've heard what Dr. Ransford has to say," replied Mary.

Bryce disliked that ready retort. He was beginning to feel that he was being met by some force stronger than his own.

"That's all very well," he remarked. "I don't say that I wouldn't do the same. But I'm only explaining the police position, and showing you the danger likely to arise from it. The police theory is this, as far as I can make it out: Ransford, years ago, did Braden a wrong, and Braden certainly swore revenge when he could find him. Circumstances prevented Braden from seeking him closely for some time; at last they met here, by accident. Here the police aren't decided. One theory is that there was an altercation, blows, a struggle, in the course of which Braden met his death; the other is that Ransford deliberately took Braden up into the gallery and flung him through that open doorway—"

"That," observed Mary, with something very like a sneer, "seems so likely that I should think it would never occur to anybody but the sort of people you're telling me of! No man of any real sense would believe it for a minute!"

"Some people of plain common sense do believe it for all that!" retorted Bryce. "For it's quite possible. But as I say, I'm only repeating. And of course, the rest of it follows on that. The police theory is that Collishaw witnessed Braden's death at Ransford's hands, that Ransford got to know that Collishaw knew of that, and that he therefore quietly removed Collishaw. And it is on all that that they're going, and will go. Don't ask me if I think they're right or wrong! I'm only telling you what I know so as to show you what danger Ransford is in."

Mary made no immediate answer, and Bryce sat watching her. Somehow—he was at a loss to explain it to himself—things were not going as he had expected. He had confidently believed that the girl would be frightened, scared, upset, ready to do anything that he asked or suggested. But she was plainly not frightened. And the fingers which busied themselves with the fancy-work had become steady again, and her voice had been steady all along.

"Pray," she asked suddenly, and with a little satirical inflection of voice which Brice was quick to notice, "pray, how is it that you—not a policeman, not a detective!—come to know so much of all this? Since when were you taken into the confidence of Mitchington and the mysterious person from London?"

"You know as well as I do that I have been dragged into the case against my wishes," answered Bryce almost sullenly. "I was fetched to Braden—I saw him die. It was I who found Collishaw—dead. Of course, I've been mixed up, whether I would or not, and I've had to see a good deal of the police, and naturally I've learnt things."

Mary suddenly turned on him with a flash of the eye which might have warned Bryce that he had signally failed in the main feature of his adventure.

"And what have you learnt that makes you come here and tell me all this?" she exclaimed. "Do you think I'm a simpleton, Dr. Bryce? You set out by saying that Dr. Ransford is in danger from the police, and that you know more—much more than the police! what does that mean? Shall I tell you? It means that you—you!—know that the police are wrong, and that if you like you can prove to them that they are wrong! Now, then isn't that so?"

"I am in possession of certain facts," began Bryce. "I—"

Mary stopped him with a look.

"My turn!" she said. "You're in possession of certain facts. Now isn't it the truth that the facts you are in possession of are proof enough to you that Dr. Ransford is as innocent as I am? It's no use your trying to deceive me! Isn't that so?"

"I could certainly turn the police off his track," admitted Bryce, who was growing highly uncomfortable. "I could divert—"

Mary gave him another look and dropping her needlework continued to watch him steadily.

"Do you call yourself a gentleman?" she asked quietly. "Or we'll leave the term out. Do you call yourself even decently honest? For, if you do, how can you have the sheer impudence—more, insolence!—to come here and tell me all this when you know that the police are wrong and that you could—to use your own term, which is your way of putting it—turn them off the wrong track? Whatever sort of man are you? Do you want to know my opinion of you in plain words?"

"You seem very anxious to give it, anyway," retorted Bryce.

"I will give it, and it will perhaps put an end to this," answered Mary. "If you are in possession of anything in the way of evidence which would prove Dr. Ransford's innocence and you are willfully suppressing it, you are bad, wicked, base, cruel, unfit for any decent being's society! And," she added, as she picked up her work and rose, "you're not going to have any more of mine!"

"A moment!" said Bryce. He was conscious that he had somehow played all his cards badly, and he wanted another opening. "You're misunderstanding me altogether! I never said—never inferred—that I wouldn't save Ransford."

"Then, if there's need, which I don't admit, you acknowledge that you could save him?" she exclaimed sharply. "Just as I thought. Then, if you're an honest man, a man with any pretensions to honor, why don't you at once! Any man who had such feelings as those I've just mentioned wouldn't hesitate one second. But you—you!—you come and—talk about it! As if it were a game! Dr. Bryce, you make me feel sick, mentally, morally sick."

Bryce had risen to his feet when Mary rose, and he now stood staring at her. Ever since his boyhood he had laughed and sneered at the mere idea of the finer feelings—he believed that every man has his price—and that honesty and honor are things useful as terms but of no real existence. And now he was wondering—really wondering—if this girl meant the things she said: if she really felt a mental loathing of such minds and purposes as he knew his own were, or if it were merely acting on her part. Before he could speak she turned on him again more fiercely than before.

"Shall I tell you something else in plain language?" she asked. "You evidently possess a very small and limited knowledge—if you have any at all!—of women, and you apparently don't rate their mental qualities at any high standard. Let me tell you that I am not quite such a fool as you seem to think me! You came here this afternoon to bargain with me! You happen to know how much I respect my guardian and what I owe him for the care he has taken of me and my brother. You thought to trade on that! You thought you could make a bargain with me; you were to save Dr. Ransford, and for reward you were to have me! You daren't deny it. Dr. Bryce—I can see through you!"

"I never said it, at any rate," answered Bryce.

"Once more, I say, I'm not a fool!" exclaimed Mary. "I saw through you all along. And you've failed! I'm not in the least frightened by what you've said. If the police arrest Dr. Ransford, Dr. Ransford knows how to defend himself. And you're not afraid for him! You know you aren't. It wouldn't matter twopence to you if he were hanged tomorrow, for you hate him. But look to yourself! Men who cheat, and scheme, and plot, and plan as you do come to bad ends. Mind yours! Mind the wheel doesn't come full circle. And now, if you please, go away and don't dare to come near me again!"

Bryce made no answer. He had listened, with an attempt at a smile, to all this fiery indignation, but as Mary spoke the last words he was suddenly aware of something that drew his attention from her and them. Through an opening in Ransford's garden hedge he could see the garden door of the Folliots' house across the Close. And at that moment out of it emerge Folliot himself in conversation with Glassdale!

Without a word, Bryce snatched up his hat from the table of the summerhouse, and went swiftly away—a new scheme, a new idea in his mind.

XXIV - Finesse

Glassdale, journeying into Wrychester half an hour after Bryce had left him at the Saxonsteade Arms, occupied himself during his ride across country in considering the merits of the two handbills which Bryce had given him. One announced an offer of five hundred pounds reward for information in the Braden-Collishaw matter; the other, of a thousand pounds. It struck him as a curious thing that two offers should be made—it suggested, at once, that more than one person was deeply interested in this affair. But who were they?—no answer to that question appeared on the handbills, which were, in each case, signed by Wrychester solicitors. To one of these Glassdale, on arriving in the old city, promptly proceeded—selecting the offerer of the larger reward. He presently found himself in the presence of an astute-looking man who, having had his visitor's name sent in to him, regarded Glassdale with very obvious curiosity.

"Mr. Glassdale?" he said inquiringly, as the caller took an offered chair. "Are you, by any chance, the Mr. Glassdale whose name is mentioned in connection with last night's remarkable affair?"

He pointed to a copy of the weekly newspaper, lying on his desk, and to a formal account of the discovery of the Saxonsteade jewels which had been furnished to the press, at the Duke's request, by Mitchington. Glassdale glanced at it—unconcernedly.

"The same," he answered. "But I didn't call here on that matter—though what I did call about is certainly relative to it. You've offered a reward for any information that would lead to the solution of that mystery about Braden—and the other man, Collishaw."

"Of a thousand pounds—yes!" replied the solicitor, looking at his visitor with still more curiosity, mingled with expectancy. "Can you give any?"

Glassdale pulled out the two handbills which he had obtained from Bryce.

"There are two rewards offered," he remarked. "Are they entirely independent of each other?"

"We know nothing of the other," answered the solicitor. "Except, of course, that it exists. They're quite independent."

"Who's offering the five hundred pound one?" asked Glassdale.

The solicitor paused, looking his man over. He saw at once that Glassdale had, or believed he had, something to tell—and was disposed to be unusually cautious about telling it.

"Well," he replied, after a pause. "I believe—in fact, it's an open secret—that the offer of five hundred pounds is made by Dr. Ransford."

"And—yours?" inquired Glassdale. "Who's at the back of yours—a thousand?"

The solicitor smiled.

"You haven't answered my question, Mr. Glassdale," he observed. "Can you give any information?"

Glassdale threw his questioner a significant glance.

"Whatever information I might give," he said, "I'd only give to a principal—the principal. From what I've seen and known of all this, there's more in it than is on the surface. I can tell something. I knew John Braden—who, of course, was John Brake—very well, for some years. Naturally, I was in his confidence."

"About more than the Saxonsteade jewels, you mean?" asked the solicitor.

"About more than that," assented Glassdale. "Private matters. I've no doubt I can throw some light—some!—on this Wrychester Paradise affair. But, as I said just now, I'll only deal with the principal. I wouldn't tell you, for instance—as your principal's solicitor."

The solicitor smiled again.

"Your ideas, Mr. Glassdale, appear to fit in with our principal's," he remarked. "His instructions—strict instructions—to us are that if anybody turns up who can give any information, it's not to be given to us, but to—himself!"

"Wise man!" observed Glassdale. "That's just what I feel about it. It's a mistake to share secrets with more than one person."

"There is a secret, then!" asked the solicitor, half slyly.

"Might be," replied Glassdale. "Who's your client?"

The solicitor pulled a scrap of paper towards him and wrote a few words on it. He pushed it towards his caller, and Glassdale picked it up and read what had been written—Mr. Stephen Folliot, The Close.

"You'd better go and see him," said the solicitor, suggestively. "You'll find him reserved enough."

Glassdale read and re-read the name—as if he were endeavoring to recollect it, or connect it with something.

"What particular reason has this man for wishing to find this out?" he inquired.

"Can't say, my good sir!" replied the solicitor, with a smile. "Perhaps he'll tell you. He hasn't told me."

Glassdale rose to take his leave. But with his hand on the door he turned.

"Is this gentleman a resident in the place?" he asked.

"A well-known townsman," replied the solicitor. "You'll easily find his house in the Close—everybody knows it."

Glassdale went away then—and walked slowly towards the Cathedral precincts. On his way he passed two places at which he was half inclined to call—one was the police-station; the other, the office of the solicitors who were acting on behalf of the offerer of five hundred pounds. He half glanced at the solicitor's door—but on reflection went forward. A man who was walking across the Close pointed out the Folliot residence—Glassdale entered by the garden door, and in another minute came face to face with Folliot himself, busied, as usual, amongst his rose-trees.

Glassdale saw Folliot and took stock of him before Folliot knew that a stranger was within his gates. Folliot, in an old jacket which he kept for his horticultural labours, was taking slips from a standard; he looked as harmless and peaceful as his occupation. A quiet, inoffensive, somewhat benevolent elderly man, engaged in work, which suggested leisure and peace.

But Glassdale, after a first quick, searching glance, took another and longer one—and went nearer with a discreet laugh.

Folliot turned quietly, and seeing the stranger, showed no surprise. He had a habit of looking over the top rims of his spectacles at people, and he looked in this way at Glassdale, glancing him up and down calmly. Glassdale lifted his slouch hat and advanced.

"Mr. Folliot, I believe, sir?" he said. "Mr. Stephen Folliot?"

"Aye, just so!" responded Folliot. "But I don't know you. Who may you be, now?"

"My name, sir, is Glassdale," answered the other. "I've just come from your solicitor's. I called to see him this afternoon—and he told me that the business I called about could only be dealt with—or discussed—with you. So—I came here."

Folliot, who had been cutting slips off a rose-tree, closed his knife and put it away in his old jacket. He turned and quietly inspected his visitor once more.

"Aye!" he said quietly. "So you're after that thousand pound reward, eh?"

"I should have no objection to it, Mr. Folliot," replied Glassdale.

"I dare say not," remarked Folliot, dryly. "I dare say not! And which are you, now?—one of those who think they can tell something, or one that really can tell? Eh?"

"You'll know that better when we've had a bit of talk, Mr. Folliot," answered Glassdale, accompanying his reply with a direct glance.

"Oh, well, now then, I've no objection to a bit of talk—none whatever!" said Folliot. "Here!—we'll sit down on that bench, amongst the roses. Quite private here—nobody about. And now," he continued, as Glassdale accompanied him to a rustic bench set beneath a pergola of rambler roses, "who are you, like? I read a queer account in this morning's local paper of what happened in the Cathedral grounds yonder last night, and there was a person of your name mentioned. Are you that Glassdale?"

"The same, Mr. Folliot," answered the visitor, promptly.

"Then you knew Braden—the man who lost his life here?" asked Folliot.

"Very well indeed," replied Glassdale.

"For how long?" demanded Folliot.

"Some years—as a mere acquaintance, seen now and then," said Glassdale. "A few years, recently, as what you might call a close friend."

"Tell you any of his secrets?" asked Folliot.

"Yes, he did!" answered Glassdale.

"Anything that seems to relate to his death—and the mystery about it?" inquired Folliot.

"I think so," said Glassdale. "Upon consideration, I think so!"

"Ah—and what might it be, now?" continued Folliot. He gave Glassdale a look which seemed to denote and imply several things. "It might be to your advantage to explain a bit, you know," he added. "One has to be a little—vague, eh?"

"There was a certain man that Braden was very anxious to find," said Glassdale. "He'd been looking for him for a good many years."

"A man?" asked Folliot. "One?"

"Well, as a matter of fact, there were two," admitted Glassdale, "but there was one in particular. The other—the second—so Braden said, didn't matter; he was or had been, only a sort of cat's-paw of the man he especially wanted."

"I see," said Folliot. He pulled out a cigar case and offered a cigar to his visitor, afterwards lighting one himself. "And what did Braden want that man for?" he asked.

Glassdale waited until his cigar was in full going order before he answered this question. Then he replied in one word.

"Revenge!"

Folliot put his thumbs in the armholes of his buff waistcoat and leaning back, seemed to be admiring his roses.

"Ah!" he said at last. "Revenge, now? A sort of vindictive man, was he? Wanted to get his knife into somebody, eh?"

"He wanted to get something of his own back from a man who'd done him," answered Glassdale, with a short laugh. "That's about it!"

For a minute or two both men smoked in silence. Then Folliot—still regarding his roses—put a leading question.

"Give you any details?" he asked.

"Enough," said Glassdale. "Braden had been done—over a money transaction—by these men—one especially, as head and front of the affair—and it had cost him—more than anybody would think! Naturally, he wanted—if he ever got the chance—his revenge. Who wouldn't?"

"And he'd tracked 'em down, eh?" asked Folliot.

"There are questions I can answer, and there are questions I can't answer," responded Glassdale. "That's one of the questions I've no reply to. For—I don't know! But—I can say this. He hadn't tracked 'em down the day before he came to Wrychester!"

"You're sure of that?" asked Folliot. "He—didn't come here on that account?"

"No, I'm sure he didn't!" answered Glassdale, readily. "If he had, I should have known. I was with him till noon the day he came here—in London—and when he took his ticket at Victoria for Wrychester, he'd no more idea than the man in the moon as to where those men had got to. He mentioned it as we were having a bit of lunch together before he got into the train. No—he didn't come to Wrychester for any such purpose as that! But—"

He paused and gave Folliot a meaning glance out of the corner of his eyes.

"Aye—what?" asked Folliot.

"I think he met at least one of 'em here," said Glassdale, quietly. "And—perhaps both."

"Leading to—misfortune for him?" suggested Folliot.

"If you like to put it that way—yes," assented Glassdale.

Folliot smoked a while in more reflective silence.

"Aye, well!" he said at last. "I suppose you haven't put these ideas of yours before anybody, now?"

"Present ideas?" asked Glassdale, sharply. "Not to a soul! I've not had 'em—very long."

"You're the sort of man that another man can do a deal with, I suppose?" suggested Folliot. "That is, if it's made worth your while, of course?"

"I shouldn't wonder," replied Glassdale. "And—if it is made worth my while."

Folliot mused a little. Then he tapped Glassdale's elbow.

"You see," he said, confidentially, "it might be, you know, that I had a little purpose of my own in offering that reward. It might be that it was a very particular friend of mine that had the misfortune to have incurred this man Braden's hatred. And I might want to save him, d'ye see, from—well, from the consequence of what's happened, and to hear about it first if anybody came forward, eh?"

"As I've done," said Glassdale.

"As—you've done," assented Folliot. "Now, perhaps it would be in the interest of this particular friend of mine if he made it worth your while to—say no more to anybody, eh?"

"Very much worth his while, Mr. Folliot," declared Glassdale.

"Aye, well," continued Folliot. "This very particular friend would just want to know, you know, how much you really, truly know! Now, for instance, about these two men—and one in particular—that Braden was after? Did—did he name 'em?"

Glassdale leaned a little nearer to his companion on the rose-screened bench.

"He named them—to me!" he said in a whisper. "One was a man called Falkiner Wraye, and the other man was a man named Flood. Is that enough?"

"I think you'd better come and see me this evening," answered Folliot. "Come just about dusk to that door—I'll meet you there. Fine roses these of mine, aren't they?" he continued, as they rose. "I occupy myself entirely with 'em."

He walked with Glassdale to the garden door, and stood there watching his visitor go away up the side of the high wall until he turned into the path across Paradise. And then, as Folliot was retreating to his roses, he saw Bryce coming over the Close—and Bryce beckoned to him.

XXV - The Old Well House

When Bryce came hurrying up to him, Folliot was standing at his garden door with his hands thrust under his coat-tails—the very picture of a benevolent, leisured gentleman who has nothing to do and is disposed to give his time to anybody. He glanced at Bryce as he had glanced at Glassdale—over the tops of his spectacles, and the glance had no more than mild inquiry in it. But if Bryce had been less excited, he would have seen that Folliot, as he beckoned him inside the garden, swept a sharp look over the Close and ascertained that there was no one about, that Bryce's entrance was unobserved. Save for a child or two, playing under the tall elms near one of the gates, and for a clerical figure that stalked a path in the far distance, the Close was empty of life. And there was no one about, either, in that part of Folliot's big garden.

"I want a bit of talk with you," said Bryce as Folliot closed the door and turned down a side-path to a still more retired region. "Private talk. Let's go where it's quiet."

Without replying in words to this suggestion, Folliot led the way through his rose-trees to a far corner of his grounds, where an old building of grey stone, covered with ivy, stood amongst high trees. He turned the key of a doorway and motioned Bryce to enter.

"Quiet enough in here, doctor," he observed. "You've never seen this place—bit of a fancy of mine."

Bryce, absorbed as he was in the thoughts of the moment, glanced cursorily at the place into which Folliot had led him. It was a square building of old stone, its walls unlined, unplastered; its floor paved with much worn flags of limestone, evidently set down in a long dead age and now polished to marble-like smoothness. In its midst, set flush with the floor, was what was evidently a trap-door, furnished with a heavy iron ring. To this Folliot pointed, with a glance of significant interest.

"Deepest well in all Wrychester under that," he remarked. "You'd never think it—it's a hundred feet deep—and more! Dry now—water gave out some years ago. Some people would have pulled this old well-house down—but not me! I did better—I turned it to good account." He raised a hand and pointed upward to an obviously modern ceiling of strong oak timbers. "Had that put in," he continued, "and turned the top of the building into a little snuggery. Come up!"

He led the way to a flight of steps in one corner of the lower room, pushed open a door at their head, and showed his companion into a small apartment arranged and furnished in something closely approaching to luxury. The walls were hung with thick fabrics; the carpeting was equally thick; there were pictures, books, and curiosities; the two or three chairs were deep and big enough to lie down in; the two windows commanded pleasant views of the Cathedral towers on one side and of the Close on the other.

"Nice little place to be alone in, d'ye see?" said Folliot. "Cool in summer—warm in winter—modern fire-grate, you notice. Come here when I want to do a bit of quiet thinking, what?"

"Good place for that—certainly," agreed Bryce.

Folliot pointed his visitor to one of the big chairs and turning to a cabinet brought out some glasses, a syphon of soda-water, and a heavy cut-glass decanter. He nodded at a box of cigars which lay open on a table at Bryce's elbow as he began to mix a couple of drinks.

"Help yourself," he said. "Good stuff, those."

Not until he had given Bryce a drink, and had carried his own glass to another easy chair did Folliot refer to any reason for Bryce's visit. But once settled down, he looked at him speculatively.

"What did you want to see me about?" he asked.

Bryce, who had lighted a cigar, looked across its smoke at the imperturbable face opposite.

"You've just had Glassdale here," he observed quietly. "I saw him leave you."

Folliot nodded—without any change of expression.

"Aye, doctor," he said. "And—what do you know about Glassdale, now?"

Bryce, who would have cheerfully hobnobbed with a man whom he was about to conduct to the scaffold, lifted his glass and drank.

"A good deal," he answered as he set the glass down. "The fact is—I came here to tell you so!—I know a good deal about everything."

"A wide term!" remarked Folliot. "You've got some limitation to it, I should think. What do you mean by—everything?"

"I mean about recent matters," replied Bryce. "I've interested myself in them—for reasons of my own. Ever since Braden was found at the foot of those stairs in Paradise, and I was fetched to him, I've interested myself. And—I've discovered a great deal—more, much more than's known to anybody."

Folliot threw one leg over the other and began to jog his foot.

"Oh!" he said after a pause. "Dear me! And—what might you know, now, doctor? Aught you can tell me eh?"

"Lots!" answered Bryce. "I came to tell you—on seeing that Glassdale had been with you. Because—I was with Glassdale this morning."

Folliot made no answer. But Bryce saw that his cool, almost indifferent manner was changing—he was beginning, under the surface, to get anxious.

"When I left Glassdale—at noon," continued Bryce, "I'd no idea—and I don't think he had—that he was coming to see you. But I know what put the notion into his head. I gave him copies of those two reward bills. He no doubt thought he might make a bit—and so he came in to town, and—to you."

"Well?" asked Folliot.

"I shouldn't wonder," remarked Bryce, reflectively, and almost as if speaking to himself, "I shouldn't at all wonder if Glassdale's the sort of man who can be bought. He, no doubt, has his price. But all that Glassdale knows is nothing—to what I know."

Folliot had allowed his cigar to go out. He threw it away, took a fresh one from the box, and slowly struck a match and lighted it.

"What might you know, now?" he asked after another pause.

"I've a bit of a faculty for finding things out," answered Bryce boldly. "And I've developed it. I wanted to know all about Braden—and about who killed him—and why. There's only one way of doing all that sort of thing, you know. You've got to go back—a long way back—to the very beginnings. I went back—to the time when Braden was married. Not as Braden, of course—but as who he really was—John Brake. That was at a place called Braden Medworth, near Barthorpe, in Leicestershire."

He paused there, watching Folliot. But Folliot showed no more than close attention, and Bryce went on.

"Not much in that—for the really important part of the story," he continued. "But Brake had other associations with Barthorpe—a bit later. He got to know—got into close touch with a Barthorpe man who, about the time of Brake's marriage, left Barthorpe and settled in London. Brake and this man began to have some secret dealings together. There was another man in with them, too—a man who was a sort of partner of the Barthorpe man's. Brake had evidently a belief in these men, and he trusted them—unfortunately for himself he sometimes trusted the bank's money to them. I know what happened—he used to let them have money for short financial transactions—to be refunded within a very brief space. But—he went to the fire too often, and got his fingers burned in the end. The two men did him—one of them in particular—and cleared out. He had to stand the racket. He stood it—to the tune of ten years' penal servitude. And, naturally, when he'd finished his time, he wanted to find those two men—and began a long search for them. Like to know the names of the men, Mr. Folliot?"

"You might mention 'em—if you know 'em," answered Folliot.

"The name of the particular one was Wraye—Falkiner Wraye," replied Bryce promptly. "Of the other—the man of lesser importance—Flood."

The two men looked quietly at each other for a full moment's silence. And it was Bryce who first spoke with a ring of confidence in his tone which showed that he knew he had the whip hand.

"Shall I tell you something about Falkiner Wraye?" he asked. "I will!—it's deeply interesting. Mr. Falkiner Wraye, after cheating and deceiving Brake, and leaving him to pay the penalty of his over-trustfulness, cleared out of England and carried his money-making talents to foreign parts. He succeeded in doing well—he would!—and eventually he came back and married a rich widow and settled himself down in an out-of-the-world English town to grow roses. You're Falkiner Wraye, you know, Mr. Folliot!"

Bryce laughed as he made this direct accusation, and sitting forward in his chair, pointed first to Folliot's face and then to his left hand.

"Falkiner Wraye," he said, "had an unfortunate gun accident in his youth which marked him for life. He lost the middle finger of his left hand, and he got a bad scar on his left jaw. There they are, those marks! Fortunate for you, Mr. Folliot, that the police don't know all that I know, for if they did, those marks would have done for you days ago!" For a minute or two Folliot sat joggling his leg—a bad sign in him of rising temper if Bryce had but known it. While he remained silent he watched Bryce narrowly, and when he spoke, his voice was calm as ever.

"And what use do you intend to put your knowledge to, if one may ask?" he inquired, half sneeringly. "You said just now that you'd no doubt that man Glassdale could be bought, and I'm inclining to think that you're one of those men that have their price. What is it?"

"We've not come to that," retorted Bryce. "You're a bit mistaken. If I have my price, it's not in the same commodity that Glassdale would want. But before we do any talking about that sort of thing, I want to add to my stock of knowledge. Look here! We'll be candid. I don't care a snap of my fingers that Brake, or Braden's dead, or that Collishaw's dead, nor if one had his neck broken and the other was poisoned, but—whose hand was that which the mason, Varner, saw that morning, when Brake was flung out of that doorway? Come, now!—whose?"

"Not mine, my lad!" answered Folliot, confidently. "That's a fact?"

Bryce hesitated, giving Folliot a searching look. And Folliot nodded solemnly. "I tell you, not mine!" he repeated. "I'd naught to do with it!"

"Then who had?" demanded Bryce. "Was it the other man—Flood? And if so, who is Flood?"

Folliot got up from his chair and, cigar between his lips and hands under the tails of his old coat, walked silently about the quiet room for a while. He was evidently thinking deeply, and Bryce made no attempt to disturb him. Some minutes went by before Folliot took the cigar from his lips and leaning against the chimney-piece looked fixedly at his visitor.

"Look here, my lad!" he said, earnestly. "You're no doubt, as you say, a good hand at finding things out, and you've doubtless done a good bit of ferreting, and done it well enough in your own opinion. But there's one thing you can't find out, and the police can't find out either, and that's the precise truth about Braden's death. I'd no hand in it—it couldn't be fastened on to me, anyhow."

Bryce looked up and interjected one word.

"Collishaw?"

"Nor that, neither," answered Folliot, hastily. "Maybe I know something about both, but neither you nor the police nor anybody could fasten me to either matter! Granting all you say to be true, where's the positive truth?"

"What about circumstantial evidence," asked Bryce.

"You'd have a job to get it," retorted Folliot. "Supposing that all you say is true about—about past matters? Nothing can prove—nothing!—that I ever met Braden that morning. On the other hand, I can prove, easily, that I never did meet him; I can account for every minute of my time that day. As to the other affair—not an ounce of direct evidence!"

"Then—it was the other man!" exclaimed Bryce. "Now then, who is he?"

Folliot replied with a shrewd glance.

"A man who by giving away another man gave himself away would be a damned fool!" he answered. "If there is another man—"

"As if there must be!" interrupted Bryce.

"Then he's safe!" concluded Folliot. "You'll get nothing from me about him!"

"And nobody can get at you except through him?" asked Bryce.

"That's about it," assented Folliot laconically.

Bryce laughed cynically.

"A pretty coil!" he said with a sneer. "Here! You talked about my price. I'm quite content to hold my tongue if you'd tell me something about what happened seventeen years ago."

"What?" asked Folliot.

"You knew Brake, you must have known his family affairs," said Bryce. "What became of Brake's wife and children when he went to prison?"

Folliot shook his head, and it was plain to Bryce that his gesture of dissent was genuine.

"You're wrong," he answered. "I never at any time knew anything of Brake's family affairs. So little indeed, that I never even knew he was married."

Bryce rose to his feet and stood staring.

"What!" he exclaimed. "You mean to tell me that, even now, you don't know that Brake had two children, and that—that—oh, it's incredible!"

"What's incredible?" asked Folliot. "What are you talking about?"

Bryce in his eagerness and surprise grasped Folliot's arm and shook it.

"Good heavens, man!" he said. "Those two wards of Ransford's are Brake's girl and boy! Didn't you know that, didn't you?"

"Never!" answered Folliot. "Never! And who's Ransford, then? I never heard Brake speak of any Ransford! What game is all this? What—"

Before Bryce could reply, Folliot suddenly started, thrust his companion aside and went to one of the windows. A sharp exclamation from him took Bryce to his side. Folliot lifted a shaking hand and pointed into the garden.

"There!" he whispered. "Hell and—What's this mean?"

Bryce looked in the direction pointed out. Behind the pergola of rambler roses the figures of men were coming towards the old well-house led by one of Folliot's gardeners. Suddenly they emerged into full view, and in front of the rest was Mitchington and close behind him the detective, and behind him—Glassdale!

XXVI - The Other Man

It was close on five o'clock when Glassdale, leaving Folliot at his garden door, turned the corner into the quietness of the Precincts. He walked about there a while, staring at the queer old houses with eyes which saw neither fantastic gables nor twisted chimneys. Glassdale was thinking. And the result of his reflections was that he suddenly exchanged his idle sauntering for brisker steps and walked sharply round to the police-station, where he asked to see Mitchington.

Mitchington and the detective were just about to walk down to the railway-station to meet Ransford, in accordance with his telegram. At sight of Glassdale they went back into the inspector's office. Glassdale closed the door and favoured them with a knowing smile.

"Something else for you, inspector!" he said. "Mixed up a bit with last night's affair, too. About these mysteries—Braden and Collishaw—I can tell you one man who's in them."

"Who, then?" demanded Mitchington.

Glassdale went a step nearer to the two officials and lowered his voice.

"The man who's known here as Stephen Folliot," he answered. "That's a fact!"

"Nonsense!" exclaimed Mitchington. Then he laughed incredulously. "Can't believe it!" he continued. "Mr. Folliot! Must be some mistake!"

"No mistake," replied Glassdale. "Besides, Folliot's only an assumed name. That man is really one Falkiner Wraye, the man Braden, or Brake, was seeking for many a year, the man who cheated Brake and got him into trouble. I tell you it's a fact! He's admitted it, or as good as done so, to me just now."

"To you? And—let you come away and spread it?" exclaimed Mitchington. "That's incredible! more astonishing than the other!"

Glassdale laughed.

"Ah, but I let him think I could be squared, do you see?" he said. "Hush-money, you know. He's under the impression that I'm to go back to him this evening to settle matters. I knew so much—identified him, as a matter of fact—that he'd no option. I tell you he's been in at both these affairs—certain! But—there's another man."

"Who's he?" demanded Mitchington.

"Can't say, for I don't know, though I've an idea he'll be a fellow that Brake was also wanting to find," replied Glassdale. "But anyhow, I know what I'm talking about when I tell you of Folliot. You'd better do something before he suspects me."

Mitchington glanced at the clock.

"Come with us down to the station," he said. "Dr. Ransford's coming in on this express from town; he's got news for us. We'd better hear that first. Folliot!—good Lord!—who'd have believed or even dreamed it!"

"You'll see," said Glassdale as they went out.

"Maybe Dr. Ransford's got the same information." Ransford was out of the train as soon as it ran in, and hurried to where Mitchington and his companions were standing. And behind him, to Mitchington's surprise, came old Simpson Harker, who had evidently travelled with him. With a silent gesture Mitchington beckoned the whole party into an empty waiting-room and closed its door on them.

"Now then, inspector," said Ransford without preface or ceremony, "you've got to act quickly! You got my wire—a few words will explain it. I went up to town this morning in answer to a message from the bank where Braden lodged his money when he returned to England. To tell you the truth, the managers there and myself have, since Braden's death, been carrying to a conclusion an investigation which I began on Braden's behalf—though he never knew of it—years ago. At the bank I met Mr. Harker here, who had called to find something out for himself. Now I'll sum things up in a nutshell: for years Braden, or Brake, had been wanting to find two men who cheated him. The name of one is Wraye, of the other, Flood. I've been trying to trace them, too. At last we've got them. They're in this town, and without doubt the deaths of both Braden and Collishaw are at their door! You know both well enough. Wraye is-"

"Mr. Folliot!" interrupted Mitchington, pointing to Glassdale. "So he's just told us; he's identified him as Wraye. But the other—who's he, doctor?"

Ransford glanced at Glassdale as if he wished to question him, but instead he answered Mitchington's question.

"The other man," he said, "the man Flood, is also a well-known man to you. Fladgate!"

Mitchington started, evidently more astonished than by the first news.

"What!" he exclaimed. "The verger! You don't say!"

"Do you remember," continued Ransford, "that Folliot got Fladgate his appointment as verger not so very long after he himself came here? He did, anyway, and Fladgate is Flood. We've traced everything through Flood. Wraye has been a difficult man to trace, because of his residence abroad for a long time and his change of name, and so on, and it was only recently that my agents struck on a line through Flood. But there's the fact. And the probability is that when Braden came here he recognized and was recognized by these two, and that one or other of them is responsible for his death and for Collishaw's too. Circumstantial evidence, all of it, no doubt, but irresistible! Now, what do you propose to do?"

Mitchington considered matters for a moment.

"Fladgate first, certainly," he said. "He lives close by here; we'll go round to his cottage. If he sees he's in a tight place he may let things out. Let's go there at once."

He led the whole party out of the station and down the High Street until they came to a narrow lane of little houses which ran towards the Close. At its entrance a policeman was walking his beat. Mitchington stopped to exchange a few words with him.

"This man Fladgate," he said, rejoining the others, "lives alone—fifth cottage down here. He'll be about having his tea; we shall take him by surprise." Presently the group stood around a door at which Mitchington knocked gently, and it was on their grave and watchful faces that a tall, clean-shaven, very solemn-looking man gazed in astonishment as he opened the door, and started back. He went white to the lips and his hand fell trembling from the latch as Mitchington strode in and the rest crowded behind.

"Now then, Fladgate!" said Mitchington, going straight to the point and watching his man narrowly, while the detective approached him closely on the other side. "I want you and a word with you at once. Your real name is Flood! What have you to say to that? And—it's no use beating about the bush—what have you to say about this Braden affair, and your share with Folliot in it, whose real name is Wraye. It's all come out about the two of you. If you've anything to say, you'd better say it."

The verger, whose black gown lay thrown across the back of a chair, looked from one face to another with frightened eyes. It was very evident that the suddenness of the descent had completely unnerved him. Ransford's practiced eyes saw that he was on the verge of a collapse.

"Give him time, Mitchington," he said. "Pull yourself together," he added, turning to the man. "Don't be frightened; answer these questions!"

"For God's sake, gentlemen!" grasped the verger. "What—what is it? What am I to answer? Before God, I'm as innocent as—as any of you—about Mr. Brake's death! Upon my soul and honor I am!"

"You know all about it"; insisted Mitchington.

"Come, now, isn't it true that you're Flood, and that Folliot's Wraye, the two men whose trick on him got Brake convicted years ago? Answer that!"

Flood looked from one side to the other. He was leaning against his tea-table, set in the middle of his tidy living room. From the hearth his kettle sent out a pleasant singing that sounded strangely in contrast with the grim situation.

"Yes, that's true," he said at last. "But in that affair I—I wasn't the principal. I was only—only Wraye's agent, as it were: I wasn't responsible. And when Mr. Brake came here, when I met him that morning—"

He paused, still looking from one to another of his audience as if entreating their belief.

"As sure as I'm a living man, gentlemen!" he suddenly burst out, "I'd no willing hand in Mr. Brake's death! I'll tell you the exact truth; I'll take my oath of it whenever you like. I'd have been thankful to tell, many a time, but for—for Wraye. He wouldn't let me at first, and afterwards it got complicated. It was this way. That morning—when Mr. Brake was found dead—I had occasion to go up into that gallery under the clerestory. I suddenly came on him face to face. He recognized me. And—I'm telling you the solemn, absolute truth, gentlemen!—he'd no sooner recognized me than he attacked me, seizing me by the arm. I hadn't recognized him at first, I did when he laid hold of me. I tried to shake him off, tried to quiet him; he struggled—I don't know what he wanted to do—he began to cry out—it was a wonder he wasn't heard in the church below, and he would have been only the organ was being played rather loudly. And in the struggle he slipped—it was just by that open doorway—and before I could do more than grasp at him, he shot through the opening and fell! It was sheer, pure accident, gentlemen! Upon my soul, I hadn't the least intention of harming him."

"And after that?" asked Mitchington, at the end of a brief silence.

"I saw Mr. Folliot—Wraye," continued Flood. "Just afterwards, that was. I told him; he bade me keep silence until we saw how things went. Later he forced me to be silent. What could I do? As things were, Wraye could have disclaimed me—I shouldn't have had a chance. So I held my tongue."

"Now, then, Collishaw?" demanded Mitchington. "Give us the truth about that. Whatever the other was, that was murder!"

Flood lifted his hand and wiped away the perspiration that had gathered on his face.

"Before God, gentlemen!" he answered. "I know no more—at least, little more—about that than you do! I'll tell you all I do know. Wraye and I, of course, met now and then and talked about this. It got to our ears at last that Collishaw knew something. My own impression is that he saw what occurred between me and Mr. Brake—he was working somewhere up there. I wanted to speak to Collishaw. Wraye wouldn't let me, he bade me leave it to him. A bit later, he told me he'd squared Collishaw with fifty pounds—"

Mitchington and the detective exchanged looks.

"Wraye—that's Folliot—paid Collishaw fifty pounds, did he?" asked the detective.

"He told me so," replied Flood. "To hold his tongue. But I'd scarcely heard that when I heard of Collishaw's sudden death. And as to how that happened, or who—who brought it about—upon my soul, gentlemen, I know nothing! Whatever I may have thought, I never mentioned it to Wraye—never! I—I daren't! You don't know what a man Wraye is! I've been under his thumb most of my life and—and what are you going to do with me, gentlemen?"

Mitchington exchanged a word or two with the detective, and then, putting his head out of the door beckoned to the policeman to whom he had spoken at the end of the lane and who now appeared in company with a fellow-constable. He brought both into the cottage.

"Get your tea," he said sharply to the verger. "These men will stop with you—you're not to leave this room." He gave some instructions to the two policemen in an undertone and motioned Ransford and the others to follow him. "It strikes me," he said, when they were outside in the narrow lane, "that what we've just heard is somewhere about the truth. And now we'll go on to Folliot's—there's a way to his house round here."

Mrs. Folliot was out, Sackville Bonham was still where Bryce had left him, at the golf-links, when the pursuers reached Folliot's. A parlor maid directed them to the garden; a gardener volunteered the suggestion that his master might be in the old well-house and showed the way. And Folliot and Bryce saw them coming and looked at each other.

"Glassdale!" exclaimed Bryce. "By heaven, man!—he's told on you!"

Folliot was still staring through the window. He saw Ransford and Harker following the leading figures. And suddenly he turned to Bryce.

"You've no hand in this?" he demanded.

"I?" exclaimed Bryce. "I never knew till just now!"

Folliot pointed to the door.

"Go down!" he said. "Let 'em in, bid 'em come up! I'll—I'll settle with 'em. Go!"

Bryce hurried down to the lower apartment. He was filled with excitement—an unusual thing for him—but in the midst of it, as he made for the outer door, it suddenly struck him that all his schemings and plottings were going for nothing. The truth was at hand, and it was not going to benefit him in the slightest degree. He was beaten.

But that was no time for philosophic reflection; already those outside were beating at the door. He flung it open, and the foremost men started in surprise at the sight of him. But Bryce bent forward to Mitchington—anxious to play a part to the last.

"He's upstairs!" he whispered. "Up there! He'll bluff it out if he can, but he's just admitted to me—"

Mitchington thrust Bryce aside, almost roughly.

"We know all about that!" he said. "I shall have a word or two for you later! Come on, now—"

The men crowded up the stairway into Folliot's snuggery, Bryce, wondering at the inspector's words and manner, following closely behind him and the detective and Glassdale, who led the way. Folliot was standing in the middle of the room, one hand behind his back, the other in his pocket. And as the leading three entered the place he brought his concealed hand sharply round and presenting a revolver at Glassdale fired point-blank at him.

But it was not Glassdale who fell. He, wary and watching, started aside as he saw Folliot's movement, and the bullet, passing between his arm and body, found its billet in Bryce, who fell, with little more than a groan, shot through the heart. And as he fell, Folliot, scarcely looking at what he had done, drew his other hand from his pocket, slipped something into his mouth and sat down in the big chair behind him ... and within a moment the other men in the room were looking with horrified faces from one dead face to another.

XXVII - The Guarded Secret

When Bryce had left her, Mary Bewery had gone into the house to await Ransford's return from town. She meant to tell him of all that Bryce had said and to beg him to take immediate steps to set matters right, not only that he himself might be cleared of suspicion but that Bryce's intrigues might be brought to an end. She had some hope that Ransford would bring back satisfactory news; she knew that his hurried visit to London had some connection with these affairs; and she also remembered what he had said on the previous night. And so, controlling her anger at Bryce and her impatience of the whole situation she waited as patiently as she could until the time drew near when Ransford might be expected to be seen coming across the Close. She knew from which direction he would come, and she remained near the dining-room window looking out for him. But six o'clock came and she had seen no sign of him; then, as she was beginning to think that he had missed the afternoon train she saw him, at the opposite side of the Close, talking earnestly to Dick, who presently came towards the house while Ransford turned back into Folliot's garden.

Dick Bewery came hurriedly in. His sister saw at once that he had just heard news which had had a sobering effect on his usually effervescent spirits. He looked at her as if he wondered exactly how to give her his message.

"I saw you with the doctor just now," she said, using the term by which she and her brother always spoke of their guardian. "Why hasn't he come home?"

Dick came close to her, touching her arm.

"I say!" he said, almost whispering. "Don't be frightened—the doctor's all right—but there's something awful just happened. At Folliot's."

"What" she demanded. "Speak out, Dick! I'm not frightened. What is it?"

Dick shook his head as if he still scarcely realized the full significance of his news.

"It's all a licker to me yet!" he answered. "I don't understand it—I only know what the doctor told me—to come and tell you. Look here, it's pretty bad. Folliot and Bryce are both dead!"

In spite of herself Mary started back as from a great shock and clutched at the table by which they were standing.

"Dead!" she exclaimed. "Why—Bryce was here, speaking to me, not an hour ago!"

"Maybe," said Dick. "But he's dead now. The fact is, Folliot shot him with a revolver—killed him on the spot. And then Folliot poisoned himself—took the same stuff, the doctor said, that finished that chap Collishaw, and died instantly. It was in Folliot's old well-house. The doctor was there and the police."

"What does it all mean?" asked Mary.

"Don't know. Except this," added Dick, "they've found out about those other affairs—the Braden and the Collishaw affairs. Folliot was concerned in them; and who do you think the other was? You'd never guess! That man Fladgate, the verger. Only that isn't his proper name at all. He and Folliot finished Braden and Collishaw, anyway. The police have got Fladgate, and Folliot shot Bryce and killed himself just when they were going to take him."

"The doctor told you all this?" asked Mary.

"Yes," replied Dick. "Just that and no more. He called me in as I was passing Folliot's door. He's coming over as soon as he can. Whew! I say, won't there be some fine talk in the town! Anyway, things'll be cleared up now. What did Bryce want here?"

"Never mind; I can't talk of it, now," answered Mary. She was already thinking of how Bryce had stood before her, active and alive, only an hour earlier; she was thinking, too, of her warning to him. "It's all too dreadful! too awful to understand!"

"Here's the doctor coming now," said Dick, turning to the window. "He'll tell more."

Mary looked anxiously at Ransford as he came hastening in. He looked like a man who has just gone through a crisis and yet she was somehow conscious that there was a certain atmosphere of relief about him, as though some great weight had suddenly been lifted. He closed the door and looked straight at her.

"Dick has told you?" he asked.

"All that you told me," said Dick.

Ransford pulled off his gloves and flung them on the table with something of a gesture of weariness. And at that Mary hastened to speak.

"Don't tell any more—don't say anything—until you feel able," she said. "You're tired."

"No!" answered Ransford. "I'd rather say what I have to say now—just now! I've wanted to tell both of you what all this was, what it meant, everything about it, and until today, until within the last few hours, it was impossible, because I didn't know everything. Now I do! I even know more than I did an hour ago. Let me tell you now and have done with it. Sit down there, both of you, and listen."

He pointed to a sofa near the hearth, and the brother and sister sat down, looking at him wonderingly. Instead of sitting down himself he leaned against the edge of the table, looking down at them.

"I shall have to tell you some sad things," he said diffidently. "The only consolation is that it's all over now, and certain matters are, or can be, cleared and you'll have no more secrets. Nor shall I! I've had to keep this one jealously guarded for seventeen years! And I never thought it could be released as it has been, in this miserable and terrible fashion! But that's done now, and nothing can help it. And now, to make everything plain, just prepare yourselves to hear something that, at first, sounds very trying. The man whom you've heard of as John Braden, who came to his death—by accident, as I now firmly believe—there in Paradise, was, in reality, John Brake—your father!"

Ransford looked at his two listeners anxiously as he told this. But he met no sign of undue surprise or emotion. Dick looked down at his toes with a little frown, as if he were trying to puzzle something out; Mary continued to watch Ransford with steady eyes.

"Your father—John Brake," repeated Ransford, breathing more freely now that he had got the worst news out. "I must go back to the beginning to make things clear to you about him and your mother. He was a close friend of mine when we were young men in London; he a bank manager; I, just beginning my work. We used to spend our holidays together in Leicestershire. There we met your mother, whose name was Mary Bewery. He married her; I was his best man. They went to live in London, and from that time I did not see so much of them, only now and then. During those first years of his married life Brake made the acquaintance of a man who came from the same part of Leicestershire that we had met your mother in—a man named Falkiner Wraye. I may as well tell you that Falkiner Wraye and Stephen Folliot were one and the same person."

Ransford paused, observing that Mary wished to ask a question.

"How long have you known that?" she asked.

"Not until today," replied Ransford promptly. "Never had the ghost of a notion of it! If I only had known—but, I hadn't! However, to go back—this man Wraye, who appears always to have been a perfect master of plausibility, able to twist people round his little finger, somehow got into close touch with your father about financial matters. Wraye was at that time a sort of financial agent in London, engaging in various doings which, I should imagine, were in the nature of gambles. He was assisted in these by a man who was either a partner with him or a very confidential clerk or agent, one Flood, who is identical with the man you have known lately as Fladgate, the verger. Between them, these two appear to have cajoled or persuaded your father at times to do very foolish and injudicious things which were, to put it briefly and plainly, the lendings of various sums of money as short loans for their transactions. For some time they invariably kept their word to him, and the advances were always repaid promptly. But eventually, when they had borrowed from him a considerable sum—some thousands of pounds—for a deal which was to be carried through within a couple of days, they decamped with the money, and completely disappeared, leaving your father to bear the consequences. You may easily understand what followed. The money which Brake had lent them was the bank's money. The bank unexpectedly came down on him for his balance, the whole thing was found out, and he was prosecuted. He had no defense—he was, of course, technically guilty—and he was sent to penal servitude."

Ransford had dreaded the telling of this but Mary made no sign, and Dick only rapped out a sharp question.

"He hadn't meant to rob the bank for himself, anyway, had he?" he asked.

"No, no! not at all!" replied Ransford hastily. "It was a bad error of judgment on his part, Dick, but he—he'd relied on these men, more particularly on Wraye, who'd been the leading spirit. Well, that was your father's sad fate. Now we come to what happened to your mother and yourselves. Just before your father's arrest, when he knew that all was lost, and that he was helpless, he sent hurriedly for me and told me everything in your mother's presence. He begged me to get her and you two children right away at once. She was against it; he insisted. I took you all to a quiet place in the country, where your mother assumed her maiden name. There, within a year, she died. She wasn't a strong woman at any time. After that—well, you both know pretty well what has been the run of things since you began to know anything. We'll leave that, it's nothing to do with the story. I want to go back to your father. I saw him after his conviction. When I had satisfied him that you and your mother were safe, he begged me to do my best to find the two men who had ruined him. I began that search at once. But there was not a trace of them—they had disappeared as completely as if they were dead. I used all sorts of means to trace them—without effect. And when at last your father's term of imprisonment was over and I went to see him on his release, I had to tell him that up to that point all my efforts had been useless. I urged him to let the thing drop, and to start life afresh. But he was determined. Find both men, but particularly Wraye, he would! He refused point-blank to even see his children until he had found these men and had forced them to acknowledge their misdeeds as regards him, for that, of course, would have cleared him to a certain extent. And in spite of everything I could say, he there and then went off abroad in search of them—he had got some clue, faint and indefinite, but still there, as to Wraye's presence in America, and he went after him. From that time until the morning of his death here in Wrychester I never saw him again!"

"You did see him that morning?" asked Mary.

"I saw him, of course, unexpectedly," answered Ransford. "I had been across the Close—I came back through the south aisle of the Cathedral. Just before I left the west porch I saw Brake going up the stairs to the galleries. I knew him at once. He did not see me, and I hurried home much upset. Unfortunately, I think, Bryce came in upon me in that state of agitation. I have reason to believe that he began to suspect and to plot from that moment. And immediately on hearing of Brake's death, and its circumstances, I was placed in a terrible dilemma. For I had made up my mind never to tell you two of your father's history until I had been able to trace these two men and wring out of them a confession which would have cleared him of all but the technical commission of the crime of which he was convicted. Now I had not the least idea that the two men were close at hand, nor that they had had any hand in his death, and so I kept silence, and let him be buried under the name he had taken—John Braden."

Ransford paused and looked at his two listeners as if inviting question or comment. But neither spoke, and he went on.

"You know what happened after that," he continued. "It soon became evident to me that sinister and secret things were going on. There was the death of the laborer—Collishaw. There were other matters. But even then I had no suspicion of the real truth—the fact is, I began to have some strange suspicions about Bryce and that old man Harker—based upon certain evidence which I got by chance. But, all this time, I had never ceased my investigations about Wraye and Flood, and when the bank-manager on whom Brake had called in London was here at the inquest, I privately told him the whole story and invited his co-operation in a certain line which I was then following. That line suddenly ran up against the man Flood—otherwise Fladgate. It was not until this very week, however, that my agents definitely discovered Fladgate to be Flood, and that—through the investigations about Flood—Folliot was found to be Wraye. Today, in London, where I met old Harker at the bank at which Brake had lodged the money he had brought from Australia, the whole thing was made clear by the last agent of mine who has had the searching in hand. And it shows how men may easily disappear from a certain round of life, and turn up in another years after! When those two men cheated your father out of that money, they disappeared and separated—each, no doubt, with his share. Flood went off to some obscure place in the North of England; Wraye went over to America. He evidently made a fortune there; knocked about the world for a while; changed his name to Folliot, and under that name married a wealthy widow, and settled down here in Wrychester to grow roses! How and where he came across Flood again is not exactly clear, but we knew that a few years ago Flood was in London, in very poor circumstances, and the probability is that it was then when the two men met again. What we do know is that Folliot, as an influential man here, got Flood the post which he has held, and that things have resulted as they have. And that's all!—all that I need tell you at present. There are details, but they're of no importance."

Mary remained silent, but Dick got up with his hands in his pockets.

"There's one thing I want to know," he said. "Which of those two chaps killed my father? You said it was accident—but was it? I want to know about that! Are you saying it was accident just to let things down a bit? Don't! I want to know the truth."

"I believe it was accident," answered Ransford. "I listened most carefully just now to Fladgate's account of what happened. I firmly believe the man was telling the truth. But I haven't the least doubt that Folliot poisoned Collishaw—not the least. Folliot knew that if the least thing came out about Fladgate, everything would come out about himself."

Dick turned away to leave the room.

"Well, Folliot's done for!" he remarked. "I don't care about him, but I wanted to know for certain about the other."

When Dick had gone, and Ransford and Mary were left alone, a deep silence fell on the room. Mary was apparently deep in thought, and Ransford, after a glance at her, turned away and looked out of the window at the sunlit Close, thinking of the tragedy he had just witnessed. And he had become so absorbed in his thoughts of it that he started at feeling a touch on his arm and looking round saw Mary standing at his side.

"I don't want to say anything now," she said, "about what you have just told us. Some of it I had half-guessed, some of it I had conjectured. But why didn't you tell me! Before! It wasn't that you hadn't confidence?"

"Confidence!" he exclaimed. "There was only one reason—I wanted to get your father's memory cleared—as far as possible—before ever telling you anything. I've been wanting to tell you! Hadn't you seen that I hated to keep silent?"

"Hadn't you seen that I wanted to share all your trouble about it?" she asked. "That was what hurt me—because I couldn't!"

Ransford drew a long breath and looked at her. Then he put his hands on her shoulders.

"Mary!" he said. "You—you don't mean to say—be plain!—you don't mean that you can care for an old fellow like me?"

He was holding her away from him, but she suddenly smiled and came closer to him.

"You must have been very blind not to have seen that for a long time!" she answered.

THE END

In the Fog

By Richard Harding Davis

CHAPTER I

THE GRILL is the club most difficult of access in the world. To be placed on its rolls distinguishes the new member as greatly as though he had received a vacant Garter or had been caricatured in *Vanity Fair*.

Men who belong to the Grill Club never mention that fact. If you were to ask one of them which clubs he frequents, he will name all save that particular one. He is afraid if he told you he belonged to the Grill, that it would sound like boasting.

The Grill Club dates back to the days when Shakespeare's Theatre stood on the present site of the *Times* office. It has a golden Grill which Charles the Second presented to the Club, and the original manuscript of *Tom and Jerry in London*, which was bequeathed to it by Pierce Egan himself. The members, when they write letters at the Club, still use sand to blot the ink.

The Grill enjoys the distinction of having blackballed, without political prejudice, a Prime Minister of each party. At the same sitting at which one of these fell, it elected, on account of his brogue and his bulls, Quiller, Q. C., who was then a penniless barrister.

When Paul Preval, the French artist who came to London by royal command to paint a portrait of the Prince of Wales, was made an honorary member—only foreigners may be honorary members—he said, as he signed his first wine card, "I would rather see my name on that, than on a picture in the Louvre."

At which Quiller remarked, "That is a devil of a compliment, because the only men who can read their names in the Louvre today have been dead fifty years."

On the night after the great fog of 1897 there were five members in the Club, four of them busy with supper and one reading in front of the fireplace. There is only one room to the Club, and one long table. At the far end of the room the fire of the grill glows red, and, when the fat falls, blazes into flame, and at the other there is a broad bow window of diamond panes, which looks down upon the street. The four men at the table were strangers to each other, but as they picked at the grilled bones, and sipped their Scotch and soda, they conversed with such charming animation that a visitor to the Club, which does not tolerate visitors, would have counted them as friends of long acquaintance, certainly not as Englishmen who had met for the first time, and without the form of an introduction. But it is the etiquette and tradition of the Grill, that whoever enters it must speak with whomever he finds there. It is to enforce this rule that there is but one long table, and whether there are twenty men at it or two, the waiters, supporting the rule, will place them side by side.

For this reason the four strangers at supper were seated together, with the candles grouped about them, and the long length of the table cutting a white path through the outer gloom.

"I repeat," said the gentleman with the black pearl stud, "that the days for romantic adventure and deeds of foolish daring have passed, and that the fault lies with ourselves. Voyages to the pole I do not catalogue as adventures. That African explorer, young Chetney, who turned up yesterday after he was supposed to have died in Uganda, did nothing adventurous. He made maps and explored the sources of rivers. He was in constant danger, but the presence of danger does not constitute adventure. Were that so, the chemist who studies high explosives, or who investigates deadly poisons, passes through adventures daily. No, 'adventures are for the adventurous.' But one no longer ventures. The spirit of it has died of inertia. We are grown too practical, too just, above all, too sensible. In this room, for instance, members of this Club have, at the sword's point, disputed the proper scanning of one of Pope's couplets. Over so weighty a matter as spilled Burgundy on a gentleman's cuff, ten men fought across this table, each with his rapier in one hand and a candle in the other. All ten were wounded. The question of the spilled Burgundy concerned but two of them. The eight others engaged because they were men of 'spirit.' They were, indeed, the first gentlemen of the day. Tonight, were you to spill Burgundy on my cuff, were you even to insult me grossly, these gentlemen would not consider it incumbent upon them to kill each other. They would separate us, and tomorrow morning appear as witnesses against us at Bow Street. We have here tonight, in the persons of Sir Andrew and myself, an illustration of how the ways have changed."

The men around the table turned and glanced toward the gentleman in front of the fireplace. He was an elderly and somewhat portly person, with a kindly, wrinkled countenance, which wore continually a smile of almost childish confidence and good-nature. It was a face which the illustrated prints had made intimately familiar. He held a book from him at arm's-length, as if to adjust his eyesight, and his brows were knit with interest.

"Now, were this the eighteenth century," continued the gentleman with the black pearl, "when Sir Andrew left the Club tonight I would have him bound and gagged and thrown into a sedan chair. The watch would not interfere, the passers-by would take to their heels, my hired bullies and ruffians would convey him to some lonely spot where we would guard him until morning. Nothing would come of it, except added reputation to myself as a gentleman of adventurous spirit, and possibly an essay in the *Tatler*, with stars for names, entitled, let us say, 'The Budget and the Baronet.'"

"But to what end, sir?" inquired the youngest of the members. "And why Sir Andrew, of all persons—why should you select him for this adventure?"

The gentleman with the black pearl shrugged his shoulders.

"It would prevent him speaking in the House tonight. The Navy Increase Bill," he added gloomily. "It is a Government measure, and Sir Andrew speaks for it. And so great is his influence and so large his following that if he does"—the gentleman laughed ruefully—"if he does, it will go through. Now, had I the spirit of our ancestors," he exclaimed, "I would bring chloroform from the nearest chemist's and drug him in that chair. I would tumble his unconscious form into a hansom cab, and hold him prisoner until daylight. If I did, I would save the British taxpayer the cost of five more battleships, many millions of pounds."

The gentlemen again turned, and surveyed the baronet with freshened interest. The honorary member of the Grill, whose accent already had betrayed him as an American, laughed softly.

"To look at him now," he said, "one would not guess he was deeply concerned with the affairs of state."

The others nodded silently.

"He has not lifted his eyes from that book since we first entered," added the youngest member. "He surely cannot mean to speak tonight."

"Oh, yes, he will speak," muttered the one with the black pearl moodily. "During these last hours of the session the House sits late, but when the Navy bill comes up on its third reading he will be in his place—and he will pass it."

The fourth member, a stout and florid gentleman of a somewhat sporting appearance, in a short smoking-jacket and black tie, sighed enviously.

"Fancy one of us being as cool as that, if he knew he had to stand up within an hour and rattle off a speech in Parliament. I 'd be in a devil of a funk myself. And yet he is as keen over that book he's reading as though he had nothing before him until bedtime."

"Yes, see how eager he is," whispered the youngest member. "He does not lift his eyes even now when he cuts the pages. It is probably an Admiralty Report, or some other weighty work of statistics which bears upon his speech."

The gentleman with the black pearl laughed morosely.

"The weighty work in which the eminent statesman is so deeply engrossed," he said, "is called 'The Great Rand Robbery.' It is a detective novel, for sale at all bookstalls."

The American raised his eyebrows in disbelief.

"'The Great Rand Robbery'?" he repeated incredulously. "What an odd taste!"

"It is not a taste, it is his vice," returned the gentleman with the pearl stud. "It is his one dissipation. He is noted for it. You, as a stranger, could hardly be expected to know of this idiosyncrasy. Mr. Gladstone sought relaxation in the Greek poets, Sir Andrew finds his in Gaboriau. Since I have been a member of Parliament I have never seen him in the library without a shilling shocker in his hands. He brings them even into the sacred precincts of the House, and from the Government benches reads them concealed inside his hat. Once started on a tale of murder, robbery, and sudden death, nothing can tear him from it, not even the call of the division bell, nor of hunger, nor the prayers of the party Whip. He gave up his country house because when he journeyed to it in the train he would become so absorbed in his detective stories that he was invariably carried past his station." The member of Parliament twisted his pearl stud nervously, and bit at the edge of his mustache. "If it only were the first pages of 'The Rand Robbery' that he were reading," he murmured bitterly, "instead of the last! With such another book as that, I swear I could hold him here until morning. There would be no need of chloroform to keep him from the House."

The eyes of all were fastened upon Sir Andrew, and each saw with fascination that with his forefinger he was now separating the last two pages of the book. The member of Parliament struck the table softly with his open palm.

"I would give a hundred pounds," he whispered, "if I could place in his hands at this moment a new story of Sherlock Holmes—a thousand pounds," he added wildly—"five thousand pounds!"

The American observed the speaker sharply, as though the words bore to him some special application, and then at an idea which apparently had but just come to him, smiled in great embarrassment.

Sir Andrew ceased reading, but, as though still under the influence of the book, sat looking blankly into the open fire. For a brief space no one moved until the baronet withdrew his eyes and, with a sudden start of recollection, felt anxiously for his watch. He scanned its face eagerly, and scrambled to his feet.

The voice of the American instantly broke the silence in a high, nervous accent.

"And yet Sherlock Holmes himself," he cried, "could not decipher the mystery which tonight baffles the police of London."

At these unexpected words, which carried in them something of the tone of a challenge, the gentlemen about the table started as suddenly as though the American had fired a pistol in the air, and Sir Andrew halted abruptly and stood observing him with grave surprise.

The gentleman with the black pearl was the first to recover.

"Yes, yes," he said eagerly, throwing himself across the table. "A mystery that baffles the police of London.

"I have heard nothing of it. Tell us at once, pray do—tell us at once."

The American flushed uncomfortably, and picked uneasily at the tablecloth.

"No one but the police has heard of it," he murmured, "and they only through me. It is a remarkable crime, to, which, unfortunately, I am the only person who can bear witness. Because I am the only witness, I am, in spite of my immunity as a diplomat, detained in London by the authorities of Scotland Yard. My name," he said, inclining his head politely, "is Sears, Lieutenant Ripley Sears of the United States Navy, at present Naval Attaché to the Court of Russia. Had I not been detained today by the police I would have started this morning for Petersburg."

The gentleman with the black pearl interrupted with so pronounced an exclamation of excitement and delight that the American stammered and ceased speaking.

"Do you hear, Sir Andrew!" cried the member of Parliament jubilantly. "An American diplomat halted by our police because he is the only witness of a most remarkable crime—*the* most remarkable crime, I believe you said, sir," he added, bending eagerly toward the naval officer, "which has occurred in London in many years."

The American moved his head in assent and glanced at the two other members. They were looking doubtfully at him, and the face of each showed that he was greatly perplexed.

Sir Andrew advanced to within the light of the candles and drew a chair toward him.

"The crime must be exceptional indeed," he said, "to justify the police in interfering with a representative of a friendly power. If I were not forced to leave at once, I should take the liberty of asking you to tell us the details."

The gentleman with the pearl pushed the chair toward Sir Andrew, and motioned him to be seated.

"You cannot leave us now," he exclaimed. "Mr. Sears is just about to tell us of this remarkable crime."

He nodded vigorously at the naval officer and the American, after first glancing doubtfully toward the servants at the far end of the room, leaned forward across the table. The others drew their chairs nearer and bent toward him. The baronet glanced irresolutely at his watch, and with an exclamation of annoyance snapped down the lid. "They can wait," he muttered. He seated himself quickly and nodded at Lieutenant Sears.

"If you will be so kind as to begin, sir," he said impatiently.

"Of course," said the American, "you understand that I understand that I am speaking to gentlemen. The confidences of this Club are inviolate. Until the police give the facts to the public press, I must consider you my confederates. You have heard nothing, you know no one connected with this mystery. Even I must remain anonymous."

The gentlemen seated around him nodded gravely.

"Of course," the baronet assented with eagerness, "of course."

"We will refer to it," said the gentleman with the black pearl, "as 'The Story of the Naval Attaché.'"

"I arrived in London two days ago," said the American, "and I engaged a room at the Bath Hotel. I know very few people in London, and even the members of our embassy were strangers to me. But in Hong Kong I had become great pals with an officer in your navy, who has since retired, and who is now living in a small house in Rutland Gardens opposite the Knightsbridge barracks. I telegraphed him that I was in London, and yesterday morning I received a most hearty invitation to dine with him the same evening at his house. He is a bachelor, so we dined alone and talked over all our old days on the Asiatic Station, and of the changes which had come to us since we had last met there. As I was leaving the next morning for my post at Petersburg, and had many letters to write, I told him, about ten o'clock, that I must get back to the hotel, and he sent out his servant to call a hansom.

"For the next quarter of an hour, as we sat talking, we could hear the cab whistle sounding violently from the doorstep, but apparently with no result.

"'It cannot be that the cabmen are on strike,' my friend said, as he rose and walked to the window.

"He pulled back the curtains and at once called to me.

"'You have never seen a London fog, have you?' he asked. 'Well, come here. This is one of the best, or, rather, one of the worst, of them.' I joined him at the window, but I could see nothing. Had I not known that the house looked out upon the street I would have believed that I was facing a dead wall. I raised the sash and stretched out my head, but still I could see nothing. Even the light of the street lamps opposite, and in the upper windows of the barracks, had been smothered in the yellow mist. The lights of the room in which I stood penetrated the fog only to the distance of a few inches from my eyes.

"Below me the servant was still sounding his whistle, but I could afford to wait no longer, and told my friend that I would try and find the way to my hotel on foot. He objected, but the letters I had to write were for the Navy Department, and, besides, I had always heard that to be out in a London fog was the most wonderful experience, and I was curious to investigate one for myself.

"My friend went with me to his front door, and laid down a course for me to follow. I was first to walk straight across the street to the brick wall of the Knightsbridge Barracks. I was then to feel my way along the wall until I came to a row of houses set back from the sidewalk. They would bring me to a cross street. On the other side of this street was a row of shops which I was to follow until they joined the iron railings of Hyde Park. I was to keep to the railings until I reached the gates at Hyde Park Corner, where I was to lay a diagonal course across Piccadilly, and tack in toward the railings of Green Park. At the end of these railings, going east, I would find the Walsingham, and my own hotel.

"To a sailor the course did not seem difficult, so I bade my friend goodnight and walked forward until my feet touched the paving. I continued upon it until I reached the curbing of the sidewalk. A few steps further, and my hands struck the wall of the barracks. I turned in the direction from which I had just come, and saw a square of faint light cut in the yellow fog. I shouted 'All right,' and the voice of my friend answered, 'Good luck to you.' The light from his open door disappeared with a bang, and I was left alone in a dripping, yellow darkness. I have been in the Navy for ten years, but I have never known such a fog as that of last night, not even among the icebergs of Behring Sea. There one at least could see the light of the binnacle, but last night I could not even distinguish the hand by which I guided myself along the barrack wall. At sea a fog is a natural phenomenon. It is as familiar as the rainbow which follows a storm, it is as proper that a fog should spread upon the waters as that steam shall rise from a kettle. But a fog which springs from the paved streets, that rolls between solid house-fronts, that forces cabs to move at half speed, that drowns policemen and extinguishes the electric lights of the music hall, that to me is incomprehensible. It is as out of place as a tidal wave on Broadway.

"As I felt my way along the wall, I encountered other men who were coming from the opposite direction, and each time when we hailed each other I stepped away from the wall to make room for them to pass. But the third time I did this, when I reached out my hand, the wall had disappeared, and the further I moved to find it the further I seemed to be sinking into space. I had the unpleasant conviction that at any moment I might step over a precipice. Since I had set out I had heard no traffic in the street, and now, although I listened some minutes, I could only distinguish the occasional footfalls of pedestrians. Several times I called aloud, and once a jocular gentleman answered me, but only to ask me where I thought he was, and then even he was swallowed up in the silence. Just above me I could make out a jet of gas which I guessed came from a street lamp, and I moved over to that, and, while I tried to recover my bearings, kept my hand on the iron post. Except for this flicker of gas, no larger than the tip of my finger, I could distinguish nothing about me. For the rest, the mist hung between me and the world like a damp and heavy blanket.

"I could hear voices, but I could not tell from whence they came, and the scrape of a foot moving cautiously, or a muffled cry as someone stumbled, were the only sounds that reached me.

"I decided that until someone took me in tow I had best remain where I was, and it must have been for ten minutes that I waited by the lamp, straining my ears and hailing distant footfalls. In a house near me some people were dancing to the music of a Hungarian band. I even fancied I could hear the windows shake to the rhythm of their feet, but I could not make out from which part of the compass the sounds came. And sometimes, as the music rose, it seemed close at my hand, and again, to be floating high in the air above my head. Although I was surrounded by thousands of householders, I was as completely lost as though I had been set down by night in the Sahara Desert. There seemed to be no reason in waiting longer for an escort, so I again set out, and at once bumped against a low iron fence. At first I believed this to be an area railing, but on following it I found that it stretched for a long distance, and that it was pierced at regular intervals with gates. I was standing uncertainly with my hand on one of these when a square of light suddenly opened in the night, and in it I saw, as you see a picture thrown by a biograph in a darkened theatre, a young gentleman in evening dress, and back of him the lights of a hall. I guessed from its elevation and distance from the side-walk that this light must come from the door of a house set back from the street, and I determined to approach it and ask the young man to tell me where I was. But in fumbling with the lock of the gate I instinctively bent my head, and when I raised it again the door had partly closed, leaving only a narrow shaft of light. Whether the young man had re-entered the house, or had left it I could not tell, but I hastened to open the gate, and as I stepped forward I found myself upon an asphalt walk. At the same instant there was the sound of quick steps upon the path, and someone rushed past me. I called to him, but he made no reply, and I heard the gate click and the footsteps hurrying away upon the sidewalk.

"Under other circumstances the young man's rudeness, and his recklessness in dashing so hurriedly through the mist, would have struck me as peculiar, but everything was so distorted by the fog that at the moment I did not consider it. The door was still as he had left it, partly open. I went up the path, and, after much fumbling, found the knob of the door-bell and gave it a sharp pull. The bell answered me from a great depth and distance, but no movement followed from inside the house, and although I pulled the bell again and again I could hear nothing save the dripping of the mist about me. I was anxious to be on my way, but unless I knew where I was going there was little chance of my making any speed, and I was determined that until I learned my bearings I would not venture back into the fog. So I pushed the door open and stepped into the house.

"I found myself in a long and narrow hall, upon which doors opened from either side. At the end of the hall was a staircase with a balustrade which ended in a sweeping curve. The balustrade was covered with heavy Persian rugs, and the walls of the hall were also hung with them. The door on my left was closed, but the one nearer me on the right was open, and as I stepped opposite to it I saw that it was a sort of reception or waiting-room, and that it was empty. The door below it was also open, and with the idea that I would surely find someone there, I walked on up the hall. I was in evening dress, and I felt I did not look like a burglar, so I had no great fear that, should I encounter one of the inmates of the house, he would shoot me on sight. The second door in the hall opened into a dining-room. This was also empty. One person had been dining at the table, but the cloth had not been cleared away, and a flickering candle showed half-filled wineglasses and the ashes of cigarettes. The greater part of the room was in complete darkness.

"By this time I had grown conscious of the fact that I was wandering about in a strange house, and that, apparently, I was alone in it. The silence of the place began to try my nerves, and in a sudden, unexplainable panic I started for the open street. But as I turned, I saw a man sitting on a bench, which the curve of the balustrade had hidden from me. His eyes were shut, and he was sleeping soundly.

"The moment before I had been bewildered because I could see no one, but at sight of this man I was much more bewildered.

"He was a very large man, a giant in height, with long yellow hair which hung below his shoulders. He was dressed in a red silk shirt that was belted at the waist and hung outside black velvet trousers which, in turn, were stuffed into high black boots. I recognized the costume at once as that of a Russian servant, but what a Russian servant in his native livery could be doing in a private house in Knightsbridge was incomprehensible.

"I advanced and touched the man on the shoulder, and after an effort he awoke, and, on seeing me, sprang to his feet and began bowing rapidly and making deprecatory gestures. I had picked up enough Russian in Petersburg to make out that the man was apologizing for having fallen asleep, and I also was able to explain to him that I desired to see his master.

"He nodded vigorously, and said, 'Will the Excellency come this way? The Princess is here.'

"I distinctly made out the word 'princess,' and I was a good deal embarrassed. I had thought it would be easy enough to explain my intrusion to a man, but how a woman would look at it was another matter, and as I followed him down the hall I was somewhat puzzled.

"As we advanced, he noticed that the front door was standing open, and with an exclamation of surprise, hastened toward it and closed it. Then he rapped twice on the door of what was apparently the drawing-room. There was no reply to his knock, and he tapped again, and then timidly, and cringing subserviently, opened the door and stepped inside. He withdrew himself at once and stared stupidly at me, shaking his head.

"'She is not there,' he said. He stood for a moment gazing blankly through the open door, and then hastened toward the dining-room. The solitary candle which still burned there seemed to assure him that the room also was empty. He came back and bowed me toward the drawing-room. 'She is above,' he said; 'I will inform the Princess of the Excellency's presence.'

"Before I could stop him he had turned and was running up the staircase, leaving me alone at the open door of the drawing-room. I decided that the adventure had gone quite far enough, and if I had been able to explain to the Russian that I had lost my way in the fog, and only wanted to get back into the street again, I would have left the house on the instant.

"Of course, when I first rang the bell of the house I had no other expectation than that it would be answered by a parlor-maid who would direct me on my way. I certainly could not then foresee that I would disturb a Russian princess in her boudoir, or that I might be thrown out by her athletic bodyguard. Still, I thought I ought not now to leave the house without making some apology, and, if the worst should come, I could show my card. They could hardly believe that a member of an Embassy had any designs upon the hat-rack.

"The room in which I stood was dimly lighted, but I could see that, like the hall, it was hung with heavy Persian rugs. The corners were filled with palms, and there was the unmistakable odor in the air of Russian cigarettes, and strange, dry scents that carried me back to the bazaars of Vladivostock. Near the front windows was a grand piano, and at the other end of the room a heavily carved screen of some black wood, picked out with ivory. The screen was overhung with a canopy of silken draperies, and formed a sort of alcove. In front of the alcove was spread the white skin of a polar bear, and set on that was one of those low Turkish coffee tables. It held a lighted spirit-lamp and two gold coffee cups. I had heard no movement from above stairs, and it must have been fully three minutes that I stood waiting, noting these details of the room and wondering at the delay, and at the strange silence.

"And then, suddenly, as my eye grew more used to the half-light, I saw, projecting from behind the screen as though it were stretched along the back of a divan, the hand of a man and the lower part of his arm. I was as startled as though I had come across a footprint on a deserted island. Evidently the man had been sitting there since I had come into the room, even since I had entered the house, and he had heard the servant knocking upon the door. Why he had not declared himself I could not understand, but I supposed that possibly he was a guest, with no reason to interest himself in the Princess's other visitors, or perhaps, for some reason, he did not wish to be observed. I could see nothing of him except his hand, but I had an unpleasant feeling that he had been peering at me through the carving in the screen, and that he still was doing so. I moved my feet noisily on the floor and said tentatively, 'I beg your pardon.'

"There was no reply, and the hand did not stir. Apparently the man was bent upon ignoring me, but as all I wished was to apologize for my intrusion and to leave the house, I walked up to the alcove and peered around it. Inside the screen was a divan piled with cushions, and on the end of it nearer me the man was sitting. He was a young Englishman with light yellow hair and a deeply bronzed face.

"He was seated with his arms stretched out along the back of the divan, and with his head resting against a cushion. His attitude was one of complete ease. But his mouth had fallen open, and his eyes were set with an expression of utter horror. At the first glance I saw that he was quite dead.

"For a flash of time I was too startled to act, but in the same flash I was convinced that the man had met his death from no accident, that he had not died through any ordinary failure of the laws of nature. The expression on his face was much too terrible to be misinterpreted. It spoke as eloquently as words. It told me that before the end had come he had watched his death approach and threaten him.

"I was so sure he had been murdered that I instinctively looked on the floor for the weapon, and, at the same moment, out of concern for my own safety, quickly behind me; but the silence of the house continued unbroken.

"I have seen a great number of dead men; I was on the Asiatic Station during the Japanese-Chinese war. I was in Port Arthur after the massacre. So a dead man, for the single reason that he is dead, does not repel me, and, though I knew that there was no hope that this man was alive, still for decency's sake, I felt his pulse, and while I kept my ears alert for any sound from the floors above me, I pulled open his shirt and placed my hand upon his heart. My fingers instantly touched upon the opening of a wound, and as I withdrew them I found them wet with blood. He was in evening dress, and in the wide bosom of his shirt I found a narrow slit, so narrow that in the dim light it was scarcely discernable. The wound was no wider than the smallest blade of a pocket-knife, but when I stripped the shirt away from the chest and left it bare, I found that the weapon, narrow as it was, had been long enough to reach his heart. There is no need to tell you how I felt as I stood by the body of this boy, for he was hardly older than a boy, or of the thoughts that came into my head. I was bitterly sorry for this stranger, bitterly indignant at his murderer, and, at the same time, selfishly concerned for my own safety and for the notoriety which I saw was sure to follow. My instinct was to leave the body where it lay, and to hide myself in the fog, but I also felt that since a succession of accidents had made me the only witness to a crime, my duty was to make myself a good witness and to assist to establish the facts of this murder.

"That it might possibly be a suicide, and not a murder, did not disturb me for a moment. The fact that the weapon had disappeared, and the expression on the boy's face were enough to convince, at least me, that he had had no hand in his own death. I judged it, therefore, of the first importance to discover who was in the house, or, if they had escaped from it, who had been in the house before I entered it. I had seen one man leave it; but all I could tell of him was that he was a young man, that he was in evening dress, and that he had fled in such haste that he had not stopped to close the door behind him.

"The Russian servant I had found apparently asleep, and, unless he acted a part with supreme skill, he was a stupid and ignorant boor, and as innocent of the murder as myself. There was still the Russian princess whom he had expected to find, or had pretended to expect to find, in the same room with the murdered man. I judged that she must now be either upstairs with the servant, or that she had, without his knowledge, already fled from the house. When I recalled his apparently genuine surprise at not finding her in the drawing-room, this latter supposition seemed the more probable. Nevertheless, I decided that it was my duty to make a search, and after a second hurried look for the weapon among the cushions of the divan, and upon the floor, I cautiously crossed the hall and entered the dining-room.

"The single candle was still flickering in the draught, and showed only the white cloth. The rest of the room was draped in shadows. I picked up the candle, and, lifting it high above my head, moved around the corner of the table. Either my nerves were on such a stretch that no shock could strain them further, or my mind was inoculated to horrors, for I did not cry out at what I saw nor retreat from it. Immediately at my feet was the body of a beautiful woman, lying at full length upon the floor, her arms flung out on either side of her, and her white face and shoulders gleaming dully in the unsteady light of the candle. Around her throat was a great chain of diamonds, and the light played upon these and made them flash and blaze in tiny flames. But the woman who wore them was dead, and I was so certain as to how she had died that without an instant's hesitation I dropped on my knees beside her and placed my hands above her heart. My fingers again touched the thin slit of a wound. I had no doubt in my mind but that this was the Russian princess, and when I lowered the candle to her face I was assured that this was so. Her features showed the finest lines of both the Slav and the Jewess; the eyes were black, the hair blue-black and wonderfully heavy, and her skin, even in death, was rich in color. She was a surpassingly beautiful woman.

"I rose and tried to light another candle with the one I held, but I found that my hand was so unsteady that I could not keep the wicks together. It was my intention to again search for this strange dagger which had been used to kill both the English boy and the beautiful princess, but before I could light the second candle I heard footsteps descending the stairs, and the Russian servant appeared in the doorway.

"My face was in darkness, or I am sure that at the sight of it he would have taken alarm, for at that moment I was not sure but that this man himself was the murderer. His own face was plainly visible to me in the light from the hall, and I could see that it wore an expression of dull bewilderment. I stepped quickly toward him and took a firm hold upon his wrist.

"'She is not there,' he said. 'The Princess has gone. They have all gone.'

"'Who have gone?' I demanded. 'Who else has been here?'

"'The two Englishmen,' he said.

"'What two Englishmen?' I demanded. 'What are their names?'

"The man now saw by my manner that some question of great moment hung upon his answer, and he began to protest that he did not know the names of the visitors and that until that evening he had never seen them.

"I guessed that it was my tone which frightened him, so I took my hand off his wrist and spoke less eagerly.

"'How long have they been here?' I asked, 'and when did they go?'

"He pointed behind him toward the drawing-room.

"'One sat there with the Princess,' he said; 'the other came after I had placed the coffee in the drawing-room. The two Englishmen talked together and the Princess returned here to the table. She sat there in that chair, and I brought her cognac and cigarettes. Then I sat outside upon the bench. It was a feast day, and I had been drinking. Pardon, Excellency, but I fell asleep. When I woke, your Excellency was standing by me, but the Princess and the two Englishmen had gone. That is all I know.'

"I believed that the man was telling me the truth. His fright had passed, and he was now apparently puzzled, but not alarmed.

"'You must remember the names of the Englishmen,' I urged. 'Try to think. When you announced them to the Princess what name did you give?'

"At this question he exclaimed with pleasure, and, beckoning to me, ran hurriedly down the hall and into the drawing-room. In the corner furthest from the screen was the piano, and on it was a silver tray. He picked this up and, smiling with pride at his own intelligence, pointed at two cards that lay upon it. I took them up and read the names engraved upon them."

The American paused abruptly, and glanced at the faces about him. "I read the names," he repeated. He spoke with great reluctance.

"Continue!" cried the Baronet, sharply.

"I read the names," said the American with evident distaste, "and the family name of each was the same. They were the names of two brothers. One is well known to you. It is that of the African explorer of whom this gentleman was just speaking. I mean the Earl of Chetney. The other was the name of his brother, Lord Arthur Chetney."

The men at the table fell back as though a trapdoor had fallen open at their feet.

"Lord Chetney!" they exclaimed in chorus. They glanced at each other and back to the American with every expression of concern and disbelief.

"It is impossible!" cried the Baronet. "Why, my dear sir, young Chetney only arrived from Africa yesterday. It was so stated in the evening papers."

The jaw of the American set in a resolute square, and he pressed his lips together.

"You are perfectly right, sir," he said, "Lord Chetney did arrive in London yesterday morning, and yesterday night I found his dead body."

The youngest member present was the first to recover. He seemed much less concerned over the identity of the murdered man than at the interruption of the narrative.

"Oh, please let him go on!" he cried. "What happened then? You say you found two visiting cards. How do you know which card was that of the murdered man?"

The American, before he answered, waited until the chorus of exclamations had ceased. Then he continued as though he had not been interrupted.

"The instant I read the names upon the cards," he said, "I ran to the screen and, kneeling beside the dead man, began a search through his pockets. My hand at once fell upon a card-case, and I found on all the cards it contained the title of the Earl of Chetney. His watch and cigarette-case also bore his name. These evidences, and the fact of his bronzed skin, and that his cheekbones were worn with fever, convinced me that the dead man was the African explorer, and the boy who had fled past me in the night was Arthur, his younger brother.

"I was so intent upon my search that I had forgotten the servant, and I was still on my knees when I heard a cry behind me. I turned, and saw the man gazing down at the body in abject horror.

"Before I could rise, he gave another cry of terror, and, flinging himself into the hall, raced toward the door to the street. I leaped after him, shouting to him to halt, but before I could reach the hall he had torn open the door, and I saw him spring out into the yellow fog. I cleared the steps in a jump and ran down the garden walk but just as the gate clicked in front of me. I had it open on the instant, and, following the sound of the man's footsteps, I raced after him across the open street. He, also, could hear me, and he instantly stopped running, and there was absolute silence. He was so near that I almost fancied I could hear him panting, and I held my own breath to listen. But I could distinguish nothing but the dripping of the mist about us, and from far off the music of the Hungarian band, which I had heard when I first lost myself.

"All I could see was the square of light from the door I had left open behind me, and a lamp in the hall beyond it flickering in the draught. But even as I watched it, the flame of the lamp was blown violently to and fro, and the door, caught in the same current of air, closed slowly. I knew if it shut I could not again enter the house, and I rushed madly toward it. I believe I even shouted out, as though it were something human which I could compel to obey me, and then I caught my foot against the curb and smashed into the sidewalk. When I rose to my feet I was dizzy and half stunned, and though I thought then that I was moving toward the door, I know now that I probably turned directly from it; for, as I groped about in the night, calling frantically for the police, my fingers touched nothing but the dripping fog, and the iron railings for which I sought seemed to have melted away. For many minutes I beat the mist with my arms like one at blind man's bluff, turning sharply in circles, cursing aloud at my stupidity and crying continually for help. At last a voice answered me from the fog, and I found myself held in the circle of a policeman's lantern.

"That is the end of my adventure. What I have to tell you now is what I learned from the police.

"At the station-house to which the man guided me I related what you have just heard. I told them that the house they must at once find was one set back from the street within a radius of two hundred yards from the Knightsbridge Barracks, that within fifty yards of it someone was giving a dance to the music of a Hungarian band, and that the railings before it were as high as a man's waist and filed to a point. With that to work upon, twenty men were at once ordered out into the fog to search for the house, and Inspector Lyle himself was dispatched to the home of Lord Edam, Chetney's father, with a warrant for Lord Arthur's arrest. I was thanked and dismissed on my own recognizance.

"This morning, Inspector Lyle called on me, and from him I learned the police theory of the scene I have just described.

"Apparently I had wandered very far in the fog, for up to noon today the house had not been found, nor had they been able to arrest Lord Arthur. He did not return to his father's house last night, and there is no trace of him; but from what the police knew of the past lives of the people I found in that lost house, they have evolved a theory, and their theory is that the murders were committed by Lord Arthur.

"The infatuation of his elder brother, Lord Chetney, for a Russian princess, so Inspector Lyle tells me, is well known to everyone. About two years ago the Princess Zichy, as she calls herself, and he were constantly together, and Chetney informed his friends that they were about to be married. The woman was notorious in two continents, and when Lord Edam heard of his son's infatuation he appealed to the police for her record.

"It is through his having applied to them that they know so much concerning her and her relations with the Chetneys. From the police Lord Edam learned that Madame Zichy had once been a spy in the employ of the Russian Third Section, but that lately she had been repudiated by her own government and was living by her wits, by blackmail, and by her beauty. Lord Edam laid this record before his son, but Chetney either knew it already or the woman persuaded him not to believe in it, and the father and son parted in great anger. Two days later the marquis altered his will, leaving all of his money to the younger brother, Arthur.

"The title and some of the landed property he could not keep from Chetney, but he swore if his son saw the woman again that the will should stand as it was, and he would be left without a penny.

"This was about eighteen months ago, when apparently Chetney tired of the Princess, and suddenly went off to shoot and explore in Central Africa. No word came from him, except that twice he was reported as having died of fever in the jungle, and finally two traders reached the coast who said they had seen his body. This was accepted by all as conclusive, and young Arthur was recognized as the heir to the Edam millions. On the strength of this supposition he at once began to borrow enormous sums from the money lenders. This is of great importance, as the police believe it was these debts which drove him to the murder of his brother. Yesterday, as you know, Lord Chetney suddenly returned from the grave, and it was the fact that for two years he had been considered as dead which lent such importance to his return and which gave rise to those columns of detail concerning him which appeared in all the afternoon papers. But, obviously, during his absence he had not tired of the Princess Zichy, for we know that a few hours after he reached London he sought her out. His brother, who had also learned of his reappearance through the papers, probably suspected which would be the house he would first visit, and followed him there, arriving, so the Russian servant tells us, while the two were at coffee in the drawing-room. The Princess, then, we also learn from the servant, withdrew to the dining-room, leaving the brothers together. What happened one can only guess.

"Lord Arthur knew now that when it was discovered he was no longer the heir, the money-lenders would come down upon him. The police believe that he at once sought out his brother to beg for money to cover the post-obits, but that, considering the sum he needed was several hundreds of thousands of pounds, Chetney refused to give it him. No one knew that Arthur had gone to seek out his brother. They were alone. It is possible, then, that in a passion of disappointment, and crazed with the disgrace which he saw before him, young Arthur made himself the heir beyond further question. The death of his brother would have availed nothing if the woman remained alive. It is then possible that he crossed the hall, and with the same weapon which made him Lord Edam's heir destroyed the solitary witness to the murder. The only other person who could have seen it was sleeping in a drunken stupor, to which fact undoubtedly he owed his life. And yet," concluded the Naval Attaché, leaning forward and marking each word with his finger, "Lord Arthur blundered fatally. In his haste he left the door of the house open, so giving access to the first passer-by, and he forgot that when he entered it he had handed his card to the servant. That piece of paper may yet send him to the gallows. In the meantime he has disappeared completely, and somewhere, in one of the millions of streets of this great capital, in a locked and empty house, lies the body of his brother, and of the woman his brother loved, undiscovered, unburied, and with their murder unavenged."

In the discussion which followed the conclusion of the story of the Naval Attaché the gentleman with the pearl took no part. Instead, he arose, and, beckoning a servant to a far corner of the room, whispered earnestly to him until a sudden movement on the part of Sir Andrew caused him to return hurriedly to the table.

"There are several points in Mr. Sears's story I want explained," he cried. "Be seated, Sir Andrew," he begged. "Let us have the opinion of an expert. I do not care what the police think, I want to know what you think."

But Sir Henry rose reluctantly from his chair.

"I should like nothing better than to discuss this," he said. "But it is most important that I proceed to the House. I should have been there some time ago." He turned toward the servant and directed him to call a hansom.

The gentleman with the pearl stud looked appealingly at the Naval Attaché. "There are surely many details that you have not told us," he urged. "Some you have forgotten."

The Baronet interrupted quickly.

"I trust not," he said, "for I could not possibly stop to hear them."

"The story is finished," declared the Naval Attaché; "until Lord Arthur is arrested or the bodies are found there is nothing more to tell of either Chetney or the Princess Zichy."

"Of Lord Chetney perhaps not," interrupted the sporting-looking gentleman with the black tie, "but there'll always be something to tell of the Princess Zichy. I know enough stories about her to fill a book. She was a most remarkable woman." The speaker dropped the end of his cigar into his coffee cup and, taking his case from his pocket, selected a fresh one. As he did so he laughed and held up the case that the others might see it. It was an ordinary cigar-case of well-worn pig-skin, with a silver clasp.

"The only time I ever met her," he said, "she tried to rob me of this."

The Baronet regarded him closely.

"She tried to rob you?" he repeated.

"Tried to rob me of this," continued the gentleman in the black tie, "and of the Czarina's diamonds." His tone was one of mingled admiration and injury.

"The Czarina's diamonds!" exclaimed the Baronet. He glanced quickly and suspiciously at the speaker, and then at the others about the table. But their faces gave evidence of no other emotion than that of ordinary interest.

"Yes, the Czarina's diamonds," repeated the man with the black tie. "It was a necklace of diamonds. I was told to take them to the Russian Ambassador in Paris who was to deliver them at Moscow. I am a Queen's Messenger," he added.

"Oh, I see," exclaimed Sir Andrew in a tone of relief. "And you say that this same Princess Zichy, one of the victims of this double murder, endeavored to rob you of—of—that cigar-case."

"And the Czarina's diamonds," answered the Queen's Messenger imperturbably. "It's not much of a story, but it gives you an idea of the woman's character. The robbery took place between Paris and Marseilles."

The Baronet interrupted him with an abrupt movement. "No, no," he cried, shaking his head in protest. "Do not tempt me. I really cannot listen. I must be at the House in ten minutes."

"I am sorry," said the Queen's Messenger. He turned to those seated about him. "I wonder if the other gentlemen—" he inquired tentatively. There was a chorus of polite murmurs, and the Queen's Messenger, bowing his head in acknowledgment, took a preparatory sip from his glass. At the same moment the servant to whom the man with the black pearl had spoken, slipped a piece of paper into his hand. He glanced at it, frowned, and threw it under the table.

The servant bowed to the Baronet.

"Your hansom is waiting, Sir Andrew," he said.

"The necklace was worth twenty thousand pounds," began the Queen's Messenger. "It was a present from the Queen of England to celebrate—" The Baronet gave an exclamation of angry annoyance.

"Upon my word, this is most provoking," he interrupted. "I really ought not to stay. But I certainly mean to hear this." He turned irritably to the servant. "Tell the hansom to wait," he commanded, and, with an air of a boy who is playing truant, slipped guiltily into his chair.

The gentleman with the black pearl smiled blandly, and rapped upon the table.

"Order, gentlemen," he said. "Order for the story of the Queen's Messenger and the Czarina's diamonds."

CHAPTER II

"THE NECKLACE was a present from the Queen of England to the Czarina of Russia," began the Queen's Messenger. "It was to celebrate the occasion of the Czar's coronation. Our Foreign Office knew that the Russian Ambassador in Paris was to proceed to Moscow for that ceremony, and I was directed to go to Paris and turn over the necklace to him. But when I reached Paris I found he had not expected me for a week later and was taking a few days' vacation at Nice. His people asked me to leave the necklace with them at the Embassy, but I had been charged to get a receipt for it from the Ambassador himself, so I started at once for Nice The fact that Monte Carlo is not two thousand miles from Nice may have had something to do with making me carry out my instructions so carefully. Now, how the Princess Zichy came to find out about the necklace I don't know, but I can guess. As you have just heard, she was at one time a spy in the service of the Russian government. And after they dismissed her she kept up her acquaintance with many of the Russian agents in London. It is probable that through one of them she learned that the necklace was to be sent to Moscow, and which one of the Queen's Messengers had been detailed to take it there. Still, I doubt if even that knowledge would have helped her if she had not also known something which I supposed no one else in the world knew but myself and one other man. And, curiously enough, the other man was a Queen's Messenger too, and a friend of mine. You must know that up to the time of this robbery I had always concealed my dispatches in a manner peculiarly my own. I got the idea from that play called *A Scrap of Paper*. In it a man wants to hide a certain compromising document. He knows that all his rooms will be secretly searched for it, so he puts it in a torn envelope and sticks it up where any one can see it on his mantel shelf. The result is that the woman who is ransacking the house to find it looks in all the unlikely places, but passes over the scrap of paper that is just under her nose. Sometimes the papers and packages they give us to carry about Europe are of very great value, and sometimes they are special makes of cigarettes, and orders to court dressmakers. Sometimes we know what we are carrying and sometimes we do not. If it is a large sum of money or a treaty, they generally tell us. But, as a rule, we have no knowledge of what the package contains; so, to be on the safe side, we naturally take just as great care of it as though we knew it held the terms of an ultimatum or the crown jewels. As a rule, my confreres carry the official packages in a dispatch-box, which is just as obvious as a lady's jewel bag in the hands of her maid. Everyone knows they are carrying something of value. They put a premium on dishonesty. Well, after I saw the *Scrap of Paper* play, I determined to put the government valuables in the most unlikely place that any ne would look for them. So I used to hide the documents they gave me inside my riding-boots, and small articles, such as money or jewels, I carried in an old cigar-case. After I took to using my case for that purpose I bought a new one, exactly like it, for my cigars. But to avoid mistakes, I had my initials placed on both sides of the new one, and the moment I touched the case, even in the dark, I could tell which it was by the raised initials.

"No one knew of this except the Queen's Messenger of whom I spoke. We once left Paris together on the Orient Express. I was going to Constantinople and he was to stop off at Vienna. On the journey I told him of my peculiar way of hiding things and showed him my cigar-case. If I recollect rightly, on that trip it held the grand cross of St. Michael and St. George, which the Queen was sending to our Ambassador. The Messenger was very much entertained at my scheme, and some months later when he met the Princess he told her about it as an amusing story. Of course, he had no idea she was a Russian spy. He didn't know anything at all about her, except that she was a very attractive woman.

"It was indiscreet, but he could not possibly have guessed that she could ever make any use of what he told her.

"Later, after the robbery, I remembered that I had informed this young chap of my secret hiding-place, and when I saw him again I questioned him about it. He was greatly distressed, and said he had never seen the importance of the secret. He remembered he had told several people of it, and among others the Princess Zichy. In that way I found out that it was she who had robbed me, and I know that from the moment I left London she was following me and that she knew then that the diamonds were concealed in my cigar-case.

"My train for Nice left Paris at ten in the morning. When I travel at night I generally tell the *chef de gare* that I am a Queen's Messenger, and he gives me a compartment to myself, but in the daytime I take whatever offers. On this morning I had found an empty compartment, and I had tipped the guard to keep everyone else out, not from any fear of losing the diamonds, but because I wanted to smoke. He had locked the door, and as the last bell had rung I supposed I was to travel alone, so I began to arrange my traps and make myself comfortable. The diamonds in the cigar-case were in the inside pocket of my waistcoat, and as they made a bulky package, I took them out, intending to put them in my hand bag. It is a small satchel like a bookmaker's, or those hand bags that couriers carry. I wear it slung from a strap across my shoulder, and, no matter whether I am sitting or walking, it never leaves me.

"I took the cigar-case which held the necklace from my inside pocket and the case which held the cigars out of the satchel, and while I was searching through it for a box of matches I laid the two cases beside me on the seat.

"At that moment the train started, but at the same instant there was a rattle at the lock of the compartment, and a couple of porters lifted and shoved a woman through the door, and hurled her rugs and umbrellas in after her.

"Instinctively I reached for the diamonds. I shoved them quickly into the satchel and, pushing them far down to the bottom of the bag, snapped the spring lock. Then I put the cigars in the pocket of my coat, but with the thought that now that I had a woman as a travelling companion I would probably not be allowed to enjoy them.

"One of her pieces of luggage had fallen at my feet, and a roll of rugs had landed at my side. I thought if I hid the fact that the lady was not welcome, and at once endeavored to be civil, she might permit me to smoke. So I picked her hand bag off the floor and asked her where I might place it.

"As I spoke I looked at her for the first time, and saw that she was a most remarkably handsome woman.

"She smiled charmingly and begged me not to disturb myself. Then she arranged her own things about her, and, opening her dressing-bag, took out a gold cigarette case.

"'Do you object to smoke?' she asked.

"I laughed and assured her I had been in great terror lest she might object to it herself.

"'If you like cigarettes,' she said, 'will you try some of these? They are rolled especially for my husband in Russia, and they are supposed to be very good.'

"I thanked her, and took one from her case, and I found it so much better than my own that I continued to smoke her cigarettes throughout the rest of the journey. I must say that we got on very well. I judged from the coronet on her cigarette-case, and from her manner, which was quite as well-bred as that of any woman I ever met, that she was some one of importance, and though she seemed almost too good looking to be respectable, I determined that she was some *grande dame* who was so assured of her position that she could afford to be unconventional. At first she read her novel, and then she made some comment on the scenery, and finally we began to discuss the current politics of the Continent. She talked of all the cities in Europe, and seemed to know everyone worth knowing. But she volunteered nothing about herself except that she frequently made use of the expression, 'When my husband was stationed at Vienna,' or 'When my husband was promoted to Rome.' Once she said to me, 'I have often seen you at Monte Carlo. I saw you when you won the pigeon championship.' I told her that I was not a pigeon shot, and she gave a little start of surprise. 'Oh, I beg your pardon,' she said; 'I thought you were Morton Hamilton, the English champion.' As a matter of fact, I do look like Hamilton, but I know now that her object was to make me think that she had no idea as to who I really was. She needn't have acted at all, for I certainly had no suspicions of her, and was only too pleased to have so charming a companion.

"The one thing that should have made me suspicious was the fact that at every station she made some trivial excuse to get me out of the compartment. She pretended that her maid was travelling back of us in one of the second-class carriages, and kept saying she could not imagine why the woman did not come to look after her, and if the maid did not turn up at the next stop, would I be so very kind as to get out and bring her whatever it was she pretended she wanted.

"I had taken my dressing-case from the rack to get out a novel, and had left it on the seat opposite to mine, and at the end of the compartment farthest from her. And once when I came back from buying her a cup of chocolate, or from some other fool errand, I found her standing at my end of the compartment with both hands on the dressing-bag. She looked at me without so much as winking an eye, and shoved the case carefully into a corner. 'Your bag slipped off on the floor,' she said. 'If you've got any bottles in it, you had better look and see that they're not broken.'

"And I give you my word, I was such an ass that I did open the case and looked all through it. She must have thought I was a Juggins. I get hot all over whenever I remember it. But in spite of my dullness, and her cleverness, she couldn't gain anything by sending me away, because what she wanted was in the hand bag and every time she sent me away the hand bag went with me.

"After the incident of the dressing-case her manner changed. Either in my absence she had had time to look through it, or, when I was examining it for broken bottles, she had seen everything it held.

"From that moment she must have been certain that the cigar-case, in which she knew I carried the diamonds, was in the bag that was fastened to my body, and from that time on she probably was plotting how to get it from me. Her anxiety became most apparent. She dropped the great lady manner, and her charming condescension went with it. She ceased talking, and, when I spoke, answered me irritably, or at random. No doubt her mind was entirely occupied with her plan. The end of our journey was drawing rapidly nearer, and her time for action was being cut down with the speed of the express train. Even I, unsuspicious as I was, noticed that something was very wrong with her. I really believe that before we reached Marseilles if I had not, through my own stupidity, given her the chance she wanted, she might have stuck a knife in me and rolled me out on the rails. But as it was, I only thought that the long journey had tired her. I suggested that it was a very trying trip, and asked her if she would allow me to offer her some of my cognac.

"She thanked me and said, 'No,' and then suddenly her eyes lighted, and she exclaimed, 'Yes, thank you, if you will be so kind.'

"My flask was in the hand bag, and I placed it on my lap and with my thumb slipped back the catch. As I keep my tickets and railroad guide in the bag, I am so constantly opening it that I never bother to lock it, and the fact that it is strapped to me has always been sufficient protection. But I can appreciate now what a satisfaction, and what a torment too, it must have been to that woman when she saw that the bag opened without a key.

"While we were crossing the mountains I had felt rather chilly and had been wearing a light racing coat. But after the lamps were lighted the compartment became very hot and stuffy, and I found the coat uncomfortable. So I stood up, and, after first slipping the strap of the bag over my head, I placed the bag in the seat next me and pulled off the racing coat. I don't blame myself for being careless; the bag was still within reach of my hand, and nothing would have happened if at that exact moment the train had not stopped at Arles. It was the combination of my removing the bag and our entering the station at the same instant which gave the Princess Zichy the chance she wanted to rob me.

"I needn't say that she was clever enough to take it. The train ran into the station at full speed and came to a sudden stop. I had just thrown my coat into the rack, and had reached out my hand for the bag. In another instant I would have had the strap around my shoulder. But at that moment the Princess threw open the door of the compartment and beckoned wildly at the people on the platform. 'Natalie!' she called, 'Natalie! here I am. Come here! This way!' She turned upon me in the greatest excitement. 'My maid!' she cried. 'She is looking for me. She passed the window without seeing me. Go, please, and bring her back.' She continued pointing out of the door and beckoning me with her other hand. There certainly was something about that woman's tone which made one jump. When she was giving orders you had no chance to think of anything else. So I rushed out on my errand of mercy, and then rushed back again to ask what the maid looked like.

"'In black,' she answered, rising and blocking the door of the compartment. 'All in black, with a bonnet!'

"The train waited three minutes at Aries, and in that time I suppose I must have rushed up to over twenty women and asked, 'Are you Natalie?' The only reason I wasn't punched with an umbrella or handed over to the police was that they probably thought I was crazy.

"When I jumped back into the compartment the Princess was seated where I had left her, but her eyes were burning with happiness. She placed her hand on my arm almost affectionately, and said in a hysterical way, 'You are very kind to me. I am so sorry to have troubled you.'

"I protested that every woman on the platform was dressed in black.

"'Indeed I am so sorry,' she said, laughing; and she continued to laugh until she began to breathe so quickly that I thought she was going to faint.

"I can see now that the last part of that journey must have been a terrible half hour for her. She had the cigar-case safe enough, but she knew that she herself was not safe. She understood if I were to open my bag, even at the last minute, and miss the case, I would know positively that she had taken it. I had placed the diamonds in the bag at the very moment she entered the compartment, and no one but our two selves had occupied it since. She knew that when we reached Marseilles she would either be twenty thousand pounds richer than when she left Paris, or that she would go to jail. That was the situation as she must have read it, and I don't envy her her state of mind during that last half hour. It must have been hell.

"I saw that something was wrong, and in my innocence I even wondered if possibly my cognac had not been a little too strong. For she suddenly developed into a most brilliant conversationalist, and applauded and laughed at everything I said, and fired off questions at me like a machine gun, so that I had no time to think of anything but of what she was saying. Whenever I stirred she stopped her chattering and leaned toward me, and watched me like a cat over a mouse-hole. I wondered how I could have considered her an agreeable travelling companion. I thought I would have preferred to be locked in with a lunatic. I don't like to think how she would have acted if I had made a move to examine the bag, but as I had it safely strapped around me again, I did not open it, and I reached Marseilles alive. As we drew into the station she shook hands with me and grinned at me like a Cheshire cat.

"'I cannot tell you,' she said, 'how much I have to thank you for.' What do you think of that for impudence!

"I offered to put her in a carriage, but she said she must find Natalie, and that she hoped we would meet again at the hotel. So I drove off by myself, wondering who she was, and whether Natalie was not her keeper.

"I had to wait several hours for the train to Nice, and as I wanted to stroll around the city I thought I had better put the diamonds in the safe of the hotel. As soon as I reached my room I locked the door, placed the hand bag on the table and opened it. I felt among the things at the top of it, but failed to touch the cigar-case. I shoved my hand in deeper, and stirred the things about, but still I did not reach it. A cold wave swept down my spine, and a sort of emptiness came to the pit of my stomach. Then I turned red-hot, and the sweat sprung out all over me. I wet my lips with my tongue, and said to myself, 'Don't be an ass. Pull yourself together, pull yourself together. Take the things out, one at a time. It's there, of course it's there. Don't be an ass.'

"So I put a brake on my nerves and began very carefully to pick out the things one by one, but after another second I could not stand it, and I rushed across the room and threw out everything on the bed. But the diamonds were not among them. I pulled the things about and tore them open and shuffled and rearranged and sorted them, but it was no use. The cigar-case was gone. I threw everything in the dressing-case out on the floor, although I knew it was useless to look for it there. I knew that I had put it in the bag. I sat down and tried to think. I remembered I had put it in the satchel at Paris just as that woman had entered the compartment, and I had been alone with her ever since, so it was she who had robbed me. But how? It had never left my shoulder. And then I remembered that it had—that I had taken it off when I had changed my coat and for the few moments that I was searching for Natalie. I remembered that the woman had sent me on that goose chase, and that at every other station she had tried to get rid of me on some fool errand.

"I gave a roar like a mad bull, and I jumped down the stairs six steps at a time.

"I demanded at the office if a distinguished lady of title, possibly a Russian, had just entered the hotel.

"As I expected, she had not. I sprang into a cab and inquired at two other hotels, and then I saw the folly of trying to catch her without outside help, and I ordered the fellow to gallop to the office of the Chief of Police. I told my story, and the ass in charge asked me to calm myself, and wanted to take notes. I told him this was no time for taking notes, but for doing something. He got wrathy at that, and I demanded to be taken at once to his Chief. The Chief, he said, was very busy, and could not see me. So I showed him my silver greyhound. In eleven years I had never used it but once before. I stated in pretty vigorous language that I was a Queen's Messenger, and that if the Chief of Police did not see me instantly he would lose his official head. At that the fellow jumped off his high horse and ran with me to his Chief,—a smart young chap, a colonel in the army, and a very intelligent man.

"I explained that I had been robbed in a French railway carriage of a diamond necklace belonging to the Queen of England, which her Majesty was sending as a present to the Czarina of Russia. I pointed out to him that if he succeeded in capturing the thief he would be made for life, and would receive the gratitude of three great powers.

"He wasn't the sort that thinks second thoughts are best. He saw Russian and French decorations sprouting all over his chest, and he hit a bell, and pressed buttons, and yelled out orders like the captain of a penny steamer in a fog. He sent her description to all the city gates, and ordered all cabmen and railway porters to search all trains leaving Marseilles. He ordered all passengers on outgoing vessels to be examined, and telegraphed the proprietors of every hotel and pension to send him a complete list of their guests within the hour. While I was standing there he must have given at least a hundred orders, and sent out enough *commissaires, sergeants de ville*, gendarmes, bicycle police, and plain-clothes Johnnies to have captured the entire German army. When they had gone he assured me that the woman was as good as arrested already. Indeed, officially, she was arrested; for she had no more chance of escape from Marseilles than from the Chateau D'If.

"He told me to return to my hotel and possess my soul in peace. Within an hour he assured me he would acquaint me with her arrest.

"I thanked him, and complimented him on his energy, and left him. But I didn't share in his confidence. I felt that she was a very clever woman, and a match for any and all of us. It was all very well for him to be jubilant. He had not lost the diamonds, and had everything to gain if he found them; while I, even if he did recover the necklace, would only be where I was before I lost them, and if he did not recover it I was a ruined man. It was an awful facer for me. I had always prided myself on my record. In eleven years I had never mislaid an envelope, nor missed taking the first train. And now I had failed in the most important mission that had ever been entrusted to me. And it wasn't a thing that could be hushed up, either. It was too conspicuous, too spectacular. It was sure to invite the widest notoriety. I saw myself ridiculed all over the Continent, and perhaps dismissed, even suspected of having taken the thing myself.

"I was walking in front of a lighted cafe, and I felt so sick and miserable that I stopped for a pick-me-up. Then I considered that if I took one drink I would probably, in my present state of mind, not want to stop under twenty, and I decided I had better leave it alone. But my nerves were jumping like a frightened rabbit, and I felt I must have something to quiet them, or I would go crazy. I reached for my cigarette-case, but a cigarette seemed hardly adequate, so I put it back again and took out this cigar-case, in which I keep only the strongest and blackest cigars. I opened it and stuck in my fingers, but instead of a cigar they touched on a thin leather envelope. My heart stood perfectly still. I did not dare to look, but I dug my finger nails into the leather and I felt layers of thin paper, then a layer of cotton, and then they scratched on the facets of the Czarina's diamonds!

"I stumbled as though I had been hit in the face, and fell back into one of the chairs on the sidewalk. I tore off the wrappings and spread out the diamonds on the cafe table; I could not believe they were real. I twisted the necklace between my fingers and crushed it between my palms and tossed it up in the air. I believe I almost kissed it. The women in the cafe stood tip on the chairs to see better, and laughed and screamed, and the people crowded so close around me that the waiters had to form a bodyguard. The proprietor thought there was a fight, and called for the police. I was so happy I didn't care. I laughed, too, and gave the proprietor a five-pound note, and told him to stand everyone a drink. Then I tumbled into a fiacre and galloped off to my friend the Chief of Police. I felt very sorry for him. He had been so happy at the chance I gave him, and he was sure to be disappointed when he learned I had sent him off on a false alarm.

"But now that I had found the necklace, I did not want him to find the woman. Indeed, I was most anxious that she should get clear away, for if she were caught the truth would come out, and I was likely to get a sharp reprimand, and sure to be laughed at.

"I could see now how it had happened. In my haste to hide the diamonds when the woman was hustled into the carriage, I had shoved the cigars into the satchel, and the diamonds into the pocket of my coat. Now that I had the diamonds safe again, it seemed a very natural mistake. But I doubted if the Foreign Office would think so. I was afraid it might not appreciate the beautiful simplicity of my secret hiding-place. So, when I reached the police station, and found that the woman was still at large, I was more than relieved.

"As I expected, the Chief was extremely chagrined when he learned of my mistake, and that there was nothing for him to do. But I was feeling so happy myself that I hated to have any one else miserable, so I suggested that this attempt to steal the Czarina's necklace might be only the first of a series of such attempts by an unscrupulous gang, and that I might still be in danger.

"I winked at the Chief and the Chief smiled at me, and we went to Nice together in a saloon car with a guard of twelve carabineers and twelve plain-clothes men, and the Chief and I drank champagne all the way. We marched together up to the hotel where the Russian Ambassador was stopping, closely surrounded by our escort of carabineers, and delivered the necklace with the most profound ceremony. The old Ambassador was immensely impressed, and when we hinted that already I had been made the object of an attack by robbers, he assured us that his Imperial Majesty would not prove ungrateful.

"I wrote a swinging personal letter about the invaluable services of the Chief to the French Minister of Foreign Affairs, and they gave him enough Russian and French medals to satisfy even a French soldier. So, though he never caught the woman, he received his just reward."

The Queen's Messenger paused and surveyed the faces of those about him in some embarrassment.

"But the worst of it is," he added, "that the story must have got about; for, while the Princess obtained nothing from me but a cigar-case and five excellent cigars, a few weeks after the coronation the Czar sent me a gold cigar-case with his monogram in diamonds. And I don't know yet whether that was a coincidence, or whether the Czar wanted me to know that he knew that I had been carrying the Czarina's diamonds in my pigskin cigar-case. What do you fellows think?"

CHAPTER III

SIR ANDREW rose with disapproval written in every lineament.

"I thought your story would bear upon the murder," he said. "Had I imagined it would have nothing whatsoever to do with it I would not have remained." He pushed back his chair and bowed stiffly. "I wish you good night," he said.

There was a chorus of remonstrance, and under cover of this and the Baronet's answering protests a servant for the second time slipped a piece of paper into the hand of the gentleman with the pearl stud. He read the lines written upon it and tore it into tiny fragments.

The youngest member, who had remained an interested but silent listener to the tale of the Queen's Messenger, raised his hand commandingly.

"Sir Andrew," he cried, "in justice to Lord Arthur Chetney I must ask you to be seated. He has been accused in our hearing of a most serious crime, and I insist that you remain until you have heard me clear his character."

"You!" cried the Baronet.

"Yes," answered the young man briskly. "I would have spoken sooner," he explained, "but that I thought this gentleman"—he inclined his head toward the Queen's Messenger—"was about to contribute some facts of which I was ignorant. He, however, has told us nothing, and so I will take up the tale at the point where Lieutenant Sears laid it down and give you those details of which Lieutenant Sears is ignorant. It seems strange to you that I should be able to add the sequel to this story. But the coincidence is easily explained. I am the junior member of the law firm of Chudleigh & Chudleigh. We have been solicitors for the Chetneys for the last two hundred years. Nothing, no matter how unimportant, which concerns Lord Edam and his two sons is unknown to us, and naturally we are acquainted with every detail of the terrible catastrophe of last night."

The Baronet, bewildered but eager, sank back into his chair.

"Will you be long, sir!" he demanded.

"I shall endeavor to be brief," said the young solicitor; "and," he added, in a tone which gave his words almost the weight of a threat, "I promise to be interesting."

"There is no need to promise that," said Sir Andrew, "I find it much too interesting as it is." He glanced ruefully at the clock and turned his eyes quickly from it.

"Tell the driver of that hansom," he called to the servant, "that I take him by the hour."

"For the last three days," began young Mr. Chudleigh, "as you have probably read in the daily papers, the Marquis of Edam has been at the point of death, and his physicians have never left his house. Every hour he seemed to grow weaker; but although his bodily strength is apparently leaving him forever, his mind has remained clear and active. Late yesterday evening word was received at our office that he wished my father to come at once to Chetney House and to bring with him certain papers. What these papers were is not essential; I mention them only to explain how it was that last night I happened to be at Lord Edam's bed-side. I accompanied my father to Chetney House, but at the time we reached there Lord Edam was sleeping, and his physicians refused to have him awakened. My father urged that he should be allowed to receive Lord Edam's instructions concerning the documents, but the physicians would not disturb him, and we all gathered in the library to wait until he should awake of his own accord. It was about one o'clock in the morning, while we were still there, that Inspector Lyle and the officers from Scotland Yard came to arrest Lord Arthur on the charge of murdering his brother. You can imagine our dismay and distress. Like everyone else, I had learned from the afternoon papers that Lord Chetney was not dead, but that he had returned to England, and on arriving at Chetney House I had been told that Lord Arthur had gone to the Bath Hotel to look for his brother and to inform him that if he wished to see their father alive he must come to him at once. Although it was now past one o'clock, Arthur had not returned. None of us knew where Madame Zichy lived, so we could not go to recover Lord Chetney's body. We spent a most miserable night, hastening to the window whenever a cab came into the square, in the hope that it was Arthur returning, and endeavoring to explain away the facts that pointed to him as the murderer. I am a friend of Arthur's, I was with him at Harrow and at Oxford, and I refused to believe for an instant that he was capable of such a crime; but as a lawyer I could not help but see that the circumstantial evidence was strongly against him.

"Toward early morning Lord Edam awoke, and in so much better a state of health that he refused to make the changes in the papers which he had intended, declaring that he was no nearer death than ourselves. Under other circumstances, this happy change in him would have relieved us greatly, but none of us could think of anything save the death of his elder son and of the charge which hung over Arthur.

"As long as Inspector Lyle remained in the house my father decided that I, as one of the legal advisers of the family, should also remain there. But there was little for either of us to do. Arthur did not return, and nothing occurred until late this morning, when Lyle received word that the Russian servant had been arrested. He at once drove to Scotland Yard to question him. He came back to us in an hour, and informed me that the servant had refused to tell anything of what had happened the night before, or of himself, or of the Princess Zichy. He would not even give them the address of her house.

"'He is in abject terror,' Lyle said. 'I assured him that he was not suspected of the crime, but he would tell me nothing.'

"There were no other developments until two o'clock this afternoon, when word was brought to us that Arthur had been found, and that he was lying in the accident ward of St. George's Hospital. Lyle and I drove there together, and found him propped up in bed with his head bound in a bandage. He had been brought to the hospital the night before by the driver of a hansom that had run over him in the fog. The cab-horse had kicked him on the head, and he had been carried in unconscious. There was nothing on him to tell who he was, and it was not until he came to his senses this afternoon that the hospital authorities had been able to send word to his people. Lyle at once informed him that he was under arrest, and with what he was charged, and though the inspector warned him to say nothing which might be used against him, I, as his solicitor, instructed him to speak freely and to tell us all he knew of the occurrences of last night. It was evident to any one that the fact of his brother's death was of much greater concern to him, than that he was accused of his murder.

"'That,' Arthur said contemptuously, 'that is damned nonsense. It is monstrous and cruel. We parted better friends than we have been in years. I will tell you all that happened—not to clear myself, but to help you to find out the truth.' His story is as follows: Yesterday afternoon, owing to his constant attendance on his father, he did not look at the evening papers, and it was not until after dinner, when the butler brought him one and told him of its contents, that he learned that his brother was alive and at the Bath Hotel. He drove there at once, but was told that about eight o'clock his brother had gone out, but without giving any clue to his destination. As Chetney had not at once come to see his father, Arthur decided that he was still angry with him, and his mind, turning naturally to the cause of their quarrel, determined him to look for Chetney at the home of the Princess Zichy.

"Her house had been pointed out to him, and though he had never visited it, he had passed it many times and knew its exact location. He accordingly drove in that direction, as far as the fog would permit the hansom to go, and walked the rest of the way, reaching the house about nine o'clock. He rang, and was admitted by the Russian servant. The man took his card into the drawing-room, and at once his brother ran out and welcomed him. He was followed by the Princess Zichy, who also received Arthur most cordially.

"'You brothers will have much to talk about,' she said. 'I am going to the dining-room. When you have finished, let me know.'

"As soon as she had left them, Arthur told his brother that their father was not expected to outlive the night, and that he must come to him at once.

"'This is not the moment to remember your quarrel,' Arthur said to him; 'you have come back from the dead only in time to make your peace with him before he dies.'

"Arthur says that at this Chetney was greatly moved.

"'You entirely misunderstand me, Arthur,' he returned. 'I did not know the governor was ill, or I would have gone to him the instant I arrived. My only reason for not doing so was because I thought he was still angry with me. I shall return with you immediately, as soon as I have said good-by to the Princess. It is a final good-by. After tonight, I shall never see her again.'

"'Do you mean that?' Arthur cried.

"'Yes,' Chetney answered. 'When I returned to London I had no intention of seeking her again, and I am here only through a mistake.' He then told Arthur that he had separated from the Princess even before he went to Central Africa, and that, moreover, while at Cairo on his way south, he had learned certain facts concerning her life there during the previous season, which made it impossible for him to ever wish to see her again. Their separation was final and complete.

"'She deceived me cruelly,' he said; 'I cannot tell you how cruelly. During the two years when I was trying to obtain my father's consent to our marriage she was in love with a Russian diplomat. During all that time he was secretly visiting her here in London, and her trip to Cairo was only an excuse to meet him there.'

"'Yet you are here with her tonight,' Arthur protested, 'only a few hours after your return.'

"'That is easily explained,' Chetney answered. 'As I finished dinner tonight at the hotel, I received a note from her from this address. In it she said she had but just learned of my arrival, and begged me to come to her at once. She wrote that she was in great and present trouble, dying of an incurable illness, and without friends or money. She begged me, for the sake of old times, to come to her assistance. During the last two years in the jungle all my former feeling for Zichy has utterly passed away, but no one could have dismissed the appeal she made in that letter. So I came here, and found her, as you have seen her, quite as beautiful as she ever was, in very good health, and, from the look of the house, in no need of money.

"'I asked her what she meant by writing me that she was dying in a garret, and she laughed, and said she had done so because she was afraid, unless I thought she needed help, I would not try to see her. That was where we were when you arrived. And now,' Chetney added, 'I will say good-by to her, and you had better return home. No, you can trust me, I shall follow you at once. She has no influence over me now, but I believe, in spite of the way she has used me, that she is, after her queer fashion, still fond of me, and when she learns that this good-by is final there may be a scene, and it is not fair to her that you should be here. So, go home at once, and tell the governor that I am following you in ten minutes.' "'That,' said Arthur, 'is the way we parted. I never left him on more friendly terms. I was happy to see him alive again, I was happy to think he had returned in time to make up his quarrel with my father, and I was happy that at last he was shut of that woman. I was never better pleased with him in my life.' He turned to Inspector Lyle, who was sitting at the foot of the bed taking notes of all he told us.

"'Why in the name of common sense,' he cried, 'should I have chosen that moment of all others to send my brother back to the grave!' For a moment the Inspector did not answer him. I do not know if any of you gentlemen are acquainted with Inspector Lyle, but if you are not, I can assure you that he is a very remarkable man. Our firm often applies to him for aid, and he has never failed us; my father has the greatest possible respect for him. Where he has the advantage over the ordinary police official is in the fact that he possesses imagination. He imagines himself to be the criminal, imagines how he would act under the same circumstances, and he imagines to such purpose that he generally finds the man he wants. I have often told Lyle that if he had not been a detective he would have made a great success as a poet, or a playwright.

"When Arthur turned on him Lyle hesitated for a moment, and then told him exactly what was the case against him.

"'Ever since your brother was reported as having died in Africa,' he said, 'your Lordship has been collecting money on post obits. Lord Chetney's arrival last night turned them into waste paper. You were suddenly in debt for thousands of pounds— for much more than you could ever possibly pay. No one knew that you and your brother had met at Madame Zichy's. But you knew that your father was not expected to outlive the night, and that if your brother were dead also, you would be saved from complete ruin, and that you would become the Marquis of Edam.'

"'Oh, that is how you have worked it out, is it?' Arthur cried. 'And for me to become Lord Edam was it necessary that the woman should die, too!'

"'They will say,' Lyle answered, 'that she was a witness to the murder—that she would have told.'

"'Then why did I not kill the servant as well!' Arthur said.

"'He was asleep, and saw nothing.'

"'And you believe that?' Arthur demanded.

"'It is not a question of what I believe,' Lyle said gravely. 'It is a question for your peers.'

"'The man is insolent!' Arthur cried. 'The thing is monstrous! Horrible!'

"Before we could stop him he sprang out of his cot and began pulling on his clothes. When the nurses tried to hold him down, he fought with them.

"'Do you think you can keep me here,' he shouted, 'when they are plotting to hang me? I am going with you to that house!' he cried at Lyle. 'When you find those bodies I shall be beside you. It is my right. He is my brother. He has been murdered, and I can tell you who murdered him. That woman murdered him. She first ruined his life, and now she has killed him. For the last five years she has been plotting to make herself his wife, and last night, when he told her he had discovered the truth about the Russian, and that she would never see him again, she flew into a passion and stabbed him, and then, in terror of the gallows, killed herself. She murdered him, I tell you, and I promise you that we will find the knife she used near her—perhaps still in her hand. What will you say to that?'

"Lyle turned his head away and stared down at the floor. 'I might say,' he answered, 'that you placed it there.'

"Arthur gave a cry of anger and sprang at him, and then pitched forward into his arms. The blood was running from the cut under the bandage, and he had fainted. Lyle carried him back to the bed again, and we left him with the police and the doctors, and drove at once to the address he had given us. We found the house not three minutes' walk from St. George's Hospital. It stands in Trevor Terrace, that little row of houses set back from Knightsbridge, with one end in Hill Street.

"As we left the hospital Lyle had said to me, 'You must not blame me for treating him as I did. All is fair in this work, and if by angering that boy I could have made him commit himself I was right in trying to do so; though, I assure you, no one would be better pleased than myself if I could prove his theory to be correct. But we cannot tell. Everything depends upon what we see for ourselves within the next few minutes.'

"When we reached the house, Lyle broke open the fastenings of one of the windows on the ground floor, and, hidden by the trees in the garden, we scrambled in. We found ourselves in the reception-room, which was the first room on the right of the hall. The gas was still burning behind the colored glass and red silk shades, and when the daylight streamed in after us it gave the hall a hideously dissipated look, like the foyer of a theatre at a matinee, or the entrance to an all-day gambling hell. The house was oppressively silent, and because we knew why it was so silent we spoke in whispers. When Lyle turned the handle of the drawing-room door, I felt as though some one had put his hand upon my throat. But I followed close at his shoulder, and saw, in the subdued light of many-tinted lamps, the body of Chetney at the foot of the divan, just as Lieutenant Sears had described it. In the drawing-room we found the body of the Princess Zichy, her arms thrown out, and the blood from her heart frozen in a tiny line across her bare shoulder. But neither of us, although we searched the floor on our hands and knees, could find the weapon which had killed her.

We Found the Body of The Princess Zichy

"'For Arthur's sake,' I said, 'I would have given a thousand pounds if we had found the knife in her hand, as he said we would.'

"'That we have not found it there,' Lyle answered, 'is to my mind the strongest proof that he is telling the truth, that he left the house before the murder took place. He is not a fool, and had he stabbed his brother and this woman, he would have seen that by placing the knife near her he could help to make it appear as if she had killed Chetney and then committed suicide. Besides, Lord Arthur insisted that the evidence in his behalf would be our finding the knife here. He would not have urged that if he knew we would not find it, if he knew he himself had carried it away. This is no suicide. A suicide does not rise and hide the weapon with which he kills himself, and then lie down again. No, this has been a double murder, and we must look outside of the house for the murderer.'

"While he was speaking Lyle and I had been searching every corner, studying the details of each room. I was so afraid that, without telling me, he would make some deductions prejudicial to Arthur, that I never left his side. I was determined to see everything that he saw, and, if possible, to prevent his interpreting it in the wrong way. He finally finished his examination, and we sat down together in the drawing-room, and he took out his notebook and read aloud all that Mr. Sears had told him of the murder and what we had just learned from Arthur. We compared the two accounts word for word, and weighed statement with statement, but I could not determine from anything Lyle said which of the two versions he had decided to believe.

"'We are trying to build a house of blocks,' he exclaimed, 'with half of the blocks missing. We have been considering two theories,' he went on: 'one that Lord Arthur is responsible for both murders, and the other that the dead woman in there is responsible for one of them, and has committed suicide; but, until the Russian servant is ready to talk, I shall refuse to believe in the guilt of either.'

"'What can you prove by him!' I asked. 'He was drunk and asleep. He saw nothing.'

"Lyle hesitated, and then, as though he had made up his mind to be quite frank with me, spoke freely.

"'I do not know that he was either drunk or asleep,' he answered. 'Lieutenant Sears describes him as a stupid boor. I am not satisfied that he is not a clever actor. What was his position in this house! What was his real duty here? Suppose it was not to guard this woman, but to watch her. Let us imagine that it was not the woman he served, but a master, and see where that leads us. For this house has a master, a mysterious, absentee landlord, who lives in St. Petersburg, the unknown Russian who came between Chetney and Zichy, and because of whom Chetney left her. He is the man who bought this house for Madame Zichy, who sent these rugs and curtains from St. Petersburg to furnish it for her after his own tastes, and, I believe, it was he also who placed the Russian servant here, ostensibly to serve the Princess, but in reality to spy upon her. At Scotland Yard we do not know who this gentleman is; the Russian police confess to equal ignorance concerning him. When Lord Chetney went to Africa, Madame Zichy lived in St. Petersburg; but there her receptions and dinners were so crowded with members of the nobility and of the army and diplomats, that among so many visitors the police could not learn which was the one for whom she most greatly cared.'

"Lyle pointed at the modern French paintings and the heavy silk rugs which hung upon the walls.

"'The unknown is a man of taste and of some fortune,' he said, 'not the sort of man to send a stupid peasant to guard the woman he loves. So I am not content to believe, with Mr. Sears, that the servant is a boor. I believe him instead to be a very clever ruffian. I believe him to be the protector of his master's honor, or, let us say, of his master's property, whether that property be silver plate or the woman his master loves. Last night, after Lord Arthur had gone away, the servant was left alone in this house with Lord Chetney and Madame Zichy. From where he sat in the hall he could hear Lord Chetney bidding her farewell; for, if my idea of him is correct, he understands English quite as well as you or I. Let us imagine that he heard her entreating Chetney not to leave her, reminding him of his former wish to marry her, and let us suppose that he hears Chetney denounce her, and tell her that at Cairo he has learned of this Russian admirer—the servant's master. He hears the woman declare that she has had no admirer but himself, that this unknown Russian was, and is, nothing to her, that there is no man she loves but him, and that she cannot live, knowing that he is alive, without his love. Suppose Chetney believed her, suppose his former infatuation for her returned, and that in a moment of weakness he forgave her and took her in his arms. That is the moment the Russian master has feared. It is to guard against it that he has placed his watchdog over the Princess, and how do we know but that, when the moment came, the watchdog served his master, as he saw his duty, and killed them both? What do you think?' Lyle demanded. 'Would not that explain both murders?'

"I was only too willing to hear any theory which pointed to anyone else as the criminal than Arthur, but Lyle's explanation was too utterly fantastic. I told him that he certainly showed imagination, but that he could not hang a man for what he imagined he had done.

"'No,' Lyle answered, 'but I can frighten him by telling him what I think he has done, and now when I again question the Russian servant I will make it quite clear to him that I believe he is the murderer. I think that will open his mouth. A man will at least talk to defend himself. Come,' he said, 'we must return at once to Scotland Yard and see him. There is nothing more to do here.'

"He arose, and I followed him into the hall, and in another minute we would have been on our way to Scotland Yard. But just as he opened the street door a postman halted at the gate of the garden, and began fumbling with the latch.

"Lyle stopped, with an exclamation of chagrin.

"'How stupid of me!' he exclaimed. He turned quickly and pointed to a narrow slit cut in the brass plate of the front door. 'The house has a private letter-box,' he said, 'and I had not thought to look in it! If we had gone out as we came in, by the window, I would never have seen it. The moment I entered the house I should have thought of securing the letters which came this morning. I have been grossly careless.' He stepped back into the hall and pulled at the lid of the letterbox, which hung on the inside of the door, but it was tightly locked. At the same moment the postman came up the steps holding a letter. Without a word Lyle took it from his hand and began to examine it. It was addressed to the Princess Zichy, and on the back of the envelope was the name of a West End dressmaker.

"'That is of no use to me,' Lyle said. He took out his card and showed it to the postman. 'I am Inspector Lyle from Scotland Yard,' he said. 'The people in this house are under arrest. Everything it contains is now in my keeping. Did you deliver any other letters here this morning!'

"The man looked frightened, but answered promptly that he was now upon his third round. He had made one postal delivery at seven that morning and another at eleven.

"'How many letters did you leave here!' Lyle asked.

"'About six altogether,' the man answered.

"'Did you put them through the door into the letter-box!'

"The postman said, 'Yes, I always slip them into the box, and ring and go away. The servants collect them from the inside.'

"'Have you noticed if any of the letters you leave here bear a Russian postage stamp!' Lyle asked.

"The man answered, 'Oh, yes, sir, a great many.'

"'From the same person, would you say!'

"'The writing seems to be the same,' the man answered. 'They come regularly about once a week—one of those I delivered this morning had a Russian postmark.'

"'That will do,' said Lyle eagerly. 'Thank you, thank you very much.'

"He ran back into the hall, and, pulling out his penknife, began to pick at the lock of the letter-box.

"'I have been supremely careless,' he said in great excitement. 'Twice before when people I wanted had flown from a house I have been able to follow them by putting a guard over their mail-box. These letters, which arrive regularly every week from Russia in the same handwriting, they can come but from one person. At least, we shall now know the name of the master of this house. Undoubtedly it is one of his letters that the man placed here this morning. We may make a most important discovery.'

"As he was talking he was picking at the lock with his knife, but he was so impatient to reach the letters that he pressed too heavily on the blade and it broke in his hand. I took a step backward and drove my heel into the lock, and burst it open.

The lid flew back, and we pressed forward, and each ran his hand down into the letterbox. For a moment we were both too startled to move. The box was empty.

"I do not know how long we stood staring stupidly at each other, but it was Lyle who was the first to recover. He seized me by the arm and pointed excitedly into the empty box.

"'Do you appreciate what that means?' he cried. 'It means that someone has been here ahead of us. Someone has entered this house not three hours before we came, since eleven o'clock this morning.'

"'It was the Russian servant!' I exclaimed.

"'The Russian servant has been under arrest at Scotland Yard,' Lyle cried. 'He could not have taken the letters. Lord Arthur has been in his cot at the hospital. That is his alibi. There is someone else, someone we do not suspect, and that someone is the murderer. He came back here either to obtain those letters because he knew they would convict him, or to remove something he had left here at the time of the murder, something incriminating,—the weapon, perhaps, or some personal article; a cigarette-case, a handkerchief with his name upon it, or a pair of gloves. Whatever it was it must have been damning evidence against him to have made him take so desperate a chance.'

"'How do we know,' I whispered, 'that he is not hidden here now?'

"'No, I'll swear he is not,' Lyle answered. 'I may have bungled in some things, but I have searched this house thoroughly. Nevertheless,' he added, 'we must go over it again, from the cellar to the roof. We have the real clew now, and we must forget the others and work only it.' As he spoke he began again to search the drawing-room, turning over even the books on the tables and the music on the piano. "'Whoever the man is,' he said over his shoulder, 'we know that he has a key to the front door and a key to the letter-box. That shows us he is either an inmate of the house or that he comes here when he wishes. The Russian says that he was the only servant in the house. Certainly we have found no evidence to show that any other servant slept here. There could be but one other person who would possess a key to the house and the letter-box—and he lives in St. Petersburg. At the time of the murder he was two thousand miles away.' Lyle interrupted himself suddenly with a sharp cry and turned upon me with his eyes flashing. 'But was he?' he cried. 'Was he? How do we know that last night he was not in London, in this very house when Zichy and Chetney met?'

"He stood staring at me without seeing me, muttering, and arguing with himself.

"'Don't speak to me,' he cried, as I ventured to interrupt him. 'I can see it now. It is all plain. It was not the servant, but his master, the Russian himself, and it was he who came back for the letters! He came back for them because he knew they would convict him. We must find them. We must have those letters. If we find the one with the Russian postmark, we shall have found the murderer.' He spoke like a madman, and as he spoke he ran around the room with one hand held out in front of him as you have seen a mind-reader at a theatre seeking for something hidden in the stalls. He pulled the old letters from the writing-desk, and ran them over as swiftly as a gambler deals out cards; he dropped on his knees before the fireplace and dragged out the dead coals with his bare fingers, and then with a low, worried cry, like a hound on a scent, he ran back to the waste-paper basket and, lifting the papers from it, shook them out upon the floor. Instantly he gave a shout of triumph, and, separating a number of torn pieces from the others, held them up before me.

"'Look!' he cried. 'Do you see? Here are five letters, torn across in two places. The Russian did not stop to read them, for, as you see, he has left them still sealed. I have been wrong. He did not return for the letters. He could not have known their value. He must have returned for some other reason, and, as he was leaving, saw the letter-box, and taking out the letters, held them together—so—and tore them twice across, and then, as the fire had gone out, tossed them into this basket. Look!' he cried, 'here in the upper corner of this piece is a Russian stamp. This is his own letter—unopened!'

"We examined the Russian stamp and found it had been cancelled in St. Petersburg four days ago. The back of the envelope bore the postmark of the branch station in upper Sloane Street, and was dated this morning. The envelope was of official blue paper and we had no difficulty in finding the two other parts of it. We drew the torn pieces of the letter from them and joined them together side by side. There were but two lines of writing, and this was the message: 'I leave Petersburg on the night train, and I shall see you at Trevor Terrace after dinner Monday evening.'

"'That was last night!' Lyle cried. 'He arrived twelve hours ahead of his letter—but it came in time—it came in time to hang him!'"

The Baronet struck the table with his hand.

"The name!" he demanded. "How was it signed? What was the man's name!"

The young Solicitor rose to his feet and, leaning forward, stretched out his arm. "There was no name," he cried. "The letter was signed with only two initials. But engraved at the top of the sheet was the man's address. That address was 'THE AMERICAN EMBASSY, ST. PETERSBURG, BUREAU OF THE NAVAL ATTACHÉ,' and the initials," he shouted, his voice rising into an exultant and bitter cry, "were those of the gentleman who sits opposite who told us that he was the first to find the murdered bodies, the Naval Attaché to Russia, Lieutenant Sears!"

A strained and awful hush followed the Solicitor's words, which seemed to vibrate like a twanging bowstring that had just hurled its bolt. Sir Andrew, pale and staring, drew away with an exclamation of repulsion. His eyes were fastened upon the Naval Attaché with fascinated horror. But the American emitted a sigh of great content, and sank comfortably into the arms of his chair. He clapped his hands softly together.

"Capital!" he murmured. "I give you my word I never guessed what you were driving at. You fooled me, I'll be hanged if you didn't—you certainly fooled me."

The man with the pearl stud leaned forward with a nervous gesture. "Hush! be careful!" he whispered. But at that instant, for the third time, a servant, hastening through the room, handed him a piece of paper which he scanned eagerly. The message on the paper read, "The light over the Commons is out. The House has risen."

The man with the black pearl gave a mighty shout, and tossed the paper from him upon the table.

"Hurrah!" he cried. "The House is up! We've won!" He caught up his glass, and slapped the Naval Attaché violently upon the shoulder. He nodded joyously at him, at the Solicitor, and at the Queen's Messenger. "Gentlemen, to you!" he cried; "my thanks and my congratulations!" He drank deep from the glass, and breathed forth a long sigh of satisfaction and relief.

"But I say," protested the Queen's Messenger, shaking his finger violently at the Solicitor, "that story won't do. You didn't play fair—and—and you talked so fast I couldn't make out what it was all about. I'll bet you that evidence wouldn't hold in a court of law—you couldn't hang a cat on such evidence. Your story is condemned tommy-rot. Now my story might have happened, my story bore the mark—"

In the joy of creation the story-tellers had forgotten their audience, until a sudden exclamation from Sir Andrew caused them to turn guiltily toward him. His face was knit with lines of anger, doubt, and amazement.

"What does this mean!" he cried. "Is this a jest, or are you mad? If you know this man is a murderer, why is he at large? Is this a game you have been playing? Explain yourselves at once. What does it mean?"

The American, with first a glance at the others, rose and bowed courteously.

"I am not a murderer, Sir Andrew, believe me," he said; "you need not be alarmed. As a matter of fact, at this moment I am much more afraid of you than you could possibly be of me. I beg you please to be indulgent. I assure you, we meant no disrespect. We have been matching stories, that is all, pretending that we are people we are not, endeavoring to entertain you with better detective tales than, for instance, the last one you read, *The Great Rand Robbery*."

The Baronet brushed his hand nervously across his forehead.

"Do you mean to tell me," he exclaimed, "that none of this has happened? That Lord Chetney is not dead, that his Solicitor did not find a letter of yours written from your post in Petersburg, and that just now, when he charged you with murder, he was in jest?"

"I am really very sorry," said the American, "but you see, sir, he could not have found a letter written by me in St. Petersburg because I have never been in Petersburg. Until this week, I have never been outside of my own country. I am not a naval officer. I am a writer of short stories. And tonight, when this gentleman told me that you were fond of detective stories, I thought it would be amusing to tell you one of my own—one I had just mapped out this afternoon."

"But Lord Chetney is a real person," interrupted the Baronet, "and he did go to Africa two years ago, and he was supposed to have died there, and his brother, Lord Arthur, has been the heir. And yesterday Chetney did return. I read it in the papers."

"So did I," assented the American soothingly; "and it struck me as being a very good plot for a story. I mean his unexpected return from the dead, and the probable disappointment of the younger brother. So I decided that the younger brother had better murder the older one. The Princess Zichy I invented out of a clear sky. The fog I did not have to invent. Since last night I know all that there is to know about a London fog. I was lost in one for three hours."

The Baronet turned grimly upon the Queen's Messenger.

"But this gentleman," he protested, "he is not a writer of short stories; he is a member of the Foreign Office. I have often seen him in Whitehall, and, according to him, the Princess Zichy is not an invention. He says she is very well known, that she tried to rob him."

The servant of the Foreign Office looked unhappily at the Cabinet Minister, and puffed nervously on his cigar.

"It's true, Sir Andrew, that I am a Queen's Messenger," he said appealingly, "and a Russian woman once did try to rob a Queen's Messenger in a railway carriage—only it did not happen to me, but to a pal of mine. The only Russian princess I ever knew called herself Zabrisky. You may have seen her. She used to do a dive from the roof of the Aquarium."

Sir Andrew, with a snort of indignation, fronted the young Solicitor.

"And I suppose yours was a cock-and-bull story, too," he said. "Of course, it must have been, since Lord Chetney is not dead. But don't tell me," he protested, "that you are not Chudleigh's son either."

"I'm sorry," said the youngest member, smiling in some embarrassment, "but my name is not Chudleigh. I assure you, though, that I know the family very well, and that I am on very good terms with them."

"You should be!" exclaimed the Baronet; "and, judging from the liberties you take with the Chetneys, you had better be on very good terms with them, too."

The young man leaned back and glanced toward the servants at the far end of the room.

"It has been so long since I have been in the Club," he said, "that I doubt if even the waiters remember me. Perhaps Joseph may," he added. "Joseph!" he called, and at the word a servant stepped briskly forward.

The young man pointed to the stuffed head of a great lion which was suspended above the fireplace.

"Joseph," he said, "I want you to tell these gentlemen who shot that lion. Who presented it to the Grill?"

Joseph, unused to acting as master of ceremonies to members of the Club, shifted nervously from one foot to the other.

"Why, you—you did," he stammered.

"Of course I did!" exclaimed the young man. "I mean, what is the name of the man who shot it! Tell the gentlemen who I am. They wouldn't believe me."

"Who you are, my lord?" said Joseph. "You are Lord Edam's son, the Earl of Chetney."

"You must admit," said Lord Chetney, when the noise had died away, "that I couldn't remain dead while my little brother was accused of murder. I had to do something. Family pride demanded it. Now, Arthur, as the younger brother, can't afford to be squeamish, but personally I should hate to have a brother of mine hanged for murder."

"You certainly showed no scruples against hanging me," said the American, "but in the face of your evidence I admit my guilt, and I sentence myself to pay the full penalty of the law as we are made to pay it in my own country. The order of this court is," he announced, "that Joseph shall bring me a wine-card, and that I sign it for five bottles of the Club's best champagne." "Oh, no!" protested the man with the pearl stud, "it is not for you to sign it. In my opinion it is Sir Andrew who should pay the costs. It is time you knew," he said, turning to that gentleman, "that unconsciously you have been the victim of what I may call a patriotic conspiracy. These stories have had a more serious purpose than merely to amuse. They have been told with the worthy object of detaining you from the House of Commons. I must explain to you, that all through this evening I have had a servant waiting in Trafalgar Square with instructions to bring me word as soon as the light over the House of Commons had ceased to burn. The light is now out, and the object for which we plotted is attained."

The Baronet glanced keenly at the man with the black pearl, and then quickly at his watch. The smile disappeared from his lips, and his face was set in stern and forbidding lines.

"And may I know," he asked icily, "what was the object of your plot!"

"A most worthy one," the other retorted. "Our object was to keep you from advocating the expenditure of many millions of the people's money upon more battleships. In a word, we have been working together to prevent you from passing the Navy Increase Bill."

Sir Andrew's face bloomed with brilliant color. His body shook with suppressed emotion.

"My dear sir!" he cried, "you should spend more time at the House and less at your Club. The Navy Bill was brought up on its third reading at eight o'clock this evening. I spoke for three hours in its favor. My only reason for wishing to return again to the House tonight was to sup on the terrace with my old friend, Admiral Simons; for my work at the House was completed five hours ago, when the Navy Increase Bill was passed by an overwhelming majority."

The Baronet rose and bowed. "I have to thank you, sir," he said, "for a most interesting evening."

The American shoved the wine-card which Joseph had given him toward the gentleman with the black pearl.

"You sign it," he said.

THE END

The Wooden Hand

A Detective Story

By Fergus Hume

I - MISERY CASTLE

"AH WELL, Miss Eva, I 'spose your pa'ull come home to spile things as he allays have done. It ain't no wonder, I ses, as you sits moping by the winder, looking double your age, and you only twenty, as has no right to look forty, whatever you may say, though I took my dying alfred-david on its blessed truth."

This slightly incoherent and decidedly pessimistic speech was moaned, rather than spoken, by a lean-bodied, hard-faced, staring-eyed woman to a pretty girl, who did not look at the speaker. And small wonder. Mrs. Merry--inappropriate name--was unattractive to the eye. She was angular, grey-skinned, grey-eyed, grey-haired, and had thin, drooping lips almost as grey as the rest of her. In her black stuff gown--she invariably wore the most funereal dresses--with uneasy hands folded under a coarse apron, she stood before Eva Strode, uttering lamentations worthy of Jeremiah at his worst. But such dumpishness was characteristic of the woman. She delighted in looking on the black side of things, and the blacker they were, the more she relished them. Out of wrong-doing, and grief and things awry, she extracted a queer sort of pleasure, and felt never so happy as when the worst came to the worst. It seemed unfit that such a walking pageant of woe should be called Merry.

Eva, already depressed by the voice and sentiment of this lamentable dame, continued to look at the gaudy hollyhocks, even while she answered calmly, "I expect my father is the same as he was when he went to South Africa five years ago. I don't hope to find him an angel. I am certain he has not changed."

"If you're thinking of black angels," said the lively Merry, "you can have satisfactions from thinking him Beelzebub, for him he are."

"Don't call my father names. It does no good, Mrs. Merry."

"Beg pardon, miss, but it do relieve the heart and temper. And I will call him a leper, if that's a name, seeing as he'll never change his spots, however persuaded."

"What's the time?"

Mrs. Merry peered into the dial of a clock on the mantelpiece. "You might call it six, Miss Eva, and a lovely evening it is, though rain may spile it unexpected. Your pa 'ull be seated at the table in the next room at eight, let us hope, if nothing do happen to him, and I do pray on my bended knees, Miss Eva, as he won't growl at the meal, his habit allays when your poor dear ma--her ladyship was alive. Ah well," said Mrs. Merry with emphasis, "she's an angel now, and your pa ain't likely to trouble her again."

"Why, don't you think my father may come home? I mean, why do you fancy anything may happen to him?"

"Oh, I ain't got no cause, but what you might call the uncertainties of this vale of tears, Miss Eva. He have to drive ten mile here from the Westhaven station, and there's tramps about them lonely roads. Coming from South Africa, your pa 'ull naturally have diamonds to tempt the poor."

"I don't know what he has got," said Eva rather pettishly. "And no one, save you and me, know he is returning from Africa."

"No one, Miss Eva?" questioned the woman significantly.

Miss Strode colored. "I told Mr. Hill."

"And he told his pa, and his pa who have a long tongue told all the village, I don't doubt. If ever there was a man as fiddled away his days in silliness," cried Merry, "it's that pink and white jelly-fish as you call Hills."

"Hill," corrected Miss Strode; then added coloring: "His son doesn't take after him."

"No," admitted the other grudgingly, "I will say as Mr. Allen is a tight lad. His mother gave him her blood and sense and looks; not that I say he's worthy of you, Miss Eva."

"Mrs. Merry," said Eva quietly, "you let your tongue run on too freely about my friends."

"Not the father Hills, if I die in saying it. He's no friend of yours, seeing he's your pa's; and as to Mr. Allen, I never had a sweetheart as I called friend, when you could call him something better."

Eva took no notice of this speech, but continued, "You are my old nurse, Mrs. Merry, and I allow you to talk openly."

"For your good, Miss Eva," put in Merry.

"For my good, I know," said the girl; "but you must not run down Allen's father or mine."

"As to his father, I say nothing but that he's a driveling jelly-fish," said Mrs. Merry, who would not be suppressed; "but your own pa I know, worse luck, and I don't think much of him as a man, whatever I say about his being Beelzebub, which he is. Fifty years and more he is, fine-looking at that, though wickedness is in his aching bones. Not that I know of their aching," explained Mrs. Merry, "but if sin would make 'em smart, ache they do. You've been happy with me, Miss Eva, dear, in spite of a humble roof and your poor ma's death, four and a half year back. But your pa's come home to make trouble. Satan let loose is what I call him, and if I could stop his coming by twisting his wicked neck, I would."

"Mrs. Merry!" Eva rose quickly and flushed. "You forget yourself."

"There," said Mrs. Merry, casting up her eyes, "and I fed her with my own milk."

Eva, who was tenderly attached to the angular, dismal, chattering woman, could not withstand this remark. "Dear Nanny," she said, comforting the wounded heart, "I know you mean well, but my father is my father after all."

"Worse luck, so he is," sobbed Mrs. Merry, feeling for Eva's hand.

"I wish to think of him as kindly as I can, and----"

"Miracles won't make you do that," interrupted the woman, dropping her apron from her eyes, and glaring. "Miss Eva, I knew your pa when he was a bad boy, both him and me being neighbors, as you might say, though I did live in a cottage and he in a Manor House not two mile from here. He and that jelly-fish of a Hills were always together doing mischief, and setting neighbors by the ears, though I do say as your pa, being masterful, led that jelly-fish away. Then your pa ran away with Lady Jane Delham, your ma, as is dead, and treated her shameful. She come here to me, as an old friend, for friend I was, tho' humble," sobbed Mrs. Merry weeping again, "and you were born. Then your pa takes you away and I never set eyes on you and my lady till five years ago when he brought you here. To settle down and make you happy? No! Not he. Away he goes gallivanting to South Africa where the blacks are, leaving a lady born and bred and his daughter just a bud, meaning yourself, to live with a common woman like me!"

"I have been very happy, Nanny, and my mother was happy also, when she was alive."

"Ah," said Mrs. Merry bitterly, "a queer sort of happiness, to be that way when your husband goes. I've had a trial myself in Merry, who's dead, and gone, I hope, where you'll find your pa will join him. But you'll see, Miss Eva, as your pa will come and stop your marrying Mr. Allen."

"I think that's very likely," said Eva sadly.

"What," said Mrs. Merry under her breath, and rising, "he's at it already is he? I thought so."

"I received a letter from him the other day," explained Eva; "knowing your prejudice against my father, I said nothing."

"Me not to be trusted, I 'spose, Miss Eva?" was the comment.

"Nonsense. I trust you with anything."

"And well you may. I fed you with my heart's blood, and foster sister you are to my boy Cain, though, Lord knows, he's as bad as his father was before him--the gipsy whelp that he is. Not on my side, though," cried Mrs. Merry. "I'm true English, and why I ever took up with a Romany rascal like Giles Merry, I don't know. But he's dead, I hope he is, though I never can be sure, me not knowing where's his grave. Come now," Mrs. Merry gave her face a wipe with the apron, "I'm talking of my own troubles, when yours is about. That letter----?"

"It is one in answer to mine. I wrote to Cape Town three months ago telling my father that I was engaged to Allen Hill. He wrote the other day--a week ago--from Southampton, saying he would not permit the marriage to take place, and bade me wait till he came home."

"Trouble! trouble," said Mrs. Merry, rocking; "I know the man. Ah, my dear, don't talk. I'm thinking for your good."

It was hot outside, though the sun was sinking and the cool twilight shadowed the earth. The hollyhocks, red and blue and white and yellow, a blaze of color, were drooping their heads in the warm air, and the lawn looked brown and burnt for want of rain. Not a breath of wind moved the dusty sycamore trees which divided the cottage from the high-road, and the crimson hue of the setting sun steeped everything in its sinister dye. Perhaps it was this uncanny evening that made Eva Strode view the home-coming of her father with such uneasiness, and the hostility and forebodings of Mrs. Merry did not tend to reassure her. With her hand on that dismal prophetess's shoulder, she stood silently looking out on the panting world bathed in the ruddy light. It was as though she saw the future through a rain of blood.

Misery Castle was the name of the cottage, and Mrs. Merry was responsible for the dreary appellation. Her life had been hard and was hard. Her husband had left her, and her son, following in his father's footsteps, was almost constantly absent in

London, in more than questionable company. Mrs. Merry therefore called the cottage by as dismal a name as she could think of. Even Eva, who protested against the name, could not get the steadfastly dreary woman to change it. "Misery dwells in it, my dear lamb," said Mrs. Merry, "and Misery it shall be called. Castle it ain't from the building of it, but Castle it is, seeing the lot of sorrow that's in it. Buckingham Palace and the Tower wouldn't hold more, and more there will be, when that man comes home with his wicked sneering face, father though he be to you, my poor young lady."

It was a delightful cottage, with whitewashed walls covered with creepers, and a thatched roof, grey with wind and weather and the bleaching of the sun. The rustic porch was brilliant with red roses, and well-kept garden-beds bloomed with rainbow-hued flowers seasonable to the August month. To the right this domain was divided from a wide and gorse-covered common by an ancient wall of mellow-hued brick, useful for the training of peach-trees: to the left a low hedge, with unexpected gaps, ran between the flower-beds and a well-stocked orchard. This last extended some distance, and ended in a sunken fence, almost buried in nettles and rank weeds. Beyond stretched several meadows, in which cows wandered, and further still, appeared fields of wheat, comfortable farm-houses, clumps and lines of trees, until the whole fertile expanse terminated at the foot of low hills, so far away that they looked blue and misty. A smiling corn-land, quite Arcadian in its peace and beauty.

Along the front of the cottage and under the dusty sycamore trees ran a highroad which struck straightly across the common, slipped by Misery Castle, and took its way crookedly through Wargrove village, whence it emerged to twist and turn for miles towards the distant hills and still more distant London town. Being the king's highway it was haunted by tramps, by holiday vans filled with joyous folk, and by fashionable motor-cars spinning noisily at illegal speed. But neither motor-cars, nor vans, nor tramps, nor holidaymakers stopped at Wargrove village, unless for a moment or two at the one public-house on thirsty days. These went on ten miles further across the common to Westhaven, a rising watering-place at the Thames mouth. So it will be seen that the publicity of the highway afforded Eva a chance of seeing the world on wheels, and diversified her somewhat dull existence.

And it was dull, until a few months ago. Then Allen Hill came home from South America, where he had been looking after mines. The young people met and subsequently fell in love. Three months before the expected arrival of Mr. Strode they became engaged with the consent of Allen's parents but without the knowledge of Eva's father. However, being a dutiful daughter to a man who did not deserve such a blessing, she wrote and explained herself. The reply was the letter, mention of which she had made to Mrs. Merry. And Mrs. Merry prognosticated trouble therefrom.

"I know the man--I know the man," moaned Mrs. Merry, rocking herself, "he'll marry you to someone else for his ambitions, drat him."

"That he shall never do," flashed out Eva.

"You have plenty of spirit, Miss Eva, but he'll wear you out. He wore out Lady Jane, your ma, as is now where he will never go. And was it this that set you moping by the winder, my dear lamb?"

Eva returned to her former seat. "Not altogether." She hesitated, and then looked anxiously at her old nurse, who stood with folded arms frowning and rigid. "You believe in dreams, Mrs. Merry?"

"As I believe that Merry was a scoundrel, and that my boy will take after him, as he does," said the woman, nodding sadly; "misery ain't surer nor dreams, nor taxes which allays come bringing sorrow and summonses with 'em. So you dreamed last night?"

"Yes. You know I went to bed early. I fell asleep at eight and woke at nine, trembling."

"Ah!" Mrs. Merry drew nearer--"'twas a baddish dream?"

"A horrible dream--it was, I think, two dreams."

"Tell it to me," said the old woman, her eyes glittering.

Eva struck her closed fist on the sill. "No," she cried passionately, "it's impossible to tell it. I wish to forget."

"You'll remember it well enough when the truth comes."

"Do you think anything will come of it?"

"It's as sure as sure," said Mrs. Merry.

Eva, less superstitious, laughed uneasily, and tried to turn the subject. "Allen will be at the gate soon," she said. "I'm walking to the common with him for an hour."

"Ah well," droned Mrs. Merry, "take your walk, Miss Eva. You won't have another when he comes home."

"Nurse!" Eva stamped her foot and frowned. "You make my father out to be a----"

"Whatever I make him out to be, I'll never get near what he is," said Mrs. Merry viciously. "I hate him. He ruined my Giles, not as Giles was much to boast of. Still, I could have talked him into being a stay-at-home, if your pa--there--there--let him be, say I. If his cup is full he'll never come home alive."

Eva started and grew deathly pale. "My dream--my dream," she said.

"Ah yes!" Mrs. Merry advanced and clutched the girl's wrist. "You saw him dead or dying, eh, eh?"

"Don't, nurse; you frighten me," said Miss Strode, releasing her wrist; then she thought for a moment. "My dream or dreams," said she after a pause, went something after this fashion. "I thought I was in the Red Deeps----"

"Five miles from here," muttered Mrs. Merry, hugging herself. "I know the place--who better? Red clay and a splash of water, however dry."

"Ah, you are thinking of the spring!" said Eva starting; "it was there I saw--oh no--no," and she closed her eyes to shut out the sight.

"What was it--what was it?" asked Mrs. Merry eagerly; "death?"

"He was lying face downward in the moist red clay beside the spring of the Red Deeps!"

"Who was lying?"

"I don't know. I seemed to see the place and the figure of a man in dark clothes lying face downward, with his hands twisted helplessly in the rank grasses. I heard a laugh too--a cruel laugh, but in my dream I saw no one else. Only the dead man, face downward," and she stared at the carpet as though she saw the gruesome sight again.

"How do you know 'twas your father's corpse?" croaked the old woman.

"I didn't think it was--I didn't tell you it was," panted Eva, flushing and paling with conflicting emotions.

"Ah," interpreted Mrs. Merry, "someone he killed, perhaps."

"How dare you--how dare----? Nurse," she burst out, "I believe it was my father lying dead there--I saw a white-gloved right hand."

"Your pa, sure enough," said the woman grimly. "His wooden hand, eh? I know the hand. He struck me with it once. Struck me," she cried, rising and glaring, "with my own husband standing by. But Giles was never a man. So your pa was dead, wooden hand and all, in the Red Deeps? Did you go there to see, this day?"

"No, no," Eva shuddered, "it was only a dream."

"Part of one, you said."

Miss Strode nodded. "After I saw the body and the white glove on the wooden hand glimmering in the twilight--for twilight it was in my dream--I seemed to sink into darkness, and to be back in my bed--yes, in my bed in the room across the passage."

"Ah! you woke then?" said Mrs. Merry, disappointed.

"No, I swear I was not awake. I was in my bed asleep, dreaming, for I heard footsteps--many footsteps come to the door--to the front door, then five knocks----"

"Five," said the woman, surprised.

"Five knocks. One hard and four soft. Then a voice came telling me to take in the body. I woke with a cry, and found it was just after nine o'clock."

"Well, well," chuckled the old woman, "if Robert Strode is dead----"

"You can't be sure of that," said Eva fiercely, and regretted telling this dismal woman her dream.

"You saw the gloved hand--the wooden hand?"

"Bah! It is only a dream."

"Dreams come true. I've known 'em to come true," said Mrs. Merry, rising, "and tomorrow I go to the Red Deeps to see."

"But my father comes home tonight."

"No," said Mrs. Merry, with the mien of a sibyl, "he'll never come home agin to the house where he broke a woman's heart."

And she went out laughing and muttering of the Red Deeps.

II - LOVE'S YOUNG DREAM

EVA STRODE was an extremely pretty blonde. She had golden-brown hair which glistened in the sunshine, hazel eyes somewhat meditative in expression, and a complexion that Mrs. Merry, in her odd way, compared to mixed roses and milk. Her nose was delicate and straight, her mouth charming and sensitive, and if it drooped a trifle at the corners, she had good cause for so melancholy a twist. Her figure was so graceful that envious women, less favoured by Nature, suggested padding: but these same depreciators could say nothing against her hands and feet, which were exquisitely formed. Usually Eva, cunning enough to know that her beauty needed no adornment, dressed in the very plainest fashions. At the present moment she was arrayed in a pale blue dress of some coarse material, and wore a large straw hat swathed in azure tulle. An effective touch of more pronounced color appeared in the knot of red ribbon at her throat and the bunch of crimson roses thrust into her waistband. She looked dainty, well-bred, charming, and even the malignant female eye would have found little to blame. But the female eye generally did find fault. Eva was much too pretty a girl to escape remark.

This vision of loveliness walked demurely down the garden path to gladden the eyes of a young man lingering at the gate. He, eagerly expecting the descent of Venus, quickly removed his Panama hat, and looked at the goddess with admiring eyes, eloquent of unspoken praise. Eva, feeling, rather than meeting, their fervid gaze, halted within the barrier and blushed as red as the roses in her belt. Then she ventured to look at her lover, and smiled a welcome.

Certainly the lover was not unworthy of the lass, so far as looks went. Allen Hill was as dark as Eva was fair. Indeed, he more resembled a Spaniard than an Englishman. His oval face, smooth and clean-shaven save for a small, smartly pointed moustache, was swarthy, his eyes were wonderfully black and large, and his closely clipped hair might be compared to the hue of the raven's wing. His slim figure was clothed in white flannels, so well cut and spotless that they conveyed a suspicion that the young gentleman was something of a dandy. He looked more like a poet than a mining engineer.

Yet an engineer he was, and had travelled over the greater part of the world with his eyes open. These looked languid enough as a rule, but they could blaze with a fighting light, as his associates in the lands at the back of Beyond knew. At thirty years of age Allen knew quite as much as was good for him, and knew also how to utilize his knowledge. In many lands he had seen fair women, but none had captured his heart as had this dewy, fragrant English rose.

Six months earlier the two had met at a garden party. Allen came and saw, and Eva--as women always do--conquered. The engineer's heart, being tinder, caught fire easily and began to blaze with a fiery flame not to be extinguished by reason. Eva herself, not being tame either, rather liked this Sabine courtship, and did not leave Allen long in doubt as to the way in which she regarded his audacious advances. The result was that in a few months they became engaged, and the flower-time of their love came almost as speedily as did that of Romeo and Juliet. But now, as Eva well knew, the common sense of the world was about to chill their ardor. She had this very evening to inform this eager, whole-hearted lover that her father refused to sanction the engagement. No easy task, seeing she loved the man with her whole heart and soul.

"My dear, my love," murmured Allen, as the gate closed behind the girl: and he would have embraced her in the public road, but that she dexterously evaded his widely spread arms.

"Not here--not here," she whispered hurriedly, and with a fine color; "it's too public, you stupid boy."

The stupid boy, cheated of his treat, glared up and down the road, "I don't see any one," he grumbled.

"Eyes at those windows," said Eva, waving a slim hand towards a row of thatched cottages, "and tongues also."

"I am not ashamed of our love. I wish the whole world knew of it."

"The whole world probably does," rejoined Miss Strode, a trifle drily; "if any one saw you with those eyes and that look, and--oh, you ridiculous boy!" and she shook her finger at him.

"Oh, you coquette. Can't we----"

"On the common we can talk, if that is what you mean," said Eva, turning away to trip up the dusty road; "the common," she cried with a backward look which should have drawn the young man after her at a fine pace.

But Allen lingered for a moment. Deeply in love as he was, he had his own ideas regarding the management of the fair sex. He knew that when a woman is sure of her swain she is apt to be exacting, so as to check his ardor. On the other hand, if the swain hangs back, the maid comes forward with winsome looks. Hitherto, Allen had been all passion and surrender. Now he thought he would tease Eva a little, by not coming immediately to her beck and call. Therefore, while she skipped ahead--and without looking back, so sure was she that Allen followed--the young man lighted a cigarette, and when the smoke perfumed the air, looked everywhere save in the direction he desired to look. North, south, west looked Allen, but never east, where could be seen the rising sun of his love. But passion proved to be stronger than principle, and finally his eyes fastened on the shadowy figure of Eva pausing on the edge of the common. She was looking back now, and beckoned with persuasive finger. Allen made a step forward to follow the siren, then halted. A strange feeling took possession of him. Allen's mother was Scotch, and having the impressionable Celtic nature, he was quick to feel the influences of that unseen world which lies all round, invisible to dull eyes, and unfelt by material souls. At the moment, in spite of the warmth, he had what the Scotch call a "grue," and shivered where he stood. At his back sank the sun red and angry, peering through lines of black cloud suggestive of prison bars. The scarlet light flooded the landscape in a sinister manner, and dyed the flitting figure of Eva in crimson hues. She looked as though bathed in blood, and--as she was now speeding towards the trysting place--as though she fled from justice. Also, she ran from the red west into the gloom of the east, already shadowy with the coming night. Was there no parable in this? considered Allen, and shivered again.

"Indigestion," thought Allen, striving to throw off that weird feeling and trying to explain it in the most commonplace way. But he knew well that he had never in his life suffered from indigestion, and that the feeling--which had now passed away--was a hint of coming evil. "To me, I hope," murmured the young man, stepping out briskly, "not to Eva, poor darling."

When he joined the girl, he was quite his old fervid self, and felt his premonitions pass away in the charm of the hour. Even the sunset was less scarlet and more of a rosy tint like his new thoughts. He threw himself at the feet of his beloved, cast away his cigarette, and took her hand within his. For the moment Dan Cupid was king.

But was he? Eva did not appear to think so. She allowed her hand to remain in Allen's warm grip, but he felt no responsive pressure. The two were seated on a rustic bench within a circle of flowering gorse. The sward was green and smooth, worthy of the dancing feet of Titania's elves, and perhaps it might have been one of their ballrooms the lovers had invaded. In that case it would certainly prove unhappy ground to them. The fairies do not like mortals, however loving, who intrude on their privacy. The elves, however, not yet awakened by the moon, made no sign, and in that still place no sound could be heard. Overhead was the flushed sky, underfoot the emerald sward, and there were the lovers supplied with an admirable stage on which to play their parts. Allen was willing enough, and looked up adoringly into the face of his Juliet. But Eva's gaze was fixed on the orange-hued blossom of the gorse with a far-away look. And when she spoke, it certainly was not of love.

"Allen," she said, in a calm, level voice, "we have known each other for nearly a year."

"Call it a century," said Allen, kissing her hand. "I love you and you love me. Why talk of time? Love like ours lives in eternity."

"Hum," said Eva, although the ejaculation was not a pretty one, the question is, "Will it live at all?"

"Eva!" He raised himself on his elbow and stared; but the girl continued to speak without looking at him.

"Do you know my history, Allen?" she asked; then without waiting for his reply, went on in a passionless way: "My father is the last Strode of Wargrove. The manor house of our race is only a few miles away, and there the Strodes lived for centuries. My grandfather, however, was an extravagant man, and lost all the money. When my father returned from Oxford to take up his position in the world, he found that his father was dead and that the estate would have to be sold to pay the debts. In that way, Allen, the manor passed from our family."

"I have heard something of this, Eva," said the perplexed young man; "but why waste time in telling me of it now?"

"You will find the time will not be wasted," rejoined Eva, glancing down with something like pity; "let me go on. My father, brought up in a luxurious way, took what money there was left and went to seek work in London. He speculated, and knowing nothing about speculation he lost everything. Then your father, who was his friend at school and college, lent him some thousands, and my father, to better his position, married Lady Jane Delham, daughter of the Earl of Ipsen. I understand that the money which she brought with her, was lost also--in speculation."

"But why did your father speculate so much?" asked Allen.

"His one desire was to buy back the manor," said Eva. "He has much pride of race, and wants to end his days under the roof where he was born. But let me go on once more. The money was lost, and Lord Ipsen died. His title went to a distant cousin, who did not like my mother, consequently there was no chance of my father getting more money in that quarter. I was born under Mrs. Merry's roof; but till the age of seven I lived with my mother in a small Hampstead cottage. My father went on speculating. Sometimes he made money, at other times he lost it; but always, he followed the will-o'-the-wisp of fortune, hoping to get back his old home. He then went to South America, and took my mother with him. I was placed at school, and until I was fifteen I never saw my parents."

"Poor Eva, how lonely you must have been!"

"I was lonely, and yet--having seen so little of my parents I don't know that I missed them so very much. My father stopped in Peru till I was fifteen, and my mother with him. He came back poor, but with sufficient money to speculate again. He therefore placed my mother and me in Misery Castle."

"Ridiculous name," muttered Allen uneasily.

"A very appropriate name," said Eva with some bitterness, seeing how unhappy Mrs. Merry is. "She had a bad husband and has a bad son. My mother was also unhappy. Meeting her again after all those years, I did my best to comfort her. But her heart was broken."

"Your father?" asked Allen in a low voice.

"Who else?" replied Eva, flushing, and the water came to her eyes. "Oh! Allen, I do not wish to speak ill, or to think ill, of my father; but--no," she broke off, suppressing herself. "I cannot speak from what I have seen, and I judge no one, let alone my father, on what I have heard. Mrs. Merry thinks badly of my father, and my poor mother--ah! my poor mother! she said as little as she could. But her heart was broken, Allen; she died of a broken heart and a crushed spirit. I lost her five months after my father went to seek his fortune in South Africa, and since then I have lived alone with Mrs. Merry."

"Poor Eva!" said Hill tenderly, and repossessed himself of the hand which she had withdrawn. "But Mrs. Merry is good to you?"

"Very--very good," said Miss Strode with emphasis. "She was my nurse and foster-mother, Allen. When I was born my father came here for a time before taking the Hampstead cottage. Well, Allen, that is my history. My father all these five years has paid Mrs. Merry for my board and lodging, and has sent home pocket-money for me. But all that time he has never written me a tender. letter."

"Not even when his wife died?"

"No. He wrote a few words of sympathy, but not those which a father should have written to a motherless girl. From what I know of him, and from what Mrs.

Merry says, he is a hard, cold, self-concentrated man. I dread his coming more than I can tell you, Allen."

"If he ever does come," said the young man softly.

Eva started and looked down. "What do you mean by that?" she asked anxiously.

Allen met her gaze frankly and laughed. "Oh, you need not disturb yourself, my dear," he said with a shrug, "only you know my father and yours were always chums. Why, I don't know, as my father is certainly not the kind of man to suit such a one as you describe Mr. Strode to be. But they were chums at school and college, and my father knows a lot about yours. When I mentioned that your father was expected tonight, my father--it was at breakfast--said that Mr. Strode might not arrive after all. I did not ask him what he meant."

"Could Mr. Hill have heard from my father?"

"I can't say, and even if he did, I don't know why my father should suggest that Mr. Strode would not come home. But, Eva, you are pale."

"I feel pale," she said in a low voice. "Allen, sit beside me. I want to talk seriously--to tell you a dream."

The young man, nothing loath, promptly seated himself by her side and slipped a strong, tender arm round her slender waist. Eva's heart beat stronger when she found herself in such an assured haven. It seemed as though Allen, noble and firm and loving, would be able to shelter her from the coming storm. "And the storm will come," she said aloud.

"What is that?" asked Hill, not catching her meaning.

"It is my dream," she answered; and then, with her head on his shoulder, she told about her vision of the night. Allen was inclined to make light of it.

"You superstitious little darling," he said fondly, "the dream is easily accounted for. You were thinking of your father, and, being anxious about his arrival, dreamed what you did."

Eva released herself, rather offended. "I was thinking of my father, I admit," she said, "but I was not at all anxious. My father has been all over the world, and in wild parts, so he can look after himself very well. Besides, I never thought of the Red Deeps. And remember, Allen, I saw the right hand, gloved."

"That would seem to intimate that the dead man you saw in your dream was Mr. Strode," said Allen, kissing her; "but it's all nonsense, Eva."

"You don't think anything will happen?" she demanded, anxious to be reassured after Mrs. Merry's gloomy talk.

"No, I don't. I have known of lots of dreams quite vivid which never came true. I'm not a scientific chap," added Allen, laughing, "or I would be able to prove that this dream is only a reflex of your waking thoughts. Mr. Strode will arrive all right."

"And then we must part," sighed Eva.

This time it was Hill who started, and his face flushed. "I don't quite understand."

"You will soon. I told you the history of my life, Allen, so that I might lead up to this. I wrote to my father at Cape Town, telling him I loved you, and that Mr. Hill was pleased we should be engaged."

"My father was delighted," put in Allen quickly.

"So I said. My father never replied to my letter save in sending a cablegram stating he was coming home in the Dunoon Castle.. When he was at Southampton, he wrote, saying I was not to think of marrying you, and that he would tell me of his plans for my future when he returned to Wargrove. He decided to remain for a week in London, and yesterday he wired that he was coming home tonight. So you see, Allen," Eva rested her head on her lover's shoulder, "he will part us."

"No!" cried Hill, rising and looking very tall and strong and determined, "he will never do that. What reason----"

"My father is a man who will refuse to give his reason."

"Not to me," rejoined the other hotly. "Mr. Strode will not dare to dismiss me in so easy and off-hand a fashion. I love you, Eva, and I marry you, whatever your father may say. Unless," he caught her hands as she rose, and stared deep into her eyes, "unless you leave me."

"No! no! I never will do that, Allen. Come what may, I'll be true."

Then followed an interlude of kisses, and afterwards the two, hand in hand, walked across the common on their way to Misery Castle. It was not seven o'clock, but the twilight was growing darker. "Do you know what your father's plans are?" asked Allen, as they stepped out on to the deserted and dusty road.

"No. I know nothing save what I tell you. And my dream----"

"Dearest, put the dream out of your head. If it is any comfort to you, I'll go to the Red Deeps tonight. Do you think I'll find a dead body there?" he asked, laughing.

"Not if you go before nine o'clock. The dream was at nine last night."

"But your father will be home at eight, Eva?"

"I hope so," she murmured.

"You are so foolishly superstitious," said Allen, pressing her arm which was within his own; "you dear little goose, don't you see that if your father comes to Misery Castle at eight, he can't possibly be lying dead in the Red Deeps at nine. When did you last hear from him, Eva?"

"Yesterday morning. He wired that he would be down at eight this evening."

"Well then, he was alive then, and is stopping in town on business as you said. He will come to Westhaven by the train arriving at six-thirty and will drive over."

"The road passes the Red Deeps," insisted Eva.

"How obstinate you are, Eva," said Allen, contracting his forehead; "I tell you what I'll do to set your mind at rest; you know he is alive now?"

"Yes, I suppose so. I got that wire yesterday morning."

"Well then, I'll set off to the Red Deeps at once, and will get there just at eight. I may meet Mr. Strode coming along in the fly, and if so I'll follow it back to Misery Castle, so as to see him safely home. If I don't, I'll go to the Red Deeps, and if any attack is made on him, I'll be there to give him a hand."

"Thank you, Allen. I should be more at ease if you did that."

"Then it shall be done," said Allen, kissing her, "but I feel that I am encouraging you in superstitious fancies."

"My dream was so vivid."

"Pooh. Indigestion."

"Then Mr. Hill hinted that my father might not return."
"Well then, I'll ask him what he meant, and explain when we meet again."
"If we ever do meet," sighed Eva, stopping at the gate.
"You will be true to me, Eva?"
"Always--always--always. There--there," she kissed him under the friendly shelter of the sycamore and ran indoors.

Allen turned on his heel in high spirits, and set out for the Red Deeps. At first he laughed at Eva's dream and Eva's superstition. But as he walked on in the gathering darkness, he felt as though the future also was growing more gloomy. He recalled his own feelings of the girl's dress dappled with blood, and of her flying form. Again he felt the "grue," and cursed himself for an old woman. "I'll find nothing--nothing," he said, trying to laugh.

But the shadow of the dream, which was also the shadow of the future, fell upon him darker than ever.

III - THE NE'ER-DO-WEEL

ANXIOUS to make the best impression on her father, Eva Strode ran up to her room to put on an evening gown. Mr. Strode supplied her liberally with money, for whatever his faults may have been, he certainly was not mean; therefore she possessed a fairly extensive wardrobe. She did not see Mrs. Merry on entering the cottage, as that good lady was occupied in looking after the dinner in the little back-kitchen. The table was laid, however, and after making herself smart, Eva descended to add a few finishing touches in the shape of flowers.

Cheered by the view Allen took of her dream, and still more by the fact that he had gone to the Red Deeps, Eva arranged many roses, red and white, in a great silver bowl which had belonged to her mother. As a matter of fact, Eva had been born in Misery Castle, and being sickly as a baby, had been christened hurriedly in the cottage out of the bowl, an heirloom of the Delham family. Mrs. Merry had taken possession of it, knowing, that if Lady Jane took it away, her husband would speedily turn it into money. Therefore, Mrs. Merry being a faithful guardian, the bowl was still in the cottage, and on this night Eva used it as a centerpiece to the prettily decorated table. And it did look pretty. The cloth was whiter than snow, the silver sparkled and the crystal glittered, while the roses blooming in the massive bowl added a touch of needed color.

There were evidences of Eva's taste in the small dining-room. Mrs. Merry had furnished it, certainly, but Eva had spent much of her pocket-money in decorating the room. Everything was charming and dainty and intensely feminine. Anyone could see at a glance that it was a true woman's room. And Eva in her black gauze dress, bare-necked and bare-armed, flitted gracefully about the tiny apartment. Her last act was to light the red-shaded lamp which hung low over the table. The window she left open and the blind up, as the night was hot, and the breeze which cooled the room made the place more bearable.

"It's quite pretty," said Eva, standing back against the door to get the effect of the glittering table and the red light and the flowers. "If father is dissatisfied he must be hard to please," she sighed, "and from what Nanny says, I fear he is. A quarter to eight, he'll be here soon. I'd better see when the dinner will be ready."

But before doing so, she went to the front door and listened for the sound of wheels. She certainly heard them, but the vehicle was driving towards, and not from, the common. Apparently Mr. Strode was not yet at hand, so she went to the kitchen. To her surprise she heard voices. One was that of Mrs. Merry, querulous as usual, and the other a rich, soft, melodious voice which Eva knew only too well. It was that of her foster-brother Cain.

This name was another of Mrs. Merry's eccentricities. Her husband, showing the brute within him a year after marriage, had disillusioned his poor wife very speedily. He was drunk when the boy was born, and still drunk when the boy was christened; Mrs. Merry therefore insisted that the boy would probably take after his father, and requested that the name of Cain should be given to him. The curate objected, but Mrs. Merry being firm and the curate weak, the boy was actually called after Adam's eldest son. Had the rector been at home such a scandal--as he regarded it--would not have occurred, but Mr. Quain was absent on a holiday, and returned to find an addition to his flock in the baby person of Cain Merry. The lad grew up handsome enough, but sufficiently wild and wicked to justify his mother's choice of a name. Yet he had his good moments, and might have improved had not his mother nagged him into wrong-doing.

"Well, Cain," said Eva, entering the kitchen, "so you're back?"

"Like a bad penny," cried Mrs. Merry, viciously stabbing some potatoes with a fork; "six months he's been away, and----"

"And I'd remained longer if I'd thought of getting this welcome, mother," growled Cain sulkily. "But I might have known."

He was a remarkably handsome lad of eighteen, almost as dark as Allen Hill. As Mr. Merry had gipsy blood in his veins, it was probable that Cain inherited the nature and looks of some splendid Romany ancestor. With his smooth dark skin, under which the rich red blood mantled, his eyes large and black as night, and clearly-cut features, Cain looked as handsome as a picture. Not even the rough dress he wore, which was that of a laborer, could disguise his fine figure and youthful grace. He looked like a young panther, sleek, beautiful, and dangerous. Cap on head, he leaned against the jamb of the outer door--his mother would not allow him to come further--and seemed a young Apollo, so slim and graceful did he appear. But Mrs. Merry, gesticulating with the fork, had no eye for his good looks. He reminded her too much of the absent Merry, who was just such a splendid outlaw, when he won her to a bitterly regretted marriage. Cain, meeting with so unpleasant a reception, was sulky and inclined to be defiant, until Eva entered. Then he removed his cap, and became wonderfully meek. He was fond of his foster-sister, who could do much with him.

"When did you come back, Cain?" she asked.

"Ten minutes ago, and mother's been ragging me ever since," he replied; "flesh and blood can't stand it, Miss Eva, I'll go."

"No you won't," struck in Mrs. Merry, "you'll stop and give the mother who bore you--worse luck--the pleasure of your company."

Cain grinned in a sleepy manner. "Not much pleasure for me."

"Nor for me, you great hulking creature," said Mrs. Merry, threatening him with a fork. "I thought you'd grow up to be a comfort to me, but look at you----"

"If you thought I'd be a comfort, why did you call me Cain, mother?"

"Because I knew what you'd turn out," contradicted Mrs. Merry, "just like your father, oh, dear me, just like him. Have you seen anything of your father, Cain?"

"No," said Cain stolidly, "and I don't want to."

"That's right, deny the author of your being. Your father, who was always a bad one, left me fifteen years ago, just after you were born. The cottage was not then my own, or he'd never have left me. But there, thank heaven," cried Mrs. Merry, throwing up her eyes to the smoky ceiling, "father didn't die and leave me well off, till Giles went! Since that I've heard nothing of him. He was reported dead----"

"You said you heard nothing of him, mother," put in Cain, smiling.

"Don't show your teeth in that way at your mother," snapped Mrs. Merry, "what I say, I say, and no mistake. Your father was reported dead, and as he's left me for seven years and more, I could marry again, if I were such a fool. But I haven't, hoping you'd be a comfort to the mother who brought you into the world. But you were always a bad boy, Cain. You played truant from school, you ran away to become a navvy at thirteen, and again and again you came back in rags."

"I'm not in rags now," said Cain, restive under this tongue.

"Then you must have stolen the clothes," retorted his mother, "I'll be bound you didn't come by them honestly: not as they're much."

While this pleasant conversation was going on Eva stood mute. She knew of old how impossible it was to stop Mrs. Merry's tongue, and thought it best to let her talk herself out. But the last speech made Cain laugh, and he was cool enough to wink at Eva. She knew Cain so intimately and really liked him so much in spite of his wickedness, that she did not take offence, but strove to turn from him the wrathful speech of his mother.

"I am sure Cain has turned over a new leaf," she said, smiling.

"He's turned over volumes of 'em," groaned Mrs. Merry, dashing down a pot on the range, "but each page is worst nor the last. Oh, I know what I'm saying," she went on triumphantly. "I was a farmer's daughter and had three years' schooling, not to speak of having mixed with the aristocracy in the person of your dear ma, Miss Eva, and your own blessed self as is always a lady. But Cain--oh, look at him."

"He looks very well," said Eva, "and he looks hungry. Don't you think you might give him a meal, Mrs. Merry?"

"Kill the fatted calf, as you might say," suggested Cain impudently.

"Calf!" screeched Mrs. Merry, "you're one yourself, Cain, to talk like that with Miss Eva present. Ain't you got no respect?"

"Miss Eva knows I mean no harm," said the goaded Cain.

"Of course you don't," said Miss Strode; "come, Mrs. Merry, the boy's home for good now."

"For bad, you mean."

"I'm not home at all," said Cain unexpectedly. "I'm working at Westhaven, but I came over just to see my mother. If she don't want me I can go back to those who do," and he turned to go.

"No. Stop," cried Mrs. Merry, whose bark was worse than her bite. "I shan't let a growing lad like you tramp back all them ten miles with a starving inside. Wait till I get this dinner off my mind, and the pair of us will sit down like Christians to eat it."

Eva stared and laughed. "You forget nurse: this dinner is for my father. He should be here in a few minutes."

Mrs. Merry turned grey. "I ain't forgot your dream, my dear. He'll never eat it for want of breath, nor you for sorrow. Now, Cain----"

Miss Strode, who had a temper of her own, stamped a pretty slippered foot imperiously. "Hold your tongue, Mrs. Merry," she cried, the color rising in her cheeks, "my father will arrive."

The old woman glanced at the American clock which stood on the mantelpiece. The small hand pointed to eight. "He ain't come yet."

"Cain," said Eva, turning, still flushed, to the lad, "you came along the Westhaven road?"

Cain nodded. "Twenty minutes ago, Miss Eva," said he.

"Did you see my father? No, you don't remember my father. Did you see a fly coming along?"

"No. But then I didn't come along the road all the time. I took a short cut across country, Miss Eva. I'll just have a meal with mother, and then go back to my business."

"And what is your business, I'd like to know?" questioned Mrs. Merry sharply; "a fine business it must be to take you from your mother."

"I'm in a circus."

"What, riding on horses in tights!" cried Mrs. Merry aghast.

"No such luck. I'm only a groom. I got the billet when I was in London, and glad enough I was, seeing how hard up I've been. It's Stag's Circus and a good show. I hope you'll come over to Shanton tomorrow, Miss Eva; there's a performance at night, and you'll see some riding. Ah, Miss Lorry can ride a bit!"

"Miss who?" asked Eva, who, with the kitchen door open, was straining her ears to hear if Mr. Strode was coming.

"Some low female, I'll be bound," snorted Mrs. Merry. "I've seen 'em dancing in pink stockings and raddling their brazen cheeks with paint. She's no better than she ought to be, not she, say what you like."

Cain grew angry. "You're quite wrong, mother," said he. "Miss Lorry is very much respected. She rides her own horse, White Robin, and has appeared before crowned heads. She's billed as the Queen of the Arena, and is a thing of beauty."

"Ha!" said Mrs. Merry sharply, "and you love her. Ho! You that told me you loved that freckle-faced, snub-nosed Jane Wasp, the daughter o' that upsetting Wasp policeman, with his duty-chatter, and----"

"I don't love any one," said Cain, putting on his cap; "and if you talk like that I'll go."

"To marry a circus rider. Never enter my doors again if you do. I've got this cottage and fifty pounds a year, inherited from my father, to leave, remember."

"Dear nurse," said Eva soothingly, "Cain has no idea of marrying."

"Miss Lorry wouldn't have me if I had," said Cain sadly, though his black eyes flashed fire; "why, Lord Saltars is after her."

"What!" shrieked Mrs. Merry, turning sharply. "Miss Eva's cousin?"

Cain looked astonished. "Is he your cousin?" he asked.

"Yes, Cain--a distant cousin. He is the eldest son of Lord Ipsen. My mother was the daughter of the last Earl. Is he in Westhaven?"

"Yes, miss. He follows the circus everywhere, for love of her." "We don't want to hear about those things," said Mrs. Merry sharply; "leave your Lorries and rubbish alone, and go and wash in my room. I'll get the dinner ready soon, and then we can sit down for a chat."

"Another bullying," grumbled Cain, throwing down his cap and preparing to take a seat. But he never did. At that moment there came a long shrill whistle with several modulations like a bird's note. Cain started, and cocked his handsome head on one side. The whistle was repeated, upon which, without a word either to his mother or Miss Strode, he dashed out of the kitchen.

"There," said Mrs. Merry, waving the fork, "to treat his own lawful mother in that way--to say nothing of you, Miss Eva."

"He'll come back soon," replied Eva.

"Oh, he will, if there's money and food about. But he'll get neither, after behaving in that way. That my son should belong to a circus! Ah, I always said Cain was born for the gallows, like his father."

"But you don't know if his father----"

"I know what I know," replied Mrs. Merry with dignity, "which is to say, nothing. But Giles is what Giles was, and has everything likely to bring him to a rope's end. I'll be the wife of one hanged man," added the old woman with relish, "and the mother of another. Then my cup of misery will be full enough. But, bless me, Miss Eva, don't stay here, getting that pretty dress all greasy. Go and wait for your pa in the doring-room, and I'll bring in the dinner as soon as I hear him swearing--for swear he will, if he arrive."

"Of course he'll arrive," said Eva impatiently, looking at the clock, which now indicated five minutes past eight; "he's a little late."

Mrs. Merry shook her head. "He'll not come. He's in the Red Deeps, lying face downward in the mud."

Eva grew angry at this persistent pessimism, but nothing she could say or do, was able to change Mrs. Merry's opinion. Finding that more talk with the prophetess only made her angry, Eva returned to the front of the house, and, sitting in the drawing-room, took up the last fashionable novel which she had borrowed. But not all the talent of the author was able to enchain her attention. She kept thinking of her father and of the Red Deeps, and kept also looking at the clock. It was drawing to nine when she went again to the front door, subsequently to the gate.

There was no sign of Cain coming back. He had appeared like a ghost and had vanished as one. Why the whistle should have made him turn pale and take so abrupt a departure, Eva was not able to say. Moreover, the non-arrival of her father fully occupied her attention. She could not believe that her dream, vivid as it had been, would prove true and set down her nervous fears, which were now beginning to get the upper hand, to Mrs. Merry's chatter. That old woman appeared at her elbow while she leaned over the gate, looking down the road.

"He ain't come," croaked Mrs. Merry. "Bless you, deary, of course he ain't. I know where he is, and you saw him in your dream."

"Nonsense," said Eva, and ran out on to the road. A few people were passing--mostly villagers, but Eva was well known and no one was surprised at seeing her hatless. Even if anyone had expressed surprise, she was too anxious to trouble much about public opinion.

"Aaron," she asked an old man who came trudging down from the common, "did you see my father coming along in a fly?"

"Why, miss," said Aaron scratching his shock head, "it's a matter of five year since I saw your father, and I don't rightly know as I'd tell him. But I ain't seen nothing but carts this evening, ay, and you might say bicycles."

"No fly?"

"Not one, miss. Good-evening. I dare say your father will walk, miss, by reason of the hot evening."

This suggestion was the very reverse of what Mr. Strode would do, he being a gentleman mindful of his own comfort. However, after the rustic had departed, Eva ran up as far as the common. There was no sign of any vehicle, so she returned to the cottage. Mrs. Merry met her at the door.

"The dinner spiling," said Mrs. Merry crossly; "do come and eat some, Miss Eva, and I'll keep the dishes hot."

"No, I'll wait till my father comes. Is Cain back?"

"Not a sign of him. But, lor bless you, deary, I never expected it, not me. He's gone to his circuses; to think that a son of mine----"

But the girl was in no humour to hear the lamentations of Mrs. Merry over the decay of her family, and returned to the drawing-room. There she sat down again and began to read--or try to.

Mrs. Merry came in at half-past nine, and brought a cup of tea, with a slice of toast. Eva drank the tea, but declined the toast, and the old woman retired angrily, to remove the spoilt dinner. Then Eva played a game of patience, and at ten threw down the cards in despair. The non-arrival of her father, coupled with her dream, made her restless and uneasy. "I wish Allen would return," she said aloud. But Allen never appeared, although by now he had ample time to reach the Red Deeps and to return therefrom. It was in Eva's mind to go to Mr. Hill's house, which was at the further end of Wargrove village, but a mindful thought of Mr. Hill's jokes, which were usually irritating, made her hesitate. She therefore went back to the kitchen, and spoke to Mrs. Merry, who was crooning over the fire.

"What are you doing?" she asked snappishly, for her nerves, poor girl, were worn thin by this time.

"I'm waiting for the body," said Mrs. Merry grimly.

Eva bit her lip to keep down her anger, and returned to the drawing-room, where she wandered hopelessly up and down. While straining her ears she heard footsteps and ran to the door. It proved to be a telegraph boy, dusty and breathless. Eva snatched the wire from him, although she was surprised at its late arrival. As she opened the envelope, the boy explained needlessly--

"It come at four," he said, "and I forgot to bring it, so the Head sent me on all these ten mile, miss, at this hour by way of punishment. And I ain't had no supper," added the injured youth.

But Eva did not heed him. She was reading the wire, which said that Mr. Strode had postponed his departure from town till the morrow, and would then be down by mid-day. "There's no reply," said Eva curtly, and went to the kitchen for the fifth time that evening. The messenger boy grumbled at not getting a shilling for his trouble, quite forgetting that the late arrival of the wire was due to his own carelessness. He banged the front gate angrily, and shortly rode off on his red-painted bicycle.

"My father's coming tomorrow," said Eva, showing the telegram.

Mrs. Merry read it, and gave back the pink paper. "Let them believe it as does believe," said she, "but he'll not come."

"But the wire is signed by himself, you stupid woman," said Eva.

"Well and good," said Mrs. Merry, "but dreams are dreams, whatever you may say, deary. Your pa was coming before and put it off; now he put it off again, and----"

"Then you believe he sent the wire. There, there, I know you will contradict me," said Miss Strode crossly, "I'm going to bed."

"You'll be woke up soon," cried Mrs. Merry after her; "them knocks----"

Eva heard no more. She went to her room, and, wearied out by waiting and anxiety, retired speedily to bed. Mrs. Merry remained seated before the kitchen fire, and even when twelve struck she did not move. The striking of the clock woke Eva. She sat up half asleep, but was speedily wide awake. She heard footsteps, and listened breathlessly. A sharp knock came to the front door. Then four soft knocks. With a cry she sprang from her bed, and ran to the door. Mrs. Merry met her, and kept her back.

"They've brought him home, miss," she said; "the dream's come true."

IV - MYSTERY

MR. HILL'S house at the far end of the village was an eccentric building. Originally it had been a laborer's cottage, and stood by itself, a stone-throw away from the crooked highway which bisected Wargrove. On arriving in the neighborhood some twenty-five years before, Mr. Hill had bought the cottage and five acres of land around. These he enclosed with a high wall of red brick, and then set to work to turn the cottage into a mansion. As he was his own architect, the result was a strange mingling of styles.

The original cottage remained much as it was, with a thatched roof and whitewashed walls. But to the left, rose a round tower built quite in the medieval style, to the right stretched a two-story mansion with oriel windows, a terrace and Tudor battlements. At the back of this, the building suddenly changed to a bungalow with a tropical verandah, and the round tower stood at the end of a range of buildings built in the Roman fashion with sham marble pillars, and mosaic encrusted walls. Within, the house was equally eccentric. There was a Spanish patio, turned, for the sake of the climate, into a winter garden and roofed with glass. The dining-room was Jacobean, the drawing-room was furnished in the Louis Quatorze style, Mr. Hill's library was quite an old English room with casements and a low roof. There were many bedrooms built in the severe graceful Greek fashion, a large marble swimming-bath after the ancient Roman type, and Mr. Hill possessed a Japanese room, all bamboo furniture and quaintly pictured walls, for his more frivolous moods. Finally there was the music-room with a great organ, and this room was made in the similitude of a church. On these freaks and fancies Mr. Hill spent a good deal of money, and the result was an olla-podrida of buildings, jumbled together without rhyme or reason. Such a mansion--if it could be called so--might exist in a nightmare, but only Mr. Hill could have translated it into fact. Within and without, the place was an example of many moods. It illustrated perfectly the mind of its architect and owner.

Allen's father was a small, delicate, dainty little man with a large head and a large voice, which boomed like a gong when he was angry. The man's head was clever and he had a fine forehead, but there was a streak of madness in him, which led him to indulge himself in whatever mood came uppermost. He did not exercise the least self-control, and expected all around him to give way to his whims, which were many and not always agreeable. Someone called Mr. Hill a brownie, and he was not unlike the pictures of that queer race of elves. His body was shapely enough, but as his legs were thin and slightly twisted, these, with his large head, gave him a strange appearance. His face was clean-shaven, pink and white, with no wrinkles. He had a beautifully formed mouth and a set of splendid teeth. His fair hair, slightly--very slightly--streaked with grey, he wore long, and had a trick of passing his hand through it when he thought he had said anything clever. His hands were delicate--real artistic hands--but his feet were large and ill-formed. He strove always to hide these by wearing wide trousers. Both in winter and summer he wore a brown velvet coat and white serge trousers, no waistcoat, and a frilled shirt with a waist-band of some gaudy Eastern stuff sparkling with gold thread and rainbow hues. When he went out, he wore a straw hat with a gigantic brim, and as he was considerably under the ordinary height, he looked strange in this headgear. But however queer his garb may have been in the daytime, at night Mr. Hill was always accurately attired in evening dress of the latest cut, and appeared a quiet, if somewhat odd, English gentleman.

This strange creature lived on his emotions. One day he would be all gaiety and mirth; the next morning would see him silent and sad. At times he played the organ, the piano, the violin; again he would take to painting; then he would write poems, and anon his mood would change to a religious one. Not that he was truly religious. He was a Theosophist, a Spiritualist, sometimes a Roman Catholic, and at times a follower of Calvin. Lately he fancied that he would like to be a Buddhist. His library, a large one, was composed of various books bought in different moods, which illustrated--like his house--the queer jumbled mind of the man. Yet with all his eccentricity Mr. Hill was far from being mad. He was clever at a bargain, and took good care of the wealth, which he had inherited from his father, who had been a stockbroker. At times Mr. Hill could talk cleverly and in a businesslike way; at others, he was all fantasy and vague dreams. Altogether an irritating creature. People said they wondered how Mrs. Hill could put up with such a changeling in the house.

Mrs. Hill put up with it--though the general public did not know this--simply for the sake of Allen, whom she adored. It was strange that Allen, tall, stalwart, practical, and quiet, with a steadfast mind and an open nature, should be the son of the freakish creature he called father. But the young man was in every way his mother's son. Mrs. Hill was tall, lean, and quiet in manner. Like Mrs. Merry, she usually wore black, and she moved silently about the house, never speaking, unless she was spoken too. Originally she had been a bright girl, but marriage with the brownie had sobered her. Several times during her early married life she was on the point of leaving Hill, thinking she had married a madman, but when Allen was born, Mrs. Hill resolved to endure her lot for the sake of the boy. Hill had the money, and would not allow the control of it to pass out of his hands. Mrs. Hill had come to him a pauper, the daughter of an aristocratic scamp who had gambled away a fortune. Therefore, so that Allen might inherit his father's wealth, which was considerable, the poor woman bore with her strange husband. Not that Hill was unkind. He was simply selfish, emotional, exacting, and irritating. Mrs. Hill never interfered with his whims, knowing from experience that interference would be useless. She was a cypher in the house, and left everything to her husband. Hill looked after the servants, arranged the meals, ordered the routine, and danced through life like an industrious butterfly.

As to Allen, he had speedily found that such a life was unbearable, and for the most part remained away. He had early gone to a public school, and had left it for college; then he had studied in London to be an engineer and took the first opportunity to procure work beyond the seas. He wrote constantly to his mother, but hardly ever corresponded with his father. When he came to England he stopped at "The Arabian Nights"--so the jumbled house was oddly named by its odd owner-- but always, he had gone away in a month. On this occasion the meeting with Eva kept him in Wargrove, and he wished to be sure of her father's consent to the match before he went back to South America. Meantime his partner carried on the business in Cuzco. Mr. Hill was not ill pleased that Allen should stop, as he was really fond of his son in his own elfish way. Also he approved of the engagement to Eva, for whose beauty he had a great admiration.

On the morning after Mr. Strode's expected arrival, the three people who dwelt in "The Arabian Nights' were seated in the Jacobean dining-room. Mr. Hill, in his invariable brown velvet coat with a rose in his buttonhole and a shining morning face, was devouring pâté-de-foie-gras sandwiches, and drinking claret. At times he took a regular English egg-and-bacon coffee and marmalade breakfast, but he varied his meals as much as he did his amusements. One morning, bread and milk; the next he would imitate Daniel and his friends to the extent of living on pulse and water; then a Continental roll and coffee would appeal to him; and finally, as on the present occasion, he would eat viands more suited to a luncheon than to a breakfast. However, on this especial morning he announced that he was in a musical mood, and intended to compose during the day.

"Therefore," said Mr. Hill, sipping his claret and trifling with his sandwiches, "the stomach must not be laden with food. This," he touched the sandwiches, "is nourishment to sustain life, during the struggle with melody, and the wine is of a delicate thin nature which maketh the heart glad without leading to the vice of intoxication. Burgundy, I grant you, is too heavy. Champagne might do much to raise the airy fancy, but I believe in claret, which makes blood; and the brain during the agonies of composition needs a placid flow of blood."

Mrs. Hill smiled wearily at this speech and went on eating. She and Allen were engaged in disposing of a regular English meal, but neither seemed to enjoy the food. Mrs. Hill, silent and unemotional, ate like one who needs food to live, and not as though she cared for the victuals. Allen looked pale and haggard. His face was white, and there were dark circles under his eyes as though he had not slept.

"Late hours," said his father, staring at him shrewdly; "did I not hear you come in at two o'clock, Allen?"

"Yes, sir;" Allen always addressed his parent in this stiff fashion. "I was unavoidably late."

Mrs. Hill cast an anxious look at his face, and her husband finished his claret before making any reply. Then he spoke, folding up his napkin as he did so. "When I gave you a latchkey," said Mr. Hill in his deep, rich voice, "I did not expect it to be used after midnight. Even the gayest of young men should be in bed before that unholy hour."

"I wasn't very gay," said Allen listlessly; "the fact is, father, I sprained my ankle last night four miles away."

"In what direction."

"The Westhaven direction. I was going to the Red Deeps, and while going I twisted my ankle. I lay on the moor--I was half way across when I fell--for a long time waiting for help. As none came, I managed to crawl home, and so reached here at two. I came on all fours."

"Humph," said Hill, "it's lucky Wasp didn't see you. With his ideas of duty he would have run you in for being drunk."

"I think I could have convinced Wasp to the contrary," said Allen drily; "my mother bathed my ankle, and it is easier this morning."

"But you should not have come down to breakfast," said Mrs. Hill.

"It would have put my father out, had I not come, mother."

"Quite so," said Mr. Hill; "I am glad to hear that you try to behave as a son. Besides, self-denial makes a man," added Mr. Hill, who never denied himself anything. "Strange, Allen, I did not notice that you limped--and I am an observant man."

"I was seated here before you came down," his son reminded him.

"True," said Mr. Hill, rising; "it is one of my late mornings. I was dreaming of an opera. I intend, Allen, to compose an opera. Saccharissa," thus he addressed Mrs. Hill, who was called plain Sarah, "do you hear? I intend to immortalize myself."

"I hear," said Saccharissa, quite unmoved. She had heard before, of these schemes to immortalize Mr. Hill.

"I shall call my opera 'Gwendoline,'" said Mr. Hill, passing his hand through his hair; "it will be a Welsh opera. I don't think anyone has ever composed a Welsh opera, Allen."

"I can't call one to mind, sir," said Allen, his eyes on his plate.

"The opening chorus," began Mr. Hill, full of his theme, "will be----"

"One moment, sir," interrupted Allen, who was not in the mood for this trifling, "I want to ask you a question."

"No! no! no! You will disturb the current of my thoughts. Would you have the world lose a masterpiece, Allen?"

"It is a very simple question, sir. Will you see Mr. Strode today?"

Hill, who was looking out of the window and humming a theme for his opening chorus, turned sharply. "Certainly not. I am occupied."

"Mr. Strode is your oldest and best friend," urged Allen.

"He has proved that by taking money from me," said Hill, with a deep laugh. "Why should I see him?"

"I want you to put in a good word for me and Eva. Of course," Allen raised his eyes abruptly and looked directly at his father, "you expected to see him this morning?"

"No, I didn't," snapped the composer. "Strode and I were friends at school and college, certainly, but we met rarely in after life. The last time I saw him was when he brought his wife down here."

"Poor Lady Jane," sighed Mrs. Hill, who was seated with folded hands.

"You may well say that, Saccharissa. She was wedded to a clown----"

"I thought Mr. Strode was a clever and cultured man," said Allen drily.

"He should have been," said Mr. Hill, waving his hand and then sticking it into the breast of his shirt. "I did my best to form him. But flowers will not grow in clay, and Strode was made of stodgy clay. A poor creature, and very quarrelsome."

"That doesn't sound like stodgy clay, sir."

"He varied, Allen, he varied. At times the immortal fire he buried in his unfruitful soil would leap out at my behest; but for the most part Strode was an uncultured yokel. The lambent flame of my fancy, my ethereal fancy, played on the mass harmlessly, or with small result. I could not submit to be bound even by friendship to such a clod, so I got rid of Strode. And how did I do it? I lent him two thousand pounds, and not being able to repay it, shame kept him away. Cheap at the price-- cheap at the price. Allen, how does this theme strike you for an opening chorus of Druids--modern Druids, of course? The scene is at Anglesea----"

"Wait, father. You hinted the other morning that Mr. Strode would never come back to Wargrove."

"Did I?" said Mr. Hill in an airy manner; "I forget."

"What grounds had you to say that?"

"Grounds--oh, my dear Allen, are you so commonplace as to demand grounds. I forget my train of thought just then--the fancy has vanished: but I am sure that my grounds were such as you would not understand. Why do you ask?"

"I may as well be frank," began Allen, when his father stopped him.

"No. It is so obvious to be frank. And today I am in an enigmatic mood--music is an enigma, and therefore I wish to be mysterious."

"I may as well be frank," repeated Allen doggedly, and doggedness was the only way to meet such a trifler as Mr. Hill. "I saw Eva last night, and she related a dream she had."

"Ah!" Mr. Hill spun round vivaciously--"now you talk sense. I love the psychic. A dream! Can Eva dream?--such a matter-of-fact girl."

"Indeed she's no such thing, sir," said the indignant lover.

"Pardon me. You are not a reader of character as I am. Eva Strode at present possesses youth, to cover a commonplace soul. When she gets old and the soul works through the mask of the face, she will be a common-looking woman like your mother."

"Oh!" said Allen, at this double insult. But Mrs. Hill laid her hand on his arm, and the touch quietened him. It was useless to be angry with so irresponsible a creature as Mr. Hill. "I must tell you the dream," said Allen with an effort, "and then you can judge if Eva is what you say."

"I wait for the dream," replied Mr. Hill, waving his arm airily; "but it will not alter my opinion. She is commonplace, that is why I agreed to your engagement. You are commonplace also--you take after your mother."

Mrs. Hill rose quite undisturbed. "I had better go," she said.

"By all means, Saccharissa," said Hill graciously; "today in my music mood I am a butterfly. You disturb me. Life with me must be sunshine this day, but you are a creature of gloom."

"Wait a moment, mother," said Allen, catching Mrs. Hill's hand as she moved quietly to the door, "I want you to hear Eva's dream."

"Which certainly will not be worth listening to," said the butterfly. Allen passed over this fresh piece of insolence, although he secretly wondered how his mother took such talk calmly. He recounted the dream in detail. "So I went to the Red Deeps at Eva's request," he finished, "to see if her dream was true. I never thought it would be, of course; but I went to pacify her. But when I left the road to take a short cut to the Red Deeps, about four miles from Wargrove, I twisted my ankle, as I said, and after waiting, crawled home, to arrive here at two o'clock."

"Why do you tell me this dream--which is interesting, I admit?" asked Mr. Hill irritably, and with a rather dark face.

"Because you said that Mr. Strode would never come home. Eva's dream hinted at the same thing. Why did you----?"

"Oh, that's it, is it?" said Mr. Hill, sitting down with a smile. "I will endeavor to recall my mood when I spoke." He thought for a few minutes, then touched his forehead. "The mood taps here," said he playfully. "Allen, my son, you don't know Strode; I do. A truculent ruffian, determined to have money at any cost."

"I always heard he was a polished gentleman," objected Allen.

"Oh, quite so. The public school life and university polish gave him manners for society: I don't deny that. But when you scratched the skin, the swashbuckler broke out. Do you know how he came to lose his right hand, Allen? No. I could tell you that, but the story is too long, and my brain is not in its literary vein this day. If I could sing it, I would, but the theme is prosaic. Well, to come to the point, Allen, Strode, though a gentleman, is a swashbuckler. Out in Africa he has been trying to make money, and has done so at the cost of making enemies."

"Who told you so?"

"Let me see--oh, his lawyer, who is also mine. In fact, I introduced him to Mask, my solicitor. I went up a few months ago to see Mask about some business, and asked after Strode; for though the man is a baron of the middle ages and a ruffian, still he is my friend. Mask told me that Strode was making money and enemies at the same time. When you informed me, Allen, that Strode was coming home in the Dunoon Castle, and that he had arrived at Southampton, I thought some of his enemies might have followed him, and might have him arrested for swindling. In that case, he certainly would not arrive."

"But how do you know that Mr. Strode would swindle?"

"Because he was a man with no moral principles," retorted Mr. Hill; "your mother here will tell you the same."

"I did not like Mr. Strode," said Mrs. Hill calmly; "he was not what I call a good man. Eva takes after Lady Jane, who was always a delightful friend to me. I was glad to hear you were engaged to the dear girl, Allen," she added, and patted his hand.

"It is strange that your observation and Eva's dream should agree."

"Pardon me," said Mr. Hill, rising briskly, "they do not agree. I suggested just now that Strode might be followed by his Cape Town enemies and arrested for swindling. Eva dreamed that he was dead."

"Then you don't agree with her dream?" asked Allen, puzzled.

"Interesting, I admit; but--oh no"--Hill shrugged his shoulders--"Strode can look after himself. Whosoever is killed, he will be safe enough. I never knew a man possessed of such infernal ingenuity. Well, are you satisfied? If not, ask me more, and I'll explain what I can. Ah, by the way, there's Wasp coming up the garden." Hill threw open the window and hailed the policeman. "I asked Wasp to come and see me, Allen, whenever he had an interesting case to report. I intend to write a volume on the physiology of the criminal classes. Probably Wasp, wishing to earn an honest penny, has come to tell me of some paltry crime not worth expending five shillings on--that's his price. Ah, Wasp, what is it?"

The policeman, a stout little man, saluted. "Death, sir."

"How interesting," said Mr. Hill, rubbing his hands; "this is indeed news worth five shillings. Death?"

"Murder."

Allen rose and looked wide-eyed at the policeman. "Mr. Strode?"

"Yes, sir. Mr. Strode. Murdered--found dead at the Red Deeps."

"Face downward in the mud?" whispered Allen. "Oh, the dream--the dream!" and he sank back in his chair quite overwhelmed.

"You seem to know all about it, Mr. Allen," said Wasp, with sudden suspicion.

V - A STRANGE LOSS

WASP WAS a bulky little man with a great opinion of his own importance. In early years he had been in the army, and there, had imbibed stern ideas of duty. Shortly after joining the police force he was sent to Wargrove, and, with an underling, looked after the village and the surrounding district. Married while young, he now possessed a family of ten, who dwelt with Mrs. Wasp in a spick-and-span house on the verge of the common. Everything about Wasp's house was spotless. The little policeman had drilled his wife so thoroughly, that she performed her duties in quite a military way, and thought Wasp the greatest of men mentally, whatever he may have been physically. The ten children were also drilled to perfection, and life in the small house was conducted on garrison lines. The family woke early to the sound of the bugle, and retired to bed when 'Lights out' was sounded. It was quite a model household, especially as on Sunday, Wasp, a fervid churchman, walked at the head of his olive-branches with Mrs. Wasp to St. Peter's church.

The pay was not very large, but Wasp managed to make money in many ways. Lately he had been earning stray crowns from Mr. Hill by detailing any case which he thought likely to interest his patron. Hitherto these had been concerned with thieving and drunkenness and poaching--things which Mr. Hill did not care about. But on this occasion Wasp came to 'The Arabian Nights' swelling with importance, knowing that he had a most exciting story to tell. He was therefore not at all pleased when Allen, so to speak, took the words out of his official mouth. His red face grew redder than ever, and he drew up his stiff little figure to its full height, which was not much. "You seem to know all about it, Mr. Allen," said Wasp tartly.

"It is certainly strange that Miss Strode should dream as she did," said Hill, who had turned a trifle pale; "what do you think, Saccharissa?"

Mrs. Hill quoted from her husband's favorite poet: "'There are more things in heaven and earth----'"

"That's poetry, we want sense," said Hill interrupting testily; "my music mood has been banished by this news. I now feel that I am equal to being a Vidocq. Allen, henceforth I am a detective until the murderer of my friend Strode is in the dock. Where is the criminal," added Hill, turning to the policeman, "that I may see him?"

"No one knows who did it, sir," said Wasp, eyeing Allen suspiciously.

"What are the circumstances?"

"Mr. Allen, your son here, seems to know all about them," said Wasp stiffly.

Allen, who was resting his head on the white cloth of the table, looked up slowly. His face seemed old and worn, and the dark circles under his eyes were more marked than ever. "Didn't Miss Strode tell you her dream, Wasp?" he asked.

The policeman snorted. "I've got too much to do in connection with this case to think of them rubbishy things, sir," said he; "Mrs. Merry did say something, now you mention it. But how's a man woke up to dooty at one in the morning to listen to dreams."

"Were you woke at one o'clock, Wasp?" asked Mr. Hill, settling himself luxuriously; "tell me the details, and then I will go with you to see Miss Strode and the remains of one, whom I always regarded as a friend, whatever his shortcomings might have been. Allen, I suppose you will remain within and nurse your foot."

"No," said Allen rising painfully. "I must see Eva."

"Have you hurt your foot, sir?" asked Wasp, who was paying particular attention to Allen.

"Yes; I sprained it last night," said Allen shortly.

"Where, may I ask, sir?"

"On Chilvers Common."

"Ho!" Wasp stroked a ferocious moustache he wore for the sake of impressing evil-doers; "that's near the Red Deeps?"

"About a mile from the Red Deeps, I believe," said Allen, trying to ease the pain of his foot by resting it.

"And what were you doing there, may I ask, sir?" This time it was not Allen who replied, but his mother. The large, lean woman suddenly flushed and her stolid face became alive with anger. She turned on the little man--well named Wasp from his meddlesome disposition and desire to sting when he could--and seemed like a tigress protecting her cub. "Why do you ask?" she demanded; "do you hint that my son has anything to do with this matter?"

"No, I don't, ma'am," replied Wasp stolidly, "but Mr. Allen talked of the corpse being found face downward in the mud. We did find it so--leastways them as found the dead, saw it that way. How did Mr. All----"

"The dream, my good Wasp," interposed Hill airily. "Miss Strode dreamed a dream two nights ago, and thought she saw her father dead in the Red Deeps, face downward. She also heard a laugh--but that's a detail. My son told us of the dream before you came. It is strange it should be verified so soon and so truly. I begin to think that Miss Strode has imagination after all. Without imagination," added the little man impressively, "no one can dream. I speak on the authority of Coleridge, a poet," he smiled pityingly on the three--"of whom you probably know nothing."

"Poets ain't in the case," said Wasp, "and touching Mr. Allen----"

The young engineer stood up for himself. "My story is short," he said, "and you may not believe it, Wasp."

"Why shouldn't I?" demanded the policeman very suspiciously.

Allen shrugged his shoulders. "You have not imagination enough," he answered, copying his father; "it seems to me that you believe I am concerned in this matter."

"There ain't no need to incriminate yourself, sir."

"Spare me the warning. I am not going to do so. If you want to know the truth it is this: Miss Strode dreamed the other night that her father was lying dead in the Red Deeps. After vainly endeavoring to laugh her out of the belief that the dream was true, I went last night to the Red Deeps to convince her that all was well. I struck across the moor from the high-road, and catching my foot in some bramble bushes I twisted my ankle. I could not move, and my ankle grew very painful. For hours I waited, on the chance that someone might come past, but Chilvers Common being lonely, as you know, I could not get help. Therefore, shortly before midnight-

-though I can hardly tell the exact time, my watch having been stopped when I fell--I managed to crawl home. I arrived about two o'clock, and my mother was waiting up for me. She bathed my ankle and I went to bed."

"It couldn't have been very bad, sir, if you're down now," said Wasp bluntly, and only half satisfied with Allen's explanation.

"I forced myself to come down, as my father does not like any one to be absent from meals," was the reply.

"Right, Mr. Wasp--right," said Hill briskly, "you need not go on suspecting my son. He has nothing to do with this matter, the more so as he is engaged to Miss Strode."

"And I certainly should end all my chances of marrying Miss Strode by killing her father," said Allen sharply; "I think you take too much upon yourself, Wasp."

The policeman excused himself on the plea of zeal, but saw that he had gone too far, and offered an apology. "But it was your knowing the position of the body that made me doubtful," he said.

"That is the dream," said Mrs. Hill quietly; "but you can now tell us all that has taken place."

Hill looked astonished at his wife and a trifle annoyed. She was not usually given to putting herself forward--as he called it--but waited to take her tune from him. He would have interposed and asked the question himself, so as to recover the lead in his own house, but that Wasp, anxious to atone for his late error, replied at once, and addressed himself exclusively to Mrs. Hill.

"Well, ma'am, it's this way," he said, drawing himself up stiffly and saluting apologetically. "I was wakened about one o'clock by a message that I was wanted at Misery Castle,--a queer name as you know, ma'am----"

"We all know about Mrs. Merry and her eccentricities," said Mrs. Hill, who, having an eccentric person in the house, was lenient towards the failings of others; "go on."

"Well, ma'am, Jackson, who is under me, was at the other end of the village before midnight, but coming past Misery Castle on his rounds he saw Mrs. Merry waiting at the gate. She said that Mr. Strode had been brought home dead by three men--laborers. They, under the direction of Miss Eva, took the body in and laid it on a bed. Then Miss Eva sent them away with money. That was just about twelve o'clock. The men should have come to report to me, or have seen Jackson, but they went back to their own homes beyond the common, Westhaven way. I'm going to ask them what they mean by doing that and not reporting to the police," said Wasp sourly. "Well then, ma'am, Jackson saw the body and reported to me at one in the morning. I put on my uniform and went to Misery Castle. I examined the remains and called up Jackson. We made a report of the condition of the body, and sent it by messenger to Westhaven. The inspector came this morning and is now at Misery Castle. Being allowed to go away for a spell, having been on duty all night over the body, I came here to tell Mr. Hill, knowing he'd like to hear of the murder."

"I'm glad you came," said Hill, rubbing his hands, "a fine murder; though," his face fell, "I had rather it had been any one but my old friend. I suppose you don't know how he came by his death?"

"He was shot, sir."

"Shot?" echoed Allen, looking up, "and by whom?"

"I can't say, nor can anyone, Mr. Allen. From what Mrs. Merry says, and she asked questions of those who brought the body home, the corpse was found lying face downward in the mud near the Red Deeps spring. Why he should have gone there--the dead man, I mean, sir--I can't say. I hear he was coming from London, and no doubt he'd drive in a fly to Wargrove. But we'll have to make inquiries at the office of the railway station, and get to facts. Someone must hang for it."

"Don't, Wasp; you're making my mother ill," said Allen quickly.

And indeed Mrs. Hill looked very white. But she rallied herself and smiled quietly in her old manner. "I knew Mr. Strode," she said, "and I feel his sad end keenly, especially as he has left a daughter behind him. Poor Eva," she added, turning to Allen, "she is now an orphan."

"All the more reason that I should make her my wife and cherish her," said Allen quickly. "I'll go to the cottage," he looked at his father; "may I take the pony chaise?--my foot----"

"I was thinking of going myself," said Hill hesitating, "but as you are engaged to the girl, it is right you should go. I'll drive you." Allen looked dubious. Mr. Hill thought he could drive in the same way that he fancied he could do all things: but he was not a good whip, and Allen did not want another accident to happen. However, he resolved to risk the journey, and, thanking his father, went out of the room. While the chaise was getting ready, Allen, looking out of the window, saw his father leave the grounds in the company of Wasp. Apparently both were going to Misery Castle. He turned to his mother who was in the room. "What about my father driving?" he asked. "I see he has left the house."

"Probably he has forgotten," said Mrs. Hill soothingly; "you know how forgetful and whimsical he is."

"Do I not?" said Allen with a sigh, "and don't you?" he added, smiling at the dark face of his mother. "Well, I can drive myself. Will you come also, mother, and comfort Eva?"

"Not just now. I think that is your task. She is fond of me, but at present you can do her more good. And I think, Allen," said Mrs. Hill, "that you might bring her back. It is terrible that a young girl should be left alone in that small cottage with so dismal a woman as Mrs. Merry. Bring her back."

"But my father?"

"I'll make it right with him," said Mrs. Hill determinedly.

Allen looked at her anxiously. His mother had a firm, dark face, with quiet eyes steady and unwavering in their gaze. It had often struck him as wonderful, how so strong a woman--apparently--should allow his shallow father to rule the house. On several occasions, as he knew, Mrs. Hill had asserted herself firmly, and then Hill, after much outward anger, had given way. There was a mystery about this, and on any other occasion Allen would have asked his mother why she held so subordinate a position, when, evidently, she had all the strength of mind to rule the house and her husband and the whole neighborhood if necessary. But at present he was too much taken up with the strange fulfilment of Eva's dream, and with the thought of her sorrow, to trouble about so petty a thing. He therefore remained silent and only spoke when the chaise came to the door in charge of a smart groom.

"I'll tell you everything when I return," he said, and hastily kissing his mother he moved slowly out of the room. Mrs. Hill stood smiling and nodding at the window as he drove away, and then returned to her needlework. She was always at needlework, and usually wrought incessantly, like a modern Penelope, without displaying any emotion. But today, as she worked in the solitude of her own room, her tears fell occasionally. Yet, as she did not like Strode, the tears could not have been for his untimely death. A strange, firm, self-reliant woman was Mrs. Hill; and although she took no active part in the management of the house, the servants secretly looked on her as the real ruler. Mr. Hill, in spite of his bluster, they regarded as merely the figurehead.

On the way to Misery Castle, Allen chatted with Jacobs, a smart-looking lad, who had been transformed from a yokel into a groom by Mr. Hill. Jacobs had heard very little of the affair, but admitted that he knew the crime had been committed. "My brother was one of them as brought the corpse home, sir," he said, nodding.

"Why did your brother and the others not report to Wasp?"

Jacobs grinned. "Mr. Wasp have himself to thank for that, sir," said he, "they were all frightened as he'd say they did it, and don't intend to come forward unless they have to."

"All zeal on Mr. Wasp's part, Jacobs," said Allen, smiling faintly, "I can quite understand the hesitation, however. How did your brother find the body?"

"Well, sir," Jacobs scratched his head, "him and Arnold and Wake was coming across Chilvers Common last night after they'd been to see the circus at Westhaven, and they got a thirst on them. There being no beer handy they went to the spring at the Red Deeps to get water. There they found Mr. Strode's body lying in the mud. His face was down and his hands were stretched. They first saw the corpse by the white glove, sir, on the right hand."

"The wooden hand," said Allen absently.

"What, sir? Is it a wooden hand?" asked Jacobs eagerly.

"Yes. Didn't you know?--no----" Allen checked himself, "of course you wouldn't know. You can't remember Mr. Strode when he was here last."

"It's not that, sir," began Jacobs thoughtfully, "but here we are at the gate. I'll tell you another time, Mr. Allen."

"Tell me what?" asked Allen, as he alighted painfully.

"No matter, sir. It ain't much," replied the lad, and gathering up the reins he jumped into the trap. "When will I come back?"

"In an hour, and then you can tell me whatever it is."

"Nothing--nothing," said the groom, and drove off, looking thoughtful.

It seemed to Allen that the lad had something to say to him relating to the wooden hand, but, thinking he would learn about the matter during the homeward drive, he dismissed the affair from his mind and walked up the path.

He found the front door closed, and knocked in vain. Finding that no one came, he strolled round to the back, and discovered Mrs. Merry talking to a ragged, shock-headed, one-eyed boy of about thirteen. "Just you say that again," Mrs. Merry was remarking to this urchin.

The boy spoke in a shrill voice and with a cockney accent. "Cain sez to me, as he'll come over and see you tomorrer!"

"And who are you to come like this?" asked Mrs. Merry.

"I'm Butsey, and now you've as you've heard twice what Cain hes t'saiy, you can swear, without me waiting," and after this insult the urchin bolted without waiting for the box on the ear, with which Mrs. Merry was prepared to favor him. Allen, quick in his judgments, saw that this was a true specimen of a London gamin, and wondered how such a brat had drifted to Wargrove. As a rule the London guttersnipe sticks to town as religiously as does the London sparrow.

"If I had a child like that," gasped Mrs. Merry as the boy darted round the corner of the cottage, "I'd put him in a corner and keep him on bread and water till the sin was drove out of him. Ah, Mr. Allen, that's you. I'm glad you've come to the house of mourning, and well may I call this place Misery Castle, containing a corpse as it do. But I said the dream would come true, and true it came. Five knocks at the door, and the corpse with three men bearing it. Your pa's inside, looking at the body, and Miss Eva weeping in the doring-room."

Allen brushed past the garrulous woman, but halted on the doorstep, to ask why she had not come to the front door. Mrs. Merry was ready at once with her explanation. "That door don't open till the corpse go out," she said, wiping her hands on her apron. "Oh, I know as you may call it superstition whatever you may say, Mr. Allen, but when a corpse enter at one door nothing should come between its entering and its going out. If anything do, that thing goes with the corpse to the grave," said Mrs. Merry impressively; "police and doctor and your pa and all, I haven't let in by the front, lest any one of them should die. Not as I'd mind that Wasp man going to his long home, drat him with his nasty ways, frightening Miss Eva."

Waiting to hear no more, Hill went through the kitchen and entered the tiny drawing-room. The blinds were down and on the sofa he saw Eva seated, dressed in black. She sprang to her feet when she saw him. "Oh, Allen, I am so glad you have come. Your father said you could not, because of your foot."

"I sprained it, Eva, last night when----"

"Yes. Your father told me all. I wondered why you did not come back, Allen, to relieve my anxiety. Of course you did not go to the Red Deeps?"

"No," said Allen sitting down, her hand within his own, "I never got so far, dearest. So your dream came true?"

"Yes. Truer than you think--truer than you can imagine," said Eva in a tone of awe. "Oh, Allen, I never believed in such things; but that such a strange experience should come to me,"--she covered her face and wept, shaken to the core of her soul; Allen soothed her gently, and she laid her head on his breast, glad to have such kind arms around her. "Yes, my father is dead," she went on, "and do you know, Allen, wicked girl that I am, I do not feel so filled with sorrow as I ought to be? In fact"--she hesitated, then burst out, "Allen, I am wicked, but I feel relieved----"

"Relieved, Eva?"

"Yes! had my father come home alive everything would have gone wrong. You and I would have been parted, and--and--oh, I can't say what would have happened. Yet he is my father after all, though he treated my mother so badly, and I knew so little about him. I wish--oh, I wish that I could feel sorry, but I don't--I don't."

"Hush, hush! dearest," said Allen softly, "you knew little of your father, and it's natural under the circumstances you should not feel the loss very keenly. He was almost a stranger to you, and----"

While Allen was thus consoling her, the door opened abruptly and Hill entered rather excited. "Eva," he said quickly, "you never told me that your father's wooden hand had been removed."

"It has not been," said Eva, "it was on when we laid out his body."

"It's gone now, then," said Hill quietly, and looking very pale; "gone."

VI - THE WARNING

ON HEARING this announcement of the loss, Eva rose and went to the chamber of death. There, under a sheet, lay the body of her father looking far more calm in death, than he had ever looked in life. But the sheet was disarranged on the right side, and lifting this slightly, she saw that what Mr. Hill said was true. The wooden hand had been removed, and now there remained but the stump of the arm. A glance round the room showed her that the window was open, but she remembered opening it herself. The blind was down, but someone might have entered and thieved from the dead. It was an odd loss, and Eva could not think why it should have taken place.

When she returned to the tiny drawing-room, Allen and his father were in deep conversation. They looked up when the girl entered.

"It is quite true," said Eva, sitting down; "the hand is gone."

"Who can have stolen it?" demanded Allen, wrinkling his brow.

"And why should it be stolen?" asked Hill pointedly.

Eva pressed her hands to her aching head. "I don't know," she said wearily. "When Mrs. Merry and I laid out the body at dawn this morning the hand was certainly there, for I noted the white glove all discolored with the mud of the Red Deeps. We pulled down the blind and opened the window. Someone may have entered."

"But why should someone steal?" said Hill uneasily; "you say the hand was there at dawn?"

"Yes." Eva rose and rang the bell. "We can ask Mrs. Merry."

The old woman speedily entered, and expressed astonishment at the queer loss. "The hand was there at nine," she said positively. "I went to see if everything was well, and lifted the sheet. Ah, dear me, Mr. Strode, as was, put a new white glove on that wooden hand every morning, so that it might look nice and clean. Whatever would he have said, to see the glove all red with clay? I intended," added Mrs. Merry, "to have put on a new glove, and I sent Cain to buy it."

"What?" asked Eva, looking up, "is Cain back?"

"Yes, deary. He came early, as the circus is passing through this place on to the next town, Shanton. Cain thought he'd pick up the caravans on the road, so came to say good-bye."

Eva remembered Cain's odd behavior, and wondered if he had anything to do with the theft. But the idea was ridiculous. The lad was bad enough, but he certainly would not rob the dead. Moreover--on the face of it--there was no reason he should steal so useless an object as a wooden hand. What with the excitement of the death, and the fulfilment of the dream, not to mention that she felt a natural grief for the death of her father, the poor girl was quite worn out. Mr. Hill saw this, and after questioning Mrs. Merry as to the theft of the glove, he went away.

"I shall see Wasp about this," he said, pausing at the door, "there must be some meaning in the theft. Meanwhile I'll examine the flower-bed outside the window."

Mrs. Merry went with him, but neither could see any sign of foot-marks on the soft mold. The thief--if indeed a thief had entered the house, had jumped the flower-bed, and no marks were discoverable on the hard gravel of the path. "There's that boy," said Mrs. Merry.

"What boy?" asked Hill, starting.

"A little rascal, as calls himself Butsey," said the old woman, folding her hands as usual under her apron. "London street brat I take him to be. He came to say Cain would be here tomorrow."

"But Cain is here today," said Mr. Hill perplexed.

"That's what makes me think Butsey might have stolen the wooden hand," argued Mrs. Merry. "Why should he come here else? I didn't tell him, as Cain had already arrived, me being one as knows how to hold my tongue whatever you may say, Mr. Hills"--so Mrs. Merry named her companion. "I would have asked questions, but the boy skipped. I wonder why he stole it?"

"You have no proof that he stole it at all," said Hill smartly; "but I'll tell Wasp what you say. When does the inquest take place?"

"Tomorrow, as you might say," snapped Mrs. Merry crossly; "and don't bring that worriting Wasp round here, Mr. Hills. Wasp he is by name and Wasp by nature with his questions. If ever you----"

But Mr. Hill was beyond hearing by this time. He always avoided a chat with Mrs. Merry, as the shrillness of her voice--so he explained--annoyed him. The old woman stared after his retreating figure and she shook her head. "You're a bad one," she soliloquized; "him as is dead was bad too. A pair of ye--ah--but if there's trouble coming, as trouble will come, do what you may--Miss Eva shan't suffer while I can stop any worriting."

Meanwhile Eva and Allen were talking seriously. "My dream was fulfilled in the strangest way, Allen," the girl said. "I dreamed, as I told you, the night before last at nine o'clock----"

"Well?" questioned the young man seeing she hesitated.

Eva looked round fearfully. "The doctor says, that, judging by the condition of the body, my father must have been shot at that hour."

"Last night you mean," said Allen hesitatingly.

"No. This is Friday. He was shot on Wednesday at nine, and the body must have lain all those long hours at the Red Deeps. Of course," added Eva quickly, "no one goes to the Red Deeps. It was the merest chance that those laborers went last night and found the body. So you see, Allen, my father must have been killed at the very time I dreamed of his death."

"It is strange," said young Hill, much perturbed. "I wonder who can have killed him?"

Eva shook her head. "I cannot say, nor can anyone. The inspector from Westhaven has been here this morning making inquiries, but, of course, I can tell him nothing--except about the telegram."

"What telegram?"

"Didn't I mention it to you?" said the girl, raising her eyes which were fixed on the ground disconsolately; "no--of course I didn't. It came after you left me--at nine o'clock--no it was at half-past nine. The wire was from my father, saying he would be down the next day. It had arrived at Westhaven at four, and should have been delivered earlier but for the forgetfulness of the messenger."

"But, Eva, if the wire came from your father yesterday, he could not have been shot on Wednesday night."

"No, I can't understand it. I told Inspector Garrit about the wire, and he took it away with him. He will say all that he learns about the matter at the inquest tomorrow. And now my father's wooden hand has been stolen--it is strange."

"Very strange," assented Allen musingly. He was thinking of what his father had said about Mr. Strode's probable enemies. "Eva, do you know if your father brought any jewels from Africa--diamonds, I mean?"

"I can't say. No diamonds were found on his body. In fact his purse was filled with money and his jewelry had not been taken."

"Then robbery could not have been the motive for the crime."

"No, Allen, the body was not robbed." She rose and paced the room. "I can't understand my dream. I wonder if, when I slept, my soul went to the Red Deeps and saw the crime committed."

"You did not see the crime committed?"

"No; I saw the body, however, lying in the position in which it was afterwards found by Jacobs and the others. And then the laugh--that cruel laugh as though the assassin was gloating over his cruel work--the man who murdered my father was laughing in my dream."

"How can you tell it was a man?"

"The laugh sounded like that of a man."

"In your dream? I don't think a jury will take that evidence."

Eva stopped before the young man and looked at him determinedly. "I don't see why that part of my dream should not come true, if the other has already been proved true. It's all of a piece."

To this remark young Hill had no answer ready. Certainly the dream had come true in one part, so why not in another? But he was too anxious about Eva's future to continue the discussion. "What about you, darling?" he asked.

"I don't know," she replied, and sat down beside him again. "I can think of nothing until the inquest has taken place. When I learn who has killed my father, I shall be more at ease."

"That is only right and natural; but----"

"Don't mistake me, Allen," she interrupted vehemently. "I saw so little of my father, and, through my mother, knew so much bad about him, that I don't mourn his death as a daughter ought to. But I feel that I have a duty to perform. I must learn who killed him, and have that person sent to the scaffold."

Allen colored and looked down. "We can talk about that when we have further facts before us. Inspector Garrit, you say, is making inquiries?"

"Yes; I have given him the telegram, and also the address of my father's lawyer, which I found in a letter in his pocket."

"Mr. Mask?"

"Yes; Sebastian Mask--do you know him?"

"I know of him. He is my father's lawyer also, and so became Mr. Strode's man of business. Yes, it is just as well Garrit should see him. When your father arrived in London he probably went to see Mask, to talk over business. We might learn something in that quarter."

"Learn what?" asked Eva bluntly.

Allen did not answer at once. "Eva," he said after a pause, "do you remember I told you that my father said Mr. Strode might not arrive. Well, I asked him why he said so, and he declared that from what he knew of your father, Mr. Strode was a man likely to have many enemies. It struck me that this crime may be the work of one of these enemies. Now Mask, knowing all your father's business, may also know about those who wished him ill."

"It may be so," said Eva reflectively; "my father," from what Mrs. Merry says, "was a most quarrelsome man, and would stop at nothing to make money. He doubtless made enemies in Africa as your father suggests, but why should an enemy follow him to England to kill him? It would have been easier to shoot him in Africa."

Allen shrugged his shoulders. "It's all theory on our parts," he said. "We don't know yet if Mr. Strode had any virulent enemies, so we cannot say if he was shot out of malice."

"As the contents of his pockets were not touched, Allen, it looks as though malice might have led to the crime."

"True enough." Allen rose wearily to go, and Eva saw that he limped. "Oh," she cried with true womanly feeling, springing forward to help him, "I forgot about your sprain; is it very painful?"

"Oh no, not at all," said Allen, wincing; "help me to the door, Eva, and I'll get into the chaise. It must be here by this time. We must go round by the back."

In spite of her sorrow, Eva smiled. "Yes, Mrs. Merry won't allow the front door to be opened until my father's corpse passes through. I never thought she was so superstitious."

"The realization of your dream is enough to make us all superstitious," said Allen as they passed through the kitchen. "Oh, by the way, Eva, my mother wants to know if you will stop with her till the funeral is over?"

"No, Allen, thanking your mother all the same. My place is here. Mrs. Palmer asked me also."

Mrs. Palmer was a gay, bright young widow who lived at the other end of the village, and whom Mrs. Merry detested, for some unknown reason. The sound of the name brought her into the conversation, as she was just outside, when the couple arrived at the kitchen door.

"Mrs. Palmer indeed," cried Mrs. Merry, wiping her red eyes; "the idea of her asking Miss Eva to stop with her. Why, her father was a chemist, and her late husband made his money out of milk and eggs!"

"She is very kind to ask me, Nanny, all the same."

"She's no lady," said Mrs. Merry, pursing up her lips, "and ain't the kind for you to mix with, Miss Eva."

"My mother wishes Miss Strode to come to us," said Allen.

"Well, sir," said the old nurse, "I don't say as what it wouldn't be good for my dear young lady: that is," added Mrs. Merry with emphasis, "if she keeps with your ma."

"My father won't trouble her if that's what you mean," said the young man drily, for Mrs. Merry made no secret of her dislike for Mr. Hill.

"People have their likings and no likings," said the old dame, "but if your ma will take Miss Eva till we bury him," she jerked her head in the direction of the death chamber, "it would be happier for her than sticking in the house along with her pa and me. If Cain was stopping I'd say different, but he's going after his circus, and two women and a corpse as ain't lived well, isn't lively, whatever you may say, Mr. Allen."

"I intend to stop here," said Eva sharply, "so there's no need for you to say anything more, Nanny. Ah, here's Cain. Help Mr. Hill, Cain."

The dark-eyed youth doffed his cap and came forward with alacrity to aid Allen. "Jacobs is at the gate with the pony, miss," he said, "but I hope our horses won't run over him."

"What do you mean?" asked Allen, limping round the corner.

"The circus is coming, on its way to Shanton. I told Mr. Stag--he owns it, Miss Eva--that murder had been committed, so the circus band won't play when the horses pass."

"Oh," said Eva stopping short, for already she saw a crowd of people on the road. "I'd better remain within."

"Yes, do, Eva," said Allen. "Cain will help me to the chaise. I'll come and see you again; and Eva," he detained her, "ask Inspector Garrit to see me. I want to know what can be done towards discovering the truth."

While Allen whispered thus, a procession of golden cars and cream-colored horses was passing down the road amongst a sparse gathering of village folk. These had come to look at the house in which the body of the murdered man lay, although they knew Misery Castle as well as they knew their own noses. But the cottage had acquired a new and terrible significance in their eyes. Now another sensation was provided in the passing of Stag's Circus on its way to Shanton fifteen miles further on. What between the tragedy and the circus the villagers quite lost their heads. At present, however, they looked at the cages of animals, at the band in a high red chariot, and at many performers prancing on trained steeds. With the music of the band it would have been even more exciting, but Stag, with extraordinary good taste, forbore to play martial melodies while passing through the village. Cain had not told him about the cottage, so the equestrians were unaware that Misery Castle contained the remains of the man whose death had caused such excitement in Westhaven.

Just as Eva turned to go in, and thus avoid the gaze of the curious, she heard a deep voice--a contralto voice--calling for Cain. On turning her head, she saw a handsome dark woman mounted on a fine white horse. "It's Miss Lorry," said Cain, leaving Allen's arm and running to the gate, with his face shining.

The young man, still weak in his ankle, lurched, so sudden had been Cain's departure, and Eva, with a cry of anger, ran forward to stop him from falling. "Cain, how could you!" cried Eva; "hold up, Allen."

"Go back and help the gentleman," said the dark woman, fixing her bold eyes on the girl's white face with a look of pity. "Miss Strode!"

Eva turned indignantly--for Cain by this time was helping Allen, and she was returning to the house--to see why the woman dare address her. Miss Lorry was reining in her rearing, prancing horse, and showing off her fine figure and splendid equestrian management. She was dressed plainly in a dark blue riding-habit, and wore a tall silk hat. With these, and white collar and cuffs and neat gloves, she looked very well turned out. By this time the procession had passed on towards the village, and the people, drawn by the superior attraction of the circus, streamed after it. Only a few hung about, and directed curious eyes towards the cottage and towards Eva, who paused near the fence in response to Miss Lorry's cry. Allen, who was now in the chaise, and had gathered up the reins, also waited to hear what this audacious woman had to say to Eva.

"Come here, please," said Miss Lorry, with a fine high color in her cheeks. "I'm not going to bite you. You are Miss Strode, aren't you?--else that lad," she pointed to Cain, "must have lied. He said you lived in his mother's cottage and----"

"I am Miss Strode," said Eva sharply. "What is it? I don't know you."

Miss Lorry laughed in an artificial manner. "Few people can say that," she said; "Bell Lorry is known everywhere as the Queen of the Arena. No, Miss Strode, you don't know me; but I know you and of you. Your cousin Lord Saltars----"

"Oh!" cried Eva, turning red, and walked up towards the house.

"Come back," cried Miss Lorry, "I want to whisper--it's about the death," she added in a lower tone. But Eva was out of hearing, and round the corner walking very fast, with her haughty head in the air.

Miss Lorry, who had not a good temper, ground her fine white teeth. "I've a good mind to hold my tongue," she said.

"What is it about the murder?" asked Allen quickly; "I am engaged to marry Miss Strode."

"Oh, are you? Then tell her to be careful of the wooden hand!"

VII - THE INQUEST

THERE WAS great excitement when the inquest was held on the remains of Mr. Strode. Although he belonged to the old family of the neighborhood, and should have lived in the manor as the lord of the village, he had been absent from Wargrove for so long, that few people were well acquainted with him. Some ancient villagers remembered him as a gay, sky-larking young man, when with Mr. Hill the two had played pranks during vacation. Then came the death of the old squire and the sale of the manor by his son. At times Strode had come to Wargrove with his wife, and at Misery Castle Eva had been born. But he usually stopped only a short time, as the slow life of the country wearied his restless spirit. But always, when he came to his old haunts, he went to look at the home of his race. Everyone knew that it was his desire to be Strode of Wargrove again, in fact as well as in name.

Many people remembered him when he came to Wargrove for the last time, to place his wife and daughter under the roof of Mrs. Merry. Strode had always been stiff and cold in manner, but, being of the old stock, this behavior was esteemed right, as no lord of the soil should be too familiar, the wiseacres thought. "A proud, haughty gentleman," said some, "but then he's a right to be proud. Ain't the Strodes been here since the Conquest? 'Tis a wonder he took up with that Mr. Hill, whose father was but a stockbroker."

So it will be guessed that Strode's return to his native place to meet with a violent death at unknown hands, created much excitement. The jury surveyed the body in Misery Castle, and then went to the one inn of the village to hear the evidence. A few people were in the coffee-room where the proceedings took place, but Inspector Garrit gave orders that the crowd should be kept out. The street therefore was filled with people talking of Strode and of his terrible end. One old man, who had seen eighty summers, gave it as his opinion, that it was no wonder Mr. Strode had died so.

"And what do you mean by that?" asked Wasp, who, full of importance, was making things unpleasant with over-zeal.

The ancient pulled his cap to the majesty of the law. "Whoy," said he, chewing a straw, "Muster Robert--by which I means Muster Strode--was a powerful angery gent surely. He gied I a clip on th' 'ead when I was old enough to be his father, though to be sure 'twas in his colleging days. Ah, I mind them two well!"

"What two?" asked Wasp, on the alert to pick up evidence.

"Muster Strode as was, an' Muster Hill as is. They be very hoity-toity in them days, not as 'twasn't right fur Muster Robert, he being lard an' master of the village. But Muster Hill"--the ancient spat out the straw to show his contempt--"Lard, he be nothin'!"

"He's very rich, Granfer."

"What's money to blood? Muster Strode shouldn't ha' taken him up, and given he upsettin' notions. He an' Giles Merry, as run away from his wife, and Muster Strode, ah--them did make things lively-like."

"I don't see what this has to do with the death," said Wasp snappishly.

"Never you mind," said Granfer, valiant through over-much beer. "I knows what I knows. Muster Robert--'twas a word an' a blow with him, and when he clips me on the 'ead, I ses, 'Sir, 'tis a red end as you'll come to,' and my words have come true. He've bin shot."

"And who shot him?" asked the blacksmith.

"One of 'em as he clipped on the 'ead same as he did me," said Granfer.

Wasp dismissed this piece of gossip with contempt, and entered the coffee-room to watch proceedings. The little policeman was very anxious to bring the murderer to justice, in the hopes that he would be rewarded for his zeal by a post at Westhaven. Hitherto he had found nothing likely to lead to any discovery, and Inspector Garrit had not been communicative. So, standing stiffly at the lower end of the room, Wasp listened with all his red ears to the evidence, to see what he could gain therefrom likely to set him on the track. A chance like this was not to be wasted, and Wasp's family was very large, with individual appetites to correspond.

Eva was present, with Allen on one side of her, and Mrs. Palmer on the other. Behind sat Mrs. Merry, sniffing because Mrs. Palmer was offering Eva her smelling-bottle. The widow was blonde and lively, well dressed, and of a most cheerful disposition. Her father certainly had been a chemist, but he had left her money. Her husband undoubtedly had been an egg and butter merchant, but he also had left her well off. Mrs. Palmer had been born and brought up in Shanton, and her late husband's shop had been in Westhaven. Therefore she lived at neither place now that she was free and rich, but fixed her abode at Wargrove, midway between the two towns. She went out a good deal, and spent her money freely. But she never could get amongst the county families as was her ambition. Perhaps her liking for Eva Strode was connected with the fact that the girl was of aristocratic birth. With the Lord of the Manor--as he should have been--for a father, and an Earl's daughter for a mother, Eva was as well-born as anyone in the county. But apart from her birth, Mrs. Palmer kindly and genial, really liked the girl for her own sake. And Eva also was fond of the merry, pretty widow, although Mrs. Merry quite disapproved of the friendship.

Inspector Garrit was present, and beside him sat a lean, yellow-faced man, who looked like a lawyer and was one. He had presented himself at the cottage that very morning as Mr. Mask, the solicitor of the deceased, and had been brought down by Garrit to give evidence as to the movements of Mr. Strode in town, since his arrival from Africa. Eva had asked him about her future, but he declined to say anything until the verdict of the jury was given. When this matter was settled, and when Strode was laid in the family vault beside his neglected wife, Mask said that he would call at Misery Castle and explain.

The case was opened by Garrit, who detailed the facts and what evidence he had gathered to support them. "The deceased gentleman," said Garrit, who was stout and short of breath, "came to Southampton from South Africa at the beginning of August, a little over a week ago. He had been in South Africa for five years. After stopping two days at Southampton at the Ship Inn, the deceased had come to London and had taken up his quarters in the Guelph Hotel, Jermyn Street. He went to the theatres, paid visits to his tailors for a new outfit, and called also on his lawyer, Mr. Mask, who would give evidence. On Wednesday last, the deceased wired from London that he would be down at eight o'clock on Thursday evening. The wire was sent to Miss Strode, and was taken from the hotel by the porter who sent it, from the St. James's telegraph office."

"Why are you so precise about this telegram?" asked the coroner.

"I shall explain later, sir," panted Garrit, wiping his face, for it was hot in the coffee room. "Well then, gentlemen of the jury, the deceased changed his mind, as I learned from inquiries at the hotel. He came down on Wednesday evening instead of Thursday, and arrived at the Westhaven station at six-thirty."

"That was the train he intended to come by on Thursday?" asked a juryman.

"Certainly. He changed the day but not the train."

"Didn't he send another wire to Miss Strode notifying his change of plan?"

"No. He sent no wire saying he would be down on Wednesday. Perhaps he desired to give Miss Strode a pleasant surprise. At all events, Miss Strode did not expect him till Thursday night at eight. She will give evidence to that effect. Well, gentlemen of the jury, the deceased arrived at Westhaven by the six-thirty train on Wednesday, consequent on his change of plan. He left the greater part of his luggage at the Guelph Hotel, and came only with a small bag, from which it would seem that he intended to stop only for the night. As the bag was easily carried, Mr. Strode decided to walk over----"

"But if he arrived by the six-thirty he would not get to the cottage at eight," said a juryman.

"No. I can't say why he walked--it's ten miles. A quick walker could do the distance in two hours, but Mr. Strode not being so young as he was, was not a quick walker. At all events, he walked. A porter who offered to take his bag, and was snubbed, was the last person who saw him."

"Didn't any one see him on the road to Wargrove?"

"I can't say. As yet I have found no one who saw him. Besides, Mr. Strode did not keep to the road all the time. He walked along it for some distance and then struck across Chilvers Common, to go to the Red Deeps. Whether he intended to go there," added the Inspector, wiping his face again, "I can't say. But he was found there dead on Thursday night by three men, Arnold, Jacobs, and Wake. These found a card in the pocket giving the name of the deceased, and one of them, Jacobs, then recognized the body as that of Mr. Strode whom he had seen five years previous. The men took the body to the cottage and then went home."

"Why didn't they inform the police?" asked the coroner.

Garrit stole a glance at Wasp and suppressed a smile. "They will tell you that themselves, sir," he said; "however, Mrs. Merry found the policeman Jackson on his rounds, late at night, and he went to tell Mr. Wasp, a most zealous officer. I came over next morning. The doctor had examined the body, and will now give his evidence."

After this witness retired, Dr. Grace appeared, and deposed that he had been called in to examine the body of the deceased. The unfortunate gentleman had been shot through the heart, and must have been killed instantaneously. There was also a flesh wound on the upper part of the right arm; here the doctor produced a bullet: "This I extracted from the body, gentlemen, but the other bullet cannot be found. It must have merely ripped the flesh of the arm, and then have buried itself in the trees."

"This bullet caused the death?" asked the coroner.

"Certainly. It passed through the heart. I expect the assassin fired twice, and missing his victim at the first shot fired again with a surer aim. From the nature of the wound in the arm, gentlemen," added Grace, "I am inclined to think that the deceased had his back to the assassin. The first bullet--the lost one, mind--skimmed along the flesh of the arm. The pain would make the deceased turn sharply to face the assassin, whereupon the second shot was fired and passed through the heart. I think, from the condition of the body, that the murder was committed at nine o'clock on Wednesday night. Mr. Strode may have gone to the Red Deeps to meet the assassin and thus have----"

"This isn't evidence," interrupted the coroner abruptly; "you can sit down, Dr. Grace."

This the doctor did, rather annoyed, for he was fond of hearing himself chatter. The three laborers, Arnold, Wake, and Jacobs, followed, and stated that they went to the Red Deeps to get a drink from the spring. It was about half-past ten when they found the body. It was lying near the spring, face downwards. They took it up and from a card learned it was that of Mr. Strode. Then they took it to the cottage and went home.

"Why didn't you inform the police?" a juryman asked Jacobs.

The big man scratched his head and looked sheepish. "Well, you see, sir, policeman Wasp's a sharp one, he is, and like as not he'd have thought we'd killed the gent. We all three thought as we'd wait till we could see some other gentleman like yourself."

There was a smile at this, and Wasp grew redder than he was. "A trifle too much zeal on the part of policeman Wasp," said the coroner drily, "but you should have given notice. You carried the body home between you, I suppose?"

"Yes. There was Arnold, myself, and Wake--then there was the boy," added the witness with hesitation.

"Boy?" questioned the coroner sharply, "what boy?"

Jacobs scratched his head again. "I dunno, sir. A boy joined us on the edge of the common near Wargrove, and, boy-like, when he saw we'd a corpse he follered. When we dropped the body at the door of Misery Castle"--the name of Mrs. Merry's abode provoked a smile--"the boy said as he'd knock. He knocked five times."

"Why five times?" questioned a juryman, while Eva started.

"I can't say, sir. But knock five times he did, and then ran away."

"What kind of a boy was he?"

"Just an ordinary boy, sir," grunted the witness, save that he seemed sharp. "He'd a white face and a lot of red hair----"

"Lor!" cried Mrs. Merry, interrupting the proceedings, "it's Butsey."

"Do you know the boy?" asked the coroner. "Come and give your evidence, Mrs. Merry."

The old woman, much excited, kissed the book. "Know the boy?" she said in her doleful voice. "Lord bless you, Mr. Shakerley, that being your name, sir, I don't know the boy from a partridge. But on Friday morning he came to me, and told me as Cain--my boy, gentlemen, and a wicked boy at that--would come and see me Saturday. As Cain was in the house, gentlemen, leastways as I'd sent him for a glove for the wooden hand of the corpse, the boy--Butsey, he said his name was--told a lie, which don't astonish me, seeing what boys are. I think he was a London boy, being sharp and ragged. But he just told the lie, and before I could clout his head for falsehoods, he skipped away."

"Have you seen him since?"

"No, I ain't," said Mrs. Merry, "and when I do I'll clout him, I will."

"Does your son know him?"

"That he don't. For I asked Cain why he told the boy to speak such a falsehood seeing there was no need. But Cain said he'd told no one to say as he was coming, and that he intended to see me Friday and not Saturday, as that lying boy spoke."

Here Inspector Garrit rose, and begged that Miss Strode might be called, as she could tell something, bearing on the boy. Eva looked somewhat astonished, as she had not seen Butsey. However, she was sworn and duly gave her evidence.

"My father came home from South Africa over a week ago in the Dunoon Castle. He wrote to me from Southampton saying he would be down. He then went to London and stopped there a week. He did not write from London, but sent two telegrams."

"Two telegrams," said the coroner. "One on Wednesday----"

"Yes," said the witness, "and one on Thursday night."

"But that's impossible. He was dead then, according to the medical evidence."

"That's what I cannot understand," said Eva, glancing at the Inspector. "I expected him on Thursday night at eight and had dinner ready for him. After waiting till after nine I was about to go to bed when a telegraph messenger arrived. He gave me the wire and said it arrived at four, and should have been sent then. It was from my father, saying he had postponed his departure till the next day, Friday. I thought it was all right and went to bed. About twelve I was awakened by the five knocks of my dream----"

"What do you mean by your dream, Miss Strode?"

Eva related her dream, which caused much excitement. "And the five knocks came. Four soft and one hard," she went on. "I sprang out of bed, and ran into the passage. Mrs. Merry met me with the news that my father had been brought home dead. Then I attended to the body, while Mrs. Merry told Jackson, who went to see Mr. Wasp."

"What did you do with the wire?" asked the coroner, looking perplexed at this strange contradictory evidence, as he well might.

"I gave it to Inspector Garrit."

"Here it is," said the inspector producing it; "when I was in town, I went to the office whence this had been sent. It was the St. James's Street office where the other wire had been sent from. I learnt from a smart operator that the telegram had been brought in by a ragged, red-haired boy----"

"Butsey," cried Mrs. Merry, folding her shawl tightly round her lean form.

"Yes," said Garrit, nodding, "apparently it is the same boy who joined the three men when they carried the body home, and knocked five times."

"And the same boy as told me a lie about Cain," cried Mrs. Merry; "what do you make of it all, gentlemen?"

Mrs. Merry was rebuked, but the jury and coroner looked puzzled. They could make nothing of it. Inquiry showed that Butsey had vanished from the neighborhood. Wasp deposed to having seen the lad. "Ragged and white-faced and red-haired he was," said Wasp, "with a wicked eye----"

"Wicked eyes," corrected the coroner.

"Eye," snapped Wasp respectfully, "he'd only one eye, but 'twas bright and wicked enough to be two. I asked him--on the Westhaven road--what he was doing there, as we didn't like vagrants. He said he'd come from London to Westhaven with a Sunday school treat. I gave him a talking to, and he ran away in the direction of Westhaven. Oh, sir," added Wasp, obviously annoyed, "if I'd only known about the knocking, and the lying to Mrs. Merry, and the telegram, I'd have taken him in charge."

"Well, you couldn't help it, knowing no reason why the lad should be detained," said the coroner; "but search for him, Wasp."

"At Westhaven? I will, sir. And I'll see about the Sunday school too. He'd be known to the teachers."

Mrs. Merry snorted. "That's another lie. I don't believe the brat has anything to do with Sunday schools, begging your pardon, Mr. Shakerley. He's a liar, and I don't believe his name's Butsey at all."

"Well, well," said the coroner impatiently, "let us get on with the inquest. What further evidence have you, inspector?"

"I have to speak," said Mr. Mask rising and looking more yellow and prim than ever as he took the oath. "I am Mr. Strode's legal adviser. He came to see me two or three times while he was in town. He stated that he was going down to Wargrove."

"On what day did he say?"

"On no particular day. He said he would be going down some time, but he was in no hurry."

"Didn't he tell you he was going down on Thursday?"

"No. He never named the day."

"Had he any idea of meeting with a violent death?"

"If he had, he certainly would not have come," said Mask grimly; "my late client had a very good idea of looking after his own skin. But he certainly hinted that he was in danger."

"Explain yourself."

"He said that if he couldn't come himself to see me again he would send his wooden hand."

The coroner looked puzzled. "What do you mean?"

"Mr. Strode," said Mask primly, "talked to me about some money he wished to place in my keeping. I was to give it back to him personally, or when he sent the wooden hand. I understood from what he hinted that there was a chance he might get into trouble. But he explained nothing. He always spoke little and to the point."

"And have you got this money?"

"No. Mr. Strode didn't leave it with me."

"Then why did he remark about his wooden hand?"

"I expect he intended to leave the money with me when he returned from Wargrove. So it would seem that he did not expect anything to happen to him on his visit to his native place. If he had expected a tragedy, he would have left the money; and the wooden hand would have been the token for me to give it."

"To whom, sir?"

"To the person who brought the wooden hand."

"And has it been brought?"

"No. But I understand from Inspector Garrit that the hand has been stolen."

"Dear me--dear me." Mr. Shakerley rubbed his bald head irritably. "This case is most perplexing. Who stole the hand?"

Mr. Hill came forward at this point and related how he had gone into the death chamber to find the hand gone. Eva detailed how she had seen the hand still attached to the arm at dawn, and Mrs. Merry deposed that she saw the hand with the body at nine o'clock. These witnesses were exhaustively examined, but nothing further could be learned. Mr. Strode had been shot through the heart, and the wooden hand had been stolen. But who had shot him, or who had stolen the hand, could not be discovered.

The coroner did his best to bring out further evidence: but neither Wasp nor Garrit could supply any more witnesses. The further the case was gone into, the more mysterious did it seem. The money of the deceased was untouched, so robbery could not have been the motive for the commission of the crime. Finally, after a vain endeavor to penetrate the mystery, the jury brought in a verdict of "Willful murder against some person or persons unknown."

VIII - A NEW LIFE

NOTHING NEW was discovered after the inquest, although all inquiries were made. Butsey had vanished. He was traced to Westhaven after his interview with Wasp, and from that place had taken the train to London. But after landing at Liverpool Street Station, he disappeared into the world of humanity, and not even the efforts of the London police could bring him to light. No weapon had been found near the Red Deeps spring, nor could any footmarks be discerned likely to lead to a detection of the assassin. Mr. Strode had been shot by some unknown person, and it seemed as though the affair would have to be relegated to the list of mysterious crimes. Perhaps the absence of a reward had something to do with the inactivity displayed by Garrit and Wasp.

But how could a reward be offered when Eva had no money? After the funeral, and when the dead man had been bestowed in the Strode vault under St. Peter's Church, the lawyer called to see the girl. He told her coldly, and without displaying any sympathy, that her father had left no money in his hands, and that he could do nothing for her. Eva, having been brought up in idleness, was alarmed at the prospect before her. She did not know what to do.

"I must earn my bread in some way," she said to Mrs. Merry a week later, when consulting about ways and means. "I can't be a burden on you, Nanny."

"Deary," said the old woman, taking the girl's hand within her withered claws, "you ain't no burden, whatever you may say. You stay along with your old nurse, who loves you, an' who has fifty pound a year, to say nothing of the castle and the land."

"But, Nanny, I can't stay on here forever."

"And you won't, with that beauty," said Mrs. Merry sturdily, "bless you, deary, Mr. Allen will marry you straight off if you'll only say the word; I saw him in the village this very day, his foot being nearly well. To be sure he was with his jellyfish of a pa; but I took it kind of him that he stopped and spoke to me. He wants to marry you out of hand, Miss Eva."

"I know," said the girl flushing; "I never doubted Allen's love. He has asked me several times since the funeral to become his wife. But my poor father----"

"Poor father!" echoed Mrs. Merry in tones of contempt; "well, as he was your pa after all, there ain't nothing to be said, whatever you may think, Miss Eva. But he was a bad lot."

"Mrs. Merry, he's dead," said Eva rebukingly. The old woman rubbed her hands and tucked them under her apron. "I know that," said she with bright eyes, "and put 'longside that suffering saint your dear ma: but their souls won't be together whatever you may say, deary. Well, I'll say no more. Bad he was, and a bad end he come to. I don't weep for him," added Mrs. Merry viciously; "no more nor I'd weep for Giles if he was laid out, and a nasty corpse he'd make."

Eva shuddered. "Don't speak like that."

"Well then, deary, I won't, me not being wishful to make your young blood run cold. But as to what you'll do, I'll just tell you what I've thought of, lying awake. There's the empty room across the passage waiting for a lodger; then the cow's milk can be sold, and there's garden stuff by the bushel for sale. I might let out the meadow as a grazing ground, too," said Mrs. Merry, rubbing her nose thoughtfully, "but that the cow's as greedy a cow as I ever set eyes on, an' I've had to do with 'em all my born days, Miss Eva. All this, rent free, my dear, and fifty pounds in cash. You'll be as happy as a queen living here, singing like a bee. And then when the year's mourning is over--not as he deserves it--you'll marry Mr. Allen and all will be gay."

"Dear Nanny," said the girl, throwing her arms round the old woman's neck, "how good you are. But, indeed I can't."

"Then you must marry Mr. Allen straight away."

"I can't do that either. I must earn my bread."

"What," screeched Mrs. Merry, "and you a born lady! Never; that saint would turn in her grave--and I wonder she don't, seeing she's laid 'longside him as tortured her when alive. There's your titles, of course, Lord Ipsen and his son."

"I wouldn't take a penny from them," said Eva coloring. "They never took any notice of me when my father was alive, and----"

"He didn't get on well with 'em," cried Mrs. Merry; "and who did he get on with, I ask you, deary? There's Lady Ipsen--she would have made much of you, but for him."

"I don't like Lady Ipsen, Nanny. She called here, if you remember, when my mother was alive. I'm not going to be patronized by her."

"Ah, Miss Eva," said the old dame admiringly, "it's a fine, bright, hardy spirit of your own as you've got. Lady Ipsen is as old as I am, and makes herself up young with paint and them things. But she has a heart. When she learned of your poverty----"

Eva sprang to her feet. "No! no! no!" she cried vehemently, "never mention her to me again. I would not go to my mother's family for bread if I was starving. What I eat, I'll earn."

"Tell Mr. Allen so," said Mrs. Merry, peering out of the window; "here he comes. His foot 'ull get worse, if he walk so fast," she added, with her usual pessimism.

Allen did not wait to enter in by the door, but paused at the open window before which Eva was standing. He looked ill and white and worried, but his foot was better, though even now, he had to use a stick, and walked slowly. "You should not have come out today," said Eva, shaking her finger at him.

"As Mrs. Mountain would not go to Mr. Mahomet," said Allen, trying to smile, "Mr. Mahomet had to come to Mrs. Mountain. Wait till I come in, Eva," and he disappeared.

The girl busied herself in arranging an arm-chair with cushions, and made her lover sit down when he was in the room. "There! you're more comfortable." She sat down beside him. "I'll get you a cup of tea."

"Don't bother," murmured Allen, closing his eyes.

"It's no bother. In any case tea will have to be brought in. Mrs. Palmer is coming to see me soon. She wants to talk to me."

"What about?"

"I can't say; but she asked me particularly to be at home today. We can have our talk first, though. Do smoke, Allen."

"No. I don't feel inclined to smoke."

"Will you have some fruit?"

"No, thank you," he said, so listlessly that Eva looked at him in alarm. She noted how thin his face was, and how he had lost his color.

"You do look ill, Allen."

He smiled faintly. "The foot has pulled me down."

"Are you sure it's only the foot?" she inquired, puzzled.

"What else should it be?" asked Allen quietly; "you see I'm so used to being in the open air, that a few days within doors, soon takes my color away. But my foot is nearly well. I'll soon be myself again. But, Eva," he took her hand, "do you know why I come."

"Yes," she said looking away, "to ask me again to be your wife."

"You have guessed it the first time," replied Allen, trying to be jocular; "this is the third time of asking. Come, Eva," he added coaxingly, "have you considered what I said?"

"You want me to marry you at once," she murmured.

"Next week, if possible. Then I can take you with me to South America, and we can start a new life, far away from these old vexations. Come, Eva. Near the mine, where I and Parkins are working, there's a sleepy old Spanish town where I can buy the most delightful house. The climate is glorious, and we would be so happy. You'll soon pick up the language."

"But why do you want me to leave England, Allen?"

Hill turned away his head as he answered. "I haven't enough money to keep you here in a proper position," he said quietly. "My father allows me nothing, and will allow me nothing. I have to earn my own bread, Eva, and to do so, have to live for the time being in South America. I used to think it exile, but with you by my side, dearest, it will be paradise. I want to marry you: my mother is eager to welcome you as her daughter, and----"

"And your father," said Eva, seeing he halted. Allen made a gesture of indifference. "My father doesn't care one way or the other, darling. You should know my father by this time. He is wrapped up in himself. Egotism is a disease with him."

Eva twisted her hands together and frowned. "Allen, I really can't marry you," she said decisively; "think how my father was murdered!"

"What has that to do with it?" demanded Allen almost fiercely.

"Dear, how you frighten me. There's no need to scowl in that way. You have a temper, Allen, I can see."

"It shall never be shown to you," he said fondly. "Come, Eva."

But she still shook her head. "Allen, I had small cause to love my father, as you know. Still, he has been foully murdered: I have made up my mind to find out who killed him before I marry."

Allen rose in spite of his weak ankle and flung away her hand. "Oh, Eva," he said roughly, "is that all you care for me? My happiness is to be settled in this vague way----"

"Vague way----?"

"Certainly!" cried Hill excitedly; "you may never learn who killed your father. There's not a scrap of evidence to show who shot him."

"I may find Butsey," said Eva, looking obstinate.

"You'll never find him; and even if you do, how do we know that he can tell?"

"I am certain that he can tell much," said Miss Strode determinedly. "Think, Allen. He sent the telegram probably by order of my father's enemy. He came suddenly on those men at midnight when they were carrying the body. What was a child like that doing out so late, if he wasn't put up to mischief by some other person? And he knocked as happened in my dream, remember," she said, sinking her voice; "and then he came here with a lying message on the very day my father's wooden hand was stolen."

"Do you think he stole it?"

"Yes, I do; though why he should behave so I can't say. But I am quite sure that Butsey is acting on behalf of some other person--probably the man who killed my father."

Allen shrugged his shoulders frowningly. "Perhaps Butsey killed Mr. Strode himself," he said; "he has all the precocity of a criminal."

"We might even learn that," replied Eva, annoyed by Allen's tone; "but I am quite bent on searching for this boy and of learning who killed my father and why he was killed."

"How will you set about it?" asked Allen sullenly.

"I don't know. I have no money and no influence, and I am only a girl. But I'll learn the truth somehow."

Hill walked up and down the little room with a slight limp, though his foot was much better and gave him no pain. He was annoyed that Eva should be so bent on avenging the murder of her father, for he quite agreed with Mrs. Merry that the man was not worth it. But he knew that Eva had a mulish vein in her nature, and from the look on her face and from the hard tones of her voice, he was sure she would not be easily turned from her design. For a few minutes he thought in silence, Eva watching him intently. Then he turned suddenly: "Eva, my dear," he said, holding out his hands, "since you are so bent upon learning the truth leave it in my hands. I'll be better able to see about the matter than you. And if I find out who killed your father----"

"I'll marry you at once!" she cried, and threw herself into his arms.

"I hope so," said Allen in a choked voice. "I'll do my best, Eva; no man can do more. But if I fail, you must marry me. Here, I'll make a bargain with you. If I can't find the assassin within a year, will you give over this idea and become my wife?"

"Yes," said Eva frankly; "but I am certain that the man will be found through that boy Butsey."

"He has to be found first," said Allen with a sigh, "and that is no easy task. Well, Eva, I'll settle my affairs and start on this search."

"Your affairs!" said Eva in a tone of surprise.

"Ah," said the young man smiling, "you have seen me idle for so long that you think I have nothing to do. But I have to get back soon to Bolivia. My friend Parkins and I are working an old silver mine for a Spanish Don. But we discovered another and richer mine shown to me by an Indian. I believe it was worked hundreds of years ago by the Inca kings. Parkins and I can buy it, but we have not the money. I came home to see if my father would help me. But I might have spared myself the trouble: he refused at once. Since then I have been trying all these months to find a capitalist, but as yet I have not been successful. But I'll get him soon, and then Parkins and I will buy the mine, and make our fortunes. I wish you'd give up this wild goose chase after your father's murderer, and let us go to Bolivia."

"No," said Eva, "I must learn the truth. I would never be happy if I died without knowing who killed my father, and why he was killed."

"Well, then, I'll do my best. I have written to Parkins asking him to give me another six months to find a capitalist, and I shall have to take rooms in London. While there I'll look at the same time for Butsey, and perhaps may learn the truth. But if I don't----"

"I'll marry you, if you don't find the assassin in a year," said Eva embracing him. "Ah, Allen, don't look so angry. I don't want you to search all your life: but one year--twelve months----"

"Then it's a bargain," said Allen kissing her: "and, by the way, I shall have the assistance of Parkins's brother."

"Who is he?" asked Eva; "I don't want everyone to----"

"Oh, that's all right. Parkins tells me his brother is shrewd and clever. I may as well have his assistance. Besides, I got a letter from Horace Parkins--that's the brother, for my man is called Mark--and he is in town now. He has just come from South Africa, so he may know of your father's doings there."

"Oh," Eva looked excited, "and he may be able to say who killed him!"

Allen shrugged his shoulders. "I don't say that. Your father may have had enemies in England as well as in Africa. But we'll see. I have never met Horace Parkins, but if he's as good a fellow as his brother Mark, my chum and partner, he'll do all he can to help me."

"I am sure you will succeed, Allen," cried Eva joyfully; "look how things are fitting in. Mr. Parkins, coming from Africa, is just the person to know about my father."

Young Hill said nothing. He fancied that Horace Parkins might know more about Mr. Strode than Eva would like to hear, for if the man was so great a scamp in England, he certainly would not settle down to a respectable life in the wilds. However he said nothing on this point, but merely reiterated his promise to find out who murdered Robert Strode, and then drew Eva down beside him. "What about yourself?" he asked anxiously.

"I don't know. Mrs. Merry wants me to stop here."

"I should think that is the best thing to do."

"But I can't," replied Eva, shaking her head; "Mrs. Merry is poor. I can't live on her."

"I admire your spirit, Eva, but I don't think Mrs. Merry would think you were doing her anything but honor."

"All the more reason I should not take advantage of her kindness."

Allen laughed. "You argue well," he said indulgently. "But see here, dearest. My mother is fond of you, and knows your position. She wants you to come to her."

"Oh, Allen, if she were alone I would love to. I am very devoted to your mother. But your father----"

"He won't mind."

"But I do," said Eva, her color rising. "I don't like to say so to you, Allen, but I must."

"Say what?"

"That I don't like your father very much."

235

"That means you don't like him at all," said the son coolly. "Dear me, Eva, what unpleasant parents you and I have. Your father and mine--neither very popular. But you won't come?"

"I can't, Allen."

"You know my father is your dead father's dearest friend."

"All the same I can't come."

"What will you do, then?" asked Allen vexed.

"Go out as a governess."

"No; you must not do that. Why not----"

Before Allen could propose anything the door opened and Mrs. Merry, with a sour face, ushered in Mrs. Palmer. The widow looked prettier and brighter than ever, though rather commonplace. With a disdainful sniff Mrs. Merry banged the door.

"Eva, dear," said Mrs. Palmer. "Mr. Hill, how are you? I've come on business."

"Business?" said Eva surprised.

"Yes. Pardon my being so abrupt, but if I don't ask you now I'll lose courage. I want you to come and be my companion."

IX - THE MYSTERIOUS PARCEL

SO HERE was a way opened by Providence in an unexpected direction. Mrs. Palmer, with a high color and rather a nervous look, stood waiting for Eva's reply. The girl looked at her lover, but Allen, very wisely, said nothing. He thought that this was a matter which Eva should settle for herself. But he was secretly amused at the abrupt way in which the little widow had spoken. It seemed as though she was asking a favor instead of conferring one. Miss Strode was the first of the three to recover, and then she did not reply immediately. She first wanted to know why Mrs. Palmer had made so generous an offer.

"Do sit down," she said, pushing forward a chair, "and then we can talk the matter over. I need not tell you that I am very thankful for your kind offer."

"Oh, my dear;" Mrs. Palmer sank into the chair and fanned herself with a lace handkerchief, "if you accept it, it is I who shall be thankful. I do hate living by myself, and I've never been able to find a companion I liked. But you, dear Eva, have always been a pet of mine. I have known you for four years, and I always did think you the very dearest of girls. If you will only come we shall be so happy."

"But what makes you think that I want to be any one's companion?"

Mrs. Palmer colored and laughed nervously. She was very pretty, but with her pink and white complexion and flaxen hair and pale blue eyes she looked like a wax doll. Anyone could see at a glance that she was perfectly honest. So shallow a nature was incapable of plotting, or of acting in a double fashion. Yet Eva wondered all the same that the widow should have made her so abrupt a proposal. So far as she knew, no one was aware that she was in want of money, and it seemed strange if providential that Mrs. Palmer should come in the very nick of time to help her in this way.

"Well, my dear," she said at length and looking at her primrose-hued gloves, "it was Lord Saltars who led me to make the offer."

"My cousin." Eva frowned and Allen looked up. "Do you know him?"

"Oh yes. Didn't I mention that I did?"

"No. I was not aware that you had ever met."

"We did in town about a year ago. I met him only once when I was at Mr. Mask's to dinner. Since then I have not seen him until the other day, and perhaps that was why I said nothing. I remember you told me he was your cousin, Eva, but I quite forgot to say that I knew him."

"Do you know Mr. Mask?" asked Hill.

"Of course I do. You know I quarreled with my old lawyer about the money left by Palmer. He was most disagreeable, so I resolved to change for a nicer man. I spoke to your father about it, and he kindly gave me the address of his own lawyer. I went up and settled things most satisfactorily. Of course Mr. Mask is a fearful old mummy," prattled on Mrs. Palmer in her airy fashion, "but he is agreeable over legal matters, and understands business. Palmer's affairs were rather complicated, you know, so I placed them all in Mr. Mask's hands. He has been my lawyer ever since, and I have every reason to be pleased."

"And you met my cousin there?" said Eva doubtfully.

"Lord Saltars? Yes. I was dining with Mr. Mask and his wife in their Bloomsbury Square house, a doleful old place. Lord Saltars came in to see Mr. Mask on business after dinner, so Mr. Mask asked him in to drink coffee. I was there, and so we met."

"Did he mention my name?" asked Miss Strode stiffly.

"Oh dear, no. He was unaware that I lived in the same village as you did. We talked about general things. But he mentioned it to me the other night at the circus, when I went to see the performance at Shanton."

"Did you go there?"

"Yes, my dear, I did," said Mrs. Palmer laughing. "I'm sure this place is dull enough. Any amusement pleases me. I didn't know at the time that your father was dead, Eva, or I should not have gone--not that I knew Mr. Strode, but still, you are my friend, and I should have come to comfort you. But you know I'm at the other end of the village, and the news had not time to get to me before I started for Shanton to luncheon with some friends. I remained with them for the night, and we went to the circus. Lord Saltars sat next to me, and we remembered that we had met before. In the course of conversation I mentioned that I lived at Wargrove, and he asked if I knew you. I said that I did."

"How did Lord Saltars know of the murder?" asked Allen hastily.

"I believe he learned it from one of the performers called Miss----"

"Miss Lorry," said Eva coloring--"I remember. Cain told her, and she had the audacity to speak to me."

Allen said nothing, remembering the message Miss Lorry had delivered relative to the wooden hand. He had not spoken of it to Eva hitherto, and thought wisely that this was not the time to reveal his knowledge. He preferred to listen to Mrs. Palmer, who as yet had not shown how she came to know that Eva needed the offer of a situation.

"So Miss Lorry spoke to you?" said Mrs. Palmer with great curiosity; "such a bold woman, though handsome enough. Lord Saltars seems to think a lot of her. Indeed I heard a rumor that he was about to marry her. My friends told me. But people will gossip," added Mrs. Palmer apologetically.

"Lord Saltars and his doings do not interest me," said Eva coldly. "We have only met once, and I don't like him. He is too fast for me. I could never enjoy the company of a man like that. I think as he was related by marriage to my father, he might have called to see me about the matter, and offered his assistance."

"We can do without that," cried Allen quickly.

"Lord Saltars doesn't know that we can," replied Eva sharply; "however, I understand how you met him, Mrs. Palmer, and how he came to know about the murder through Miss Lorry, who heard of it from Cain. But what has all this to do with your asking me to be your companion?"

Mrs. Palmer colored again and seemed embarrassed. "My dear," she said seriously, "I shall have to tell you about Mr. Mask first, that you may know all. After the inquest he called to see me----"

"But he came here," put in Eva.

"Quite so, and told you that your father had left no money."

"How do you know that?"

"Mr. Mask told me," said the widow simply, and laid her hand on Eva's hand; "don't be angry, my dear. Mr. Mask came to me and told me you were poor. He asked me if I would help you in what way I could, as he said he knew I was rich and kind hearted. I am the first, but I really don't know if I'm the last."

"I think you are," said Miss Strode softly. "I never gave Mr. Mask leave to talk of my business, and I don't know why he should have done so, as he did not seem to care what became of me."

"Oh, but I think he intended to help you if he could, and came to tell me of your dilemma for that purpose, Eva."

"Apparently he wished to play the part of a good Samaritan at your expense, Mrs. Palmer," said Eva drily; "however, I understand how you came to know that I needed assistance, but Lord Saltars----"

"Ah!" cried the widow vivaciously, "that is what puzzles me. Lord Saltars seems to think you are rich."

"Rich?" echoed Allen, while Eva also looked surprised.

"Yes. He said you would no doubt inherit your father's money. I answered--pardon me, Eva--that Mr. Strode was not rich, for I heard so in another quarter."

Eva looked at Allen, and Allen at Eva. Both guessed that the quarter indicated was Mr. Hill, who had a long tongue and small discretion. Mrs. Palmer, however, never noticed the exchange of glances, and prattled on. "Lord Saltars insisted that your father had brought home a fortune from Africa."

"How did he know that?" asked Allen quickly.

"I don't know, he didn't say. I of course began to believe him, for when I hinted doubts, Lord Saltars said that if I offered to help you, I would learn that you were poor. I really thought you were rich, Eva, till Mr. Mask came to me, or I should have come before to make you this offer. But Mr. Mask undeceived me. I told him what Lord Saltars had said, but Mr. Mask replied that his lordship was quite wrong--that Mr. Strode had left no money, and that you would not be able to live. I therefore came to ask you to be my companion at the salary of one hundred a year. I don't know how I dare offer it, my dear," said the good-hearted widow; "and if I hadn't spoken just when I came in, I should not have had the courage. But now I have made the offer, what do you say?"

"I think it is very good and kind of you--"

"And bold. Yes, I can see it in your eyes--very speaking eyes they are--that you think I am bold in meddling with your private affairs. But if you really think so, please forgive me and I'll go away. You may be sure I'll hold my tongue about the matter. If everyone thinks you are rich--as they do--it is not for me to contradict them."

Eva laughed rather sadly. "I really don't know why people think I am rich," she said in a low voice; "my father has always been poor through speculation. What his money affairs were when he came home I don't know. He said nothing to me, and no papers were found at the hotel or in his pockets, likely to throw light on them. He never told Mr. Mask he was rich----"

"I thought at the inquest Mr. Mask said something about money being left in his charge, Eva?" said Allen.

Miss Strode nodded. "My father mentioned that later he might give Mr. Mask some money to hold for him, and that he would come again himself to get it. If not, he would send his wooden hand as a sign that the money should be handed over to anyone who brought it."

"Humph," said Allen pulling his moustache, "it seems to me that the hand has been stolen for that purpose."

"If so, it will be taken to Mr. Mask, and then we will learn who stole it. But of course Mr. Mask will not be able to give any money, as my father--so he said--never left any with him."

"This is all most interesting and mysterious," said Mrs. Palmer. "Oh dear me, I wonder who killed your poor father? Don't look anxious, Eva; what you and Mr. Hill say, will never be repeated by me. All I come for is to make this offer, and if you think me rude or interfering I can only apologize and withdraw."

Eva caught the widow by the hand. "I think you are very kind," she said cordially, "and I thankfully accept your offer."

"Oh, you dear girl!" and Mrs. Palmer embraced her.

"Have you quite decided to do that, Eva?" asked Allen.

"Quite," she answered firmly. "Mrs. Palmer likes me----"

"I quite adore you, Eva, dear!" cried the widow.

"And I am fond of her."

"I know you are, dear, though you never would call me Constance."

"Later I may call you Constance," said Eva, smiling at the simple way in which Mrs. Palmer talked. "So you may look upon it as settled. I shall come to be your companion whenever you like."

"Come at once, dear."

"No, I must wait here a few days to reconcile my old nurse to my departure."

"Mrs. Merry? Oh, Eva, I am afraid she will hate me for this. She doesn't like me as it is. I don't know why," added Mrs. Palmer dolefully; "I am always polite to the lower orders."

"Mrs. Merry is an odd woman," said Eva rising, "but her heart is in the right place."

"Odd people's hearts always are," said the widow. "Wait here and talk to Allen," said Eva going to the door. "I'll see about tea."

But the fact is Eva wanted to talk to Mrs. Merry, anxious to get over a disagreeable interview, as she knew there would be strenuous opposition. To her surprise, however, Mrs. Merry was in favor of the scheme, and announced her decision when Eva came to the kitchen.

"Don't tell me about it, Miss Eva," she said, "for I had my ear to the keyhole all the time."

"Oh, Nanny!"

"And why do you say that?" asked the old woman bristling; "if I ain't got the right to look after you who has? I never cared for that Mrs. Palmer, as is common of commonest, so I listened to hear what she'd come about."

"Then you know all. What do you say?"

"Go, of course."

"But, Nanny, I thought----"

"I know you did, deary," said Mrs. Merry penitently. "I'm always calling folk names by reason of my having bin put on in life. And Mrs. Palmer is common--there's no denying--her father being a chemist and her late husband eggs and butter. But she's got a kind heart, though I don't see what right that Mask thing had to talk to her of your being poor when I've got this roof and fifty pound. Nasty creature, he wouldn't help you. But Mrs. Palmer is kind, Miss Eva, so I say, take what she offers. You'll be near me, and perhaps you'll be able to teach her manners, though you'll never make a silk purse out of a swine's ear."

Eva was surprised by this surrender, and moreover saw that Mrs. Merry's eyes were red. In her hands she held a letter, and Eva remembered that the post had called an hour before. "Have you had bad news, Nanny?" she asked anxiously.

"I got a letter from Giles," said Mrs. Merry dully; "he writes from Whitechapel, saying he's down on his luck and may come home. That's why I want you to go to Mrs. Palmer, deary. I can't keep you here with a nasty, swearing jail-bird in the house. Oh dear me," cried Mrs. Merry, bursting into tears, "and I thought Giles was dead, whatever you may say, drat him!"

"But, Nanny, you needn't have him in the house if he treats you badly. This place is your own."

"I must have him," said the old woman helplessly, "else he'll break the winders and disgrace me before every one. You don't know what an awful man he is when roused. He'd murder me if I crossed him. But to think he should turn up after all these years, when I thought him as dead and buried and being punished for his wickedness."

"Nanny," said Eva kissing the poor wrinkled face, "I'll speak to you later about this. Meanwhile I'll tell Mrs. Palmer that I accept her offer."

"Yes do, deary. It goes to my heart for you to leave. But 'tis better so, and you'll have your pride satisfied. And it will be Christian work," added Mrs. Merry, "to dress that widder properly. Rainbows ain't in it, with the colors she puts on."

Eva could not help smiling at this view of the matter, and withdrew to excuse herself offering tea to Mrs. Palmer. Nanny was not in a state to make tea, and Eva wished to return and learn more, also to comfort her. She therefore again told Mrs. Palmer that she accepted the offer and would come to her next week. Then taking leave of Allen, Eva went back to the kitchen. Mrs. Palmer and her companion walked down the road.

"I hope you think I've acted rightly, Mr. Hill," said the widow.

"I think you are most kind," said Allen, "and I hope you will make Eva happy."

"I'll do my best. She shall be a sister to me. But I think," said Mrs. Palmer archly, "that someone else may make her happier."

"That is not to be my fate at present," said Allen a little sadly. "Good-bye, Mrs. Palmer. I'll come and see you and Eva before I go to town."

"You'll always be welcome, Mr. Hill, and I can play the part of gooseberry." So they parted laughing.

Allen, thinking of this turn in Eva's affairs which had given her a home and a kind woman to look after her, walked towards the common to get a breath of fresh air before returning to "The Arabian Nights." Also he wished to think over his plans regarding meeting Horace Parkins and searching for Butsey, on whom seemed to hang the whole matter of the discovery of Strode's assassin. At the end of the road the young man was stopped by a tall, fresh-colored girl neatly dressed, who dropped a curtsey.

"Well, Jane, and how are you?" asked Allen kindly, recognizing the girl as Wasp's eldest daughter.

"I'm quite well, and, please, I was to give you this," said Jane.

Allen took a brown paper parcel and looked at it with surprise. It was directed to 'Lawrence Hill.' "My father," said Allen. "Why don't you take it to the house?"

"I saw you coming, sir, and I thought I'd give it to you. I've just walked from Westhaven, and father will be expecting me home. I won't have time to take the parcel to 'The Arabian Nights.'"

"Where did this come from?" asked Allen, tucking the parcel under his arm.

"I got it from Cain, sir, at Colchester."

"Have you been there?" asked Hill, noting the girl's blush. He knew that Cain and Jane Wasp admired one another, though the policeman was not at all in favor of Cain, whom he regarded, and with some right to do so, as a vagabond.

"Yes, sir. Mother sent me over with a message to a friend of hers. I walked to Westhaven and took the train to Colchester. Stag's Circus is there, and I met Cain. He brought that parcel and asked me to take it to Mr. Hill."

"But why should Cain send parcels to my father?" asked Allen.

"I don't know, sir. But I must get home, or father will be angry."

When the girl marched off--which she did in a military way suggestive of her father's training--Allen proceeded homeward. The parcel was very light and he could not conjecture what was inside it. He noted that the address had been written by someone to whom writing was a pain, for the calligraphy sprawled and wavered lamentably. Cain had been to a board school and could write very well, so apparently it was not his writing. Allen wondered who could be corresponding with his father, but as the matter was really none of his business, he took the parcel home. At the gate of "The Arabian Nights" he met his father.

Mr. Hill was as gay and as airy as ever, and wore his usual brown velvet coat and white trousers. Also he had on the large straw hat, and a rose bloomed in his buttonhole. He saluted his son in an offhand manner. "I've been walking, Allen," he said lightly, "to get inspiration for a poem on the fall of Jerusalem."

"I think some Italian poet has written on that subject, sir."

"But not as it should be written, Allen. However, I can't waste time now in enlightening your ignorance. What have you here?"

"A parcel for you," and Allen gave it.

"For me, really." Mr. Hill was like a child with a new toy, and sat down on the grass by the gate to open it. The removal of the brown paper revealed a cardboard box. Hill lifted the lid, and there were two dry sticks tied in the form of a cross with a piece of grass. But Allen looked at this only for a moment. His father had turned white, and after a moment quietly fainted away. The young man looked down with a haggard face. "Am I right after all?" he asked himself.

X - MRS. HILL EXPLAINS

AN HOUR later Allen was conversing with his mother. Mr. Hill, carried into the house by Allen, had been revived; but he steadfastly refused to speak as to the cause of his fainting; and put it down to the heat of the weather and to his having taken too long a walk. These excuses were so feeble that the son could not help his lip curling at their manifest untruth. Hill saw this and told Allen he would lie down for an hour or so. "When I rise I may tell you something," he said feebly.

"I think we may as well understand one another," said Allen coldly.

"Bring in here those things which came in the parcel," said Hill.

"Only one thing came," replied his son--"a rough cross----"

"Yes--yes--I know. Bring it in--paper and box and all. Where did you get it?"

Allen explained how Jane Wasp received it from Cain at Colchester, and Mr. Hill listened attentively. "I understand now," he said at length. "Put the things in my study. I'll see you later--say in two hours."

The young man, wondering what it all meant, departed and left his father to take--on the face of it--a much needed sleep. He went outside and picked up the cross, the box, and the paper, which still remained on the grassy bank near the gate. These he brought into the study, and examined them. But nothing was revealed to his intelligence. The box was an ordinary cardboard one; he did not recognize the ill-formed writing, and the cross was simply two sticks tied together by a wisp of dry grass. Why the contents of the box should have terrified his father Allen could not say. And that the sight of the symbol did terrify him, he was well assured, since Mr. Hill was not a man given to fainting. The box came from someone who knew Mr. Hill well, as the name Lawrence was on it, and this was his father's second name rarely used. Mr. Hill usually called himself Harold, and suppressed the Lawrence. But Allen had seen the middle name inscribed in an old book, which had been given by Strode to Hill in their college days. This coincidence made Allen wonder if the sending of the cross and the use of the rarely used name had anything to do with the murder.

While he thus thought, with his face growing darker and darker, the door opened and Mrs. Hill entered. She had been working in her own room, and knew nothing of the affair. But some instinct made her aware that Allen was in the house, and she never failed to be with him when he was at home. Indeed, she was hardly able to bear him out of her sight, and seized every opportunity to be in his presence. With this love it was strange that Mrs. Hill should be content that Allen should remain in South America for so long, and pay only flying visits to the paternal roof.

"You are back, Allen," she said softly, and came forward to lay her hand on his wrinkled forehead. "My dear boy, why that frown? Has Eva been unkind?"

"Oh no," said Allen, taking his mother's hand and kissing it, "she will not marry me yet."

"Foolish girl. What does she intend to do--stop with Mrs. Merry, I suppose, which is a dull life for her? Far better if she came to me, even if she will not marry you at once."

"She has accepted the position of companion to Mrs. Palmer."

"Indeed," said Mrs. Hill, looking surprised; "I should have thought her pride would have prevented her placing herself under an obligation."

Allen shrugged his shoulders. "There is no obligation," he said; "Eva is to be paid a salary. Besides, she likes Mrs. Palmer, and so do I."

"She is not a lady," said Mrs. Hill, pursing up her lips.

"Nevertheless she has a kind heart, and will make Eva very happy. I think, mother, it is the best that can be done. Eva doesn't want to come here, and she will not marry me until the murderer of her father is discovered."

"Why won't she come to me?" asked Mrs. Hill sharply.

Allen looked down. "She doesn't like my father," he said.

"Very rude of her to tell you that. But I know my poor Harold is not popular."

"He is whimsical," said Allen, "and, somehow, Eva can't get on with him. She was not rude, mother, but simply stated a fact. She likes my father well enough to meet him occasionally, but she would not care to live with him. And if it comes to that," added Allen frowning, "no more should I. He is too eccentric for me, mother, and I should think for you, mother."

"I am fond of your father in my own way," said Mrs. Hill, looking down and speaking in a low voice, as though she made an effort to confess as much. "But does Eva expect to find out who murdered Mr. Strode?"

"Yes. She refuses to marry me until the assassin is found and punished. As she was bent on searching for the man herself, I offered to search for her."

Mrs. Hill frowned. "Why did you do that?" she asked sharply; "Strode is nothing to you, and you have to return to America. Far better find that capitalist you want, than waste your time in avenging the death of that man."

"You don't seem to like Mr. Strode, mother."

"I hate him," said the woman harshly and clenching her fist: "I have cause to hate him."

"Had my father cause also?" asked Allen pointedly.

She looked away. "I don't know," she answered gloomily. "Strode and your father were very intimate all their lives, till both married. Then we saw very little of him. He was not a good man--Strode, I mean, Allen. If my word has any weight with you, stop this search."

The young man rose and began to pace the library. "Mother, I must take up the search," he said in an agitated voice, "for my father's sake. No one but myself must search for the assassin."

"What do you mean by that?" questioned Mrs. Hill, sitting very upright and frowning darker than ever.

Allen replied by asking a question. "Who knows that my father is called Lawrence, mother?"

Mrs. Hill uttered an ejaculation of surprise and grew pale. "Who told you he was called so?"

"I found the name in an old book of Cowper's poems given by Mr. Strode to my father in their college days. It was presented to Harold Lawrence Hill."

"I remember the book," said Mrs. Hill, recovering her composure. "But what is odd about your father having two names? He certainly has dropped the Lawrence and calls himself simply, Harold Hill--but that is for the sake of convenience. Only those who knew him in his young days would know the name of Lawrence."

"Ah!" said Allen, thoughtfully turning over the brown paper, "then this was sent by someone who knew him in his young days."

Mrs. Hill looked at the brown paper covering, at the box, and at the roughly-formed cross. "What are these?" she asked carelessly.

"That is what I should like to know," said her son; "at least I should like to know why the sight of this cross made my father faint."

Mrs. Hill gasped, and laid her hand on her heart as though she felt a sudden pain. "Did he faint?" she asked--"did Lawrence faint?" The young man noticed the slip. Usually his mother called his father Mr. Hill or Harold, but never till this moment had he heard her call him Lawrence. Apparently the memory of old events was working in her breast. But she seemed genuinely perplexed as to the reason of Hill's behavior at the sight of the cross. "Where did he faint?"

"Outside the gate," said Allen quickly, and explained how he had received the parcel from Jane Wasp, and the circumstance of its delivery, ending with the query: "Why did he faint?"

"I can't say," said Mrs. Hill, pushing back the cross and box pettishly; "there is no reason so far as I know. We'll ask your father when he awakens."

"He said he would explain," said Allen sadly; "and between you and me, mother, we must have an explanation."

"Your father won't like the use of the word 'must,' Allen."

"I can't help that," said the young man doggedly, and went to the door of the library. He opened it, looked out, and then closed it again. His mother saw all this with surprise, and was still more surprised when Allen spoke again. "Do you know, mother, why I say I must undertake this investigation?"

"No," said Mrs. Hill calmly; "I don't know."

"It is because I wish to save my father's good name."

"Is it in danger?" asked the woman, turning pale again.

"It might be--if anyone knew he met Mr. Strode at the Red Deeps on the night of the murder."

Mrs. Hill leaped to her feet and clutched her son's arm. "Allen," she gasped, and the ashen color of her face alarmed him, "how dare you say that--it is not possible--it cannot--cannot--"

"It is possible," said Allen firmly. "Sit down, mother, and let me explain. I held my tongue as long as I could, but now my father and I must have an explanation. The fact of his fainting at the sight of this cross makes me suspicious, and the fact that Eva wants to investigate the case makes me afraid of what may come out."

"Has the cross anything to do with the affair?"

"Heaven, whose symbol it is, only knows," said the young man gloomily. Mother, "I am moving in the darkness, and I dread to come into the light. If I undertake this search I may be able to save my father."

"From what--from--from----"

Allen nodded and sank his voice. "It may even come to that. Listen, mother, I'll tell you what I know. On that night I went to the Red Deeps to prove the falsity of Eva's dream, I found it only too true."

"But you never got to the Red Deeps," said Mrs. Hill, looking steadily into her son's face, "you sprained your ankle."

"So I did, but that was after I knew the truth."

"What truth?"

"That Eva's dream was true; that her father was lying dead by the spring of the Red Deeps."

Mrs. Hill looked still more searchingly at him. "You saw that?"

"I did--in the twilight. I reached there before it grew very dark. I found the body, and, as in Eva's dream, I recognized it by the gloved right hand----"

"The wooden hand," moaned Mrs. Hill, rocking herself. "Oh, heavens!"

"Yes! The whiteness of the glove caught my eyes. From what Eva had told me, I had no need to guess who was the dead man. The wooden hand explained all. The corpse was that of Strode, shot through the heart."

"But there was a slight flesh wound on the arm, remember," said Mrs. Hill.

"I know, but I did not notice that at the time," said Allen quickly. "At first, mother, I intended to give the alarm, and I was hurrying back to Wargrove to tell Wasp and Jackson, when I caught sight of a revolver lying in the mud. I took it up--there was a name on the silver plate on the butt. It was----" Allen sank his voice still lower. "It was my own name."

"The revolver was yours?"

"Yes. I brought it with me from South America, and kept it in my portmanteau, since a weapon is not needed in England. But one day I took it out to shoot some birds and left it in this library. I never thought about it again, or I should have put it away. The next sight I got of it was in the Red Deeps, and I thought----"

"That your father took it to shoot Strode!" burst out Mrs. Hill. "You can't be certain of that--you can't be certain. No, no, Lawrence!" again she used the unaccustomed name. "Lawrence would never commit a murder--so good--so kind--no, no."

Allen looked surprised. He never expected his mother to stand up for his father in this way. Hill, so far as the son had seen, was not kind to any one, and he certainly was not good. Why Mrs. Hill, who seemed to have no particular affection for him, should defend him in this way puzzled the young man. She saw the effect her speech had produced and beckoned Allen to sit down. "You must know all," she said--"you must know how I came to marry your father; and then you will know why I speak as I do, Allen." She laid a trembling hand on his shoulder. "You never thought I was fond of your father?"

Allen looked embarrassed. "Well, no, mother. I thought you tolerated him. You have strength to rule the house and the whole county if you chose to exert it, but you let my father indulge in his whims and fancies, and allow him to speak to you, as he certainly should not do. Oftentimes I have been inclined to interfere when hearing how disrespectfully he speaks, but you have always either touched me, or have given me a look."

"I would let no one lay a finger on your father, Allen, no one--let alone his son. I don't love your father, I never did, but"--she drew herself up--"I respect him."

The young man looked aghast. "I don't see how anyone can respect him," he said. "Heaven only knows I should like to be proud of my father, but with his eccentricities----"

"They cover a good heart."

"Well, mother, you know best," said Allen soothingly. He did not think his father possessed a good heart by any manner of means. The young fellow was affectionate, but he was also keen sighted, and Mr. Hill had never commanded his respect in any way.

"I do know best," said Mrs. Hill in a strong tone, and looked quite commanding. "Allen, are you aware why I am so fond of Eva?"

"Because she is the most charming girl in the world," said the lover fondly. "Who could help being fond of Eva?"

"Women are not usually fond of one another to that extent," said Mrs. Hill drily; "and a mother does not always love the girl who is likely to take her son away. No, Allen, I don't love Eva so much for her own sake as because she is the daughter of Robert Strode."

"I thought you disliked him--you said he was not a good man."

"Neither he was, Allen. He was the worst of men--but I loved him all the same. I should have married him, but for a trouble that came. I have never told anyone what I am about to tell you, but you must know. I don't believe your father killed Strode, and you must do your best to keep him out of the investigation. With your father's sensitive nature he would go mad if he were accused of such a crime."

"But my revolver being found in----"

"That can be explained," said Mrs. Hill imperiously. "I shall ask Harold"--she went back to the old name being calmer. "I shall ask him myself to explain. He is innocent. He is whimsical and strange, but he would not kill a fly. He is too good-hearted."

Allen wondered more and more that his mother should be so blind. "I am waiting to hear," he said resignedly.

"You will not repeat what I say to Eva?"

"To no one, mother. Great heavens, do you think I would?"

"If you took after your father, poor, babbling soul, you would."

"Ah," Allen kissed her hand, "but I am your own son, and know how to hold my tongue. Come, mother, tell me all."

"Then don't interrupt till I end; then you can make your comments, Allen." She settled herself and began to speak slowly. "Both my parents died when I was a young girl, and like Eva Strode I was left without a penny. I was taken into the house of Lord Ipsen as a nursery governess----"

"What! Eva's mother----"

"I did not teach her, as she was my own age, but I taught her younger brother, who afterwards died. You promised not to interrupt, Allen. Well, I was comparatively happy there, but Lady Ipsen did not like me. We got on badly. There was a large house-party at the family seat in Buckinghamshire, and I was there with my charge. Amongst the guests were Mr. Strode and your father. They were both in love with Lady Jane Delham."

"What! my father also? I never knew----"

"You never shall know if you interrupt," said his mother imperiously; "wait and listen. I loved Mr. Strode, but as he was favoured by Lady Jane I saw there was no chance for me. Your father then had not come in for his money, and his father, ambitious and rich, was anxious that he should make an aristocratic match. That was why he asked Lady Jane to be his wife. She refused, as she loved Robert Strode. I felt very miserable, Allen, and as your father was miserable also, he used to console me. He was much appreciated for his talents in the house, and as he was a great friend of Mr. Strode's his lack of birth was overlooked. Not that I think Lord Ipsen would have allowed him to marry Lady Jane. But he never guessed that Harold lifted his eyes so high. Well, things were in this position when the necklace was lost--yes, the necklace belonging to Lady Ipsen, a family heirloom valued at ten thousand pounds. It was taken out of the safe." Mrs. Hill dropped her eyes and added in a low voice, "I was accused."

Allen could hardly believe his ears, and rose, filled with indignation: "Do you mean to say that any one dared to accuse you?"

"Lady Ipsen did. She never liked me, and made the accusation. She declared that she left the key of the safe in the school-room. As I was very poor, she insisted that I had taken it. As it happened I did go to London shortly after the robbery and before it was found out. Lady Ispen said that I went to pawn the necklace. I could not prove my innocence, but the Earl interfered and stood by me. He insisted that the charge was ridiculous, and made the detectives which Lady Ipsen had called in, drop the investigation. I was considered innocent by all save Lady Ipsen. The necklace was never found, and has not been to this day. I was discharged with hardly a penny in my pocket and certainly with no friend. In spite of people saying I was innocent I could not get another situation. I should have starved, Allen, and was starving in London when your father came like an angel of light and--married me."

"Married you? Did he love you?"

"No, he loved Lady Jane, but she married Mr. Strode. But your father was so angered at what he considered an unjust charge being made against me, that he risked his father's wrath and made me his wife."

"It was noble of him," said Allen, "but----"

"It was the act of a saint!" cried Mrs. Hill, rising. "His father cut him off with a shilling for what he did. I was penniless, deserted, alone. I would have died but for Lawrence. He came--I did not love him, nor he me, but I respect him for having saved a broken-hearted woman from a doom worse than death. Allen, Allen, can I ever repay your father for his noble act? Can you wonder that I tolerate his whims--that I let him do what he likes? He saved me--he surrendered all for me."

"He did act well," admitted Allen, puzzled to think that his whimsical, frivolous father should act so nobly, "but you made him happy, mother. There is something to be said on your side."

"Nothing! nothing!" cried Mrs. Hill with the martyr instinct of a noble woman; "he gave up all for me. His father relented after a time, and he inherited a fortune, but for a year we almost starved together. He married me when I was under a cloud. I can never repay him; never, never, I tell you, Allen," she said, facing him with clenched fists, "if I thought that he committed this crime, I would take the blame on myself rather than let him suffer. He saved me. Shall I not save him?"

"Was the person who stole the necklace ever discovered, mother?"

"No, the necklace vanished and has never been found to this day. I met Lady Jane Strode when she came here. She did not believe me to be guilty, and we were good friends. So you see, Allen, it is small wonder that I let your father do what he likes. Why should I cross the desires of a man who behaved so nobly? Sometimes I do interfere, as you know, for at times Harold needs guidance--but only rarely."

"Well, mother, I understand now, and can say nothing. But as to how the revolver came to the Red Deeps----"

"Your father shall explain," said Mrs. Hill, moving to the door; "come with me."

The two went to the room at the back of the house where Hill had lain down. It was one of the Greek apartments where the little man sometimes took his siesta. But the graceful couch upon which Allen had left him lying an hour previous was empty, and the window was open on to the Roman colonnade. There was no sign of Mr. Hill.

"He must have gone into the garden," said the wife, and stepped out.

But there was no sign of him there. The gardener was working in the distance, and Mrs. Hill asked him where his master was.

"Gone to London, ma'am," was the unexpected answer; "Jacobs drove him to the Westhaven Station."

Allen and his mother looked at one another with dread in their eyes. This sudden departure was ominous in the extreme.

XI - ALLEN AS A DETECTIVE

MR. HILL left no message behind him with the groom. Jacobs returned and said that his master had gone to London; he did not state when he would return. Allen and his mother were much perplexed by this disappearance. It looked very much like a flight from justice, but Mrs. Hill could not be persuaded to think ill of the man to whom she owed so much. Like many women she took too humble an attitude on account of the obligation she had incurred. Yet Mrs. Hill was not humble by nature.

"What will you do now, Allen?" she asked the next morning.

"I intend to learn why Cain sent that parcel to my father. If he can explain I may find out why my father is afraid."

"I don't think he is afraid," insisted Mrs. Hill, much troubled.

"It looks very like it," commented her son; "however, you had better tell the servants that father has gone to London on business. I expect he will come back. He can't stop away indefinitely."

"Of course he'll come back and explain everything. Allen, your father is whimsical--I always admitted that, but he has a heart of gold. All that is strange in his conduct he will explain on his return."

"Even why he took my revolver to the Red Deeps?" said Allen grimly.

"Whatever he took it for, it was for no ill purpose," said Mrs. Hill. "Perhaps he made an appointment to see Strode there. If so I don't wonder, he went armed, for Strode was quite the kind of man who would murder him."

"In that case Mr. Strode has fallen into his own trap. However, I'll see what I can do."

"Be careful, Allen. Your father's good name must not suffer."

"That is why I am undertaking the investigation," replied the young man, rising. "Well, mother, I am going to see Mrs. Merry and ask where Cain is to be found. The circus may have left Colchester."

"You might take the brown paper that was round the box," suggested Mrs. Hill. "Mrs. Merry may be able to say if the address is in her son's writing."

"I don't think it is--the hand is a most illiterate one. Cain knows how to write better. I have seen his letters to Eva."

"What!" cried Mrs. Hill, scandalized, "does she let a lad in that position write to her?"

"Cain is Eva's foster-brother, mother," said Allen drily, "and she is the only one who can manage him."

"He's a bad lot like his father was before him," muttered Mrs. Hill, and then went to explain to the servants that Mr. Hill would be absent for a few days.

Allen walked to Misery Castle, and arrived there just before midday. For some time he had been strolling on the common wondering how to conduct his campaign. He was new to the detective business and did not very well know how to proceed. At first he had been inclined to seek professional assistance; but on second thoughts he decided to take no one into his confidence for the present. He dreaded what he might learn concerning his father's connection with the crime, as he by no means shared his mother's good opinion of Mr. Hill. Allen and his father had never got on well together, as their natures were diametrically opposed to each other. Allen had the steady good sense of his mother, while the father was airy and light and exasperatingly frivolous. Had not Mrs. Hill thought herself bound, out of gratitude, to live with the man who had done so much for her, and because of her son Allen, she certainly would not have put up with such a trying husband for so many years. Allen was always impatient of his father's ways; and absence only confirmed him in the view he took of his evergreen sire. He could scarcely believe that the man was his father, and always felt relieved when out of his presence. However, he determined to do his best to get to the bottom of the matter. He could not believe that Mr. Hill had fired the fatal shot, but fancied the little man had some knowledge of who had done so. And whether he was an accessory before or after the fact was equally unpleasant.

On arriving at Mrs. Merry's abode he was greeted by that good lady with the news that Eva had gone to spend the day with Mrs. Palmer. "To get used to her, as you might say," said Mrs. Merry. "Oh, Mr. Allen, dear," she spoke with the tears streaming down her withered face, "oh, whatever shall I do without my deary?"

"You'll see her often," said Allen soothingly.

"It won't be the same," moaned Mrs. Merry. "It's like marrying a daughter, not that I've got one, thank heaven--it's never the same."

"Well--well--don't cry, there's a good soul. I have come to see you about Cain."

Mrs. Merry gave a screech. "He's in gaol! I see it in your eyes! Oh, well I knew he'd get there!"

"He hasn't got there yet," said the young man impatiently; "come into the drawing-room. I can explain."

"Is it murder or poaching or burglary?" asked Mrs. Merry, still bent on believing Cain was in trouble, "or horse-stealing, seeing he's in a circus?"

"It's none of the three," said Allen, sitting down and taking the brown paper wrapping out of his pocket. "Jane Wasp saw him in Colchester, and he's quite well."

"And what's she been calling on my son there, I'd like to know?" asked Mrs. Merry, bridling. "He shan't marry her, though he says he loves her, which I don't believe. To be united with that meddlesome Wasp policeman. No, Mr. Allen, never, whatever you may say."

"You can settle that yourself. All I wish to know is this," he spread out the paper. "Do you know whose writing this is?"

Mrs. Merry, rather surprised, bent over the paper, and began to spell out the address with one finger. "Lawrence Hill," she said, "ah, they used to call your father that in the old days. I never hear him called so now."

"Never mind. What of the writing?"

Mrs. Merry looked at it at a distance, held it close to her nose, and then tilted it sideways. All the time her face grew paler and paler. Then she took an envelope out of her pocket and glanced from the brown paper to the address. Suddenly she gave a cry, and threw her apron over her head. "Oh, Giles--Giles--whatever have you bin up to!"

"What do you mean?" asked Allen, feeling inclined to shake her.

"It's Giles's writing," sobbed Mrs. Merry, still invisible; "whatever you may say, it's his own writing, he never having been to school and writing pothooks and hangers awful." She tore the apron from her face and pointed, "Look at this Lawrence, and at this, my name on the envelope. He wrote, saying he's coming here to worry me, and I expect he's sent to your pa saying the same. They was thick in the old days, the wicked old days," said Mrs. Merry with emphasis, "I mean your pa and him as is dead and my brute of a Giles."

"So Giles Merry wrote this?" said Allen thoughtfully, looking at the brown paper writing. "I wonder if the cross is a sign between my father and him, which has called my father to London?"

"Have you seen Giles, sir?" asked Mrs. Merry dolefully, "if so, tell him I'll bolt and bar the house and have a gun ready. I won't be struck and bullied and badgered out of my own home."

"I haven't seen your husband," explained Allen, rising, "this parcel was sent to my father by your son through Jane Wasp." Mrs. Merry gave another cry. "He's got hold of Cain--oh, and Cain said he hadn't set eyes on him. He's ruined!" Mrs. Merry flopped into a chair. "My son's ruined--oh, and he was my pride! But that wicked father of his would make Heaven the other place, he would."

"I suppose Cain must have got the parcel from his father?" said Allen.

"He must have. It's in Giles's writing. What was in the parcel, sir?"

"A cross made of two sticks tied with a piece of grass. Do you know what that means?"

"No, I don't, but if it comes from Giles Merry, it means some wicked thing, you may be sure, Mr. Allen, whatever you may say."

"Well, my father was much upset when he got this parcel and he has gone to London."

"To see Giles?" asked Mrs. Merry.

"I don't know. The parcel came from Colchester."

"Then Giles is there, and with my poor boy," cried Mrs. Merry, trembling. "Oh, when will my cup of misery be full? I always expected this."

"Don't be foolish, Mrs. Merry. If your husband comes you can show him the door."

"He'd show me his boot," retorted Mrs. Merry. "I've a good mind to sell up, and clear out. If 'twasn't for Miss Eva, I would. And there, I've had to part from her on account of Giles. If he came and made the house, what he do make it, which is the pit of Tophet, a nice thing it would be for Miss Eva."

"I'll break his head if he worries Eva," said Allen grimly; "I've dealt before with that sort of ruffian. But I want you to tell me where Cain is to be heard of. I expect the circus has left Colchester by this time."

"Cain never writes to me, he being a bad boy," wailed Mrs. Merry, "an' now as his father's got hold of him he'll be worse nor ever. But you can see in the papers where the play-actors go, sir."

"To be sure," said Allen, "how stupid I am. Well, good-day, Mrs. Merry, and don't tell Miss Eva anything of this."

"Not if I was tortured into slices," said Mrs. Merry, walking to the door with Allen, "ah, it's a queer world. I hope I'll go to my long home soon, sir, and then I'll be where Merry will never come. You may be sure they won't let him in."

This view of the case appeared to afford Mrs. Merry much satisfaction, and she chuckled as Allen walked away. He went along the road wondering at the situation. His father was not a good husband to his mother--at least Allen did not think so. Giles was a brute to his wife, and the late Mr. Strode from all accounts had been a neglectful spouse. "And they were all three boon companions," said Allen to himself; "I wonder what I'll find out about the three? Perhaps Giles has a hand in the death of Strode. At all events the death has been caused by some trouble of the past. God forgive me for doubting my father, but I dread to think of what I may learn if I go on with the case. But for my mother's sake I must go on."

Allen now directed his steps to Wasp's abode, as he knew at this hour the little policeman would be at home. It struck Allen that it would be just as well to see the bullet which had pierced the heart of Mr. Strode. If it was one from his own revolver--and Allen knew the shape of its bullets well--there would be no doubt as to his father's guilt. But Allen fancied, that from the feeble nature of the wound on the arm, it was just the kind of shaky aim which would be taken by a timid man like his father. Perhaps (this was Allen's theory) the three companions of old met at the Red Deeps--Mr. Strode, Giles, and his father. Mr. Hill, in a fit of rage, might have fired the shot which ripped the arm, but Giles must have been the one who shot Strode through the heart. Of course Allen had no grounds to think in this way, and it all depended on the sight of the bullet in the possession of Wasp as to the truth of the theory. Allen intended to get Wasp out of the room on some pretext and then fit the bullet into his weapon. He had it in his pocket for the purpose. This was the only way in which he could think of solving the question as to his father's guilt or innocence.

Wasp was at home partaking of a substantial dinner. Some of the children sat round, and Mrs. Wasp, a grenadier of a woman, was at the head of the table. But three children sat out with weekly journals on their laps, and paper and pencil in hand. They all three looked worried. After greeting Allen, Wasp explained.

"There's a prize for guessing the names of European capitals," he said; "it's given in the Weekly Star., and I've set them to work to win the prize. They're working at it now, and don't get food till each gets at least two capitals. They must earn money somehow, sir."

"And they've been all the morning without getting one, sir," said Mrs. Wasp plaintively. Apparently her heart yearned over her three children, who looked very hungry. "Don't you think they might eat now in honor of the gentleman's visit?"

"Silence," cried Wasp, "sit down. No talking in the ranks. Wellington, Kitchener, and Boadicea"--these were the names of the unhappy children--"must do their duty. Named after generals, sir," added Wasp with pride.

"Was Boadicea a general?" asked Allen, sorry for the unfortunate trio, who were very eagerly searching for the capitals in a school atlas.

"A very good one for a woman, sir, as I'm informed by Marlborough, my eldest, sir, as is at a board school. Boadicea, if you don't know the capital of Bulgaria you get no dinner."

Boadicea whimpered, and Allen went over to the three, his kind heart aching for their hungry looks. "Sofia is the capital. Put it down."

"Right, sir," said Wasp in a military fashion, "put down Sofia."

"What capital are you trying to find, Wellington?" asked Allen.

"Spain, sir, and Kitchener is looking for Victoria."

"The Australian country, sir, not Her late Majesty," said Wasp smartly.

"Madrid is the capital of Spain, and Melbourne that of Victoria."

The children put these down hastily and simply leaped for the table.

"Silence," cried the policeman, horrified at this hurry; "say grace."

The three stood up and recited grace like a drill sergeant shouting the standing orders for the day. Shortly, their jaws were at work. Wasp surveyed the family grimly, saw they were orderly, and then turned to his visitor.

"Now, Mr. Allen, sir, I am at your disposal. Come into the parlor."

He led the way with a military step, and chuckles broke out amongst the family relieved of his presence. When in the small room and the door closed, Allen came artfully to the subject of his call. It would not do to let Wasp suspect his errand. Certainly the policeman had overcome his suspicion that Allen was concerned in the matter, but a pointed request for the bullet might reawaken them. Wasp was one of those hasty people who jump to conclusions, unsupported by facts.

"Wasp," said Allen, sitting down under a portrait of Lord Roberts, "Miss Strode and myself are engaged, as you know."

"Yes, sir." Wasp standing stiffly saluted. "I give you joy."

"Thank you. We have been talking over the death of her father, and she is anxious to learn who killed him."

"Natural enough," said the policeman, scratching his chin, "but it is not easy to do that, especially"--Wasp looked sly--"as there is no reward."

"Miss Strode is not in a position to offer a reward," replied Allen, "so, for her sake, I am undertaking the search. I may want your assistance, Wasp, and I am prepared to pay you for the same. I am not rich, but if ten pounds would be of any use----"

"If you'd a family of ten, sir, you'd know as it would," said Wasp, looking gratified. "I'm not a haggler, Mr. Allen, but with bread so dear, and my children being large eaters, I'm willing to give you information for twenty pounds."

"I can't afford that," said Allen decidedly.

"I can tell you something about Butsey," said Wasp eagerly.

"Ten pounds will pay you for your trouble," replied Allen, "and remember, Wasp, if you don't accept the offer and find the culprit on your own, there will be no money coming from the Government."

"There will be promotion, though, Mr. Allen," said Wasp, drawing himself up, "and that means a larger salary. Let us say fifteen."

"Very good, though you drive a hard bargain. When the murderer is laid by the heels I'll pay you fifteen pounds. No, Wasp," he added, seeing what the policeman was about to say, "I can't give you anything on account. Well, is it a bargain?"

"It must be, as you won't do otherwise," said Wasp ruefully. "What do you want to know?"

"Tell me about this boy."

"Butsey?" Wasp produced a large note-book. "I went to Westhaven to see if there was truth in that Sunday school business he told me about when I met him. Mr. Allen, there's no Sunday school; but there was a treat arranged for children from London."

"Something of the Fresh Air Fund business?"

"That's it, sir. This was a private business, from some folk as do kindnesses in Whitechapel. A lot of children came down on Wednesday----"

Allen interrupted. "That was the day Mr. Strode came down?"

"Yes, sir, and on that night he was shot at the Red Deeps. Well, sir, Butsey must have been with the ragged children as he looks like that style of urchin. But I can't be sure of this. The children slept at Westhaven and went back on Thursday night."

"And Butsey saw Mrs. Merry in the morning of Thursday?"

"He did, sir, and me later. Butsey I fancy didn't go back till Saturday. But I can't be sure of this."

"You don't seem to be sure of anything," said Allen tartly. "Well, I can't say your information is worth much, Wasp."

"Hold on, sir. I've got the address of the folk in Whitechapel who brought the children down. If you look them up, they may know something of Butsey."

"True enough. Give me the address."

Wasp consented, and wrote it out in a stiff military hand, while Allen went on artfully, "Was any weapon found at the Red Deeps?"

"No, sir," said Wasp, handing his visitor the address of the Whitechapel Mission, which Allen put in his pocket-book. "I wish the revolver had been found, then we'd see if the bullet fitted."

"Only one bullet was found."

"Only one, sir. Dr. Grace got it out of the body. It is the bullet which caused the death, and I got Inspector Garrit to leave it with me. Perhaps you'd like to see it, sir?"

"Oh, don't trouble," said Allen carelessly. "I can't say anything about it, Wasp."

"Being a gentleman as has travelled you might know something, Mr. Allen," said Wasp, and went to a large tin box, which was inscribed with his name and the number of his former regiment, in white letters. From this he took out a packet, and opening it, extracted a small twist of paper. Then he placed the bullet in Allen's hand.

"I should think it came from a Derringer," said Wasp.

Allen's heart leaped, for his revolver was not a Derringer. He turned the bullet in his hand carelessly. "It might," he said with a shrug. "Pity the other bullet wasn't found."

"The one as ripped the arm, sir? It's buried in some tree trunk, I guess, Mr. Allen. But it would be the same size as this. Both were fired from the same barrel. First shot missed, but the second did the business. Hold on, sir, I've got a drawing of the Red Deeps, and I'll show you where we found the corpse," and Wasp left the room.

Allen waited till the door was closed, then hastily took the revolver from his breast-pocket. He tried the bullet, but it proved to be much too large for the revolving barrel, and could not have been fired therefrom. "Thank heaven," said Allen, with a sigh of relief, "my father is innocent."

XII - LORD SALTARS

MRS. PALMER dwelt in a large and imposing house, some little distance from the village, and standing back a considerable way from the Shanton Road. It had a park of fifteen acres filled with trees, smooth lawns, a straight avenue, imposing iron gates, and a lodge, so that it was quite an impressive mansion. The building itself was square, of two stories, painted white, and had many windows with green shutters. It somewhat resembled an Italian villa, and needed sunshine to bring out its good points; but in wet weather it looked miserable and dreary. It was elevated on a kind of mound, and a stone terrace ran round the front and the side. At the back were large gardens and ranges of hot-houses. Everything was kept as neat as a new pin, for Mrs. Palmer had many servants. Being rich, she could afford to indulge her fancies, and made full use of her money.

"La, dear," said Mrs. Palmer, when Eva was settled with her as companion, "what's the use of five thousand a year if you don't make yourself comfortable? I was brought up in a shabby way, as poor dead pa was a small--very small--chemist at Shanton. Palmer had his shop in Westhaven and was also in a grubbing way of business till people took to coming to Westhaven. Then property rose in value, and Palmer made money. He used to call on pa and commiserate with him about the dull trade in Shanton, where people were never sick. He advised him to move to Westhaven, but pa, losing heart after the death of ma, would not budge. Then Palmer proposed to me, and though I was in love with Jimmy Eccles at the Bank, I thought I'd marry money. Oh, dear me," sighed Mrs. Palmer looking very pretty and placid, "so here I am a widow."

"A happy widow," said Eva, smiling.

"I don't deny that, dear. Though, to be sure, the death of poor pa, and of Palmer, were blows. I was fond of both. Jimmy Eccles wanted to marry me when Palmer went, but I sent him off with a flea in his ears. It was only my money he wanted. Now he's married a freckled-faced girl, whose pa is a draper."

"I suppose you will marry again, Mrs. Palmer?"

"I suppose I will, when I get the man to suit. But I do wish, Eva dear, you would call me Constance. I'm sure you might, after being three days in the house. Call me Constance, and I'll tell you something which will please you."

"What is it, Constance?"

"There's a dear. I shan't tell you yet--it's a surprise, and perhaps you may be angry with me. But someone is coming to dinner."

"Allen?" asked Eva, her face lighting up.

"No! He's in town. At least you told me so."

Eva nodded. "Yes; he went up to town last week, after seeing Wasp."

"About that horrid murder?"

"Certainly. Allen is trying to learn who killed my father."

"It's very good of him," said the widow, fanning herself vigorously, "and I'm sure I hope he'll find out. The man who shot Mr. Strode should be hanged, or we won't sleep in our beds safe. Why, Eva, you have no idea how I tremble here at nights. This is a lonely house, and these holiday trippers might bring down burglars amongst them."

"I don't think you need fear, Constance. There have been no burglars down here. Besides, you have a footman, and a coachman, and a gardener. With three men you are quite safe."

"I'm sure I hope so, dear. But one never knows. When do you expect Mr. Hill back?"

"In a few days. I don't know what he's doing. He refuses to tell me anything until he finds some definite clue. But I have his address, and can write to him when I want to."

"His father is in town also--so Mrs. Hill told me."

"Yes, Mr. Hill went up before Allen. I believe he has gone to some sale to buy ancient musical instruments."

"Dear me," said Mrs. Palmer, "what rubbish that man does spend his money on. What's the use of buying instruments you can't play on? I dare say he'll try to, though, for Mr. Hill is the queerest man I ever set eyes on."

"He is strange," said Eva gravely. She did not wish to tell Mrs. Palmer that she disliked the little man, for after all he was Allen's father, and there was no need to say anything. "But Mr. Hill is very clever."

"So they say. But he worries me. He's always got some new idea in his head. I think he changes a thousand times a day. Mrs. Merry doesn't like him, but then she likes no one, not even me."

"Poor nurse," said Eva sadly, "she has had an unhappy life."

"I don't think you have had a bright one, dear; but you shall have, if I can make it so. Are you sure you have everything you want?"

"Everything," said Eva affectionately; "you are more than kind, Mrs.----"

"Constance!" cried the pretty widow in a high key.

"Constance, of course. But tell me your surprise."

Mrs. Palmer began to fidget. "I don't know if you will be pleased, after all, Eva. But if you don't like to meet him say you have a headache, and I'll entertain him myself."

"Who is it?" asked Eva, surprised at this speech.

"Lord Saltars," said Mrs. Palmer in a very small voice, and not daring to look at her companion.

Miss Strode did not reply at once. She was ill-pleased that the man should come to the house, because she did not wish to meet him. Her mother's family had done nothing for her, and even when she lost her father, Saltars, although in the neighborhood, had not been kind enough to call. Eva met him once, and, as she had told Mrs. Palmer, did not like his free and easy manner. However, it was not her place to object to Saltars coming. This was not her house, and she was merely a paid companion. This being the case, she overcame her momentary resentment and resolved to make the best of the position. She did this the more especially as she knew that Mrs. Palmer had only been actuated in inviting Saltars by her worship of rank. "I shall be quite pleased to meet my cousin," said Eva.

"I hope you are not annoyed, Eva."

"I am not exactly pleased, but this is your house, and----"

"Oh, please--please don't speak like that," cried the widow, "you make me feel so cheap. And the fact is--I may as well confess it--Lord Saltars, knowing you were with me, for I told my Shanton friends and they told him, asked if I would invite him to dinner."

"To meet me, I suppose?"

"I fancy so. But why don't you like him, Eva He's a very nice man."

"Not the kind of man I care about," replied Eva, rising; "however, Mrs. Palmer, I'll meet him. It's time to dress now." She glanced at the clock. "At what time does he arrive?"

"At seven. He's at Shanton."

"Ah! Is the circus there again?"

"Yes. It is paying a return visit. But I know you're angry with me, dear--you call me Mrs. Palmer."

"Very well, then, Constance," said Eva, and kissing the pouting widow she escaped to her own room.

Mrs. Palmer was kind and generous, and made her position more pleasant than she expected. But Mrs. Palmer was also foolish in many ways, particularly in her worship of rank. Because Lord Saltars had a title she was willing to overlook his deficiencies, though he was neither intellectual nor amusing. Eva really liked Mrs. Palmer and felt indebted to her, but she wished the widow's good taste had led her to refuse Saltars permission to call. But there--as Mrs. Merry would say--Mrs. Palmer not being a gentlewoman had no inherent good taste. But for her kind heart she would have been intolerable. However, Eva hoped to improve her into something better, by gentle means, though Constance with her loud tastes and patent tuft-hunting was a difficult subject.

As she was in mourning for her father, Eva dressed in the same black gauze gown in which she had hoped to welcome him, but without any touch of color on this occasion. As she went down the stairs, she hoped that Mrs. Palmer would be in the room to welcome her noble visitor, so as to save the embarrassment of a tête-à-tête.. But Mrs. Palmer was one of those women who never know the value of time, and when Eva entered the drawing-room she found herself greeted by a short, square-built jovial-looking man of forty. Saltars was perfectly dressed and looked a gentleman, but his small grey eyes, his red, clean-shaven face and remarkably closely clipped hair did not, on the whole, make up a good-looking man. As soon as he saw Eva, he strolled forward calmly and eyed her critically.

"How are you, Miss Strode?--or shall I say Cousin Eva?"

"I think Miss Strode is sufficient," said Eva, seating herself. "I am sorry Mrs. Palmer is not down yet."

"By Jove, I'm not," said Saltars, taking possession of a near chair. "I want to have a talk with you."

"This is hardly the hour or the place."

"Come now, Miss Strode--if you will insist on being so stiff--you needn't be too hard on a chap. I know I should have called, and I quite intended to do so, but I had reasons----"

"I don't ask for your reasons, Lord Saltars."

The man clicked his tongue against the roof of his mouth. "We don't seem to get on," he said at length, "yet I wish to be friendly. See here, I want my mother to call and see you."

"If Lady Ipsen calls, I shall be pleased."

"In a society way, but you won't be heart-pleased."

"No," said Eva, very decidedly; "how can you expect me to? Your family has not treated me or my dead father well."

"Your father----" Saltars clicked again and seemed on the point of saying something uncomplimentary of the dead; but a gleam in his companion's eye made him change his mind. "I know you've been a bit neglected, and I'm very sorry it should be so," said he bluntly. "I assure you that it was always my wish you should be invited to stop with us in Buckinghamshire. And my father was in favor of it too."

"But Lady Ipsen wasn't," said Eva coolly; "don't trouble to apologize, Lord Saltars, I should not have gone in any case."

"No, by Jove, I can see that. You're as proud as a peacock--just like the portrait of Lady Barbara Delham who lived in Queen Anne's reign. And she was a Tartar."

Eva began to smile. Saltars was amusing. She saw that he was simply a thoughtless man, who lived for himself alone. He apparently wished to be friendly, so as Eva had no real grudge against him, she unbent.

"I don't think we need quarrel," she said.

"No, by Jove. But I shan't. Any quarrelling that is to be done must be on your side. There's enough in our family as it is. You should hear how my mother and the dowager Lady Ipsen fight: but then the dowager is a dreadful old cat," he finished candidly.

"I have never seen her."

"You wouldn't forget her if you did. She's beaked like a parrot, and talks like one. She and I don't hit it off. She's one of what they call the old school, whatever that means, and she thinks I'm a low person--like a groom. What do you think?"

Lord Saltars was not unlike a groom in some ways, but his good nature and candor amused Eva. "I am not a person to judge," she said, smiling.

"By Jove, you might have been, though," said he, fixing his small grey eyes on her; "supposing you became Lady Saltars?"

"There's not the slightest chance of that," said Eva coldly.

"There isn't now: but there might have been. And after all, why not now, if things are what your father said they were?"

Miss Strode drew herself up. She thought he was going too far. "I really don't know what you mean. I am engaged to be married."

"I know; to a fellow called Hill. Your father told me."

"Lord Saltars, did you meet my father after he came home?"

"Of course I did. He called to see me when he came to London, and corresponded with me long before that. I say, do you remember when I came to see you at Wargrove?"

"Yes. We did not get on well together."

"By Jove, no more we did! That was a pity, because I came to see what kind of a wife you'd make."

"You're very kind," said Eva indignantly, "but I'm not on the market to be examined like a horse."

"Haw--haw," laughed the other, slapping his knee, "that's the kind of thing the dowager would say. Don't get waxy, Eva--Miss Strode then, though I wish you'd call me Herbert and I'd call you Eva."

"I shall call you Lord Saltars."

"Saltars without the confounded lord," urged the man pertinaciously.

"No; go on. What were you saying? Yes, that you came to see what sort of a wife I'd make. Who told you to?"

"Your father."

"I don't believe it."

"It's true, though. Your father wanted you to marry me. He kept writing to me from South Africa to keep me up to the scratch, and said he was gathering a fortune for us both. When he came home he called on me and told me you had some folly in your head about this chap Hill, and----"

Eva rose indignantly, "Lord Saltars," she said calmly and distinctly, "I don't allow anyone to talk to me in this way. My engagement to Mr. Allen Hill is not a folly. And I don't see why my father should have talked to you about it."

"Because he wanted me to marry you," said Saltars, rising and following her to the fireplace.

Eva placed one slippered foot on the fender, and an elbow on the mantelpiece. She looked angry, but extremely pretty and well-bred. Saltars adopted the same attitude opposite her and looked more like a groom than ever. But the expression of his face was so good-natured that Eva could not feel as angry as she ought to have done.

"I should never have married you," she said, her color deepening. "I understand that you have other views."

Saltars grew red in his turn. "It's that boy Cain's been talking," he said; "I'll break his head."

"That is for you and Cain to decide," said Miss Strode indifferently, "but you can quite understand why I don't discuss these things."

Saltars kicked the fender sulkily. "I wish you would be more friendly, Eva," he said. "I need a friend, and so, by Jove, do you."

"How can I befriend you?"

"Well, I'm in love with Miss Lorry, and there will be a shine if I marry her. She's perfectly straight and----"

"I don't want to hear about her," said Eva angrily, "and if you were a gentlemen you wouldn't talk to me of that sort of person."

"She's a perfectly decent sort," said Saltars, angry in his turn, "I intend to make her my wife."

"That has nothing to do with me. And I wish you'd drop this conversation, Lord Saltars. It doesn't interest me. I am quite willing to be friends. Your manner is absurd, but you mean well. Come," and she held out her hand.

Saltars took it with a long breath. "Just like the dowager," said he, "just as nippy. I'd like to see you have a turn up with old Lady Ipsen."

"Well, then," said Eva, "now we are friends and you promise not to talk nonsense to me, tell me what you mean by my father making a fortune for me."

"For both of us, by Jove," said his lordship; "you were to be Lady Saltars, and then we were to have forty thousand pounds."

"But my father didn't leave me a penny," said Eva.

"That's what I wish to see you about," said Saltars earnestly. "I heard from Mrs. Palmer's friends that you were without money, and were her companion, so I wrote asking to come tonight. I want to be your friend and help you. You ought to have forty thousand pounds."

"How do you know that?"

"Because I saw your father twice before he was killed: within the last six weeks. He told me that he had brought home forty thousand pounds. Twice he told me that; but he did not say how it was invested. I expect his lawyer, Mask, can tell you. He's my lawyer too."

"Mr. Mask told me that I inherited no money."

"Yet your father saw him," said the perplexed Saltars.

"I know he did; but he said nothing about forty thousand pounds. I know that he told Mr. Mask he would place some money in his keeping, without mentioning the amount, but he never did so."

"Didn't you find the money in his portmanteau or box, or----?"

"We found nothing; nor did we find any papers mentioning that such a sum of money was in existence."

"Then he must have been robbed of it, when dead."

Eva shook her head. "Nothing was taken out of his pockets. His money, his jewelry, his watch--nothing was taken."

"Queer," said Saltars. "Did you find in his pockets a large blue pocket-book with his crest on it, stamped in gold?"

"No. When did you see that?"

"When he was talking to me. I was hard up. I don't mind saying," said Saltars frankly, "that I'm always hard up. As your father looked upon me as his intended son-in-law, he gave me a pony, and took the notes out of the blue pocket-book. He carried his money there."

"He would scarcely carry forty thousand pounds there."

"No; but he might have carried a letter of credit for that amount. Or at least he would have some memorandum of such a large sum. If any notes were stolen with the pocket-book, you can trace those by the numbers when the murderer presents them, and then the beast will be caught. But the forty thousand----"

"Stop--stop," said Eva, my head is in a whirl. "Are you sure?"

"Perfectly; I was to marry you, and then we were to get the money. And I may tell you that your father said, more would come to us when he died. Depend upon it, Eva, the murder was committed for the sake of that money."

"I wonder if my father meant diamonds?" said Eva.

Saltars started. "By Jove, I shouldn't wonder," he said eagerly, "he would bring diamonds from South Africa as the easiest way to carry such a large sum. Perhaps he had the diamonds in his pocket and they were stolen."

"I must tell Allen this."

"Who is Allen?--oh, young Hill! Don't deny it. I can see it in your face, it's the lucky man. And by Jove he is. I don't see why I should surrender you. Your father wished us to marry----"

"You go too fast, Lord Saltars. Remember Miss Lorry."

Saltars would have said something more but that the door opened and Mrs. Palmer, fastening her glove, sailed in. "Not a word of the diamonds to anyone," said Eva hurriedly.

"Not a word," said Saltars in a low voice, then raised it gaily--"How are you, Mrs. Palmer? My cousin and I have been talking"--he looked at Eva inquiringly, his invention failing him--"About--about----"

"Chinese metaphysics," said the feminine intellect.

XIII - THE OTHER WOMAN

LORD SALTARS spent a very enjoyable evening in the company of two pretty women. Eva had no chance of further conversation, as Mrs. Palmer made the most of her noble guest. She sang to him, she chattered to him, she did all that a lively woman could do to amuse him. In fact, it seemed to Eva as though the widow was trying to fascinate his lordship. Saltars, no fool, saw this also.

"But it won't do," chuckled the guest, as he drove back to Shanton in a smart dog-cart. "She's a pretty, saucy little woman that widow, and has money, too, though not enough for me to marry her on. Then Eva's worth a dozen of her, for looks and breeding. But then she's got no money, and I can't afford to marry poverty. Of course that forty thousand pounds might turn up, but on the other hand it might not. Finally, there's Bell Lorry! Ugh!" his lordship shivered. "I'm not so gone on her as I was; yet there's something infernally taking about Bell. She's a fine woman--with a temper. But she's got no money, and no birth, and precious little character, I should say. I'm not going to marry her, though she thinks so. But it will be the deuce's own job to get rid of her."

Saltars argued this way until he arrived at Shanton. Then he delivered the reins to his groom at the door of the Queen's Hotel, where he was stopping, and rang the bell. It was after twelve o'clock, and a fine starry night. But the chill in the air made Saltars pull up the collar of his overcoat and grumble. He was anxious for his bed and a glass of steaming grog. He got the last, but he was prevented from getting to the first by reason of a visitor. On ascending to his sitting-room he was met by a sleepy waiter.

"Your lordship," said this individual, "there's a lady waiting to see your lordship in your lordship's room."

"What, at this hour! It's not respectable."

"So the landlady told her, your lordship, but she said that she would do what she liked, and threatened to make a scene. Mrs. Cowper then thought it would be best to let her stay. She's waiting upstairs--the lady, I mean, your lordship--and is in a fine rage."

"It sounds like Bell," thought Saltars, and dismissed the old waiter, who went back to tell the night-porter he was going to bed. But the night-porter persuaded him to remain up for a time.

"There's going to be a row with that wench," said the night-porter; "she's a circus-rider--Miss Lorry by name, and has a temper of her own. I think she'll give it to his lordship hot. I wonder Mrs. Cowper don't object to such goings on."

So the two men, waiter and night-porter, remained below while Saltars, fully aware from the description that his visitor was Miss Lorry, entered the room prepared for a storm. The lady was seated in a chair near the table, and was drinking champagne which she had ordered at his expense. She was a fine-looking woman of mature age, and was expensively dressed in blue silk. Her arms and neck were bare, and she wore many jewels. As she was of the Junoesque order of woman, she looked remarkably well. Her cheeks were flushed, but whether from the champagne or from rage it was impossible to say. Probably a mixture of both gave her the high color she wore, when she looked up to see Saltars enter.

In spite of this description and of the lateness of the hour, and of the lady's loud manner, it must not be thought that Miss Lorry was anything but a thoroughly decent woman--if somewhat of a Bohemian. She was known as an accomplished rider throughout the length and breadth of the three kingdoms, and no one had a word to say against her character. She was certainly fond of wine, but kept her liking for that within due bounds, as a rule. She was also kind-hearted, charitable, and generous. Many a man and woman connected with the circus, and with the sawdust profession as a whole, had cause to remember Miss Lorry's kind heart. Bohemian as she was, the woman was really good and true and had many noble instincts. Saltars might have done worse than marry her, in spite of her birth, and profession, and years--for she certainly was older than he was. But Saltars, with his shallow instincts, looked on the outward beauty of Bell Lorry somewhat coarsened by age and her hard life. He had not the penetration to see the real, true, kindly, noble soul she possessed.

And then it must be confessed that Miss Lorry masked her many good qualities by indulging on the least provocation in royal rages. When blind with passion, she was capable of anything.

"Oh," said she, tossing her head, "so you're back!"

"Just so," replied Saltars, taking off his overcoat and tossing it on to the sofa. "I didn't expect to find you here--it's after twelve--really you should not, you know, for your own sake. People will talk, and the landlady here is no angel."

Miss Lorry snapped her fingers and drank some wine. "That for the landlady," she said coolly, "so long as my conscience is clear, I'm not afraid of what people say. And I couldn't go to bed without seeing you. The circus leaves for Chelmsford tomorrow."

"But you needn't go with it," said Saltars, lighting a cigarette. "I daresay we can have a talk tomorrow before you go?"

"We must have a talk tonight and an understanding too," snapped the woman, her eyes blazing. "Look here, Lord Saltars, what do you mean by going after that girl?"

"What girl?" asked his lordship, taking a seat.

"You know well enough. You've been over to Wargrove to dine with that Mrs. Palmer, and Miss Strode is with her as a companion."

"You seem to know all about it, Bell."

"Don't call me Bell. I've never given you permission to call me by my Christian name. I always call you Lord Saltars and not Herbert. You can't say a word against me."

"I don't want to, but----"

"I shan't listen to your remarks," said Miss Lorry in a rage; "you think because I'm a circus-rider that I've got no pride and no decency. But I'd have your lordship know that I'm a respectable woman, and there's no mud can be thrown at me. You asked me to marry you, and I said I would. Is that so?"

"Yes, but----"

"Hold your tongue. If that is so, what right have you to go after that girl? She's a nice girl and a decent girl, and a lady, which I am not. All the same, you shan't spoil her life."

Saltars raised his eyebrows. "I have no intention of spoiling her life. She's my cousin, if you remember----"

"Oh, I know. But you're just the sort of man to make love to her, and break her heart. And as you're engaged to marry me, I shan't have it. So you look out, Mr. Herbert Delham, or Lord Saltars, or whatever you call yourself."

"I wouldn't get in a rage over nothing, if I were you," said Saltars coolly, "and I shouldn't drink more of that wine either. It only excites you. Try this," he tossed her a cigarette, "it may calm your nerves."

"My nerves are my own to do what I like with. And if you had my nerves you might talk. It isn't a nervous woman who can ride and control a savage stallion like White Robin."

"That horse will kill you some day," said Saltars; "he's got the temper of a fiend."

"So have I when roused, so don't you make me angry."

"You're not very good-tempered now. Try the cigarette."

"I'll smoke if you hand me one properly and light it for me. I do not take things thrown to me as if I were a dog."

Lord Saltars rose and produced another cigarette--the one he threw was lying on the table. He offered this to Miss Lorry with a bow, and then gravely lighted a match. In another minute the smoke was curling from her full lips, and she calmed down. Saltars returned to his seat and lighted a new roll of tobacco with the stump of his old cigarette. "How did you know I went to Shanton tonight?"

"Cain told me. Yes, and he told me about Miss Strode being Mrs. Palmer's companion. He went today to see his mother, with whom Miss Strode lived. She--the mother, I mean--knew that you were going to Mrs. Palmer's tonight, as Mrs. Palmer told her."

"I wonder Mrs. Palmer took the trouble," said Saltars coolly. "My movements seem to interest her, and this Mrs. Merry and Cain. I'll break that young man's head if he spies on me."

"You'll have to reckon with Signor Antonio if you do, and, as he's the Strong Man of our show, you'll get the worst of it."

"Great strength doesn't usually mean science. And I think I can put up my flippers with any man."

"You're a brute," said Miss Lorry, with an admiring glance at Saltars' sullen strength, which was what attracted her; "no one would take you to be a nobleman."

"As to Signor Antonio," went on Saltars, taking no notice of the compliment, "he's not an Italian in spite of his dark looks and broken English. He's a half-bred gipsy mumper, and a blackguard at that. You seem to know him pretty well, Miss Lorry. I can't say I admire your choice of acquaintances."

"I know you," she retorted, "so you're the last person to talk. As to Antonio, he's been with the show for years, and I'm always friendly with fellow artistes. He's a brute, as you are: but he daren't show his teeth to me."

"He shows them to Cain often enough."

"He's fond of the boy all the same, and he's the----" here Miss Lorry checked herself; "well it doesn't matter. I didn't come here to talk about Antonio. It's getting late, and I want to go to my room. I'm lodging in the next house."

"You should have left a message asking me to call."

"I dare say, and you'd have come, wouldn't you?"

"But here at this hour your reputation----"

"Leave my reputation alone," cried Miss Lorry in a rage, "it's better than yours. I'd like to see anyone say a word again me. I'd have the law of him or her--if you're thinking of that white-faced cat the landlady. But see here, about Miss Strode----"

"Don't say anything about Miss Strode. I called, as her cousin. There's no chance of my marrying her."

"Mr. Strode said otherwise."

"You didn't know Strode," said Saltars, starting and looking puzzled.

"Oh, didn't I though?" jeered Miss Lorry; "well, I just did. Six years ago I knew him. He came to the circus, behind the scenes, I mean, to see Signor Antonio. He spotted Antonio performing in the ring and recognized an old friend. So he called after the performance and was introduced to me. I knew him again when he came to the circus when we were near London. He came to see you then."

"I know he did. Strode called at my digs and found from my man that I'd gone to the circus. As he wished to see me before he went to Wargrove, he followed me to the show. But I didn't know you spoke to him, or even knew him."

"He came to see me on his own," said Miss Lorry, frowning, "when you were talking to Stag. We had a conversation, and he said you were going to marry Miss Strode----"

"Well, I wasn't engaged to you then."

"You're not engaged now unless I choose to," said the woman coolly, "but you were making love to me, and I told Mr. Strode that I had a claim on you. He lost his temper and said you had promised to marry his daughter."

"If I had, I would hardly have proposed to you," said Saltars diplomatically.

"Oh, I don't know. You do exactly what suits you. And if Mr. Strode had lived he might have induced you to throw me over and marry Miss Strode. But he's dead, whosoever killed him, poor man, and you're engaged to me. Do you intend to marry me or not?"

"Well I want to, but there's no money."

"How do you know there's no money? I've got my savings. Yes, you may look; but I'm no spendthrift. I have enough invested to bring me in five hundred a year, and many a year I've worked to get the money together. We can live on that and with what your father will allow you."

"My father won't allow me a penny if I marry you."

Miss Lorry rose calmly. "Very good. If you're going to take that line, let us part. I shan't see you again after tonight."

But Saltars was not going to let her go so easily. He really loved this woman, while his liking for Eva was only a passing fancy begotten of her dead father's schemes. Often, when away from Miss Lorry did he curse himself for a fool, and decide to break his chains, but when in her presence the magnetism of the woman asserted itself. Her bold, free, fiery spirit appealed to Saltars greatly: also she was a splendid horsewoman and could talk wisely about the stables. Saltars loved horses more than anything in life save this woman, and her conversation was always within his comprehension. Moreover, during all the time of their courting she had never allowed him to even kiss her, always asserting that she was a respectable woman. Consequently as the fruit was dangling just out of Saltars' reach and only to be obtained by marriage, he was the more anxious to pluck it. Finally, Bell was really a magnificent-looking woman in a bold way, and this also appealed to the susceptible nature of Saltars.

"Don't go, Bell," he said, catching her dress as she moved to the door. Whereat she turned on him.

"Leave me alone, Lord Saltars, and call me Miss Lorry. I won't have you take liberties. Either you love me and will marry me openly in a decent church, or we part. I'm not going to have mud thrown on my good name for you or any one."

"You know that I love you----"

"I know nothing of the sort. If you did, you'd not go after your cousin; not that I've a word to say against her, though she did treat me like dirt when we spoke at Wargrove."

"I only went to see my cousin about the money left by her father."

Miss Lorry turned and leaned against the wall near the door. "There was no money left," she said sharply. "Mrs. Merry told Cain, and he told me. The poor girl has to go out as a companion."

"I know. But there is money. Strode told me that he would give her and me forty thousand pounds if we married."

"Very well, then," said Miss Lorry, her eyes flashing; "why don't you go and marry her? I won't stop you."

"Because, in the first place, I love you; in the second, she has not got the money and don't know where it is; and in the third, she is engaged to a fellow called Hill."

"Allen Hill?" said Miss Lorry; "yes, I remember him. He told me he was engaged when we spoke at the gate of the cottage. A nice young fellow and quite the man. I love a man," said Miss Lorry admiringly, "and that chap has a man's eye in his head, I can tell you."

"What about me?"

"Oh, you're a man right enough, or I shouldn't have taken up with you. But I say, if Miss Strode's engaged to Hill why doesn't she marry him now that the father's dead and there's no obstacle?"

"I don't know why the marriage doesn't take place," said Saltars pondering, "but I think it is because there's no money."

"There's the forty thousand pounds."

"That can't be found, and there's no memorandum amongst the papers of Strode likely to say where it is. I expect he brought the money home from Africa in the form of diamonds, and hid them somewhere."

Miss Lorry changed color. "Oh," she said thoughtfully, and then went on rapidly, "If this forty thousand pounds comes to Miss Strode, I suppose she'd marry Hill."

"Rather. She seems very fond of him."

"He's worth being fond of! he's a man I tell you, Saltars. Humph! I wonder if the money can be found?"

"There doesn't seem to be much chance."

"Do you think the money is locked up in diamonds?"

"It might be. As no money was found, Strode might have brought home his fortune in that form."

"I read the papers about the inquest," said Miss Lorry, staring at the ground; "what about that lawyer?"

"Mask? Oh, he knows nothing. He said so at the inquest."

"I wonder if the wooden hand has anything to do with the matter?"

"Well," said Saltars, rising and yawning, "it was certainly stolen, so it would seem it had a value. Of course if the hand was sent to Mask it was to be a sign that he had to give up any money he might have. It might have been stolen for that purpose."

"Yes, and the man might have been murdered to obtain possession of it."

"I don't think so. If Strode had been murdered on that account, the hand would have been stolen when the body was lying in the Red Deeps."

"It was stolen when it lay in the cottage," said Miss Lorry, "I remember. And Mask said that he had no money of Strode's, so there's not much use of the hand being sent to him. It's all very queer."

"Do you intend to try and unravel the mystery of the death?"

"Why not? I'd like that girl married to Hill and out of my way. I don't intend to let her marry you. So good-night," and Miss Lorry marched off without a word more.

XIV - SIGNOR ANTONIO

CAIN MERRY was a particular pet of Miss Lorry's, and the lad felt grateful to her for the attention. He admired her exceedingly, and at one time had fancied himself in love with her. But Miss Lorry, experienced in admirers, laughed at him the moment she descried the early symptoms, and told him she was old enough to be his mother. It was creditable to Cain that he took the hint thus given, and devoted himself to Jane Wasp, with whom he had been in love ever since they attended the same board school. And after his passing fancy for Miss Lorry, the lad's love for the policeman's daughter became even more marked, much to the joy of Jane, who adored the dark-eyed scamp, and lost no opportunity of meeting him.

But Cain was such a Bohemian, that this was no easy matter. Owing to the nagging of his mother, he stayed away from Misery Castle as much as he could, and got jobs in the surrounding country and in London. Also there was some influence at work on Cain's character, which Jane could not understand: something that made him moody and inclined him to despair. In her simple way Jane tried to learn what it was, that she might comfort him, but Cain always baffled her.

On the morning after Miss Lorry's interview with Saltars, the lad was more dismal than usual, and was rather listless in his work. As the circus was packing up to move on to Chelmsford, there was little time to be lost, and Cain came in for many a hard word. At length the manager became exasperated at his indolence, and sent him off with a message to Miss Lorry, who had rooms near the Queen's Hotel. Nothing loath to be relieved from moving heavy beams, and taking down the large tent, Cain set off in better spirits.

On passing through the market place about ten o'clock he saw Jane, perched on a light market cart, and ran towards her with a bright face. The girl received him with a joyful cry, and explained that she had been looking for him for the past hour.

"Mrs. Whiffles drove me over," she explained, getting down to speak more freely; "she keeps the Wargrove inn, you know----"

"Of course I know," said Cain quickly; "I'm Wargrove as well as you, Jane. But how did your father let you go. I thought he was keeping you in, to help your mother."

"Ah, he does that," said Jane with a sigh; "father's a hard one, Cain, and hates you like poison. You see he's all for the law, and you----"

"And I'm a vagabond, as my mother says. Well, Jane, don't you fret, I'm getting a higher law than that your father serves. I'll tell you about it someday. How did you come over?"

"I told you. I came with Mrs. Whiffles. Mother wanted some things here, and as Mrs. Whiffles was going, she thought I might come too. I shan't tell father anything, nor will mother. He's out till two, and we must be back before then. But mother wouldn't have let me come had she known the circus was here, Cain. She says I'm not to think of you at all. I'm to go out to service."

"We may marry before you do that," said Cain quickly; "how did you know the circus was here?"

"Mr. Hill's groom Jacobs told me."

"Oh!" Cain frowned. "You're too thick with that Harry Jacobs."

"I've known him all my life, Cain."

"So have I, and I don't like him. He thinks he's every one, because he wears a smart livery. I wear just as smart a one in the circus."

"Yes, but the circus ain't decent, Cain. I could never marry you if you kept on there. I couldn't go about as you do, and if you're to be my husband I'd like to be near you."

"You shall be near me, and we'll marry to take service in something better than a circus," said Cain, his face lighting up.

"What's that?"

Cain drew near and was about to speak, when his ear was suddenly seized by a large dark man, who frowned. "Why aren't you seeing Miss Lorry, you young scamp?" said the stranger. "I've got to do your business. Mr. Stag asked you particularly to give that note. Hand it over."

"I'll take it now," said Cain, getting free; "leave my ear alone."

"You give the note to me, Cain. Who is this?" and he looked at Jane.

"She's a friend of mine from Wargrove," said Cain sulkily; "get back into the cart, Jane."

"From Wargrove?" said the dark man with a queer smile; "and her name?"

"I'm Jane Wasp, sir," said the girl, looking into the man's somewhat brutal face.

The man laughed. "Policeman Wasp's daughter, as I'm a sinner. How's your fool of a father? Catching every one he shouldn't catch, I suppose? He was always too clever."

Cain interposed. "Leave her alone fa----, I mean Signor Antonio," he said, "she's going home."

Signor Antonio turned on him with a snarl. "Hold your tongue, you whelp," he said, "I'll talk to whom I like and as long as I like. I want to know what Policeman Wasp's doing now?"

"He's looking after the murderer of Mr. Strode," said Jane politely.

The man started and laughed. "I hope he'll catch him: but it's a business rather beyond his powers, I fancy. Stop, you're the girl who delivered the package to Mr. Hill."

"To young Mr. Hill," said Jane, climbing into Mrs. Whiffles cart, "not to the father."

Signor Antonio turned on the boy with a frown. "I told you it was to be given to Mr. Hill himself."

"Well, he got it right enough," said Cain impatiently. "I gave it to Jane at Colchester, and she took it to Mr. Allen, who gave it to his father."

"And what happened?"

"I don't know," said Jane. "I didn't see Mr. Hill get it."

"You fool," cried Antonio turning on Cain with another snarl. "I wanted the girl to report how Hill looked when he opened the package, and now----"

"Jane's got nothing to do with this business," said Cain resolutely, "and I won't have her mixed up in your affairs."

"Do you know who I am?" demanded the man, black with anger.

"Yes," replied the boy with a queer look; "you're Signor Antonio."

Jane thought she would interfere as there seemed to be a chance of a quarrel. "Mr. Hill went to London after he got the parcel."

"On the same day?" asked the man eagerly.

"Yes, sir. Jacobs, who drives him, told me he went within two hours after he opened the parcel. He's gone up to attend a sale----"

"Oh," sneered Signor Antonio, "so he's gone to attend a sale? Very good, that's all right. The parcel was a notice about a sale----"

"Of musical instruments, I know, sir. Jacobs told me."

"You speak too much to Jacobs," cried Cain; "remember you're engaged to marry me, Jane."

"Stuff and nonsense," said Signor Antonio, who in spite of his Italian name and looks did not speak his own language; "you'll not marry the girl."

"But I shall," said Cain, setting his teeth; "mind your own business."

"This is my business, you brat----"

"Jane," said Cain pointing to the hotel, "yonder is Mrs. Whiffles waving to you. Drive over. I'll send you my address, and you can write to me. Goodbye, dear."

He would have climbed on the cart and kissed her, but that the so-called Italian drew him back. Jane, rather started and puzzled by the dominion this stranger seemed to exercise over Cain, drove hastily away to the curb where fat Mrs. Whiffles stood waving her fat arms. She looked back to see Cain and Antonio in fierce conversation, and dreaded a quarrel.

And indeed there would have been a quarrel but for the boy's self-possession. Cain appeared to have far more command of his temper than the older man, and spoke quietly enough. "See here," he said, "I won't have you interfering with my affairs."

"Do you know who I am?" demanded Antonio again.

"You asked me that before and in public," said Cain, "and I told you, you were Signor Antonio. But you know well enough what you are and so do I."

"And what am I?" jeered Antonio.

"You're the man that deserted his wife and child, and your name is Giles Merry."

"Yes, it is, and don't you talk of deserting, you brat. I'm your father, so you look out. I'll thrash you."

"Oh no, you won't," said Cain boldly, "I'm quite equal to standing up to you, father. Leave my business alone, I've put up with you ever since we met a year ago, and I did what you wanted because you promised me not to go near my mother. I learn that you have written that you intend to call on her."

"What if I do? She's my wife as you're my son. She's got a house over her head, and money, and I've got a right to share both."

"No, you haven't," said Cain sharply, "you're no father of mine, as you deserted me and mother when we were poor. Now that we've got money, you'd come and make mother miserable. I kept my part of the bargain, so you keep to yours. If you write mother again or go near her, I'll make things hot."

Antonio made a dash at the boy--they were now in a quiet side street--and gasped with rage. "You unnatural young cuckoo----"

"Leave me alone, father, or I'll sing out for the police."

"What!" Antonio, finding force would not do, began to whine, "you'd run in your poor old father?"

"I don't want to," said Cain, "but if you force me to, I must. All I ask is for you to keep away from mother, and leave me alone. If you don't, I'll tell Wasp something he may like to hear."

The older man turned pale through his swarthy skin. "What will you tell him?" he asked in a thick voice.

"Never you mind. But I know you saw Mr. Strode when he came to the circus that night after Lord Saltars. Then there's Butsey----"

"What about Butsey?" asked the father uneasily, and glaring.

"Nothing. Only he's a bad lot. I'm no great shakes myself," admitted Cain sadly, "but I'm beginning to see how wicked I am. If I was as bad as Butsey, father, I'd not treat you like this. You sent Butsey with a lying message to mother----"

"I wanted to know how she looked."

"No, you didn't. I believe you sent Butsey to steal that wooden hand."

"It's a lie. I don't know who took it."

"I believe Butsey did, though why you wanted it I don't know. And what is there between you and Mr. Hill, father, seeing you sent him that cross?"

"That's my business," growled Antonio, finding his son knew too much for him; "you hold your tongue."

"I will, as long as you keep away from my mother."

"Lord, I'll keep away," said Antonio good-humoredly. "I don't want to live with her nagging and whimpering. You're her son, sure enough--a young prig going against your lawful father."

"Only for my mother's sake. And you want me to do wrong. I'm seeing light, father, and I'm changing."

"What do you mean by seeing light? You're always saying that."

"I've been to the Salvation Army meetings," said Cain solemnly, "and I see what a sinner I am."

"Oh, you're going to turn parson, are you? Well, you can do what you like, but hold your tongue about my business."

"I'll do so. But tell me, father?" Cain looked anxiously into the brutal face, "had you anything to do with that murder?"

Antonio glared and looked like a devil. He made another dash at the boy, but at that moment three or four men came round the corner, and amongst them a policeman. At once Antonio burst out into a loud laugh and took to his broken English. "Ver' goot, my leetle boy, gif me the letter. I go to Mees Lorry. Ah, Dio!"

Cain saw that he would not receive a reply to his terrible question just then, so, glad to get away on the chance of having another talk with Jane, he escaped. Hardly had he turned the corner when his father was after him, and a deep voice breathed in his ear:

"I had nothing to do with that," said Antonio anxiously; "I'm bad, but not so bad as that. I don't know who killed the man. Go"--a push sent the boy reeling--"and hold your tongue. I'll keep my part of the bargain and leave your mother alone. Keep yours," and before Cain could recover his breath Antonio was ringing the bell of Miss Lorry's lodgings.

That lady was just up and at breakfast. Antonio was shown into her sitting-room, and found her drinking coffee. She saluted him with a smile. "Well, Giles, what's brought you here at this hour?"

"This letter from Stag," said Antonio, giving the note he had received from Cain; "and don't call me Giles, Bell."

"You seem very much afraid of people knowing you," she jeered, opening the envelope, and running her eyes over the letter. "Stag wants me to make another contract for the North." She threw down the note. "Well then, I won't."

"What are you going to do, then?"

"Go to London and marry Lord Saltars."

"He means business, then?"

Miss Lorry rose, and looked as though she would slap Antonio's face. "You hound," she hissed, "do you think I'd let any man play fast and loose with me. Not a word," she added, seeing a grim smile on the strong man's face. "I know what you would say. Leave the past alone, or it will be the worse for you. And see here, what's become of that boy Butsey?"

"He's in London at Father Don's."

"Poor little wretch. Being made into a devil such as you are. Then, you send for him to come to Chelmsford. I want him to deliver a letter, and the sooner it's delivered the better."

"Can't I deliver it?"

"No, you can't. I can trust Butsey. I can't trust you."

"Who is the letter to?"

"That's my business," flashed out Miss Lorry, returning to her interrupted breakfast; "tell Stag I'll see him about the note at my own time."

"But, Bell, if you leave the show, how will you live?"

"I've got money saved. You need not ask how much," she added, seeing the cupidity flash into the man's eyes, "for I am not going to tell you. I leave the show at the end of October, and then I remain in town till I become Lady Saltars."

"A nice bargain he'll get with you," growled Antonio. "I know you."

"As we've been together in the circus for years, you ought to----"

"I wasn't thinking of the circus, but of----"

"Hold your tongue," she cried, rising again, "mind your own business."

"You don't make it worth my while. Suppose I spoil your game with Lord Saltars?"

Miss Lorry's face became hard and her eyes glittered. "You dare to interfere, and I'll send to that policeman at Wargrove to tell him I saw you at Westhaven speaking to a pair of the biggest blackguards in London."

"And what will that do? I've got a right to speak to whom I choose."

"You can for all I care," said Miss Lorry, sitting down once more, "your business has nothing to do with me so long as you leave me alone. Why don't you go home to your poor wife?"

"My poor wife don't want me. And I wouldn't live with her for gold untold, seeing how she nags and moans. My wife?" sneered the man with an ugly look; "you're a nice one to talk of her."

"I tell you what, Giles Merry," said Miss Lorry, with great deliberation, "you'd better keep a civil tongue, or you'll have a bad time. I'll horsewhip you before the company, strong man as you are."

Antonio scowled. "You wouldn't dare."

"Wouldn't I? You talk like that and you'll see. You always were a brute and you always will be. I only hope," added Miss Lorry, suddenly looking into his eyes, "that you aren't something worse."

Antonio met the look with great composure. "Meaning a murderer?" he said. "Cain asked me if I did kill Strode."

"And how do I know you didn't?"

"Because I did not," cried the man, rising and looking fierce.

"Well," said Miss Lorry, after a pause, "I daresay you didn't. But you know who did." She looked at him searchingly.

"I swear by all that's holy, I don't!"

Miss Lorry laughed disagreeably. "Fancy Giles Merry talking of holy things. Cain's worth a dozen of you."

"The young fool! He's going to join the Salvationists!"

"And a good job too," cried Miss Lorry, with a pleased look, "he may convert you."

"Let him try," said the affectionate father, "and I'll smash him."

"Perhaps you'd rather Cain joined Father Don, and Red Jerry and Foxy. Oh, I saw you talking to Jerry and Foxy at Westhaven. It's my belief," added Miss Lorry, crushing her egg-shell, "that those two have something to do with Strode's end."

"Why don't you tell the police so?"

"Because I've got my own fish to fry," retorted Miss Lorry, rising and wiping her mouth; "but the presence of London thieves at Westhaven when a gentleman was murdered and robbed, looks queer. If the police knew they'd collar Jerry and Foxy and Father Don too. I fancy you would be brought into the matter."

"Look here," cried Antonio with an oath, "do you charge me, or any of those three with murder?"

"No, I don't. I only know that you were Strode's pal in the old days, and that you did a lot of dirty work for him. You're in with a bad lot, Giles, and will come to a bad end. I only wish I could rescue that poor little brat of a Butsey from you, but the boy's past reforming. I know nothing of him, save that he has an admiration for me, and ran my errands, so that is why I want him to deliver this letter. You'll try and learn who the letter is written to, Giles: but you won't. I can trust Butsey. But why don't you turn honest, man, and make money?"

"How can I? Honest men don't make money. And I gain my living honestly enough as a strong man with Stag."

"Ah, that's a blind to cloak your real character. You're in with Father Don's gang. Why not split on them?" Miss Lorry leaned forward and spoke softly. "For instance, why not call on Mr. Strode's lawyer and tell him Red Jerry came home from Africa about the same time that Strode did?"

"What good would that do?"

"I can't say. Mask knows something, and I want that something told, so that Miss Strode may marry Allen Hill, and be put out of my way, for me to marry Saltars. He admires her, and I want her safely married, beyond his reach. If you told about Red Jerry, Mask might be able to get back Miss Strode's fortune."

"What!"--Giles pricked up his ears--"Fortune?"

"Forty thousand pounds, Giles, in diamonds, I fancy."

Antonio sat down. "I never knew Strode was so rich," he said. "Why, the liar told me at Brentwood that he'd made no money."

"I don't wonder at that," said Miss Lorry; "he knew you'd blackmail him if he confessed to having money."

"I knew enough to make things hot for him," said Giles, biting his large, square fingers, "but I never knew he was rich. Lord, forty thousand pounds! If I'd known that----"

"You'd have killed him to get it."

"I don't say that," growled Giles, putting on his hat, "and as I didn't kill him, there's no more to be said. Where's the money now?"

Miss Lorry looked curiously at him. "You should know!"

"What the blazes do you mean?"

"Oh, if you don't know there's no more to be said. As Strode is dead, you can't get the money now. Your blackmailing is of no value. Miss Strode will get the diamonds and marry Mr. Allen Hill."

"Hill?" said Giles thoughtfully; "does he take after that fool of a father of his?"

"No; he's a man and not a whimpering ass like Lawrence Hill."

Giles stood musing at the door. "So Miss Strode will get the diamonds?" he said; "blest if I don't see her, and----"

Miss Lorry whirled round. "You leave her alone or I'll make things unpleasant for you. The poor girl has sorrow enough, and she's a good girl."

"Keep your hair on, I'll do nothing--at present," added Antonio significantly: and with an ironical bow he departed.

Miss Lorry clutched her breast with a frown. "I'll write that letter and send it by Butsey," she said determinedly.

XV - AN UNEXPECTED MEETING

MR. MASK had a dark little office in the city down a long narrow lane which led from Cheapside. In the building he inhabited were many offices, mostly those of the legal profession, and Mr. Mask's rooms were on the ground floor. He had only two. In the outer one a clerk almost as old as Mr. Mask himself scribbled away in a slow manner, and showed in clients to the inner room. This was a gloomy little dungeon with one barred window looking out on to a blank wall, damp and green with slime. Light was thrown into the room through this window by means of a silvered glass, so the actual illumination of the apartment was very small indeed, even in summer. In winter the gas glared and flared all the day.

Here Mr. Mask sat like a spider in his den, and the place was so full of cobwebs that it really suggested spiders in plenty. There was a rusty grate in which a fire was never lighted, an old mahogany book-case filled with uninviting-looking volumes, and a tin wash-stand which was hidden behind a screen of shabby Indian workmanship. The walls were piled to the dingy ceiling with black japanned deed-boxes, with the names of various clients inscribed on them in white letters. Before the window--and dirty enough the glass of that was--stood a large mahogany table covered untidily with papers, deeds, briefs, memoranda, and such-like legal documents. A small clearing in front was occupied by red blotting paper, and a large lead ink bottle with a tray of pens. There was one chair for Mr. Mask and one for a client. Finally, as there was no carpet on the floor it may be guessed that the office was not an inviting-looking sanctum. Into this hole--as it might fitly be termed--Allen was shown one morning. He had not called immediately on Mr. Mask when he came to town, as he had been searching for his father for the last five days. But all inquiries proved futile. Allen went to the hotel at which Mr. Hill usually stayed, but could not find him there. He had not been stopping in the place for months. Allen sought the aid of the police, but they could not find Mr. Hill. Finally he put an advertisement in the paper, which remained unanswered. Also Allen had called on Mr. Hill's bankers, but found that he had not been near the place. It was so strange that Allen was beginning to feel afraid. The message conveyed in the symbol sent through Cain must be a very serious one, to make his father cut himself off from those who knew him, in this way.

As a last resource, Allen came to see Mr. Mask, feeling he should have done this before. Mask had a large business, but on the face of it appeared to do very little in the dingy office. But he was a man who could be trusted with a secret, and many people who knew this entrusted him with affairs they wished kept quiet. Consequently Mask's business was sometimes rather shady, but he made a great deal of money by it, and that was all he cared about.

A silent, cold man was Mask, and even in his own home at Bloomsbury he was secretive. Still the man had his good points, and had an undercurrent of good nature of which he was somewhat ashamed, heaven only knows why. If he had been as hard as he looked, he certainly would not have asked Mrs. Palmer to give poor Eva a home.

"Well, Mr. Allen," said Mask, who called him thus to distinguish him from his father, whom he had known many years, "so you have come at last?" Allen, who was placing his hat on the floor, as there was no table to put it on, started and stared. "Did you expect me?"

"Long ago," said Mask, putting his fingers together and leaning back with crossed legs; "in fact, you should have come to me five days ago. There was no necessity for you to consult the police as to your father's whereabouts, or to call at his bank and hotel, or to put that very injudicious advertisement into the paper."

"You seem to know all about my doings?"

"Quite so. I know a great many things. To be frank, Mr. Allen, I have had you watched by a private detective, ever since you came to town."

Allen rose in a towering rage. "How dare you do that, Mr. Mask?"

"I did so at your father's request," said the lawyer, on whom the young man's rage produced not the least effect.

"You have seen him?"

"I have. He came to me when he arrived."

"Do you know where he is?"

"I do--but I am not at liberty to tell you."

"Do you know why he is acting in this way?"

Mr. Mask's calm face suddenly wrinkled. "No," he said, looking perplexed, "frankly, Mr. Allen, I don't, and I am glad you have called. I wish to talk the matter over with you."

"Why didn't you send for me, then?"

"Because it is never my wish to take the initiative. People come to me. I don't go to them. I get a lot of business by waiting, Mr. Allen. People are only too glad to find a man who can keep a secret; I have made a fine business out of nothing, simply by holding my tongue."

"And do you intend to do so in this instance?"

Mask shrugged his spare shoulders. "That depends. Johnstone!"

He raised his voice rather, and the door opened to admit a small clerk with a large red beard and a bald head, and a face lined with wrinkles. What his age was no one could tell, and he said as little as he could, being as secretive as his master. Without a word he stood at the door, seen dimly in the half light of the office, for the day was dark. "Johnstone," said Mr. Mask. "I'll be engaged with this gentleman for some time. Let no one in, till I call again."

Johnstone bowed and departed without a word, while Mr. Mask went on in a smooth tone, "I sit in this office from ten in the morning till six at night. Johnstone comes at nine and leaves at four."

"Why before you?" asked Allen, wondering why this information was supplied.

"Because I like the office to myself to see nervous clients. The lawyers in the other offices of the building do not stay late, and frequently I am perfectly alone with clients who wish their business kept so secret that they don't want even to be seen entering this place."

"Are you not afraid?"

Mr. Mask shrugged his shoulders again. "No. Why should I be?"

"Some rough client might do you some harm."

"Oh, I don't think so. Anyone who comes here finds it to his interest to conciliate me, not to threaten. But I confess that I was rather startled the other night."

"What do you mean?"

"I'll come to the story in time. Because I intend to tell it, I drew your attention to my hours. Well, Mr. Allen," Mask leaned back again, "and what can I do for you?"

"Tell me where my father is."

"I can't do that. I have not your father's permission to do so."

"How long will he be away?"

"Until I can induce him to return," said Mask blandly.

Allen leaned forward, and looked the lawyer in the eyes. "Is my father afraid of being arrested?"

Mask started. "No. Why do you say that?"

"Because--but before I tell you, may I ask his reason for staying away?"

Mask looked perplexed again. "I can't exactly tell you," he said. "I may as well be frank, Mr. Allen, as I don't like the situation. Your father, whom I have known all his life, came to me over a week ago in great agitation. He said that he was in danger, but what the danger was, he refused to confess. I insisted on an explanation, and he promised to tell me some day. Meantime he wanted to be hidden away for the time being. I arranged that for him."

"I don't think that was wise of you, Mr. Mask."

"My good Allen--I can call you so as I've known you since you were a lad--there is no reason why I should not help your father. He may have done something against the law, for all I know, but as he is my client, it is my duty to help him. He is a good client to me, and I am not such a fool as to lose him. It is my business to keep secrets, and here is one I have not found out. But I don't intend to let your father go away till I do find out," said Mask grimly. "On that condition I helped him. And after all," added the lawyer, "your father is quite in his sane senses, and I have no right to dictate to him, even when he acts in so eccentric a manner."

"He is always eccentric," said the son wearily; "but this behavior is beyond a joke. How is my mother to live?"

"I can't send her money. Your father will see to that."

"But why am I shut out from my father's confidence?"

"I can't say. Remember," said Mask in a slightly irritable tone, "I am shut out also."

Allen, much perplexed over the situation which was sufficiently annoying and mysterious, thought for a moment. "Did my father tell you of the cardboard box he received?"

"He did not. He said nothing, save that he wished to hide for a time, and would reveal his reason later."

"Then I must tell you everything I know," said Allen in desperation. "If my father won't trust you, I must. My mother is in a great state of alarm, and for her sake I must get him to come back."

Mr. Mask looked doubtful. "I don't know whether he'll hear reason," he said, after a pause. "However, what you tell me will go no further."

"Well then, Mr. Mask, I know why my father is afraid."

"It's more than I do. Why is he afraid?"

"Because he thinks he may be arrested for the murder of Strode."

Mask pushed back his chair and rose quickly. It was not an easy matter to astonish a man, who, in that very room, had heard tales worthy of the Arabian Nights., but Allen had certainly managed to do so. "Do you mean to say he killed Strode?" he asked.

"No. But he thinks he did."

"How can that be?"

Allen related the episode of the pistol, and how he found that the bullet which killed Strode would not fit the barrel. "So you see my father thought he had killed him, and when this cross was sent----"

"What cross?" asked Mask, looking up quickly.

"I forgot. I thought you knew." And Allen related everything in detail. Mask heard the story with his chin on his hand, and in silence. Even when in full possession of the facts he did not speak. Allen grew impatient. "What do you think?"

Mask moved a few papers hither and thither, but did not look straight at his visitor. "It's a mystery," he said. "I know not what to say. But I am perfectly sure of one thing," he added with emphasis, "that your father never shot Strode----"

"I said so. The bullet that went through the heart did not fit the barrel of my revolver."

"You misunderstand me. I don't even believe that your father fired the shot which ripped the flesh of the arm. Why, Strode was his best friend and he was devoted to him."

"My father to Strode, or Strode to my father?"

"Both ways you can take it. Why, it was Strode brought about the marriage between your parents."

"My mother told me how the marriage came about," said Allen quickly, "but I understood that my father acted from a chivalrous motive."

Mask's lip curled. "I fear not," he said, "there were circumstances connected with your mother----"

Allen shifted himself uneasily and grew red. "I know--I know," he said sharply, "my mother told me about the necklace. Surely you did not believe her guilty, Mr. Mask?"

"No," said the lawyer emphatically, "I certainly did not. I can't say who stole the necklace, but it was lost and the thief has never been found. As to the marriage"--he waved his hand--"Strode brought it about--at least he told me so. How he managed I can't say, unless it was that he used his influence over your father."

"My mother believes----"

"I know. All the more credit to her. But we can discuss this on some more fitting occasion. Meantime we must talk of your father. I don't see why you shouldn't see him," said Mask musingly.

"Give me his address."

"Humph," said the lawyer, smiling slightly. "I'll see. But about this murder? Your father did not kill the man."

"No," said Allen sharply, "I swear he did not."

"Quite so. Well, who did, and what was the motive?"

"Robbery was the motive," said Allen, taking a letter out of his pocket. "Read this, I received it from Miss Strode."

Mask took the letter, but did not read it immediately. "I don't believe the motive was robbery," he declared deliberately; "Strode had little money. He certainly brought a hundred or so from Africa and I cashed his letters of credit."

"Did you give him the money in notes?"

"Yes; and what is more I have the numbers of the notes. I see what you mean: you fancy the notes were stolen and that the criminal can thus be traced."

"Read the letter," said Allen impatiently.

The lawyer did so, and thus became possessed of a faithful report of Saltars' communications to Eva which she had detailed for Allen's benefit. On ending he placed the letter on the table. "A blue pocket-book," said Mask musingly. "Yes, he had such a one. I remember he placed the notes in it. I wonder I didn't ask about that at the inquest. It's stolen. Humph! Looks like a commonplace robbery after all. Allen," he raised his eyes, "I gave Strode two hundred in ten pound Bank of England notes. As I have the numbers, I may be able to trace how much of this sum has been spent by inquiring at the Bank. The numbers that are missing will be those that Strode had in the blue pocket-book when he went on that fatal journey to Westhaven. If the murderer stole the book and has cashed the notes he may be traced by the numbers."

"I agree. But what about the forty thousand pounds?"

Mask shook his head. "I can't say. Strode certainly never mentioned to me that he had such a sum."

"Did he say he had diamonds?"

"No. Perhaps, as Miss Strode suggests, the forty thousand pounds may have been locked up in diamonds as a portable way to carry such a sum. But we found no diamonds amongst his effects, so it is probable he carried them on his person."

"And was murdered for the sake of them?"

"Perhaps. It was strange, though, that Strode should have spoken to me about his wooden hand. He promised that he would return from Wargrove to place a large sum of money in my hands--probably the forty thousand pounds, though he did not mention the amount."

"I dare say he intended to turn the diamonds into money and then give it to you."

"Perhaps," said Mask carelessly, "but we are not yet sure if the money was in diamonds. However, Strode said, that when he wanted the promised money, he would get it from me personally, and, if he did not apply in person, he would send the wooden hand. As he certainly would not have let the hand be taken from him while alive, it was a very safe token to send."

Allen looked down. "It seems as though he was afraid of being killed," he said musingly; "and he was killed, and the wooden hand was stolen."

"Not only that," said Mask, "but it was brought to me."

"What!" Allen started to his feet, "here! Why didn't you have the man who brought it arrested?"

"Because I could not," said Mask drily; "this is why I told you of my habits. It was after four when Johnstone and everyone in the place was away. In fact, it was nearly six, and when I was getting ready to go, that this man came."

"What kind of a man was he?"

"A venerable old man, who looked like the Wandering Jew, with a long white beard, and a benevolent face. He asked if he could speak to me, and we talked. I must remind you that everyone in this building is away at the hour of six."

"I understand. But what was the old man's name?"

"He gave none. He simply asked if I had a sum of money in my possession belonging to Mr. Strode. I said I had not; so he asked if Mr. Strode had left a packet of diamonds with me."

"Then there are diamonds!" cried Allen; "and you knew?"

"Now you mention it, I did know," said Mask coolly; "all in good time, Allen. I wished to learn how much you knew before I spoke out. I am a man who keeps secrets, mind you, and I don't say more than is needful. Well, this old man, when I said that I had no diamonds, told me in so many words that I was a liar, and insisted that I should give them up. To test him, I jokingly asked him if he had the wooden hand, which was to be the token to deliver the money or diamonds. He then produced the article."

"Why didn't you arrest him?"

"Let me remind you that I was alone with the Wandering Jew, and that he brought two men of whom I caught a glimpse. They remained in the outer room during our conversation. I asked the old man how he became possessed of the wooden hand. He refused to tell me, but insisted that I should hand over the diamonds. I protested that I had none, and told him what I tell you, as to what Strode said about giving me money later."

"What did the old man say then?"

"He began to believe me, and muttered something about the diamonds being in Strode's possession. Then he sang out, 'No go, Jerry,' to a red-headed ruffian outside. After that, he left."

"You should have followed, Mr. Mask, and have had him arrested."

"I could scarcely do that," said the lawyer drily, "the old gentleman was too clever. He went with one man, and left the red-headed Jerry to keep watch. I had to remain in this room till seven, or else Jerry threatened to shoot me."

"He would never have dared."

"Oh yes, he would, and in this lonely building no one could have stopped him. Well I agreed, and remained in here doing some work. At seven I opened the outer door. Jerry had decamped, but where he and his friends went I can't say?"

"Have you told the police?"

"No. I think it is wiser to remain quiet. These men will try again to get the money through the wooden hand; but they must first learn who killed Strode, and stole the diamonds--for I now agree with you, Allen, that the forty thousand pounds are locked up in diamonds. But now we have talked on this point and it seems clear, let us talk on another in the presence of a third person."

"Who?" asked Allen anxiously.

"Your father," said Mask. "Johnstone!"

The red-bearded clerk entered, and when within, removed a false beard and a wig.

"Father," cried Allen, rising. It was indeed Mr. Hill, pale and trembling.

XVI - MR. HILL'S STORY

ALLEN WAS so thunderstruck at the sight of his father, who had so unexpectedly appeared, that he could only stand silently staring. Mr. Hill gave a nervous titter, and tried to appear at his ease. But the sight of his pale face and trembling limbs shewed that the man was possessed by terror. Also he locked the door while Allen gaped. It was Mask who spoke first.

"You are surprised to find your father as my clerk," he said smoothly to Allen; "but when he came to me asking to be concealed, I arranged that Johnstone should take a much-needed holiday at the sea-side. I believe he is at Brighton," said Mr. Mask deliberately. "In the meantime, your father, by means of a clever disguise, adopted Johnstone's name, and personality, and looks. In the dim light of the office everyone thinks he is Johnstone, and to tell you the truth," said Mr. Mask, smiling, "my clients are so possessed by their own fears, that they take very little notice of my clerk."

Allen scarcely listened to the half of this explanation. "Father," he cried, "whatever is the meaning of all this?"

Hill tittered again, and looked about for a seat as his limbs would hardly support him. As Mr. Mask had one chair, and Allen the other, it looked as though Hill would have to sink on the floor. But Allen pushed forward his own chair and made his father sit down. Then, so white was the man, that he produced his flask, and gave him a nip of brandy. "I never travel without this," said Allen, alluding to the flask. "It comes in handy at times," and he spoke this irrelevantly so as to put Hill at his ease.

The little man, under the grotesque mask of Johnstone, grew braver after the brandy, with Dutch courage. "You did not expect to find me here, Allen?" he said, with his nervous titter.

"I certainly did not," said his son bitterly; "and I don't know why you need disguise yourself in this way. I know you did not murder Strode."

"But I intended to," cried Hill, suddenly snarling, and showing his teeth, "the black-hearted villain."

"I thought Strode was your friend, father?"

"He was my enemy--he was my evil genius--he was a tyrant who tried to crush all the spirit out of me. Oh," Hill beat his fist on the table in impotent rage, "I'm glad he's dead. But I wish he'd died by torture--I wish he'd been burnt--sliced to atoms. I wish----"

"Stop," said Mask, seeing Allen turn white and faint, at the sight of this degrading spectacle, "there's no need to speak like this, Lawrence. Tell us how you came to be at the Red Deeps."

"How do you know I was at the Red Deeps?" asked Hill, shivering, and with the sudden rage dying out of him.

"Well, you took your son's revolver, and----"

"You said you didn't believe I fired the shot, Mask," cried the miserable creature. "I heard you say so, I had my ear to the keyhole all the time----

"Father--father," said Allen, sick with disgust at the sight of his parent behaving in this way.

"And why not?" cried Hill, turning fiercely on him. "I am in danger. Haven't I the right to take all measures I can for my own safety? I did listen, I tell you, and I overheard all. Had you not proved to Mask here, that the bullet which caused the death could not have been fired out of your revolver, I'd not have come in. I should have run away. But you know I am innocent----"

"Quite so," said Mask, looking searchingly at the speaker, "therefore the reason for your disguise is at an end."

Hill passed his tongue over his dry lips and crouched again. "No, it isn't," he said faintly, "there's something else."

"In heaven's name, what is it?" asked Allen.

"Leave me alone," snarled his father, shrinking back in his chair and looking apprehensively at his tall, white-faced son, "it's got nothing to do with you."

"It has everything to do with me," said his son with calm firmness, "for my mother's sake I intend to have an explanation."

"If my wife were here she would never let you treat me in this way, Allen," whimpered the miserable father. "Sarah"--he did not call his wife Saccharissa now, the situation being too serious--"Sarah is always kind to me."

Allen with folded arms leaned against the bookcase and looked at his father with deep pity in his eyes. Hill was alternately whimpering and threatening: at one moment he would show a sort of despairing courage, and the next would wince like a child fearful of a blow. The young man never loved his father, who, taken up with himself and his whims, had done nothing to make the boy love him. He had never respected the man, and only out of regard for his mother had he refrained from taking strong measures to curb the pronounced eccentricities of Hill. But the man, miserable coward as he seemed, was still his father, and it behoved him to deal with him as gently as possible. In his own mind, Allen decided that his father's troubles--whatever they were--had driven him insane. But the sight of that cringing, crawling figure begot a mixture of pity and loathing--loathing that a human creature should fall so low, and pity that his own father should suddenly become a 'thing' instead of a man.

"I want to be kind to you, father," he said after a pause; "who will you trust if not your own son?"

"You were never a son to me," muttered Hill.

"Was that my fault?" asked Allen strongly. "I would have been a son to you, if you had let me. But you know, father, how you kept me at arm's length--you know how you ruled the house according to your whims and fancies, and scorned both my mother and myself. Often you have spoken to her in such a manner that it was only the knowledge that you are my father which made me refrain from interfering. My mother says she owes much to you----"

"So she does--so she does."

"Then why take advantage of her gratitude? She gives everything to you, father, and you treat her in a way--faugh," Allen swept the air with his arm, as though to banish the subject. "Let us say no more on that point. But I have come up here to get to the bottom of this affair, father, and I don't leave this place till I know all."

Hill tried to straighten himself. "You forget I am your father," he said, with an attempt at dignity.

"No; I do not forget. Because you are my father I wish to help you out of this trouble, whatever it is. I can save you from being accused of Strode's murder, but the other thing----"

"I never said there was anything else," said Hill quickly.

"Yes, you did, Lawrence," said Mask. "I have taken a note of it."

"Oh," whimpered Hill, "if you turn against me too---"

"Neither one of us intend to turn against you," said Allen in deep disgust, for the man was more like a jelly-fish than ever, and constantly evaded all attempts to bring him to the point. "For heaven's sake, father, summon up your manhood and let us know the worst!"

"I won't be spoken to in this way," stuttered Hill, growing red.

Allen made one stride forward, and looked down from his tall height at the crouching figure in the chair--the figure in its shameful disguise, with the white face and wild eyes. "You shall be spoken to in a perfectly quiet way," he said calmly, although inwardly agitated, "but you shall do what you are told. I have put up with this state of things long enough. In future, my mother shall govern the house, and you shall come back to it to indulge in whatever whims you like within reason. But master you shall not be."

"Who will prevent me?" said Hill, trying to bluster.

"I shall," said Allen decisively; "you are not fit to manage your own affairs or to rule a house. If you come back--as you shall--my mother, who loves you, will do all she can to make you happy. I also, as your son, will give you all respect due to a father."

"You're doing so now, I think," sneered Hill, very white.

"God help me, what else can I do?" cried Allen, restraining himself by a violent effort; "if you could see yourself you would know what it costs me to speak to you like this. But, for your own sake, for my mother's sake, for my own, I must take the upper hand."

Hill leaped panting from his seat. "You dare!----"

"Sit down," said his son imperiously, and pushed him back in his chair; "yes, I dare, father. As you are not responsible, I shall deal with you as I think is for your good. I know how to deal with men," said Allen, looking very tall and very strong, "and so I shall deal with you."

"You forget," panted Hill, with dry lips, "I have the money."

"I forget nothing. I shall have a commission of lunacy taken out against you and the money matters shall be arranged----"

"Oh," Hill burst into tears, and turned to the quiet, observant Mask, "can you sit and hear all this?"

"I think your son is right, Lawrence."

"I shall go to law," cried Hill fiercely.

"Can a man in hiding go to law?" hinted Mask significantly.

The miserable man sank back in his seat and wept. Sick at heart, Allen looked at the old lawyer. "You are my father's friend, sir," he said gently, "try and bring him to reason. As for me, I must walk for a time in the outer room to recover myself. I can't bear the sight of those tears. My father--oh, God help me, my father!" and Allen, unlocking the door, walked into the outer room sick at heart. He was not a man given to melodrama, but the sight of his wretched father made him sick and faint. He sat down in the clerk's chair to recover himself, and leaned his aching head on his hand.

What passed between Mask and Hill he never knew, but after half an hour the old lawyer called Allen in. Hill had dried his tears, and was still sitting hunched up in the chair. But he was calmer, and took the words which Mask would have spoken out of the lawyer's mouth. "I am much worried, Allen," said he softly, "so you must excuse my being somewhat unstrung. If you think it wise, I'll go back."

"So far as I know, I do think it wise."

"Let us hear the story first," said Mask.

"What story?" asked Allen sharply.

"My miserable story," said Hill; "I'll tell it all. You may be able to help me. And I need help," he ended piteously.

"You shall have all help, father. Tell me why you went to the Red Deeps and took my revolver."

Hill did not answer at once. His eyelids drooped, and he looked cunningly and doubtfully at his son. Apparently he did not trust him altogether, and was thinking as to what he would say, and what leave unsaid. The two men did not speak, and after a pause, Hill, now more composed, began to speak slowly:

"I have known Strode all my life, and he always treated me badly. As a boy I lived near his father's place at Wargrove, and my father liked me to associate with him, as he was of better birth than I. We studied at the same school and the same college, and, when we went into the world, Strode's influence introduced me into aristocratic circles. But my own talents aided me also," said Hill, with open vanity, "I can do everything and amuse any one. When I stopped at Lord Ipsen's----"

"My mother told me of that," said Allen with a gesture of repugnance, "and I don't want to hear the story again."

"I'm not going to tell it," retorted his father tartly, "my idea was to explain a popularity you will never attain to, Allen. However, I'll pass that over. I married your mother, and Strode married Lady Jane Delham, with whom I also was in love-- and I would have made her a much better husband than Strode," said the little man plaintively.

"Go on, please," said Mask, glancing at his watch. "There isn't much time. I have to go out to luncheon."

"Always thinking of yourself, Mask," sneered Hill, "you always did, you know. Well, I saw little of Strode for some time. Then I lent him money and saw less of him than ever. Then he----"

"You told me all this before," interposed Allen, who began to think his father was merely playing with him.

"I'll come to the point presently," said Hill with great dignity; "let me say, Allen, that although I hated Strode, and had good cause too--yes, very good cause--I liked Eva. When you wished to marry her, I was pleased. She wrote to her father about the marriage. He sent her a cablegram saying he was coming home----"

"And when he did arrive at Southampton he told her she was not to think of the marriage."

"He told me also," said Hill, "and long before. He wrote from the Cape telling me he would not allow you to marry Eva."

"Allow me!" said Allen indignantly.

"Yes, and told me I was to stop the marriage. I wrote, and urged the advisability of the match. When Strode reached Southampton, he wrote again saying he intended Eva to marry Lord Saltars---"

"Did he make any mention of money?"

"No. He simply said that if I did not stop the marriage he would disgrace me," here Hill changed color, and looked furtively at both his listeners.

"How disgrace you?" asked Mask sharply.

"I shan't tell you that," was the dogged reply, "all you need know is, that Strode could disgrace me. I--I--made a mistake when I was a young man," said Hill, casting down his eyes, so as not to meet the honest gaze of his son, "and Strode took advantage of it. He made me sign a document confessing what I had done----"

"And what in heaven's name had you done?" questioned Allen, much troubled.

"That's my business. I shan't say--it has nothing to do with you," said Hill hurriedly, "but Strode had the document and always carried it about with him. I wanted to get it and destroy it, so I asked him when he came to Wargrove to meet me at the Red Deeps, and then I would tell him how the marriage with you could be prevented. I also said that I knew something about Lord Saltars----"

"What is that?"

"Nothing," said Hill, this time frankly. "I really knew nothing, but I wanted Strode to come to the Red Deeps. He made an appointment to meet me there on Wednesday at nine."

"In that case, why did he wire to Eva he would be down on Thursday?"

"Because he wanted to come down quietly to see me. And," added Hill hesitating, "he had to see someone else. I don't know who, but he hinted that he had to see someone."

"When you spoke to him at the Red Deeps?"

"Yes. I went there on Wednesday and he was waiting. It was getting dark, but we saw plainly enough. I urged him to give up the document. He refused, and told me that he required more money. I grew angry and left him."

"Alive?"

"Yes. But I had your revolver with me, Allen. I took it with the idea of shooting Strode, if he didn't give up the document----"

"Oh," cried Allen, shrinking back. It seemed horrible to hear his father talk like this. "But you didn't----"

"No. I got behind a bush and fired. My shot touched his arm, for he clapped his hand to the wound. Then he turned with a volley of abuse to run after me. At that moment there came another shot from a clump of trees near me, and Strode fell face downward. I was so afraid at the idea of any one having been near me, and of having overheard our conversation----"

"And of seeing your attempt at murder," interpolated Mask.

"Yes--yes--that I dropped Allen's revolver and ran away."

"I found the revolver and took it home," said Allen; "so the way you acted the next morning when Wasp came was----"

"It was the morning after that," said his father drily, "on Friday, and Strode was shot on Wednesday. I never went near the Red Deeps again. I didn't know if Strode was dead, but I knew that he had been shot. I steeled myself to bear the worst, but did not make any inquiries out of policy. When Wasp came that morning at breakfast, I knew what he had to say. Strode was dead. I dreaded lest Wasp should say that the revolver had been found, in which case you might have got into trouble, Allen: but I was thankful nothing was said of it."

The young man was astounded at this cool speech: but he passed it over, as it was useless to be angry with such a man. "I picked up the revolver as I said," he replied; "but about the document?"

"I hadn't time to get it. The shot frightened me."

"Did you see who fired the shot?"

"No. I was too afraid. I simply ran away and never looked back."

At this point Mask held up his hand. "I hear someone in the outer office," he said, and rose to open the door. Hill slipped behind the table quivering with fear. However, Mask returned to his seat. "I am wrong," he said, "there's no one there. Go on."

"What else do you want to know?" questioned Hill irritably.

"Why you fainted and left the house, when you got that cross from Giles Merry?"

Hill stared. "You knew it was Giles?" he stammered; "what do you know of Giles?"

"Nothing. But Mrs. Merry recognized the direction on the brown paper as being in her husband's writing. Why did you faint?"

Hill looked down and then looked up defiantly. He was still standing behind the desk. "I stole the wooden hand!"

"What!" cried Mask and Allen, both rising.

"Yes. I had my reasons for doing so. I took it from the body, when I was in the death-chamber. I had it in my pocket when I saw you and Eva, and said it was stolen. And then," went on Mr. Hill very fast, so that Allen should not give expression to the horror which was on his face, "I took it home. But I feared lest my wife should find it and then I would get into trouble. Sarah was always looking into my private affairs," he whined, "so to stop that, I went and buried the hand on the common. Someone must have watched me, for I put that cross to mark the spot. When I opened the parcel and saw the cross I knew someone must have dug up the wooden hand and that my secret----"

"What has the wooden hand to do with your secret?"

Hill shuffled, but did not reply to the question. "It was Giles's writing. I knew he'd got the wooden hand, and my secret--Hark!" There was certainly the sound of retreating footsteps in the other room. Allen flung open the door, while his father cowered behind the desk. The outer door was closing. Allen leaped for it: but the person had turned the key in the lock. They heard a laugh, and then retreating footsteps. Mask, who had followed Allen, saw something white on the floor. He picked it up. It was a letter addressed to Sebastian Mask. Opening this he returned to the inner office. "Let us look at this first," said Mask, and recalled Allen: then he read what was in the envelope. It consisted of one line. "Open the wooden hand," said the mysterious epistle.

"No," shrieked Hill, dropping on his knees; "my secret will be found out!"

XVII - A FRIEND IN NEED

ALLEN WAS stopping in quiet rooms near Woburn Square, which was cheaper than boarding at a hotel. He was none too well off, as his father allowed him nothing. Still, Allen had made sufficient money to live fairly comfortable, and had not spent much, since his arrival in England, owing to his residence at "The Arabian Nights."

It had been Allen's intention to escort his father back to Wargrove, whither Hill consented to go. But, on explaining to Mask his desire to trace out Butsey by using the address of the Fresh Air People in Whitechapel, Mask had agreed to take the old man home himself. He thought that it was just as well Allen should find the boy, who might know much.

"He didn't steal the wooden hand," said Mask, when he parted from Allen, "but he is evidently in with the gang."

"What gang, Mr. Mask?"

"That headed by the old gentleman who called on me. Jerry is one of the gang, and this boy Butsey another. He sent that telegram, remember. If you can find the lad you may learn much, and perhaps may get back the hand."

"But what good will that do?" asked Allen, puzzled; "from what my father said when you read the anonymous letter, he evidently knew that the hand can be opened. If, as he says, it contains his secret, he must have opened it himself when he took it home, and before he buried it."

Mask wrinkled his brows and shook his head. "I confess that I cannot understand," he remarked hopelessly, "nor will I, until your father is more frank with me.

This is one reason why I am taking him myself to Wargrove. When I get him there I may induce him to tell me his secret."

"It must be a very serious secret to make him behave as he does."

Mask sighed. "I repeat that I can't understand. I have known your father all his life. We were boys together, and I also knew Strode. But although your father was always foolish, I can't think that he would do anything likely to bring him within reach of the law."

"He stole the wooden hand, at all events," said Allen grimly.

"Out of sheer terror, I believe, and that makes me think that his secret, for the preservation of which he robbed the dead, is more serious than we think. However I'll see what I can learn, and failing your father, I shall ask Giles Merry."

"Do you think he knows?"

"I fancy so. The parcel with the cross was addressed in his writing, so it is he who has the hand. He must have given it to the old scoundrel who called on me, so I think, Mr. Allen, we are justified in adding Merry to the gang."

"But the hand must have been empty when my father buried it on the common, so how could Giles know his secret?"

"I can only say that I don't understand," said Mask with a gesture of hopelessness; "wait till I get your father to speak out. Then we may learn the truth."

"I dread to hear it," said the son gloomily.

"Well," replied Mask in a comforting tone, "at all events we know it has nothing to do with this murder. It is your task to learn who committed that, and you may do so through Butsey."

After this conversation Mr. Mask took Hill back to Wargrove, whither the old man went willingly enough. He seemed to think himself absolutely safe, when in the company of his legal adviser and old friend. Allen returned to his rooms, and sent a message to Mr. Horace Parkins that he would see him that afternoon. It was necessary that he should keep faith with his friend Mark Parkins in South America, and find a capitalist; and Allen thought that Horace, whom Mark reported shrewd, might know of some South African millionaire likely to float the mine in Bolivia. As to the search after Butsey, Allen had not quite made up his mind. He could learn of Butsey's whereabouts certainly, but if it was some low den where the lad lived, he did not want to go alone, and thought it might be necessary to enlist the service of a detective. For his father's sake, Allen did not wish to do so. But he must have someone to go with him into the depths of London slums, that was certain. Allen knew the life of the Naked Lands, and there could more than hold his own, but he was ignorant of the more terrible life of the submerged tenth's dens.

It was at three o'clock that Allen appointed the meeting with Parkins, and at that hour precisely a cab drove up. In a few minutes Parkins was shown in by the landlady, and proved to be a giant of over six feet, lean, bright-eyed, and speaking with a decided American accent. He was smartly dressed in a Bond Street kit, but looked rather out of place in a frock-coat and silk hat and patent leather boots.

"Well, I'm glad to see you," said the giant, shaking hands with a grip which made Allen wince--and he was no weakling. "Mark's been firing in letters about what a good sort you are, and I was just crazy to meet you. It isn't easy finding a pal in this rotten planet of ours, Mr. Hill, but I guess from what Mark says, you fill the bill, so far as he's concerned, and I hope you'll cotton on to me, for I'm dog-sick with loneliness in this old city."

Allen laughed at this long speech and placed a chair for his visitor. "You'd like a drink, I know," he said, ringing the bell.

"Milk only," said Parkins, hitching up the knees of his trousers, and casting his mighty bulk into the deep chair; "I don't hold with wine, or whisky, or tea, or coffee, or anything of that sort. My nerves are my own, I guess, and all I've got to hang on to, for the making of bargains. I'm not going to play Sally-in-our-Alley with them. No, sir, I guess not. Give me the cow's brew."

So a glass of milk was brought, and Mr. Parkins was made happy. "I suppose you don't smoke, then?" said Allen, amused.

"You bet--a pipe." He produced a short clay and filled it. "I'm of the opinion of that old chap in Westward Ho., if you know the book?"

"I haven't read it for years."

"Y'ought to. I read it every year, same as I do my Bible. Had I my way, sir," he emphasized with his pipe, "I'd give every English boy a copy of that glorious book to show him what a man should be."

"You're English, I believe, Mr. Parkins?"

"Born, but not bred so. Fact is, my mother and father didn't go well in double harness, so mother stopped at home with Mark, and I lighted out Westward-ho with father. You'd never take me for Mark's brother?"

"I should think not. You're a big man and he's small: you talk with a Yankee accent, and he speaks pure English. He's----"

"Different to me in every way. That's a fact. I'm a naturalized citizen of the U.S.A. and Mark's a Britisher. We've met only once, twice, and again, Mr. Hill, but get on very well. There's only two of us alive of the Parkins gang, so I guess we'd best be friendly, till we marry and rear the next generation. I'm going to hitch up with an English girl, and Mark--if I can persuade him--will marry an American dollar heiress. Yes, sir, we'll square accounts with the motherland that way."

All the time Parkins talked, he pulled at his pipe, and enveloped himself in a cloud of smoke. But his keen blue eyes were constantly on Allen's face, and finally he stretched out a huge hand. "I guess I've taken to you, some," said he, "catch on, and we'll be friends."

"Oh," said Allen, grasping the hand, "I'm sure we shall. I like Mark."

"Well then, just you like the American side of him, which is Horace Parkins. I guess we'll drop the misters and get to business, Hill."

"I'm ready. What do you want to see me about?"

"Well, Mark wrote to me as you'd got a mine of sorts, and wanted a capitalist. I'm not a millionaire, but I can shell out a few dollars, if y'think you can get the property cheap."

"Oh, I think so. The Spaniard that owns it wants money and isn't very sure of its value."

"Tell me about that right along."

Whereupon Hill detailed the story of the Indian and how the mine had been worked by the Inca kings. He described the locality and the chances of getting the silver to the coast: also spoke of the labour required and the number of shares he and Mark intended to divide the mine into. Horace listened, nodding gravely.

"I see you've figured it out all right, Hill," said Parkins, "and I guess I'll take a hand in the game. Give me a share and I'll engineer the buying."

"Good," said Allan, delighted, "we'll divide the mine into three equal shares. You buy it, and Mark and I will work it."

"Good enough. We won't want anyone else to chip in. It's a deal."

They shook hands on this, and then had a long talk about the West Indies, which Horace, who had never been there, knew chiefly through the glowing pages of Westward Ho.. "Though I guess the place has changed since then," said he, "but the gold and silver's there right enough, and maybe, if we looked long enough, we'd chance on that golden Manoa Kingsley talks about."

The talk drifted into more immediate topics, and Allen, much amused at his gigantic companion's naïve ways of looking at things, asked him about his life. Thereupon Horace launched out into a wild tale of doings in Africa. He had been all through the war and had fought therein. He had been up the Shire River, and all over the lion country. He made money and lost it, so he said, and finally managed to find a fortune. It was five o'clock before he ended, and later he made a remark which made Allen jump: "So I just thought when I got Mark's letter telling me you were in the old country and about the mine, that I'd come home and see what kind of man you were. I'm satisfied--oh yes, you bet. I'll trust you to the death, for I size up folk uncommon quick, and you?"

"I'll trust you also," said Allen, looking at the man's clear eyes and responding to his true-hearted grip, "and in fact I need a friend now, Mr. Parkins."

"Call me Parkins, plain, without the Mister. Well, here I am, ready to be your pal, while Mark's over the herring-pond. What's up? Do you want me to cut a throat? Just say the word, and I'll do it. Anything for a change, for I'm dead sick of this place ever since I left the Dunoon Castle.."

It was this speech which made Allen jump. "What, did you come home in the Dunoon Castle?"

"You bet I did, and a fine passage we had."

"Did you know a passenger called Strode?"

Parkins raised his immense bulk slightly, and looked sharply at the questioner. "Do you mean the man who was murdered?"

"Yes. I suppose you read about the crime in the papers?"

"That's so. Yes, I knew him very well. Better than anyone on board, I guess. We got along finely. Not a man I trusted," added Parkins musingly, "but a clever sort of chap. Well?"

"Did he ever tell you of his daughter?"

"No. He never spoke of his private relations."

"Well, he has a daughter, Miss Eva Strode. You must have read her name in the papers when the case was reported."

"I did," said Parkins after a pause; "yes?"

"I'm engaged to her."

Parkins rose and looked astonished. "That's a queer start."

"You'll hear of something queerer if you will answer my questions."

"What sort of questions?"

Allen debated within himself if he should trust Parkins all in all. It seemed a rash thing to do, and yet there was something about the man which showed that he would not break faith. Horace was just the sort of companion Allen needed to search after Butsey in the slums of Whitechapel. It was no good telling him anything, unless all were told, and yet Allen hesitated to bring in the name of his father. Finally he resolved to say as little as he could about him, and merely detail the broad facts of the murder, and of the theft of the hand, without mentioning names. "Parkins," he said frankly and with a keen look, "can I trust you?"

"I guess so," said the big man serenely. "I mean what I say. You can take my word without oaths, I reckon."

"Very well, then," said Allen with a sudden impulse to make a clean breast of it; "sit down again and answer a few questions."

Horace dropped down heavily and loaded his pipe. While he was lighting up, he listened to Allen's questions. But Allen did not begin before he had explained the purpose of his inquiries.

"I am engaged to Miss Strode," said Allen, "but she refuses to marry me until I learn who killed her father."

"Very right and just," nodded Parkins.

"Well, I'm trying to hunt out the criminal, and I should like you to help me."

"I'm with you right along, Hill. Fire away with your questions."

Allen began: "Did Mr. Strode ever tell you he had money?"

"Yes. He made a lot in South Africa and not in the most respectable way. I don't like talking ill of the dead, and of the father of the girl you're going to make Mrs. Hill, but if I am to be truthful----"

"I want you to be, at all costs. The issues are too great for anything false to be spoken."

"Well then, I heard a lot about Strode in Africa before we steamed together in the Dunoon Castle.. He made his money in shady ways."

"Humph!" said Allen, "I'm not surprised, from what I've heard."

"He was an I. D. B. if you want to get to facts."

"What's that?" demanded Allen.

"An illicit diamond buyer."

"Can you explain?"

"I guess so. Strode bought diamonds from anyone who had them. If a Kaffir stole a jewel, and many of them do steal, you bet, Strode would buy it from him at a small price. He was on this lay for a long time, but was never caught. And yet I don't know," said Parkins half to himself, "that brute Jerry Train knew something of his doings!"

Allen almost leaped from his seat. "Jerry! was he a big red-headed man--a ruffian?"

"He was a bad lot all through--a horse-thief and I don't know what else in the way of crime. He made South Africa too hot for him, and came home steerage in the Dunoon Castle.. I saw him at times, as I knew a heap about him, and he thieved from a pal of mine up Bulawayo way. He seemed to suspect Strode of yanking diamonds out of the country."

"Did Strode tell you he possessed diamonds?"

"No. He said he'd made money to the extent of forty thousand pounds."

"Did he carry the money with him?"

Parkins shook his head. "I can't say. I should think he'd have letters of credit. He'd a pocketbook he was always dipping into, and talked of his money a lot."

"A blue pocket-book with a crest?"

"That's so. Do you know it?"

"No. But that pocket-book was stolen from the body. At least it was not found, so it must have been stolen."

"Oh, and I guess Strode was murdered for the sake of the pocket-book. But see here," said Horace shrewdly, "I've told you a heap. Now, you cut along and reel out a yarn to me."

The other man needed no second invitation. He laid aside his pipe and told the story of the crime, suppressing only the doings of his father. Horace listened and nodded at intervals.

"I don't see clear after all," he said when Allen ended, "sure you've told me everything?"

The young man looked uneasy. "I've told you what I could."

Parkins rose and stretched out his hand. "What you've told me will never be repeated. Good-bye."

"What for?" asked Allen, also rising.

"Because you won't trust me. I can't straighten out this business, unless you do."

"The other thing I might tell isn't my own."

"No go. If it concerns the murder it must be told. I don't work half knowledge with any one. You can trust me."

Allen hesitated. He wanted to tell all, for he felt sure that Parkins would help him. But then it seemed terrible to reveal his father's shame to a stranger. What was he to do?

"See here, I'll tell--you everything, suppressing names."

"Won't do," said the inflexible Parkins; "good-bye."

"Will you give me a few hours to think over the matter?"

"No. If I'm not to be trusted now, I'm not to be trusted at all."

The young man bit his fingers. He couldn't let Parkins go, for he knew about Strode and Red Jerry, and might aid the case a lot. It was imperative that the truth should be discovered, else it might be that his father would be put to open shame. Better, Allen thought, to tell Parkins and get his aid, than risk the arrest of his father and see the whole story in the papers. "I'll tell all," he said.

"Good man," growled Parkins, his brow clearing.

When in possession of all the facts, Parkins thought for a moment and delivered his opinion: "Strode I take it was followed to the Red Deeps by Jerry Train, and Jerry shot him and stole the pocket-book."

"But the wooden hand?"

"Merry's got it and he's in the gang. Hold on," said Parkins, "I'll not give a straight opinion till I see this boy. We'll go down and hunt him up. He'll give the show away."

"But my father?" asked Allen, downcast.

"He's a crank. I don't believe he mixed up in the biznai at all."

XVIII - THE FINDING OF BUTSEY

IT DID not take Allen long to learn something about Butsey. An inquiry at the offices of the philanthropic people, who dealt with the transfer of ragged boys to the country for fresh air, brought out the fact that Butsey was a thief, and a sparrow of the gutter, who lived in a certain Whitechapel den--address given--with a set of the greatest ruffians in London.

"It was a mere accident the boy came here," said the spectacled gentleman who supplied the information; "we were sending out a number of ragged children to Westhaven for a couple of days, and this boy came and asked if he could go too. At first, we were not inclined to accept him, as we knew nothing about him. But the boy is so clever and amusing, that we consented he should go. He went with the rest to Westhaven, but did not keep with those who looked after the poor creatures. In fact, Mr. Hill," said the gentleman frankly, "Butsey took French leave."

"Where did he go?"

"I can't tell you. But one of our men caught sight of Father Don, and Red Jerry, at Westhaven--those are the ruffians Butsey lives with. He might have gone with them."

"Did you take the children down on a Wednesday?"

"Yes. And then they came back, late the next day."

Allen reflected that if Butsey sent the wire before four o'clock, he must have gone back to London, and wondered where he got the money for the fare. Then he must have come down again, in order to give the lying message to Mrs. Merry. However, he told the philanthropist nothing of this, but thanked him for his information. "I intend to look this boy up," he said, when taking his leave.

"Has he got into trouble?" asked the gentleman anxiously.

"Well, not exactly. But I want to learn something from him relative to a matter about which it is not necessary to be too precise. I assure you, sir, Butsey will not come to harm."

"He has come to harm enough already, poor lad." I tell you, Mr. Hill, "that I should like to drag that boy out of the gutter, and make him a decent member of society. He is sharp beyond his years, but his talents are utilized in the wrong way---_"

"By Father Don, Red Jerry, and Co.," said Allen drily; "so I think."

"One moment, Mr. Hill; if you go to the Perry Street den, take a plain clothes policeman with you. Father Don is dangerous."

"Oh, I'll see to that," said Allen, confident in his own muscles and in those of Parkins. "You couldn't get Butsey to come here?"

"I fear not--I sadly fear not, Mr. Hill. The boy has never been near us since he came back with the children from Westhaven."

"He did come back with them, then?"

"Oh yes," said the philanthropist frankly, by the late train; "but what he did in the meantime, and where he went, I can't say. He refused to give an account of himself."

"Shrewd little devil," said Allen; "but I think I know."

"I trust it has nothing to do with the police," said the gentleman anxiously; "a detective asked after Butsey. I gave him the address of Father Don in Perry Street, but the lad could not be found. The detective refused to say why the lad was wanted, and I hope he'll not come to harm. If you find him, bring him to me, and I'll see what I can do to save him. It's a terrible thing to think that an immortal soul and a clever lad should remain in the depths."

Allen assented politely, promised to do what he could towards bringing about the reformation of Butsey, and went his way. He privately thought that to make Butsey a decent member of society would be next door to impossible, for the lad seemed to be quite a criminal, and education might only make him the more dangerous to the well-being of the community. However he reserved his opinion on this point, and got back to his Woburn rooms to explain to Horace. The big American-- for he virtually was a Yankee--nodded gravely.

"We'll go down this very night," he said. "I guess we'd best put on old togs, leave our valuables at home, and carry six-shooters."

"Do you think that last is necessary?" asked Allen anxiously.

"It's just as well to be on the safe side, Hill. If this boy is employed by Father Don and his gang, he won't be let go without a fight. Maybe he knows too much for the safety of the gang."

"That's very probable," assented Hill drily; "however, we'll take all precautions, and go to Perry Street."

"This is what I call enjoyment," said Horace, stretching his long limbs. "I'm not a quarrelsome man, but, by Gosh, I'm just spoiling for a fight."

"I think there's every chance we'll get what you want, Parkins."

So the matter was arranged, and after dinner the two men changed into shabby clothes. It was raining heavily, and they put on overcoats, scarves, and wore slouch hats. Both carried revolvers, and thus they felt ready for any emergency. As Allen knew London comparatively well, he took the lead, and conducted Horace to Aldgate Station by the underground railway. Here they picked up a cab and went to Whitechapel. The driver knew Perry Street but refused to go near it, on the plea that it was a dangerous locality. However, he deposited the two near the place, and drove away in the rain, leaving Allen and Horace in a somewhat dark street. A search for a guide produced a ragged boy of the Butsey type, who volunteered to show the way to Father Don's den. "You've got some swag to send up the spout, gents both?" leered the brat, looking up to the big men as they stood under a lamp-post.

"Just so," said Horace quickly, thinking this a good excuse; "you engineer us along, sonny, and we'll give you a shilling."

"A bob?--that's good enough," said the urchin, and scampered down a back street so quickly that they had some difficulty in keeping up with him. Later on, when they caught him at the end of a cul-de-sac., Allen gripped the guide by his wet shoulder. "Do you know a boy called Butsey?"

"Oh my eyes and ears, don't I just? Why, he's Father Don's pet. But he's in disgrace now."

"Why?" asked Horace coolly.

"Father Don sent him down the country, and he didn't turn up at the hour he was told to. He's been whacked and put on bread and water," said the brat, grinning, "worse luck for Father Don. Butsey'll put a knife into him for that."

"Good," whispered Allen to the American as they went on in the darkness. "Butsey will have a grudge against Father Don, and will be all the more ready to tell."

"Humph! I'm not so sure. There's honor amongst thieves."

They had no further time for conversation, for the guide turned down a narrow lane leading off the cul-de-sac., and knocked at the door of a ruined house with broken windows. A shrill voice inside asked who was there.

"Swell mobsmen with swag for the patrico," said the guide, whistling shrilly. "Show us a light."

The door opened, and a small pinched-looking girl appeared with a candle. She examined the two men and then admitted them. When they ventured within, she shut the door, which seemed to be very strong. But Horace noticed a door on the left of the passage leading into an empty room. He knew that one of the broken windows set in the street wall gave light to this room, and resolved to make it a line of retreat should they be too hardly pressed. Meantime the boy and girl led the way along the passage and towards a trap-door. Here, steps leading downward brought them to a large cellar filled with ragged people of both sexes. There was a fire in a large chimney, which seemed to have been constructed to roast an ox, and round this they sat, their damp garments steaming in the heat. A curtain portioned off a corner of the cellar, and when the strangers entered two shrill voices were heard talking together angrily. But the thieves around paid no attention.

"Red Jerry," said Horace, touching Allen's arm, and he pointed to a truculent-looking ruffian, almost as big as himself, who was lying on a bed composed of old newspapers and day-bills. He seemed to be drunk, for he breathed heavily and his pipe had fallen from his fevered lips. "Nice man to tackle," muttered Horace.

"Come along," said the guide, tugging at Allen's hand. "Father Don's got someone in there, but he'll see you. What's the swag--silver?"

"Never you mind," said Horace; "you find Butsey and I'll make it worth your while."

"Give us a sov. and I'll do it," said the brat. "I'm Billy, and fly at that."

"Good. A sov. you shall have."

The boy whistled again and some of the thieves cursed him. He then pushed Horace towards the ragged curtain behind which the shrill voices sounded, and vanished. The two were now fully committed to the adventure.

Curiously enough, the ruffians in the cellar did not take much notice of the strangers. Perhaps they were afraid of Father Don, seeing that the two came to dispose of swag, and at all events they apparently thought that Father Don could protect himself. Meanwhile the keen ears of Horace heard a deeper voice, something like a man's, mingling with the shrill ones of the other speakers. Without a moment's hesitation, and anxious to get the business over, the big American dragged aside the curtain and entered.

Allen and he found themselves before a narrow door. On entering this, for it was open, they saw an old man with a white beard sitting at a small table with papers before him. Near, was a small sharp-faced man, and at the end of the table sat a woman dressed in black.

"It won't do, Father Don," the woman was saying in deep tones; "you told that brat to rob me. Give it up, I tell you."

"Give up what?" asked Father Don sharply. "How can I give up anything, when I don't know what it is?"

"Butsey knows," said the woman. "Where is he?"

"On bread and water in the attic," said the small man with a shrill laugh; "he's having his pride brought down."

"You'd better take care of Butsey," said the woman drily, "or he'll sell you."

"Let him try," snarled the benevolent-looking old gentleman. "Red Jerry's his father and will break his back."

This much the two gentlemen heard, and it was then that the American appeared in the narrow doorway. The woman started and looked at him. He eyed her in turn and saw a fine-looking creature with dark eyes, and of a full voluptuous beauty hardly concealed by the plain dark robes she wore. Allen glanced over Parkins's shoulder and uttered an ejaculation. "Why, Miss Lorry," he said.

The woman started and rose quickly, overturning the table. The small lamp on it, fell and went out. There were a few curses from Father Don and a shrill expostulation from the small man. In the hot darkness a dress brushed past the two men who were now in the room, and a strong perfume saluted their nostrils. Horace could have stopped Miss Lorry from going, but he had no reason to do so, and she slipped out while Father Don was groping for the lamp, and the other man struck a match. As the blue flare spurted up, the man saw the two who had entered. "What's this?" he cried with an oath, which it is not necessary to set down; "who are you?"

"We've come about business," said Horace; "don't you move till the old man's got the lamp alight, or you'll get hurt."

"It's the 'tecs," said Father Don savagely.

"I guess not. We've come to do business."

This remark seemed to stimulate the curiosity of the two men, and they refrained from a shout which would have brought in all the riff-raff without. Allen congratulated himself, that Parkins had roused this curiosity. He had no desire to fight in a dark cellar with his back to the wall against a score of ruffians. In a few minutes the lamp was lighted. "Turn it up, Foxy," said Father Don; "and now, gentlemen," he added politely, "how did you get here?"

"A boy called Billy brought us," said Allen stepping forward. "I fear we've frightened the lady away."

"Let her go, the jade," said Foxy shrilly; "there would have been a heap of trouble if she'd remained," and he confirmed this speech with several oaths.

Father Don did not swear. He spoke in a clear, refined, and educated voice, and apparently was a well-educated man who had fallen into the depths through some rascality. But his face looked most benevolent, and no one would have suspected him of being a ruffian of the worst. He eyed Allen piercingly, and also his companion. "Well, gentlemen," he asked quietly, "and what can I do for you?" Horace sat down heavily and pulled out his pipe. "We may as well talk comfortably," he said. "Sit down, Hill."

"Hill?" said Father Don with a start, while Foxy opened his small eyes--"not of Wargrove?"

"The same," said Allen quietly. "How do you know me?"

"I know a good many things," said Father Don calmly.

"Do you know who shot Strode?"

Foxy rose as though moved by a spring. "You're on that lay, are you?" said he shrilly; "then you've come to the wrong shop."

"Oh, I guess not, said Horace lazily--to the right shop. You see, Mister," he went on to the elder ruffian, "we want that wooden hand."

"What wooden hand?" asked Father Don. "If you mean----"

"Yes, I do mean that," said Allen quickly; "you brought it to Mr. Mask to get the money."

"Did I?" said Father Don coolly and eyeing the young man; "well, maybe I did. But I didn't take it from the dead?"

Allen colored. "Merry took it," he said.

"Oh no, he didn't," sneered Foxy. "Merry got it from Butsey, who dug it up after it had been planted by----"

"Stop," said Allen, rising. "Father Don," he added, turning to the old man, "you seem to be a gentleman----"

"I was once. But what's that got to do with this?"

"Stop this man," he pointed to Foxy, "from mentioning names."

"I'll stop everything, if you'll tell us where the diamonds are to be found," said Father Don.

"I don't know what you mean," said Allen.

"Oh yes, you do. You know everything about this case, and you've come here to get the hand. Well then, you won't. Only while I hold that hand can I get the diamonds."

"Where will you get them?"

"That's what I want you to tell me."

"I guess Red Jerry knows," said Horace sharply; "he took the diamonds from the dead body of the man he shot."

"Meaning Strode," said Foxy, with a glance at Father Don.

"Jerry didn't shoot him," said that venerable fraud.

"I surmise he did," said Parkins. "Ask him in."

"How do you know about Jerry?" asked Father Don uneasily.

"I sailed along o' him, and saved him from being lynched as a horse-thief. If you won't call him in, I'll do so myself."

"Hold your tongue," said Father Don, rising and looking very benevolent, "you take too much upon yourself. I'm king here, and if I say the word neither of you will go out alive."

"Oh, I guess so," said Horace coolly, "we don't come unprepared," and in a moment he swung out his Derringer. "Sit still, Father Christmas," said Parkins, levelling this, "or you'll get hurt."

Seeing Parkins's action, Allen produced his weapon and covered Foxy, so there sat the kings of the castle, within hail of their ruffianly crew, unable to call for assistance.

"And now we'll call in Jerry," said Allen coolly. "Sing out, Parkins."

But before the big American could raise a shout there was a sudden noise outside. A shrill voice was heard crying that the police were coming, and then ensued a babel. Father Don seized the opportunity when Parkins's eye was wavering to knock the revolver out of his hand. The American thereupon made a clutch at his throat, while Allen tripped Foxy up. A small boy dashed into the room. He was white-faced, stunted, red-haired, and had but one eye. At once he made for Parkins, squealing for the police. When he got a grip of Horace's hand he dropped his voice:

"Ketch t'other cove's hand, and mine," said the boy, and then with a dexterous movement overturned the table, whereby the lamp went out again for the second time. Parkins seized the situation at once, and while Father Don, suddenly released, scrambled on the floor, and made use for the first time of bad language, he grabbed Allen's hand and dragged him toward the door. Horace in his turn was being drawn swiftly along by the small boy. The outer cellar was filled with a mass of screaming, squalling, swearing humanity, all on the alert for the advent of the police. The boy drew the two men through the crowd, which did not know whence to expect the danger. Horace hurled his way through the mob by main strength, and Allen followed in his devastating wake. Shortly, they reached the trap-door, and ran along the passage. The boy pulled them into the side-room Horace had noted when he came to the den.

"Break the winder," said the boy to Parkins.

The American did not need further instructions, and wrapping his coat round his arm he smashed the frail glass. From below came confusedly the noise of the startled thieves. But Horace first, Allen next, and the boy last, dropped on to the pavement. Then another lad appeared, and all four darted up the street. In ten minutes they found themselves blown but safe, in the chief thoroughfare and not far from a policeman, who looked suspiciously at them.

"There," said the last-joined boy, "you're saif. Butsey saived y'."

"Butsey?" said Allen, looking at the stunted, one-eyed lad.

"That's me," said Butsey with a grin; "y'were near being scragged by th' ole man. If y'd called Red Jerry, he'd ha' done fur y'. Miss Lorry told me t'get you out, and I've done it."

"But I reckon the old Father Christmas told us you were locked up."

"Was," said Butsey laconically; "in th' attic--bread an' water. I ain't goin' to work fur sich a lot anymore, so I dropped out of th' winder, and climbed the roof--down the spout. In the street I met Miss Lorry--she told me there was fightin' below, so'--he winked.

"Then there was no police?" said Allen, admiring the boy's cleverness.

"Not much. But they're allays expecting of th' peelers," said Butsey coolly; "'twasn't difficult to get 'em rizzed with fright. But you look here, Misters, you clear out now, or they'll be after you."

"You come also, Butsey."

"Not me. I'm agoin' to doss along o' Billy here. I'll come an' see you at Wargrove and bring the wooden hand with me."

"What," said Allen, "do you know----?"

"I knows a lot, an' I'm going to split," said Butsey. "Give us a bob"; and when Allen tossed him one, he spat on it for luck. "See y' m' own time," said Butsey. "I'm goin' to turn respectable an' split. Th' ole man ain't goin' to shut me up for nix. 'Night," and catching his companion's arm, both boys ran off into the darkness.

XIX - MRS. MERRY'S VISITORS

THE VISIT to the den was certainly a fiasco. Those who had ventured into those depths, had, on the face of it, gained nothing. What would have happened had not Butsey raised the false alarm it is impossible to say. According to the boy, Jerry would have turned disagreeable, and probably there would have been a free fight. As it was, Allen and Horace came back without having achieved their object. They were as far as ever from the discovery of the truth.

"And yet, I don't know," said Allen hopefully, "somehow I feel inclined to trust Butsey. He's got some scheme in his head."

"Huh," said Horace heavily, "y' can't trust a boy like that. He's got his monkey up because the old man dropped on him, but like as not, he'll change his tune and go back. Father Don 'ull make things square. He can't afford to lose a promising young prig like Butsey."

"I believe the boy will come to Wargrove as he said," insisted Allen.

"In that case I guess we'd better go down too. Would you mind putting me up for a few days?"

"I'll be glad, and I don't think my father will object. It is just as well you should see him."

"That's why I want to come down," said Parkins cheerfully; "y'see, Hill, the business has to be worked out somehow. I think your father's got a crazy fit, and there isn't anything he's got to be afraid of. But he's shivering about someone, and who that someone is, we must learn. Better we should sift the matter ourselves than let the police handle it."

Allen turned pale. "God forbid," said he; "I want the authorities kept away."

So Allen wrote a letter to his father, asking if he could bring down Parkins for a few days. The reply, strange to say, came from Mrs. Hill, and the reading of it afforded Allen some thought.

"There is no need to ask your father anything," she wrote, "he has given everything into my hands, even to the money. What the reason is I can't say, as he refuses to speak. He seems very much afraid, and remains in his own rooms--the Japanese apartments. Mr. Mask also refused to speak, saying my husband would tell me himself if he felt inclined, but I can learn nothing. I am glad you are coming back, Allen, as I am seriously anxious. Of course you can bring Mr. Parkins. The house is large and he will not need to go near your father, though, it may be, the sight of a new face would do your father good. At all events come down and let us talk over things."

So Allen and Horace went to Westhaven and drove over to Wargrove. On the way Allen stopped the brougham, which was driven by Harry Jacobs, and took Horace to the Red Deeps to see the spot where the murder had been committed. When they got back--as the day was wet--their boots were covered with the red mud of the place. Jacobs saw this, and begged to speak to Allen before he got in.

"I say, Mr. Allen," he whispered, so that Parkins, now in the brougham, should not hear, "do you remember when I drove you to Misery Castle I said I'd tell you something?"

"Yes. What is it?"

"Well, you know I clean the boots, sir? Well, master's boots were covered with that red mud, on the day after----"

"I know all about that," interrupted Allen, feeling his blood run cold as he thought what trouble might come through the boy's chatter; "my father explained. You need not mention it."

"No, sir," said Jacobs obediently enough. He was devoted to Allen, for a queer reason that Allen had once thrashed him for being impertinent. There was no danger that he would say anything, but on the way to Wargrove the groom wondered if his master had anything to do with the commission of the crime. Only in the direction of the Red Deeps could such mud be found, and Jacobs had no doubt but that Mr. Hill senior had been to the place.

When they arrived at "The Arabian Nights" Mr. Hill at first refused to see Allen, but consented to do so later. When the young man entered the Japanese rooms, he was alarmed to see how ill his father looked. The man was wasting to skin and bone, his face was as white as death, and he started nervously at every noise.

"You must see Dr. Grace," said Allen.

"No," said Hill, "I won't--I shan't--I can't. How can you ask me to see any one when I'm in such danger?"

"You're in no danger here," said his son soothingly.

"So your mother says, and I can trust her. Let me keep to my own rooms, Allen, and leave me alone."

"You don't mind Parkins being in the house?"

"Why should I?--the house has nothing to do with me. I have given everything over to your mother's care. Mask has drawn up my will--it is signed and sealed, and he has it. Everything has been left to your mother. I left nothing to you," he added maliciously.

"I don't want anything, so long as my mother is safe."

"She is safe," said his father gloomily, "but am I? They'll find me out and kill me----"

"Who will?" asked Allen sharply.

"Don't speak like that--your voice goes through my head. Go away and amuse your friend. Your mother is mistress here--I am nothing, I only want my bite and sup--leave me alone--oh, how weary I am!"

So the miserable man maundered on. He had quite lost his affectations and looked worn out. He mostly lay on the sofa all day, and for the rest of the time he paced the room ceaselessly. Seeing him in this state Allen sought his mother.

"Something must be done," he said.

"What can be done?" said Mrs. Hill, who looked firmer than ever. "He seems to be afraid of something. What it is I don't know--the illness is mental, and you can't minister to a mind diseased. Perhaps you can tell me what this all means, Allen."

"I'll tell you what I know," said Allen wearily, for the anxiety was wearing out his nerves, and he thereupon related all that had taken place since he left Wargrove. Mrs. Hill listened in silence.

"Of course, unless your father speaks we can do nothing," she said at last; "do you think he is in his right mind, Allen?"

"No. He has always been eccentric," said the son, "and now, as he is growing old he is becoming irresponsible. I am glad he has given everything over to you, mother, and has made his will."

"Mr. Mask induced him to do that," said Mrs. Hill thankfully; "if he had remained obstinately fixed about the money I don't know what I should have done. But now that everything is in my hands I can manage him better. Let him stay in his rooms and amuse himself, Allen. If it is necessary that he should see the doctor I shall insist on his doing so. But at present I think it is best to leave him alone."

"Well, mother, perhaps you are right. And in any case Parkins and I will not trouble him or you much. I'll introduce him to Mrs. Palmer, and she'll take him off our hands."

"Of course she will," said Mrs. Hill rather scornfully; "the woman's a born flirt. So you don't know yet who killed Eva's father, Allen?"

"No," said he, shaking his head. "I must see Eva and tell her of my bad fortune."

No more was said at the time, and life went on fairly well in the house. Under Mrs. Hill's firm sway the management of domestic affairs was much improved, and the servants were satisfied, which they had never been, when Lawrence Hill was sole master. Parkins was much liked by Mrs. Hill, and easily understood that Mr. Hill, being an invalid, could not see him. She put it this way to save her husband's credit. She was always attending to him, and he clung to her like a frightened child to its mother. There was no doubt that the fright over the parcel had weakened a mind never very strong.

Allen and Parkins walked, rode, golfed on the Shanton Links, and paid frequent visits to Mrs. Palmer's place. Allen took the American there within a couple of days of his return, and the widow forthwith admired Parkins. "A charming giant," she described him, and Horace reciprocated. "I like her no end," he confided to Allen; "she's a clipper. Just the wife for me."

Eva laughed when Allen told her this, and remarked that if things went on as they were doing there was every chance that Mrs. Palmer would lose her heart.

"But that's ridiculous, Eva," said Allen, "they have known each other only five days."

"Well, we fell in love in five minutes," said Eva, smiling, which provocative remark led to an exchange of kisses.

The two were seated in the drawing-room of the villa. They had enjoyed a very good dinner, and had now split into couples. Allen and Eva remained in the drawing-room near the fire, while Parkins and Mrs. Palmer played billiards. It was a chill, raw evening, but the room looked bright and cheerful. The lovers were very happy being together again, and especially at having an hour to themselves. Mrs. Palmer was rather exacting, and rarely let Eva out of her sight.

"But she is really kind," said Eva, turning her calm face to Allen; "no one could be kinder."

"Except me, I hope," said Allen, crossing the hearth-rug and seating himself by her side. "I want to speak seriously, Eva."

"Oh dear," she said in dismay; "is it about our marriage?"

"Yes. I have arranged the money business with Horace Parkins, and it is necessary I should go to South America as soon as possible. If I don't, the mine may be sold to someone else."

"But can't Mr. Mark Parkins buy it?"

"Well, he could, but Horace wants to go out, so as to be on the spot, and I must go with him. It's my one chance of making a fortune, for the mine is sure to turn out a great success. As I want to marry you, Eva, I must make money. There's no chance, so far as I can see, of your getting that forty thousand pounds Lord Saltars spoke of."

"Then you really think, Allen, that there is money?"

"I am certain of it--in the form of diamonds. But we'll talk of that later. Meantime I want to say that, as you wish it, we'll put off our marriage for a year. You can stay here with Mrs. Palmer, and I'll go next month to South America with Horace Parkins."

"But what about my father's death?"

"I hope that we'll learn the truth within the next three weeks," said Allen. "Everything turns on this boy Butsey. He knows the truth."

"But will he tell it?"

"I think he will. The lad is clever but venomous. The way in which he has been treated by his father and Don has made him bitter against them. Also, after the false alarm he gave the other night to get Parkins and me out of the mess, he can't very well go back to that place. The old man would murder him; and I don't fancy the poor little wretch would receive much sympathy from his father."

"What do you think of him, Allen?"

"My dear, I don't know enough about him to speak freely. From what the philanthropist in Whitechapel says, I think the boy is very clever, and that his talents might be made use of. He is abominably treated by the brutes he lives with--why, his eye was put out by his father. But the boy has turned on the gang. He burnt his boats when he raised that alarm, and I am quite sure in his own time, he will come down here and turn King's evidence."

"About what?"

"About the murder. The boy knows the truth. It's my opinion that Red Jerry killed your father, Eva."

"How do you make that out?" she asked anxiously.

"Well, Red Jerry knew of your father in Africa and knew that he was buying diamonds." Allen suppressed the fact of Strode's being an I. D. B. "He followed him home in the Dunoon Castle., and then went to tell Foxy and Father Don at Whitechapel. They came down to Westhaven and tracked your father to the Red Deeps, and there shot him. I can't understand why they did not take the wooden hand then, though."

"Who did take the hand?" asked Eva.

"My father. Yes," said Allen sadly, "you may look astonished and horrified, Eva, but it was my unhappy father. He is not in his right mind, Eva, for that is the only way to account for his strange behavior;" and then Allen rapidly told Eva details.

"Oh," said the girl when he finished, "he must be mad, Allen. I don't see why he should act in that way if he was not. Your father has always been an excitable, eccentric man, and this trouble of my father's death has been too much for him. I quite believe he intended to kill my father, and thank God he did not--that would have parted us forever. But the excitement has driven your father mad, so he is not so much to blame as you think."

"I am glad to hear you say so, darling," said the poor young fellow, "for it's been like a nightmare, to think that my father should behave in such a manner. I dreaded telling you, but I thought it was best to do so."

"I am very glad you did," she replied, putting her arms round him; "oh, don't worry, Allen. Leave my father's murder alone. Go out to Bolivia, buy this mine, and when you have made your fortune come back for me. I'll be waiting for you here, faithful and true."

"But you want to know who killed Mr. Strode?"

"I've changed my mind," she answered quickly, "the affair seems to be so mysterious that I think it will never be solved. Still I fancy you are right: Red Jerry killed my father for the sake of the diamonds."

"He did not get them if he did," said Allen, "else he and Father Don would not have gone to see Mask and thus have risked arrest. No, my dear Eva, the whole secret is known to Butsey. He can tell the truth. If he keeps his promise, and comes here we shall know all: if he does not, we'll let the matter alone. I'll go to Bolivia about this business, and return to marry you."

"And then we'll bury the bad old past," said Eva, "and begin a new life, darling. But, Allen, do you think Miss Lorry knows anything?"

"What, that circus woman? I can't say. It was certainly queer she should have been in that den. What a woman for your cousin to marry."

"I don't know if he will marry after all," said Eva.

"I believe old Lady Ipsen will stop the marriage."

"How do you know?"

"Because she wrote to say she was coming to see me. She says she will come unexpectedly, as she has something to tell me."

Allen colored. He hoped to avoid old Lady Ipsen as he did not forget that she had accused his mother of stealing the Delham heirloom. However, he merely nodded and Eva went on: "Of course I am willing to be civil to her and shall see her. But she's a horrid old woman, Allen, and has behaved very badly to me. I am her granddaughter, and she should have looked after me. I won't let her do so now. Well, Allen, that's one piece of news I had to tell you. The next is about Giles Merry."

"What about him?"

"I received a letter from Shanton written by Miss Lorry. That was when you were away. She sent it over by Butsey."

"What! Was that boy here?"

"Yes. When you were away. He delivered it at the door and went. I only knew it was Butsey from the description, and by that time the boy was gone. Had I seen him I should have asked Wasp to keep him here, till you came back."

"I understand," said Allen thoughtfully. "Miss Lorry sent for Butsey. He was told to return to Perry Street, Whitechapel, within a certain time and did not. For that, Father Don shut him up in the attic and fed him on bread and water. The treatment made Butsey rebellious. But what had Miss Lorry to say?"

"She wrote that if Giles Merry worried me I was to let her know and she'd stop him doing so."

Allen looked astonished. "Why should Giles worry you?" he asked indignantly.

"I can't say. He hasn't come to see me yet, and if he does, of course I would rather you dealt with him than Miss Lorry. I want to have nothing to do with her."

"Still, she's not a bad sort," said Allen after a pause, "she saved our lives on that night by sending Butsey to get us out of the den. Humph! If she met Butsey on that night I wonder if she asked him to return what he'd stolen?"

"What was that?" asked Eva.

"I don't know. Horace Parkins and I overheard her complaining, that Butsey, when down seeing her, had stolen something. She refused to say what it was and then bolted when she saw me. But what has Giles Merry to do with her?"

"Cain told me that Giles was the 'strong man' of Stag's Circus."

"Oh, and Miss Lorry knows him as a fellow artiste. Humph! I daresay she is aware of something queer about him. From the sending of that parcel, I believe Giles is mixed up with Father Don's lot, and by Jove, Eva, I think Miss Lorry must have something to do with them also! We've got to do with a nice lot, I must say. And they're all after the diamonds. I shouldn't wonder if Butsey had them, after all. He's just the kind of young scamp who would get the better of the elder ruffians. Perhaps he has the diamonds safely hidden, and is leaving the gang, so as to turn respectable. He said he wanted to cut his old life. Yes"--Allen slapped his knee-- "Eva, I believe Butsey has the diamonds. For all I know he may have shot your father."

"Oh, Allen," said Eva, turning pale, "that lad."

"A boy can kill with a pistol as surely as if he were a man, and Butsey has no moral scruples. However, we'll wait till he comes and then learn what we can. Once I get hold of him he shan't get away until I know everything. As to Merry, if he comes, you let me know and I'll break his confounded neck."

"I believe Nanny would thank you if you did," said Eva; the poor woman is in a terrible fright. "He wrote saying he was coming to see her."

"She needn't have anything to do with him."

"I told her so. But she looks on the man as her husband, bad as he is, and has old-fashioned notions about obeying him. If he wasn't her husband she wouldn't mind, but as it is----" Eva shrugged her shoulders.

They heard the sound of footsteps approaching the door. Shortly the footman entered. "There's a woman to see you, miss," he said to Eva, holding the door open. "Mrs. Merry, miss."

"What!" cried Eva; "show her in."

"She won't come, miss. She's in the hall."

"Come, Allen," said the girl, and they went out into the hall, where Mrs. Merry with a scared face was sitting. She rose and came forward in tears, and with sopping clothes, owing to her walk through the heavy rain.

"I ran all the way", Miss Eva. "I'm in such sorrow. Giles has come."

"What, your husband?" said Allen.

"Yes, and worse. I found this on the doorstep." She drew from under her shawl the wooden hand!

XX - AN AMAZING CONFESSION

MR. AND MRS. MERRY were seated the next day in the kitchen having a long chat. It was not a pleasant one, for Mrs. Merry was weeping as usual, and reproaching her husband. Giles had been out to see his old cronies in the village, and consequently had imbibed sufficient liquor to make him quarrelsome. The first thing he did, when he flung himself into a chair, was to grumble at the kitchen.

"Why should we sit here, Selina?" he asked; "it's a blamed dull hole, and I'm accustomed to drawing-rooms."

"You can't go into the drawing-room," said Mrs. Merry, rocking and dabbing her red eyes with the corner of her apron. "Miss Eva is in there with a lady. They don't want to be disturbed."

"Who is the lady?" demanded Signor Antonio, alias Mr. Merry.

"Lady Ipsen. She's Miss Eva's grandmother and have called to see her. What about, I'm sure I don't know, unless it's to marry her to Lord Saltars, not that I think much of him."

"Lady Ipsen--old Lady Ipsen?" said Giles slowly, and his eyes brightened; "she's an old devil. I knew her in the days when I and Hill and Strode enjoyed ourselves."

"And bad old days they were," moaned Mrs. Merry; "you'd have been a better man, Giles, if it hadn't been for that Strode. As for the jelly-fish, he was just a shade weaker than you. Both of you were under the thumb of Strode, wicked man that he was, and so cruel to his wife, just as you are, Giles, though you mayn't think so. But if I die----"

"You will, if you go on like this," said Merry, producing his pipe; "this is a nice welcome. Old Lady Ipsen," he went on, and laughed in so unpleasant a manner, that his wife looked up apprehensively.

"What wickedness are you plotting now?" she asked timidly.

"Never you mind. The marriage of Lord Saltars," he went on with a chuckle. "Ho! he's going to marry Miss Lorry."

"So they say. But I believe Lady Ipsen wants to stop that marriage, and small blame to her, seeing what a man he----"

"Hold your jaw, Selina. I can't hear you talking all day. You get me riz and you'll have bad time, old girl. So go on rocking and crying and hold that red rag of yours. D'ye hear?"

"Yes, Giles--but Lord Saltars----"

"He's going to marry Miss Lorry, if I let him."

Mrs. Merry allowed the apron to fall from her eyes in sheer amazement. "If you let him?" she repeated; "lor', Giles, you can't stop his lordship from----"

"I can stop her," said Merry, who seemed determined never to let his wife finish a sentence; "and I've a mind to, seeing how nasty she's trying to make herself." He rose. "I'll see Miss Eva and make trouble."

"If you do, Mr. Allen will interfere," said Mrs. Merry vigorously. "I knew you'd make trouble. It's in your nature. But Miss Lorry wrote to Miss Eva and said she'd interfere if you meddled with what ain't your business."

Giles shook off the hand his wife had laid on his arm, and dropped into a chair. He seemed dumfounded by the information. "She'll interfere, will she?" said he, snarling, and with glittering eyes. "Like her impudence. She can't hurt me in any way----"

"She may say you killed Strode," said Mrs. Merry.

Giles raised a mighty fist with so evil a face, that the woman cowered in her chair. Giles smiled grimly and dropped his arm.

"You said before, as I'd killed Strode. Well then, I didn't."

"How do I know that?" cried his wife spiritedly; "you can strike me, but speak the truth I will. Bad as you are, I don't want to see you hanged, and hanged you will be, whatever you may say. I heard from Cain that you talked to Strode on the Wednesday night he was killed. You met him at the station, when he arrived by the six-thirty, and----"

"What's that got to do with the murder?" snapped Giles savagely. "I talked to him only as a pal."

"Your wicked London friends were there too," said Mrs. Merry; "oh, Cain told me of the lot you're in with; Father Don, Foxy, and Red Jerry--they were all down at Westhaven, and that boy Butsey too, as lied to me. You sent him here to lie. Cain said so."

"I'll break Cain's head if he chatters. What if my pals were at Westhaven? what if I did speak to Strode----?"

"You was arranging to have him shot," said Mrs. Merry, "and shot him yourself for all I know."

Signor Antonio leaped, and taking his wife by the shoulders, shook her till her head waggled. "There," he said, while she gasped, "you say much more and I'll knock you on the head with a poker, you poll-parrot. I was doing my turn at the circus at the time Strode was shot, if he was shot at nine on Wednesday as the doctor said. I saw the evidence in the paper. You can't put the crime on me."

"Then your pals did it."

"No, they didn't. They wanted the diamonds, it's true----"

"They struck him down and robbed him."

"You said they shot him just now," sneered Giles with an evil face, "don't know your own silly mind, it seems. Gar'n, you fool, there was nothing on him to rob. If my pals had shot him, they'd have collared the wooden hand. That was the token to get the diamonds, as Red Jerry said. But Mask hasn't got them, and though Father Don did open the hand he found nothing."

"Open the hand?" questioned Mrs. Merry curiously.

"Yes. We found out--I found out, and in a way which ain't got nothing to do with you, that the hand could be opened. It was quite empty. Then Father Don put it aside, and that brat Butsey prigged it. Much good may it do him."

"The wooden hand was put on the doorstep last night," said Mrs. Merry, "and I gave it to Miss Eva."

The man's face grew black. "Oh, you did, did you," he said, "instead of giving it to your own lawful husband? I've a mind to smash you," he raised his fist again, and his poor wife winced; then he changed his mind and dropped it. "But you ain't worth a blow, you white-faced screeching cat. I'll see Miss Eva and make her give up the hand myself. See if I don't."

"Mr. Allen will interfere."

"Let him," snarled Merry; "I know something as will settle him. I want that hand, and I'm going to have it. Get those diamonds I will, wherever they are. I believe Butsey's got 'em. He's just the sort of little devil as would have opened that hand, and found the paper inside, telling where the diamonds were."

"But did he have the hand?"

"Yes, he did. He dug up the hand--never mind where--and brought it to me. It was empty then. Yes, I believe Butsey has the diamonds, so the hand will be no go. Miss Eva can keep it if she likes, or bury it along with that infernal Strode, who was a mean cuss to round on his pals the way he did."

"Ah! he was a bad man," sighed Mrs. Merry; "and did he----?"

"Shut up and mind your own business," said Giles in surly tones. He thought he had said too much. "It's that Butsey I must look for. He stole the hand from Father Don and left it on your doorstep, for Miss Eva, I suppose. He must be in the place, so I'll look for him. I know the brat's playing us false, but his father's got a rod in pickle for him, and----"

"Oh, Giles, Giles, you'll get into trouble again. That Wasp----"

"I'll screw his neck if he meddles with me," said the strong man savagely; "see here, Selina, I'm not going to miss a chance of making a fortune. Those diamonds are worth forty thousand pounds, and Butsey's got them. I want money to hunt him down and to do--other things," said Giles, hesitating, "have you got five hundred?"

"No," said Mrs. Merry with spirit, "and you shouldn't have it if I had. You're my husband, Giles, worse luck, and so long as you behave yourself, I'll give you roof and board, though you are not a nice man to have about the house, but money you shan't have. I'll see Mr. Mask first. He's looking after my property, and if you----"

"I'll do what I like," said Giles, wincing at the name of Mask; "if I wasn't your husband, you'd chuck me, I 'spose."

"I would," said Mrs. Merry, setting her mouth, "but you're married to me, worse luck. I can't get rid of you. See here, Giles, you go away and leave me and Cain alone, and I'll give you five pounds."

"I want five hundred," said Giles, "I'll stop here as long as I like. I'm quite able to save myself from being accused of Strode's murder. As to Cain," Giles chuckled, "he's taken up with a business you won't like, Selina?"

"What is it?--oh, what is it?" gasped Mrs. Merry, clasping her hands.

"The Salvation Army."

"What! Has he joined the Salvation Army?"

"Yes," sneered the father; "he chucked the circus at Chelmsford, and said it was a booth of Satan. Now he's howling about the street in a red jersey, and talking pious."

Mrs. Merry raised her thin hands to heaven. "I thank God he has found the light," she said solemnly, "I'm Methodist myself, but I hear the Army does much good. If the Army saves Cain's immortal soul," said the woman, weeping fast, "I'll bless its work on my bended knees. I believe Cain will be a comfort to me after all. Where are you going, Giles--not to the drawing-room?"

"As far as the door to listen," growled Merry. "I'm sick of hearing you talk pious. I'll come and stop here, and twist Cain's neck if he prays at me."

"Trouble--trouble," wailed Mrs. Merry, wringing her hands, "I wish you'd go. Cain and me would be happier without you, whatever you may say, Giles, or Signor Antonio, or whatever wickedness you call yourself. Oh, I was a fool to marry you!"

Giles looked at her queerly. "Give me five hundred pounds, and I won't trouble you again," he said, "meanwhile"--he moved towards the door. Mrs. Merry made a bound like a panther and caught him.

"No," she said, "you shan't listen."

Giles swept her aside like a fly, and she fell on the floor. Then with a contemptuous snort he left the kitchen and went into the passage which led to the front. On the right of this was the door of the drawing-room, and as both walls and door were thin, Mr. Merry had no difficulty in overhearing what was going on within. Could his eyes have seen through a deal board, he would have beheld an old lady seated in the best arm-chair, supporting herself on an ebony crutch. She wore a rich black silk, and had white hair, a fresh complexion, a nose like the beak of a parrot, and a firm mouth. The expression of the face was querulous and ill-tempered, and she was trying to bring Eva round to her views on the subject of Saltars' marriage. The girl sat opposite her, very pale, but with quite as determined an expression as her visitor.

"You're a fool," said Lady Ipsen, striking her crutch angrily on the ground. "I am your grandmother, and speak for your good."

"It is rather late to come and speak for my good, now," said Eva with great spirit; "you have neglected me for a long time."

"I had my reasons," said the other sharply. "Jane, your mother, married Strode against my will. He was of good birth, certainly, but he had no money, and besides was a bad man."

"There is no need to speak evil of the dead."

"The man's being dead doesn't make him a saint, Eva. But I'll say no more about him, if you'll only listen to reason."

"I have listened, and you have my answer," said Eva quietly; "I am engaged to Allen Hill, and Allen Hill I intend to marry."

"Never, while I have a breath of life," said the old woman angrily. "Do you think I am going to let Saltars marry this circus woman? No! I'll have him put in gaol first. He shall not disgrace the family in this way. Our sons take wives from theatres and music-halls," said Lady Ipsen grimly, "but the sawdust is lower than either. I shan't allow the future head of the house to disgrace himself."

"All this has nothing to do with me," said Eva.

"It has everything to do with you," said Lady Ipsen quickly; "don't I tell you that Saltars, since he saw you at that Mrs. Palmer's, has taken a fancy to you? It would take very little for you to detach him from this wretched Miss Lorry."

"I don't want to, Lady Ipsen!"

"Call me grandmother."

"No. You have never been a grandmother to me. I will be now," Lady Ipsen tried to soften her grim face; "I wish I'd seen you before," she added, "you're a true Delham, with very little of that bad Strode blood in you, unless in the obstinacy you display. I'll take you away from this Mrs. Palmer, Eva----"

"I have no wish to leave Mrs. Palmer."

"You must. I won't have a granddaughter of mine remain in a situation with a common woman."

"Leave Mrs. Palmer alone, Lady Ipsen. She is a good woman, and when my relatives forsook me she took me up. If you had ever loved me, or desired to behave as you should have done, you would have come to help me when my father was murdered. And now," cried Eva, rising with flashing eyes, "you come when I am settled, to get me to help you with your schemes. I decline."

The old woman, very white and with glittering eyes, rose. "You intend then to marry Allen Hill?"

"Yes, I do."

"Well then, you can't," snapped the old woman; "his mother isn't respectable."

"How dare you say that?" demanded Eva angrily.

"Because I'm accustomed to speak my mind," snapped Lady Ipsen, glaring; "it is not a chit like you will make me hold my peace. Mrs. Hill was in our family as a governess before your father married my daughter Jane."

"What of that?"

"Simply this: a valuable diamond necklace was lost--an heirloom. I believe Mrs. Hill stole it."

Eva laughed. "I don't believe that for one moment," she said scornfully. "Mrs. Hill is a good, kind, sweet lady."

"Lady she is, as she comes of good stock. Sweet I never thought her, and kind she may be to you, seeing she is trying to trap you into marrying her miserable son----"

"Don't you call Allen miserable," said Eva, annoyed; "he is the best man in the world, and worth a dozen of Lord Saltars."

"That would not be difficult," said Lady Ipsen, sneering; "Saltars is a fool and a profligate."

"And you expect me to marry him?"

"To save him from disgracing the family."

"The Delham family is nothing to me," said Eva proudly; "look after the honor of the family yourself, Lady Ipsen. As to this talk about Mrs. Hill, I don't believe it."

"Ask her yourself, then."

"I shall do so, and even, if what you say is true, which I don't believe, I shall still marry Allen."

"Eva," the old lady dropped into her seat, "don't be hard on me. I am old. I wish you well. It is true what I say about Mrs. Hill. You can't marry her son."

"But I can, and I intend to."

"Oh, this marriage--this disgraceful marriage!" cried the old woman in despair, "how can I manage to stop it. This Miss Lorry will be married to Saltars soon, if I can't put an end to his infatuation."

Eva shrugged her shoulders. "I can give you no help."

"You might plead with Saltars."

"No. I can't do that. It is his business, not mine. Why don't you offer Miss Lorry a sum of money to decline the match?"

"Because she's bent upon being Lady Saltars, and will stop at nothing to achieve her end. I would give five hundred--a thousand pounds to stop the marriage. But Miss Lorry can't be bribed."

It was at this point that Giles opened the door softly and looked in. "Make it fifteen hundred, your ladyship, and I'll stop the marriage," he said impudently.

"Giles," cried Eva, rising indignantly, "how dare you----?"

"Because I've been listening, and heard a chance of making money."

Mrs. Merry burst in at her husband's heels. "And I couldn't stop him from listening, Miss Eva," she said, weeping; "he's a brute. Don't give him the money, your ladyship; he's a liar."

"I'm not," said Giles coolly, "for fifteen hundred pounds I can stop this marriage. I have every reason to hate Miss Lorry. She's been playing low down on me, in writing to you, Miss Strode, and it's time she learned I won't be put on. Well, your ladyship?"

The old woman, who had kept her imperious black eyes fixed on Giles, nodded. "Can you really stop the marriage?"

"Yes I can, and pretty sharp too."

"Then do so and you'll have the fifteen hundred pounds."

"Will you give me some writing to that effect?"

"Yes," said Lady Ipsen, becoming at once a business woman; "get me some ink and paper, Eva."

"Stop," said Giles politely--so very politely that his poor wife stared. "I don't doubt your ladyship's word. Promise me to send to this address," he handed a bill containing the next place where Stag's Circus would perform, "one thousand five hundred in notes, and I'll settle the matter."

"I'll bring the money myself," said Lady Ipsen, putting away the bill; "you don't get the money till I know the truth. How can you stop the marriage? Tell me now."

"Oh, I don't mind that," said Giles, shrugging. "I'm sure you won't break your word, and even if you were inclined to you can't, if you want to stop the marriage. You can't do without me."

"Speak out, man," said Lady Ipsen sharply.

"Well then----" began Giles and then hesitated, as he looked at poor faded Mrs. Merry in her black stuff dress. "Selina, you give me fifteen hundred pounds and I'll not speak."

"What have I got to do with it?" asked his wife, staring.

"It will be worth your while to pay me," said Merry threateningly.

"I can't and I won't, whatever you may say. Tell Lady Ipsen what you like. Your wickedness hasn't anything to do with me."

"You'll see," he retorted, turning to the old lady. "I've given you the chance. Lady Ipsen, I accept your offer. Lord Saltars can't marry Miss Lorry, because that lady----"

"Well, man--well."

"That lady," said Giles, "is married already."

"Who to?" asked Eva, while Lady Ipsen's eyes flashed.

"To me," said Merry; "I married her years ago, before I met Selina."

"Then I am free--free," cried Eva's nurse; "oh, thank heaven!" and she fell down on the floor in a faint, for the first and last time in her life.

XXI - THE DIAMONDS

AT SEVEN o'clock that same evening Allen and his American friend were walking to Mrs. Palmer's to dine. As yet, Allen knew nothing of what had transpired at Misery Castle, for Eva was keeping the story till they met. But as the two men passed the little inn they saw Giles Merry descend from a holiday-making char-à-banc.. Two or three men had just passed into the inn, no doubt to seek liquid refreshment. Allen knew Merry's face, as Mrs. Merry had shown him a photograph of Signor Antonio in stage dress, which she had obtained from Cain. The man was a handsome and noticeable blackguard, and moreover his good looks were reproduced in Cain. Therefore young Hill knew him at once, and stepped forward.

"Good evening, Mr. Merry," he said; "I have long wished to meet you."

Giles looked surly. "My name is Signor Antonio, monsieur," he said.

"Oh," mocked Allen, "and being Italian you speak English and French badly?"

"What do you want?" demanded Giles savagely, and becoming the English gipsy at once. "I've no time to waste?"

"Why did you send that cross to Mr. Hill?"

Giles grinned. "Just to give him a fright," he said. "I knew he was a milk-and-water fool, as I saw a lot of him in the old days, when I did Strode's dirty work."

"You dug up the wooden hand?"

"No, I didn't. Butsey, who was on the watch, saw Hill plant it, and dug it up. He brought it to me, and I gave it to Father Don. Then Butsey stole it back, and passed it along to that young woman you're going to marry."

"I guess," said Horace at this point, "you'd best speak civil of Miss Strode. I'm not taking any insolence this day."

Allen nodded approval, and Giles cast a look over the big limbs of the American. Apparently, strong man as he was, he thought it would be best not to try conclusions with such a giant. "I wish I'd met you in Father Don's den," he said. "I'd have smashed that handsome face of yours."

"Two can play at that game," said Allen quietly; "and now, Mr. Merry, or Signor Antonio, or whatever you choose to call yourself, why shouldn't I hand you over to Wasp?"

"You can't bring any charge against me."

"Oh, can't I? You know something about this murder----"

"I was playing my turn at the circus in Westhaven when the shot was fired," said Giles coolly.

"I didn't say you shot the man yourself; but you know who did."

"No, I don't," said Merry, his face growing dark; "if I did know the man, I'd make him a present. I'd like to have killed Strode myself. He played me many a dirty trick, and I said I'd be even with him. But someone else got in before me. As to arrest," he went on sneeringly, "don't you think I'd be such a fool as to come down here, unless I was sure of my ground. Arrest me indeed!"

"I can on suspicion. You're in with the Perry Street gang."

Giles cast a look towards the inn and laughed. "Well, you've got to prove that I and the rest have done wrong, before you can run us all in."

"The wooden hand----"

"Oh, we know all about that, and who stole it," said Giles meaningly.

Allen started. He saw well enough that he could not bring Giles to book without mentioning the name of his father. Therefore he changed his mind about calling on Wasp to interfere, and contented himself with a warning. "You'd best clear out of this by tomorrow," said he angrily. "I shan't have you, troubling your wife."

"My wife! Ha--ha!" Merry seemed to find much enjoyment in the remark.

"Or Miss Strode either."

"Oh," sneered the man insolently, "you'd best see Miss Strode. She may have something interesting to tell you. But I can't stay talking here forever. I'm going back to Shanton tonight. Come round at eleven," he said to the driver of the char-à-banc.. "We'll drive back in the moonlight."

"I think you'd better," said Allen grimly; "you stop here tomorrow, and whatever you may know about a person, whose name need not be mentioned, I'll have you run in."

"Oh, I'll be gone by tomorrow," sneered Merry again, and took his cap off with such insolence that Horace longed to kick him, "don't you fret yourself. I'm a gentleman of property now, and intend to cut the sawdust and go to South Africa--where the diamonds come from," he added with an insolent laugh, and then swung into the inn, leaving Allen fuming with anger. But there was no use in making a disturbance, as the man could make things unpleasant for Mr. Hill, so Allen walked away with Horace to Mrs. Palmer's.

It would have been wiser had he entered the inn, for in the coffee-room were three men, whom he might have liked to meet. These were Father Don smartly dressed as a clergyman, Red Jerry as a sailor, and Foxy in a neat suit of what are known as hand-me-downs. The trio looked most respectable, and if Jerry's face was somewhat villainous, and Foxy's somewhat sly, the benevolent looks of Father Don were above suspicion. Giles sat down beside these at a small table, and partook of the drinks which had been ordered. The landlord was under the impression that the three men were over on a jaunt from Shanton, and intended to return in the moonlight. Merry had met them at the door, and now came in to tell them his plans.

"I've arranged matters," he said in a low voice to Father Don, "the groom Jacobs is courting some young woman he's keeping company with, and the women servants have gone to a penny reading the vicar is giving."

"What of young Hill and his friend?"

"They are dining with Mrs. Palmer. The house is quite empty, and contains only Mr. and Mrs. Hill. I have been in the house before, and know every inch of it. I'll tell you how to get in."

"You'll come also?" said Foxy suspiciously.

"No," replied Giles. "I'll stop here. I've done enough for the money. If you're fools enough to be caught, I shan't be mixed up in the matter."

"We won't be caught," said Father Don with a low laugh; "Jerry will keep guard at the window, and Foxy and I will enter."

"How?" asked the sharp-faced man.

"By the window," said Giles. "I explained to Father Don here, in London. Hill has taken up his quarters in a Japanese room on the west side of the house, just over the wall. There are French windows opening on to the lawn. You can steal up and the grass will deaden the sound of footsteps. It goes right up to the window. That may be open. If not, Jerry can burst it, and then you and Don can enter."

"But if Hill isn't alone?"

"Well then, act as you think best. Mrs. Hill's twice the man her husband is. She might give the alarm. But there's no one in the house, and she'll have to sing out pretty loudly before the alarm can be given to the village."

"There won't be any alarm," said Father Don calmly. "I intend to make use of that paper I got from you. Where did you get it, Merry?"

"From Butsey. I found him with Strode's blue pocket-book, and made a grab at it. I saw notes. But Butsey caught those and bolted. I got the book and some papers. The one I gave you, Don, will make Hill give up the diamonds, if he has them."

"He must have them," said Don decidedly, "we know from the letter sent to Mask, and which was left at his office by Butsey, that the hand could be opened. I did open it and found nothing. I believe that Strode stored the diamonds therein. If Hill stole the hand, and took it home, he must have found the diamonds, and they are now in his possession. I expect he looked for them."

"No," said Merry grimly, "he was looking for that paper you intend to show him. He'll give up the diamonds smart enough, when he sees that. Then you can make for Westhaven----"

"What of the charry-bang?" asked Jerry in heavy tones.

"That's a blind. It will come round at eleven, but by that time we will all be on our way to Westhaven. If there is pursuit, Wasp and his friend will follow in the wrong direction. Then Father Don can make for Antwerp, and later we can sell the diamonds. But no larks," said Merry, showing his teeth, "or there will be trouble."

"Suppose young Hill and his friend tell the police?"

"Oh," said Giles, grinning, "they will do so at the risk of the contents of that paper being made public. Don't be a fool, Don, you've got the whole business in your own hands. I don't want a row, as I have to meet a lady in a few days," Giles grinned again, when he thought of Lady Ipsen, "and we have to do business."

So the plan was arranged, and after another drink Father Don and stroll in the village to "see the venerable church in the moonlight," as the pseudo clergyman told the landlord. But when out of sight, the trio changed the direction of their walk, and made for "The Arabian Nights" at the end of the village. Departing from the highroad they stole across a large meadow, and, in a dark corner, climbed the wall. Father Don was as active as any of them, in spite of his age. When the three rascals were over the wall and standing on a smoothly-shaven lawn, they saw the range of the Roman pillars, but no light in the windows. "It's on the west side," said Don in a whisper; "come along, pals."

The three crept round the black bulk of the house and across the drive. All was silent and peaceful within the boundary of the wall. The moonlight silvered the lawns and flower-beds and made beautiful the grotesque architecture of the house.

A few steps taken in a cat-like fashion brought the thieves to the west side. They here saw a light glimmering through three French windows which opened on to a narrow stone terrace. From this, the lawn rolled smoothly to the flower-beds, under the encircling red brick wall. Father Don pointed to the three windows.

"The middle one," he said quietly; "see if it's open, Foxy. If not, we'll have to make a certain noise. And look inside if you can."

Foxy stole across the lawn and terrace and peered in. After a time, he delicately tried the window and shook his head. He then stole back to report, "Hill is lying on the sofa," he said, "and his wife is seated beside him. He's crying about something."

"We'll give him something to cry about soon," said Father Don, feeling for the paper which he had received from Giles. "Smash the middle window in, Jerry."

Without the least concealment the huge man rushed up the slope and hurled his bulk against the window. The frail glass gave way and he fairly fell into the center of the room. With a shrill cry of terror, Hill sprang from the sofa, convulsively clutching the hand of his wife, while Mrs. Hill, after the first shock of alarm, faced the intruders boldly. By this time Father Don with Foxy behind him was bowing to the disturbed couple. Jerry took himself out of the room, and guarded the broken window.

"Who are you? what do you want?" demanded Mrs. Hill. "If you don't go I'll ring for the servants."

"I am afraid you will give yourself unnecessary trouble," said Don suavely. "We know the servants are out."

"What do you want?"

"We'll come to that presently. Our business has to do with your husband, Mr. Hill"--Father Don looked at the shivering wretch.

"I never harmed you--I don't know you," mumbled Hill. "Go away--leave me alone--what do you want?"

"We'll never get on in this way.--No, you don't," added Don, as Mrs. Hill tried to steal to the door, "Go and sit down by your good husband," and he enforced this request by pointing a revolver.

"I am not to be frightened by melodrama," said Mrs. Hill scornfully.

"Sit down, Sarah--sit down," said Hill, his teeth chattering.

The woman could not help casting a contemptuous look on the coward, even though she fancied, she owed so much to him. But, as she was a most sensible woman, she saw that it would be as well to obey. "I am ready to hear," she said, sitting by Hill, and putting her strong arm round the shivering, miserable creature.

"I'll come to the point at once," said Don, speaking to Hill, "as we have not much time to lose. Mr. Hill, you have forty thousand pounds' worth of diamonds here. Give them up!"

Hill turned even paler than he was. "How do you know that?" he asked.

"It can't be true," put in Mrs. Hill spiritedly. "If you are talking of Mr. Strode's diamonds, my husband hasn't got them."

"Your husband stole the wooden hand from the dead," said Foxy, with his usual snarl. "He took it home and opened it."

"I did not know it contained the diamonds," babbled Hill.

"No. You thought it contained a certain document," said Don, and produced a paper from his pocket, "a blue paper document, not very large--of such a size as might go into a wooden hand, provided the hand was hollow as it was. Is this it?"

Hill gave a scream and springing up bounded forward. "Give it to me--give it!' he cried.

"For the diamonds," said Father Don, putting the paper behind him.

"You shall have them. I hid them in this room--I don't want them, but that paper--it is mine."

"I know that--signed with your name, isn't it? Well, bring out the diamonds, and, when you hand them over----"

"You'll give me the paper?"

Foxy shook his head as Father Don looked inquiringly at him. "No, we must keep that paper, so as to get away--otherwise you'll be setting the police on our track."

"I swear I won't--I swear----" Hill dropped on his knees, "I swear----"

His wife pulled him to his feet. "Try and be a man, Lawrence," she said. "What is this document?"

"Nothing--nothing--but I must have it," cried Hill jerking himself away. He ran across the room, and fumbled at the lock of a cabinet. "See--see--I have the diamonds! I found them in the hand--I put them into a canvas bag--here--here--" his fingers shook so that he could hardly open the drawer. Foxy came forward and kindly helped him. Between the two, the drawer was opened. Hill flung out a mass of papers, which strewed the floor. Then from beneath these, he hauled a small canvas bag tied at the mouth and sealed. "All the diamonds are here," he said, bringing this to Don and trying to open it. "Forty thousand pounds--forty--for God's sake--" he broke off hysterically--"the paper, the paper I signed!"

Don took possession of the bag and was about to hand over the document, when Foxy snatched it. "We'll send this from the Continent," he said, "while we have this, you won't be able to set the peelers on us."

Hill began to cry and again fell on his knees, but Father Don took no notice of him. He emptied the contents of the bag on the table and there the jewels flashed in the lamp-light, a small pile of very fine stones. While he gloated over them, Mrs. Hill laid her hand on Foxy's arm: "What is in that paper?" she asked sternly.

"Don't tell her--don't tell her!" cried Hill.

"Lawrence!"

But he put his hands to his ears and still cried and groveled. "I shall go mad if you tell her! I shall--ah--oh--ugh--!" he suddenly clutched at his throat and reeled to the sofa.

Mrs. Hill took little notice of him. "Read me the document," she said.

"I can almost repeat it from memory," said Foxy, putting the paper into his pocket; "it's simply a confession by your husband that he stole a certain necklace belonging to----"

"The Delham heirloom!" cried Mrs. Hill, turning grey, and recoiling.

"Yes, and also a promise to withdraw from seeking to marry Lady Jane Delham, and to marry you."

"Oh!" Mrs. Hill turned such a withering look on her miserable husband, that he shrank back and covered his eyes. "So this is the real reason of your chivalry?"

"Yes," said Father Don, who had placed the diamonds again in his bag, and stood up, "I heard some of the story from Giles Merry, and read the rest in the signed document. It was Hill who stole the necklace. He took the key from the schoolroom, where it had been left by Lady Ipsen. He opened the safe, and collared the necklace. Near the door, he left a handkerchief of yours, Mrs. Hill, so that, if there was danger, you might be accused. Strode found the handkerchief, and knowing Hill had possessed it, made him confess. Then he made Hill sign the confession that he had stolen the necklace, and also made him promise to marry you."

Mrs. Hill sank down with a stern, shamed look, "So this was your chivalry," she said, looking again at her husband, "you stole the necklace--you let me bear the shame--you tried to incriminate me--you pretended to wed me to save me from starvation, and--oh, you--you shameless-creature!" she leaped, and made as though she would have struck Hill; the man cowered with a cry of alarm like a trapped rabbit.

"What became of the necklace?" she asked Don sharply.

"Strode made Hill sell it, and they divided the profits."

"Eva's father also," moaned Mrs. Hill, covering her face, "oh, shame--shame--shall I ever be able to look on this man's face again!"

Hill attempted to excuse himself, "I didn't get much money," he wailed. "I let Strode take the lot. He carried the confession in his wooden hand--that's why I took it. I stole the hand and opened it--but the confession wasn't in it--I found the diamonds, and I have given them to you--let me have the paper!" he bounded to his feet, and snatching a dagger from a trophy of arms on the wall made for Foxy, "I'll kill you if you don't give it to me!"

Father Don dodged behind a chair, while Foxy, who was right in the center of the room, ran for the window, and, bursting past Jerry, raced down the lawn with Hill after him, the dagger upraised. Round and round they went, while Mrs. Hill stood on the terrace, looking on with a deadly smile. Had Hill been struck down, she would have rejoiced. Don twitched the arm of Jerry.

"Let's cut," he said; "I've got the swag, Foxy can look after himself," and these two gentlemen left the house hurriedly.

Mrs. Hill saw them disappear without anxiety. The blow she had received seemed to have benumbed her faculties. To think that she had been so deceived and tricked. With a stony face she watched Foxy flying round the lawn, with the insane man--for Hill appeared to be mad--after him. Foxy, in deadly terror of his life, seeing his pals disappear, tore the document from his pocket, threw it down, and ran panting towards the wall. While he scaled it, Hill picked up the paper and tore it, with teeth and hands, into a thousand shreds. The three scoundrels had disappeared, and Mrs. Hill looked down coldly on her frantic husband. Hill danced up to the terrace, and held out his hands. "Happiness--happiness, I am safe."

"Coward," she said in a terrible voice. Her husband looked at her, and then began to laugh weirdly. Then with a cry, he dropped.

"I hope he is dead," said Mrs. Hill, looking down on him with scorn.

XXII - BUTSEY'S STORY

THERE WAS no excitement in Wargrove next day over the burglars who had entered "The Arabian Nights," for the simple reason that the village knew nothing about the matter. But a rumor was current, that Mr. Hill had gone out of his mind. No one was astonished, as he had always been regarded as queer. Now, it appeared, he was stark, staring mad, and no longer the harmless eccentric the village had known for so long. And the rumor was true.

"It is terrible to think of the punishment which has befallen him, Allen," said Mrs. Hill the next morning; "but can we call it undeserved?"

"I suppose not," answered her son gloomily. "I wish I had remained at home last night, mother."

"Things would have been worse, had you remained. There would have been a fight."

"I would have saved Eva's diamonds, at all events."

"Let the diamonds go, Hill," chimed in Parkins, who formed a third in the conversation, "they were come by dishonestly, and would have brought no luck. You come out to Bolivia, and fix up the mine. Then you can make your own coin, and marry Miss Strode."

"But you forget, Mr. Parkins," said Mrs. Hill, "I am now rich, and Allen need not go to America."

"No, mother," said Allen hastily, "I'll go. You will do much more good with my father's money than I can. Besides----" he hesitated, and looked at Horace. The American interpreted the look.

"Guess you want a little private conversation," he said; "well I'll light out and have a smoke. You can call me when you want me again," and Mr. Parkins, producing his pipe, left the room.

"My poor mother," said Allen, embracing her, "don't look so sad. It is very terrible and----"

"You can't console me, Allen," said the poor woman bitterly, "so do not try to. To think that I should have believed in that man all these years. He was a thief-- doubly a thief; he not only robbed the Delhams of the necklace, but robbed the dead, and me of my good name."

"I almost think the dead deserved to be robbed," said Allen; "I begin to believe, mother, that Strode was my father's evil genius as he said he was. Why should my father steal this necklace, when he had plenty of money?"

"He had not at the time. I think his father kept him short. He took the necklace, I expect, under the strong temptation of finding the key in the schoolroom."

"I believe Strode urged him to steal it," said Allen, "and at all events Strode was not above profiting by the theft. And it was Strode who brought about the marriage----"

"By threats," said Mrs. Hill grimly, "I expect, Strode swore he would reveal the truth, unless Lawrence married me. And I thought Lawrence acted so, out of chivalry."

"But if Strode had revealed the truth he would have incriminated himself."

"Ah, but, as I learn, he waited till after I was married before he disposed of the necklace. Then he sold it through Father Don, who was his associate in villainy. However, Strode is dead and your father is mad. I wonder what fate will befall Merry and those wretches he associates with?"

"Oh, their sins will come home to them, never fear," said Allen, in a prophetic vein. "I suppose it is best to let the matter rest."

"Certainly. Father Don and his two associates have got away. What about Merry?"

"He went almost at once to Shanton, and did not pay for the char-à-banc.. The owner is in a fine rage and drove back to Shanton at midnight, vowing to summons Merry, who was responsible for its ordering."

"Well, they are out of our life at last," said his mother, "we now know the secret which caused your unhappy father to try and murder Strode, and did make him steal the hand. The confession has been destroyed, so no one can say anything. Merry will not speak----"

"No; that's all right. Merry is going to receive money from old Lady Ipsen, for stopping the marriage of Saltars with Miss Lorry. I expect he will go to Africa as he says. He'll hold his tongue and so will the others. But they have the diamonds, and poor Eva receives nothing."

"I agree with Mr. Parkins," said Mrs. Hill quickly, "the jewels were come by dishonestly, and would have brought no good fortune. Will you tell Eva anything, Allen?"

"No. I'll tell her as little as possible. No one, but you, I, and Parkins, know of the events of last night. My poor father has been reported ill for some time and has always been so eccentric, so it will surprise no one to hear he has gone mad. We will place him in some private asylum, and----"

"No, Allen," said Mrs. Hill firmly, "the poor soul is harmless. After all, wickedly as he has acted, he has been severely punished, and is my husband. I'll keep him here and look after him till the end comes--and that won't be long," sighed Mrs. Hill.

"Very good, mother, you shall act as you think fit. But we know the truth now."

"Yes, save who murdered Mr. Strode."

"I believe Jerry did, or Giles."

"They both deny doing so."

"Of course," said Allen contemptuously, "to save their own skins. I shall go up to London, mother, and tell Mr. Mask what has taken place."

But there was no need for Allen to go to town. That afternoon the lawyer arrived and with him a small boy with one eye. The lad was neatly dressed, he had his hair cut, and his face washed. In spite of his one eye and white cheeks he looked a very smart youngster, and grinned in a friendly manner at Allen and Horace.

"This," said Mr. Mask, leading the lad into the room, where the young men were smoking after luncheon, "is Master Train----"

"Butsey?" said Allen.

"Oh no," replied Mask gravely, "he is a gentleman of property now and is living on his money. You mustn't call him by so low a name as Butsey."

The boy grinned and shrugged his shoulders. "I say, how long's this a-goin' on?" he inquired; "you've been shying fun at me all day."

"We won't shy fun anymore," said Mr. Mask in his melancholy voice. "I have brought you here to make a clean breast of it."

"About the diamonds?"

"We know about the diamonds," said Horace. "I guess Father Don's got them."

"Saikes! He's he?" said Butsey regretfully; "that comes of me tellin' about the letter I guv to you"--this was to Mask--"if he hadn't opened the hand, he wouldn't have got 'em."

"You are quite wrong, Butsey," said Allen, rising. "Horace, I'll leave the boy in your keeping. Mr. Mask, will you come with me into the next room?"

Rather surprised, Mask did so, and was speedily put in possession of the terrible story. He quite agreed that the matter should be kept quiet. "Though I hope it won't be necessary to rake it up when Butsey is tried for murder."

"What! did that boy shoot Mr. Strode?"

"I think so," said the lawyer, looking puzzled; "but to tell you the truth I'm not sure. I can't get the boy to speak freely. He said he would do so, only in the presence of you and Parkins. That is why I brought him down."

"How did you get hold of him?"

"Through one of the stolen notes. Butsey presented himself at the bank and cashed ten pounds. He was arrested and brought to me. I gave bail for him, and brought him to explain."

"Where did he get the notes?"

"Out of the blue pocket-book, he says--in which case he must have committed the murder. Not for his own sake," added Mask quickly. "I fear the poor little wretch has been made a cat's-paw by the others."

"Well," said Allen, drawing a long breath of astonishment, "wonders will never cease. I never thought Butsey was guilty."

"I can't be sure yet if he is. But, at all events, he certainly knows who is the culprit, and, to save his own neck, he will confess."

"But would the law hang a boy like that even if guilty?"

"I don't think Butsey will give the law the chance of trying the experiment. He's a clever little reptile. But we had better return and examine him. Your mother----?"

"She is with my poor father."

"Is that quite safe?" asked Mask anxiously. "Perfectly. He is harmless."

Mask looked sympathetic, although he privately thought that madness was the best thing which could have befallen Mr. Hill, seeing he had twice brought himself within the clutches of the law. At least there was now no danger of his being punished for theft or attempted murder, whatever might be said by those who had escaped with the diamonds; and certainly Mrs. Hill would be relieved of a very troublesome partner. Had Hill remained sane, she would not have lived with him after discovering how he had tricked her into marriage, and had traded on her deep gratitude all these years. Now, by tending him in his hopeless state, she was heaping coals of fire on his head, and proving herself to be, what Mask always knew she truly was, a good woman.

So, in Allen's company, he returned to the room where Parkins was keeping watch over Master Train, and found that brilliant young gentleman smoking a cigarette. "Produced it from a silver case too," said the amused American. "This is a mighty smart boy. I guess you got rid of a lot of that money, bub?"

"I cashed two notes," said Butsey coolly, "but the third trapped me. But I don't care. I've had a good time!"

"And I expect you'll pass the rest of your life in gaol."

"What's that?" said Butsey, not turning a hair; "in gaol?--not me. I've been in quod once and didn't like it. I ain't a-goin' again. No, sir, you give me some cash, Mr. Hill, and I'll go to the States."

"They'll lynch you there, as sure as a gun," said Horace, grinning.

Allen was quite taken aback by the coolness of the prisoner, for a prisoner Butsey virtually was. Mask leaned back nursing his foot, and did not take much part in the conversation. He listened to Allen examining the culprit, and only put a word in now and then.

"You don't seem to realize your position," said Hill sharply.

"Oh yuss, I does," said Butsey, calmly blowing a cloud of smoke, "you wants to get the truth out of me. Well, I'll tell it, if you'll let me go. I dessay our friend here"--he nodded to Mask--"can arrange with the peelers about that note."

"It's probable I can," said Mask, tickled at the impudence of the boy; "but wouldn't you rather suffer for stealing, than for murder?"

The boy jumped up and became earnest at once. "See here," he said, wetting his finger, "that's wet," and then he wiped it on his jacket, "that's dry, cut my throat if I tell a lie. I didn't shoot the old bloke. S'elp me, I didn't!"

"Who did, then? Do you know?"

"I might know; but you've got to make it worth my while to split."

Allen took the boy by the collar and shook him. "You young imp," he said, "you'll tell everything you know, or pass some time in gaol."

"Make me tell, then," said Butsey, and put out his tongue.

"Suppose I hand you over to Father Don and your own parent?"

"Can't, sir. Th' gang's broke up. They'll go abroad with them diamonds, and start in some other country. 'Sides, I ain't going in for that business again. I'm going to be respectable, I am. And I did git you out of the den, sir," said Butsey more earnestly.

Allen dropped his hand from the boy's collar. "You certainly did that--at the request of Miss Lorry. What of her?"

"Nothing but good," said Butsey, flushing; "she's the best and kindest laidy in the world. I ain't a-goin' to saiy anything of her."

"I don't want you to talk of people who have nothing to do with the matter in hand," said Hill; "but you must tell us about the murder. If you don't----"

"What am I a-goin' to get fur splitting?" asked Butsey in a businesslike way.

"I'll arrange that you won't go to gaol. You must remember, Master Train," said Mask with deliberation, "that you are in a dangerous position. The note you cashed was taken from a pocket-book which the murdered man had on his person, when he was shot. How did you get it, eh? The presumption is that you shot him."

Butsey whistled between his teeth. "You can't frighten me," said he, his one eye twinkling savagely; "but I'll tell you everything, 'cept who shot the bloke."

"Huh," said Horace. "I guess we can ravel out that, when we know what you have to say. But you speak straight, young man, or I'll hide you proper."

"Lor," said Butsey coolly, "I've bin hided by father and old Don much wuss than you can hammer. But I'll tell--jest you three keep your ears open. Where 'ull I begin?"

"From the beginning," said Allen; "how did the gang come to know that Strode had the diamonds?"

"It wos father told 'em," said Butsey candidly. "Father's Red Jerry, an' a onener at that--my eye! He got into trouble here, and cuts to furrein parts some years ago. In Africay he saw the dead bloke."

"Strode?"

"Well, ain't I a-saiyin' of him?" snapped Butsey; "yuss--Strode. Father comes 'ome in the saime ship es Strode and knows all about 'im having prigged diamonds in Africay."

"What do you mean by prigged?"

"Wot I saiy, in course. Strode got them diamonds wrong----"

"I. D. B.," said Parkins. "I told you so, Hill."

"Well then," went on Butsey, looking mystified at the mention of the letters, "father didn't see why he shouldn't git the diamonds, so he follered the dead bloke to this here country and come to tell old Father Don in the Perry Street ken. Father Don and Foxy both went in with father----"

"To murder Strode?" said Allen.

"Not much. They wanted to rob him, but didn't want to dance on nothink. Father Don's a fly one. I was told about the job, an' sent to watch the dead bloke. I watched him in London, and he wos never out of my sight. He wos coming down to this here plaice on Thursdaiy---"

"How do you know that?" asked Mask.

"Cause I knows the 'all porter at the Guelph Hotel, an' he tells me," said Butsey calmly. "I cuts an' tells Father Don, and him and father an' Foxy all come to Westhaven on Wednesday to see him as is called Merry."

"He's another of the gang?"

"Rather. He's bin in with us fur years, he he's. And he wos doin' the strong man at Stag's circus at Westhaven. Father Don, he come down, knowing Merry 'ated Strode, to try and get him to do the robbin'."

"Did Merry agree?"

"In course he did, only too glad to get a shot at Strode----"

"Do you mean to say Merry shot him?"

"Naow," said Butsey, making a gesture of irritation, "let a cove talk. I'll tell you if he shot him, if you'll let me. I saiy we wos all down to fix things on Wednesdaiy, and I come along with a blessed ragged kids' fresh air fund, so as to maike m'self saife, if the police took a hand. I didn't want to be mixed with no gang, having my good name to think of."

Horace grinned and rubbed his hands, but Allen frowned. "Go on," he said sharply, "and don't play the fool."

"Oh, I'm a-goin' on," was the unruffled reply, "and I don't plaiy th' fool without cause, d'ye see. Well, I wos at the station at Westhaven, an' I sees Strode come. I went off to tell Merry, and he comes to the station and talks to Strode."

"That was on Wednesday?"

"Yuss. Strode sold 'us and come down, though we didn't 'ope to 'ave the pleasure of his company till Thursday. Well, I tried to 'ear what Giles wos a-saiying, but he guves me a clip on the ear and sends me spinnin', so I couldn't 'ear. I goes to complain to Father Don, an' when I gits back, Strode's away and Merry too. He'd started walkin' to Wargrove, a porter tole me. I wos about to foller, when Merry, he comes up and tells me, he'll go himself."

"That's a lie," said Allen; "Merry was doing the strong man that night in the circus."

"No, he wasn't," grinned the boy. "I went to the circus, havin' nothin' to do, and I saw the strong man. It wos Cain Merry, his son, he's like his father, and could do the fakements. No one knew but the circus coves."

"Then Merry----?"

"He went after Strode. I told Father Don an' Foxy, an' they swore awful. They couldn't start after him, as they didn't know what 'ud happen, and Merry's an awful one when put out, so they waited along o' me, d'ye see? Next daiy Merry come back, but said he'd left Strode a-goin' to the Red Deeps."

"What did Father Don do?"

"He went to the Red Deeps an' found the dead bloke. Then he come back and saw Merry. What he said to 'im I don't know: but Father Don sent me with a telegram to send from the St. James's Street orfice, saiying that Strode wouldn't be down till Friday. I think Father Don did that, to give toime to Merry to get awaiy."

"That was the telegram received by Miss Strode after nine on Thursday, I think?" said Mask.

"Yuss," said Butsey. "I sent it early an' the kid es took it to Wargrove forgot it till laite. I comes down again from town, gits back with the fresh air kids, saime night, to sell the peelers, an' nex' mornin' I comes down agin to tell Mrs. Merry es Cain would be over th' nex' daiy."

"Why did you do that? Cain was in the house."

"I knowed he wos. But Merry sent me to see if Miss Eva hed heard o' the death. Then I cuts----"

"One moment," said Allen, "if Father Don saw the man dead, why didn't he take the wooden hand?"

"Cause he didn't know it wos worth anythin' till Mr. Masks here spoke at the inquest."

"About its being delivered to get the diamonds?" said Mask; "quite so. And you saw Mr. Hill bury it?"

"Yuss. I wos told to watch him, es Merry said he knew a lot about Strode, and if the wust come he might be accused----"

"A clever plot. Well?"

"I follered him and saw him bury something. I digs it up and takes the cross es he put over it to mark it. Then I gives the 'and to Father Don an' the cross to Merry. He sends it to Hill to frighten him, and sends it through Cain. Then Father Don sees Mr. Mask, and you knows the rest."

"Not all, I guess," said Horace, stretching a long arm and shaking the boy, "say straight, you--you imp. Did Merry shoot?"

"Of course he did," replied Butsey cheerfully, "he hated Strode, an' wanted to git them diamonds. Merry hed the blue pocket-book, fur when I come down to see Miss Lorry at Shanton, I took the book from Merry's box which wos in his room. He found me with it and took it back, hammerin' me fur stealin'. But I got the notes," added Butsey with satisfaction, "and I spent three."

"Merry seems to be guilty," said Mr. Mask; "he was absent from the circus on that night and let his son--who resembles, him closely--take his place. He had the pocket-book and----"

"Got the diamonds? No, he didn't," said Butsey briskly, "he didn't know es the hand would open. I found that out from a letter I guv you, Mr. Mask, and tole ole Father Don. He opened the hand--that wos arter he saw you, Mr. Mask--but he foun' nothin'. Then he guessed es Hill--your father, Mr. Allen--had got the diamonds, seein' he had the han', while looking fur some paiper. An' Merry got the paiper out of the pocket-book," said Butsey, "an' showed it to Don. Wot Don did with it I dunno."

"He got the diamonds with it," said Allen grimly, "and has escaped. But I don't think Merry will. He's at Shanton now, as the circus is again there by particular request of the townsfolk. We'll go over tonight, Parkins, and see him perform: then we'll catch him and make him confess."

"Will you have him arrested?" asked Horace coolly.

"We'll see when the time comes," said Allen shortly. "Mask----?"

"I'll remain here and look after this boy, Master Train."

Butsey made a grimace, but so the matter was arranged.

XXIII - MISS LORRY'S LAST APPEARANCE

THERE WAS no doubt that Stag's Circus was a great success at Shanton. Within a comparatively short period it had played three engagements in the little town, two performances each time, and on every occasion the tent was full. Now it was the very last night, as Stag announced; the circus would next turn its attention towards amusing the North. Consequently the tent was crammed to its utmost capacity, and Stag, loafing about in a fur coat, with a gigantic cigar, was in a very good humour.

Not so Miss Lorry. That lady was already dressed in riding-habit and tall hat to show off the paces of her celebrated stallion White Robin, and she sat in her caravan dressing-room fuming with anger. Miss Lorry always insisted on having a dressing-room to herself, although the accommodation in that way was small. But she had such a temper and was such an attraction that the great Stag consented she should be humored in this way. She had a bottle of champagne beside her and was taking more than was good for her, considering she was about to perform with a horse noted for its bad temper. In her hand Miss Lorry held an open letter which was the cause of her wrath. It was from Saltars, written in a schoolboy hand, and announced that he could never marry her, as he was now aware, through the dowager Lady Ipsen, that she, Miss Lorry, was a married woman. "I have been with the dowager to the church in London," said the letter, "so I know there's no mistake. I think you've treated me very badly. I loved you and would have made you my wife. Now everything is off, and I'll go back and marry my cousin Eva Strode."

There were a few more reproaches to the effect that the lady had broken the writer's heart, and although these were badly expressed and badly written, yet the accent of truth rang true. Miss Lorry knew well that Saltars had really loved her, and would not have given her up unless the result had been brought about by the machinations of the dowager. She ground her teeth and crushed up the letter in her hand.

"I'm done for," she said furiously. "I'd have given anything to have been Lady Saltars, and I could have turned that fool round my finger. I've risked a lot to get the position, and here I'm sold by that brute I married when I was a silly girl! I could kill him--kill him," she muttered, "and as it is, I've a good mind to thrash him," and so saying she grasped a riding-whip firmly. It was used to bring White Robin to subjection, but Miss Lorry was quite bold enough to try its effect on the human brute.

Shortly she sent a message for Signor Antonio, and in a few minutes Giles presented himself with a grin. He was ready to go on for his performance, and the fleshings showed off his magnificent figure to advantage. He looked remarkably handsome, as he faced the furious woman coolly, and remarkably happy when he thought of a certain parcel of notes he had that afternoon placed in the safe keeping of the Shanton Bank.

"Well, Bell," said he coolly, "so you know the worst, do you? You wouldn't look in such a rage if you didn't."

Miss Lorry raised her whip and brought it smartly across the eyes of Signor Antonio. "You hound!" she said, in a concentrated voice of hate, "I should like to kill you."

Merry snatched at the whip, and, twisting it from her grip, threw it on the floor of the caravan. "That's enough," he said in a quietly dangerous voice. "You've struck me once. Don't do it again or I twist your neck."

"Oh no, you won't," said Miss Lorry, showing her fine white teeth; "what do you mean by splitting?"

"I was paid to do so," said Merry coolly; "so, now you know the worst, don't keep me chattering here all night. I 'ave to go on soon."

"I have my turn first," said Miss Lorry, glancing at a printed bill pinned against the wall of the van. "I must speak out, or burst," she put her hand to her throat as though she were choking. "You beast," she cried furiously, "have I not suffered enough at your hands already?"

"You were always a tigress," growled Merry, shrinking back before her fury; "I married you when you was a slip of a girl----"

"And a fool--a fool!" cried the woman, beating her breast; "oh, what a fool I was! You know my father was a riding-master, and----"

"And how you rode to show off to the pupils?" said Merry with a coarse laugh. "I just do. It was the riding took me."

"You came as a groom," panted Miss Lorry, fixing him with a steelly glare, "and I was idiot enough to admire your good looks. I ran away with you, and we were married----"

"I did the straight thing," said Giles, "you can't deny that."

"I wish I had died, rather than marry you," she said savagely. "I found myself bound to a brute. You struck me--you ill-treated me within a year of our marriage."

Merry lifted a lock of his black hair and showed a scar. "You did that," he said; "you flew at me with a knife."

"I wish I'd killed you," muttered Miss Lorry. "And then you left me. I found out afterwards you had married that farmer's daughter in Wargrove because you got a little money with her. Then you left her also, you brute, and with a baby. Thank God, I never bore you any children! Ah, and you were in with that bad lot of Hill, and Strode, and Father Don, who was kicked out of the army for cheating at cards. You fell lower and lower, and when you found I was making money in the circus you would have forced me to live with you again, but that I learned of your Wargrove marriage. It was only my threat of bigamy that kept you away."

"You intended to commit bigamy too, with Lord Saltars," said Merry sullenly, "and I was willing enough to let you. But you wrote to Miss Strode saying you'd stop me going to Wargrove----"

"So I could by threatening to prosecute you for bigamy."

Merry shrugged his shoulders. "Well, what good would that do?" he asked brutally. "I have confessed myself, and now you can do what you like. Old Lady Ipsen paid me fifteen hundred pounds for stopping your marriage with Saltars, and now it's off. I'm going to South Africa," finished the man.

"I'll prosecute you," panted his wife.

"No, you won't," he turned and looked at her sharply, "I know a little about you, my lady----"

Before he could finish his sentence, the name of Miss Lorry was called for her turn. She picked up the riding-whip and gave Giles another slash across the eyes, then with a taunting laugh she bounded out of the van. Giles, left alone, set his teeth and swore.

He was about to leave the caravan, intending to see Miss Lorry no more, and deciding to go away from Shanton next day with his money, for London en route to South Africa, when up the steps came Allen. Behind him was a veiled lady.

"What are you doing here?" demanded Merry, starting back; "get away. This place is for the performers."

"And for murderers also," said Allen, blocking the way resolutely, in spite of the splendid specimen of physical strength he saw before him. "I know you, Mr. Giles Merry?"

"What do you know?" asked Merry, turning pale. "I know that you shot Strode----"

"It's a lie," said Merry fiercely. "I was at the circus----"

"Cain was at the circus. He performed in your stead on that night at Westhaven. You followed Strode to the Red Deeps where he met my unhappy father, and you shot him. The boy Butsey has confessed how he found the blue pocket-book, taken from Strode's body, in your box. You took it back: but the boy retained the notes and was traced thereby. Butsey is in custody, and you also will be arrested."

Merry gasped and sat down heavily. "It's a lie. I saw Butsey with the pocket-book, and took it from him. It was in the book I found the paper which Don showed to your father; I never knew there was any notes. I don't know where Butsey stole the book."

"He took it from you."

"It's a lie, I tell you," cried Merry frantically, and seeing his danger. "I was never near the Red Deeps. Ask Cain, and he'll tell you, I and not he performed. He perform my tricks!" said Merry with a sneer; "why he couldn't do them--he hasn't the strength. I swear, Mr. Hill, by all that's holy I was not at the Red Deeps."

"You were," said the woman behind Allen, and Eva Strode pushed past her lover. "Allen and I came to this circus to see Cain and get him to speak about his appearing for you at Westhaven. We came round to the back, by permission of Mr. Stag. When we were passing here, I heard you laugh. It was the laugh I heard in my dream--a low, taunting laugh----"

"The dream?" said Merry aghast; "I remember reading what you said at the inquest, Miss Strode, and then my silly wife--the first wife," said Merry, correcting himself, "talked of it. But dreams are all nonsense."

"My dream was not, Giles. The body was brought home, and the five knocks were given----"

"By Butsey?" said Merry contemptuously; "bless you, Miss Eva, the boy was hidden on the verge of the common when you and Mr. Allen were walking on the night your father's body was brought home. You told Mr. Allen your dream."

"Yes, Eva, so you did," said Allen.

"Well then, Butsey heard you, and being a little beast as he always is, when he met those three men with the body he came too, and knocked five times as you described to Mr. Allen. That for dreams," said Merry, snapping his fingers.

Eva was slightly disconcerted. "That is explained away," she said, "but the laugh I heard in my dream, and heard just now in this caravan, isn't. It was you who laughed, Giles, and you who shot my father."

Merry started, and a red spot appeared on his cheek. "I wonder if Bell did kill him after all?" he murmured to himself; "she's got a vile temper, and perhaps----"

Allen was about to interrupt him, when there came a cry of dismay from the circus tent, and then a shrill, terrible scream. "There's an accident!" cried Merry, bounding past Eva and Allen, "White Robin's done it at last," and he disappeared.

The screams continued, and the noise in the tent. Suddenly there was the sound of two shots, and then a roar from the audience. A crowd of frightened women and children came pouring out. From the back came Stag and Merry and Horace and others carrying the mangled body of Miss Lorry. She was insensible and her face was covered with blood.

The tears were streaming down Stag's face. "I knew that brute would kill her someday," he said. "I always warned her--oh, poor Bell! Take her into the van, gentlemen. She'll have the finest funeral;--send for a doctor, can't you!"

Eva shrank back in horror at the sight of that marred face. The woman opened her eyes, and they rested on the girl. A flash of interest came into them and then she fell back unconscious. Stag and Merry carried her into the van, but Horace, surrendering his place to another bearer, joined Allen and Miss Strode.

"It was terrible," he said, wiping his face, which was pale and grave, "after you left me to see Cain, Miss Lorry entered on her white stallion. She was not very steady in the saddle--drink, I fancy. Still she put the horse through some of his tricks all right. But he seemed to be out of temper, and reared. She began to strike him furiously with her whip, and quite lost her self-control. He grew more savage and dashed her against the pole of the tent. How it happened I can't say, but in a moment she was off and on the ground, with the horse savaging her. Oh, the screams," said Horace, biting his lips, "poor woman! I had my Derringer in my pocket and almost without thinking I leaped into the ring and ran up to put a couple of bullets through the brute's head. White Robin is dead, and poor Miss Lorry soon will be," and he wiped his face again.

Allen and Eva heard this recital horror-struck, and then a medical man pushed past them. He was followed by a handsome boy in a red jersey. "Cain--Cain," cried Eva, but he merely turned for a moment and then disappeared into the van. Merry came out almost immediately, still in his stage dress and looking ashy white.

"She's done for," he whispered to Allen, "she can't live another hour," the doctor says. "I'll change, and come back. Miss Eva," he added, turning to the horror-struck girl, "you want to know who laughed in the van? It was Miss Lorry."

"Your wife?" said Eva, with pale lips; "then she----"

"If you believe in that dream of yours, she did," said Merry, and moved away before Allen could stop him. Cain appeared at the top of the van steps.

"Miss Eva?" he said, "she saw you, and she wants you."

"No, no!" said Allen, holding the girl back.

"I must," said Eva, breaking away; "you come too, Allen. I must learn the truth. If Miss Lorry laughed"--she paused and looked round, "oh, my dream--my dream!" she said, and ran up the steps.

Miss Lorry was lying on the floor, with her head supported by a cushion. Her face was pale and streaked with blood, but her eyes were calm, and filled with recognition of Eva. The doctor, kneeling beside the dying woman, was giving her some brandy, and Cain, in his red jersey, with a small Bible in his hand, waited near the door. Allen and Horace, with their hats off, stood behind him.

"I'm--glad," said Miss Lorry, gasping; "I want to speak. Don't you let--Saltars--marry you," she brought out the words with great force, and her head fell back.

"You mustn't talk," said the doctor faintly.

"Am I dying?" she asked, opening her splendid eyes.

The doctor nodded, and Cain came forward with the tears streaming down his face, "Oh, let me speak, dear Miss Lorry," he said, "let me pray----"

"No," said the woman faintly, "I must talk to Miss Eva. I have much to say. Come and kneel down beside me, dear."

Eva did so, and took Miss Lorry's hand. The dying woman smiled. "I'm glad to have you by me, when I pass," she said; "Mr. Hill, White Robin--he didn't mean to. I was not well--I should not have struck him."

"He's dead," said the deep voice of the American; "I shot him."

"Shot him!" said Miss Lorry, suddenly raising herself; "shot who?--not Strode. It was I--it was I who----"

"Miss Lorry--let me pray," cried Cain vehemently; "make your peace with our dear, forgiving Master."

"You're a good boy, Cain. You should have been my son. But I must confess my sins before I ask forgiveness. Mr. Hill, have you paper and a pencil?--ah, give me some brandy----"

While the doctor did so, Horace produced a stylographic pen, and a sheet of paper torn from his pocket-book. He passed these to Allen, who also came and knelt by Miss Lorry. He quite understood that the miserable creature was about to confess her crime. Stag appeared at the door, but did not venture further. Cain saw him, and pushed him back, "Let her die in peace," he said, and took Stag away.

"Do you want us to remain?" said the doctor gently.

"Yes. I want to tell everyone what I did. Mr. Hill, write it down. I hope to live to sign it."

"I am ready," said Allen, placing the paper, and poising the pen.

Miss Lorry had some more brandy. A light came into her eyes, and her voice also became stronger.

"Hold my hand," she said to Eva. "If you keep holding it, I'll know you forgive me. I--I shot your father."

"You--but why?" asked Eva, aghast.

"Don't take away your hand--don't. Forgive me. I was mad. I knew your father many years ago. He was cruel to me. Giles would have been a better husband but for your father. When Strode--I can call him Strode, can't I?--when he came back from South Africa, he came to the circus, when we were near London. He found out my address from Giles, with whom he had much to do, and not always doing the best things either. Strode said he wanted to marry you to Saltars, and he heard that Saltars wanted to marry me. He told me that he would stop the marriage, by revealing that I was Giles's wife--ah!----"

Another sup of brandy gave her strength to go on, and Allen set down all she said.--"I was furious. I wanted to be Lady Saltars: besides, I loved him. I always loved him. I had such a cruel life with Giles--I was so weary of riding--I thought I might die poor. I have saved money--but not so much as I said. I told Saltars I had five hundred a year: but I have only two hundred pounds altogether. When that was gone, I thought I might starve. If my beauty went--if I met with an accident--no, I could not face poverty. Besides, I loved Saltars, I really loved him. I implored your father to hold his tongue. Giles could say nothing, as I could stop him by threatening to prosecute him for bigamy. Only your father knew----"

Again she had to gasp for breath, and then went on rapidly as though she feared she would not last till she had told all. "Your father behaved like a brute. I hated him. When he came that night to Westhaven, I heard from Butsey of his arrival, and that he had gone to the Red Deeps. How Butsey knew, I can't say. But I was not on in the bills till very late--at the very end of the program--I had a good, quick horse, and saddled it myself--I took a pistol--I intended to shoot your father, and close his mouth forever. It was his own fault--how could I lose Saltars, and face poverty and--disgrace?"

There was another pause while Allen's pen set down what she said, and then with an effort she continued: "I went to the Red Deeps and waited behind some trees. It was close on nine. I saw your father waiting by the spring. It was a kind of twilight, and, hidden by the bushes, I was really quite near to him. He was waiting for someone. At first I thought I would speak to him again, and implore his pity; but I knew he would do nothing--I knew also he was going to Wargrove, and would tell Mrs. Merry that I was her husband's wife. I waited my chance to fire. I had tethered the horse some distance away. As I looked there came a shot which evidently hit Strode on the arm, for he put his hand up and wheeled round. I never stopped to think that someone was trying to kill him also, or I should have let the work be done by that person."

"Did you know who the person was?"

"No, I did not see," said Miss Lorry faintly; "I had no eyes save for Strode. Oh, how I hated him!" a gleam of anger passed over her white face. "When he wheeled to face the other person who shot, I saw that his breast was turned fairly towards me. I shot him through the heart. I was a good shot," added Miss Lorry proudly, "for I earned my living in the circus at one time by shooting as the female cowboy"--the incongruity of the phrase did not seem to strike her as grotesque. "I heard someone running away, but I did not mind. I sprang out of the bush and searched his pockets.

I thought he might have set down something about my marriage in his papers. I took the blue pocket-book and then rode back quickly to Westhaven, where I arrived in time for my turn. That's all. Let me sign it."

She did so painfully, and then Allen and Horace appended their names as witnesses.

"How came the pocket-book into Merry's possession?" It was Allen who asked, and Miss Lorry replied drowsily--

"Butsey stole the pocket-book from my rooms. He saw the notes which I left in it, and when I was out he found where I kept it. I believe Merry took it from him, and then--oh, how weary I am!----"

The doctor made a sign, and Allen, putting the confession into his pocket, moved away with Horace. Eva bent down and kissed the dying woman. "I forgive you," she said, "indeed I forgive you. You acted under a sudden impulse and----"

"Thank God you forgive me," said Miss Lorry.

Eva would have spoken but that Cain drew her back. "Ask our Lord and Master to forgive you," he said in piercing tones. "Oh, pray, Miss Lorry--pray for forgiveness!"

"I have been too great a sinner."

"The greatest sinner may return; only ask Him to forgive!"

Eva could bear the sight no longer; she walked quickly out of the tent and almost fainted in Allen's arms as she came down the steps. And within they heard the dying woman falteringly repeating the Lord's prayer as Cain spoke it:

"For-give us our tres-passes as we forgive those who----"

Then the weaker voice died away, and only the clear tones of the lad could be heard finishing the sublime petition.

XXIV - THE WINDING OF THE SKEIN

A YEAR after the death of Miss Lorry, two ladies sat in Mrs. Palmer's drawing-room. One was the widow herself, looking as pretty and as common as ever, although she now dressed in more subdued tints, thanks to her companion's frequent admonitions. Eva was near her, with a bright and expectant look on her face, as though she anticipated the arrival of some one. It was many months since Allen had gone out to Bolivia, and this day he was expected back with Mr. Horace Parkins. Before he departed again for South America, a ceremony would take place to convert Eva Strode into Mrs. Hill.

"I'm sure I don't know what I shall do without you, Eva dear," said the widow for the tenth time that day.

"Oh, you'll have Mr. Parkins to console you, Constance."

"Mr. Parkins, indeed?" said Mrs. Palmer tossing her head.--She and Eva were both in evening-dress, and were waiting for the guests. Allen was coming, also his mother and Mr. Parkins.--"I don't know why you should say that, dear."

Eva laughed. "I have seen a number of letters with the Bolivian stamp on them, Constance----"

"Addressed to you. I should think so. But something better than letters is coming this evening, Eva."

"Don't try to get out of the position," said Miss Strode, slipping her arm round the waist of the widow; "you created it yourself. Besides, Allen told me in his letter that Mr. Parkins talked of no one and nothing but you. And think, dear, you won't have to alter your initials, Constance Parkins sounds just as well as Constance Palmer."

"Better, I think. I don't deny that I like Mr. Parkins."

"Call him Horace----"

"He hasn't given me the right. You forget I saw him only for a month or so, when he was home last."

"You saw him long enough to fall in love with him."

"I don't deny that--to you; but if he dares to ask me to be his wife, I'll tell him what I think."

"Quite so, and then we can be married on the same day;--I to Allen, and you to Horace Parkins. Remember Horace is rich now--the mine has turned out splendidly."

"I'm rich enough without that," said Mrs. Palmer with a fine color; "if I marry, it will be to please myself. I have had quite enough of marrying for money, and much good it's done me."

"You have done every one good," said Eva, kissing her; "think how kind you were to me, throughout that terrible time, when----"

"Hark!" said Mrs. Palmer, raising a jeweled finger; "at last!"

Shortly the door opened and Mrs. Hill entered, followed by Allen and Horace and by Mr. Mask. Eva had already seen Allen, and Mrs. Palmer had asked him and Horace to dinner, but both ladies were astonished when they saw the lawyer. "Well, this is a surprise," said the widow, giving her hand.

"I thought I would come, as this is Allen's welcome home," said Mr. Mask; "you don't mind?"

"I am delighted."

"And you, Miss Strode?"

"I am pleased too. I look on you as one of my best friends," said Eva, who did not forget that she owed Mrs. Palmer's protection to the lawyer's kindness. "Mrs. Hill, how are you?"

"I think you can call me mother now," said the old lady as she greeted her son's promised wife with a kiss.

"Oh!" said Allen, who looked bronzed and very fit, "I think, mother, you are usurping my privilege."

"Why should it be a privilege?" said Horace, casting looks at the widow; "why not make it a universal custom?"

"In that case I should----" began Mrs. Palmer.

"No, you shouldn't," said Horace, "the world wouldn't let you."

"Let me what? You don't know what I was about to say."

Horace would have responded, but the gong thundered.

"You were about to say that you hoped we were hungry," said Mask slyly; "that is what a hostess usually says."

"That," said Mrs. Palmer in her turn, "is a hint. Mr. Hill, will you take in Eva?--Mr. Mask----"

"I offer my arm to Mrs. Hill," said the old lawyer.

"In that case," said the widow, smiling, and with a look at the big American, "I must content myself with you."

Horace said something which made her smile and blush, and then they all went into a dainty meal, which everyone enjoyed. After the terrible experiences of a year ago, each person seemed bent upon enjoyment, and the meal was a very bright one. When it was ended, the gentlemen did not sit over their wine, but joined the ladies almost immediately. Mrs. Palmer and Mrs. Hill were in the drawing-room talking in low tones, but Eva was nowhere to be seen. Allen looked around, and Mrs. Palmer laughed at the sight of his anxious face. "You'll find her in the garden," she said; "it's quite a perfect night of the Indian summer, therefore----"

Allen did not wait for further information. He departed at once and by the quickest way, directly through the French window, which happened to be open. A few steps along the terrace, under a full moon, showed him Eva walking on the lawn. At once he sprang down the steps. "Don't walk on the grass, you foolish child," he said, taking her arm, "you'll get your feet damp."

"It's too delicious a night for that," said Eva, lifting her lovely face to the silver moon; "but we can sit in the arbor----"

"Don't you think Parkins will want that? He's bound to come out with Mrs. Palmer, and then----"

"Does he really mean to propose?"

"He's been talking of nothing else for the last few months, and has come home for that precise purpose. But for that, he would have remained with Mark at the mine. Poor Mark has all the work, and we have all the fun. But I was determined to come to you and make sure that you hadn't married Saltars after all."

"Poor Saltars," said Eva, smiling, "he did come and ask me; but his heart was not in the proposal. That terrible grandmother of mine urged him to the breach. He seemed quite glad when I declined."

"What bad taste," said Allen laughing.

"I think he really loved that poor woman who died," said Eva in low tones, "and she certainly loved him, when she committed so daring a crime for his sake."

"It might have been ambition as well as love, Eva, and it certainly was a fear of starvation in her old age. Miss Lorry wanted to make herself safe for a happy time, and so when she found your father was likely to rob her of an expected heaven, she shot him."

"I wish the truth had not been made public, though," said Eva.

"My dear, it was necessary, so as to remove all blame from anyone who may have been suspected. Poor Stag, however, was not able to give Miss Lorry the splendid funeral he wished to give, out of respect. As you know, she was buried very quietly. Only Horace and I and Saltars followed her to her grave."

"Didn't her husband?"

"Giles Merry? No: he never came back, even to see her die. The man was a brute always. He went off to Africa, I believe, with the money he borrowed--that's a polite way of putting it--from old Lady Ipsen. I suppose Mrs. Merry was glad when she heard he was out of the country?"

Eva nodded. "And yet I think if he had come back, she would have faced him. Ever since she knew he was not her husband, she seemed to lose her fear of him. She still calls herself Mrs. Merry for Cain's sake. No one knows the truth, save you and I and Lady Ipsen."

"Well it's best to let things remain as they are. I trust Mrs. Merry is more cheerful?"

"Oh yes; the fact is, Cain has converted her."

"Oh, has Cain taken up his residence in Misery Castle?"

Eva laughed. "It is called the House Beautiful now," she said; "Cain got the name out of the Pilgrim's Progress., and he lives there with his mother and his wife."

"What, did he marry Jane Wasp after all?"

"He did, some months after you left. Wasp was very much against the match, as he called Cain a vagabond."

"Well he was, you know."

"He is not now. After he joined the Salvation Army he changed completely and is quite a different person. But even then, Wasp would not have allowed the match to take place, but that Cain inherited two hundred pounds from Miss Lorry."

"Ah, poor soul," said Allen sympathetically, "she talked of that sum when she was dying. Why did she leave it to Cain?"

"She always liked Cain, and I think she was sorry for the slur on his birth cast by his father. But she left him the money, and then Wasp found out that Cain was a most desirable son-in-law."

"Does he still belong to the Army?"

"No. Wasp insisted he should leave. So Cain lives at the House Beautiful and preaches throughout the country. I believe he is to become a Methodist minister shortly. At all events, Allen, he is making his poor mother happy, after all the misery she has had."

"And how do Mrs. Merry and Wasp get along?"

"Oh, they rarely see one another, which is just as well. Wasp has been moved to Westhaven at a higher salary, and is getting along capitally."

"I suppose he drills his household as much as ever," laughed Allen; "let us walk, Eva. We can sit on the terrace."

Eva pinched Allen's arm, and he looked, to see Horace sauntering down the path with Mrs. Palmer. They were making for the arbor. The other lovers therefore sat on the terrace, so as to afford Horace plenty of time to propose. And now, Allen, said Eva, I must ask you a few questions. "What of Father Don and his gang?"

"No one knows. I heard that Red Jerry had been caught by the Continental police for some robbery. But Foxy and Father Don have vanished into space with their loot. I regret those diamonds."

"I don't," said Eva proudly; "I would much rather live as your wife on your money, Allen."

"On my own earnings, you mean?"

"Yes, though you will be very rich when your mother dies."

"I hope that won't be for a long time," said Allen gravely; "poor mother, she had a sad life with my father."

"Why did he go mad so suddenly, Allen?"

"The shock of those diamonds being carried off, I suppose, Eva. But he was mad when he stole that wooden hand. Where is it?"

"Buried in the vault. We put it there," said Eva, shuddering; "I never wish to see it again. Look at the misery it caused. But why did your father steal it?"

"Never mind. He was mad, and that's the best that can be said. It was just as well he died while I was away. He would only have lingered on, an imbecile. I wish my mother would give up the house and come out with us to Bolivia, Eva."

"We might be able to persuade her. But there's one question I want to ask: What's become of Butsey? I haven't heard of him, since he left Mr. Mask."

Allen laughed. "Yes; he gave Mask the slip very smartly," he said, "a dangerously clever lad is Butsey. I heard he was in America. A fine field for his talents he'll find there."

"Why did he tell lies about Giles Merry?"

"Because he hated Merry, and wanted to save Miss Lorry. He knew all the time that Miss Lorry was guilty, but would have hanged Giles to save her. Had she not confessed, Giles, with that brat lying in the witness-box, would have been in a strange plight."

"Would they have tried Butsey, had he not got away?"

"I can't say. Perhaps they would. I am not a good lawyer. You had better ask Mask. However, the boy's gone, and I dare say he'll someday be lynched in the States. People like him always come to a bad end, Eva. Well, any more questions?"

"I can't think of any. Why do you ask?"

Allen took her hands, and looked into her eyes. "Because I want to put the old bad past out of our minds. I want you to ask what you wish to ask, and I'll answer. Then we'll drop the subject forever."

"There's nothing more I want to know," said Eva after a pause; "tell me about our house, Allen."

He kissed her, and then told of the quaint Spanish house in the sleepy old Spanish town, and told also of the increasing wealth of the silver mine. "We'll all be millionaires in a few years, Eva, and then we can return to Europe and take a house in London."

"Certainly not in Wargrove," said Eva, shivering. "I want to forget this place with all its horrors. My dream----"

"Don't talk of it, Eva. We'll be married next week, and then life will be all joy for us both. Ah, here is Mrs. Palmer!----"

"Mrs. Parkins that is to be," said the male figure by the widow's side; "we're going to travel together."

"I am so glad, Constance," said Eva, kissing her.

"What about me, Miss Strode?" asked the envious American.

"I'll salute you by proxy in this way," said Eva, and kissed Allen.

"Oh, Horace!" sighed Mrs. Palmer, and sank into her lover's arms.

So all four were happy, and the troubles of the past gave place to the joys of the present. The evil augury of Eva's dream was fulfilled--the dark night was past, and joy was coming in the morning. So after all, good had come out of evil.

THE END

The Maxwell Mystery

By Carolyn Wells

I: CONCERNING OPPORTUNITIES

"PETER KING—Please—Peter King—Peter King!"
With a telegram on his tray, the bell-boy traversed the crowded hotel dining-room, chanting his monotonous refrain, until I managed to make him realize that I owned the above name, and persuaded him to hand over the message.

It was short, and extremely characteristic of the sender.

House party. Take afternoon train Saturday. Stay Tuesday.
I. G.
PHILIP MAXWELL.

I was more than willing to take the designated train, and looked forward with satisfaction to a few days of pleasure. Philip had a decided genius for arranging parties of congenial people, and, moreover, the telegram assured me that at least one of my fellow guests would prove attractive.

For the letters "I. G." meant nothing more nor less than that Irene Gardiner would be there. Though I had met this young woman only twice, she already exerted a fascination over me such as I had never before experienced.

As I had hoped, she too went down to Hamilton on the afternoon train, and the four hours' journey gave me an opportunity to cultivate her acquaintance more informally than at our previous meetings.

This pleased me, and yet when we were comfortably settled in our chairs, and rushing swiftly through the monotonous and uninteresting landscapes of central and southern New Jersey, I was conscious of a certain disappointment regarding my fair companion.

In the daylight, and on a railroad train, she lost the subtle charm which perhaps had been imparted by the glamour and artificial light of a ballroom; and she looked older and less ingenuous than I had thought her.

And yet she was a beautiful woman.

Her clear dark eyes were straightforward without being piercing; nor were they soulful or languishing, but capable of a direct gaze that was both perceptive and responsive. Her clear-cut mouth and chin betokened not only a strong will, but a strong character and a capable nature.

No, seen by day light there was no glamour about Irene Gardiner, but the very lack of it, where I had expected to find it, interested me.

She was entirely at her ease as we pursued our journey, and with a ready, graceful tact adapted herself to all the exigencies of the situation. Perhaps it would be more nearly true of Irene Gardiner to say that she adapted situations to herself. Without seeming to dictate, she anticipated my wishes, and made just such suggestions as I wished to carry out.

Within an hour of our leaving New York, I found myself enjoying a cigar in the smoker, and wondered how I had managed it. When I realized that I had come there at her advice and even insistence, I gave her immediate credit for tactful cleverness—woman's most admirable trait.

Yet somehow I felt a certain chagrin. To be sure I did want a smoke, but I didn't want to be made to smoke;—and to obey the suggestion unconsciously at that!

There was no one in the smoker that I knew, and after I had finished my cigar, I began to feel a strong inclination to return to Miss Gardiner's society, and with a sudden intuition I felt sure that this was just the result she had intended to bring about, and that she had dismissed me in order that we might not both become bored by a long and uninterrupted téte-a-téte.

This very thought determined me not to go back; but such is the perversity of the human will, that the more I stayed away, the more I felt inclined to go.

So half angry at myself I returned to my chair in the parlor-car, and was greeted by a bright smile of welcome.

"I've been reading a detective story," she said, as she turned down a leaf and closed the paper covered book she held. "I don't often affect that style of literature, but the train-boy seemed of the opinion that this book was the brightest gem of modern fiction, and that no self-respecting citizen could afford to let it go unread."

"Don't scorn detective fiction as a class," I begged. "It's one of my favorite lines of light reading. I have read that book, and though its literary style is open to criticism, it advances a strong and tenable theory of crime."

"I haven't finished the story," said Miss Gardiner, "but I suppose you mean the idea that innocence is only the absence of temptation."

"That is perhaps putting it a little too strongly, but I certainly think that often opportunity creates a sinner."

"It is not a new idea," said Miss Gardiner thoughtfully; "I believe Goethe said 'We are all capable of crime—even the best of us.' And while he would doubtless have admitted exceptions to his rule, he must have thought it applicable to the great majority."

"It's impossible to tell," I observed, "for though we often know when a man succumbs to temptation we cannot know how often he resists it."

"But we can know about ourselves," exclaimed Miss Gardiner with a sudden energy.

"Honestly, now, if the motive were sufficient and a perfect opportunity presented itself unsought, could you imagine yourself committing a great crime?"

"Oh, I have a vivid imagination," I replied gaily, "and it isn't the least trouble to imagine myself cracking a safe or kidnapping a king. But when it came to the point, I doubt if I'd do it after all. I'd be afraid of the consequences."

"Now you're flippant. But I'm very much in earnest. I really believe if the motive were strong enough, I mean if it were one of the elemental motives, like love, jealousy, or revenge, I could kill a human being without hesitation. Of course it would be in a moment of frenzy, and I would doubtless regret it afterward, and even wonder at my own deed. But the point I'm trying to make is only that, in proportion to the passions of which we are capable, we possess an equivalent capability of executing the natural consequences of those passions."

I looked at Miss Gardiner curiously.

She certainly was in earnest, yet she gave me the impression of a theorist rather than one speaking from personal conviction.

And, too, it shocked me. She couldn't mean it, and yet the positiveness of her speech and the earnestness of her look indicated sincerity. With her animated dark beauty she looked just then like Judith and Jael and Zenobia all in one. It was not at all difficult, at that moment, to imagine her giving way to an elemental emotion, but the thought was far from pleasant and I put it quickly away from me.

"Let us leave ourselves out of the question," I said, "and merely admit that crimes have been committed by persons innocent up to the moment when strong temptation and opportunity were present at the same time."

"You will not be serious," she retorted, "so we'll drop the subject. And now, unless you make yourself very entertaining, I'll return to my story book and leave you to your own devices."

"That would be a crime, and you would commit it because you see your opportunity," I replied, whereupon Miss Gardiner laughed gaily, and abandoned her discussion of serious theories.

I must have proved sufficiently entertaining, for she did not reopen her novel, and we chatted pleasantly during the rest of the journey.

"Is it a large and a gay party we're travelling toward?" I asked, as we neared Hamilton.

"I don't really know," said Miss Gardiner; "Miss Maxwell invited me, and the only other guests she mentioned in her letter, beside yourself, were Mildred Leslie and the Whitings."

"You mean Mildred's sister Edith, and her husband?"

"Yes, you know Edith married Tom Whiting. He's a most delightful man and the Leslies are dear girls."

"I remember Edith as a beauty, but I haven't seen Mildred since she was a youngster."

"Prepare yourself for a surprise, then; she's grown up to be the most fascinating little witch you ever saw."

"At any rate, Philip thinks so," I said, smiling, and Miss Gardiner returned an understanding glance.

"Yes," she agreed, "Philip is perfectly daft about her, but I don't think Miss Maxwell is altogether pleased at that. She's awfully fond of Mildred, but I think she would rather Philip should choose a different type for a wife."

"But I doubt if Philip will ask his aunt's advice in such a matter."

"Indeed he won't; nor his uncle's either. Phil's a dear fellow, but those two old people have spoiled him by humoring him too much; and now they can't be surprised if he insists upon his own way."

"Do you approve the match?" I asked, rather pointedly.

"No; I can't. Milly is a perfect darling, but she would lead Philip a dance all his life. She's a born coquette and she can't help flirting with everybody."

"She may try it with me, if she likes," I said, nonchalantly, and Miss Gardiner responded, "Have no doubts of that! She's bound to do so. I only wish you would involve her, or let her involve you in so deep a flirtation that Philip would lose his interest."

"My dear Miss Gardiner, don't you know that that would be just the way to pique Philip's interest, and defeat your own very admirable intent?"

"I suppose it would," said Irene, with a little sigh, and then our train drew into the Hamilton station.

Philip met us at the train with his automobile.

"I say, but you're late!" he shouted. "We've been waiting twenty minutes." He led the way to his big touring car, as shinily spick-and-span as a steam yacht, and bundled us into it.

"You sit back, Peter," he directed, "with Mrs. Whiting and Miss Leslie, and I'll take Miss Gardiner with me. We'll run around the country a bit before we go home."

I hadn't seen Mildred Leslie for several years and I was all unprepared for the change which had transformed the shy schoolgirl into one of the most beautiful women I had ever seen. She was of the apple-blossom type, and her frivolous, dimpled face was adorably pink and white, with big pansy-blue eyes, and a saucy, curved mouth. A riotous fluff of golden hair escaped from her automobile-veil, and the first glance proved the girl to be a coquette to her fingertips.

Her sister, Mrs. Whiting, was totally unlike her. She was a solid, sensible little woman, whose sole occupation in life seemed to be a protracted futile attempt to keep Mildred in order.

I took my seat between these two ladies, feeling that, for the next few days at least, my lines had fallen in pleasant places.

"I do love a house party at the Maxwells," said Mildred, "because the party never stays in the house. There are so many lovely, outdoorsy things to do that if it weren't for meals we'd never see the inside of the beautiful old mansion."

"It is a beautiful house," said Mrs. Whiting. "I almost wish it would rain tomorrow so that we might stay in and enjoy it."

"Oh, Edith, not tomorrow!" cried Mildred; "we've too many things planned. Why, Mr. King, there's a different picnic arranged for every hour in the day, and you can pick out whichever ones you like best to go to."

"I've such faith in your taste," I replied, "that I'll just follow you, and go to the ones you attend."

"I'm going to send regrets to several of the picnics," announced Irene Gardiner, "and ramble around the house. I've never seen it, but I've often heard of its glories."

"We must stay indoors long enough to have some music," said Mrs. Whiting; "I want to hear Irene sing some of her old songs again."

"I cannot sing the old songs," Irene said, laughing; "but I know a lot of new ones."

"I'll stay home from any picnic to hear them," said Mildred promptly.

"I'll stay, too," said I, but though this sounded as if a compliment to Miss Gardiner's music, a flash of appreciation from Mildred's blue eyes proved to me that she read my intent.

II: "MAXWELL CHIMNEYS"

"OH, how stunning!" cried Irene Gardiner, for just then we whizzed up the driveway to the Maxwell house, and though perhaps not the word a purist would have chosen, "stunning" did seem to express the effect. The white pillars and porticoes of the mansion gleamed through the evergreen trees that dotted the broad lawn; the sunset in progress was of the spectacular variety, and a nearby lake reflected its gorgeous colorings.

Alexander Maxwell had chosen to call his beautiful home "Maxwell Chimneys," and the place was as picturesque and unusual as its name. It had chimneys of the reddest of red brick, and these stuck up all over the roof of the many-gabled house, and also ran up the sides and down the back, and nestled in corners, and even presented the novel spectacle of a fireplace right out on the broad front veranda.

Though Philip had laughed at this addition to the heating facilities of the mansion, it proved to be a great success, and on cool summer evenings the open fire lit up the atmosphere gaily and, incidentally, warmed a small portion of it.

The truth was, Miss Maxwell did not herself like outdoor life; so, by filling her home with cozy fireplaces, she often enticed her guests indoors, which thoroughly pleased her hospitable soul. For the great house was always filled with guests, and one house-party followed close on the heels of another all summer long. "Maxwell Chimneys" occupied one of the most desirable locations in Fairmountain Park, and the views from its various windows and balconies were like a series of illuminated post-cards. Or, at least, that was the remark made by seven out of every ten of the guests who visited there.

As we neared the veranda, a cheery voice shouted "Hello," and Tom Whiting ran down the steps to meet us. The big, good-natured chap was a general favorite, and I cordially returned his hearty greeting. Then the wide front door swung open, and the old doorway made a fitting frame for the gentle lady of the house who stood within it.

Miss Miranda Maxwell was Philip's aunt and, incidentally, was his devoted slave. She and her brother Alexander had lived in the old house for many years, beloved and respected by the townspeople of Hamilton, though deemed perhaps a shade too quiet and old-fogy for the rising generation.

But this was all changed when their nephew Philip came to live with them, and filled the house with young life and new interests. He had been there about three years now, and though the village gossips had concluded that he would never make the gentleman of the old school that his uncle was, yet he had won his own place in their regard, and his gay, sunny nature had gained many friends for him.

Phil was a good-looking chap of about twenty-three and had been an orphan since childhood. After his school and college days, his uncle had invited him to make his permanent home at "Maxwell Chimneys," and Philip had accepted the invitation. It was generally understood that he would eventually inherit the place, together with Alexander Maxwell's large fortune, and though not avaricious, Philip looked forward complacently to a life of ease and luxury.

So far as social life went, he was practically master of Maxwell Chimneys; he invited guests whenever he chose, and entertained them elaborately. Though Mr. Maxwell joined but seldom in the young people's festivities, he paid the bills without a murmur, and smiled indulgently at his merry-hearted nephew.

I had known Philip all through our college days, and I had made long and frequent visits at Maxwell Chimneys, where the hours of quiet enjoyment were often varied by delightful impromptu entertainments, the product of Philip's ingenuity.

I was a favorite with both the old people, and I fully returned their regard. Mr. Maxwell was a collector in a modest way, and I was always gratified when I could assist him in his quest or researches.

Miss Maxwell had such a kind, motherly heart that I think she was a friend to everybody, but she, too, seemed specially to like me, and so my visits to Hamilton were always pleasant occasions.

"How do you do, Peter? I'm very glad to see you," she said, so cordially, that the warm welcome of her tone made the commonplace salutation a heartfelt one.

"How do you do, Miss Miranda?" I responded, with equal cordiality. "I'm most happy to be here again. It is a long time since I've enjoyed your hospitality. Ah! here is Mr. Maxwell; how do you do, sir?"

I raised my voice to speak to my elderly host, for I remembered his deafness. He shook hands, and greeted me warmly, expressing his pleasure that I was with them once again.

I counted this brother and sister among my best friends, and aside from their kindness and hospitality they represented the best type of our American people. Educated, cultured and refined, they imbued their home with an atmosphere of pleasantest good humor.

The house was luxurious, and their manner of living, though rather elaborate, was not formal and not uncomfortably conventional.

Miss Maxwell herself showed me to my room, and as she left me at the door, she gave a motherly little pat to my shoulder, saying: "Now, Peter, dear boy, Philip's man will look after you, but if everything isn't just to your liking let me know, won't you?"

"Sure he will, Aunt Miranda," broke in Philip's gay voice, as he passed us in the hall; "look alive, now, Peter, old boy, and tog yourself for dinner at once; and drop down to the terrace as soon as you're ready."

But after I was dressed, I stepped out onto the balcony through my own window, lured by the beauty of the scene before me. The distant hills were purple in the late twilight, and the crisp air of early autumn was pleasant after the warmth of the house. I stood at the balcony rail, and as I looked down I saw two people strolling along the terrace just beneath me. In the dusk, I was uncertain who they were, and then I heard Philip's clear, deep voice:

"You're a rattle-brained, butterfly-minded and extremely conceited young person," he declared, "but I have the misfortune to love you as I love life itself; so, once more, Mildred, darling, won't you marry me?"

Mildred laughed.

"Philip," she said, "I do believe that's the thousandth time you've asked me that question. Please don't do it again. My answer is—No."

"Milly," and Philip's voice took on a new tone, "I shall ask you that question just once more. Not now; and only once more. Remember, dear, only once. Come, let us go back to the house."

I felt no compunction at my involuntary eavesdropping, for these people were speaking in casual tones, and any one on the verandas might have overheard them. And, too, what they said was no secret. Miss Gardiner had told me that Philip wanted to marry Mildred, and I felt sure that the laughing reply she had given him was merely coquetry, and that he would again ask her the same question and get another answer.

I went downstairs and met the pair just entering the house, and then we went in to dinner. Later on, as was the custom at Maxwell Chimneys, we all gathered on the front veranda to watch the moon rise. Now, moonrise over Fairmountain was of the nature of a solemn function, and by no means to be lightly treated. The feminine members of the party, therefore, had selected their places with a view to their own picturesque effect in connection with the view and the men naturally fell into position near the women they most admired.

This, of course, meant that Philip Maxwell should establish himself in the near vicinity of Mildred Leslie. But the young man had learned by experience that Mildred's nature was possessed of a certain butterfly quality, that often caused her to hover about from one place to another, before settling on a final choice. And as he could not, with dignity, jump up and run about after her, he wisely paused, and stood carelessly leaning against a pillar, watching her as she fluttered about.

The young man had certainly shown no error in taste in admiring Mildred. She was without doubt the prettiest girl present, and prettier than any girl one would meet in many a long summer day. Her piquant, merry little face was always smiling, and her deep blue eyes seemed to be full of half-hidden sunshine. Her hair was just on the darker side of golden, and owing to a bewitching waviness seemed to look prettier every new way she arranged it.

Mildred was not quite twenty, and had not outgrown a certain childish willfulness that was inherent in her nature.

But though sometimes provokingly saucy, she was so winsomely attractive that her friends declared her adorable, in spite of the fact that she was a spoiled child.

Philip's devotion to her was an open secret, and though there were others whose devotion was equally evident, the somewhat strong-willed young man had determined to win her, and of late had felt that he might consider his case hopeful.

In her dainty white evening gown, befrilled with fluffy laces, Mildred was a picture as she flitted about, from one group to another, the filmy blue scarf trailing around her, never in place, but always picturesque.

"Dear Miss Maxwell," she said, pausing a moment by her hostess' chair, "mayn't we have a picnic to Heatherwood, someday, soon?"

"Oh, do let us," chimed in Irene Gardiner, "a real old-fashioned picnic, with devilled eggs and lemon pie."

"My dear girls," replied Miss Maxwell, "you may have a picnic at Land's End if you choose, provided you don't ask me to go to it." For though Miss Miranda wanted young people about her, she didn't fancy running around much.

"Dear old Dearie," said Mildred, patting her shoulder, "she shall stay at home if she wants to, and toast her toes at her own fire-side, so she shall. Edith, you'll chaperon us, won't you?" she asked of the young matron of the party.

"I'll be chaperon in name only," said Mrs. Whiting, laughing; "but as to exercising any real authority over you rollicking creatures, I shouldn't like to promise it."

"Now, Mrs. Whiting," exclaimed Irene, "that's too bad! Milly, we all know, is difficult, but I'm as good as gold. At least, I have my good days; they're Tuesdays and Sundays this summer, and as tomorrow is Sunday you needn't worry at all about me."

"That's a lovely plan of yours," said Mildred, "to have days on which to be good. I wish I had one. I think one would be enough for me."

"You!" exclaimed Gilbert Crane, a neighbor who had strolled over; "you'd have to choose Tib's Eve, or the thirty-first of February."

"How delightfully rude you are," said Mildred, her dimples deepening, as she slowly drawled out the words at him; then, as if it were an afterthought —" I love rude men."

"It's nice of you to put it that way," he responded, "and as a reward I'll take you for a walk. Come on, we'll go and hunt up that moon. I don't believe it's ever going to rise over that mountain. Must have slipped a cog, or something."

"Thank you so much," said Mildred settling herself complacently in a rustic chair beside Miss Maxwell, "but I'm not going out this evening."

"Oh, yes, you are!" declared Crane in a gaily commanding tone, "just gather up that undecided blue wrap that seems to be detaching itself from your personality, and come along with me."

"Observe me go," said Mildred calmly, as she sat motionless in her big rattan easy chair.

Gilbert Crane laughed, and sat down beside her, and began to chat in low tones, paying no attention to Philip's haughty look. Presently their attention was arrested by what Miss Maxwell was saying.

"Yes, he's coming tomorrow," declared that lady, with a note of triumph in her voice. She had been reading a telegram which a servant had just brought her, and as she folded it away, Mildred asked:

"Who is coming tomorrow?"

"Clarence, Earl of Clarendon," was the proud reply.

"Goodness! What a name! He ought to have it dramatized. But I suppose we can call him Clare or Clarry. Is he a real live earl, and what's he coming for?"

"Yes, indeed, he's real," said Miss Maxwell, in reply to the first question. "I was so afraid he wouldn't come, that I didn't tell you I had asked him. But he is coming, and all you girls must make yourselves particularly charming, and give him a good time. His people were perfectly lovely to us in England, so we must reciprocate. He'll be here in time for your picnic, Milly."

"He won't like me," said Mildred, pensively. "I'm too Stars and Stripesy to please an English earl. He'll succumb to Irene's statuesque charm and Vere de Verean repose of manner."

"Yes, of course, Clarence will think Irene the gem of this collection," agreed Edith Whiting; "but let's put up a brave fight, Milly. If we can't charm the belted gentleman, let's at least impress him with our free-born Americanism. We can attract his attention in some way, unless he's hunting an heiress."

"Why are earls always belted?" asked Mildred, drowning Miss Maxwell's protest at Edith's last words.

"They deserve to be belted for coming over here and bothering our girls," said Philip.

"I sha'n't bother with him," declared Mildred. "United States boys are good enough for me"; and she cast an approving glance at the good-looking young American men standing about.

"That's all very well," said Gilbert Crane, "and I hope you won't bother with his Earlship; but, I say, Milly, if you cast those big blue soup-plates of eyes of yours at him, I shouldn't like to answer for the consequences. You know English girls stare, they don't dart fascinating glances through a regular Niagara Falls of eyelashes; and I prophesy that his Belted Highness won't know where he's at, when you've smiled at him a few."

"Nonsense," said Mildred; "he won't give me a chance to look at him. Those English grandees are awfully stuck up, and they only come to quiz us and write us up. What does he look like, Miss Miranda? I suppose, as Lord Fauntleroy says, he doesn't wear his coronet all the time."

"I won't tell you anything more about him," rejoined Miss Maxwell, decidedly. "It isn't fair for you to know about him when he doesn't know anything about you."

"I think," said Tom Whiting, "I shall draw up a sort of descriptive catalogue of you girls, and nail it on the inside of his door. It will save him lots of trouble. Something like this, you know: Miss Irene Gardiner, raving beauty of the Burne-Jones type; classic features, amiable disposition, great tennis player and all-round athlete."

"There's no use going any further than Irene," interrupted Edith, with a disheartened sigh; "after that description, Clarence won't read any more."

"Wait and see," said her husband, laughingly.

"Next, we have Mrs. Whiting; a perfect blonde, of the peaches and cream variety. Sings like an angel and plays the mandolin to beat the band."

"That ought to charm any old earl," declared Crane; "now hit off Milly, though no mere words can do her justice."

"Ah, there's the rub!" exclaimed Tom. "If anyone can describe Mildred Leslie they're welcome to do it. *I* can't."

"I'll try," said Crane, "and if my descriptive powers give out, somebody else can take up the tale. To begin with, I should say Miss Mildred Leslie is a mischievous, roguish, saucy, adorable bit of humanity, who flirts with everybody within hailing distance—"

"I don't!" put in Milly, making a *moue.*

"You do," asserted Philip.

"Go on, Gilbert; a willful, perverse, spoiled child, who always has her own way --"

"Because everybody is so good to her," interrupted Milly again.

"Because everybody loves her," said Miss Maxwell, looking affectionately at the young girl. At which Mildred kissed that lady's hand, and suddenly jumped up and ran away.

Later, when their hostess declared it was growing chilly, and they would go indoors and have some music, Philip came upon Milly and myself in a vine draped corner of the veranda.

"See here, Milly," he said, "you're not to let that foreign popinjay tie himself to your apron strings."

"Oh, do you suppose that's what he is coming over here for?" asked the girl, dropping her voice to an awestruck tone.

"If you weren't you, Milly, I should say you are a goose!" and Philip's tone actually sounded vexed.

Mildred's manner became coldly dignified, but her eyes gleamed as she said, "Why, that's what I wanted to say to you."

At that Philip laughed genially.

"Then let me beg you again not to let the Britisher tie himself up with any of your danglers."

"I certainly sha'n't ask him to," said Mildred carelessly, "but if he sees fit to tie himself, I can't help it. And you must admit, Phil, it would be a novel experience to have a real earl at my beck and call! Oh, I'd love to be proposed to by a nobleman! How do you suppose they do it, Philip?"

"You ought to know all there is to know about how men propose; you've been through it often enough."

"Yes, but it's almost always you, you know."

"I only wish that were true."

"Well, it is—almost," Mildred sighed. "But anyway, I like you better than most of the others; you're a lot nicer than Gilbert Crane, for instance."

"Well, I am glad you think so!" and Philip squared his shoulders with an unconscious air of superiority.

"You needn't act so conceited over it!" Mildred exclaimed. "Of course, you're big and handsome—and he's insignificant looking; but he can't help that, and you oughtn't to be vain."

Philip tried to look modest and self-depreciatory, but only succeeded in achieving a satisfied grin, whereat we all laughed.

"But you know," Mildred went on, "it isn't everything to be big and handsome and rich, as you are; and if I promised to marry you, I might afterward see someone I liked better."

"An earl, perhaps," said Philip, not noticing me, but looking at her steadily.

"Yes," said Mildred, returning his look with an unflinching gaze, "an earl, perhaps."

"Well," said Philip, giving her a curious look, "you might do worse."

"Indeed I might," she responded, a little curtly; "very much worse."

And, laughing a little at their foolish banter, I left them and went into the house.

III: THE BELTED EARL

CLARENCE, Earl of Clarendon, was arriving. Wherefore, the feminine guests at Maxwell Chimneys were peeping with careful discretion through curtains and window blinds, in their impatience to comment upon the appearance of the distinguished visitor.

But from their vantage ground they could see only a big, heavy-coated figure emerging from a motor-car, followed by a quantity of foreign-looking luggage.

"He's gone to his rooms," announced Milly, after a skirmishing peep into the hall, "and of course we won't see him until dinner time. Come on, Irene, let's go and put on our very bestest frocks. I wish I had a tiara or a coronet! Do you think I'd better wear feathers in my hair or just a wreath of roses?"

"I'm sure I don't know about earls," I put in, "but I'm sure, Miss Leslie, that most men prefer natural flowers to those fanciful confections that you young ladies sometimes perch on your heads."

"You tell us, Mr. Maxwell," said Irene Gardiner, as our host entered the room, "do you suppose earls prefer made-up hair ornaments or natural flowers?"

"Bless my soul! I'm sure I don't know," declared the bewildered old gentleman; "I never was an earl!"

"You ought to be," said Mildred, smiling at him; "your manners are courtly enough to grace any,—any—what do earls grace, anyway?"

"Well, as one will grace our dinner table pretty soon, it would be wise for you girls to run away and get ready to do your part of the gracing," said Miss Maxwell, smiling at pretty Milly, who was in her most roguish mood.

"I simply can't dress, Miss Miranda, until I decide between my silver filigree headdress and a wreath of pink roses."

"Nor I," said Edith; "I believe I'll wear a single rosebud."

"Yes, do," said Mildred; "do wear the simple little blossom, dear; it will make you look younger!"

As Edith was only two years older than her sister this could not be called an unkind sarcasm.

"Baby-face!" she retorted; "nothing could make *you* look younger, unless, perhaps, you carry a Teddy Bear in your arm."

"I've a notion to do just that!" said Mildred, laughing.

"I must shock that English prig, somehow."

"How do you know he's a prig?"

"All Englishmen are. I've never met any, but I'm sure they're snippy and critical, and not a bit like our own brave lads. I've lost interest in him anyhow. You may have him, Irene, if you want to."

"That's all very well, now, but as soon as you see him, you'll appropriate him."

"No, I won't, honest; I hereby make over to you whatever interest I may have had in the noble Earl of Clarendon, and promise not to interfere with your game, if you choose to add his very likely bald scalp to your other trophies of the chase."

"Oh, pshaw, that won't do a scrap of good if you even talk to him or look at him at all," said Irene, putting on a rueful look. "Just as Mr. Crane said, if you sweep your eyelashes round once, he'll be done for."

"All right," said Mildred; "then, furthermore, I promise not to talk or converse with the above mentioned Clarence beyond the ordinary civilities of the house; never to smile at him voluntarily and never to wave my eyelashes at him across the table. "And now," she rattled on, "I know I'll be late for dinner!" and then she ran away to her own room.

Presumably, she took great pains with her toilette, for it happened that she was the latest to enter the drawing-room. She had elected to wear a gown of palest blue organdy, which, though of simple effect, was in reality a marvelous confection, born of art and science.

Her hair was massed in a curly top-knot, secured by shining combs, and on her soft fair neck rested a string of wax beads, which she chose to call "The Leslie Pearls."

Her cheeks were a little flushed with the exertion of her hasty dressing, and fear of tardiness lent her an apologetic air, half timid and half-cajoling, as she crossed the room to her hostess.

Miss Maxwell stood near the fireplace and smiled indulgently at the pretty dismay of her young guest.

Mildred smiled, too, and then, raising her eyes, suddenly discovered that at Miss Maxwell's side stood six feet two of man, with the broadest shoulders she had ever seen!

"Oh," she almost gasped; "I thought..." and then she seemed to realize that a formal introduction was being made.

She dropped a slight and very dainty curtsey, and as she was about to raise her eyes to the face which she naturally assumed surmounted this column of humanity, she remembered she had promised not to wave her eyelashes at him.

Convulsed with the ridiculousness of the situation, she stammered a greeting which meant nothing, and resolutely turned her face away.

"What's the matter, Mildred; are you ill?" said Miss Maxwell solicitously.

"Oh, no, indeed," said Mildred, raising her blue eyes to meet the elder lady's glance, and just giving the Earl a three-quarter view of her really wonderful lashes.

"No—I—I, that is, I was afraid I would be late for dinner, you know."

"Nonsense, child; don't be foolish. Talk to Lord Clarence for a few minutes, before we go to the dining-room."

So Mildred dutifully talked, but, in a moment dinner was announced, and it fell to her lot to be escorted to the dining-room by my humble self.

"What's the matter?" I asked after we were seated at the dinner table. "Why did you turn down his Noble Nibs so soon? You scarcely spoke to him."

"Too English for me," said Mildred briefly, not wishing to discuss his lordship. "He's a handsome chap," I went on. "And he's a good, all-round fellow, too. I've been talking with him, and he's broad-minded and fair, with a keen sense of humor. Go in and win, Milly; I'll give you my blessing."

"No, thank you," said Mildred, turning her eyes resolutely away from the stranger. "Columbia is the 'Gem of the Ocean,' for me."

"Why don't you announce your engagement to Philip, and have done with it?" I said audaciously.

"One reason is, that I'm not engaged to him," said Mildred calmly.

"But you will be. He has every chance in the world."

"That's where you're wrong. There's only one chance in the world that I shall marry Philip Maxwell." She smiled as she remembered Philip's emphatic assurance that he should ask her once more only. "But I'm not going to marry anybody for *years* yet. Let's talk about something more interesting. Look at Phil, now! He's devotedly reciting poetry to Irene."

"Oho, that's your more interesting topic, is it? But, wait, the noble Britisher is making good. Just listen to that yarn he's telling. He's a ripping good story-teller." And Mildred, listening, was forced to agree.

On the terrace, after dinner, the party broke up into small groups of two or three, and Mildred, quite unintentionally, found herself talking to Lord Clarendon, or rather he was talking to her.

"Don't run away," he said, as she tried to edge off toward another group; "stay and talk to me."

"I can't talk to you," she said, stammering a little, "because—because—" and as he smiled at her, she continued, in sheer desperation, "because— because I don't know what to call you!"

"Don't you know my name?"

"Yes; but I don't know whether to address you as 'my lord' or 'your lordship.' "

She knew she was talking nonsense, but she was honestly trying to get away, and so said anything at random.

The Earl stood looking down at her, with his half-mocking smile.

"Either would succeed in attracting my attention, if I heard you; but why not call me Clarence?"

"It's a stunning name," said Mildred, "but I couldn't use it so soon. Indeed I never can."

With a sudden determination she turned abruptly and walked away, leaving him standing there.

"By Jove!" said his lordship to me as he looked after her; "I can't make her out at all; but she's a dear little enigma."

The evening wore away, and it was quite late when Mildred and I, again together for a moment, saw someone coming near. Then a kind voice over her shoulder said, "Is it possible that this little lady's afraid of me?

There was a laughing note in the voice, an amused, yet self-assured tone that seemed joyously confident and contradictory to the words.

I wondered what reply she would make, for the terrace in the moonlight was a dangerous place. Acting on a sudden impulse, whether courage or cowardice I didn't know, she whispered in a broken voice, "yes, I am afraid of you," and turned swiftly and suddenly away from him.

Philip was never very far away from Mildred's side, and though he was glad to notice her apparent lack of interest in the Earl, he was at a loss to understand her persistent rejection of the nobleman's advances.

"What's the matter with the Belted One, Milly?" he asked; "I'm sure I don't want you to churn with him, but why treat him with such desperate scorn?"

"I don't scorn him, but he doesn't interest me," said Mildred, a little impatiently, for she was beginning to be tired of her own game.

But Philip was not entirely unversed in the whims and ways of the Eternal Feminine, and he responded, "Oho! piqued, are you?"

"Indeed I'm not, and, pray, why should I be?"

"Oh, for many reasons. Perhaps because Clarence is so devoted to Irene. She'd look well wearing a coronet, wouldn't she? It would suit her tall stateliness a lot better than it would your petite effects."

"Don't talk any more about that horrid Earl. I'm tired of the thought of him."

"That's your attitude toward everything," said I.

"Oh, no, it isn't," she responded saucily.

"I never get tired of myself, and I'm not yet tired of you."

"Don't think of him, then," said Philip. "I'm truly glad, if you don't like him. But you're overdoing it so it made me a bit suspicious. You see, I know your tricks and your manners!"

"Am I very bad, Philip?" said Mildred, a little wistfully.

"You are indeed. You're a heartless little witch, and you'd not only flirt with a wooden Indian, but you'd know just the best way to go about it."

"Thank you for the subtle compliment. And yet—with all my faults, you?"

"Of course I do, and always shall! Does it please you to know it?"

"Not especially," said Mildred, her mocking eyes smiling gaily into Philip's handsome, earnest face. "And I sha'n't talk to you any more now, for you seem to have only two subjects of conversation—yourself and the Earl of Clarendon. And I don't care a straw for either."

Philip only smiled, for though Mildred's words sounded indifferent, the glance that reached him from beneath the long lashes belied the words, and, I am sure, strengthened his conviction that the butterfly heart was really his.

I left the pair then, and strolled away in the direction of Irene Gardiner.

IV: SAUCY MILDRED

"I'M so glad we're going to have a dance tonight," said Edith Whiting at luncheon next day.

"Oh, so am I," declared Mildred, "I'd rather dance than eat; and we haven't had a real party dance since we've been here."

"Give me four two-steps, won't you, Miss Leslie?" said I.

"Why don't you ask for eight steps; can't you multiply? Indeed I won't give you four two-steps, Mr. King."

"Oh, I so hoped you would!" I responded, in mock dejection.

"Why, how can you expect it?" she exclaimed.

"There'll be a lot of strange men here from all the country round, and I'm going to give them all my dances. I can dance any day with you men who are staying in the house."

"Do you mean that, Miss Leslie?" exclaimed Clarendon, in such apparent consternation that everybody laughed.

"On second thoughts, I'll give you one apiece, all round," said Mildred gaily.

Philip sat next to her at the table.

"You'll give me more than that," he said in a low tone, "or else you needn't give me any."

"Very well," said Mildred airily, "you needn't have any. Lord Clarendon, if you care for two dances tonight, I have an extra one that has just been returned with thanks, which you may have."

"I accept it gladly, fair lady, but don't let it be one of your American two-steps, for I have not yet mastered their intricacies."

"They shall be any ones you choose," said Mildred, with a glance at the Earl, that was deliberately intended to delight him and to anger Philip, and succeeded perfectly in both cases.

"Mildred," said Tom Whiting, under his breath, as they left the table, "you are playing with fire."

"Perhaps I wish to get burnt," she retorted saucily, and ran laughing away.

That afternoon Philip and I chanced to find ourselves alone for a time. I was glad, for I hadn't had an opportunity to talk much with him.

We sat in a shady corner of the veranda and he looked moody and glum. Finally he threw his cigar away, and said, frankly, "What would you do with her, Peter?"

"Do you want me to answer you seriously," I said, "or flippantly?"

"Seriously, please."

"Then I think you'll have to teach her a lesson. You let her go too far, Philip; and you may find, when you try to curb her, you can't do it."

"I know I can't, King; she's reached that point already."

"Then begin as soon as possible. Tell her that she must either be engaged to you or not. And if she is engaged to you, she must stop flirting with the Earl."

"Good Heavens, Peter! it isn't the Earl that bothers me. It's someone quite different."

"Who?" I asked in astonishment, but just then we were interrupted, and I had no answer to my question. But it bothered me for a time; and I couldn't help wondering if by any possibility Philip could be jealous of me! It seemed absurd, for though of course I admired Milly Leslie, as everybody did, yet I wouldn't for the world have intruded upon Philip's rights. I could get no opportunity to speak to Philip again on the matter until that evening after dinner. The ladies had all gone away to dress for the dance, and Philip and I chose to stroll and smoke in the rose garden. But again my intention came to nought, for Earl Clarence joined us. Philip seemed in better spirits than in the afternoon, and he chaffed the Earl gaily, in an unusually merry mood.

It was after dark, but by the faint light of a moon which had not yet risen, we saw what seemed almost like a fairy being coming toward us. It was Mildred, and she was wrapped in a voluminous cloak of pale blue, beneath which showed a pair of dainty white dancing slippers.

"Oh," she exclaimed, drawing back as she recognized us, "I thought you were the gardener!"

"To which one of us did you pay that compliment?" inquired Philip, laughing.

"Oh, I won't be partial, I thought you were all gardeners," said Mildred drawing her cloak around her and seeming about to leave us,—though I felt sure she had no such intention, and was coquetting as usual.

"Do you want a gardener?" said I; "won't I do for one?"

"Well," and Mildred hesitated, "I was just dressing for the dance you know, and I found I must have,—simply must have some of those tiny yellow roses, that grow over there.

I would have sent the maid for them, but I know she wouldn't select the very tiniest ones, and those are the ones I must have.

So I thought I'd just run down and get them myself,—I never dreamed I'd meet anybody!"

Though the big blue eyes looked babyishly innocent above the closely held blue wrap, I felt a secret conviction that those same eyes had seen the group of men in the rose garden, and did not mistake us for a group of gardeners.

"I knew everybody was dressing for the dance," she went on, "so I thought I couldn't possibly meet anybody."

She pouted a little, as if we were to blame for interfering with her plan.

"It doesn't matter that you have met us, dear," said Philip, gently; "I'll cut some roses for you,—which ones do you want?"

Milly was a tease, there was no doubt about it. She smiled at Philip, and then turning deliberately to the Earl, said, "You're nearest to the yellow rose tree,—won't you cut me some, please?"

Philip spoke no word, but stood for a moment looking at the girl he loved. Then, in a tense, unnatural voice, he said, "Clarendon, will you look after Miss Leslie?" and, turning on his heel, walked rapidly away.

"Milly," said the Earl, eagerly stepping toward her. It was the first time he had ever addressed her so, but Mildred had no intention of precipitating matters in this unconventional situation, and, too, she was troubled at the remembrance of Phil's disapproving glance.

"Lord Clarendon," she said coldly, "will you be so very kind as to pick me a few yellow roses, and let me hasten back to the house?"

"There is plenty of time," he said quietly; "please give me a few moments."

"No," said Mildred, stamping her foot impatiently, "I wish to return at once."

"Very well," said Clarendon gently, "I will not detain you. Will you have this spray?"

He selected a charming cluster of roses, and taking his penknife from his pocket cut them for her, and stood trimming off the thorns.

"I wish I might have given you flowers to wear this evening," he said.

His manner was gentle and deferential, and I was sure Mildred felt perhaps she had been too brusque, as she said kindly, "I wish so, too; but how could you have bought any flowers way off here in the country?"

"I could have sent to town for them, or gone myself for them."

"But I oughtn't to accept real hothouse flowers from you –"

"Why not? Because it would mean a special favor on your part? But that is just what I want it to mean, dear little girl –"

"Oh, Lord Clarendon, please don't! Please give me my flowers and let me go."

"Will you consider them a gift from me, as I can't get any others now? And will you let them mean –"

"Oh no, they don't mean anything—not anything at all—yet."

He had taken her hands and placed the spray of roses between them, and still held the two little hands, roses and all, close clasped in his own.

Her long cloak, released, fell away, and the vision in the pale silken robe seemed to the noble Englishman quite the most beautiful thing he had ever seen. He caught his breath, as he looked at the baby face, with its troubled, beseeching eyes.

"Please let me go, Lord Clarendon—please!"

Then she gently disengaged her hands from his, and gathering up the folds of her blue cloak, prepared to run away.

But be detained her a moment. "Miss Leslie," he said, and his choking voice betrayed his passion, "I won't keep you now—but to-night you will give me an opportunity, won't you, to tell you –"

"Tonight, my lord, you are to have one dance with me, you know."

"One? You promised me two!"

"Oh, I never keep dance promises. I'm not at all sure I shall give you one."

"But I'm sure you will, you tantalizing baby! Now which shall be the first one that I may call mine?"

"Choose for yourself, my lord," said Mildred, in her most demure way.

"Seven is a lucky number, may I have number seven?"

"Yes, I'll save that for you," and, with a laughing glance over her shoulder, she ran away.

"What a little witch she is, to be sure, eh?" and Earl Clarence gave a short laugh.

"I beg your pardon if I offend," I said, a little stiffly; "but I think you,—that is we,—ought to remember that she is pledged to Philip."

"Ah, I did not know it was announced."

"Nor is it, officially. But in this country, we accept such a situation, without words,—if we are friendly with the people concerned."

"Indeed!" was the cool response; "but the men of my country have their own code of honor, and it is not to be impugned."

This was a fine opening for a quarrel, but as I had no intention of indulging in a dispute with our titled visitor, I said only, "I have no criticism to make of the English code of honor,—I'm sure!" and turning on my heel, I left his lordship among the yellow roses.

Soon after, standing in the lower hall, I watched Mildred Leslie come dancing down the stairs. She wore a short dancing gown of palest yellow chiffon, and in her shining curls nestled the tiny yellow roses.

It was an unusual color for a pronounced blonde to wear, but it suited her dainty beauty, and she looked like a spring daffodil.

Of course she was immediately surrounded by would-be partners, but Philip Maxwell was not among them.

"Sulky," said naughty Mildred, as I asked her where he was. "Well, it will do him good to worry a little."

As was usually the case, pretty Mildred was the belle of the ball.

She halved most of her dances, and changed her mind so frequently about her partners that she soon tore up her program, declaring it bothered her, and she should accept invitations only as each dance began.

She finished the sixth dance with me, and as we sauntered about after the music ceased, we met Philip apparently looking for her.

"The next dance is ours," he said looking at her in an unsmiling way.

"Indeed it isn't!" declared Mildred, who had by no means forgotten to whom she had promised the seventh dance.

"It is," said Philip sternly, "come!"

"Better go," I whispered in Mildred's ear; "he's in an awful huff!"

Meekly she allowed herself to be led away, and Philip took her out on the veranda.

"Now," he said, as they passed out of hearing, "with whom are you going to dance this next dance, with me or with that confounded foreigner?"

"With him, Philip," said Mildred, very quietly.

"I promised it to him before the party began."

I was thoroughly angry at the little coquette, and I turned away and strolled idly through the rooms. I did not feel like dancing, for the moment; and seeing Miss Maxwell, sitting alone in a corner of the drawing-room, I went and sat by her for a few moments' chat.

She seemed preoccupied, and after some perfunctory answers to my trivial remarks, she said:

"Peter"—she always called me by my first name, and somehow her soft, sweet voice gave the ugly word a pleasant sound—"there is something wrong with Philip. I can't imagine what it is, but for a week or more he has been so different. It began all at once.

"One day last week he came to luncheon looking so harassed and worried that my heart ached for him. I said nothing about it—we are not confidential as a family, you know—I only tried to be especially gentle and tender toward him. But he didn't get over it. He spoke sharply to his uncle, he failed to show his usual deferential courtesy to me, and he behaved altogether like a man stunned and bewildered by some sudden misfortune.

"I talked to his uncle about it when we were alone, and he, too, had noticed it, but could not account for it in any way. He though perhaps it might be money difficulties of some sort, and he offered to increase Philip's allowance. But Philip refused to accept an increase, and said he had no debts and plenty of spending money. So we are at our wits' end to understand it."

"Could it have anything to do with Miss Leslie?" I asked.

"I think so," replied Miss Miranda, looking about to make sure we were not overheard. "He is very much in love with her, and I think she cares for him, but she is such a coquettish little rogue that one cannot be sure of her. Besides, this trouble of Philip's began before he planned this house party, and before he thought of inviting Miss Leslie and her sister down here."

"Does he talk frankly to you about Mildred?"

"Oh, yes, he hopes to win her—indeed, he says he feels confident of succeeding. But I think he tries to persuade himself that he will succeed, while really she is breaking his heart over her flirtation with Gilbert Crane."

"Gilbert Crane!" I exclaimed, greatly surprised.

"Why, I thought she was flirting so desperately with the Earl."

"Nonsense! Mildred is just teasing Philip with him. When she flirts so openly, there is no danger. But she conceals her liking for Gilbert Crane. He's here tonight, and I'm sure I don't know what will happen."

"But Gilbert Crane! why he's a friend of Philip's."

"Yes, our fellow townsman, and one of Philip's best friends."

"But he can't hold a candle to Philip."

"I know it. Philip is rich, or will be, and Philip is handsome and talented, while Gilbert is none of these. But somehow he has a queer sort of fascination over Mildred, and she is certainly very gracious to him."

"Philip and Gilbert are as good friends as ever, aren't they?"

"Yes, I think so, lately. At least they were until lately. But Mildred's evident preference for Gilbert's society has wounded Philip, and though he treats Gilbert as kindly as ever, I've seen him look at him as if he wondered how he could play such an unfriendly part."

"You think, then, to put it plainly, that Gilbert is trying to win Mildred away from Philip?"

"I do, and I think Philip is as much hurt by Gilbert's treachery as by Mildred's fickleness. But I cannot think that it is this affair that worried Philip so last week. For then, Mildred hadn't come, and Gilbert was right here all the time, and he and Philip were inseparable. No, it's something else, and I can't imagine what."

"Phil seems about as usual to me," I said.

"Yes, he is much brighter since you young people came. More like his old self. But when he's alone, even now, he drops into an attitude of absolute despair. I've seen him, and it is something very dreadful that has come to my boy. Oh, Peter, can't you find out what it is, and then I'm sure we can help him."

I assured Miss Miranda that I would try in every possible way to do all I could to help, but I felt convinced that no one could help Philip at the present time, except Mildred Leslie herself.

Then Mr. Maxwell came in and joined us, and the tenor of our conversation changed.

I should have been glad to talk with him about Philip, but owing to his deafness I couldn't carry on such a conversation in the drawing-room.

But notwithstanding his affliction, Mr. Maxwell had a fine ear for music, and greatly enjoyed it. A piano, violin and harp furnished the music on this occasion, and as it was of exceedingly good quality. Mr. Maxwell sat and listened, tapping his foot gently in time with the rhythm. I saw him glance at Philip several times, and, if the boy was smiling, the old gentleman's anxiety seemed relieved, but if Phil was over-quiet or sober-looking, Mr. Maxwell sighed and glanced away again.

The drawing-room was the front room on the left, as one entered the great hall that ran through the center of the house. Back of it was the billiard room; back of that, Mr. Maxwell's study and behind that a well-filled conservatory.

On the right of the wide hall, the front room was the music-room; behind it was the dining-room, and back of that a short cross hall and a butler's pantry,—the kitchen being still farther back.

The large library was on the second floor, and was in many ways the most attractive room in the house. There were bedrooms on both the second and third floors, so that Maxwell Chimneys was well adapted for generous hospitality.

A broad veranda ran all around three sides of the house both on the ground floor and second story, and on it, from most of the rooms, opened long French windows.

After watching the dancers for a while Miss Miranda urged that I join them, and though I would have quite willingly remained with her, I did as she bade me.

"And, Miss Miranda," I said, as I left her, "don't worry about Philip's affairs. I hope—I'm sure you exaggerate to yourself his despondency, and I can't help thinking that soon matters will be brighter for him."

V: THE TRAGEDY

I WAS fortunate in finding Miss Gardiner free to give me a dance, and in a moment we were circling the polished floor. She said little or nothing during the dance, and when it was over I took her for a stroll on the upper balcony, where, standing at the front railing we looked out on the beautiful country spread before us in the moonlight.

Irene Gardiner puzzled while she attracted me. I never could feel quite sure whether or not she was as frank as she seemed.

Perhaps it was only the natural effect of her dark, almost Oriental beauty, but she somehow seemed capable of diplomacy or intrigue.

Tonight, however, she was simply charming, and whether assumed or not, her attitude was sincere and confidential.

We traversed the three long sides of the house on the upper balcony and then, turning, retraced our steps. Frequently we met or passed other couples or groups of young people, and exchanged merry, bantering words.

At last Irene paused at the southeast end of the balcony, and we sat down on a wicker settee.

"Mr. King," she said, almost abruptly, "don't you think it's a shame, the way Mildred treats Mr. Maxwell?"

I was surprised at the question, but had no intention of committing myself to this mystifying young woman.

"Who can criticize the ways of such an enchanting fairy as Miss Leslie?" I replied lightly.

"Do you think her so fascinating?"

The question was wistful and very earnestly asked.

"She is both beautiful and charming, and she has completely bewitched Philip," I said.

"Yet she does not really care for him," cried Irene, passionately. "She adores Gilbert Crane, but she leads Philip on, and is breaking his noble, splendid heart, merely for her own amusement."

My eyes were opened.

"Oho, my lady," I thought to myself. "You are in love with the handsome Philip. Sits the wind in that quarter?" But I only said, "Gilbert Crane! do you really think so? Why I thought she was lavishing all her favors on our titled guest."

"Oh, he's only an incident. Milly sees that it teases Philip for her to flirt with the Earl, and she does so openly. But her liking for Mr. Crane is another matter. You men are so blind! can't you see that just because she doesn't flirt openly with Gilbert Crane, it proves that she's really interested in him?"

"She is only a child after all," I said, "and we must forgive her a great deal."

"On account of her youth and beauty!" said Miss Gardiner, in a tone that was positively bitter; "that's always the way! A baby face and golden hair and big blue eyes will excuse any amount of fickleness and treachery and deceit!"

"Those are strong words, Miss Gardiner," I said, amazed at her unkindness; "are you sure they are deserved by our little friend?"

"Yes; I know Mildred Leslie as she is! You men only know her as she chooses to appear to you!"

"I don't think I can agree with you, Miss Gardiner. If Mildred Leslie were of a deeper nature, I might think you are right. But she is as open as the day; a superficial, butterfly sort of girl, who cares only for the pleasure of the passing moment. I mean no disparagement, but I think that the lightheartedness of her nature is her best defense against your charges. I think she cares for Phil. And truly, in her heart. Who could help preferring that splendid fellow to young Crane?"

"I know it seems so," went on Irene, "but she does like Mr. Crane better. She told me so herself, only today. She said Philip is egotistical and purse-proud, and that Mr. Crane has a true poet soul."

"Perhaps she didn't mean her confidences for me, Miss Gardiner," I said a little stiffly, for I was of no mind to discuss these things.

"I don't care," cried Irene, her eyes blazing, "I'm telling you because I want you to know how matters really stand, and then I want you to warn Mr. Maxwell against such a fickle, shallow little thing as Mildred is."

"I can't consent to do that," I answered. "Philip is old enough to know what he is about. If Miss Leslie prefers Gilbert Crane, Phil will certainly find it out for himself, and soon. But I think he will convince her that she has only a passing fancy for Crane, and that he himself is really her destined fate."

I tried to speak gaily, for I did not wish to take the subject seriously. But in a low, tense voice Irene exclaimed:

"It shall never be! Philip Maxwell shall not throw himself away on a heartless little coquette who doesn't know how to value him! Since you refuse to help me, I will take matters into my own hands!"

I was amazed at her intensity of speech, but still trying to treat it all lightly, I said:

"That is your privilege, fair lady. Come, let us return to the dancing-room,—sha'n't we?"

"You go down, please, Mr. King," she said, and her voice was quieter. "Leave me here for a little, and I will rejoin you soon." As she seemed to be very much in earnest, I did her bidding, and sauntering around, I entered the house by the long French window into the front hall. As I passed through the hall, I met Miss Miranda just going to her own room.

"Leaving us?" I inquired, smiling at her.

"Yes," she said. "I am very weary tonight, and I have excused myself. Mrs. Whiting will look after you young folks, and I am sure she will ably represent me."

She looked not only tired, but worried, and I felt sure Miss Leslie's behavior was grieving her dear old heart.

"Don't worry, dear lady," I said, earnestly; "you know we must allow a certain latitude to frivolous, butterfly-minded little girls."

"Yes, I know it," and she smiled, slightly; "And I hope there is a true womanly heart under that mischievous nature."

"I'm sure there is,—and I'm sure it is devoted to our Philip. Don't take it too seriously; remember that Philip is not a weak sort of a man, and he is able to control his own affairs."

"But he is simply wax in Mildred's hands; she can do anything she likes with him. She can send him into the seventh heaven of joy or into the depths of despair by her smile or frown."

"I know it; but that has been lovely woman's privilege through all the world's history. We can't expect our Phil to escape the common fate. So cheer up, and let us hope that he will yet capture the pretty little rogue, and that they will live happy ever after."

"Thank you, Peter; you have cheered me up, as you always do; and I shall sleep better for your words of hope. Good night."

"Good night," I said gently, "and I trust you will rise tomorrow morning refreshed and happy."

"I hope so," she said. "Good night, Peter."

As I turned to go downstairs, I heard voices in the library, which I realized were those of Philip and Miss Leslie.

With no intention of eavesdropping, I couldn't help hearing him say: "Don't trifle with me tonight, Mildred; I am desperate." The tone, more than the words, struck a chill to my heart, and I hastened downstairs lest I should hear more of a conversation not meant for me.

There were groups of merry people in the music room and in the drawing-room, but somehow I didn't feel like joining them, and I wandered back through the long hall, and looked in at the open door of Mr. Maxwell's study. This attractively furnished room could have been called a "den" by a younger man, but my host was conservative in his language, and adhered to old-fashioned customs.

I well knew it was his habit to devote an hour or two after dinner to his evening paper, which, naturally, never reached Maxwell Chimneys until late.

The household always refrained from intrusion on him at this time, and so, when I saw him intently studying the market reports, I turned away.

But he had seen me, and laying down his paper, he said cordially:

"Come in, my boy, come in and smoke a pipe with me, if you are tired of your young and somewhat noisy contemporaries."

"No," said I, going into the room, "not now, Mr. Maxwell. You finish your paper, and later, I'll drop in for a smoke. I'd very much like to have a talk with you."

"About Philip?" he asked, looking at me with a concerned air.

"Yes," I said, "but don't be apprehensive. Indeed, I think we may have cause to congratulate the boy before the evening is over. He and Miss Leslie are even now in the library, and I hope that they will arrive at a happy understanding."

"Good, Mr. King, good," said the old man in his kindly, pleasant way. "Let us hope for the best, and I trust it will all come out right."

"I'm sure it will," said I, and was about to go on, when he detained me a moment longer.

"What about that decorated Britisher?" he asked, looking at me intently.

"Oh, I'm told he isn't in the running," I replied, lightly; for, as Mr. Maxwell was deaf, I didn't care to discuss this matter in tones loud enough to be heard in other rooms.

"I dare say,—I dare say," Mr. Maxwell replied, but the blank look on his face made me think he hadn't heard me clearly. However, I went on through the study, and, lifting the portiére, passed into the billiard-room.

Here I found Gilbert Crane, alone, and sitting with his face buried in his hands in an attitude of deepest dejection.

I suddenly realized that, as I was obliged to speak to Mr. Maxwell in a loud, clear voice, Mr. Crane must necessarily have heard what I said.

He looked up as I entered, and his face showed bitter despair.

He said nothing, however, and as I had nothing in particular to say to him, I went on through the drawing-room, across the main hall and into the music-room.

Pretty Edith Whiting was dancing with a Mr. Hunt, whom I knew, and as I passed Tom Whiting, I praised his wife's grace. His kindly, good-natured face lighted up. "She is a beautiful dancer," he said, "try to get a turn with her, King."

"I will," I responded, and went on. I soon found a partner, and later, another, so that two or three dances passed before I had a chance to ask Edith Whiting.

But I finally did so, and with a pretty gesture she laid her hand on my arm and we whirled away.

It chanced that we were just opposite the door into the hall, when suddenly, Gilbert Crane appeared in the doorway. His face was white with terror and wild with fright, and he cried:

"Dr. Sheldon, Philip and Mildred have shot each other! Come up to the library. Quick!"

Although Dr. Sheldon was quick in his response to Gilbert Crane's summons, I was quicker, and, dashing upstairs, I reached the library door first, with Edith and Tom Whiting close behind me. Of course Gilbert's statement that they had shot each other was manifestly improbable, and was doubtless the irresponsible speech of frenzy.

My first glance at the tragedy showed me Philip stretched on the floor, apparently dead, and Mildred fallen in a heap, a few feet away.

I did not touch them, but I saw she had a pistol grasped in her right hand.

In a moment Dr. Sheldon and several others came hastening in. I had expected to see the whole crowd, but as I learned afterward, Lord Clarence, with rare good judgment and presence of mind, had insisted on most of the guests remaining downstairs until more particulars of the accident were learned.

Dr. Sheldon gave a quick look at Philip, flung open his clothing, placed his hand on his heart, and after a moment, said gently:

"He is dead."

Then he turned to Mildred, and stooping, took her unconscious form in his arms.

"She is not," he said eagerly. "Telephone for my assistant, Dr. Burton, to come at once and bring my instruments. I think we can yet save her life. Tell him to fly. Tell him what has happened, but don't delay him."

Dr. Sheldon, who was acting as rapidly as he talked, took the weapon from Mildred's hand and laid it on the table.

"Let no one touch that," he ordered, "and let no one touch Philip Maxwell's body. Send for the coroner at once. Mr. Crane, will you keep guard in this room? And, Mr. King, will you dismiss the guests, and inform Mr. Maxwell and his sister what has happened? Mr. and Mrs. Whiting will assist me with Miss Leslie."

Tom Whiting and the doctor bore Mildred to her room, and I, not at all liking the part assigned to me, went toward Miss Maxwell's door. But I suddenly thought of Irene Gardiner, and resolved to tell her first, thinking she could break the news to the dear old lady with a better grace than I could.

I stepped out on the front balcony, wondering if I would find her around the corner where I had left her, but to my surprise she was seated near the front window, and was weeping violently.

"Irene," I said, as I touched her shoulder,

"Miss Gardiner, do you know what has happened?"

"What?" she said, still shaking with convulsive sobs.

I told her, and her piercing shriek brought Miss Maxwell to her door.

"What is it?" she cried, as she flung open the door.

"What is the matter?"

Suddenly Miss Gardiner grew calm, and with a return to her own tactful manner, she took the old lady in her arms, and told her the sad news. Miss Maxwell's face turned white with grief and shock; she tottered, but she did not faint. Then her loyal heart prompted her to cry out:

"My brother! Does he know? Has he been told?"

"No," I said, "but I will tell him."

"Do," she said, "you know and love him."

Then, supported by Irene, she returned to her room. I hurried downstairs, and found Mr. Maxwell still alone and undisturbed in his study. It was the hardest task I had ever had to do in my life. The old man laid down his paper, stretched his arms, and said:

"Well, have you come for our smoke?"

"No, Mr. Maxwell," I said, "I am the bearer of sad news. Philip has been hurt."

"Eh?" he said, not quite hearing my words.

"Philip has been hurt," I repeated, "shot."

"Shot!" and the old man's face grew ashy pale, as he leaned back in his chair.

I had heard hints of heart disease, and I was thoroughly frightened. But just then Dr. Burton came in, and I begged him to take a look at Mr. Maxwell, even before he went upstairs to Mildred Leslie.

Dr. Burton gave the old gentleman a stimulant of some sort, and I resumed my awful errand. He was very quiet, seemingly stunned by the news, and after a few moments, his sister came into the room. I believe I never was so glad to see any one in my life, and feeling now that they were better alone, I left them.

VI: "HE SHOT ME!"

I WENT next to the music-room, where Lord Clarence was dismissing the guests who, less than a half-hour before, had been so hilarious.

The Earl acted like a splendid fellow, and his cool head and capable management proved to be just what was needed for the sorry situation.

In a short time nearly all the guests had gone.

Gilbert Crane remained, and Mr. Hunt, who was a sort of society detective, asked to be allowed to stay.

The coroner arrived just then, and learning in a few words the facts of the case, he advised Hunt to stay, for a time, at least. Miss Lathrop, a trained nurse, who had been sent for by Dr. Sheldon, also came, and she was taken at once to Mildred's apartment.

"Mysterious case," said the coroner, after a long look at the room and its contents. "Might be an attempt at double suicide, or suicide and murder."

"Or double murder," said Mr. Hunt.

The coroner gave him a quick glance.

"We must work on evidence," he said, "not imagination."

"What evidences do you see?" asked Gilbert Crane.

"Very little, I confess," replied the coroner, who was a frank, straightforward sort of a man, and whose name, as I afterward learned, was Billings.

"But," he went on, "when a gentleman is found dead, and a wounded lady nearby, with a pistol in her hand, it doesn't require an unusual intellect to deduce that she probably shot him. Unless, as I said, it is a double suicide, and he shot himself first, and then she shot herself."

"Is Philip's wound one that could have been self-inflicted?" I asked.

"Without a doubt," replied Mr. Billings.

"He is shot directly through the heart, and that could have been done by himself or another."

"But of course we shall have medical evidence as to that."

"How about the powder marks?" asked the quiet voice of Mr. Hunt, who was already examining the room and taking notes.

"It is difficult to judge," answered Mr. Billings.

"The shot went through both coat and waistcoat, and while the powder marks would seem to prove that the shot was fired from a distance of three or four feet, yet I cannot say so positively."

I felt a certain relief at this, for while it was bad enough to think of poor Philip shooting himself, somehow it was worse to imagine Mildred shooting him.

Soon Dr. Burton came into the library. He talked with Mr. Hunt and Mr. Billings, and then said:

"As soon as you have completed all necessary investigations, Dr. Sheldon requests that the body shall be removed to Mr. Philip Maxwell's room and laid upon the bed, in order that it may seem less shocking to his aunt and uncle."

I liked this young doctor. He had Dr. Sheldon's clean-cut, assured ways, but he spoke and moved with rather more grace and gentleness. Dr. Sheldon had been a guest at the dance, which was fortunate, as it may have been the means of saving Mildred's life.

But Dr. Burton looked as if he were not at all inclined toward gayeties.

Serious, grave, he gave Dr. Sheldon's message, and then turned away, knowing he could do nothing more.

The coroner agreed to his suggestions, and later, I saw Mr. Maxwell and Miss Miranda go together to the room that had always been Philip's. As I look back upon that night now, it seems to me like a horrible dream—so many people coming and going, the servants beside themselves with grief and fright, and the dreadful facts themselves so mysterious and so difficult to realize.

It seemed impossible that Philip could be dead—merry, light-hearted Phil, who, except for the last week or so, had always been so gay and joyous.

And Mildred Leslie's life hung in the balance.

Dr. Burton's news of her had been this: she had been shot in the right shoulder, and the wound was dangerous but not necessarily fatal.

Partially paralyzed by the shot, or perhaps only fainting from fright, she had fallen to the floor, and struck her temple as she fell, presumably against the corner of the table near which she stood.

It was this blow which had made her unconscious, and which had left its mark in a huge, swollen discoloration on her fair brow.

She had as yet uttered no word, for she had been placed as soon as possible under the influence of ether, while the doctors probed for the bullet. It had been successfully extracted, and was now in Dr. Sheldon's possession.

Dr. Burton thought that Miss Leslie would soon regain consciousness, but deemed it exceedingly unwise to question her, or excite her in any way for some time to come.

Indeed, he said he was sure Dr. Sheldon would allow no one to see her for several days except the nurse, and possibly her sister.

At last Mr. Maxwell and Miss Miranda were persuaded to retire, and the rest of us were advised to do so.

But Gilbert Crane announced his intention of staying at the house all night.

He said someone should be in general charge, and as Philip's best friend he considered he had the right to assume such a position.

He established himself in Mr. Maxwell's study, and told the servants and the doctors to call on him in any emergency.

Seeing that Mr. Hunt sat down there too, with the evident intention of discussing the affair, I delayed my retiring and joined them.

Lord Clarence looked in, and seemed to hesitate to intrude.

"Come in," I said; "as one of the house guests you surely have a right."

He came in, and almost immediately after, Mrs. Whiting and Irene came, and we went over and over the mysterious details.

"What were Mr. Philip Maxwell's sentiments toward Miss Leslie?" inquired the detective.

No one seemed inclined to reply, and as I thought it my duty to shed all the light possible on the case, I said: "I have good reason to believe that, at or about the time of his death, Mr. Maxwell was asking Miss Leslie to marry him."

"Did she favor his suit?" pursued Mr. Hunt.

"No," broke in Irene, "she did not. She told me so only this morning."

"But that would be no reason for her shooting him and then shooting herself," wailed Edith Whiting.

"Oh, I am sure Mildred never did it. Or, at least, not intentionally. I've reasoned it all out, and I think he must have been showing her his pistol, or explaining it to her, and it went off accidentally, and then, in her grief and fright, she turned the weapon on herself."

"Was it Philip's pistol?" asked Irene.

"Yes," said the detective, "that is, it had P. M. engraved on the handle."

"Oh, it was Phil's pistol," said Gilbert Crane.

"I know it well. And he always keeps it in the top drawer of that big table-desk they were standing by."

"How do you know they were standing by it?"

This question came from the Earl, who, though he had not spoken before, had been intently listening, and who now spoke in a curt, sharp voice, almost as if he were making an accusation.

"Because," said Gilbert quietly, "there were no chairs near the desk. They both fell near the desk. Philip could not have walked a step after that shot through his heart, and Mildred must have been standing near the desk to fall and hit her head on it. Am I clear?"

"Perfectly," said the Englishman, but his voice sounded ironical.

"Mildred never shot Philip intentionally," reiterated Mrs. Whiting. "She is a rattle-pated girl—a coquette, I admit—and she was not in love with Philip Maxwell; but truly she was no more capable of a murderous thought or instinct than I am. You know that, don't you, Irene?"

Irene Gardiner gave me one quick glance, and like a flash I remembered our conversation in the train about opportunity creating a criminal.

Could it be that pretty Mildred, holding a pistol in her hand, and alone with an unwelcome suitor could—no, I could no more believe it than Edith, and I flashed a look of amazed disapproval at Irene.

But she was already speaking.

"I'm sure Mildred didn't shoot Philip at all, Edith," she said. "I think he shot himself and she tried to wrest the pistol from him, and in doing so wounded herself."

This explanation struck us all as so plausible that we gladly accepted it—all of us except Gilbert Crane—and wondered we hadn't thought of it before.

Gilbert said slowly:

"There could have been no struggle after that shot entered Philip's heart. If he shot himself, and Miss Leslie then took the pistol from him, it was after he had ceased to breathe."

"Was death, then, absolutely instantaneous?" I asked.

"Yes," said Mr. Hunt, "both doctors are sure of that."

Just here Tom Whiting came downstairs and joined us in the study. His face wore a peculiar expression. One of awe and perplexity, yet tinged with a certain relief.

"I think you ought to know," he said, "that Mildred is coming out of the ether's influence, and has spoken several times, but only to repeat the same thing over and over. She continually cries:

" 'He shot me. Oh, to think he should shoot me!' I tell you this in justice to my wife's sister."

"I knew Mildred didn't do it!" cried Edith, almost fainting in her husband's arms. "I don't care how black the evidence looked against her, I knew she never did it."

The next morning it was a sad party that gathered around the Maxwell breakfast table. After we were seated, the nurse, Miss Lathrop, glided in and took her place among us. It may have been prejudice, but I took an instant dislike to the woman from the way she glided in. Many trained nurses show a sense of their own importance, indeed, it seems to be a part of their uniform. But aside from this, Miss Lathrop gave an impression of knowing far more about the whole affair than any of the rest of us.

It was by no means what she said that carried this impression, but rather, what she didn't say.

If one of us made an observation or expressed an opinion, she turned suddenly to the speaker, gave him a sharp look, and then dropped her eyes again, but with a little superior smile hovering round her thin lips.

It exasperated me beyond endurance, though I had no real reason to resent her attitude. In response to the queries we put to her, her definite news of Mildred was not encouraging. "She will have brain fever," announced Miss Lathrop; "Doctor Sheldon fears it, but I am sure of it. I have had great experience with patients of her temperament, and I know it cannot be averted."

She shut her lips together, giving the impression that since she so willed it, Mildred should have brain fever in spite of anybody.

"Has she talked at all?" asked Miss Maxwell.

"She has said nothing," replied Miss Lathrop, "except to repeat over and over again: 'Oh, to think that he should shoot me!' in surprised and agonized tones."

Probably from her enjoyment of a dramatic sensation, Miss Lathrop's voice and expression were almost theatrical, and though this jarred on all of us, it was especially harrowing for Miss Maxwell and her brother, who of course were the ones most deeply affected by Philip's death.

Poor old Mr. Maxwell was crushed, and unless someone spoke directly to him, paid little heed to anything that was said.

Miss Miranda, on the other hand, tried to forget herself and her troubles in caring for her guests.

It was pathetic to see her efforts to be cheerful and unselfish, and she seemed to me like a lovely saint ministering to unworthy mortals.

As Mr. Hunt had remained over night, he was at breakfast with us. It seemed a strange coincidence that he should have been present the night before, for surely he would be of help in unravelling the mystery.

While not a professional detective, he had proved successful in many difficult cases in which he had chosen to interest himself.

"I can't help thinking," Mr. Hunt observed, "that when Miss Leslie is rational again, what she tells us may throw a new light on the matter."

"I quite agree with you, Mr. Hunt," said Miss Lathrop, in her cold, concise way; "I have reason to think that Miss Leslie will yet make further revelations. And I'm sure we are very fortunate in having an able detective right here in the house."

Miss Lathrop flashed a glance at Hunt, which obviously implied she knew more than she cared to tell, and then, with her odious little smile, calmly proceeded to extract the seeds from her grapes.

Mr. Maxwell looked up with a pained face.

Miss Lathrop's speech had seemed to rouse him almost to indignation.

"It is no case for a detective," he said, with a severity of manner I had never noticed in him before. "If, as Miss Leslie asserts, my poor boy shot her, that is all that is necessary for us to know about the affair. As to motive, my nephew has been seriously troubled of late, and doubtless his worry so disturbed his mind that he was irresponsible for his act. At any rate, I choose to consider him so."

"I'm sure we all agree to that," said Lord Clarence, in his kind voice; "not one of us can believe for a moment, that Philip Maxwell would commit such a deed, if he were sane at the time."

Miss Lathrop gave the Earl the benefit of one of her mysterious glances, and though she said no word, she clearly did not agree with him.

To my secret gratification, his lordship caught her up. "Have you definite reasons for not agreeing, Miss Lathrop?" he said.

Miss Lathrop was taken by surprise.

She colored slightly, and then pursing her mouth, said primly; "Professional ethics will not allow me to say."

"Professional ethics are out of place at this moment," said Mr. Maxwell, sternly. "If you know anything, Miss Lathrop, that will cast any light on this subject, it is your duty to tell us at once."

"I know nothing," Miss Lathrop said, shortly, and I, for one, believed she spoke truly.

VII: A SEARCH FOR CLUES

AFTER breakfast when Mr. Hunt started to go home, I accompanied him to the gate. Lord Clarence was also with us, and we both urged him not to go.

"I think it better that I should," Hunt responded; "Mr. Maxwell objects to seeing a detective about, and I can't blame the poor old man."

"I suppose it is a natural feeling," said Lord Clarence; "and, too, if Philip Maxwell did the shooting in a moment of temporary insanity, then, as Mr. Maxwell says, there is no occasion for detective work. But do you think that is the true explanation of the matter?"

"It is a possibility," I said, "though it's a new theory to me. But Philip was very much upset, indeed, deeply troubled for some unknown cause; and I, for one, do not think that cause was connected with Miss Leslie."

"Then why did he shoot her?" demanded Hunt.

"He didn't, intentionally. But if his mind was unbalanced, who can hold him responsible for his deed?"

"That's true," said Hunt. "Well, I suppose it will be all cleared up at the inquest. But since the perpetrator of this murder is not alive, it will doubtless be a mere matter of form."

"Where will it be held?" I inquired.

"Right here in the house, probably. Today or tomorrow, I should think; as the funeral will be on Thursday, and they can't bury him without a permit."

I shuddered at the dreadfulness of it all. Hitherto I had thought an ordinary death and burial sad enough, but how much worse with these attendant circumstances.

"Queer, nobody heard the shots," went on Mr. Hunt.

"Did nobody hear them?" I exclaimed. "I hadn't thought of that at all."

"And, yet your questions and opinions in the matter seem to imply a detective bent," said he, glancing at me a bit quizzically.

"I do take a great interest in detective work," I replied, "but I feel like Mr. Maxwell in this case. I see no occasion to detect anything beyond what we already know. It seems mysterious, I admit, but we know that one or both of the two victims did the shooting, and truly, to me, it doesn't much matter which."

"It does to me," said Gilbert Crane, who had joined us as we stood by the gate, and had heard my last remark.

"Well," said Mr. Hunt, with what seemed to me like a brutal cheerfulness, "if Miss Leslie gets well, we'll know all about it; and if she doesn't, we'll never know any more than we do now."

"If she fired either ball, she did it accidentally," declared Crane.

"Didn't you hear the shots either?" asked the Earl, turning on him suddenly.

"No," said Gilbert, "and I can't find anyone who did hear them."

"But you were first on the scene?"

"Yes, so far as I know."

"How did you happen to go up to the library just then?" asked Hunt.

"I didn't start for the library," said Gilbert slowly. "I was feeling pretty blue and forlorn, and the gay music jarred on me, so I thought I'd go home. I went upstairs for my banjo, which I had left on the upper front balcony in the afternoon."

"Was there any one on the balcony?" said Hunt, casually.

"I didn't see anybody," said Crane, "though I think I heard voices around the corner. But I didn't notice them; you know the house was full of people."

"I can't understand," pursued the Earl, thoughtfully, "why nobody heard the shots."

"Oh, I don't think that's so strange," returned Crane. "Mr. Maxwell is quite deaf, and Miss Maxwell is slightly so. And as for the young people, with the music and dancing, they wouldn't be apt to hear them."

"And you came directly downstairs after coming in from the balcony?" went on Hunt.

"As I reached the top of the stairs, I couldn't help looking toward the library, and as I heard no sounds, though I had been told Philip and Mildred were in there, I glanced in, I suppose from sheer curiosity."

"Who told you they were in there?"

"I did," said I, "or rather, I told Mr. Maxwell, in Mr. Crane's hearing. I saw them there when I went downstairs. That was, I should think, about half an hour before Mr. Crane gave the alarm."

"Can either of you fix the time of these occurrences?" said Mr. Hunt. He was very polite, even deferential in his manner, and I saw no harm in accommodating him.

"I can tell you only this," I said. "After I passed the library, where I both heard and saw Philip and Miss Leslie, I went on down-stairs and looked into Mr. Maxwell's study.

"He asked me to sit down. I did not do so; but after a word or two, I went on through to the billiard-room. I looked at the clock in the study as I passed, and it was exactly ten. I can't say, though, at just what time the general alarm was given; I should think less than a half hour later."

"I can tell you," said Gilbert. "When I concluded to go home, I looked between the portiéres into Mr. Maxwell's study, and it was twenty minutes past ten. Mr. Maxwell was nodding over his paper; he is a little deaf, so he probably didn't hear me.

"At any rate, he didn't look up. Then I went immediately upstairs, and it could not have been more than two minutes before I called Dr. Sheldon."

"All this is of interest, and I thank you," said Detective Hunt. "Although, as you say, since there is no criminal to discover, there is small use of collecting evidence."

"Queer chap, isn't he?" I said to Gilbert, as the detective went away.

"Yes, but I think he's clever."

"I don't; if there were any occasion for detective work on this case, I believe I could give him cards and spades, and then beat him at his own game."

"Perhaps you could," said Gilbert, but he spoke without interest.

There was plenty for all to do that day. I had expected to return to New York, but both Mr. Maxwell and Miss Miranda begged me to stay with them till after the funeral. As there was no reason for my immediate presence in the city, I was glad to be of service to my good friends. I assisted Mr. Maxwell to write letters to the various relatives, and together we looked over poor Philip's effects. The boy had no business papers to speak of, for he had no money except what was given him by his uncle, and apparently he kept no account of its expenditures.

"I paid all his bills," said Mr. Maxwell, in explanation of this, "and kept the receipts. I allowed Philip such ready cash as he wanted, and, I may say, I never stinted him. Whatever his recent trouble may have been, it could not have arisen from lack of funds."

"Unless he had been speculating privately," I suggested.

"I can't think so," replied his uncle. "Philip wasn't that sort, and, too, had that been the case, we would surely find papers of some sort to show it."

This was true enough, and as Philip's papers consisted entirely of such documents as scented notes addressed in feminine hands, letters from college chums, circulars of outing goods and cigars, and old dance-orders, I agreed that there was no indication of financial trouble.

Mr. Maxwell was very careful and methodical in his search. In a business-like way he went rapidly through the papers, replacing the contents of each pigeon-hole or drawer after rapidly looking them over. He showed no curiosity concerning the social notes or the circulars, but seemed searching for some letter or document that might throw light on Philip's recent despondency.

"It was about two weeks ago that Philip began to act differently," mused Mr. Maxwell, as he scanned the dates on various papers, "but I can find nothing here that would show any reason for it. The poor boy must have had some secret trouble; and doubtless, after all, it was either directly or indirectly concerned with Mildred Leslie."

The old gentleman seemed almost relieved that no letters or documents were found that showed a reason for Philip's trouble. And I could understand this, for surely it was better that a love affair should be the explanation, than some secret and perhaps dishonorable reason.

The desk we had been searching was in Philip's dressing-room, a small room off his bedroom. With the systematic thoroughness that was characteristic of him, Mr. Maxwell opened the drawers of the chiffonier, and examined the contents of a few small cabinets and boxes that stood about. He even glanced over the crumpled papers that were in the waste-basket, and then declared himself satisfied that we could find no written evidence bearing upon the secret of the boy's recent strange behavior.

Mr. Maxwell returned to his study, and I went for a stroll with Irene Gardiner. The girl looked so pale and wan, that I hoped a brisk walk would do her good.

"Do you believe in the 'accidental' theory?" she asked, as soon as we were started.

"No," I replied. "Philip was too well used to firearms to shoot anybody accidentally, or allow anyone to shoot him. But I now fully believe in Mr. Maxwell's theory that the boy's brain was temporarily affected, and that he shot himself in a moment of insanity."

"But if he shot himself first, how did he then shoot Mildred?"

"I've puzzled over that, I confess, and I think he shot her first—as I said—not being responsible for his actions. And then, overcome by grief at what he had done, he killed himself in his sudden despair."

"Yes," said Irene. "I suppose that must have been the way of it. But, granting all that, I don't see how Mildred came to have the pistol in her hand."

"Nor I. It is all most mysterious. Let us hope that Mildred will soon recover, and then we will know all."

"Mr. King, I suppose you will think very hardly of me, but I have looked at this matter in all lights, and I want to ask you if this isn't a possible case. Mightn't Philip have shot Mildred, and, since she is not very severely wounded, might she not have then snatched the pistol from him and shot at him in return."

I looked at Miss Gardiner in amazement. I felt horrified that she should imagine this, and yet there was a shadow of plausibility in it.

"It seems almost impossible," I said slowly, "that a wounded girl could have energy enough to secure a pistol and shoot her assailant. And yet, I admit, I can think of no other way to explain Miss Leslie's repeated expressions of grieved amazement that Philip should have shot her."

"You don't think it possible, then, that Mildred may not be as unconscious as she seems, and that she is making this repeated statement for reasons of her own."

"Miss Gardiner!" I exclaimed, now thoroughly aroused, "I am surprised at you. Even if you suspect Miss Leslie of absolute crime, pray give the poor girl the benefit of the doubt until she can defend herself, or—is beyond all need of defense."

"You do me injustice," said Irene, raising her head haughtily. "My logical mind necessitates the consideration of every possible solution of this puzzle. I look upon Mildred impersonally, merely as one of the actors in a tragic drama."

"You have indeed a logical mind," I said coldly, "if you can entirely eliminate the personal element from your estimate of Miss Leslie."

"I see no reason why I should not. I judge her fairly, and without prejudice. But I fail to see why the ravings of a mind affected by the consequences of an anesthetic should be accepted as unquestioned truth."

"On the contrary, the revelations made by a brain just reviving from the unconsciousness produced by ether, are conceded by all medical authorities invariably to be true statements. Many secrets have been revealed in this way."

"That fact is new to me," said Irene thoughtfully, "and it is very interesting. I am always willing to accept authoritative facts, but I decline to accept unproved theories."

"At any rate," I ventured, "you have no word of blame for Philip." She turned flashing eyes toward me, and in a moment I realized the situation. She was in the grip of two strong emotions. Grief for the man she had loved, and jealousy of her rival.

"Never speak of him to me!" she exclaimed. "I claim that much consideration from you."

"And you shall certainly receive it," I said gently. "But, on the other hand, let me beg of you not to do an innocent girl an injustice, which your better nature will surely regret later."

Irene looked at me.

She had never seemed more beautiful, and her wonderful eyes expressed contrition, gratitude, and a deep and hopeless sadness.

She held out her hand.

"I thank you," she said, "you have saved me from a grave mistake."

Still I didn't understand her, but I realized she was beginning to fascinate me in her mysterious way, and I abruptly turned our steps toward home.

When we reached Maxwell Chimneys, we found Dr. Sheldon, and the Whitings, with Mr. Maxwell and Miss Miranda in the study.

Evidently something had happened.

Each one looked excited; Mr. Maxwell was writing rapidly, and Tom Whiting was hastily turning the leaves of the telephone book.

"What is it?" I inquired. "Is Mildred…"

"No," said Dr. Sheldon, "Miss Leslie is no worse. On the contrary, she is much better. Her mind is entirely cleared, and she talks rationally, though I am not willing she should be questioned much as yet. I am very glad you have come, for there is a new and startling development in the case, and there is much to be done."

"What is it?" I asked.

"Simply this. Miss Leslie, being perfectly rational, you understand, says that neither she nor Philip fired any shots at all. They were both shot by an intruder who came in at the library window."

"But," I exclaimed, "then what did she mean by saying 'He shot me!' in such a grieved tone?"

"She tells us," said Dr. Sheldon, "that those were the last words uttered by Philip as he fell, and that they rang in her brain to the exclusion of all else. That is why she repeated them, parrot-like, during her unconsciousness."

"This changes the whole situation," said I, thinking rapidly.

"It does," said Mr. Maxwell. "It is now a case for a detective." Then he added, in a manly way, "I am sorry I spoke so shortly to Mr. Hunt this morning, and I am ready to tell him so, and to ask him to return and help us."

"But what—" I began.

"You know all that we do," interrupted the doctor. "If Miss Leslie is questioned further, or in any way excited at present, I will not answer for the consequences. My first duty is to my patient.

"This afternoon, and in my presence, she may be interviewed by someone who can do it gently and discreetly. Tomorrow, in all probability, she will be quite herself, and may be questioned by a detective or any one empowered by Mr. Maxwell."

And with this, we were obliged to be content.

VIII: THE INQUEST

THE situation was indeed changed. My latent detective instinct was now fully roused, and I determined to do all I could toward solving the mystery.

I said as much to Mr. Maxwell, and he thanked me for my sympathy and interest.

He also asked whether I thought Mr. Hunt a skilled detective, or whether I advised sending to New York for a more expert man. This annoyed me, for it proved that he considered my services as well-meant, but not especially valuable.

However, I showed no irritation, and answered simply that I thought Mr. Hunt quite capable of discovering all that could be discovered.

"You see," I went on, "we are at a disadvantage in having lost so many hours already. Had we known last night there was an intruder from outside, we could perhaps have caught him. As it is, he has probably made good his escape."

"That is true," said Mr. Maxwell with a sigh.

"But we must do our best, and leave no stone unturned in our endeavor to find Philip's assailant."

Miss Maxwell also agreed to this. "Peter," she said, and her look at me was pathetic, "you will help us, won't you? You loved Philip, I know; and you are clever and intelligent. Can't you help Mr. Hunt, and between you find the villain who murdered our boy?"

The usually timid and gentle lady was stirred, as I had never seen her, by her righteous indignation.

I was touched by her confidence in me, and I assured her that such capability as I possessed should be devoted toward the tracking of the criminal.

I determined to go at once to the library, the scene of the crime, and make a thorough search for clues before Mr. Hunt should arrive.

All the detective literature I had ever read, had taught me that it is next to impossible for a human being to enter a room and go out again, without leaving a trace of some sort, though visible only to a trained detective.

So to the library I went, and subjected the room and all its contents to a minute and systematic scrutiny. Contrary to all precedent, literary and reportorial, I found nothing.

Again I went over the room, even more diligently, remembering Sherlock Holmes' wise advice to discriminate carefully between vital and incidental clues.

But, alas, I could find neither, except the very doubtful one of a small and shiny black spangle, a tiny disk, which might have fallen from the trimmings of some lady's gown. I remembered no one who had worn such a decoration the night before, but then, I take little note of ladies' dress. In lieu of anything more interesting, I put the spangle carefully away in my note-book, and proceeded with my examinations.

All to no purpose.

The room had been put in order by the servants that morning—dusted, and possibly swept—so it was absurd to look for anything on the floor or furniture.

Sighing to think of the opportunities we had lost, I turned my attention to the window by which the intruder must have entered. It was a long French window reaching from floor to ceiling. It was in three divisions, each of which was really a door, and opened out on the balcony, which as I have said, ran around both sides and the front of the house without barrier.

The panes were of ground glass, in a diamond pattern; and I knew that at night, with lights inside the room, an outsider might look in through the glass unseen by those within.

I opened the middle door, stepped out on the balcony, and endeavored to scrutinize in a scientific way.

Signs of a scuffle there certainly were.

Just outside the library window, in the dust of the balcony, I observed many long, sweeping marks, that had every appearance of being the tracks of men who scraped their feet around in a wrestle, or struggle of some sort. From the shape of these streaks in the dust, I could not gather the size of the shoes that made them, nor the style of their toes; but as even the paint of the balcony floor was scratched by the marks, I felt sure that a tussle of some sort had taken place there.

I looked for a continuation of these tracks, but found none, save the scratches that were to be seen everywhere over the balcony floor. As many people had walked there the night before, this was of no importance, but unless someone had danced a clog dance outside the library window, I saw no reason for changing my first conclusion.

I found nothing else of note, save two more of those little black spangles—one in the outside library blind, and another farther front on the balcony. These I put away with my first one, determined to find out who wore such trimmings the evening before.

By this time Mr. Hunt had arrived.

The coroner had come, too, bringing his jury, for it had been decided to begin the inquest that very afternoon.

How strange it seemed, to hold an inquest in Miss Miranda's stately drawing-room!

But that was not more strange than realizing that Philip's dead body lay upstairs, and that we had not the faintest idea whose hand wrought this evil.

I paused in the library to talk to Mr. Hunt. He was not mysterious and uncommunicative like the regulation detective, but was frankly at his wits' end.

When I saw this, and knew that I was similarly unenlightened, I wondered if I had done wisely in advising Mr. Maxwell against getting a man from the city.

"Very little to work on, eh, Hunt?" I said.

"Just about nothing at all," he said, moodily staring at the carpet. "Look here, Mr. King, who is that foreigner staying here?"

"The Earl of Clarendon? Oh, he's a noble Britisher, all right. Don't try to stir up anything against him!"

"I'm not; don't be absurd. But, have they known him long?"

"When Mr. Alexander Maxwell and Miss Miranda traveled abroad a few years ago, I believe he entertained them in London, or at his country house. He's the real thing, Hunt, don't get any notions about that."

"I can't get any notions anywhere; there's nothing to work on."

"But the inquest may bring out some important facts."

"I doubt it. If anyone knew anything, he would have told it at once. Why shouldn't he? We are all of one interest. The deed was doubtless done by a burglar who was trying to effect an entrance, and who was frightened away by his own shots."

"Well," I responded, "I'm willing to suspend judgment until I have something more definite to base my opinions on. Come, let us go downstairs."

A crowd had assembled in the lower rooms, for the inquest was, in a way, a public function. I was sure the Maxwells were terribly annoyed at this invasion of their beautiful home, but I was also sure that such thoughts were swallowed up in their eagerness to discover and punish the murderer of Philip.

Mr. Billings was calm and business-like. He had impaneled his jury, and was already examining the first witness. Mr. Maxwell's own lawyer was present, also the district attorney and several other gentlemen of legal aspect who were strangers to me.

The first witness was Gilbert Crane.

To my surprise he appeared agitated and ill at ease. In one way, this was not astonishing, for, as the first one to discover the tragedy, his testimony would be of great importance. But he had been so cool and self-possessed all day that I couldn't understand his present demeanor.

"Will you tell us," said the coroner, not unkindly, "the circumstances which led to your going to the library last evening?"

"I was alone in the billiard-room," said Gilbert.

"I had been there alone for some time, as I was troubled and did not care to join the merry crowd in the drawing-room. I heard Mr. King come downstairs, go into Mr. Maxwell's study and talk to him for a few moments. After this I heard Mr. King tell Mr. Maxwell that Philip Maxwell and Miss Leslie were in the library.

"After this, Mr. King walked through the room I was in, but we said nothing to each other, and he went on to the drawing-room. I stayed exactly where I was for some time longer, and then I concluded I would go home.

"Not wishing to make my adieux to the guests, I thought I would merely say good night to Mr. Maxwell. I lifted the portiére and looked into his study, but as he was asleep, I thought I wouldn't disturb him, but would just run upstairs for my banjo, and then slip away unnoticed.

"I went upstairs and I admit it was curiosity concerning the two people inside that led me to pause and look toward the library door. I heard no sound of voices, so I took another step or two in that direction, and, looking, saw Philip's figure stretched on the floor.

"Then, of course, I went into the room. It has no door, and the portieres were but partly drawn. Seeing what was evidently a serious accident of some sort, I immediately ran down-stairs and called Dr. Sheldon to the scene."

"You saw no one else in the room?"

"N—no," said Gilbert, but he seemed to hesitate.

"You are quite sure?" asked the coroner.

"I am positive I saw no one else in the room," said Gilbert, decidedly this time.

"Can you fix the time of your going upstairs?"

"I can. When I looked into Mr. Maxwell's study, I noticed by his large clock that it was twenty minutes after ten. In less than a minute after that I was upstairs."

"That will do," said Mr. Billings, and Gilbert was dismissed.

Dr. Sheldon was called next, and testified that he had responded immediately to Mr. Crane's call, and on reaching the library found Philip Maxwell's dead body on the floor, and Miss Leslie, wounded and unconscious, a few feet away.

"She was shot?" asked the coroner.

"Yes, shot in the shoulder. She had fallen, and in so doing had hit her temple. This rendered her unconscious. I extracted the ball, and found it to be a thirty-eight caliber. The revolver found in Miss Leslie's hand is also thirty-eight caliber."

"And has the ball been extracted from Mr. Philip Maxwell's body?"

"Yes; that is also a thirty-eight caliber. He was shot through the heart, and must have died instantly."

"In your opinion, how long had he been dead, when you examined the body?"

"Not long, as the body was still warm. Not more than half an hour at the most."

"The pistol found in Miss Leslie's hand, and which is now in my possession," said Mr. Billings, "has two empty chambers. In view of Miss Leslie's statement that the shooting was done by a person who came in by the window, it would seem that the intruder might have placed the weapon in Miss Leslie's hand after she was wounded. In your opinion, Dr. Sheldon, would this be possible?"

"Possible, yes, but highly improbable, as I myself took the pistol from her hand, and she was holding it in a tight grasp. This would scarcely have been the case, had it been thrust into her hand while she lay unconscious."

"We will not pursue this line of investigation further, until we can hear Miss Leslie's story," said Mr. Billings. "Dr. Sheldon, you are excused."

Mr. Maxwell's testimony was merely to the effect that he had spent the evening in the drawing room until about half past nine, at which time he went to his study, and remained there, reading and occasionally dozing, until he had been told the dreadful news.

He corroborated my statement about my looking in on him at ten o'clock, though he didn't notice the time, and he said that he neither saw nor heard Gilbert Crane look in later. Asked if he heard any shots, he said he did not, owing, doubtless, to his deafness, and the fact that he was asleep part of the time. He was excused, and Mr. Billings then inquired if anyone had heard any shots.

We who were in the drawing-room during the half-hour between ten and ten-thirty (when the murder was judged to have taken place) declared we heard no shots; and this was but natural, as the library was upstairs and some distance away, and the music was, at that time, of a noisy variety.

Gilbert Crane said he heard no shots, but said that he was so deeply immersed in his own thoughts, that he doubted if he would have heard a cannon fired.

Then Miss Maxwell's gentle voice was heard, saying:

"I heard two shots, and they were fired at exactly ten o'clock."

"This is most important, madam," said the coroner. "Will you kindly take the witness chair?"

Then Miss Miranda testified that she was in her own room preparing for bed. Her doors were closed, and the water was running for her bath, so that she could not hear distinctly, but at ten o'clock she heard two sounds that seemed to her like pistol shots. At the time, however, she hardly thought they were shots, but she opened her hall door and looked out. Seeing nothing unusual, and hearing the gay music downstairs, she assumed it was the slamming of doors or some other unimportant noise, and so thought no more of it, until informed of what had happened.

"This, then," said Mr. Billings, "fixes the firing of the two shots at ten o'clock. That coincides with your diagnosis, Dr. Sheldon?"

"Yes, sir," said the doctor.

"I went upstairs at about half past ten, and found the body still warm."

"It is fortunate that we are able thus to fix the time so accurately," said the coroner, "as it may be helpful in discovering the criminal."

IX: FURTHER TESTIMONY

THE next witness called was Irene Gardiner.

For some unaccountable reason, I trembled as I saw her take the stand.

There was no knowing what sort of an impression this strange girl might create, and there were certain bits of evidence which I would feel sorry to have brought out in reference to her.

"Where were you between ten and ten-thirty last evening?" asked Mr. Billings.

Although the tone was courteous, the question had somewhat the sound of a challenge.

"On the upper balcony," replied Irene, her head held high, and her red lips curled in a haughty expression.

"Which part of the balcony?" The coroner's voice was a little more gentle.

"The south end of the east side."

That was where I had left her when I came down-stairs at ten o'clock. The library opened on the southern end of the west balcony.

"Were you there alone? "

"Mr. King was with me part of the time. Also there were others in different parts of the balcony. After Mr. King left me I was alone."

"Were not the others you mentioned there?"

"I don't know; I could see no one from where I sat."

"How long did you remain there?"

"I cannot tell the exact time. When I came into the house again, I was met by Mr. King, who told me what had happened, and asked me to break the news to Miss Maxwell."

"While sitting on the balcony alone did you see any strangers, or any one, around the grounds, or on the driveway?"

"None."

"Did you stay in the same place all the time you were on the balcony, after Mr. King left you?"

"No—that is, yes."

"What do you mean by that answer?"

"I walked a few steps back and forth."

"Not around the corner into the north side?"

"N—no. Not so far as that."

As Irene made this statement, her face grew ashen pale, and I thought I saw her glance in the direction of Gilbert Crane. But I was not sure of this, and I was most anxious to make all allowance for the girl, who was certainly pitiably nervous and disturbed.

"You are quite sure, Miss Gardiner, that you did not walk round on the north or west sides of the balcony until the time you came into the house?"

"Quite certain," said Irene, but her voice was so low as scarcely to be heard, and her eyes were cast down.

I didn't know what to make of her strange manner, and just then I chanced to look at Gilbert Crane. To my surprise, he was equally pale and agitated in appearance. No one else seemed to notice this, so I kept my own counsel concerning it.

Miss Gardiner was dismissed, and the Earl of Clarendon was next called.

Mr. Billings inquired rather definitely as to the title and pedigree of the English nobleman, and, seemingly satisfied with the replies, he asked the witness to tell what he could of the tragedy.

"I can tell very little," the Earl responded. "I was dancing with a young lady in the drawing room, when I heard Mr. Crane announce from the doorway that somebody had been shot. I realized at once that unless restrained, the guests would all rush to the scene. I took the young lady who was with me to a sofa, and then I spoke to all the people at once, advising them to remain in the drawing-room. I may have taken upon myself undue authority, but I did it in an endeavor to avoid a scene of confusion. After a time, we all learned what had happened, and of course the guests for the most part went away at once."

"Where had you been just before the dance during which you heard the news?"

"I had been on the lower veranda."

"With whom?"

"I was alone. I wanted to smoke a cigarette, and I strolled round the verandas, toward the back of the house."

"On the same side of the house as the library, upstairs?"

"Yes, the same side."

"Did you see any person or persons other than the guests of the house?"

"No, that is, not that I could distinguish. But I saw a motor car which came swiftly up the drive, passed me, and went on round the house."

"Did you notice the car especially?"

"I gave it little thought, as it might have been bringing or taking guests, or might have had to do with the caterers or servants."

"Can you describe the car?"

"Though I didn't see it clearly, it gave me the impression of being long and low, and of a gray color. Also, it was going rapidly."

"That would scarcely seem to indicate the motor vehicle of a caterer."

"Nor do I say that it did. I have no reason to give the car any thought whatever; and I have merely a memory of the car passing me as I finished my cigarette and returned to the dancing-room. I can tell you no more of it."

"You didn't notice its occupants?"

"No; nor could I see them distinctly. I fancy, however, there were three or four men in it; but again, that is merely an impression I gained from the fleeting vision. I turned away from it, even as it passed me."

After a few more inquiries the Earl was dismissed, and other witnesses followed. None was important, in the sense of throwing any further light on the incidents of the evening before.

The Whitings and other guests who had been in the drawing-room, simply repeated what was already known.

The servants had heard no shots, but as they were at that time in the outer kitchen, busily engaged in preparations for supper, that was not surprising. The coachman and gardener had rooms in the barn buildings, and said they heard nothing unusual until notified of the catastrophe. There were now no more witnesses to be heard from, save the most important one of all, Mildred Leslie. Dr. Sheldon consented that she should be interviewed, but requested a delay of an hour or so.

The coroner, therefore, announced a brief recess, and as we had all given our testimony, we were not required to remain in the drawing-room with the jury and the officials. But as we were all more than anxious to be on hand to hear Mildred's statement, we did not drift far away.

Gilbert Crane and I strolled on the front lawn, smoking and discussing the inquest. I was most curious to know the reason of his extraordinary hesitation at some points of his testimony, but not caring to inquire directly, I resolved to find out in a roundabout way.

"What did you think of Miss Gardiner's testimony?" I asked.

"I think the poor girl was so agitated she did not know what she was saying," he replied somewhat shortly, and as if he did not wish to dwell on the subject.

But I was not to be turned from it.

"It is not like Miss Gardiner," I went on, "to lose her poise in an emergency. She is usually so calm and self-possessed."

"I do not consider Miss Gardiner's a calm temperament," said Crane; "I think she is decidedly emotional."

"Emotional, yes; but she has a wonderful control over her emotions. And aside from that, she positively contradicted herself this morning. I wonder if she did walk around to the west side of the balcony and look in at the library window."

This was mere idle speculation on my part, but it had a strange effect on Gilbert Crane.

"What do you mean?" he cried angrily. "Are you insinuating anything against Miss Gardiner's veracity, or do you perhaps consider her implicated in the affair?"

"I have no thought of Miss Gardiner, save such as are most honorable and loyal," I said; "but, by the way, Crane, what sort of a gown did she wear last night?"

"I don't know, I'm sure. I'm no authority on ladies' dress. I never notice their furbelows."

Somehow, the emphasis with which he said this made me think he was overdoing it, and that perhaps he was not so ignorant as he wished me to suppose. But I had no desire to antagonize him, so I dropped the discussion of Irene altogether.

He was amiable enough then, and we returned to the house, chatting affably.

Determined to settle a certain point, I went in search of Miss Maxwell, and found that good lady in the study with her brother.

"Miss Miranda," I said, without subterfuge, "what sort of a gown did Miss Gardiner wear last evening?"

"Irene? Why, she had on a lovely rose-colored silk-gauze—a sort of pineapple material."

"Was it trimmed with black spangles?"

"No, Peter, it was all pin."

'She didn't inquire why I wished to know; indeed, I think she scarcely realized what she was talking about, for she spoke almost automatically. I understood this, for all day she had seemed dazed and bewildered, and unable to concentrate her mind.

"What is it, Peter?" asked Mr. Maxwell, "have you learned anything new?"

They were very pathetic, these two old people, who had lost their only link to the world of youth and happiness, but the brother seemed to me especially to be pitied. Owing to his deafness, he heard nothing except what was directly addressed to him, and was naturally anxious for any side-lights on the affair.

"No, sir," I replied, "nothing new. But I think we shall soon hear Miss Leslie's statement, and then we will know where to begin our work."

"Leave no stone unturned, my boy; call on me for any money you may need, and spare no trouble or expense in your efforts. You're something of a detective yourself, aren't you, Peter? Can't you ferret this thing out?"

"I mean to try, sir," I replied. "But we have lost so much time, and there is so little evidence, I have small hope of success."

"Have you any theory or suspicion?" asked Mr. Maxwell.

I couldn't tell him of my finding the spangles, and I hadn't a thought of Irene that could deserve the name suspicion, but he seemed to notice my hesitation.

"You needn't answer that," he said in a kind way, "only remember this, my boy. Be careful how you proceed on suspicion, unless your proof is pretty positive. Trace your clues carefully, and don't let them mislead you."

It seemed as if he must have read my thought—or had he too found some spangles?

Well, at any rate, I would follow his advice, and be very careful before I let even my own thoughts doubt Irene.

And now we heard the people coming down from upstairs, and all hastened back to the drawing-room.

Since Mildred's assertion that Philip was killed by an intruder, the district attorney had been called in, and had of course attended the whole inquest.

He was a Mr. Edwards, and seemed to be an alert and intelligent man.

Like the rest of us, he eagerly awaited the expected statement, and when the Coroner rose, the general excitement, though subdued, was intense.

X: MILDRED'S STRANGE STORY

"I WILL call the next witness," the coroner announced, "Miss Mildred Leslie."

There was an expectant hush all over the room, as Mildred came through the door, supported on one side by the white-capped nurse and on the other by Doctor Sheldon. Edith Whiting followed, looking very anxious, and, it seemed to me, annoyed. I knew she thought her sister was not well enough to go through this ordeal, but I knew, too, that it must be gone through, for of course this testimony was the most important of all.

Mr. Billings looked at his witness almost with consternation, when he saw how weak and fragile she appeared, and he spoke in very gentle tones.

"Miss Leslie," he said, "I will detain you no longer than is absolutely necessary. Will you tell, in your own words, the story of what occurred last evening in the library?"

Mildred stirred uneasily in the big chair, where the nurse had placed her, and grasped nervously at the hand of Miss Lathrop as she sat beside her. The nurse, the doctor and Edith Whiting were all looking anxiously at Milly as if afraid of her collapse. But seeming to nerve herself, with an effort, the girl began:

"Philip Maxwell and I were in the library, and had been there some time, when a man appeared."

"Wait a moment, Miss Leslie," interrupted Mr. Billings.

"I must ask for more details. Excuse me, but on what subjects were you and Mr. Maxwell conversing?"

"Do I have to tell that?" and Milly smiled at the coroner, looking almost like her old self again.

"I'm sorry to annoy you,"—Mr. Billings was certainly under the spell of Milly's smile,—"but I must ask you to."

"Well, then," and Milly pouted a little, "he was asking me to marry him."

"And you said?"

"Oh, I refused to. I had refused him lots of times before. He knew I didn't care for him,— that way."

"He knew then, that his was a hopeless suit?"

"He certainly did."

"Why, then, did he continue to insist upon it?"

"Well, he said that he had something to tell me that would make me change my mind."

"What was it?"

"I don't know, I'm sure. Before he had time to tell me, that awful man came, an..."

Milly put her hands up to her face, and swayed from side to side, as her thoughts flew back to the dreadful scene. Miss Lathrop put an arm around her, and offered her smelling-salts, while Edith Whiting whispered to the doctor, who only shook his head.

Indeed, all the members of the household sympathized with the poor little girl, suffering from shock and real illness. But the coroner and the District Attorney were determined to get her story if possible.

"Rest a few moments, Miss Leslie," said Mr. Billings, "and then try to continue."

"It's an outrage," murmured old Mr. Maxwell; "it's a shame to torment the poor child!"

"But better to get it over at once," said Lord Clarendon, who was gravely listening to the proceedings of the inquest.

I liked the Earl's manner; though solicitous for Mildred's comfort, he seemed to desire that the inquiry should go on as steadily as possible, toward the discovery of the truth.

"Never mind the intruder at present, Miss Leslie," went on the coroner. "What did you do then?"

"Nothing. I was so paralyzed with fright, that I couldn't move,—I couldn't even scream."

"And what did Mr. Maxwell do?"

"He seemed paralyzed too. It seemed like minutes, but I don't suppose it was, that we three stood there, looking at each other."

"And then?"

"And then," Mildred gasped as if for breath, but gripping the arms of her chair tightly, she went steadily on; "and then, Philip pulled open the top drawer of the table-desk, and grabbed out a pistol. He raised it to aim at the man, but at the same time, he said, in a low, moaning voice, 'Oh, to think he would shoot me!'"

"Then, Miss Leslie, you think Mr. Maxwell knew who shot him?"

"I think he must have known, from the way he spoke. But the man was a stranger to me. He had—"

"You may describe him later. Go on with your connected story, please."

"Well, when I saw Philip take his pistol, I had a wild desire to prevent either of the men from shooting. I suppose I was almost crazed by fright, and scarcely knew what I was doing. But my only thought was to attack the man who was threatening Philip, and so I threw..."

Mildred stopped suddenly in her recital. Both nurse and doctor leaned forward to see if she were exhausted, but she was not. She seemed to have been struck by a sudden thought, and hesitating what to say next.

I chanced to look at the Earl and found him regarding Milly intently. He had a curious look on his face, and his tightly interlaced fingers were the first sign of nervousness he had shown. He did not glance my way, but kept his gaze fixed on Milly's face, as if trying to attract her attention. If so, he succeeded, for she turned slowly and looked in his direction. She gazed straight at him for a moment, and then tossed her head with a willful little gesture peculiar to herself.

Then she turned again to the coroner.

"Proceed, Miss Leslie. You threw something at this intruder?"

"Yes; I thought if I could hit him I might prevent his shooting. I snatched up a heavy cut glass inkstand full of ink, from the desk, and threw it at him. I don't know whether it hit him or not, but the next second I picked up a bronze horse,— a paper-weight,—from the desk and threw that at him, too."

Milly was talking rapidly, and growing very much excited. Her cheeks burned, her eyes were big and shiny, and her fingers picked nervously at the arms of her chair.

Mr. Billings looked at her curiously. "You threw these heavy missiles at him?"

"Yes, I did! and it didn't take as long to do it, as it does to tell it, for my hands fairly flew. I couldn't speak or make a sound, but I felt impelled to act!"

"You are sure you threw these things, Miss Leslie?" and the coroner's tone was emphatically one of incredulity.

"Of course I'm sure!" she declared, angrily.

"And did any of these things hit him?"

"I don't know, I tell you! It's all a blur to me – the whole scene. But I remember that Philip and the man paid no attention to me, but stood with their pistols pointed at each other. Then Philip said again, in that moaning voice, 'to think he would shoot me!' and just then the man fired."

"With what result?"

"Philip fell backward, and as he fell, his pistol dropped from his hand onto the desk." Mildred's excitement had died away, and she spoke now in a tense, low voice, and seemed to be holding herself together by a desperate effort. Her eyes had a far-away look, and she went steadily on.

"I don't know what gave me courage, for I had never so much as touched a revolver before; but I suppose I was nerved up by fright, and I picked up Philip's pistol and aimed at the man, myself. With that," and Mildred's voice sank to a whisper, "he turned his own pistol toward me,—I heard the report,—and I remember falling forward. I remember nothing more."

There was a silence as Milly stopped speaking. Everyone felt the horror of the recital; everyone realized the mystery surrounding the crime. Who could have been desirous of killing both these young people?

I glanced round at our household group. The old people, Alexander Maxwell and his sister, sat hand in hand, their heads bowed with grief. Mr. Maxwell, I felt sure, had not heard all of the evidence, but of course it would be repeated to him afterwards. And perhaps after all it were well if he could be spared the harrowing details. Miss Maxwell sat with trembling lips, and though her heart was breaking, she controlled herself in her effort to be a comfort and stay to her brother.

Irene Gardiner was listening to Mildred with rapt attention and alert intelligence. She had not missed a word of all the inquiry, and I knew she was storing up in her memory every bit of testimony to be coldly considered afterward. Her air was judicial, and her calm impressed me unpleasantly. I admired the girl so much, that I resented this calculating side of her nature, which always jarred upon me.

Edith Whiting and her husband were more concerned lest the occasion prove too much for Mildred's strength and nerves, than they were in the outcome of the inquest.

The Earl sat with his eyes on the floor, now, and occasionally shook his head, as if dissatisfied with his own thoughts. Gilbert Crane was very nervous, and fidgeted incessantly with his watch chain or a lead pencil or any small object he could lay hands on.

But the coroner was continuing his questions.

"Miss Leslie," he said, "you have given a very clear and coherent statement. Now if you will describe the intruder, we will not disturb you further today."

"I can't describe him very much, except to say that he wore motoring clothes. A big coat, a cap with a visor, and goggles which covered most of his face."

"Not the lower part of his face?"

"No, but his large collar was turned up, and buttoned across in a way to hide his mouth and chin."

"Would you recognize him if you saw him again?"

"I'm sure I could not. The clothes were not peculiar in any way. Just such as all men wear motoring."

"Was it a fur coat?"

"No, not that kind. A sort of thick cloth, I think,—of medium color, but rather light than dark."

"And the cap?"

"I think that was light, too, but I couldn't say for certain."

"Did he wear gloves?"

Mildred looked perplexed.

"I can't say; I rather think he did, but my eyes rested on the pistol,—it seemed to fasciate me,—and I thought only of how I could prevent him from firing it."

"That is all, Miss Leslie," said Mr. Billings, and Mildred was allowed to be taken back to her own room. All! I should think it was enough! I felt as if I must get away to think things over by myself.

I rushed from the room and out on the veranda, where I found a secluded corner. What sort of a story had Mildred told, and why? For the doctor had sworn she was perfectly sane and rational, and quite capable of describing the affair. Why, then, did she say she threw an inkstand full of ink and a bronze horse at the intruder, when I, who had so carefully searched the room for clues, found no traces of ink? And, moreover, I especially remembered seeing that bronze horse on the desk when I first entered the library after Gilbert Crane had given the alarm!

Not for a moment did I doubt Mildred's good faith in the matter. It would be too absurd to think of her making such statements if they were not true. And yet how could they be true? How could anyone throw an inkstand full of ink, and not leave black spots somewhere? How could anyone throw a heavy bronze paper-weight, and, being shot a moment later, restore the bronze to its place on the table? Clearly she must be laboring under an hallucination regarding these things. Probably she so strongly desired to throw the inkstand or the horse that she really believed she did throw them.

Yes, that must be it. There was no other plausible explanation of her words.

XI: THE BLACK SPANGLES

AS was to be expected, the jury returned a verdict of willful murder against a person unknown; and I concluded from this, that they had accepted Mildred's story as true.

And if so, then the main thing now, was to find the man in the automobile clothes. He must be someone whom Philip knew and recognized in spite of the goggles.

He must have come in an automobile, for men do not walk around the country in such attire. But Miss Gardiner on the balcony commanded a view of the entrance and driveway, and she had seen no one enter the grounds.

Possibly then he had come from a distance, had left his machine at some point nearby, and had approached the house secretly and on foot. But how had he gained an entrance? The servants had not let him in. He couldn't have come in by the front door without being seen. The conservatory door was always locked at night.

Oh, well, while all these things were true, still there were many windows by which he might have entered, and slipped upstairs unseen. Then he could have gone out on the balcony through the little cross-hall and so reached the library window. Or, he might have climbed to the balcony by means of a veranda pillar. An agile man could easily do this—still, not so easily if dressed in a bulky automobile coat.

It was mysterious enough, but of course the first thing to do was to look for traces. If I had only known sooner that there was an intruder to be looked for, how much better a chance we should have had of finding him.

But there was no use crying over spilled milk, so I started at once to look carefully at the veranda pillars. There I found myself forestalled.

Mr. Hunt and Gilbert Crane were already examining them.

"Any scratches?" said I.

"Plenty of old ones," said Mr. Hunt, "but none that seems to have been made as recently as last night."

"How about automobile tracks?"

"There are any number of those, all over the drive; but as several people came in automobiles last night, they mean nothing definite."

"What do you make of those marks on the balcony floor that look as if made by scuffling feet?"

"They may be the marks of a scuffle," said Mr. Hunt, "or it may be that someone stood for some time looking in at the library window. A nervous person standing there might move about in a manner to leave just such traces."

For some unaccountable reason these remarks of Mr. Hunt's seemed to disturb Gilbert Crane. He turned pale and was about to speak, then set his lips firmly, and turned silently away.

"There is one circumstance that ought to be explained," I said, speaking to Mr. Hunt, and hoping that Crane would leave us.

But Gilbert turned back and seemed anxious to know what I was about to say. I watched him closely as I went on, though addressing my remarks directly to Mr. Hunt.

"I found these bits of evidence this morning," I said, taking my note-book from my pocket. "They may not be vital clues, but anything found in the library is of interest."

Even before I opened my note-book Crane showed signs of agitation which he tried vainly to suppress. His white, frightened face and his clenched hands showed that he feared the disclosure. Still watching him covertly, I produced the three black spangles.

"Do you recognize these?"

"No," said Mr. Hunt, "what are they, and where did they come from?"

"Do you recognize them?" I said, turning suddenly to Crane.

"No!" he declared, but with such emphasis that I doubted him. "But they can't possibly be of any importance."

"Perhaps not," I returned, "but I picked them up in the library, and on the balcony, and one piece I disengaged from the catch of the library window shutter."

"Well," said Gilbert Crane, trying to speak naturally, "and what does that prove to you?"

"It doesn't prove anything," I said slowly, "but it is a peculiar coincidence that they should be found just where the intruder of last night must have stood."

"Meaning that it might have been a woman?" said Hunt, quickly.

"Possibly," I returned. "But none of the ladies were on the upper balcony last evening at ten o'clock, except Miss Gardiner, and she declares that she was not in the library or on the west balcony at all."

"She says that?" said Hunt. looking up sharply, while Gilbert Crane looked more distressed than ever.

"Yes," I answered. "Did you speak, Mr. Crane?"

"No," said Gilbert, "I have nothing to say on the subject." And turning abruptly, he left us and walked rapidly across the lawn and out of the front gate.

"I don't understand Miss Gardiner's attitude," said Mr. Hunt. "I cannot think she had anything to do with the crime, but I do think she is withholding information of some sort. But I must go now, and I will return this evening. Then, if you please, Mr. King, I would like to discuss matters more at length with you."

Hunt went away, and I paced the veranda slowly, thinking things over.

I went round the house, and seeing the Earl in the billiard-room, I went in through the open French window. His lordship seemed disinclined to talk, but he was courteous enough, and by a little diplomacy I succeeded in drawing him out on the subject that absorbed us all.

"But it's better I should say nothing," he declared. "The truth is I've my own opinion of American detectives, and,—well, never mind—only you may as well give up first as last."

The Earl spoke emphatically, and Tom Whiting, coming into the room just then, heard the remark.

"No," declared Tom, "we'll never give up; not till we find that man who shot Philip, and so clear our Milly."

"Clear Milly!" I exclaimed; "why, who could possibly imagine that that child had done any wrong? She is the sufferer, not the culprit."

"I wish everybody thought so," said Tom, with but slightly concealed meaning.

"Doesn't everybody think so?" inquired the Earl, politely.

"Speak for yourself," said Whiting, in a more bitter voice than I had ever heard from the genial chap.

"I think we must admit it's all a mystery," returned the Earl, in his coldest manner; "and perhaps we must also admit that little Miss Leslie is the greatest mystery of all. It's not surprising if her brain is affected by the shock that she should tell those strange stories of throwing things around the room. But if she is rational and perfectly sane, I think we must all admit her statements are mysterious."

Tom Whiting's honest round face showed despair. He couldn't deny Lord Clarendon's assertions, though it was easily seen that he deeply resented them.

"But she sounded perfectly sane and sensible as she gave her testimony," I said. "Of course Miss Leslie is excitable, but she told a straightforward story, and we have no reason to doubt her word."

I realized as I said this that I was speaking insincerely, for I certainly couldn't help doubting Mildred's statement myself. If she had thrown those things, we couldn't have found them on the table when we all went up there immediately after.

I knew, too, that I spoke as I did, out of sympathy for Whiting, and also out of a general sense of chivalry to the girl.

And yet, after all, was it not more generous to ward her, to assume, as Lord Clarence did, that her mind must be affected?

"I think, Whiting," I said slowly, "that while Mildred's statements are untrue, they are not intentionally so. I think she had in her mind such a strong impulse to throw those heavy things that she really thought she did do it."

"Do you think so?" said the Earl, in a most unconvinced way.

"Look here, Lord Clarendon," I said, rather sharply, "are you making implications or insinuations against Miss Leslie? I had reason to think that you greatly admired her."

"So I do," returned his lordship, promptly, "and I make no implication whatever; I hold that the kindest explanation we can make of her conduct, is to believe that she is not quite in her right mind. And I hold that this should be no offence to the lady herself, or to her relatives."

He looked at Whiting as he said this, and Tom returned his glance. There was not a friendly feeling between the two men, and Tom Whiting was not one to make a pretense of such.

"Nurse Lathrop says that Milly's mind is perfectly all right," he said, doggedly, "and I have no reason to doubt her opinion."

"I don't suppose you care for my advice," said the Earl, seriously; "but don't trust that nurse too far. If I'm any reader of character she is disingenuous and not entirely to be trusted."

"We have seen no reason, Lord Clarendon, to feel any dissatisfaction with Miss Lathrop," said Tom, stiffly; "she is devoted to her patient and is exceedingly skilled in her profession."

"She is an English woman," returned the Earl, seeming not at all offended by Tom's manner.

"And though I have every regard and respect for the women of my country as a class, yet perhaps I understand them better than you do over here. And if you'll believe me, that nurse knows more than she tells, and what she tells isn't true."

"You're making grave accusations, Lord Clarendon," I said, amazed at his speech.

"Not accusations," he returned, lightly; "merely my opinions, based on my experience with English women. But it's also my opinion that you'll never know any more about this mystery than you know now. If you had a good man from Scotland Yard, he'd soon find the criminal for you; but with all due respect to the American nation, they have no detectives worthy of the name."

Tom Whiting turned on his heel and walked away. But though I was incensed at his lordship's speech, he made it with such an air of simply stating a self-evident fact, that I wondered if he mightn't be more than half right.

"You see," he went on calmly, after Whiting had gone, "Miss Leslie's story cannot be true. We must all admit that. Also she knows more than she has told. Also in her delirium, she has babbled of things that she doesn't want told, but which of course are known to Nurse Lathrop. Probably, too, Mr. and Mrs. Whiting know these things, which is why Mr. Whiting is annoyed at me."

"But, Lord Clarendon, just what sort of things do you mean? You don't think that Miss Leslie is implicated in the shooting!"

"I do not,—most emphatically I do not. But I do think that Miss Leslie knows far more than she told at the inquest."

"That leads to all sorts of conjectures," said I, thoughtfully.

"What does?" said a voice from the doorway, and Irene Gardiner walked slowly into the room. She was looking superb in a dinner gown of a thin black material, which, trailing behind her, added to her natural dignity. The soft dusky folds of her bodice threw into relief the marble whiteness of her neck and throat, and she wore a long rope of black beads.

I determined to ask her the question that was burning in my mind. "You rarely wear black, Miss Gardiner," I said, taking the risk of being too personal, "and it suits you so well. Didn't you wear a black spangled gown the night of the dance?"

In spite of my intending to ask this question most diplomatically, I had blurted it out in the least tactful way possible. And Miss Gardiner evidently thought so. She gave me first a cold stare, and then seeming to realize that I had asked the question for a definite reason, she flushed painfully and dropped her eyes.

"No," she said, but her voice trembled, "I wore a rose-colored gown, with no black trimming of any sort."

"And a charming gown it was," said the Earl, with a very evident intention of filling an awkward pause. But Irene was not willing to drop the subject. "What possible interest can you have in the details of my costume?" she asked, turning to me. She had recovered her poise, and her eyes flashed as she seemed to accuse me of a rudeness. "None," I replied, with a calmness that equaled her own. "Pardon an idle curiosity."

She gave me a glance that denoted anything but pardon, and turned to the Earl.

"It is chilly, isn't it?" she said; "the autumn will be an early one."

"Shall I close the window? May I get you a wrap?" asked the Earl, solicitously; while I stood by, ignored.

"Here is a wrap for Miss Gardiner," said a low voice, and Nurse Lathrop stepped quietly into the room. She brought a light, gauzy scarf, which she adjusted around Irene's shoulders. "I brought this down," she said, by way of explanation, "because I thought you might need it."

This sounded plausible, but after what the Earl had said, I had a dim suspicion that Miss Lathrop might have been eavesdropping and made the scarf a pretext. I fancy Miss Gardiner thought so, too, for she accepted the wrap with a cold "Thank you," and immediately left the room.

"How is your patient, Miss Lathrop?" I asked.

"I cannot say she is any better, Mr. King. It was cruel to make her go through that ordeal this afternoon. The reaction is very great, and she is weak now and shows much loss of vitality."

"Is she delirious?" asked the Earl, directly.

"She is not delirious; but her mind wanders. She tells many things which of course it would not be right for me to repeat. Still, if I thought…"

"Certainly not," said the Earl, sternly. "The secrets of a sick-room should be inviolable."

"But," I began, "if they throw any light on the mystery…"

"They don't!" the Earl again interrupted; "the ramblings of that sick girl's mind have no foundation of truth, and would only confuse the case instead of clearing it!"

"You know a great deal about it, Lord Clarendon!" said Miss Lathrop, with that annoying smile of hers.

"I know what my common sense tells me. And I advise you, nurse, not to tangle things more deeply by repeating Miss Leslie's irresponsible remarks."

"They're not entirely irresponsible; and if I told all I knew, people might look in a different direction from where they're looking now. And perhaps the high and mightiness of some people might have a sudden fall."

As Miss Lathrop glanced out on the veranda where Irene was walking up and down with Tom Whiting, it was impossible not to believe that her hint referred to

Miss Gardiner. But I also realized that Irene had not a very friendly attitude toward the nurse, and that doubtless Miss Lathrop's vague remarks were induced merely by a spirit of petty revenge.

Miss Lathrop was not an attractive woman. She was good-looking, but her spirit of self-importance and her readiness to imagine a slight cast upon her, seemed to imply a character of little sweetness and light.

The Earl of Clarendon as if struck by a sudden thought, said abruptly, "Miss Lathrop, I do not think you could tell us anything of importance. But if you do know positively any facts that bear on the case it is of course your duty to divulge them. Your opinions, however, would be entirely uncalled for."

I couldn't help wondering why the Earl treated Miss Lathrop so brusquely. However, she seemed not so much to resent it as to wish to return it in kind.

"Oh, of course I don't know anything of importance," and she smiled superiorly; "but Miss Leslie did say that she thought the motor-coat and goggles might have disguised a woman as easily as a man."

I was thunderstruck at this, but the Earl took it coolly. "Did she say that?" he asked, "or did you suggest it, and she merely acquiesce?"

The flash of surprise in Miss Lathrop's eyes proved that he had hit upon the truth, though she deigned no reply whatever.

"Moreover," he went on, "if Miss Leslie said that, or even agreed to it, it was with the intent of diverting suspicion from a man."

"You don't really think Miss Leslie knows who the intruder was!" I exclaimed, while Miss Lathrop looked at the Earl in utter astonishment.

"Of course I don't," he replied, "nor shall I think so, until she says so herself."

I knew this only meant that he considered it the part of chivalry not to admit any suspicion of Mildred's veracity and sincerity before Nurse Lathrop; though he had certainly given me to understand, that he very much doubted Milly's whole story.

The nurse went away, and her complacent air gave no sign of annoyance; but I was sure, all the same, that the Earl's straightforward talk had at least stirred her calm self-assurance.

"Don't ever try to get information from that woman," said the Earl to me, confidentially; "she would withhold the truth if it suited her purpose, or she would so distort it that it would only lead you astray. You seem to be somewhat of a detective, Mr. King, and I hope you won't take my advice amiss."

"What makes you think I'm inclined to detective work, Lord Clarendon?"

"Only because you ask questions of everybody, and then go away by yourself to puzzle out the answers."

I was inclined to feel a little chagrined at this brief description of my procedure, but the Earl's smile was friendly, and I concluded not to take exception to his good-natured chafing.

So I only said, "Well, help me out whenever you can, won't you?" And then we went away to dress for dinner.

XII: AN INTERVIEW WITH MILLY

WHEN Mr. Hunt came back that evening he found me with Mr. Maxwell in the study.

Although I did not wish to pain the old gentleman with more details than were necessary, yet I wanted him to know as nearly as possible how matters stood; and, too, I wanted the benefit of his sound judgment and good advice.

"Come in, Mr. Hunt, come in," I said to the detective. "Let us three sum up the real evidence we have and see what may be best to do next."

I closed the doors in order that we might feel more free to speak in tones which Mr. Maxwell could hear easily, and then I left it to Mr. Hunt to open the conversation.

"First," said the detective, "I would like to know Mr. Maxwell's opinion of Miss Leslie's testimony."

"I have just been reading the stenographer's report of it," said Mr. Maxwell. "I did not hear it clearly, so I asked permission to read the paper myself. I do not know Miss Leslie very well, but she impresses me as nothing more nor less than a merry, light-hearted, innocent girl. Coquettish, perhaps, but I think the depths of her nature are honest and sincere. Now, we have all agreed that her testimony regarding the inkstand and the bronze paper-weight cannot, in the very nature of things, be true testimony. For ink spilled on a carpet will remain there, and bronze horses cannot get up on a table by themselves. Personally, then, I am forced to the opinion that Miss Leslie's mind is affected—temporarily only, I trust. But surely there is no other explanation for her strange statements. And, granting this, may it not be possible that her whole story of the man in the automobile coat is but a figment of her diseased brain?"

"It is possible," said Mr. Hunt, "but they tell me that Miss Leslie is so clear-headed and rational in her conversation that I find it difficult to disbelieve her story of the intruder."

"Nor do I ask you to," said Mr. Maxwell. "I only want to call your attention to the logical point that such grave discrepancies in one part of her recital might argue doubt in other directions.

"I have a logical mind, but I have none of what is often called the 'detective instinct.' That is why I wish to put this whole affair entirely in the hands of an able detective. And again of a detective's ability I do not consider myself a judge. If you think, Mr. Hunt, that you can take care of it successfully, I have sufficient confidence in you to give you the entire responsibility. Or, should you prefer to call in an assistant or an expert from the city, I am quite willing you should do so."

"I don't want to seem egotistical, Mr. Maxwell," said Mr. Hunt, "but I can't help feeling that Mr. King and I can take care of this thing. Mr. King, though not a professional, tells me he has what you have called the 'detective instinct,' at least, in some degree. And if he will help me, I would prefer his assistance to that of a stranger."

"Then we will leave it that way," said Mr. Maxwell. "I shall be glad to have Mr. King for my guest as long as he will stay, and you may consider yourselves authorized to make such investigations as you see fit. I do not presume to advise you, but I want to ask you to take an old man's warning, and be sure of your proofs before you act upon them. Clues are often misleading; evidence may be false. But there are certain kinds of facts that point unmistakably to the truth. Those facts you must discover, and then follow where they lead, irrespective of whom they may implicate, and oblivious to any personal prejudice."

I couldn't help wondering if Mr. Maxwell shared my faint but growing suspicion that either Mr. Crane or Miss Gardiner, or both, knew more about the tragedy than they had yet told. I was sure the old gentleman's conservative habits of speech would not allow him to put this into words, but that his sense of justice demanded an intimation of the idea.

After a little further conversation with Mr. Maxwell, we left the study, and Hunt and I went for a walk.

"It's clear to my mind," said Hunt, "that this shooting was done by an intruder from outside, not a common burglar but some past acquaintance of Philip's who had some strong motive for ending the boy's existence.

"It was someone whom Philip knew and recognized. The motive he did not know, for he was both surprised and grieved that this individual should intend to kill him."

"Then you believe Mildred's story, as a whole?"

"Yes. It seems to me that we have as yet no real reason to doubt her main statement, even though the details are mystifying."

"Mystifying! They are impossible!"

"Nothing is impossible in detective work," said Mr. Hunt, "at least nothing that is mysterious."

With that we parted. Mr. Hunt went home, and I went back to Maxwell Chimneys to toss all night on a bed of wakefulness. I felt flattered that Mr. Hunt had asked me to work with him and I resolved to do something that would prove my worth as his assistant.

I thought over what the nurse had said, but dismissed it from my mind as being merely the vagary of an ill-tempered and self-centered nature. I frankly admitted to myself that had her insinuations been directed toward anyone except Irene, I might have given them a little more thoughtful consideration.

But it was out of the question to imagine Miss Gardiner in any way involved in the affair.

And then I thought, suddenly, how I had left her at her own request on the upper veranda, before I saw Philip and Mildred in the library. But I had left her far around on the other side of the house, and later when I returned to tell her of the tragedy, she was on the veranda at the front of house.

To be sure, when I found her there she was crying, or had been. But all these facts gave me no suggestion of her connection with the tragedy, but rather made me anxious to keep my knowledge of her movements to myself, lest anyone else might put on them a wrong construction.

Then I thought about what the Earl had said regarding Mildred's statements. Of course, Mildred Leslie was a frivolous-minded, mischievous girl, and more than once I had known her to make up stories out of her own fanciful brain, entirely for the purpose of astonishing her hearers. But I couldn't think she would do this, when giving witness before a jury. And yet, I well-remembered, when I dashed into the library that night after Crane's fearful announcement, that I distinctly saw the inkstand in the middle of the table.

It was one of those enormous glass and silver affairs, intended as an expensive gift and not always well adapted to practical use. It was, of course, shining and clean, and it was an absolute impossibility, if Mildred had thrown it, that she or anyone else could have replaced it in that immaculate condition in so short a time.

I mulled over the inkstand question until I felt as if my own brains were addled, and I finally fell asleep resolving to make the solution of that puzzle my definite work for the next day.

As a beginning, I begged Dr. Sheldon to allow me a short interview with Mildred the next morning. He hesitated about this, and expressed himself as doubtful of its wisdom. He said his patient was rapidly recovering from the shock sustained by her nervous system, and was now suffering mainly from the flesh wound in her shoulder, but still, he feared that any excitement might bring on fever.

"But, Doctor Sheldon," I said, "I particularly want to avoid excitement. I only want to ask her a few calm and straightforward questions. The nurse and Mrs. Whiting and yourself may all be present, and if you fear that I am alarming or over exciting your patient, I will go away at once."

It required some further persuasion, but at last Doctor Sheldon reluctantly consented to the interview.

I stepped into the sick room, trying to assume a most casual air; and sitting by the girl's bedside, I said, lightly, "I just ran in for a moment to say good morning, and to hope that you will soon be out among us again, for we miss you awfully."

Mildred Leslie may have been ill, and may have been weakened by the shock and by the wound in her shoulder, but to look at her, one would never think it. Two long braids of golden hair lay outside the coverlet, tied at the top by enormous pink bows at each side of her head. The lacy frills of her gown fell away from her baby like throat, and the piquant face with its dancing blue eyes was as saucy as ever.

One arm of course was in bandages, daintily hidden by the light folds of a lace scarf, but the other hand was held out to me in welcome.

"I'm awfully glad to see you, Mr. King," she said, smiling; "they won't let me see anybody; and going down-stairs yesterday afternoon was so perfectly horrid, that I think I ought to see somebody nice to make up for it."

I looked at the girl in secret amazement. How could she show such lightness and gayety after the fearful tragedy she had been through, and which was even yet with us?

I felt sure she had never loved Philip, but even so, his dreadful death which had appalled everybody else, must surely have affected her to some degree.

I think Edith Whiting read my thoughts, for she spoke quickly; "I'm glad you've come, too, Mr. King, to cheer Milly up. We do everything we can to keep her mind on pleasant things and away from any trouble."

It seemed to me they had succeeded in their attempts, for certainly Milly's manner was gay and care—free enough, although a little petulant at being kept in her room.

"I could just as well go down-stairs as not," she declared, pouting; "you'd carry me down, wouldn't you, Mr. King? I've one good arm that I could put round your neck."

She waved a pretty dimpled arm toward me, and then, taking her hand, as if that would help to pin down her butterfly mind to seriousness for one moment, I spoke to her quietly but decidedly.

"I will carry you downstairs, when the doctor allows it; but just now, Miss Leslie, I want to ask you one or two questions, and I know you'll be kind enough to answer them. I'm sorry that I must turn your thoughts back to a scene that you must naturally try to forget. But please tell me if you are sure that you really threw that inkstand? Might you not have intended to throw it without doing so?"

She looked at me in amazement.

"Certainly I'm sure I threw it," she said. "I distinctly remember picking it up and throwing it at the man. It did not hit him; it fell short of him, for it was heavier than I thought.

"So then I threw the bronze horse at him. That was heavy, too, and it struck the thick rug with a soft thud. That didn't hit him, either; I never could throw things very well. But I scarcely knew what I was doing, and my acts were impulsive, almost unconscious."

"That is just the point, Miss Leslie; since they were almost unconscious, might it not be that they were not acts at all, merely intention and imagination?"

"I am perfectly sure that I threw those things. Will you tell me why you doubt it?"

"Because," I said, watching her carefully, "when I entered the room where you lay unconscious, the inkstand was undisturbed on the desk, and the bronze horse also."

She drew her hand away from mine, and, as far as it was possible, her pretty baby face assumed a look of hurt dignity.

"I think," she said, "I have as much reason to doubt your statements as you have to doubt mine. For I know I threw those things. The whole affair is like a dream, a vivid dream, in one way; yet in another way every instant of it is more acutely real to me than any other moment of my life.

"I positively threw those things just as I have described to you, and if, which seems impossible, they were returned to the desk, it was done by other hands than mine, either human or supernatural."

The last words were uttered in a rising key and ended in an almost hysterical shriek. She threw her right arm across her eyes, and turning away from me, thereby greatly disturbing her bandaged left shoulder, she burst into a fit of sobbing.

"I told you so!" exclaimed Nurse Lathrop, who had stood during our conversation, with an air of disapproval on her face. She rushed to Milly, almost pushing me out of her way, and as I had promised to do in case this happened, I quickly left the room.

"Oh, Mr. King," exclaimed Edith Whiting, who had followed me, "I'm so sorry you stirred Milly up so! Now she will have brain fever, I know! I daren't go back there, for I am too much upset myself, and the doctor and nurse can take care of her best. But won't you promise me that she shall not be disturbed again?"

It was plain enough that Mrs. Whiting did not blame me, for she knew that the inquiry and investigation must go on. But she seemed to think that I could prevent the further disturbing of her sister.

"I will promise you, Mrs. Whiting," I returned, "that Miss Leslie shall not be questioned again until she is entirely well. I don't think she will have brain fever,— though she will doubtless bring on feverish conditions by that hysterical sobbing."

But even as I spoke Milly's sobs died away and there was silence in the sick room.

In a moment the nurse came out into the hall, and said dictatorially, "You people must go away from here. We have given Miss Leslie an opiate, and I shall not allow any talking, or any noise near this room. It is too bad, Mr. King, that you should have brought on this relapse."

"I'm not willing to take an individual responsibility for it, Miss Lathrop," I returned; "I went to Miss Leslie's room this morning with Doctor Sheldon's full consent."

"Yes! a consent forced from him, and which he knew was most injudicious! And now will you please go away?"

Without another word I bowed and turned away, and Mrs. Whiting went with me. We went down stairs, and finding the music-room empty, she drew me in there.

"You mustn't think Milly heartless," she said, and a sad look came over her face. "But, you see, Doctor Sheldon told us that we must not let her mind dwell on the scene of that night, or it would greatly retard her recovery. So we have not mentioned it, but have tried our best to talk of other things, and to keep her thoughts on joyful and pleasant subjects. We have read to her amusing stories, and Nurse Lathrop has been most ingenious in entertaining her. Don't think hard of us for this, for my little sister is my beloved charge, and I would do anything to help her to a quick recovery."

"I quite appreciate the situation, Mrs. Whiting, and I cannot tell you how sorry I am that it was necessary to have that interview this morning, for it was necessary, for we must continue our investigation; and I had to know whether Miss Leslie's statements were true, or whether at the inquest she was under some sort of hallucination, and detailed imaginary deeds."

"And do you feel sure now that my sister has told you the truth?"

"I must admit the way that she talked to me just now was very convincing. She seemed so entirely herself and so sure of her memory, that I feel I have no reasonable grounds to doubt her assertions."

"And you must not doubt them," said Edith Whiting, earnestly; "I'm sure Milly told you the truth, and I think you will find that out for yourself sooner or later. Will you tell me, Mr. King, why you have—why anybody has a suspicious attitude toward my sister? It seems to me that Milly is one to be avenged, almost as much as Philip. Whoever murdered him, attempted to murder her. Why, then, is his a sainted memory, and my sister talked about and looked at with doubt and uncertainty?"

"Since you ask, Mrs. Whiting, I will admit frankly that there is as yet a mystery about it all. I'd rather not discuss it with you, but, as you know, Miss Leslie is of a volatile, even erratic nature, and ..."

"I know what you're going to say," said Edith sadly; "that as Milly was found with a pistol in her hand, there is a doubt as to the truth of any of her stories! No, don't interrupt me, Mr. King,— I quite understand; and I want you to go ahead with your investigations, and find the murderer as soon as you can. It will not prove to be my sister! But the only way she can be vindicated, is to bring the real criminal to justice and prove the truth of her stories: I don't care if you did see that inkstand on the table, I am perfectly positive, after what she said this morning, that she did throw it at the man who came in at the window, exactly as she says she did! And you will yet believe this, too!"

She went away then, but she had left me something to think about; and she had made me more than ever determined to solve the mystery of the inkstand and the bronze horse before going any further.

XIII: THE MYSTERIOUS MISSILES

I WENT in search of some of the servants and learned from them two important facts: first, that the library had not been swept since Monday night, although it had been dusted; second, that the maid who dusted it distinctly remembered seeing the bronze paper-weight in its usual place, and also asserted that the large inkstand was undisturbed, and that it did not need refilling.

With this new knowledge, or, rather, with this corroboration of previously attested statements, I went to the library, determined to discover something, if I had to remain there all day.

First I looked at the bronze horse as it stood in its place on the library table.

This table, which was really a flat-topped desk, was covered with books, writing implements and bric-a-brac of various kinds.

The bronze horse was one of a half dozen different paper-weights, and was a beautiful specimen of its kind. I picked it up and gazed at it intently, wishing it could speak for itself and solve the mystery. As I stared at it I suddenly noticed that one ear was broken off.

It was a very small bit that was missing; indeed, scarcely enough to impair the beauty or value of the ornament; but if that missing ear could be found on the library floor, it would be a pretty fair proof that Mildred had thrown the horse in the way she had described.

Eagerly I went in search of the maid whose duty it was to dust the library. In response to my questions she told me that the horse had belonged to Mr. Philip; that it was one of his favorite possessions; and that it was comparatively new. She had noticed the day before that the horse's ear was broken. She could not say positively, but she thought that if it had been broken before that, she would have known it.

Excited at the prospect of something like a real clue at last, I returned to the library and began a systematic search for the missing ear. Getting down on my hands and knees in the space between the desk and the window, I searched, inch by inch, the thick Persian rug and was finally rewarded by discovering the tiny piece of bronze that I was hunting for.

Comparing it with the other ear—indeed, fitting it to the very place from which it was broken—I saw there was no doubt that I had succeeded; and though I could not imagine how the horse had been replaced on the table, I could no longer doubt the truth of Mildred's assertion regarding it.

Carefully wrapping the broken ear in a bit of tissue paper, I put it away and devoted my attention to the inkstand.

The large and elaborate affair stood in the center of the table. The inkwell itself was of heavy cut glass, and was mounted on an ornate silver standard which was also a pen-rack.

The longer I looked at it the more I felt convinced that nobody could disturb the ponderous ornament and restore it again to its place in the way Mildred told of. For it held as much as a small cupful of jet black ink, and even though the Persian rug was of an intricate design in small figures, yet it was light enough in its general coloring to make ink spots perceptible.

Helpless in the face of this assurance, my eye wandered aimlessly over the articles on the desk, when toward the right-hand end and not far from the bronze horse I spied a second inkstand. It was heavy, but not so large as the other, and had no silver standard. I opened it and looked in, and found it to be nearly half-full of red ink.

I looked again at the rug. The predominating color was red in varying shades. Instantly the thought struck me that if Mildred had thrown that inkstand and if there had not been much ink in it, the drops on the carpet would be unobservable because of the similarity of color.

Without stopping to inquire how it could be restored intact to its place, I dropped again to my knees, and again searched for traces. The pattern of the rug being so complicated and mosaic-like, it was almost impossible to discover red spots other than those which belonged there; but at last, I thought I did find on a small white figure red blotches that were not of the Persian dye.

Almost trembling with excitement, I procured from a drawer in the desk a fresh white blotter.

Moistening this, I placed it on the doubtful red spots and gently pressed it. Then lifting it, I found that it showed dull red blurs which had every appearance of being red ink.

Reserving further experiments of this nature to be done in the presence of witnesses, I went in search of Mr. Hunt. He had not yet arrived, so I telephoned him to come as soon as he could. Meanwhile, I returned to the library to think over my discoveries.

I admitted to myself that they gave us no enlightenment whatever, but they had proved the truth of the only doubtful parts of Mildred's story, and left us therefore no excuse for not believing her entire statement.

Hunt soon arrived, and was more than pleased at what I had done.

"I knew you had ingenuity," he said, in his honest, generous way. "Now, I don't believe I should ever have thought of that blotting-paper scheme."

"But what good does it do?" said I.

"Granting that she did throw them, how did they get back to the table?"

"That is another part of the problem," said Hunt, "and one which we need not consider at this moment. First, I think, if you have any more of those clean white blotters, we'll find out the route traveled by that inkstand."

I found plenty of blotters in the drawer, and, proceeding with great care, we succeeded in getting a blotting-paper impression of many more red-ink spots.

We proved to Mr. Hunt's satisfaction, and to mine, that the inkstand had reached the floor about midway between the desk and the window, and that it had then rolled toward the couch, and had stopped just under the long upholstery fringe which decorated the edge of the couch, and which reached to the floor.

"That gives a ray of light!" exclaimed Hunt, triumphantly.

"What do you mean by that?" said I wondering, for I could see no indication of light.

"I can't tell you now," said Hunt, "for someone is coming. I think, Mr. King, it will be wiser to keep these discoveries quiet for the present. Indeed, it is imperative that we should do so."

And so, though I wanted to go at once, and tell Mrs. Whiting that I had proved her sister's statements true, as she had said I would, I restrained myself because of Hunt's advice.

It was Thursday morning when one of the servants told me that Mr. Hunt wanted to see me in the library. I went there at once, and found the detective in conversation with a pretty and very much flustered Swedish parlor-maid.

"This is Emily," said Hunt, in a quiet voice, "she has been telling me of something in which you will be interested. Emily, repeat your story to Mr. King."

The girl fingered her apron nervously as she stood before us, and spoke with embarrassment and hesitation.

"It was this way, yes. I have, the day after the,—the dying of Mr. Philip,—I have to dust in this room. I sweep not, but I do the dusting. And under a chair, yes, under that great soft chair with the fringes I,—I find the jewel,—yes. And I,—oh, it is that I cannot confess!"

The girl buried her face in her apron and seemed unable to go on.

"There, there, Emily," said Hunt, gently, "you kept the jewel and said nothing about it until now. But let that go; we will forgive your stealing the jewel,—now that you have confessed,—if you will tell truly everything you know about it. This is the jewel, King."

He placed in my hand a large topaz set as a seal. It was not a ring, but seemed to me to be a pendant of a watch fob.

"It's part of a fob," said Hunt, "and I want you to look at the design."

The design, deeply cut into the stone, was a crest, coat-of-arms and motto, that I realized at once belonged to the House of Clarendon. Without a doubt it was the property of our noble visitor.

"It's the Earl's," I said simply, as I handed it back to Hunt.

"Yes, of course. And now, Emily, tell Mr. King where you found it."

Reassured by the forgiveness of her theft, the maid showed us where she had found the seal, beneath a chair near the library window. Heavy fringe hung to the floor from the upholstery, and the seal, the girl explained, she had found just inside the fringe, on the rug.

"So," she said, "I have move the chair when I dust him, and I see the sparkle stone, -- yes! I pick him up, and wickedly I put him in my pocket! It is bad, yes; but I'm tempted, and I fall! but you for give? you say so!"

I took little interest in the maid's somewhat dramatic recital, for I was intent on learning just when she had found this thing. It seemed she had found it early Wednesday morning, before I myself had looked for clues, and had found the black spangles. Since she had dusted but not swept, she had not noticed the spangles; but the seal had naturally attracted her attention as being valuable, and she had dishonestly kept it.

"Hunt," I said, "there is one thing I can swear to, and that is --"

"Wait a moment," said Hunt, giving me a warning glance. "I think that is all, Emily; you may go now, and understand, you are forgiven for this theft, only on condition that you tell nobody a single word about the matter."

"Ah, that am I only too glad to do, yes! I do not want that any one should know my baseness! I thank you much, sir, for your goodness, and never, never will I tell."

She left the room and Hunt closed the door.

"It may not mean anything, after all," he said, "for Lord Clarence may have dropped that thing in the library at any time during the day, on Monday. It doesn't implicate him in any way, but I wanted you to hear the girl's story."

"You're wrong, Hunt, it does implicate our noble friend! As I began to say, I can swear that Lord Clarence was wearing that fob himself, at about nine o'clock Monday evening."

"Great goodness!" exclaimed Hunt; "do you really mean that? How do you know?"

"Because he showed it to me, especially. We were in Mr. Maxwell's study,—I remember the people were just beginning to arrive for the dance. We happened to be speaking of seals, and Lord Clarence showed us this one, as a specially fine example of gem engraving. So, my lord was in this room that evening!"

"But it might have been before the murder, King. He might have come in here, casually, as others did, before Philip and Miss Leslie were here."

"But he said at the inquest he wasn't in this room all the evening. And, you know, he didn't come up here when we rushed up. He stayed below, and looked after the guests. I thought that was a particularly clever thing for him to do. But now…"

"And also his lordship has about half an hour on the west veranda unaccounted for, just at the time of the murder. Don't you remember, he said he was smoking a cigarette, and a long gray motor whizzed past him,—and all that. It looks a little queer, King."

"It looks more than a little queer, Hunt. But I can't help thinking there's some commonplace explanation for it, after all."

"How can there be a commonplace explanation? The man had that seal on, you say, at nine o'clock. He says he was not in the library that evening at all. Next morning early, Emily finds the seal here! What's the explanation?"

"I don't know, I'm sure; but what I say is, let's put it right up to him. I know if anybody found evidence against me, I'd rather they'd come straight to me with it, than to go nosing around. And I think that Clarence Personage is a good deal of a man."

"You know I never did share your great admiration of him."

"It isn't a great admiration; but I think he's a right good sort. And I think the fairest way, is to take this seal to him, tell him where it was found, and give him a chance to speak up for himself."

"I'm not sure that's the best plan," said Hunt, doubtfully; "but you know him better than I do, so I'll agree."

Hunt put the seal in his pocket and we went downstairs in search of Clarendon.

It was now nearly noon, and Philip's funeral was to be held that afternoon at two. Even as we went through the hall, quiet-mannered men in black were unfolding chairs and placing them in rows.

The oppressive scent of massed flowers was everywhere, and it seemed incongruous and inappropriate to pursue our errand in this sorrowful atmosphere.

In the study we found Alexander Maxwell and Miss Miranda. The brother and sister were much together, and oftenest in the study, seeming to prefer to be alone there in their grief. Miss Maxwell looked up as we entered, but, as often happened, Mr. Maxwell did not hear us, and so did not turn his head. Not wanting to intrude, I said, quietly, "We're looking for Lord Clarendon. Do you know where he is?"

"He has gone," said Miss Maxwell.

"Lord Clarendon gone! where?" I cried, unintentionally raising my voice in my surprise; and then her brother turned and saw us.

"He has gone home," said Mr. Maxwell; "he remembered an important engagement that called him to the city, and after explaining to my sister and myself that he must go at once, he went, leaving his adieux for the rest of you."

XIV: IN PURSUIT OF THE EARL

HERE was a fine state of affairs, indeed! The Earl, whom we wanted so much to see, was gone; and it seemed to me, and I was sure Hunt felt the same, that his going was, in a way, suspicious.

"Why did he go so suddenly?" I asked.

"He had to," returned Miss Maxwell; "he didn't say definitely what his engagement was, but he said it was important."

"I have an idea," said Mr. Maxwell, "that he didn't care to stay for the funeral. You know how queer Englishmen are that way, and I dare say it got on his nerves."

"Nerves nothing!" I exclaimed; "that man is mixed up in the shooting of Philip, and now we've let him get away! Hunt, tell Mr. Maxwell the circumstances."

So the detective told the two interested listeners about the finding of the letter and the conclusions we must draw from it.

"You see," I said, "I know, and you do too, Mr. Maxwell, that the Earl was in this room wearing that seal at about nine o'clock Monday evening. Early next morning it was found in the library. The Earl denied having been in the library at all that night, and so, you must admit, an explanation is called for."

"But I can't think that the explanation would prove Lord Clarendon guilty of the crime,—or even accessory," said Mr. Maxwell, looking thoughtfully at the gem he held in his hand; "he had no quarrel with our boy."

"He greatly admired Miss Leslie," I said, knowing it to be the truth.

"But he had only known her a day or two," broke in Miss Miranda's gentle voice; "he couldn't possibly become so infatuated in that short time that he would commit a crime for her! And besides, he's a nobleman."

The good lady had always been deeply impressed by the glory of the Earl's title,—a truly American weakness; and she could think no ill of one who rightfully displayed a coronet. But to my mind the fact of his being a foreigner, and a titled one at that, rather argued against him; though I realized that my prejudice was quite as illogical as Miss Maxwell's.

"Aside from any possible motive," said Hunt, "we have to explain the discrepancy between the Earl's statement that he was not in the room and the finding of a piece of his personal property there. You returned the fob to him after looking at it, I suppose?"

"Certainly I did," said Mr. Maxwell, a little shortly; "but I cannot agree that the finding of it in the library implicates his lordship in our tragedy."

"What then would be your hypothesis, sir," said Hunt, "as to finding it in the library?"

"My hypothesis, Mr. Hunt, would be, that the maid, Emily, did not tell the truth, rather than that the Earl of Clarendon did not."

"I hadn't thought of that," I said; "to be sure, that girl might have made up the story, but I can't see why she should do so. She would have kept the jewel, but that Mr. Hunt in questioning her about her dusting of the library, surprised her into a confession. She is simple-minded and emotional, and her confession, I am sure, was entirely truthful."

"It may be," said Mr. Maxwell, coldly; "but I cannot think that logically you have any more reason to assume truthfulness on her part than on the part of the Earl."

"Emily might have found it somewhere else," suggested Miss Maxwell.

"Then why make up that story?" said Hunt.

"I don't know, I'm sure, unless to make a sensation. She's a queer girl and I've never understood her."

"I'm positive that she did not make up that story, dear Miss Maxwell," said I; "and I know if you had heard her, you would agree with me. But I am willing to admit that there may be and probably is some commonplace explanation; and whatever it may be, we must know it before we go any further. Do you know where the Earl has gone?"

"Yes," said Miss Maxwell, "he went to New York. I think he is staying at the Waldorf; at least, that's where he was just before he came to us."

"Then I'm going straight there to see him," I declared, "and I shall start at once."

Hunt looked his approval of this, but the other two did not.

"I don't think you'd better, King," said Mr. Maxwell, slowly; but Miss Maxwell grasped my arm impulsively, and said, "Oh, don't go, Peter! please don't go until after the funeral, anyway."

I couldn't resist her pathetic appeal, and I agreed not to go until after the funeral, but I insisted on my plan of going then.

"Did the Earl say good-by to Miss Leslie?" I asked Miss Maxwell, pausing, as I was about to leave the room.

"Oh, no," she answered; "Milly is very ill again. The excitement of that talk with you this morning threw her into a high fever and we are all very anxious about her. I told Lord Clarendon this, and it was after that, that he told me he was going."

"Because of it?" asked Hunt, suddenly.

"No, of course not. In fact he left a message for Milly in addition to his good-by, to the effect that she would be glad he had gone."

"What could he have meant by that, Miss Maxwell?"

"I don't know, unless he felt that his attentions to her had been unwelcome, and she would be glad to know he was gone."

"No man's attentions are unwelcome to Mildred Leslie," I said, "and I don't think that's what he meant at all. I tell you, Miss Maxwell, that man is mixed up in our trouble, and Milly Leslie knows it. Suppose for a moment that it was the Earl who shot Philip, wouldn't Philip exclaim, 'Oh, to think he should shoot me!' and wouldn't Milly, if she knew or suspected it, be glad to have the Earl go away?"

"Peter," said Mr. Maxwell, somewhat sternly, "your suggestion is monstrous! I should be angry at you, were it not that your idea is so absurd! You are carried away with your desire to detect somebody or something. Now, my boy, put this all out of your mind, at least for the present. This afternoon we shall give the last honors we can to our Philip; and after that it will be time to turn our attention to avenging the crime that took him from us."

Mr. Maxwell's manner was impressive, and I felt rebuked that I should have obtruded my theories and suspicions at this moment. I said as much, in an apologetic way, and then Hunt and I withdrew.

"You're dead right, Mr. King," said Hunt, after we had left the study; "it was his Noble Nibs that turned the trick! And I hope you will track him down at once. You can take that five o'clock train to New York, but, even so, he has hours the start of you. I wish the old people would let you go now."

"No, I can't offend those gentle souls by insisting on that. But I'll go up this afternoon, Hunt, and I'll find that man, unless he has really fled from justice."

I don't care to dwell upon the sad rites of that afternoon. It was hard to realize that we were gathered there to pay the last honors to Philip Maxwell. He had always been so alert and alive, so light-hearted and debonair, that it was difficult to think of him as dead. And the mystery of his death added a peculiar horror to it all.

But at last the ceremonies were over, and I was free to go away if I chose. I hesitated about discussing the matter again with the Maxwells, for I knew they would oppose my going to New York on such an errand. And though I might persuade them that it was my duty to do so, the argument would doubtless be a long one, and I might be late for the train I wanted to take.

So I asked Hunt to tell them that I had gone, and to say that I would soon return. I advised him, too, to tell them that it was the most straight forward thing to do. For, if the Earl could give a simple and rational explanation of the question of the seal, certainly no harm would be done. And if he could not, surely the matter must be looked into.

And so I found myself in the train, returning over the road that Miss Gardiner and I had traveled a few days before.

Naturally my thoughts strayed to her, for mysterious though she was in some ways, she had made a greater impression on my heart than ever woman had done before. I ascribed her strange ways to her strength of character, and her cold logic to her high order of intellect. If a thought crept in that she knew more than she had told about the mystery, I determinedly put it away from me.

It seemed to me everybody was acting mysteriously. Mildred Leslie was inexplicable. Her rapid transitions from gay thoughtlessness to feverish hysterics surely denoted guilty knowledge of some sort. Miss Lathrop was queer enough, too; but of course, she could know nothing about the crime, except what she had heard from us, or what Mildred had revealed in her delirium.

Irene was strange; Gilbert Crane had acted very strangely, and certainly Lord Clarence's behavior was astonishing.

However, I didn't really think the nobleman had done the shooting; but I did think that he knew something about it that he preferred not to tell, and so had put himself beyond questioning.

Before ten o'clock I was at the Waldorf, inquiring for the Earl, only to be informed that he was out. He had left no word of his whereabouts at the office, but as he still retained his rooms I decided to wait for him. The clerk told me that he had come to the hotel that afternoon about four, and later had gone out, apparently to dinner.

But though I waited until midnight, his lordship did not appear.

Again I conferred with the clerk, telling him I was especially anxious to see the Earl of Clarendon. He was not greatly disturbed over my anxiety, but was willing to do what he could, and suggested that I interview his lordship's man-servant. This was a truly brilliant idea, and I directed that the valet be sent for. But the response was, that Lord Clarendon's man,—by name, Hoskins,— was not at present in the hotel.

"Did he go away with the Earl?" I inquired, but this, nobody seemed to know.

The Earl had left at about six o'clock, and as it was now twelve, all the porters and bell-boys had shifted, and no one at present on duty could give me the information I wanted. Nonplussed, I told the clerk that I would go to his lordship's rooms and wait for him there; for secretly I had a hope that I might learn something from an examination of his apartments. But permission to do this was refused me; and then, though I didn't want to hint my suspicions openly, I gave the clerk to understand, that it was in the character of a detective that I wished to see the Earl's rooms. Whereupon the clerk nonchalantly asked to see my badge. As I had none, not being a real detective at all, he seemed to consider the interview closed; and realizing I could do nothing more that night, I asked for a room and went to bed.

I rose the next morning with a firm determination to find the Earl. Surely such a personage could not drop out of civilization without leaving a trace; and he had kept his apartments at the hotel, so he evidently intended to return. But to sit and wait for him was not my plan. I went downstairs and inquired for him at the desk, but, as I had anticipated, I received no information whatever, except that he was not at present in the hotel. I thought it over, as I ate breakfast on the sunny side of the dining-room, and at last a brilliant idea came to me. I was determined to do real detective work in this matter; something more than merely making inquiries of a secretive clerk.

My brilliant plan might not prove successful, but after breakfast I put it at once to the test. Going up in the elevator, I stepped off at the fourth floor where the Earl's rooms were, instead of going on to my own on the ninth floor. I knew the Earl's apartment was numbered four ninety-two. I managed to get to its door unobserved, and then stood there, hesitating, as if just leaving the room.

I stood thus for some time, but my patience was finally rewarded by seeing a chamber-maid coming along the hall.

"Ah! there you are," I said, stepping briskly forward; "Now, look here, my good woman, I find that I put an important paper in my waste-basket by mistake. When did you empty the baskets?"

"Last evening, sir," she said, looking a little alarmed. "It should have been done earlier, sir, but I got behind-hand with my work, and -- "

"Never mind; show me the place where the papers were thrown. They're not burned yet, are they?"

She hesitated, but a powerful argument that was green and crisp induced further information.

"They're in a sack, in my broom-closet, sir. But I'd be fined if it were known..."

"It sha'n't be known, I promise you. There's no one about; show me where they are. I want to see the contents of the basket that was in four ninety-two."

"They're all together, sir, but that room is near the top. Step in here, please."

I followed the woman into her broom-closet, which proved to be a small but fairly well lighted room. She took up a large sack and tossed part of its contents out on the floor.

"Will you search, yourself, sir? I must be at my work."

"Yes, my good woman, go along. I'll find what I want, and no one will be the wiser."

She went away and I began the well-nigh hopeless task of looking over the waste paper. But after a time I began to find torn envelopes addressed to the Earl of Clarendon, and these I examined with interest. There were many invitations, advertisements and personal letters, but none seemed to bear on his present absence until I struck a note from one Mrs. Ogilby Pauncefote. This was an invitation to her country house on Long Island, at Osprey-by the-Sea. The lady asked Lord Clarendon to come the afternoon before, and as I found also a time table with the railroad station checked, I couldn't help thinking that his lordship had accepted her invitation.

At any rate I found nothing else to give me any idea of where the nobleman had gone, and I resolved to go to this place, and if he were not there, perhaps to learn from Mrs. Pauncefote where he might be. Making use of the discarded time-table, I started at once toward my destination.

But taking the first available train, it was eleven o'clock when I reached the ornate mansion at Osprey-by-the-Sea.

The footman who answered my ring informed me that Mrs. Pauncefote was not at home.

"Is the Earl of Clarendon here?" I inquired.

"No sir; he has been here all night, but he went with the party in the yacht."

"Ah, in the yacht," I said, endeavoring to assume an air of intimacy with the family. "What time did they start?"

"At ten o'clock, sir."

I looked at my watch. "Then they've been gone about an hour," I observed.

"And where are they headed for?"

"Montauk Point, sir."

"Montauk Point! why they can't reach that till late this afternoon."

"No, sir; they will lunch on board the yacht, and reach the point by dinner-time,—or I should say, perhaps at tea-time, about four o'clock, sir."

He was an amiable sort of man, and as he probably thought me a friend of the family, he was giving me all the information he could.

"H'm," I said; "I wonder how I could catch up to them. Could I get a motor-boat anywhere?"

"I don't think you could overtake the *Butterfly* that way, sir. She's a clipper. But of course you could take the train."

This seemed to be the only thing to do, and I turned away and went back to the railway station. If I had only risen earlier and started sooner, I could have found my

Lord Clarence with no trouble at all. But there was nothing for it but to keep on to Montauk Point. I had time before my train went, to send a telegram to Hunt, in which I told him that I was making progress and was on the trail of the Earl.

XV: THE EARL'S STORY

I GREW very impatient during the long ride. I had no appetite for luncheon, and occupied myself with wondering whether I were not on a wild goose chase. The yacht, *Butterfly*, might change her course and I might wait in vain on the eastern end of Long Island. But surely I was following a direct clue. Surely we wanted the Earl and I was taking the only way to find him. I reached Montauk Point and went at once to the dock where the Pauncefotes' steam-yacht might be expected to arrive. She was not in, so I waited with such patience as I could command and at last she came—a beautiful craft which seemed to be the last word in elaborate luxury.

As the party came ashore I looked in vain for my elusive nobleman, but he was certainly not with them. There were a dozen or more fashionable people, and deciding that the gray-haired, important looking lady was the hostess, I went up to her and introduced myself. With polite apologies for intruding, I inquired for the Earl of Clarendon.

Mrs. Pauncefote was exceedingly affable.

"Why, Mr. King," she said, "we did have Lord Clarence with us, but he had an engagement in New York that made it necessary for him to be there at five o'clock. So we put him off at Wading River and he took the train back to town. We hated awfully to do it, and we really came near kidnapping him and bringing him along with us; but he insisted so that we had to let him go, though it broke our hearts! didn't it, Gerry?"

Miss Geraldine Pauncefote, the daughter of the important lady, agreed that they were indeed desolate at losing the Earl, and she even suggested that I should take his place in their merry party.

"I should only be too glad to do so," I replied, glancing regretfully at the pretty girl, but it is imperative that I find the Earl as soon as possible. Can you tell me if he is going directly to his hotel?"

"I don't know, really," returned Miss Pauncefote; "I was so annoyed at him for deserting us that I wouldn't speak to him when he went away."

"He must indeed have had an important engagement to go in those circumstances," I said, smiling at her; "and I must go away I fear with a similar abruptness. But you'll speak to me, won't you?"

"Yes," she said gaily, "if you'll promise to come with us some other time. We go sailing nearly every day."

"I shall only be too glad to do so. By the way, Miss Pauncefote, may I ask you if Lord Clarence seemed anxious or troubled in any way?"

"Not that exactly," she said, thoughtfully, "but he was quiet and rather sad. He told me that a friend of his had just died, but he gave us no particulars. However, I think that was the real reason he left our merry-making, and not because of an engagement in town."

"And it was most considerate of him," said Mrs. Pauncefote; "for I'm sure there was no reason why my house party should have its pleasure spoiled by the death of somebody we didn't know. And of course, if the Earl felt sad, it was far better for him to go away than to remain, and act gloomy."

This seemed a little heartless, and yet I realized that a hostess does not like an unnecessary cloud to mar the happiness of her party. With a few more words of leave-taking, I went back to the railway station.

I was getting a little tired of railroad travel, but I had no choice save to follow the developments of my case, so I accepted it with as good a grace as possible, and seven o'clock found me back at the Waldorf, once more endeavoring to extract information from the taciturn clerk. Again he disclaimed all knowledge of the Earl or his movements, and with a feeling of utter disappointment, I stood around in the crowded lobby.

I was uncertain just what I should do next, when a cordial voice said, "Well, Mr. King, and how do you do?"

I looked up startled, to see Lord Clarence, himself, holding out his hand. In my gratitude at finding him, I grasped it and shook it warmly, but I did not tell him that I had just traveled the length of Long Island in search of him.

"Have you dined?" he asked; "no? Then dine with me, won't you? I assure you, I'd be glad of your company. Do you know, Mr. King, I can't shake off the horror of that Maxwell affair. I went off with a yachting party, by way of diversion, but it jarred too terribly, and I left the yacht somewhat abruptly, and came back to New York. I've never been through such an experience before, and that death of young Maxwell was an awful thing. Awful!"

I accepted the Earl's invitation and went with him to the dining-room, my mind in a complete chaos. If the Earl were in any way implicated in the mystery, he certainly was putting up a magnificent bluff. And if he were entirely innocent, as he seemed, then I wanted to talk matters over with him.

It was difficult to accuse him, or even to imply his possible connection with the tragedy, in the face of his straightforward and earnest sympathy.

"You stayed for the funeral, I suppose," he observed, after the first course had been served to us; "I couldn't do it. The whole affair got awfully on my nerves. What is your theory of the crime, if I may ask?"

Here was an opening, but I countered. "I'm rather at sea, Lord Clarence," I returned, "what do you think about it all? Often an outsider can get a better perspective than those more closely associated with the occurrence."

The Earl sipped his soup, thoughtfully. "I hesitate to say what I think," he said, slowly, "for I have so little on which to base any opinion. But do you mean to tell me that nothing has been accomplished by the police or the detectives?"

"It isn't really in the hands of the police," I said, a little apologetically; "You see Mr. Maxwell thinks Mr. Hunt can ferret out the truth, and I am trying to help him."

The Earl looked up at me with a flash of amusement in his eyes. "And you're helping him," he said, "by trailing me?"

I was chagrined and not a little embarrassed.

Surely a guilty man could not show that expression of indulgent amusement. Surely no one even indirectly associated with the crime, could wear such an aspect of serious concern and honest inquiry.

I concluded that frankness would be the best plan for me.

"I did come in search of you, Lord Clarendon," I said; "for I wanted to ask your explanation of a certain bit of evidence. And as I think you would prefer it, I will put the matter to you without preamble."

"I should certainly prefer direct accusation to beating about the bush."

"It isn't accusation," I responded, "and it's simply this. This seal, which is doubtless one of your belongings, was found on the floor of the library where Philip Maxwell was shot. It was found there the morning after the murder; and if you remember, you were wearing it, and in fact showing it to us, in Mr. Maxwell's study, on Monday evening before the tragedy."

I laid the seal on the table before him, and the Earl looked at it thoughtfully.

"It certainly looks like a case against me, Mr. King; and I cannot blame you or the detective, Hunt, for thinking that it implicates me very seriously in the crime. Indeed, I think that our Scotland Yard men would think it a fairly strong piece of evidence. Now, Mr. King, I take it you don't accuse me of the murder. Or, do you?"

"Certainly not," I replied; "But I ask you to remember, Lord Clarence, that you stated at the inquest that you had not been in the library that evening at all. So I merely ask you how it came about that this jewel was found there?"

"But, Mr. King, since you don't suspect me of the murder, what is it of which you do accuse me? Complicity or concealed knowledge?"

"Not necessarily complicity, but possibly concealed knowledge. But understand, I do not accuse you; I merely ask the explanation, hoping, and indeed, feeling fairly sure that you can make it."

"That's just the trouble, Mr. King; I can't give you an explanation."

"What, you mean you don't know how the seal came to be there?"

"I don't say that; but I say I cannot give you the explanation."

"Then you practically confess that you are concealing knowledge important for us to know. I think, Lord Clarence, we shall have to insist on that explanation."

"By what authority, Mr. King?"

"In the interests of right and justice."

"That is a strong argument," and the Earl looked thoughtful. "Indeed, I'm not sure but that it is my duty to tell you all I know. Of course, Mr. King, you must know why I hesitate."

"I don't," I returned, flatly.

"Well, of course you must know that I didn't kill Philip Maxwell, and that I had no interest in having him killed. Nor do I want to express any opinion, that may be wrong or unfounded, and thereby cast suspicion toward one who may be,— who must be entirely innocent."

"Meaning whom?" I asked, breathlessly.

"That's just what I hesitate to say. As you well know, a slight bit of ocular evidence goes so far, and is so difficult to suppress, though it may mean nothing."

"Lord Clarence," I said, seriously, "if you will tell me what you know, I will promise that the secret shall be carefully guarded, and put to no use whatever, unless we can feel sure that it will positively lead to the discovery of the criminal."

"Then I will tell you about this seal. As you remember, I was showing it to Mr. Alexander Maxwell in his study, and you were present. That was just before the guests arrived for the dance. Very shortly after, I danced with Miss Leslie. She told me, laughing, that a watch fob was entirely incorrect with evening clothes, and in obedience to her pretty, willful dictate, I took the fob off my watch. She admired this seal, being especially interested in the crest, and I detached it from the rest of the fob and gave it to her."

"As an out and out gift?"

"Yes; I was greatly attracted by Miss Leslie, in fact I quite lost my head over her. She attached the seal to a long neck-chain she was wearing, and seemed childishly delighted with it. She is a strange little person, isn't she?"

"She is. And since you were not in the library that night, it is to be supposed then, that she lost this seal from her chain while she was there with Philip."

"Or perhaps she purposely detached it to throw at the intruder. It is a heavy missile, you know, and the little lady seemed inclined to throw anything she could lay her hands on."

I pondered a few moments on this. The fact that the seal was found under the chair, near the window, lent a probability to the Earl's assumption.

"But why didn't she mention this, when she told her story?" I said.

"Ah, who can understand a woman? Miss Leslie declared she threw things which she couldn't possibly have thrown, and then fails to tell of a missile she could and probably did throw."

"But you don't think Mildred Leslie in any way guilty?" I exclaimed; "and besides, she did throw that horse and inkstand." And then I detailed to the Earl how we had found the red ink stains, and the broken ear of the horse.

He looked utterly astounded. "But," he said, "how could those things get back on the table again?"

"That is the mystery. To me it simply proves that someone else was in that room later who had a reason for wanting those things restored to their places."

"And you thought I did it, and left my seal by mistake," said the Earl, smiling a little; "but Mr. King, to return to your former question, I do not think Miss Leslie guilty of any part in the shooting, but I do think she knows very well who the intruder was."

"You do!" I exclaimed; "why I had never thought of that! Why do you think so?"

"Since you have promised to keep these matters confidential, at your discretion, I will tell you of the motor-car that I saw while I was on the lower veranda. That car, with four men in it, was coming in when I saw it, not going out. That would be about ten minutes after ten. I've been thinking that out. Then as you know, I returned to the dancing-room, of course, giving no further thought then to the car, and at half-past ten Mr. Crane announced to us the news of the tragedy. My theory is, Mr. King, that the murderer came in that car, shot young Maxwell and went away again. I think the whole affair was premeditated and carefully planned by the murderer. And I think, moreover, that Miss Leslie recognized the intruder in spite of his disguise, and is withholding and confusing her evidence through a desire to shield him."

I thought it over. It was all a new theory to me, and though it might not be the true one, it called for investigation. "When you were on the lower veranda, you were on the library side of the house?" I went on.

"Yes; and that car came in swiftly and passed me."

"Going around toward the back of the house?"

"Yes; there is a little staircase that runs from the lower veranda to the upper one."

"Not on the library side?"

"No, on the other side. But of course a man running up that staircase, could easily reach the library window by going around the house on the upper veranda, or by going through the house."

"If he were not intercepted. But a man in full automobile togs could hardly go around or through, unnoticed."

"I'm not explaining the details, I'm only stating a possible theory. And I think there was no one on the upper veranda at that time. We were all in the dancing-room or somewhere on the lower floor."

"Miss Gardiner was up there," I said, thoughtlessly; "I left her there as I came downstairs."

"Then if my theory is the true one, and if the man did go round the verandas and appear at the library windows in accordance with Miss Leslie's story, Miss Gardiner must have seen him."

I quickly dropped the subject of Irene Gardiner, as I did not wish her even tacitly involved in this matter. "Frankly, you do not believe Miss Leslie's story, then?" I said.

"Frankly, I do not," replied the Earl; "and that is the reason I left Maxwell Chimneys when I did. I learned that Miss Leslie had become much worse, and was growing feverish and hysterical, and I honestly thought that my departure would help her to feel more secure and less harassed. I feared it might come about that I should have to tell of this motor-car, and that it would worry or annoy Miss Leslie to think that I had seen it. And it might be the means of disclosing something that she didn't wish to have known. I felt sure she had done something with my seal, because I asked her sister the next day if it were on her chain when she was carried to her room, and Mrs. Whiting told me it was not. Altogether, Mr. King, though perhaps my reasons were not entirely logical, they were sufficiently strong to make me want to leave Maxwell Chimneys."

"To be honest, you had lost your deep interest in Miss Leslie."

"To be honest, I had. She is most attractive, an unusual type to me, and positively fascinating. But I cannot think her entirely truthful; and at any rate, I preferred to come away, lest my presence should disturb her or make harder for her the sorrow she has to bear and the part she has to endure in the tragedy. That is my story, Mr. King, and I assure you that I have no direct suspicion of anybody; and moreover, that I came away myself merely out of consideration for Miss Leslie. I trust you're convinced of my own honesty and truthfulness?"

"I am, indeed," I said, heartily; "I should apologize to you for having come to New York to find you, if I had unjustly suspected you. But I did not do that, Lord Clarendon. We found your seal in suspicious circumstances, and I deemed it only fair to us and to you to give you an opportunity to explain it. You have done so, to my entire satisfaction, and I thank you. Shall I give you back your property, or do you consider that it belongs to Miss Leslie?"

"As I really presented it to her, I don't like to take it back. Suppose you take it to her, Mr. King, and if she doesn't wish to keep it, send it to me again. But if she does, by all means let her have it."

"One thing more, Lord Clarence; since you have put thought on this matter, what in your opinion could be the motive of the man in the car for committing such a crime?"

"Of that I can form no theory. Of course he must have had some grudge against Philip Maxwell, or he must have been a jealous suitor of Miss Leslie's. But I think, Mr. King, your next move should be to discover the identity of that car and its occupants."

"We certainly shall try to do so, Lord Clarence, though I fear we have let too much time pass. It is not easy to trace a car after so many days, and with no knowledge whatever of the men in it."

"No, it will not be easy," said the Earl, "but I am sure that if she would do so, Miss Leslie could give you the information you want. Another thing, Mr. King, since you're kind enough to listen to my suggestions, I think Miss Lathrop, the nurse, knows more than she has told."

"But how can she? You remember she didn't come to the house at all, until after the crime had been committed."

"No; but she has had opportunity to hear Miss Leslie's talk in her delirium. Without a doubt, the girl told many things which the nurse, with her extreme idea of professional ethics, is not willing to reveal. This is merely a suggestion, Mr. King, but if you can find out anything from that nurse, I think it will prove of importance."

Truly the Englishman gave me food for thought. At his request, we dismissed the subject from our dinner conversation; but I had carefully laid up in my memory all he had said, and resolved to act upon it later.

XVI: THE GRAY MOTOR-CAR

SATURDAY morning I went back to Maxwell Chimneys. Though I had done very little, if anything, toward a definite solution of the mystery, yet I had eliminated the Earl as a possible factor in the case, and surely that was something.

At the luncheon table I told about it, but only in a general way, and without going into details. After luncheon, however, Mr. Hunt arrived, and we had a conference in Mr. Maxwell's study. The guests of the house were all present except Miss Leslie and her nurse.

Mr. Maxwell led the discussion. "I've been thinking it over, Peter," he said, "while you were away, and I've pretty much come to the conclusion that we may as well give up our efforts to find the man who shot Philip. I was sure, before you went away, that the Earl of Clarendon had no hand in it, and I cannot think that we shall ever learn who was in the mysterious motor-car that Lord Clarence saw that night. And should we find the car, I dare say it would turn out to be some tradesman or other equally innocent person. I, myself, am too old to take an active part in any search. Both my sister and I have a prejudice against calling in the police or applying to the detective bureau. And so, it seems to me, that my sister and I would rather bear our grief undisturbed by harrowing publicity."

"I quite appreciate your ideas, Mr. Maxwell," said Tom Whiting, respectfully; "but I want to call to your attention the fact that my wife's sister is, in a way, under a suspicion of knowing who that intruder was, and of being willing to shield him. Now we can't stand for this! Edith and I have agreed that, unless you positively forbid it, we must at least make an attempt to discover who that man was. You see, the Earl of Clarendon thinks that the man in that motor-car came up on the veranda, and shot Philip through the library window. Moreover, he distinctly implies that Milly knows who the man is, and will not tell; and that he, the Earl, went away lest his knowledge of the car and its occupants should annoy or disturb Milly. Now this is all utter poppycock! Milly isn't shielding any man. She doesn't know who that intruder was,—although Philip did. Now, I propose to track that car, and that man, whether he is the criminal or not!"

"Go ahead, Mr. Whiting, if you like," said Hunt; "but you'll find yourself on a wild goose chase. To my mind, that precious Earl is not so innocent as he makes out! He pulled the wool over Mr. King's eyes, but he doesn't fool me. And trying to hide behind a woman's skirts. is just what I should expect from a British rascal of his stamp!"

"Oh, Mr. Hunt," said Miss Miranda, looking greatly pained; "please don't talk like that about one of my guests! Why, he scarcely knew Philip, and he had no reason for wishing him ill."

"He was in love with a girl that Philip was as good as engaged to," said Hunt, bluntly; "that's enough motive for his state of mind toward Philip."

"There it is," said Mr. Maxwell, "as soon as you detectives begin to suspect anybody you let your imagination run away with you. Granting the Earl of Clarendon was attracted by Miss Leslie, it doesn't follow that he would shoot another man who happened to be in love with her, also! No, the Earl is entirely innocent, and the criminal is as far removed from our knowledge or suspicion as he ever was."

"But he won't be," said Tom Whiting, "if I can once catch that motor-car! Can't you all see clearly how a man from that car could have run up that little back staircase, around the veranda, and back again after committing the crime in a very short space of time? Of course he must have been an enemy of Philip's, and of course he must have had his plans carefully laid. But a murderer always lays his plans carefully. He doesn't go around on a casual chance!"

"But if your theory is the right one," observed Hunt, "Miss Gardiner must have seen that man, for she was on the upper veranda at the time of the crime."

"Did you see anybody, Irene?" said Edith Whiting, but she said it perfunctorily, for she knew if Miss Gardiner had seen a stranger she would have told of it before this.

"No, of course not," said Irene; "Do you suppose if I had seen Philip Maxwell's murderer I shouldn't have said so long ago? I think, with Mr. Maxwell, that he can never be found; and I see no use in keeping up a search for that motor-car. I doubt if the Earl saw one anyway."

"Good gracious!" exclaimed Tom Whiting, "why is it that everybody doubts the Earl's veracity? Surely he would have no reason for making up that story of the motor-car! Certainly he saw it; and I, for one, am determined to find out about it!"

"Yes, do," said Mrs. Whiting; "for I can never rest happy until Mildred is entirely cleared from any suspicious thought. The poor child has enough to bear, without the added insult of an unjust suspicion."

"What does she say about the Earl's seal?" I asked.

"We haven't asked her yet," returned Mrs. Whiting. "Nurse Lathrop is to ask her as soon as Milly wakens from her nap."

"Perhaps Milly has wakened already," said Miss Maxwell, and acting on that suggestion, Edith went upstairs to see.

In a few moments the nurse came down, leaving Edith with the patient. The white, stiffly-starched personage came into the room with her usual air of professional importance, and taking a chair, folded her hands primly, awaiting questions.

Miss Maxwell spoke gently: "Have you asked Milly, Miss Lathrop, about the seal the Earl gave her?"

"Yes, I have, Miss Maxwell."

"And what did she say?" went on the gentle voice, which was such a contrast to the nurse's cold, metallic tones.

"She said that the Earl gave it to her."

"Did she say she left it in the library? Tell us all she said, can't you?" This was from Mr. Maxwell, who was clearly impatient at the aggravating slowness of Miss Lathrop's story, and indeed he voiced what we all felt.

The nurse rolled her hard eyes slowly toward him. "I would rather be questioned," she said. "I might say more than would be discreet."

"Oh, bother discretion!" exclaimed Tom Whiting, whose nerves were on edge; "the Seal business doesn't amount to anything, anyway; and you're purposely trying to make it seem important."

"Why should I do that?" and Miss Lathrop smoothed her immaculate apron in a most exasperating manner.

"I don't know why you should, and I don't care," went on Whiting. "Here *I'll* question you. After Milly said the Earl gave her the seal, what did you ask her next?"

"I asked her what she did with it?"

"And what did she say?"

"She said she fastened it on her neck-chain."

"And after that?"

"She said she pulled it off her chain and threw it at the man."

"What man?"

"The man that shot Mr. Maxwell."

"Oh, she did, did she? That's just what I supposed. Did she throw it before she threw the horse or after?"

"I don't know, Mr. Whiting."

"And it doesn't make a scrap of difference anyhow! Mr. Maxwell, there's the whole seal story. The Earl gave it to Milly, and she wore it on a chain. With the impulse, which she has already described, and which is a very natural feminine instinct, to throw something at the intruder, she grabbed that heavy jewel from her chain and threw it. She probably didn't hit him, but whether she did or not, the seal fell under the edge of the chair, and was found next morning by Emily. This in no way implicates his lordship, and you can readily see that he went away, lest he should seem to know anything that might react against Milly, in an ultra-suspicious mind! Now, then, the Earl is out of the question, once for all, to my mind, and the only suspicion we have left, tends toward that motor-car, which must have brought here the man who shot both Philip and my sister. Even though you, Mr. Maxwell, do not wish to trace this man, I hold that I have a right to do so; for the fact that he did not kill Milly, in no way excuses his intent and effort to do so!"

"Do not misunderstand me, Mr. Whiting," said Mr. Maxwell; "as I said, I am unable myself to work actively in the matter. But you must surely know that I'm entirely in sympathy with your feeling, and that I wish as much as you do, to bring the villain to an accounting. If you will instigate and conduct the Search, I will defray any expenses incurred, and thus, in a way, do my share."

"All right, Mr. Maxwell," said Whiting, with enthusiasm.

"I only wanted your sanction to go ahead with my plans, King, I hope you will help me. Mr. Hunt, may I also count on you?"

"Of course," said Hunt, "but I tell you frankly, Mr. Whiting, that I cannot believe, as the rest of you do, in the entire innocence of that English Earl!"

"And I want to say," said Irene Gardiner, "that while I cannot share Mr. Hunt's actual suspicion of the Earl, I do think we ought to verify his story by some evidence other than his own."

"That's just what we're going to do, Irene," said Tom Whiting; "if we spot that car and nail the man we want, that's going to prove the Earl a real detective, and worthy of his own Scotland Yard!"

To my surprise, Miss Gardiner turned white, and trembled as if beneath a blow. Even as I watched her, I saw also that Miss Lathrop was watching her, stealthily but closely.

Irene endeavored to speak further, but was unable to do so. Her quivering lips would utter no word, and as we looked at her in amazement, unable to guess what had so stirred her, Nurse Lathrop arose and taking Irene's arm, led her from the room.

"Whatever's the matter with Irene?" exclaimed Mr. Whiting. "Anybody would think she was shielding the man in the motor-car, instead of Milly! I tell you the whole thing hinges on that man, and I'm going to find him!"

"Will it,—will it be necessary to consult the police?" said Miss Maxwell, timidly, a little alarmed at Whiting's emphatic manner.

"Certainly not," said Mr. Maxwell. "Mr. Whiting's determination, and the skilled assistance of Mr. Hunt and Mr. King, can track that car quicker than all the police in the county. Go on, my boys, and may success go with you! But I will leave all questions of method and procedure to your judgment. I'm quite sure I could not help you; and if you'll excuse me, I would rather not take part in your planning."

I felt sure that this decision of Mr. Maxwell's was largely induced by his recognition of his sister's wishes. She was shrinkingly averse to having herself or her brother drawn into the actual investigation of the crime, and I think her gentle heart would have preferred that the criminal go unpunished, rather than take part in or even have cognizance of the sordid details of the search.

And so I went with Tom Whiting and Mr. Hunt to the library to discuss what we should do first.

The memory of what had happened there made it a ghastly place to converse in, but the fact that it was the scene of the crime, seemed to stir Whiting's mind to even a more intense determination to succeed in his quest.

"I propose," he said, "that we three canvass the neighborhood, and see if we can find anyone who saw that car Monday night."

"It may be a car belonging in the neighborhood," I suggested.

"Then we must find that out. At any rate this idea will do for a start."

We agreed to this, and after some further confab, in which Tom was the main spokesman, and Hunt took a very uninterested part, we set out on our preliminary search. Later on Whiting and I returned to Maxwell Chimneys, and found there a note from Hunt, saying that he had discovered nothing of consequence.

"Let's leave him out of it," said Whiting to me; "he's no sort of a detective, anyway, unless he's working on his own individual theory. What did you find out, King?"

As we mutually discovered, we had found out considerable. Sifted out and checked up, the evidence seemed to be, that the car described by the Earl was neither fiction nor imagination.

Mr. Plattner, the neighbor on the right,—though the country houses sat some distance apart,—had seen that car come from the village of Hamilton at about ten o'clock on Monday night. He had chanced to notice it because of its great speed, and he described it as a long gray car with several men in it.

Mr. Allen, the neighbor on the other side, had seen the car pass his house, going very fast, at some time after ten. His description was the same, and we couldn't doubt the identity of the car seen by the Earl and by these two neighbors. This made it pretty positive that a fast car had come up from the village at ten, had 'turned in and stopped at the Maxwells', and had gone on along the main road by or before half-past ten. The definiteness of this seemed to Whiting to be a long step toward our goal, and my half-formed doubts had no weight with him.

"But the man in the car couldn't have gone up on the veranda by that little outside staircase, without Miss Gardiner seeing him," I said.

"Don't you be too sure that Irene didn't see him," said Whiting; "that girl knows a whole lot more than Mildred about things, but there's no earthly use in trying to get anything out of her. Irene Gardiner is a sphinx and a sibyl and a siren and all such things, but as a witness she's absolutely worthless! She doesn't want to tell anything, and wouldn't tell it if she did! But she knows! O Lord, yes, that girl knows a lot!"

"Not guilty knowledge!" I cried.

"Depends on what you mean by guilty. She didn't shoot Philip, of course, but she knows a thing or two about who did."

I made no reply to this, for I was beginning to realize that I could not speak restrainedly when I tried to defend Irene.

So Whiting went on.

"Now let's go down to the village and see if that car didn't stop at the inn before coming up toward Mr. Plattner's. It would be a most natural thing to do."

So to the inn we went, taking for the purpose a little runabout from the Maxwell garage. The ample-faced inn-keeper listened to our questions and then said thoughtfully:

"Yep, I do seem to remember that there car. It stopped here along about half-past nine or a little later on Monday night. But I never once thought of connecting that up with the Maxwell murder! Land! do you think them men did it?"

"Did the men come in? How long did they stay?" said Whiting, impatiently.

"No, they didn't come in; they didn't hardly stop, as you might say. They jus' whizzed up here, stopped a minute, and asked me where the Maxwell place was."

"They did!" we cried, in amazed duet.

"Yes sir, they did! and of course I told 'em, and never thought of it again. Good land! so they wuz the murderers, was they?"

"We don't know," said Tom, "but we're going to find out, and we want you to help us all you can. Can you describe the car?"

"Well, of course, I'm mighty used to cars, as cars go,—but I couldn't just say the make of that one. It was long, extra-long, I should say,—and gray,—darkish gray. It was a touring car, and there were four young fellows in it beside the chauffeur. Now, that's jus' about all I know about it."

"Do you know the number?"

"Well, I didn't look at it purposely, but I most always glance at a number on general principles. But all I can tell you is, that the first two figures were sixes. The other three I couldn't swear to, though I'm 'most sure one of them was a four. Of course I only caught a glimpse of it, as they swung away, but I'd know that car again anywhere!"

"Well! we may want you to identify it, if we can find it anywhere. What were the men like?"

"I didn't notice them much. It was the chap that sat by the driver that asked me where the Maxwells lived. He was a big man, one of the biggest I ever saw, and with a big, deep voice and an off-hand way,—kind of like a Westerner. The whole crowd was off-hand; kind of laughin' and carryin' on, but I didn't pay much attention to 'em. If I'd a thought anything about it, I'd a thought they was some friends of the Maxwells, but I didn't even think that. If you hadn't brought it up, I'd never have thought of that car again! How are you going to find it?"

"That's just what I don't know," said Whiting, gloomily; "you see, King, we've lost so much time. The trails are all cold, the clues all destroyed, and I confess I don't know which way to look."

The inn-keeper looked on in sympathetic silence, his bland face devoid of any idea or suggestion. But I had an inspiration. "There's one thing, Whiting," I said; "if those men left the Maxwells' as late as half-past ten, they must have gone somewhere to spend the night. Of course, they would want to get pretty well away, but I doubt if they'd travel all night. Now, let's telephone to the most likely places, and see if they know anything about them."

"Now, that's a smart idea," commented Schwartz, the inn-keeper. "I can give you a list or a map of all the hotels and inns in this part of New jersey."

"It's a pretty slim chance," said Whiting, but his face showed a gleam of hope.

"We've got to take slim chances," said I, "if we take any."

We called up a score of places on the telephone, and spent two good hours doing it. But at one of them we spotted our quarry. About midnight that gray motor-car had put up at a small hotel in Millville, a town some thirty miles away. The hotel man described the car and the party, and said that the man who registered was not the big Westerner, but one of the others, and who signed James Mordaunt and party.

We asked no further information over the wire, but determined to go to Millville early the next morning and learn what he could. Then, if we could trace our men, to go on wherever we might be led.

XVII: BIG JACK JUDSON

WE went back to the house rather elated with our success; but when we told the others what we proposed to do, our plan did not meet with entire approval.

The Maxwells thought it a hopeless quest.

Edith Whiting said it could not possibly lead to anything worthwhile; and as for Hunt, he openly ridiculed the whole thing.

Miss Gardiner, too, endeavored to dissuade us.

"Why, Mr. King," she said, "it's utterly absurd to think you can find that car or those people after nearly a week has passed!"

"But we can at least try, Miss Gardiner," I said, wondering at her persistence.

"But what's the use, when you know you can't catch them?"

"What's the use of any endeavor? and there's always a chance that it may succeed."

"Well, then, may I go with you?"

"Why certainly," I replied; "so far as I'm concerned, I should be delighted to have you. Perhaps Mrs. Whiting will go, too."

We spent most of the evening in grave discussion. There was an undercurrent of disturbance that I could not understand. At one moment we would seem to be all working harmoniously in the same direction; and then one or another would fly off at a tangent with some inexplicable remark or criticism. But since Mr. Maxwell and his sister raised no real objection to our going—though they had little hope of its successful result,—I paid scant heed to others' advices.

Miss Gardiner's attitude bothered me most. She seemed determined to persuade us not to go, but she took no definite stand in the matter. She merely implied her opinions, and made vague suggestions that we might get into trouble by interfering with what was doubtless a party of young men on a pleasure trip.

"Even if that car did come in and go around the house and out again," said Miss Gardiner, almost angrily, "that doesn't prove the men criminals! Why, they might not even have known Philip or Mildred."

"But they asked the inn-keeper where the Maxwells lived," I reminded her.

"Probably because this is the show place of the town, and they wanted to see it," she retorted.

"But they wouldn't come at ten o'clock at night to see it," exclaimed Tom Whiting; "I don't know, Irene, why you're so afraid we'll find those men."

"I'm not afraid of any such thing," responded Miss Gardiner, with a rising color at the implied accusation.

"How should I know or care who the men are?"

"You were on the upper veranda when they came," went on Tom.

"And I have told you that I saw no one," and Irene spoke coldly; and rising, immediately left the room.

"Now she's mad," said Whiting, with a sigh; "but I do think that girl is holding something back."

"Oh, surely she can't know anything about it that she won't tell," said Miss Maxwell, looking anxious; "I can't bear to think Irene deceitful."

"She isn't deceitful," I declared; "I don't believe she knows anything she hasn't told, but if she does, you may depend upon it she is withholding it from right motives."

"I can't imagine any right motive for concealing the truth in a case like this," said Whiting, sternly.

"She may be shielding somebody else." Miss Lathrop said this in her most insinuating tones, and I at once had a conviction that she only said it to involve Irene. If so, I determined to call her bluff.

"Just what do you mean by that, Miss Lathrop?" I inquired; "if you know that Miss Gardiner is shielding somebody, surely you ought not to withhold the fact."

"I know nothing about Miss Gardiner," said the nurse, pursing her lips, primly; "it is not for me to have opinions on this matter at all."

"Quite so," I returned coolly, "I admit opinions are of little value; but if you know of any facts you should not conceal them."

"When I learn of any facts I will not conceal them," returned the nurse, and a gleam in her eye made me think that she looked forward hopefully to gaining such knowledge.

Next morning we started on our trip to Millville.

Miss Maxwell proposed that we take Miss Lathrop with us to give her some fresh air; and that she herself would sit with Milly in the absence of the nurse.

Miss Leslie was slowly regaining her strength, but was still prostrated from the effects of the shock, and also by the delayed healing of her wound. She was allowed to see no one except those who took care of her. Of course this necessitated the Whitings' continued stay at Maxwell Chimneys, and as I was determined to see the case through, my stay was also indefinitely prolonged. As for Miss Gardiner, she declared each morning that she was going home that day, and each afternoon concluded to stay longer.

And so we started off for Millville; Tom Whiting and his wife in front, while I sat back with Miss Gardiner and the nurse.

It was a beautiful drive in the fresh morning air, and the roads were bordered with golden-rod and red sumac. The foliage was beginning to turn, and for a time the casual conversation was entirely regarding the weather and the scenery.

And then Miss Gardiner said abruptly, "Who is James Mordaunt?"

"I never heard of him before," I replied. "But you know he isn't the one who asked Schwartz where the Maxwells lived."

"What was his name?" demanded Irene in a nervous tone.

"I don't know I'm sure; that's what we hope to find out in Millville."

"I hope you won't," she exclaimed, and it seemed involuntary.

"Why?" I said, and Miss Lathrop said, "why?" at the same moment.

"Oh, I didn't exactly mean that, but I am so sure he can't be the criminal, that I hate to see you get on a wrong trail."

"I think that's rather a weak explanation of your speech, Miss Gardiner," said the nurse, with one of her most annoying smiles.

"Perhaps you can give a better explanation!" and Miss Gardiner's voice was coldly angry.

But I had no desire to listen to a feminine quarrel, and I said, pleasantly, "Miss Gardiner's speech doesn't need an explanation. Indeed, we're all so bewildered by our conflicting thoughts that I fear we sometimes talk at random."

"I fear some of us do," said Miss Lathrop, shortly.

But I diplomatically managed to keep peace between them, and at last we reached Millville. Our destination was the Prospect House, and we went directly there and interviewed the proprietor, Mr. Halkett, with whom we had talked over the telephone. He greeted us cordially, and took us at once to his private parlor. I told him frankly that we wanted to know the names of those men who were with Mr. Mordaunt, but I did not tell him why we were inquiring. He told us that only the one name was registered, but that during their stay he had learned the others.

There were two men named Greene, and one, the big Western man, was Judson; and the chauffeur was Hopkins.

"That Judson's the man," I declared, "whose name we want. What's his first name?"

"John," said Mr. Halkett; "John Judson. But his comrades called him Jack or Juggins. They were a hearty lot of fellows, and all in gay spirits except big Judson."

"Wasn't he?" asked Whiting, eagerly.

"No," returned Mr. Halkett, "he was moody and silent; and when the other men tried to cheer him up, he would say, 'Let me alone, boys, I'm feeling down.' "

"How long were they here?" I inquired.

"Just over the one night. They arrived before midnight, last Monday night, and went away the next morning, about ten or eleven."

"Where did they go?"

"Well, I don't know exactly; but they seemed to be making a tour along the Southern New Jersey coast. I know they were going to Atlantic City and later to Cape May. They did say they'd stop here on their way back, but I never place much dependence on those promises. Young fellows often think they'll come back the same way and then they switch off to another road."

"Where were they from?" asked Whiting.

"Mordaunt registered from Philadelphia; and that big Judson was from out West. I don't know about the others."

We asked further questions, but none brought any more definite information. We didn't want to let Mr. Halkett know that we had any sinister reason for wanting to find these men, and he probably thought they had been speeding, or some such light offence as that. As we took our leave, I fell back a little, and whispered to Mr. Halkett that if the party should return, he was to telephone me at once and privately. This he agreed to do, and then we went back to Maxwell Chimneys.

Our conference at home after this trip was more amiable than the one the night before. Miss Gardiner seemed relieved that we had not traced the men; though I by no means felt inclined to drop our search for them, and I had my own notions of what I should do next.

Miss Lathrop made no unkind remarks, but I couldn't help observing that she watched Irene stealthily, and with much the same assured expression that a cat watches a mouse.

Mr. Maxwell merely observed that he couldn't believe Mr. Mordaunt was implicated in our tragedy, as he had never heard that name before. But when I went on to tell of big Jack Judson known by his friends as Juggins, both Mr. Maxwell and his sister exclaimed in surprise.

"That's the man!" declared Miss Maxwell; "Juggins is the man who shot our Philip! oh, how dreadful! and that's why he said, 'to think he should shoot me!' Mr. King, you have indeed found the criminal!" and Miss Miranda burst into such hysterical sobbing, that Miss Lathrop at once went over and took her in her arms.

"There, there, Miranda," said her brother, "don't jump at conclusions. It couldn't have been he! Why, there wasn't time for such a thing!"

Then he turned to us, and explained, "This Judson, or Juggins, as his classmates called him, was in Philip's class at college, but they never were friends. I don't know the reason, but there was a never healed feud between them. Philip stayed away from class re-union because he didn't wish to meet Judson. I never forced my boy's confidence, and he never told me what it was all about, but I know they were enemies. My sister knows it, too, and that is why she now suspects this man of the crime. But I cannot think it. I can't believe that Judson came here secretly, and shot my boy down in cold blood! No, Mr. King, I cannot think we have the criminal yet."

This speech amazed me. If Judson were Phil's enemy, if he came to Hamilton that night and asked where the Maxwells lived, if his car, or the car he was in, was seen to enter and leave Maxwell Chimneys at the time of the murder,—what more evidence, save the man's own confession, could be required? And the hotel man in Millville had told us that Judson was sad and gloomy, though his companions were merry.

Surely then, the others didn't know it, but Judson had stopped at Maxwell Chimneys just long enough to commit his dreadful deed and had then gone on with them. I repeated all this to Mr. Maxwell, but he only shook his head. "Not likely," he said, "not likely. It was too sudden, too quickly done, to be even a possibility. And, too, though they were not friends, there could not have been such bitter hatred as to culminate in murder. And they hadn't met for years."

"You don't know that, Mr. Maxwell," I argued; "they may have met elsewhere than here, or they may have corresponded. At any rate the circumstances are too suspicious to be ignored. Judson must be found and questioned, if only to give him the chance of clearing himself."

"I suppose that is so," agreed Mr. Maxwell; beginning to take a more rational view of the case; "Go ahead then, Mr. King, in your own way. I will not interfere. But don't accuse Judson without giving him a chance to explain himself."

I promised this, and then I went away to confer with Hunt as to this new development.

It was about seven o'clock that same evening, when, as I chanced to be alone in the music-room, Miss Lathrop came to me, and as she approached put her finger to her lip in a warning manner.

"I must speak to you alone, Mr. King," she whispered. "We are alone," I answered, a little coldly, for her manner irritated me.

"Yes," she said, "if we're not interrupted. Now listen, while I tell you something."

"I am listening," I said, really annoyed by her important and mysterious manner.

"Don't be so rude! you'll change your tune when you hear what I have to tell you."

"What have you to tell me?" I asked, more gently, for I suddenly realized that if I antagonized her, I might miss some real information.

"Only this. Miss Gardiner has just mailed a letter addressed to Mr. John Judson."

"What?"

"Don't speak so loud! It is just as I tell you. So you see they are colleagues!"

"They are what?"

"Do stop asking absurd questions,—you heard me! I tell you because I think you ought to know, that Miss Gardiner is in correspondence with that man."

"She isn't in correspondence with him!"

"Well, she has just written him, at any rate; and she must be in correspondence with him or how could she know his address?"

"What is his address?"

"The letter is directed to him at Cape May."

I had recovered from my first dazed bewilderment, and though still angry, I knew it was better not to show this. Moreover, if what the nurse told me was true, as of course it must be, I must find out all I could from her.

"How do you know this? You've been prying into Miss Gardiner's private affairs!"

"Is not that allowable if one is tracking a murderer?"

I could not restrain my anger entirely. "I didn't know you were officially employed in this matter," I flung at her.

"Nor am I," she said, proudly; "if my voluntary assistance is scorned, I will discontinue it."

She turned away, and I saw I was defeating my own ends.

"Wait a moment, Miss Lathrop," I begged; "I ask your pardon if I have offended you, but I'm nearly at my wits' end in this matter, and your revelation is indeed a surprise to me. How did you discover this letter?"

"I happened to take a letter myself to the mail box in the hall, and I found the footman just emptying the box to take the letters to the post office. I chanced to see the name Judson on one of them, and naturally it caught my eye. So I looked at the letter, and saw that it was in Miss Gardiner's handwriting. I noted the address, and I said nothing to anyone else, but brought the information directly to you. Have I done right?"

"You have certainly done right in telling me about it, Miss Lathrop. May I ask you not to mention it to anyone else,—at least not for the present?"

"I will not mention it," said Miss Lathrop, and then she glided swiftly away, and I was left to ponder on her astonishing news. But after only a short consideration, I decided to go at once to Miss Gardiner and ask for the truth. There could be no ordinary or innocent reason why she should be corresponding with the man we suspected of crime.

She must have concealed knowledge of some sort, whether guilty or not. It was nearly dinner time, but I sent a message to her asking her to see me at once for a moment in the music-room.

She came down almost immediately, and as she entered, though her manner was cold and distant, I thought I had never seen her look more beautiful. Her soft, trailing, black gown was most becoming, and a gauzy black scarf that veiled her white shoulders seemed to add to her dignity and hauteur.

"You sent for me?" she said, without a smile, and in low, level tones.

"I did," I replied, "and I'm going to tell you frankly, why I did so. I have learned, Miss Gardiner, that you have just sent a letter to Mr. John Judson."

"Have I not a right to send letters to whom I choose?"

"You certainly have. But when such a letter proves that you know the address of the man we are looking for, I have a right to ask you what you know of him, and why you conceal from us the fact that you do know him."

"And if you have a right to ask those questions, I also have a right to refuse to answer them."

"You have that right, but is it wise to exercise it, Miss Gardiner? Please drop this antagonistic attitude, and if you're not willing to help us in our search, won't you tell me why?"

"I'm not willing to help you in your search, and I refuse to tell you why."

Miss Gardiner spoke deliberately, and turning slowly, left the room. It may have been my imagination, but I thought she hesitated an instant at the doorway, as if half hoping I would call her back. But I did not do so, as I knew it was but a few moments before dinner time, and I quickly concluded to wait until the evening, and then endeavor to get her alone for a more protracted interview.

All through the meal I was pre-occupied and found it difficult to control my thoughts sufficiently to take part in the general conversation. Moreover, when I lifted my eyes, I invariably found either Miss Gardiner or Miss Lathrop regarding me intently, and I found it embarrassing to meet their gaze.

XVIII: A PISTOL SHOT

DINNER was nearly over when I was called to the telephone. Excusing myself from the table, I answered the summons, only to find that it was Mr. Halkett, of the Millville Hotel, who wished to speak to me.

His message was of importance, for it told me that the gray car and the four men of Mordaunt's party had returned to the Prospect House, on their way back to Philadelphia.

"Why, I thought they had gone to Cape May," I said, impulsively.

"They did intend to," replied Mr. Halkett, "but they changed their plan, and they're here for the night. They're going to stay here until eleven o'clock or so tomorrow morning. They don't know I'm telling you this, as that's according to your orders."

"All right, Mr. Halkett," I said, seriously; "don't let them know you've telephoned me; for, understand, this is an important matter. On no account raise their suspicions in any way, but see to it that they don't leave any earlier than eleven tomorrow morning."

"All right, Mr. King; I'll see to that."

I went back to the table, intending to tell them all what I had just heard, but on second thoughts I decided not to. So I said nothing about it until after dinner, when I told Tom Whiting only.

I also told him about Irene's letter to Judson, proving that she had thought him at Cape May, whereas the party were on their return trip. He agreed with me that the situation had grown serious, and that we must move carefully.

We concluded to say nothing to anyone, but to go alone next morning over to Millville. Of course, I gave up my idea of another interview with Irene that night, as I wanted to keep her unaware of the fact that Judson was at Millville. Nor did I tell Hunt, as it seemed to me that Whiting and I could handle the case best alone. So next morning, immediately after breakfast, we started. The little runabout was a swift car, and we had ample time to reach Millville by ten o'clock. But just at the last moment, indeed, as I was getting into the car, Miss Lathrop ran out to speak to me.

"I couldn't get a chance to tell you before," she whispered; "but Miss Gardiner has sent that Judson man another letter! She had it mailed late last night, and it was addressed to Millville, and it had a special delivery stamp on it."

"Thank you, Miss Lathrop," I said, and for once I was honestly grateful to her.

"Speed her up, Tom!" I said, as I swung into the little car beside Whiting; "we've a new reason for haste. Get over to Millville as quick as you can. Irene has sent that man another letter, and he'll get away from us yet!"

"Great Scott, King!" said Tom, as we took a higher speed; "what is that girl up to? You know, King, there's nothing crooked about Irene."

"Then she's coerced or threatened by that villain Judson," I declared.

"He's the murderer, Tom, and Irene knows it!"

"Oh, no, no! not so bad as that! Well, anyhow, we'll soon find out."

We said little more as we tore along the miles. My thoughts were busy with this sudden new surprise. How had Irene discovered that Judson was in Millville, when a few hours before she had thought him at Cape May? To be sure she might have had a letter or telegram in the meantime; or,—and what was more likely the case,— she had heard enough of my telephoning to realize that the Mordaunt party were back at Millville and to act accordingly.

On we flew, and I said no word to Tom, lest I distract his attention from his driving. Moreover, I knew the situation must mystify him quite as much as it did me.

After an incredibly short trip, we whirled in at the hotel entrance. Only to be met by a distracted proprietor, who told us the car had just left with the Mordaunt party.

"But I told you not to let them get away!" I thundered, in mad disappointment.

"I know it, Mr. King," said Halkett, apologetically, "but I couldn't help it. I had to go over to the bank on an important matter and when I came back the party had just gone. Of course I couldn't forcibly restrain them."

"No, I suppose you couldn't. Which way did they go?"

"That way. The main road to Philadelphia."

"Turn around, Tom! chase them! it's our only chance."

Whiting swung the car around, and we flew out of the gate and along the main road.

"There's little hope," I shouted at him, as we whizzed madly on, "but if they've had tire trouble or anything, we might overtake them. Anyway, we'll have a try at it for a few miles,—and then give it up, if we have to."

Whiting fully entered into the spirit of the thing, and we went faster than I had ever before traveled in a motor-car.

The little machine rocked, and I involuntarily grasped at the side of the seat, lest I be flung out. Fortunately the road was clear, and of course a good one, and we kept on. I was just about ready to cry quits, when we saw a car ahead of us.

And, moreover, it was the car!

"That's it, Tom!" I shouted; "speed her!"

He couldn't speed her any more than he was already doing, but as we had gained on the big car, I believed we could continue to gain.

And we did! Of course Mordaunt's car was not going at top speed, as they didn't know they were being pursued,—a fact which I hoped they would not discover.

But they did discover it. Whether a case of a guilty conscience or not, a man rose from his seat in the tonneau, and turned to look backward.

He saw us, and must have realized that we were chasing them, for they immediately began to go faster.

The big car sped ahead, and we followed.

"Speed her, Tom!" I cried; "whoop her up!"

"Can't do any more," Tom replied; "this is our best." The poor fellow was straining every nerve, and bent to his wheel in a frenzy of excitement.

The man in the car ahead was still standing, and looking backward at us.

The space between the cars lengthened slowly, and I realized that soon they would spin ahead out of our sight. I said nothing to Tom, for I knew he could not get another ounce of speed out of our car.

The big man who stood gazing at us, as the touring car streaked ahead, was doubtless Jack Judson. He was an enormous man, and swung his arms with the free movement of a Westerner.

Though I could not see his features distinctly, I felt the triumphant smile on his face, as he took off his soft, flapping hat and waved it at us in farewell.

But even as be replaced that hat, I saw his face more clearly, and I suddenly realized that this meant a lessening of the distance between us!

"Tom!" I fairly yelled in his ear; "they're slowing down! they don't mean to,—but something has happened! we're gaining on them! Never mind, boy, don't even look up,—just saw wood! "

Obediently Tom watched his wheel, and I stared at the car, to which we were certainly creeping nearer. Yes, slowly but steadily nearer, and now I could discern Judson's face clearly, and could see his baffled expression give way to one of new resolve.

Stooping an instant, the big man straightened up again, and now in his right hand he held what was unmistakably a deadly sharp shooter!

"Tom!" I cried, actually more alarmed for my unconscious companion than for myself; "Tom,—duck! he's going to shoot us!"

In my excitement, I didn't think of ducking myself, and I sat spellbound, gazing at that weapon aimed surely at us, while Tom, after one glance, dropped his head in an effort to shield himself.

The next instant a report rang out, and as the big car passed out of sight, our pace slackened and we went along limpingly.

The big Westerner had cleverly and purposely punctured one of our front tires!

After the report, Tom's head came up, and he evidently expected, as he was unhurt, to see me wounded or dead beside him.

His look of amazement was almost comical, when I said, "He shot at the tire, Whiting, not at us, and with his blooming Western skill, he hit it!"

He had done just that, and now there was nothing for us to do, but to get out and mend the tire and then go home.

We did so, and though we talked the matter over all the way home, we could come to no other conclusion than that Judson was the murderer and that he had escaped us.

"I shall put it straight up to Miss Gardiner," I declared; "she knows about this thing and she must be made to tell."

"She must know about it," said Whiting, "but I can't believe yet that she is willfully shielding a murderer. It must be from some mistaken sense of duty or loyalty to some one."

"She's certainly very much interested in this man Judson," I returned, a little gloomily. I was really under the spell of Miss Gardiner's fascination, and of course I hoped she could clear up all these uncertainties, but certainly the Judson affair looked ominous.

After luncheon that day, I made a special request of Miss Gardiner that she would confer with Tom Whiting and myself. She agreed willingly enough, and we went to the music-room for our talk. We had thought it better not to tell the rest of the household about our morning's experience until after the conference with Irene. So I had told Mr. Maxwell that the Mordaunt party had left the hotel before we reached there and told him nothing more. But he discerned somehow, that there was more to the story, and he joined us in the music-room, uninvited. As there was no real reason why he shouldn't know all about it, I was quite willing he should be there.

In consideration of his deafness, we all sat near together and spoke distinctly.

"To begin with," I said, "I'm positive that John Judson is the man who shot Philip and Mildred."

"And I am equally positive he did not!" declared Irene, her eyes blazing; "and I can prove it!"

"You can!" exclaimed Tom Whiting; "what do you know, Irene, that the rest of us don't know? and why are you willing to defeat the efforts of right and justice?"

"First tell me what happened this morning," said the girl.

So I gave a rapid account of our pursuit of the Mordaunt car, and of Judson's shooting our tire in order to make his own escape.

"Then he got away safely?" asked Irene, eagerly.

"Yes, he is now well on toward Philadelphia. Are you glad he escaped?"

"I certainly am, as the man is absolutely innocent of any connection with our mystery."

"You know this Judson, then, Miss Gardiner?" asked Mr. Maxwell.

"Yes, I know him very well."

"Then you know he was an enemy to Philip?"

"Not exactly an enemy, though I know they never liked each other. But since Mr. Judson is safely away, I will tell you the whole story. He has been a friend of mine for some years, and though he has asked me several times to marry him, I have always refused him. Last week he went to see me at my home in New York, and they told him I was down here. He was making a motor trip with Mr. Mordaunt, and on their way to Atlantic City, they stopped here at Mr. Judson's request. He wrote me that he wanted to see me once more before he went West, but he did not care to meet Philip. So I wrote him that I would be on the upper veranda Monday night at ten o'clock, and that he might come up by the little outside staircase, and thus he need not see Philip at all. He did this, and it was Mr. Mordaunt's car that the Earl saw that night."

"Then Judson did come up on the upper veranda, Monday night at ten o'clock," said Tom Whiting; "and yet you say he had nothing to do with the shooting!"

"Absolutely nothing," said Irene. "We were on the other side of the house from the library, and he remained with me not more than two minutes."

"Why such a short stay?" asked Tom.

"Because,—because I was crying when he came, and I didn't want to see him anyway, and I begged him to go away at once."

"At what time was this?"

"I don't know exactly, but it was quite some time after ten. In fact, Mr. King came and told me about Philip and Mildred, very soon after Mr. Judson went away. But I can swear, if necessary, that he only came up to see me, stayed but a few moments and went away again. He did not go round to the library side of the house at all."

"What were you crying about?" asked Whiting, gently. "I was upset and nervous, and I couldn't control myself."

"You have heard from Mr. Judson since?" asked Mr. Maxwell, who was paying close attention to Irene's story.

"Yes,—and of course he has heard of the murder, but he has no idea he was suspected of it. But I wanted him to get away, for to detain him and make inquiries, would only mean trouble for an innocent man. So I wrote him at Millville that you were going over there, and begged him to get away before you came. I think he must have been mystified at my urging him to a speedy departure, but I'm glad to know that he did as I advised him."

"It is a strange story, Miss Gardiner," said Mr. Maxwell, thoughtfully, "but of course I do not doubt your word."

"You need not," said Irene, haughtily. "I have told only the exact truth. If I have concealed this episode, it is only because I didn't wish Mr. Judson's name brought into question at all."

We talked for some time after this, and we all agreed that as Judson was now entirely out of it, we must look in some other direction.

"I don't think Mr. Hunt is doing much," said Whiting, "and I think, Mr. Maxwell, it would be wise to put the whole affair in the hands of the police."

"If you think best," said the old gentleman, hopelessly. "I think myself, that Mr. Hunt is not discovering anything, but that may not be his fault. As I told you, Tom, whatever you and Peter agree upon, I will agree to. But I cannot seem to take any initiative. I am too old, and my deafness stands in my way, when I would question anybody."

"Certainly, Mr. Maxwell," said I, "you could not be expected to take up this matter personally. I'll see Hunt again, and if he agrees, I think we will give it over to the police."

But before I saw Hunt, I determined to do a little more investigating by myself. I went up to the library, hoping that from the scene of the crime I could get some hint of which direction to turn.

Of course, too much time had elapsed to look for further clues, but as I sat there, something brought back to my mind the black spangles I had found that next morning. The maid who had found the Earl's seal must have overlooked the tiny spangles as I found them later. But she might have found others of the same sort when she dusted the room, and I determined to ask her.

I went in search of her, and showing her the spangles I had, I inquired if she had seen any like them in the library the morning she had found the seal. At first she couldn't remember, and then she recollected having picked up two or three near the window.

"Have you any idea," I said, "where they could have come from? Did any of the ladies wear a spangled dress that night?"

"Oh, I know where they have come from," she said, quickly; "they are from the fan of Miss Gardiner."

"How do you know?"

"Because Miss Gardiner carried the black fan that evening. She left it on a seat on the veranda, and I found it and put it again in her room."

"You are certain, Emily, that Miss Gardiner carried the fan that evening?"

"I am sure, Mr. King."

"That is all, Emily, you may go."

Here was something definite. For I remembered distinctly that Miss Gardiner went to her room to get that fan just before she and I walked together on the upper veranda. Then I left her, and she remained up there, and Judson found her there, crying.

Meantime, some spangles from that fan had been dropped by the library window! It seemed to me positive proof that Irene had been around there between half past nine and half past ten that night. The more I thought it over the more I was convinced that it must be so. And yet, I did not like to face her with these facts and ask an explanation. But it seemed to me that I must do this, before going any further.

So I went on my very distasteful errand, and found Miss Gardiner in the music-room with Miss Maxwell.

"You know," I said, speaking to the girl, "it is our duty to investigate every possible clue."

"Of course," said Irene, but she trembled nervously and seemed to apprehend some new disclosure.

"Then I will show you these spangles," I said, taking them from my pocketbook, "and ask you if they could have dropped from a fan of yours."

Irene looked at them, and said, quietly, "I have a black spangled fan; they may very likely have dropped from it."

"Did you carry it the Monday night that Philip died?"

"I may have done so; I don't remember exactly. Why?"

"Because these spangles were found in the library, the morning after the shooting."

"And you think that turns suspicion toward me?" Irene rose, and stood with flashing eyes, the embodiment of indignation and anger.

"You are entirely mistaken, Mr. King, as to your suspicions! They may be spangles from my fan, they may have been dropped in the library; but I was in and out of that room during the early evening, long before the time of the tragedy."

"But you didn't have the fan with you, then," I persisted; "because I remember you went to your room for it, when you and I were together after our dance."

Miss Gardiner turned perfectly white, and swayed as if about to faint. Miss Maxwell sprang to her aid, and putting an arm about her led her from the room.

"I can't have this poor girl tortured, Peter," said the gentle old lady, and they went away leaving me to face a new suspicion that was as unwelcome as it was unexpected.

XIX: RED INK SPOTS

I RESOLVED to say nothing more about the fan or the spangles to any member of the household, but to lay the case before Hunt, when he came over to the house the next morning.

To my surprise he did not seem at all impressed with the idea of Miss Gardiner being implicated.

"You let your idea of clues run away with you, Mr. King," he said. "To be sure the spangles may point in Miss Gardiner's direction, but she certainly cannot be the intruder who came in the motor coat and cap. Now, it seems to me if we're going to look for our man through any clues, we'd better consider that red ink. When Miss Leslie threw that inkstand, and so much ink was spilled on the rug, it is extremely probable that some also spattered on the coat of the assailant."

"Well, it seems to me," I said, "that that's about the most elusive clue you could think of! We can't possibly, after all these days, trace a motor coat with red ink spots on it."

"He might have taken it to a cleaner's," said Hunt, thoughtfully.

"Then shall we advertise for a cleaner who has had such a job recently?"

But my sarcasm was lost upon Hunt. "I doubt if a cleaner could take out such spots," he went on; "red ink is almost indelible."

"Well, I have little hope of finding these mythical spots on a mythical coat belonging to a mythical man!"

"You're wrong there, for certainly the coat and the man are not mythical. Miss Leslie saw them. Perhaps she can tell us if the red ink spattered him," said Hunt, hopefully.

"She can't tell us anything at present. The doctor won't let her be spoken to on this subject. It seems to me, Hunt, the only thing to do is to call in the police. Of course if they find the man and the coat, some red ink spots on it would go a long way toward proving his guilt. But I'm sure that to find the man will require the skill of the police force, rather than our ineffectual attempts."

"Perhaps you're right," agreed Hunt, "but all the same I shall try to find that coat."

Then Tom Whiting and his wife appeared at the library door.

"We want you, Mr. King, if Mr. Hunt will excuse you," said Edith Whiting, in her pleasant way.

"Certainly," said Mr. Hunt. "I am just going home anyway."

"Have you discovered anything new?" asked Tom Whiting.

"We hope to do so," said Mr. Hunt.

"I think we are on the right track, though we have not progressed very far, as yet."

"We want you to go with us for a motor ride, Mr. King," said Edith Whiting to me.

"Tom insists on my going, and we are taking Irene with us."

We started away, but Hunt called me back to whisper a parting message.

"If you find any strangers in automobile togs," he said, "observe carefully whether there are any signs of their having tried to erase red ink spots from the lower fronts of their coats."

"That's the slimmest kind of a slim chance yet," I said, almost smiling at the idea, "but I promise you if I find an automobilist spattered with red ink, I will arrest him at once."

I found the others ready and waiting for me. It seemed pathetic to ride away in Philip's big automobile, but, as Tom Whiting had said, the ladies really needed some fresh air, and he thought the trip would do us all good.

Mr. Maxwell and Miss Miranda insisted on our going, and so we started off. Mr. and Mrs. Whiting sat in front, for Tom was quite as good a chauffeur as Philip had been; and Miss Gardiner and I sat behind. As there was ample room for another, Irene proposed that we stop for Gilbert Crane. This we did, and he seemed glad to accept the invitation.

It scarcely seemed like the same party who a few days before, accompanied by Philip, had traveled so merrily over these same roads.

On our return, Mrs. Whiting asked Mr. Crane to come in to luncheon with us, and he accepted. He alighted before I did, and as he stood waiting to help Miss Gardiner out, the midday sunlight shone full upon him.

I looked at him curiously, thinking what a large, fine-looking fellow he was physically, and how becoming his fashionable automobile coat was to him. Its color was a light brownish gray, and as my eye rested idly upon it, I suddenly noticed something that made my heart stand still.

On the front of this same coat, on the lower edge, were several small spots, visible only in the brightest sunlight, which, whatever they might be, had every appearance of being red ink.

To say I was stunned would pretty well express my feelings, but I was learning not to show surprise at unexpected developments.

I went into the house with the rest, and finding that Mr. Hunt had gone, I sent a note to him, by one of the servants, asking him to return at two o'clock.

He came just as we finished luncheon, and bidding him go in the library and await me there, I went into Mr. Maxwell's study. Finding my host there as I had hoped, and not wishing to elevate my voice, I scribbled on a bit of paper a request that Mr. Maxwell would ask Mr. Crane to come into his study, and would keep him there, securely, for twenty minutes at least.

Mr. Maxwell read the paper quietly, handed it back to me, gave me a quick nod of comprehension, and immediately went in search of Gilbert Crane. A moment later, I saw him return with Gilbert Crane. They entered the study and closed the door, so I knew that the coast was clear, and that for twenty minutes I need fear no interruption from them.

Eagerly seizing his coat from the hat-stand where he had flung it, I hastened to the library. I found Hunt there, and after closing the door I held up the coat for his inspection.

"You don't mean to say you have found the man!" he cried.

"I don't know about that," I said, very soberly, "but I have certainly found a coat that ought to be looked after. What do you make of this?"

I held the front of the coat toward the window to catch the bright sunlight, and drew Hunt's attention to the almost invisible spots on it. He looked at them in silence a moment, and then said abruptly: "Get some more blotters."

We dampened the blotters and applied them very carefully, for the spots were faint, and the surface of the cloth dusty.

But the results showed strong evidence that the stains were similar to those on the carpet.

"Whose coat is it?" said Hunt, though I think he knew.

"Gilbert Crane's," I answered, looking straight at the detective.

"But that does not prove that Gilbert Crane committed the murder," he responded, looking at me with equal directness.

"It does not," I said, emphatically, "but it is certainly a clue that must lead somewhere."

"And we must follow it wherever it leads."

"Yes," I assented, "now that we have something to work on, let us get to work. Shall I call Crane up here, and ask him if he can explain these spots on his coat? Somehow, I can't help thinking that he could do so."

"Not yet," said Mr. Hunt. "I think it wiser to straighten out a few points before we speak to Mr. Crane on the subject. He is a peculiar man, and I don't want to antagonize him. I would much rather, if you please, that you would replace the coat where you found it, let Mr. Maxwell know that he need not detain Mr. Crane any longer, and then bring Miss Gardiner back here with you for a short consultation."

I followed Mr. Hunt's suggestions to the letter, but it was with a rapidly sinking heart. Not for a moment did I think Gilbert Crane a villain, and yet there were many circumstances that looked dark against him. I was also disturbed at Mr. Hunt's request for Irene.

A strange foreboding made me fear that some dreadful revelation was about to take place.

The jury had rendered its verdict of "willful murder by a person unknown," and I fervently hoped the criminal might remain forever unknown rather than that the shadow of guilt might fall on anyone who had been hospitably received at Maxwell Chimneys.

Still, in the cause of justice, every possibility must be considered, and I knew that Mr. Hunt would shirk no duty, but would doggedly follow any clue that presented itself.

I looked in at the study door, and the merest lifting of my eye-brows was sufficient to inform Mr. Maxwell that a detention of Gilbert was no longer necessary. I looked at young Crane's inscrutable face, and was obliged to admit to myself that it was not a frank countenance in its general effect. But I resolved that this fact should not be allowed to prejudice me against him.

Finding Mrs. Whiting in the hall, and learning from her that Miss Gardiner had gone to her own room, I asked her to say to Miss Gardiner that Mr. Hunt desired to see her in the library. Mrs. Whiting promised to send Irene there at once, and, greatly dreading the interview, I returned to the library myself.

I found Hunt making a tabulated statement of certain facts.

"You see, Mr. King," he said, with a very grave face, "while these things are not positively incriminating, they are serious questions which need clearing up.

"Granting that the bronze horse was thrown at the intruder and replaced on the desk before you entered the room that night, we must allow that it was picked up and replaced by somebody. Miss Leslie was incapable of this act, the murderer was not likely to do it.

"Gilbert Crane was the first to find out that the tragedy had occurred. There is no witness to say what he might or might not have done in this room. It is possible therefore that he restored the horse to its place."

"And the inkstand?"

"You remember that Gilbert Crane insisted on spending the night in this house. Is it not, therefore, conceivable that he should have waited until everyone else had gone home, or retired to their rooms, and that he should then have come to the library, found the empty stand, refilled it, and replaced it?"

"But," said I, in utter amazement, "if he did not commit the crime why should he be so careful about these details?"

"I am not sure," said Mr. Hunt in a low voice, "that he did not commit the crime."

XX: IRENE TELLS THE TRUTH

ALTHOUGH horrified and even indignant at Mr. Hunt's assertion, I could not fail to be impressed by his arguments. I was still bewildered at the possibilities he suggested, when a tap was heard at the library door. Mr. Hunt rose quietly and admitted Miss Gardiner.

The girl looked haggard and worn. Her brilliant coloring seemed faded, and her whole attitude betrayed deep distress not unmixed with fear.

But all of this she tried to hide beneath a mask of impassivity.

I think she impressed Hunt with her appearance of calmness, though I felt sure that her turbulent spirit was far from placid.

"Sit down, Miss Gardiner," said Hunt kindly. "I wish to ask you a few questions."

Irene sat down, and with an air both haughty and dignified awaited the detective's next words. Had it not been for her restless, troubled eyes, she would have deceived me into thinking her assumed indifference real.

"In your testimony, Miss Gardiner," began Mr. Hunt, "you declared that you did not leave the spot where you were sitting, on the east end of the balcony, the night of the murder, until you came into the house at about half past ten. Are you still prepared to swear to this statement?"

"Why should I not be, Mr. Hunt?" said Irene, but her lips grew white, and her voice trembled.

"You might have since recollected that you did go around to the west side, if only for a moment."

"I have no recollections that cause me to change my sworn statement in any way," declared Irene. Her voice had sunk almost to a whisper and her eyes refused to meet mine.

Mr. Hunt continued: "Were you around on the west side, near the library window, at any time during the evening— earlier, perhaps, than the time you spent sitting alone on the east side?"

"No," said Irene, and this time her voice was stronger and her whole air more decided, as she looked the detective straight in the eye. "I was not on the west balcony earlier in the evening. I was not there at all!"

The last sentence came with a desperate burst of emphasis, that somehow did not carry conviction. For some reason the girl was under a severe tension, and I couldn't help thinking there was danger of her physical collapse.

"Then," said Mr. Hunt, suddenly producing the black spangles—"then may I ask, Miss Gardiner, how these chanced to be found in the library, and on the library window-shutter?"

Irene Gardiner gave a low cry, and hiding her face in her hands, seemed in immediate danger of the collapse I had feared.

"Miss Gardiner," I said, for though her actions were inexplicable, I was still deeply under the spell of her fascination, and greatly desired to help her— "Miss Gardiner, let me advise you, as a friend, to tell your story frankly and truthfully. I am sure it will be better for all concerned."

Raising her head, Irene Gardiner flashed a look at me so full of faith and gratitude, that, assured of her complete innocence, I determined to become her strong ally.

"Oh!" she exclaimed, "I would be so glad to tell the truth! I swore to a falsehood from a sense of duty to another."

"It is always a mistaken sense of duty that leads to false swearing," said Mr. Hunt.

"I believe that is so," said Irene earnestly, "but I had no one to advise me and I thought I was doing right. The truth is, then, that I did go around to the west end of the balcony, and that I did look in at the library window."

"At what time was this?" asked Mr. Hunt.

"I don't know," said Irene, "but it was just before Mr. Judson came, and about ten minutes later Mr. King came to me on the front balcony, and told me what had happened."

"What did you see in the library?" asked Mr. Hunt.

"Must I tell that?"

"You must."

"Then I saw Philip lying on the floor, and Mildred fallen to the floor also. But she was partly hidden by the desk."

"Is that all you saw?" asked Mr. Hunt, looking at her intently. "Was there no one else in the room?"

"Must I tell that?" asked Irene again, with an appealing glance at me.

"Yes," said Mr. Hunt sternly, "much may depend on your telling the absolute truth."

"Then," said Irene, "I saw Mr. Crane placing a pistol in Mildred's hand."

"Wait," said I, "was this occurring just as you arrived at the window?"

"Yes."

"Then," I went on, "you cannot swear that he was placing the pistol in her hand. He might have been taking it away from her, or attempting to do so."

"I never thought of that," said Irene, an expression of relief lighting up her face.

"Even so," said Mr. Hunt, "he should have told of the incident in his own testimony. What did you do next, Miss Gardiner?"

"I went away at once. I went to the east side of the veranda. I was so mystified and horrified by what I had just seen that I flung myself into a chair and cried. I was still crying when, soon after, Mr. Judson came in search of me. And I was still crying when Mr. King came later to tell me what had happened."

"She was," I said, "and crying so violently that I was alarmed. But as Miss Maxwell appeared almost immediately, I left the two ladies to look after each other."

"And had it not been for the incriminating spangles, did you not intend to correct your misstatement?" said Mr. Hunt, looking at her severely.

"No," said Irene, and her manner now was frank and self-assured, "for I felt sure Mr. Crane had done nothing wrong, and I did not wish to attract any unfounded suspicions toward him."

"A suspicion that is really unfounded can do no one any harm," said Mr. Hunt, who seemed to be in a mood for oracular utterances.

"I am glad," said Irene simply, "for I would not wish any harm to come to Mr. Crane through my testimony."

"That is as it may be," said Mr. Hunt, and the interview was at an end. Although Irene's evidence had placed Gilbert in a doubtful position, I was not yet willing to believe the man guilty, or even that he was implicated in the crime.

Indeed, I was for going straight to him, and asking him for the explanation which I felt sure he could give. But Mr. Hunt did not agree with me. He was in the grasp of a new theory, and therefore subject to the temptation which too often assails a detective, to make the facts coincide with it.

"No," he said, "don't let us go ahead too rapidly. Let us formulate a definite proposition, and then see if we are warranted in assuming it to be a true one. In the first place, whoever killed Philip Maxwell must have had a strong personal motive for the deed.

"There is no reason to suspect an ordinary burglar, for there is nothing whatever to indicate burglary in the whole affair. If Philip Maxwell had any personal enemies, the fact is not known to us. Even his uncle is unaware of the existence of any such."

"The only man we know of who might have had an ill-feeling toward Philip Maxwell—mind, I say, might have had—is Gilbert Crane. We know that an antagonism existed between the two men on account of Miss Leslie. While it would not seem to us that this antagonism was sufficient to develop a crime, yet parallel cases are not unknown. Gilbert Crane is a man of deep passions, fiery temper, and uncontrollable impulses.

"He is erratic, eccentric, and, while I do not wish to judge him too harshly, I must admit he seems to be of the stuff of which villains are made."

"But none of this is definitely incriminating," I said, appalled at the sudden directness of Hunt's attack.

"No," he replied, "and that is why I'm not willing to proceed as if. it were, or as if I so considered it."

"It is absurd anyway," I said almost angrily, "for you know that he was in the billiard-room at exactly ten o'clock. I saw him there myself. And according to Miss Maxwell, the shots were fired at ten o'clock."

"Yes, according to Miss Maxwell. But it has occurred to me that hers is the only evidence that the shots were fired at ten o'clock, and we are by no means certain that her clock or watch was exactly right."

"The clock in the study was right," I said doggedly, "it always is. Mr. Maxwell is very particular about that."

"Yes, but ladies are not apt to be so exact with their timepieces. At any rate, I shall make it my business to find out."

"Let us find out now," I said eagerly.

"If there is anything in this horrible theory I want to know it at once."

"Go yourself," said Hunt. "Go at once, and ask Miss Maxwell as to the accuracy of her clock."

I found Miss Maxwell alone, and I asked her in a casual manner how she knew it was ten o'clock when she heard, or thought she heard, the two pistol shots.

"It was ten by the little clock on my dressing table," she replied.

"I am sure of that, for it was striking at the time I heard the reports."

"And is that clock always right?" I asked.

"No," she said; "in fact, it is almost never right. For some time I have been intending to have it regulated."

"Is it slow or fast?" I asked, trying to preserve my casual manner.

"It runs slow," she said, "and that night it must have been as much as ten minutes slow, because I remember I was late for dinner, though I thought I was in ample time."

"You should have stated this discrepancy sooner, Miss Maxwell," I said, unable to keep a note of grave concern out of my voice.

"Why," she returned, in astonishment.

"I had no idea that would make any difference. In fact, I didn't think anything about it. How can it make any difference?"

"Never mind, Miss Maxwell," I said soothingly, "perhaps it won't make any difference. Don't give it any further thought. You have quite enough trouble as it is."

"Oh, I have indeed!" said the dear old lady. "I don't know what I shall do, Mr. King. Philip's death has affected my brother terribly. He was always a quiet man, but now he is so crushed and heart-broken that he is more silent than ever. And I can't seem to comfort him. I think we will have to go away from Maxwell Chimneys. We have a sister out West, and I think we will go out there. I am sure that entire and permanent change of scene is the only thing that will help Alexander at all."

I looked admiringly at the clear lady whose unselfish spirit thought of her brother's comfort, ignoring her own sorrow, and assuring her of my sincere sympathy and my assistance in every possible way, I returned to Hunt.

"I am not surprised," he said, when I told him that Miss Maxwell's clock had undoubtedly been ten minutes slow on Monday evening. "It is alarming, the way the links fit into the chain of evidence, but it must be more than mere coincidence.

"Look at it in this way for a moment—supposing, for the sake of argument, that events proceeded like this:

"You saw Gilbert Crane in the billiard-room at ten o'clock. This you are sure of. Now according to Crane's own statement he looked into Mr. Maxwell's study some twenty minutes later. But we have no other witness for this.

"Mr. Maxwell says he neither heard nor saw him, and Crane himself admits that he did not. With the exception of Miss Gardiner on the balcony, the guests were all in the music-room, not only absorbed in their music, but making a great deal of noise.

"Miss Maxwell was in her own bedroom, and the servants were busy in the kitchens, of which the doors were closed. As nearly as I can find out, Gilbert Crane came running downstairs for Dr. Sheldon a few moments before half past ten. If you have followed my reasoning, you will see that his whereabouts between ten o'clock and, say, ten twenty-five, are unaccounted for except by himself.

"His coat—the automobile coat on which we have discovered the red spots—hung on the hat stand in the back part of the hall. He, therefore, had ample opportunity to leave the billiard-room, put on his coat and the cap and goggles which he always carries in that coat pocket, go up the back staircase, and through the hall window at the head of that staircase out on to the west balcony.

"The library window is directly next to the hall window. He had therefore, I say, both time and opportunity to fire the shots at about ten minutes after ten, which would accord with Miss Maxwell's inaccurate testimony. He had also time and opportunity to return downstairs the way he came, restore his coat to its place on the hat-stand, and go back to the billiard-room.

"This yet left sufficient time for him to go upstairs again—the front stairs this time—in full view of the people in the music-room if they chanced to look, and return to make his startling announcement to Dr. Sheldon."

I had followed Hunt's words with such intense interest that I seemed to be living through the successive scenes myself. As he paused, I remarked thoughtfully:

"And that would explain why Philip cried out, 'Oh, to think that he should shoot me!' "

"Yes," said Hunt gravely, "it explains a great many things. It explains of course the spots on his coat."

"Wait," I cried eagerly, "when the ink spattered on his coat it must also have fallen on his shoes and the bottoms of his trousers."

"Not necessarily on his trousers," said Hunt, "for the coat is long and large, and would probably entirely protect them. As to his shoes, they have doubtless been blackened since, and so all trace would be lost."

"As a chain of circumstantial evidence it is certainly complete," I said, with a sigh. "But all my intuitions cry out against its being the truth."

"Have you any other theory to offer?"

"Not the shadow of one. I only wish I had. But stay. What do you make of Miss Gardiner's assertion that she saw Gilbert placing a pistol in Miss Leslie's hand?"

"I think she is mistaken as to what he was doing. I think Miss Leslie's story is true in every detail. Possibly Mr. Crane endeavored to take the pistol out of her hand, then, changing his mind for some reason, concluded not to do so."

I sat staring at Mr. Hunt, almost stunned by his convincing arguments.

"What will be your next move?" I asked.

"I shall submit this report to Inspector Davis, and he must do whatever he thinks best."

XXI: CIRCUMSTANTIAL EVIDENCE

FURTHER investigation only served to strengthen the case against Gilbert Crane.

It was discovered that he owned a thirty-eight caliber pistol. When found, this pistol was properly cleaned and loaded.

It was not rusty, and had every appearance of having been used recently, but how recently who could say?

To my mind the fact that Gilbert possessed a thirty-eight caliber pistol was not a vital bit of evidence. Anybody might possess one. But as Hunt said, it was not contradictory evidence, and, taken in conjunction with the other clues, it was of importance.

It seemed, also, to the authorities, that the motive imputed to Gilbert Crane was a strong one, and among those which most often lead to crime.

And so, Gilbert was arrested and held for trial. Though everybody at Maxwell Chimneys was shocked and astounded at the news of his arrest, it affected them in different ways.

Mildred Leslie was frantic with grief and indignation. She declared that although the intruder might have worn Gilbert's coat, it was positively not Gilbert Crane himself. She vowed she would know Gilbert in any circumstances and in any disguise, and she was sure the man who shot her was a man with whom she was unacquainted, though he was apparently well known to Philip Maxwell.

She grew so excited as to become hysterical, and the doctor ordered that she should again be remanded to absolute seclusion, and allowed to see no one save the nurse and her sister.

Irene Gardiner seemed uncertain as to the justice of the arrest. She viewed the whole matter from a stern, judicial standpoint, and seemed unable to take a personal view of it. I felt sure that she had never liked Mr. Crane, and, feeling equally sure that Mildred was very much in love with him, I could easily understand the different attitudes of the two girls.

I was conscious myself of a growing regard for Irene, and while I could wish her a little softer and more sympathetic toward the prisoner, yet I couldn't help admiring her splendid appreciation of law and justice.

As for the Maxwells, Miss Miranda was so completely crushed already, that another unexpected blow could make but little difference in her demeanor. She said she could not believe Gilbert guilty, but that it was not for her to judge.

Alexander Maxwell showed a like philosophical spirit. After the first shock of surprise, he admitted that justice must have its way, wherever that way might lead; but he again begged us not to be misled by false or incomplete clues, and to prove beyond all doubt whatever we accepted as a fact.

I fully shared the old gentleman's spirit of caution, and kept a vigilant watch on Mr. Hunt's proceedings. But I was forced to admit the evidence all pointed one way, and my only hope lay in the fact that it was purely circumstantial evidence.

Resolved, if possible, to find some weak spot in Hunt's diagnosis of the case, I obtained permission to visit Gilbert Crane in his cell.

I felt a certain embarrassment as I entered, for I expected to see a despairing, broken-down man.

But I found I did not yet know Gilbert Crane. Instead of appearing dejected, he rose to greet me with an expectant look, and held out his hand.

"Will you take it?" he said impulsively, and eagerly. "You need not hesitate. It is the hand of an honest man. I am no more guilty of Philip's death than is Philip himself."

Quite aside from his words, there was honor and truth in the sound of his voice, and the look of his eye. I am very sensitive to deceit, and in every fiber of my being I felt at that moment that an honest man stood before me.

Acting in accordance with this conviction I grasped his hand heartily, and said: "I am sure of it! I admit, and you must admit yourself, that the circumstantial evidence against you is pretty bad. But even before your denial I could not think you guilty, and now you have removed any lurking doubt I may have had."

"Thank you," said Crane simply. "And now I wonder if you can help me."

"It is what I want to do," I said, "but I fear I can do little. I have tried to get at some counter evidence, or refutation of Hunt's theories, but so far I have been unable to do so."

"That's just the point," said Gilbert, in a practical way that seemed to show me a new side of this man. "I don't know myself what to tell you to do. The whole situation is so absurd. To me it is like lightning out of a clear sky. Here am I, arrested for the murder of a man who was one of my best friends. I didn't murder him, and yet circumstances are such that I cannot prove I did not."

"Since we are speaking frankly," I said, "will you tell me if you touched the pistol that Miss Leslie held?"

Gilbert looked at me gravely. "I will," he said. "I ought to have been more straightforward about that, but I didn't mention it, because I thought it of absolutely no importance. When I saw the bodies, I thought that Philip was dead, but that Miss Leslie was still living. I went nearer to look, and on an impulse I started to take the pistol from her hand. But I at once realized that it would be better to call Dr. Sheldon before I touched anything, and I did so."

"You didn't pause to pick up the bronze horse?" I asked.

"Certainly not," was the surprised reply.

"That horse and inkstand play a most mysterious part in the matter. But there must be some explanation for them, and we must find it."

"It will be made clear," said Gilbert, "if you do what I ask."

"I am more than willing to do your bidding," I said.

"Then send for Stone. He is a New York detective, and though I do not know him personally. I know enough about him to feel sure he can unravel this tangle as no one else can."

"How shall I find him?"

"I don't know his address. You will have to go or write to Jack Hemingway; he can tell you. Stone will be expensive, but this is no time for economy. Will you get him?"

"I certainly will," I replied, "and do all in my power to help him."

"Fleming Stone won't need much help," said Gilbert, not ungratefully, but decidedly, "he is a wizard. He can see right through anybody or anything."

"Then he is the man for us, and I'll go for him myself."

"Perhaps," said Crane, after a moment's thought, "it would be wiser not to let it be generally known that he is a celebrated detective."

"All right," I replied; "but the Maxwells will have to know it, because I want to put him up there. They'll be willing, I know. Indeed, Mr. Maxwell has himself suggested that we should get a city detective down."

"I know it," said Gilbert, "but I wish you'd act as if he were just a friend of yours who has a taste for detective work."

"Very well, I'll fix it that way then. But I hate to have you staying here, even for a few days."

"That can't be helped," said Gilbert, "and mustn't be considered. If you can only get Fleming Stone to come down here, I am as good as released."

Glad that he could view the situation in this cheerful manner, I went away, prepared to go at once on Gilbert's errand.

Miss Maxwell hospitably agreed to my proposal to burden her home with another visitor, but Mr. Maxwell did not seem quite pleased.

I couldn't help wondering if he thought that a more astute detective would only succeed in proving Gilbert's guilt more conclusively. He expressed himself as thinking it wise to let well enough alone, but as he made no definite protest against my going, I went to New York that very day in search of Fleming Stone. I found him, and after some persuasion, I induced him to return to Hamilton with me in the interests of Gilbert Crane.

Never shall I forget the delight of my first long conversation with Fleming Stone.

As to personal appearance, he was a fine-looking man without being in any way remarkably handsome. He was large and well-formed, between forty and fifty years old, with iron-gray hair and a clear, healthy complexion. His eyes were his chief charm and their attraction lay largely in their expression, and in their surrounding dark lashes and brows. Mr. Stone had a kindly smile, and his face in repose seemed to denote an even temper and a gracious disposition. He was possessed of great personal magnetism, and the liking which I felt for him the first moment I saw him, grew rapidly into admiration.

On the way down, at his request, I told him everything I knew about the Maxwell mystery. He was intensely interested; and I was secretly filled with joy when he expressed a decided approval of the methods I had used in discovering the red ink.

After I had told him every detail of the story, he changed the subject courteously, but very decidedly, and talked of other matters. He was a brilliant conversationalist, which surprised me, for my mental picture of a great detective had always represented a most taciturn gentleman of sinister aspect.

When we reached Maxwell Chimneys it was nearly dinner time.

At the dinner table, Mr. Stone gave no hint of his profession either in manner or appearance. He was simply a well-bred, well-dressed gentleman, with irreproachable manners and a talent for interesting conversation.

I noticed that Mr. Maxwell looked at him with occasional furtive glances, and seemed to be mentally weighing the man's professional ability. Either he was satisfied with the result of his scrutiny, or the charm of Mr. Stone appealed to him, for he distinctly showed a liking for his new guest before the close of the meal.

As Mildred Leslie was not yet allowed to leave her room, the Whitings and Miss Gardiner made up the rest of the dinner guests.

Edith Whiting and her husband were always to be depended on for a correct demeanor of any sort that the situation might require, but I was anxious to see what attitude Irene would assume toward the newcomer.

To my surprise she showed an intense interest in him.

She seemed fairly eager lest she lose one word of his conversation, and her brilliant cheeks and shining eyes proved her vivid enjoyment of the occasion.

After dinner there was music. In addition to his other talents, Mr. Stone was a musician, and though he declined to play for us that night, he seemed thoroughly to enjoy the music we made for him.

Though quite content to leave matters in his hands, I couldn't help wondering when he intended to begin his detective work. But almost as if in answer to my thought, Mr. Stone remarked that if it met with the approval of them all, he would ask for a short but absolutely private interview with each one.

"I assume there are no secrets among us," he said, in his winning way, "and as I understand the situation, from what Mr. King has told me, I think we are all earnestly anxious to discover the person who took the life of Philip Maxwell."

This was said gravely, almost solemnly, and for a moment no one spoke. Then Miss Maxwell said, in her gentle voice, "I trust I am not too revengeful in spirit, but I own I would be glad to see the slayer of my boy brought to justice."

Fleming Stone seemed to consider this an authority to proceed in his own way. Asking Miss Maxwell to go with him to the study, he escorted her from the room with an air of courtly grace that sat well upon him.

After not more than ten minutes, Mr. Stone brought her back, and asked that he might next have a few words with Mr. Maxwell. When the two men had gone, Miss Maxwell gave voice to her admiration of her new guest and declared that she had never seen anyone who gave her such favorable first impressions. We all agreed with her, and were enthusiastic in our praise of Fleming Stone as a man, whatever he might prove to be as a detective.

When Mr. Maxwell's short interview was finished, the others were taken in turn, and I was somewhat surprised to notice that Mr. Stone detained Tom Whiting far longer than any of the rest.

When he finally rejoined the group in the music room, Fleming Stone said:

"These preliminary and perhaps not entirely necessary formalities are now over; and I think I have learned all that I need to know from you who are here. I can, of course, do nothing more tonight. Tomorrow I must ask for a short talk with Miss Leslie, and after that I will see Mr. Crane."

But later that evening, Fleming Stone and I had a short conference in the library. I showed him the horse and the inkstand; described the exact position of Philip and Mildred when they were found; showed him where the black spangles were discovered; and pointed out how the balcony floor had been marked by signs of an apparent scuffle. Mr. Stone showed an unexpected interest in this last-named clue, though I confess it had seemed to me the least important of any. The balcony had since been swept, but there were still visible slight scratches in the long, sweeping marks I have described.

"I do not deduce from these scratches that there was a scuffle," said Mr. Stone. "That is, not in the sense of there having been a struggle between two persons. I see no reason for thinking that these marks were made by more than one pair of feet."

"Mr. Stone," I said, almost timidly, "perhaps I have no right to ask, but have your suspicions fallen in any direction as yet?"

Fleming Stone looked at me with an expression of sorrow in his deep gray eyes.

"I will tell you," he said, "for I know you will not betray my confidence, that I am positively certain who the criminal is; that it is not Gilbert Crane; and that it is a person upon whom I can lay my hand at any moment."

XXII: FLEMING STONE'S DISCOVERIES

THE next morning, although Fleming Stone was the same affable, courteous gentleman that he had been the night before, yet there was a shade more of seriousness in his manner. He spoke cheerfully, but it seemed to be with an effort, and I felt a vague sense of an impending disaster which might be worse than anything that had gone before.

After breakfast, Mr. Hunt came over and in the fateful library he was introduced to Fleming Stone. I was present at their interview, and I was glad to see that the two men at once assumed cordial attitudes, and seemed prepared to work together harmoniously.

I think Hunt may have felt a natural professional jealousy of the city detective, but if so he showed no trace of it. Besides, Mr. Hunt was quite at the end of his resources—completely baffled by the case. If Gilbert Crane were not the guilty man, neither our local detective nor myself knew where to look for the criminal.

Our discussion in the library did not last long, but it was exceedingly business-like and to the point. Without losing a shade of his graceful politeness, Fleming Stone showed also the quick working of his direct, forceful mind. He approved of all that Hunt and I had done. In a few words he commended our methods and accepted our results.

Then in silence he scrutinized the library. I think nothing in the room escaped the swift, thorough glances of those dark eyes. He rose to examine the rug, and the window casing, and then stepped out on the balcony to look at the scratches of which I had told him. These latter were very faint, but with a large magnifying glass which he took from his pocket he examined them carefully and seemed satisfied with what he found.

Returning to the library, he took the waste paper basket from under the desk and examined its contents. It was empty save for a few scraps of torn paper which I had thrown there myself the day before, but I saw his action with a sudden shock of dismay.

Neither Hunt nor I had thought of looking in the waste-basket, and though I had no definite hope of anything to be found there, it was a chance we ought not to have lost.

"Did Mr. Philip Maxwell ever write letters in this room?" asked Mr. Stone.

"Sometimes he did," I replied, "but more often he wrote down in his uncle's study."

"But he might have opened letters and read them here?"

"Yes; he used this desk a great deal."

"Where are the papers from the waste-baskets thrown?"

"I don't know, Mr. Stone; but the servants can tell you. Shall I call the maid who attends to the cleaning of this room?"

"I wish you would do so; then we will consider this consultation at an end. I have no wish to be unduly secret about my plans, but I must work uninterruptedly today, for I think developments will come thick and fast."

Mr. Hunt and I left the library, and I at once sent the maid to Mr. Stone as he had requested. Less than fifteen minutes later, I saw him coming up from the cellar.

Seeing that I was alone, he said: "I found a paper that is a most important link in our chain. Will you look at it a moment?"

He drew from his pocket a paper which had evidently been smoothed out after being much crumpled, and turned down the top of the sheet so that I did not see the address. "That is Mr. Philip Maxwell's handwriting, is it not?" he said.

"Yes," I replied, and in Phil's well-known characters I read:

At last I have discovered the truth, and it has broken my heart.
Even now I could not believe it, but your...

The writing stopped abruptly, and the letter had evidently been thrown aside unfinished. I restrained my intense curiosity, and did not ask to see the name at the head of the letter, but apparently Fleming Stone divined my thoughts.

"You will know only too soon," he said with that sad note in his voice that always thrilled me. "Now I am going to see Miss Leslie."

The doctor had permitted a short interview, and I learned afterward from Edith Whiting, that though Mildred had dreaded it, she was at once put at her ease by Mr. Stone's gentleness, and gave a brief but coherent account of the affair.

It was shortly before noon that I went for a walk with Irene Gardiner. As we went away, I saw Mr. Stone and Miss Miranda Maxwell in the music room. Miss Maxwell was knitting some fleecy white-wool thing, and though she looked sad she was calm and unexcited.

They seemed to be chatting cozily, and yet I felt sure that Fleming Stone was learning some details about Philip's life or character which he considered important.

I sighed to think that the net was certainly closing in around somebody, and the amazing part was that I had not the remotest idea toward whom Fleming Stone's suspicions were directed.

Miss Gardiner and I walked down the path to the river. As was inevitable, we talked only of the all-absorbing topic, and especially of Fleming Stone.

"Isn't he wonderful?" she exclaimed.

"He is certainly the ideal detective."

"He is in his methods and his intellect," I said, "but his personal appearance is far from my preconceived notions of the regulation detective. I had always imagined them grim and sinister. This man is not only affable but positively sunny."

"He is fascinating!" declared Irene. "I have never met anyone who seemed so attractive at first sight."

I quite agreed with her, but I was suddenly conscious of an absurd pang of jealousy.

I was beginning to think that Irene Gardiner was pretty nearly necessary to the happiness of my life, and this avowed interest of hers in another man spurred me to a sudden conclusion that I cared for her very much indeed.

But this was no time or place to tell her so. At the Maxwells' invitation she had decided to remain at Maxwell Chimneys with the Whitings until Mildred was able to travel to New York. Dr. Sheldon had said that the journey might safely be taken about the middle of the following week. I had made my plans to go at the same time, but in view of the rapid developments of the past two days I had unmade those plans and had made no others.

"Doesn't it seem strange," said Irene, "that you and I were talking about crime and criminals on the way down here last week? How little we thought that we were coming straight to a tragedy."

"It is a tragedy," I said, "and it may prove even more of a one than we yet know. Irene, if Gilbert didn't shoot Philip, have you any idea who did?"

"No," she said, looking at me with a candor in her eyes which left no room for doubt.

"No, I have not the faintest idea. And yet I cannot believe Gilbert did it. I never liked him, but he does not seem to me capable of crime."

"And yet you hold the theory that, given an opportunity, we are all capable of crime."

"I know I said that," said Irene thoughtfully.

"And it does seem true in theory, but it is hard to believe it in an individual case."

"I am sure Gilbert was not the criminal," I said, "but my certainty is based on something quite apart from the question of his capability in the way of committing crime. First, I was convinced of his innocence by his own attitude. A simple assertion might be false, but Gilbert's look and voice and manner told far more than his words. No criminal could have acted as he did. Even his scornful indifference to the fact of his arrest carried conviction of his innocence. But aside from all that, Fleming Stone says he knows that Gilbert is not guilty, and moreover he knows who is."

"He knows who is!" exclaimed Irene. "Who can it be?"

"I don't know; but I am sure from what Mr. Stone says it is someone whom we all know, and whose conviction will not only surprise but sadden us."

"Do you suppose," said Irene slowly, her great eyes wide with horror, "that it could have been Mildred after all?"

So this strange girl had dared to put into words a thought which I had tried hard to keep out of my mind.

"Don't!" said I, "I cannot think of it!"

"But her whole story about the intruder may have been a fabrication."

" Don't," I said again, "such remarks are unworthy of you—are unworthy of any woman."

"You always misunderstand me," said Irene impatiently.

"I do."

"I don't mean it the way you think. If I could see Mildred myself, I would talk to her in the same way. There is no harm in asking a frank question."

"Then," I said abruptly. "I will ask you one. What did you mean last Monday night when you told me that if I wouldn't interfere between Philip and Mildred you would take matters into your own hands?"

"I am not at all offended by your question," said Irene, looking me straight in the eyes, "neither do I assume that, because you ask it, you think that I meant anything desperate. I meant only what I said—that if you wouldn't advise Philip Maxwell not to be infatuated by such a foolish, artful little coquette as Mildred Leslie, then I would warn him myself."

"Since we are speaking frankly, I must admit that it would seem to me unwarranted interference on your part."

"I suppose I am peculiar," said Irene with a sigh, "but it doesn't seem that way to me. However, this is a question capable of much discussion. Suppose we leave its consideration for some other time, and return to the house now."

We walked back, chatting in a lighter vein, and somehow my heart sank when I saw Fleming Stone sitting alone on the veranda. It may have been imagination, or perhaps intuition, but as soon as I saw him, I felt a conviction that he had accomplished his work, and that we would soon know the result.

"I've been waiting for you," he said, as I went toward him.

Irene went into the house, and Mr. Stone continued.

"I have discovered everything, and I want you to be prepared for a sad revelation."

"Did you learn anything from your interview with Miss Leslie?" I asked impulsively.

"Nothing more than I knew before I saw her," he replied, and his inscrutable face gave me no glimmer of information.

"It is almost one o'clock," he went on, "and after luncheon I will tell you all. I have asked Mr. Hunt to be present, and you will both please meet me in the library at two o'clock."

Somehow the sad foreboding that had taken possession of me made me glad of even an hour's further respite. I went to the luncheon table and made my bravest endeavor to seem my natural self.

But a depressing cloud seemed to hang over us all.

Although each one tried to be cheerful, the efforts were far from being entirely successful.

Even Mr. Maxwell seemed disturbed. Indeed, Miss Miranda was most placid of all, and I felt sure that was due to the calming effect of Mr. Stone's kindly consideration for her.

At last the meal was over, and, unable to keep up the strain any longer I went at once to the library, and awaited the others.

Mr. Hunt came first.

"Have you any idea of the disclosure Mr. Stone is about to make?" he said to me.

"No," said I, "I think I can truthfully say I haven't."

"He has asked Dr. Sheldon to be here by half past two," said Hunt.

Again my thoughts flew to Mildred Leslie, but I said nothing.

Then Fleming Stone came into the room. There was sadness still in his eyes, but he had again assumed that alert, official air which characterized his professional moments.

"Gentlemen," he said, "I came down here, as you know, an absolute stranger and entirely unprejudiced. I have listened to various accounts of the crime; I have weighed the evidence offered to me; I have made investigations on my own account and drawn my own deductions.

"I have considered the character and dispositions of all persons known to be in the vicinity of Philip Maxwell at the time of his death; have pondered over the possible motive for the crime; and, from the facts learned as a result of my investigation and consideration, I have discovered the murderer.

"Gentlemen, Philip Maxwell was shot by his uncle, Mr. Alexander Maxwell!"

XXIII: THE CONFESSION

THERE was nothing to be said.

I was silent, because I felt as if the earth had suddenly given way beneath me, and all was chaos. Not for a moment did I doubt Fleming Stone's statement, for his words compelled conviction.

But in the confused mass of sudden thoughts that surged through my brain, I seemed to see clearly nothing but Miss Miranda's placid face, and I cried out involuntarily:

"Don't let his sister know!"

Hunt sat like a man stunned. His expression was positively vacant, and I think he was trying to realize what Mr. Stone's announcement meant.

"It is terrible, I know," said Fleming Stone, "and I quite appreciate the shock it must be to you. But inexorable justice demands that we proceed without faltering. I think that, without telling you of the various steps which led me to this conclusion, I can best prove to you that it is the true one by asking you to go with me while I lay the facts before Mr. Maxwell. I think his reception of what I have to say, and the visible effect of my accusations upon him, will prove to you beyond any possible doubt his connection with the crime. Indeed, from what I know of the man I am disposed to think he will make full confession of his guilt."

Fleming Stone's words sounded to me like a voice heard in a dream; and even my own voice sounded strange and unreal, as I murmured: "It will kill him. He has heart disease."

"I know it," said Fleming Stone, "and I, too, fear the effect upon him. For that reason I have asked Dr. Sheldon to be present."

When Dr. Sheldon arrived, he came directly to us in the library, and Fleming Stone told him in a few words of the ordeal we had to undergo.

The four of us then went down to Mr. Maxwell's study. We found him there alone. We all went in, and Fleming Stone closed the door. He stood for a moment looking directly at Mr. Maxwell, and his deep eyes were filled with a great compassion.

"Mr. Maxwell," he said—and his voice though quiet was most impressive—"we have come to tell you that we have discovered that Philip Maxwell died by your hand."

If any of us had doubted Alexander Maxwell's guilt—and I think some of us had—all possibility of doubt was at once removed.

If ever I saw a face on which confession was stamped as plainly as on a printed page, it was Alexander Maxwell's face at that moment. Instinctively, I turned away, but almost immediately I heard Mr. Maxwell gasp, and I knew that Fleming Stone's expectations had been verified, and that Mr. Maxwell's heart had not been able to stand the shock.

Dr. Sheldon sprang to his side, and with the assistance of the others laid the unconscious man on the couch.

"He is not dead," said Dr. Sheldon, after a few moments. "And he will soon rally from this; but I feel sure it is a fatal attack. I think he cannot live more than a few hours."

As the doctor had surmised, Mr. Maxwell soon rallied and spoke:

"Don't let Miranda know," he said, "don't ever let Miranda know."

Fleming Stone stepped forward.

"Mr. Maxwell," he said, "if you will make a full confession in the presence of these gentlemen, I will promise you on my honor that I will use every endeavor to keep the knowledge of your guilt from your sister."

"I will not only assist Mr. Stone in his endeavor," said Dr. Sheldon, "but I think I can safely promise that Miss Miranda shall never learn the secret. You are very ill, Mr. Maxwell, and whatever you wish to say must be said at once."

"I am ready," said Alexander Maxwell, and though his voice was faint, and though he seemed to realize his own fearful position, yet his manner expressed a certainly sense of relief which I believed to be due to the relaxation of the tension of fear he had been under so long.

"I am ready," he said again, "and, to make clear to you the motive for my deed, I must begin my story many years back."

"But you must make it brief," said Dr. Sheldon. "I cannot allow you to talk long at this time."

"There will not be any other time," said Mr. Maxwell quietly.

I could not help marveling at this strange man, whose wonderful power of self-control did not desert him in this moment of mental and physical extremity.

Mr. Maxwell proceeded, and Fleming Stone took stenographic notes of his statement.

"Twenty-five years ago I lived in California and so did my brother John. Though not partners, our business interests were closely united in many ways. My brother married, and, about a year after Philip's birth, his wife died.

"Five years later, John Maxwell died, and left the whole of his large fortune with me in trust for Philip. Although it was supposed at that time that my own fortune was as large or larger than John's, the reverse was true. I had lost much money in unfortunate speculation, and it was to my surprise that I discovered the large amount of money my brother had left behind him.

"I used this money to make good my losses, trusting to replace it with further gains of my own before Philip should come of age. I was always a close-mouthed man, and neither Miranda nor my other sister, Hannah, knew anything about John's money.

"I came East to live, and after some years the lawyer who was the only one beside myself who knew the circumstances died. Having by this time become a well-known and respected citizen of Hamilton, being president of the bank, and holding, or having held, various public offices, my pride and ambition rebelled at giving up my entire fortune to Philip.

"But it would have taken all my available assets to make up the sum entrusted to me by the boy's father. For many years I struggled with this temptation, and at last, when Philip was twenty one, I succumbed.

"On his twenty-first birthday, instead of telling him the truth, I offered him a permanent home at Maxwell Chimneys and agreed to support him indulgently and even extravagantly."

Here, at the very climax of the recital, Mr. Maxwell sank back upon the couch, breathless and exhausted. But after a moment's rest he continued:

"We lived happily enough for a few years—in fact, until one day about a fortnight ago.

"That morning I was here in my study and had spread out before me the principal papers relating to the trust I had held for Philip.

"Suddenly I was called to the telephone and, thinking to return in a minute, left the papers on my desk. But I was detained at the telephone much longer than I anticipated, and, when I returned, although there was nobody in sight, it seemed to me the papers had been disturbed.

"They were tossed about, and I felt a presentiment that Philip had been in there and had read them. It would have been no breach of honor on his part, for he had always been allowed free access to my study and to my business papers.

"From that time on Philip was a changed man. His manner toward me confirmed my suspicion that he had discovered my guilt. No mention was made of the subject between us, but for more than a week Philip continued to act like a man crushed by a sudden disaster.

"Last Monday he wrote a letter to me in which he told me that he had discovered the truth, and that he felt he was entitled to an explanation. This explanation I knew I could not give, nor was I willing to face my nephew's well-deserved condemnation and the exposure of my treachery to the public.

"On Monday then, after reading Philip's letter, I determined that I would take my own life, as being a cowardly but final solution of my difficulties.

"Monday evening I sat in my study and decided that the time had come. I had placed my pistol in my pocket, and had intended to go up to my own room and there expiate my guilt toward my brother and his son.

"At this moment, Mr. King chanced to come into my study, and mentioned that Philip and Mildred were in the library. This strengthened my purpose, for I felt sure that Philip was even then telling Miss Leslie that he was in reality a rich man.

"Mr. King went on through the billiard-room and across the hall to the music-room. I left the study at once, and saw Mr. King enter the music room door.

"As I crossed the back part of the hall, I felt an impulse to look once more on Philip's face. I knew I could step out on the balcony from the hall window and look in at the library window unobserved.

"It has always been my habit when going out for a moment into the night air to catch up any coat from the hat-stand and throw it around me. I did this mechanically, and it chanced to be Gilbert Crane's automobile coat.

"I went up the back stairs, putting the coat on as I went. Instinctively putting my hands into the pockets, I felt there the cap and goggles.

"It was then that the evil impulse seized me. I saw my beautiful home with its rich appointments, its lights, and its flowers; I heard the gay music and laughter; and like a flash it came to me that Philip should be the one to give up all that, and not I.

"I realized, as by an inspiration, that the goggles and a turned-up coat-collar would be ample disguise, and I thought the crime would be attributed to an outside marauder.

"The rest you know. Philip recognized me. But Miss Leslie did not. That is all."

Mr. Maxwell fell back, and Dr. Sheldon, thinking the end had come, went toward him.

But Fleming Stone, the inexorable, leaned forward, and said distinctly to Mr. Maxwell: "Wait—did you refill the inkstand?"

"Yes," said Mr. Maxwell, with a sudden revival of strength, "yes. I returned to the room late that night, picked up the inkstand, washed it, refilled it, and replaced it. The bronze horse I picked up and replaced before leaving the room the first time."

I gazed at Alexander Maxwell, wonderingly. And yet, for a man who could live the life he had lived, who could conduct himself as he had during the past week, it was not strange that he was able thus, in the face of death, calmly to relate these details of his own crime.

"One more thing," said Mr. Stone. "Did you scrape your foot around on the balcony to efface a possible footprint?"

"Yes; I knew the dust was thick there, and I wished to eliminate all traces."

Here Mr. Maxwell's strength seemed to leave him all at once. On the verge of total collapse, he said again, "Don't let Miranda know "—and then sank into unconsciousness.

"He will probably not rally again," said Dr. Sheldon. "I think his sister should be notified at once of his illness. But we shall all agree that she must not know of his crime."

"Shall I call her?" I volunteered, as no one else moved to do so.

"Yes," said Dr. Sheldon.

"She will be startled, but it will not be entirely unexpected. I have warned her for years that the end would come like this."

In justice to the innocent, Fleming Stone and I went at once to Inspector Davis to ask that Gilbert Crane be released. The order for release was sent immediately, and at last we were free to ask Fleming Stone a few questions.

"How did you do it?" cried Hunt, in his abrupt way.

"How did you do it so soon?" cried I, no less curious.

"It was not difficult," said Fleming Stone, in that direct way of his, which was not over-modest, but simply truthful.

"Mr. King's statement, which was the first one I heard, showed me that, although Mr. Crane's alibi from ten o'clock till half past ten depended entirely upon his own uncorroborated word, yet Mr. Maxwell's alibi was equally without verification.

"Mr. King saw Mr. Maxwell in his study at ten o'clock. He was found there again some time after ten-thirty. This proved nothing but the opportunity. Then all the evidence regarding the coat, the clues found in the library, and elsewhere, would apply to him as well as to Crane. It remained, however, to find what motive, if any, could have impelled Alexander Maxwell to the deed.

"I had not talked with him ten minutes before I concluded that he was a man with a secret. Miss Maxwell supplied a clue when she told me what she knew of Philip's early history.

"Another clue was the crumpled letter found among the waste paper. This was addressed to Alexander Maxwell, and was probably begun and discarded for the one which Philip wrote and sent to his uncle.

"The fact that the inkstand had been refilled and replaced argued someone familiar with the library; even Gilbert Crane would not be apt to know where the supply of red ink was kept. Everything pointed in one direction.

"But perhaps the most convincing clue was given to me last evening by Mr. Maxwell himself. You remember, Mr. King, that I took each member of the household to the study separately. When I interviewed Mr. Maxwell there, I took care not to alarm him, but rather to put him at his ease as much as possible.

"Noticing a well-worn foot-rest, I felt sure that it was his habit to sit with his feet up on it. In hopes of his taking this position, I asked him to show me just how he was sitting when the news of the crime was brought to him.

"As I surmised, he sat down in his big armchair, and put his feet upon the foot-rest. This gave me an opportunity to examine the soles of his shoes, and I discovered on one of them a large stain of a dull, purplish red. The stain made by red ink is indelible and of a peculiar tinge, so that I felt sure this was the man at whom the inkstand had been thrown, and who had unknowingly stepped upon a wet spot of red ink.

"Owing to the awkward goggles which he wore, and, too, the excitement of the moment, he probably did not notice the ink at all. When he returned later, the spots had sunk into the crimson rug, and partly dried. The shoes were light house-shoes, and probably he did not wear them out of doors, for dampness or hard wear would have tended to obliterate the stain.

"As it was, the color could plainly be seen. I am sure that a chemical test would prove it to be a stain of red ink."

Mr. Maxwell died that night, and Dr. Sheldon at once took Miss Miranda to his own home, and kept her there, safely out of the reach of gossip until she went out to Colorado to live with her sister. Her nerves were shattered, and she begged so piteously that she might not be obliged to enter Maxwell Chimneys again, that her wishes were willingly respected. The rest of us remained at the house until the sister, Hannah, came to take charge of affairs, and to take Miss Miranda home with her.

"It is a case," I said to Irene Gardiner, "which proves your theory—the murder of Philip Maxwell was brought about solely by opportunity."

"My chance remark to Mr. Maxwell that the young people were in the library; the inadvertent snatching up of Gilbert's coat; the fact that the goggles and cap were in the pocket; the fact that Philip's uncle had a weapon with him—all these things form tiny links in a strong chain of opportunity."

"But the evil impulse must have been in his heart, or he would never have taken advantage of this opportunity," said Irene, unconsciously refuting a theory she had herself advanced.

"I would rather not think," said Fleming Stone, in his sweet, serious voice, "that opportunity creates a sinner, or even that it creates an evil impulse. I would rather believe—and I do believe—that opportunity only warms into action an evil impulse that is lying dormant; and I do not believe that dormant evil impulse is in everybody."

"Nor do I," said Irene; "it would be a sad world, indeed, if that were true. And yet," she looked at me, "I confess I used to think so. But I have learned much in the last few weeks, and I realize how difficult it is to judge what anyone would do or would not do upon occasion. And yet I would rather believe that the evil impulse was created in Mr. Maxwell's mind by the especial opportunity, than to think he had all his life been a man capable of crime."

"Perhaps you're right," said Stone; "and after all, it makes little difference. The thing is to have a strong enough character or will to resist any evil impulse or any special opportunity that may present itself. And that no one can declare he possesses, until he has been tried and proven. But let us be thankful that the opportunities are comparatively rare and the natures that succumb to them are rarer still."

"It is a satisfaction to realize that," I returned, "but that very knowledge makes it seem all the more strange and sad that an exceptional case should be this of Alexander Maxwell."

THE END

Made in the USA
Las Vegas, NV
01 June 2023